STORIES TO REMEMBER

VOLUME I

SAWYERS

STORIES TO REMEMBER

SELECTED BY

Thomas B. Costain and John Beecroft

ILLUSTRATED BY MARTHA SAWYERS AND WILLIAM REUSSWIG

Doubleday & Company, Inc., Garden City, New York, 1956

LIBRARY OF CONGRESS CATALOG CARD NUMBER 56-11620

PRINTED IN THE UNITED STATES OF AMERICA

TYPOGRAPHY BY JAMES LEACH

BOOKS BY THOMAS B. COSTAIN

Stories to Remember [*with John Beecroft*]

The Tontine

The Mississippi Bubble

The White and the Gold: *The French Regime in Canada*

The Silver Chalice

The Magnificent Century: *The Pageant of England*

Son of a Hundred Kings

The Conquerors: *The Pageant of England*

High Towers

The Moneyman

The Black Rose

Ride with Me

Joshua: A Biography [*with Rogers MacVeagh*]

For My Great Folly

BOOKS BY JOHN BEECROFT

Stories to Remember [*with Thomas B. Costain*]

A Treasury of Great Mysteries [*with Howard Haycraft*]

The Best Stories of W. Somerset Maugham

Kipling: A *Selection of His Stories and Poems*

Mr. Maugham Himself

The Modern Reader

INTRODUCTION

The word anthology meant originally a garland of flowers but by some twisting of this definition it came later to be applied to a collection of the flowers of literature. To say, therefore, that STORIES TO REMEMBER is not an anthology would be a doubtful compliment to the many supreme writers whose stories have been culled to make it up. And yet there is a distinction which the editors desire to draw. If there is one thing in the book world which is not needed at this particular moment, it is another anthology. During the last fifteen or twenty years the book presses of the country have been kept in a constant state of racketing by the demand, or what publishers hopefully assumed to be the demand, for more and more anthologies. The pages came tumbling off in countless thousands, to be bound up in huge volumes and sent off to the bookstores and there offered, again hopefully, to what should have been an avid public. Out of this feverish activity, which resulted in some splendid collections and some bad ones, a new meaning for the word seems to have emerged: an anthology is now accepted to mean a collection of the best of this or that, the best short stories, the best short novels, the best of a single author's output, or more particularly, the best love stories, or adventure stories, or ghost stories.

In this partially accepted meaning of the word, STORIES TO REMEMBER is not an anthology. The editors set themselves a much less trying but more useful, task than that of out-pontificating the highly pontifical volumes already in print. Their purpose, briefly, was this: to present a collection of stories which would (according to the nature of each) engross, excite, mystify, please, amuse, charm or satisfy our readers from the front cover of the first volume to the back of the second. Let us say at the outset that this was not as difficult as it might seem. There is plenty of gold in the literary hills, so much that the glint of "color" rewards any serious attempt at digging; there is enough, indeed, for perhaps an endless succession of volumes such as these.

Our chief difficulty came in the matter of the method of selection to be adopted. The literary stockpile built up over the ages is of such mountainous proportions that to read and analyze everything of value in it, and to set off the advantages of one item against another, would be a task of many years. It was decided to extract the desired nuggets by applying first the pick and shovel of fond memory. If we had entertained an immense liking for a story over a long span of years, and it still pleased us as much as ever, then surely this was a story which others would enjoy and remember in turn.

Proceeding on that basis, however, it was still found necessary to employ some special method in winnowing out what we wanted from such an unlimited supply. It was decided that originality would be the quality above all others to seek; originality in theme, plot, treatment or background. Authors of established stature develop from time to time ideas of rare originality, and it would be from them that we would draw most largely; for a "different" story requires the touch of a master to make it seem real. *The Jungle Books* are classics but in the hands of almost anyone but Kipling they could have been poor things indeed. Ideas that are strange and novel are a challenge to which the possessor of a sure technique always rises. It is not hard to believe that Stevenson moistened his lips and set at once to work when it occurred to him to write the story of a shot-gun wedding and tell it in a fifteenth century setting before shotguns existed (although a hangman's noose was going to serve just as well); that the persistent choice of *La Grande Bretêche* as Balzac's best tale is due to the ebullient mood with which he flung himself into the task of writing this story of a husband's macabre revenge; that Dumas sought among the cobwebs of history with an eye which glistened when he encountered such a story as the amazing impostures of one Cagliostro; that Enid Bagnold was so enamoured with the idea that a slip of a girl might conceivably win the Grand National, most gruelling of horse-races, that she adorned the telling of "*National Velvet*" with every resource of a gifted pen.

The editors were particularly happy to have each of the novels of varying lengths which are included. How great a joy it was to read again Thornton Wilder's *The Bridge of San Luis Rey* and find it still a many-splendored tale; to savor once more the charm and almost unbearable poignancy that Robert Nathan achieves in *Portrait of Jennie*; to realize what an epic use Conrad Richter made in *The Sea of Grass* of the much used western land wars; to take up after some years that truly fine piece of Americana, *The Voice of Bugle Ann* by MacKinlay Kantor; to go afield and revel in such different stories as Selma Lagerlöf's *The General's Ring* and the above mentioned "*National Velvet*" by Enid Bagnold.

These, and the shorter pieces, are vintage stories in our esteem, and we are convinced that those who read them will carry them in their memories with the same fondness and admiration that the editors have felt.

May 10, 1956

THOMAS B. COSTAIN

CONTENTS

VOLUME ONE

VOLUME TWO

A Novel

THE GENERAL'S RING

SELMA LAGERLÖF

THE GENERAL'S RING

SELMA LAGERLÖF

I

I KNOW that in former days there were plenty of people who knew not the meaning of the word "fear." I have heard of folk who loved to skate on the thinnest of ice, of others who knew no greater joy than to drive unbroken horses. There have, indeed, been even a few who would play cards with Colour Sergeant Ahlegard, although he had every trick at his fingers' ends and always managed to win. Then there are intrepid souls who have had the courage to start travelling on a Friday and to sit down thirteen to table.

But I wonder whether any even of such would have had courage to wear the fearsome ring that had belonged to old General Löwensköld of Hedeby.

It was this same old General who had won fame, property, and a title for the Löwenskölds; and so long as there was one of the family living at Hedeby, his portrait hung in the big upper drawing room, between the windows. It was a large picture, reaching from the floor to the ceiling. On glancing at it casually, you might have mistaken it for Charles the Twelfth himself, standing there firmly planted on the tessellated floor, in his blue coat, chamois leather gloves, and enormous jack boots. But, on a closer glance, you realized that it was an entirely different person.

A broad, rough peasant face rose above the coat collar. The man looked born to follow the plough all the days of his life; but, in spite of his plainness, he gave the impression of being a wise, reliable, even great, man. Had he been born in these days, he would, at least, have been on a jury, or the chairman of a Municipal Council; but living, as he did, in the reign of the great hero king, he went out and fought as a poor soldier and returned as the rich General Löwensköld, receiving as the reward of the Crown for all his service the estate of Hedeby, in the parish of Bro.

As a matter of fact, the longer you looked at the picture, the more reconciled to it you became. You seemed to realize that it was men such

Reprinted by permission of Doubleday and Company, Inc.

as this who had, under the leadership of King Charles the Twelfth, ploughed the furrow between Poland and Russia. His army had not been composed wholly of adventurers and courtiers; there had been simple, earnest men, such as the one in this picture, who had loved him, and found him a King worth living and dying for.

While studying the picture, there was generally one of the family at hand to point out that not vanity alone had prompted the General to remove the glove from his left hand, so as to display the great signet ring which he wore on his forefinger. This was the ring he had received from the King—there was only one King for him—and it was shown in the picture as a sign that Bengt Löwensköld was his faithful servant. He had been forced to listen to much bitter censure of his sovereign; there were those who even ventured to assert that, by his imprudence and recklessness, he had brought his kingdom to the verge of ruin; but the General was loyal to him through everything. The King was a man whose like had never been seen, and those who lived with him had come to realize that there are nobler and higher causes for which to fight than merely worldly honour and success.

The same reason that caused Bengt Löwensköld to display his ring in his portrait made him wish to have it buried in his grave with him. And here, too, there was no question of vanity. He had no wish, certainly, to boast of wearing a great King's jewel on his finger when he appeared in the presence of Our Lord and the Archangels, but he hoped that, when he entered the hall where Charles the Twelfth would be sitting, surrounded by his trusty swordsmen, the ring might win him recognition, so that he would spend eternity close to the man whom he had served and honoured all his life.

When the General's coffin was placed in the walled vault which he had had prepared for himself in Bro churchyard, the ring was safe on the forefinger of his left hand. Many of those present regretted that so great a treasure should go with the dead man to his grave, for the General's ring was almost as well known as the General himself, and as famous. It was said to be of sufficient value to buy a vast estate, and that the red cornelian, engraved with the King's signature, was no less valuable. People were universally agreed that it was generous of his sons not to oppose his wish, but to bury his treasure with him.

If the General's ring really resembled that represented in the picture, it must certainly have been a clumsy thing which hardly anyone nowadays could wear; but a few hundred years ago it would have been greatly valued. We must remember that all jewels and vessels of precious metals, with very few exceptions, had to be handed over to the Crown; that the nation had to struggle against "Gortz's Tokens" and national bankruptcy, so that, to many people, gold was a thing only spoken of, never seen. This is why folk could not forget the ring, so uselessly buried under the coffin lid. Its burial there was almost an injustice. It might have been taken to some foreign country, sold for a great sum to be used in procuring food for the many who now had nothing to eat save straw and the bark of trees.

Yet, though there were many who longed to possess the great treasure, there was not one who thought seriously of appropriating it. The ring lay in the coffin, with the lid screwed down, in a walled-up grave, under a heavy gravestone, out of reach of the most daring thief, and there they believed it would lie till the end of the world.

II

General Bengt Löwensköld died in the month of March, 1741, and a few months later in the same year, it happened that his eldest son, George Löwensköld, who lived generally at Hedeby, lost his little daughter from dysentery. She was buried on a Sunday immediately after the service; the whole congregation joined in the procession to the grave of the Löwenskölds, where the gravestones were standing up on end. The vault underneath had been opened by a mason in order that the dead child's little coffin might lie beside her grandfather's.

While the people were gathered round the grave listening to the burial service, it is possible that many of them remembered the royal ring and regretted that it should be lying hidden and useless in that grave, of no benefit to anyone. Perhaps here and there one whispered to his neighbour that it would not be difficult to get the ring, since the grave would not probably be closed again before the next day.

In the crowd there stood a countryman named Bard Bardsson, who lived at Mellomstuga in the village of Olsby. He, however, was not one of those who had worried themselves gray over the ring. On the contrary, when people began talking about it, he always declared that he had a good enough farm, so had no need to envy the General for taking a bushel of gold with him to his grave.

Now, as he stood in the churchyard, it occurred to him, as to so many others, how strange it was that the grave should have been opened. It did not please him, it made him uneasy. He thought to himself: "The Captain ought to have it closed this afternoon, there are many people longing for that ring."

Although it was no concern of his, nevertheless, he kept on thinking how dangerous it would be to leave the grave open all night. It was the month of August; the nights were dark, and if the grave was not shut that very day, a thief might easily creep in and carry off the treasure. He was seized with such acute anxiety that he even contemplated going himself to warn the Captain, but he knew that people considered him foolish, and he did not want to make himself a laughing stock. "You are quite right about this," he thought to himself, "but if you are too officious you will only be laughed at. The Captain, who is such a sensible man, had certainly arranged for the grave to be shut up again."

He was so absorbed with his thoughts that he did not notice that the funeral was over, but stood still beside the grave, and might have stood much longer had not his wife pulled him by the sleeve.

"What is the matter with you?" she said. "You are standing staring at one spot like a cat watching a rat hole."

The man turned round and, looking up, saw that he and his wife were alone in the churchyard.

"There's nothing the matter," he said. "I was only just wondering . . ."

He would have liked to tell his wife what he was wondering, but he knew that she was much sharper than himself. She would only think that he was worrying himself unnecessarily. She would say that if the grave were shut or not was a question that concerned nobody but Captain Löwensköld.

They turned to go home, and, as soon as Bard Bardsson had turned his back on the churchyard, he hoped he would forget the matter. But he did not, for his wife talked of nothing but the funeral, of the coffin, of the bearers, of the procession, and of the sermon; and he put in a word here and there—although he heard scarcely a word that she said—so that she should not know he was not listening. But presently her voice seemed to be reaching him from the far distance, and his brain went back to the worrying thoughts.

"This is Sunday," he thought, "perhaps the mason won't work on a day of rest. In that case, if the Captain gave him a rix-dollar, he could do it in the night. If only he could think of that!"

Presently he began to talk to himself aloud. "I ought to go to the Captain in any case. I ought not to mind whether folk laugh at me or not."

He had quite forgotten that his wife was walking beside him, but he pulled himself up when she stopped and stared at him.

"It's nothing," he said, "it's only what I was thinking of before." And so they continued their journey and soon reached their own door.

He hoped now that his troublesome thoughts would leave him; and so they might had he set about some work, but it was Sunday, and on that day the people at Mellomstuga all went to their own quarters after dinner. He remained by himself in the cottage, and immediately the same doubts recurred to his mind.

At last he got up from his seat, and, going out, began to saddle his horse, intending to ride to Hedeby and speak to the Captain.

"If I don't," he thought, "the ring will be stolen tonight."

Nevertheless, he could not bring himself to take the matter so seriously. He was too shy. He went, instead, to the farm of one of his neighbours, intending to tell the man about his anxiety; but, as the man was not alone, he again felt too shy to speak, and ended by riding home without having said a word about the matter.

As soon as the sun set, he went to bed determining to sleep till morning; but there was no sleep for him. All his restlessness came back, and he lay tossing and turning the whole night. His wife, naturally, could not sleep either, and after a time she asked him why he was so restless.

"It is nothing," he answered as usual. "Only something I am thinking about."

"You have said that several times already to-day," answered his wife, "but I think it is time now for you to tell me what you *are* thinking about. You can't have anything so dangerous in your mind that you can't tell me about it, surely."

Bard persuaded himself, on hearing his wife speak thus, that, if he told her his trouble, he would get to sleep.

"I am only wondering whether the old General's vault has been closed up," he said, "or whether it will stay open all night."

His wife laughed. "I've been thinking of that too," she said, "and I expect that everybody in church to-day was thinking the same. But you needn't let a thing like that rob you of your sleep."

Bard was glad that his wife took the matter so easily. He felt relieved and certain that now he would sleep.

But hardly had he settled himself before it all started again. He saw shadows come stealing out of every cottage, every quarter, all going on the same errand, all turning their steps toward the churchyard with the open vault. He tried to lie still so that his wife might sleep, but his head ached and his body sweated. He was forced to toss and turn. At last his wife lost all patience and blurted out, half in jest:

"Dear husband, I really think you had better go to the churchyard and see after the grave yourself, instead of tossing from side to side and never closing your eyes."

The words were hardly out of her mouth before her husband jumped out of bed and began to dress himself. He thought his wife was right. It was not more than half an hour's walk from Olsby to Bro church; he would be back within an hour, and then could have a good night's rest. But scarcely was he outside the door before it occurred to his wife that it would be a dreadful thing to let him go all alone to the churchyard; so she sprang up hastily, and she too put on her clothes.

She caught up to her husband on the slope, just below Olsby. Bard laughed as he heard her coming up behind.

"Have you come to see that I don't steal the General's ring?" he asked.

"Good gracious!" she said. "I know that you wouldn't think of such a thing. I only came to help you in case you met a ghoul or a hellhound."

They went forward at a brisk pace. Night had fallen, and it was quite dark except for a narrow streak of light in the western sky, but they were quite sure of the road. They chatted together and were in high spirits. They were only going to the churchyard to see whether the grave was still open, so that Bard could stop worrying and go to sleep.

"I can't believe that the family at Hedeby can be so rash as not to have had the ring fastened up again," said Bard.

"Well, we shall soon know," said his wife. "I believe that's the churchyard wall just close to us now."

The man stopped. He wondered why his wife's voice sounded so cheerful. Surely she could have no other reason than his own for coming on this journey.

"Before we go into the churchyard," said Bard, "we must come to some agreement as to what to do in case the grave is open."

"Whether it is open or not, I don't see that there is anything we can do, except go home and get into bed."

"No, you are right," said Bard, and went on. After a little, he said again, "I suppose we can hardly expect to find the churchyard gate unlocked at this hour."

"No, it's shut. We shall have to climb over the wall, if we want to pay a visit to the General and see how he is."

Again the man was astonished. He heard a slight rattle of falling stones, and his wife's form was outlined against the strip of bright sky toward the west. She had climbed to the top of the wall, which, after all, was not a great feat, as it was only a couple of feet high; but it was strange that she should be so eager to get in before him.

"Here," she said, "give me your hand, I will help you up."

They soon left the wall and went forward silently and carefully between the little mounds. Once Bard stumbled over a grave and nearly fell; it seemed to him as if someone had tripped him up. He was so terrified that he trembled, but he said in a loud voice, so that the dead might understand how benevolent he was:

"I should not be walking here if there was any harm in my errand."

"You may well say that!" said his wife. "You are quite right. But, do you see, there is the grave over there."

He could just see the gravestone standing on end, outlined against the dark sky. They soon reached the grave, and found it still open. The opening into the vault had not been walled up.

"I think this is dreadfully careless," said the man. "I believe it is only done to expose all the people, who know how great a treasure lies hidden here, to the greatest temptation."

"They rely on the idea that no one will dare to rob the dead," said his wife.

"It wouldn't be very pleasant, either, to go into that vault," said the man. "Getting down wouldn't be so difficult, but once in, one would stop there like a fox in a trap."

"I noticed, this afternoon, that there was a little ladder into the vault," said the woman, "but it has probably been taken away."

"I must just look and see," said the man, groping his way toward the opening. "Now, would you believe it!" he burst out, "this beats everything! The ladder is still here."

"That is very careless," chimed in his wife, "but, after all, he who dwells down there can very well protect his own property. It doesn't matter."

"If only I could be sure of that," said her husband. "Perhaps I ought at least to move the ladder away."

"I don't think we ought to move anything here. It is better that the grave should be found, to-morrow, exactly as they left it."

They stood irresolute and at a loss what to do, staring down into the vault. They ought, indeed, to have gone home now, but something mysterious, which neither of them dared to allude to, kept them rooted to the spot.

"I should let the ladder remain," said Bard, "if I were only certain that the General has the power to keep off thieves."

"You had better go down into the vault, and then you can see what power he has," said his wife.

It seemed as though Bard had been waiting for this order from his wife, for immediately he climbed down the ladder into the vault. But scarcely had he reached the floor of the death chamber when he heard a step on the ladder, and his wife stood beside him.

"So you have come down too," he said.

"I dared not let you be here alone with the dead."

"Oh, I don't believe he is so dangerous, after all," said the man. "There is no cold hand that will squeeze the life out of me."

"You see, he won't do anything to us, because he knows that we don't intend to steal the ring. But, suppose, just for fun, we were to begin to unscrew the coffin lid!"

Immediately the man approached the General's coffin, and began fumbling along the lid. He came upon a screw which had a little cross on the top.

"Everything here seems to have been prepared for a thief," said he, and began carefully and dexterously to unscrew the lid.

"Do you feel anything?" asked the wife. "Don't you feel something moving under the lid?"

"He lies as still as the grave," answered the man.

"He knows, of course, that we don't intend to remove the thing he values most," said the woman. "It would be quite a different thing if we took off the lid."

"Well, you'd better help me to do it," said the husband.

They raised the lid, and then it was impossible to restrain their longing for the treasure. They took the ring off the withered finger, replaced the lid on the coffin, and stole out of the vault in dead silence. They held each other by the hand while crossing the churchyard, and it was not until they had reclimbed the stone wall and reached the road that they dared to speak a word.

"Now I begin to think," said the woman, "that he has willed this. He understands that it isn't right of a dead man to keep such a firm death grip on a thing, and he has given it to us of his own free will."

Her husband laughed loudly. "I like that!" he said. "You will never make me believe that he let us take it willingly; we took it because he hadn't power to prevent us."

"Do you know," said his wife, "you have been very brave to-night. There aren't many people who would have ventured into the General's grave."

"I don't think I could have done it, if I were doing anything wrong, for I have never taken so much as a rix-dollar from a living man. But what harm can there be in taking something from a dead man that he does not want?"

They felt proud and happy as they walked along. They wondered why more people had not had the same thought as theirs. Bard said he intended to go to Norway and sell the ring as soon as he could see an opportunity. They believed that they would get enough money for it to keep them from want for the rest of their lives.

Suddenly the woman stood still. "What is that light I see over there, away to the east? Is the day beginning to dawn already?"

"No, it can't be the sun rising already," said the peasant. "It must be a fire—it seems to be in the direction of Olsby. Can it possibly be——"

He broke off, on hearing a wild shriek from his wife.

"It is our cottage burning," she screamed. "It is Mellomstuga burning—the General has set fire to it. . . ."

On Monday morning the sexton went hurrying to Hedeby, which lay not far from the church, to announce that when the mason and he had gone to the grave to wall up the vault, they both noticed that the coffin lid was crooked and that the stars and shields, with which it was ornamented, had been stolen.

An investigation was immediately set on foot. There was evidence of great disorder in the grave, and they found that the screws in the lid of the coffin were loose. As soon as the lid was lifted, they saw, at one glance, that the General's ring was no longer in its place on his forefinger!

III

I often think about King Charles the Twelfth and try to understand why people so loved and feared him.

I have heard that, one day toward the close of his life, he went to Karlstad church while the service was going on. He had ridden, alone and unexpectedly, into the town and, hearing that service was proceeding, he left his horse outside the gate and entered the church through the porch, in the same way as anybody else.

As soon as he got inside the door, he saw that the clergyman was in the pulpit, and, in order not to disturb anyone, he stood still and, without trying to find a seat, remained leaning against the doorpost, listening to the sermon.

But although he had entered so quietly, and although he stood in the dark, under the gallery, there was one in the last pew who recognized the King. It was probably some old soldier; he had lost an arm or a leg during the campaign, and had been sent home before the battle of Poltava, and he knew that the man with the upcombed hair and hooked nose could be no other than the King. On recognizing him, the man immediately stood up.

His neighbours in the pew wondered what he was doing, so he whispered to them that the King was in church. And positively every man in the pew immediately stood and remained standing, as is the custom when God's Word is read from the altar or the pulpit. The news spread swiftly from seat to seat, till, finally, every person present—young and old, rich and poor, strong and weak—was standing.

As already said, this happened during the latter years of Charles's life, when trouble and opposition had begun; there was, in that church, probably hardly a man who had not been bereft of his kinsmen, or lost his possessions, in the King's cause. Even if they had nothing personal to lament, there was much food for reflection over the country, which lay impoverished, over the provinces lost, and the many enemies encompassing the land.

But, always and everywhere, it was the same, and now it was enough for the whisper to go round that this man, whom they had so often cursed, stood among them in God's House, to make every person present to rise to his feet. And so they continued to stand. There was not a man among them that would have thought of sitting. They could not. There stood the King near the door, and so long as he stood, so long would they all stand. To sit would have been to dishonour the King.

It would probably be a long sermon, but they must be patient. They must not fail the man standing there at the door.

He was a soldier-king, and was accustomed to see his soldiers go willingly to death for him. But here, in the church, he was surrounded by simple peasants and artizans, by ordinary Swedish men and women, who had never aspired to sacrifice. Yet, he had but to show himself, and they were immediately under his dominion. They would go anywhere, do anything, for him, for they believed in him and worshipped him. In the whole church, there was not a person who did not that day thank God for the marvellous man who was Sweden's King.

I have tried, as I have said, to understand how this love for King Charles could fill a man's whole soul, how it could fix itself so firmly in the heart of an old, harsh, rugged man that people all expected to find it there even after death. . . .

Indeed, the thing that most astonished the people of Bro, when it was discovered that the ring had been stolen, was that anyone had had the courage to carry out the project. It was known that loving women had had their betrothal rings stolen from their coffins, and the robber had escaped scot free; a mother had been buried with a lock of her child's hair clasped in her hands; this, too, had been fearlessly reft from her. Again, a pastor had lain in his grave with a Bible for his pillow; this could have been stolen without harm to the criminal. But to steal Charles the Twelfth's ring from the finger of the dead General at Hedeby, was a crime that they could not believe any man born of woman would dare to commit.

A thorough search was carried out, but not the faintest clue could be found by which to identify the thief. He had come and gone during the dark night, without leaving any trace which could help the seekers.

Here, again, people were surprised, for they had often heard of ghosts walking night after night in order to point out the doers of far lighter crimes. No one was the least astonished, therefore, when, at last, it was found that the General had by no means left his ring to its fate, but had fought to reclaim it with the same bitter mercilessness that he would have shown had the ring been stolen from him during his lifetime.

Nor did they show any doubt about the fact, for it was exactly what they had expected.

IV

Many years had passed since the disappearance of the General's ring when it happened, one beautiful morning, that the rector of Bro was called to see a poor peasant, Bard Bardsson, who lived in the Olsby district. He was dying, and it was necessary that he should speak to the rector himself before he died.

The rector was an old man, and when he heard that it was a question of visiting a sick parishioner, living miles away in the trackless forest, it occurred to him that his curate might very well go in his stead. The message, however, had been brought by the dying man's young daughter, who, on hearing this decision, answered firmly that the rector himself must come and no one else. Father had told her to say that he wanted to tell the rector something that no one else in the world must hear.

The rector tried to throw his memory back into the past. Bard Bardsson had been a quiet man—certainly he had been rather foolish, but that was not a thing to cause a man uneasiness on his deathbed. Judged from a purely human standpoint, the rector thought he might have been one to find favour with God. During the last seven years, the man had met with every kind of misfortune. His farmhouse had been burned down; his cattle had died of disease or had been carried off by wild animals; his fields had been ruined by frost, so that he was now as poor as Job. Finally, his wife had been so distracted by all these troubles that she had drowned herself in a lake, and then Bard had gone to live at a small outlying farm, the only thing left to him now. Since that time, neither he nor his two children had ever been to church, and they had often wondered, at the Rectory, what had become of the family.

"If I judge rightly about your father, I don't think he can have done anything that he cannot confess to the curate," said the rector, looking with a friendly smile at Bardsson's daughter.

She was a girl of fourteen, tall and strong for her age. She had a broad face with rather coarse features, a somewhat foolish expression, like her father; but childish innocence and candour brightened up her face.

"Perhaps you are afraid of Strong Bengt, sir, and that is why you don't want to come to us," she said.

"What do you say, child?" returned the rector. "Who is this Strong Bengt you are talking about?"

"Oh, sir, he is the person who has made everything go wrong with us."

"Well, well," said the rector, "so there is a person called Strong Bengt, is there?"

"Don't you know it was he who burned down Mellomstuga?"

"No, I never heard that before," said the rector; at the same time getting up from his chair, he began to take out a prayer book and a little wooden chalice, which he always carried with him on his sick calls.

"He haunted my mother into the lake," continued the girl.

"Ah, that was very dreadful, poor child," said the rector. "Is this Strong Bengt still alive? Have you ever seen him?"

"No, sir, I have never seen him," said the child, "but he is still alive. It was because of him that we had to go and live in the forest on the wild fell. We have had peace from him since we went there until last week, and then Father cut his foot."

"Do you think that was Strong Bengt's fault?" asked the rector in his gentle voice, at the same time opening the door and calling his servant. He told the man to saddle his horse.

"Father says that Strong Bengt bewitched the ax, or he would never have cut himself. It wasn't a bad wound at first, but to-day Father says that mortification has set up in his foot. He says he's got to die because Strong Bengt has done for him, so he sent me to the Rectory to beg you to come yourself, sir, as quickly as you can."

"I will come," said the rector. While the girl was speaking, he had put on his hat and riding cloak. He went on:

"I can't think why this Strong Bengt should be so horrid to your father. Bard must have done something to him."

"Father doesn't deny that," said the child. "But he will never tell either me or my brother what it is. I think that is what he wants to tell you now."

"If that is the case, we cannot get there soon enough." He drew on his riding gloves and, mounting his horse, took the child on the saddle in front of him.

The rector scarcely uttered a word during the long ride to the farm. He sat pondering on the extraordinary things the girl had told him. He remembered having just met a man whom people called Strong Bengt; but it was possible that she was alluding to someone quite different.

A young man came out to meet him, as he rode into the yard; it was Ingilbert, Bard Bardsson's son. He was some years older than his sister, well grown, too, and somewhat resembling her in features, but he had deep-set eyes and lacked her candid, good-natured expression.

"You have had a long ride, sir," he said as he helped him off his horse.

"Yes," answered the old man, "but we came along faster than I expected."

"I ought to have come and fetched you," said Ingilbert, "but I was out all night fishing, and only heard when I came home just now that Father's foot was bad and that he had sent for you."

"Martha has been as good as a boy," said the rector, "and we got along famously. But how is Bard now?"

"He is very bad, but he is prepared. He was glad when I told him that you had appeared at the edge of the clearing."

The rector went straight in to Bard, and the brother and sister sat on a broad stone slab outside the cottage, to wait. They felt in a solemn mood, and talked about their dying father. They said how good he had always been to them; but he had never been happy since the fire at Mellomstuga, so perhaps it was better that he was going. Suddenly, the girl exclaimed that she was sure Father must have had something weighing on his conscience.

"He!" said her brother. "What could he have? I have never seen him lift his hand to a man or an animal."

"But there is something he wants to talk to the rector about—only to him."

"Did he tell you that? Did he say he wanted to speak to him before he died? I thought he only wanted him to give him Holy Communion."

"When he sent me off, this morning, he said I was to beg the rector himself to come, as he was the only man in the world to whom he could confess his heavy sin."

Ingilbert sat thinking for a moment. "How curious," he said. "I wonder if it is something he has imagined all the time he has been here alone. All that he has told us about Strong Bengt—I don't believe it is anything but imagination either."

"It is just about Strong Bengt that he wants to talk to the rector," said the girl.

"You can bet the whole thing is only a lie," said Ingilbert.

He got up and went to a small shutter, that stood open to let a little light and air into the windowless cottage. The sick man's bed stood so near the opening that Ingilbert could hear every word his father said; and the son stood and listened without the slightest twinge of conscience. Perhaps he had never even heard how very wrong it was to listen to a confession. Anyway, he did not believe that his father could have any very dangerous secret to confess.

After he had stood near the opening for a time, he returned to his sister.

"What did I tell you?" he began. "There is Father telling the rector that he and Mother stole the ring from old General Löwensköld."

"God be merciful to us!" cried his sister. "Do let us tell the rector that it is all a lie, that he has imagined it all."

"We can't do anything now," said Ingilbert. "Father must say what he likes, and we will tell the rector afterward."

He stole back to the opening to listen; but it was not long before he returned to his sister.

"He says now that the same night they had been to the grave, Mellomstuga was burned down. He says he believes it was the General himself who burned the house."

"You can hear it is all an invention," said his sister. "He has told us a hundred times that it was Strong Bengt who set fire to Mellomstuga."

Ingilbert was back at his post under the shutter before she had finished speaking. He stood a long time listening, and when he came back to his sister his face was ashen.

"He says it was the General who sent all his misfortunes to force him to put the ring back. He says that Mother was frightened and wanted him to go with her to the Captain at Hedeby and give him back the ring; Father wanted to obey her, but dared not go, because he thought they would both be hanged if they acknowledged that they had stolen from the dead. But Mother could bear no more, so she went and drowned herself."

It was the sister's turn to grow ashen white.

"But," she began, "Father always said it was—"

"Yes, yes, I know. He had just been explaining that he never dared to tell anyone who had brought all these misfortunes on him. Only to us, children who didn't understand, he had said it was Strong Bengt who pursued him. He says the country people always called the General Strong Bengt."

Martha crouched down where she sat on the stone slab.

"It must be true after all," she whispered, so low that it might have been her dying sigh. She gazed around in every direction. The farm stood near the edge of a forest tarn, and the tree-clad mountain ridges rose darkly on every side. There was no human dwelling within sight—there was not a soul to whom she could turn for help. Nothing reigned there but a great helpless solitude. And she thought she could see the dead man lying in wait under the gloomy trees, ready to send more misfortune.

She was still too much of a child to realize fully the shame and dishonour brought on her by her parents; but, as far as she could understand, it was a ghost, an implacable, all-powerful creature from the other world, who haunted them. She expected that she might see him at any moment, and her terror was so great that her teeth chattered. She thought how her father had lived for seven years with this same terror in his soul. She knew that seven years had passed since the fire at Mellomstuga, and all that time her father had known that he was being pursued by a dead man. Surely it was best that he should die.

Ingilbert had been listening again at the shutter, and when he returned to her, she said, making a last effort to escape from her terror:

"You don't believe it, Ingilbert, do you?" But as she looked at him, she saw that his hands shook and his eyes were wide with fear. He was as frightened as she was.

"What can I think?" whispered Ingilbert. "Father says that he tried several times to go to Norway to sell the ring, but he could never succeed. Once he fell ill, another time his horse fell and broke his leg, just as he was riding out of the gate."

"What did the rector say?" asked the girl.

"He asked why he had kept the ring all that time when he knew how dangerous it was to have it in his possession. Father said he thought the Captain would have had him hanged if he had acknowledged his crime. He had no choice but to keep it. But now that he is dying, he wants to give the ring to the rector, so that he may put it back in the General's grave, and then we children will be freed from the curse and will be able to go back to the village."

"I am glad the rector is here," said his sister, "I don't know what I shall do when he goes away. I am so frightened I believe I can see the General standing there under the pine tree. Think! he has been here every day, watching us. Perhaps Father has even seen him!"

"I am sure Father has seen him," said Ingilbert.

He went off to listen again, and when he came back he had a different expression in his eyes.

"I have seen the ring," he said. "Father has given it to the rector; it shone like a flame of fire. All red and yellow! It sparkled! The rector looked hard at it and said he recognized it as the General's ring. Go to the opening yourself—you will see it."

"I would rather hold a snake in my hand than look at that ring!" said Martha. "You surely can't think it is beautiful to look at?"

Ingilbert looked away from her. "I know very well that it has ruined us, but all the same I admire it."

Just as he pronounced these words, the rector's voice reached them; they could hear him speaking loud and clear. Hitherto, he had allowed the sick man to speak, but now it was his turn. Evidently, he did not hold with all the wild talk about the dead man's hauntings. He tried to point out to the peasant that the judgment of God had struck him for committing so gruesome a crime as to rob the dead. He absolutely refused to admit that the General had power to burn houses or to send sickness either on men or on cattle. No, the misfortunes which had ruined Bard were God's method of forcing him to repent, and to restore the ring while he was still alive, so that his sin might be forgiven, for only so could he die a blessed death.

Old Bard Bardsson lay still and listened to the rector without any apparent objection. But it did not seem to make any impression on him. He had lived through too many awful hours for him to believe that they came from God. But the two young people sitting outside and shivering with terror began to take heart.

"You hear! You hear!" said Ingilbert. "The rector says it wasn't the General."

"Yes, I hear," said his sister. She sat with her hands clasped together, drinking in every word, deep down in her soul, that the rector was saying.

Ingilbert got up. He drew a deep breath, and stretched himself up. He was free from all his terror. He looked like a new man. He walked forward quickly, opened the door of the cottage, and went in.

"What do you want?" asked the clergyman.

"I want to say a few words to Father."

"Go away! It is for me to speak to your father now!" the rector spoke sternly.

He turned again to Bard, speaking now severely, now gently and reassuringly. Ingilbert returned to his seat on the stone slab outside; but a great unrest had now seized him. He buried his face in his hands, and sat for a little, but again he returned to his father's room, and again he was sent away.

* * *

When all was over, Ingilbert was to return with the rector, to show him a way through the forest. For a time all went well, and then they came to a place in the wood where the bog was spanned by a narrow log bridge. The rector could not recollect passing over this bridge on his former journey, and he began to wonder whether Ingilbert was leading him astray. On asking him, however, Ingilbert assured him that, if they could once cross the bog, it would be a considerable short cut.

The rector cast a sharp glance at the young man. He had an impression that Ingilbert, like his father, was possessed by a love of money. He remembered how he had come to his father's room, more than once, to prevent him from parting with the ring.

"This is a very narrow, dangerous road, Ingilbert," he said. "I am afraid that the horse may fall on these slippery logs."

"I will lead the horse, sir, so that you need not be afraid." So saying, Ingilbert seized the horse by the reins.

When they reached the middle of the little bridge and were surrounded on all sides by the bog, he began to force the horse backward. It seemed as though he wanted to push it off the log bridge.

The horse reared, and the rector, who could with difficulty remain in the saddle, shouted to him, for God's sake, to let go the reins.

But Ingilbert appeared not to hear. The rector could see him, with angry face and tight-clenched teeth, struggling to force the horse over into the bog. Certain death awaited both the man and the animal, if he should succeed.

Then the rector thrust his hand into his pocket and, drawing out a little goatskin bag, he hurled it in Ingilbert's face. The latter let go the reins in order to catch the bag, and the horse, being free, galloped madly along the path.

Ingilbert remained standing where he was and made no effort to overtake them.

V

It is not to be wondered at that, after so violent a ride, the rector should feel a little giddy and light in the head; and evening had fallen before he reached the village. Neither is it to be wondered at that he did not leave the forest by the Olsby road, but went a long way round to the south and came out quite close to Hedeby.

While trying to find his way through the forest, he made up his mind that as soon as he reached home he would send a message to Carelius, the sheriff, begging him to go at once and get the ring from Ingilbert. But when he found that he was riding so near to Hedeby, he reasoned with himself whether it would not be advisable to go up to the house, see the Captain himself, and tell him who had stolen the ring from the vault.

One can hardly think that the rector need have hesitated long over so natural a course; but the fact was that no very good feeling had existed between the Captain and his father. The Captain was a man of peace; his father had certainly been a man of strife. As soon as peace had been concluded with Russia, the Captain had left the army and had used all the energies he possessed to further the well-being of his country, which had been brought to the verge of ruin during the long years of war. He was opposed to all despotism and cared little for military honours; indeed, he had even been heard to speak ill of Charles himself, and of many others whom the old man had esteemed highly. What was even worse, the Captain had taken a lively share in the parliamentary discussions on the war, but always as an adherent of the Peace Party. It may thus be seen that there was no lack of subjects for dispute between father and son.

When the General's ring had disappeared, seven years previously, the rector, together with many others, had remarked that the Captain did not greatly trouble himself to recover it. As this fact recurred to his mind now, he said to himself: "It is no good troubling to dismount at Hedeby. The Captain won't care whether Ingilbert or his father wears the ring. I had much better go straight back and let Carelius know at once about the theft."

Just as the rector had reached this conclusion, he saw that the gate leading to the Hedeby estate, swung slowly back on its hinges and remained standing open.

It struck him as curious, yet he reflected that gates often swung open if not properly fastened, and so thought no more about it. Nevertheless, he took it as a sign that he should go up to Hedeby and see the Captain.

The Captain received him more warmly than was his wont.

"It is friendly of you to come in," he said. "I wanted to see you; indeed, I decided to go to the Rectory, to-day, and speak to you about a very strange occurrence."

"You would have had your journey for nothing, Captain Löwensköld," said the rector. "I had to go, early in the forenoon, to a sick call in the Olsby district. I am only now on my way home. It has been a most exciting day for me, old friend."

"I can say the same, although I have hardly been out of my chair. I can assure you, rector, that though I am getting on for fifty and have had my fair share of adventures during the years of war, I have met with nothing so strange as my adventure of to-day."

"That being so," said the parson, "you shall begin. But I, too, have a most strange story to tell you—indeed, I think one of the strangest I have ever come across."

"Well, in that case, perhaps you won't find my story so wonderful. But I will begin by asking you one thing. Have you ever heard of Gatenhielm?"

"You mean that gruesome pirate, that senseless privateer, who was created an admiral by King Charles the Twelfth? Who hasn't heard of him?"

"While we were at dinner to-day," continued the Captain, "the conversation turned on the old war days. My sons and their tutor asked me to tell them something about the war—young people always like to hear these things. I daresay you have noticed that they prefer to hear all about those fatal wars rather than to know something of the hard, troublous years through which we Swedes had to struggle after Charles's death, or of what we suffered through bankruptcy and loss. My God! do they think it was an easy task to rebuild burned towns, to restart manufactories and workshops, to cut down forests and reclaim the lands? I believe that my sons are ashamed of me and my contemporaries because we tried to put an end to military expeditions and to the devastation of foreign countries. They seem to think that we are worse men than our fathers, and that the Swedish strength has gone out of us."

"You are perfectly right, my friend," said the rector. "These young people's love of warlike things is greatly to be deplored."

"Anyhow, I satisfied their wishes," said the Captain, "and, as they wanted to hear about a great warrior, I told them about Gatenhielm and his cruel treatment of merchants and peaceful travellers, hoping to rouse their horror and disgust. When I had succeeded in doing so, I bade them remember that this Gatenhielm was a true son of the warlike days in which he lived, and I asked them whether they would like to see the world peopled by such infernal monsters.

"But before my sons had time to answer, their tutor took up the parable, and asked my permission to tell yet another story about Gatenhielm. As he assured me that the adventure he was about to relate would only confirm what I had said about Gatenhielm's wildness and cruelty, I allowed him to proceed.

"He then began by telling us that, when Gatenhielm was dead and his body laid in Onsala church, in a marble sarcophagus that he had stolen from the Danish king, there were so many ghostly happenings in the church that the parishioners of Onsala could not endure them. They decided, therefore, that there was no other course but to lift the corpse out of the tomb and inter it on a bare rock, far out to sea.

"After that was done, peace reigned in the church; but the fishermen, whose duty took them past Gatenhielm's new resting place, described how they heard noises of all kinds and saw the foam dashing high over the unlucky rock. The fishermen believed that all the sailors and traders whom Gatenhielm had thrown overboard from the captured vessels, were now rising from their watery graves, to torment and ill-treat him; they were, therefore, very careful not to go too near the rock.

"One night, however, one of the fishermen, who had sailed rather near, found himself swept into a whirlpool; the foam lashed his face, and a voice roared at him: 'Go to Gata in Onsala, and tell my wife to send me seven hazel sticks and two cudgels!'"

So far, the rector had listened patiently and silently to the Captain;

but when he perceived that his friend had nothing better than an ordinary ghost story to relate, he could scarcely restrain a movement of impatience. The Captain, however, paid no attention to him but continued his tale.

"You can understand that there was nothing for it but to obey the command. Gatenhielm's wife also obeyed. The toughest hazel sticks and thickest cudgels were prepared, and a servant from Onsala rowed out to the rock with them."

At this point the rector made so marked an effort to interrupt him that the Captain noticed his impatience.

"I know what you are thinking, rector," he said. "Indeed, I thought the same myself when I listened to the story at dinner, but I must beg you to hear me to the end. I must say, I think that servant from Onsala must have had a stout heart and great devotion to his master, otherwise he would never have dared to carry out such an order. As he approached the burying place, the waves dashed over it as in a raging storm, and there was noise and uproar all around. But the man rowed as near as he could, and succeeded in throwing the sticks and cudgels on to the rock. Thereupon he hurried off, rowing with swift strokes to get away from the dreadful place."

"My dear Captain," began the rector, but the Captain was firm.

"He did not row very far, however, before he rested on his oars and watched to see whether anything extraordinary would happen. He had not long to wait. Suddenly the waves dashed sky-high over the rock; the noise was as the roar of guns on the battlefield; gruesome cries of distress went out across the sea. The uproar continued for a time, but with diminishing vigour, and eventually the waves ceased to rage over Gatenhielm's grave, and left the rock lying calm and peaceful like any other.

"The servant plied his oars again on his homeward journey, when suddenly he heard a loud, triumphant voice calling out: 'Go to Gata in Onsala and tell my wife that Lasse Gatenhielm triumphs over his enemies, both in life and in death!' "

The rector had been listening with bowed head, but now that the story was finished, he looked up inquiringly at the Captain.

"As the tutor said the last words," said the Captain, "I could see that my sons sympathized with that scoundrel, Gatenhielm, and enjoyed hearing about his arrogance. I recognized that the story was well constructed, but it could be nothing but a lie. I said to myself: 'If a rough pirate like Gatenhielm possessed power to assert himself, even after death, how can I explain the fact that my father, who was as great a swashbuckler as Gatenhielm but also a good and honourable man, should have let himself be robbed of his dearest possession, without doing anything to hinder the theft, or to molest the guilty person in any way since?' "

On hearing these words, the rector looked up with unwonted animation. "That is exactly my idea," he said.

"Yes, but listen to what happened next," said the Captain. "I had scarcely said these words when I heard a deep sigh just behind my chair. It was so like the tired sigh my poor old father used to give when he was suffering from the infirmities of his old age that I thought he was really there, and I got up from my chair. Of course, I saw nothing, but I was so certain that I had heard him that, instead of going back to the dinner table, I came in here, and have been sitting alone ever since, pondering over the matter.

"I should much like to hear your opinion of this, my dear old friend; was it my father whom I heard? Was he sighing over his lost treasure? If I believed that, ever since, he has been longing for it, I should go from farm to farm myself to search for the ring, rather than he should have to bear the bitter sorrow contained in that sigh."

"This is the second time to-day that I have had to answer this question —whether the dead General is still mourning over his lost ring and wishes to recover it," said the rector. "With your permission, I will now tell you my story, and we must come to some conclusion."

Therewith the rector began his story, and he soon saw that he need have no fear that the Captain would not energetically espouse his father's cause. He had never imagined that so gentle and peaceful a soul as that of the Captain could contain so much of the old Adam. But they tell us that even the little pigs grunt when the old boar suffers. He saw the veins swelling in the Captain's forehead, and he clenched his fist so that the knuckles showed white. He was seized with furious anger.

The rector, naturally, represented the case from his own point of view. He said how God's wrath had been visited on the evildoer, and would not admit that there had been any interference from the dead man.

Captain Löwensköld, however, interpreted all that he heard in quite a different way. He understood, now, that his father had been unable to rest in his grave because the ring had been removed from his finger. He felt anguish and remorse because he had hitherto taken the matter so lightly. He felt it as a pricking, aching wound in his heart.

When the rector saw how upset he was, he was almost afraid to tell him how the ring had been taken from himself by Ingilbert; however, he accepted the fact with a sort of bitter satisfaction.

"It is well that one of the pack of thieves still remains and that he is as great a scoundrel as the rest of them. The General has punished them and has hit hard; now it is my turn."

The rector noticed a merciless harshness in the Captain's voice. He grew more and more uneasy and began to fear lest the angry man should strangle Ingilbert with his own hands, or perhaps whip him to death.

"I felt it my duty to tell you of the dead man's confession, Captain," he said, "but I hope that you will not do anything hasty. I propose now to inform the sheriff about the theft of the ring from myself."

"You may do as you like about that," said the Captain. "But I will only say that you will give yourself unnecessary trouble, for I shall take the matter into my own hands now."

After this, the rector knew that there was nothing further to do at Hedeby; he therefore rode away as fast as he could, hoping to be able to send a message to the sheriff before nightfall.

Captain Löwensköld called all his men together, told them what had happened, and asked them if they were willing to accompany him next morning, at four o'clock, to hunt for the thief. There was not a man among them who refused to do such a service for the dead General and for his son; and the remainder of the evening was spent collecting all sorts of weapons, old blunderbusses, short hunting spears, long swords, cudgels, and scythes.

VI

Next morning, when the Captain started, at four o'clock, to hunt for the thief, he was accompanied by as many as fifteen men. They were all in the best possible humour. They had a just cause and the old General at their back, for if he had managed to carry the affair so far, he would certainly carry it to a successful conclusion.

They had some miles to go before reaching the real wilderness. On starting from Hedeby, they had first to traverse a wide valley, cultivated in parts, and studded with small farms. Here and there, on the surrounding ridges, there were fairly large villages. One of these was Olsby, where Bard Bardsson had lived before the General burned down his farm.

Farther on lay the great forest, spread over the earth like a thick pelt, tree after tree, without a break. But still there were signs of human activity. There were small paths which led through the forest to summer cottages and charcoal burners' clearings.

The Captain and his men seemed to take on a new mood, a new bearing, the farther they penetrated into the wood. They were out after game, and the hunting spirit sprang up within them. They cast sharp glances toward the thickets as they began to walk carefully and lightly, almost creeping as they went.

"We must arrange about one thing, boys," said the Captain. "None of you need worry about the thief—you can leave him to me. All you have to do, is to see that he doesn't escape."

This warning was not without its significance. These men who, on the

previous day, had been peacefully occupied, spreading the hay on hurdles to dry, were now on fire with a longing to give Ingilbert, the thief, something by which he should remember them.

Meanwhile, they had reached a spot where great pine trees that had stood from all eternity grew so thickly packed that they spread above their heads, like an unbroken roof; the undergrowth had ceased, and only moss covered the ground. Suddenly, they saw three men coming toward them, carrying a stretcher made of boughs, on which lay a fourth man.

The Captain and his party hastened forward to meet them, and the bearers stopped on seeing such a crowd of people. They had laid large bracken leaves over the dead man's face so that no one could see who it was; but the men of Hedeby guessed, and a shudder ran through them.

They did not see the General beside the bier. No! Not even a glimpse of him. But, anyhow, they knew he was there! He had come from the forest with the dead man—he was pointing toward him with his finger.

The three men who bore the stretcher were well-known, respectable folk. There was Eric Ivarsson, who owned a large farm at Olsby, and his brother, Ivar Ivarsson, who had never married but remained on with his brother in the old home. They were both elderly, but the third was young. He also was known to them all. He was Paul Eliasson, and was the adopted son of the two old brothers.

The Captain went up to the Ivarssons, and they set down the stretcher in order to shake hands with him. But he appeared not to notice them, he seemed unable to take his eyes off the fern leaves which covered the face of him who lay on the bier.

"Is that Ingilbert Bardsson lying there?" he asked, in a strange, hard voice. He seemed to be speaking against his will.

"Yes," answered Eric, "but how did you know, Captain? Did you recognize him by his clothes?"

"No," said the Captain, "I did not recognize him by his clothes. I have not seen him for five years."

Both his own men and the strangers regarded the Captain curiously. There seemed to be something strange and mysterious in his manner that morning. He was unlike himself. As a rule, he was polite and friendly.

He began to question the Ivarssons. What were they doing out in the forest so early, where had they found Ingilbert? The Ivarssons were well-to-do farmers, and they resented being questioned in this manner; however, he managed to extract from them the chief facts. On the previous day, they had gone to visit some of their people on an outlying farm, some miles farther on, carrying meat and provisions with them, and had slept there overnight. Very early in the morning, they had started on their homeward journey, Ivar walking in front of the two others, for having been a soldier he had caught the trick of marching.

He was a good way on in front when he saw a man coming along the path toward him. The forest was fairly open just there, no shrubs, only bare tree-stems, so he could see the man a good way off. He had not recognized him immediately, for a thin mist hovered between the trees, looking like yellow smoke when the sunshine glinted athwart it, and this had prevented his seeing the other very clearly.

Ivar said that, as soon as the man caught sight of him through the mist, he stopped in terror, stretching out his hands toward him with a beseeching gesture. As Ivar continued to approach, he called out not to come any nearer. He seemed to be insane, and Ivar thought to try and quiet him, but the other immediately fled into the wood. He had run only a few steps when suddenly he fell forward and lay motionless. By the time Ivar got up to him he was dead, but he recognized him as Ingilbert, son of that Bard Bardsson who used formerly to live at Olsby, but had moved to a smaller place after his house was burned down and his wife had drowned herself. He could not understand why Ingilbert fell dead, for no one had touched him; and, though he had tried to shake some life into him, he could do no good. As soon as the others came up, they saw that he was dead. As Bardsson had been their neighbour, when he lived at Olsby, they could not leave Ingilbert lying there in the forest, so they had knocked together a stretcher and brought him with them.

The Captain listened with a dark frown. It sounded quite probable. There lay Ingilbert, equipped for a long journey—a knapsack on his back, thick shoes on his feet. The hunting spear lying on the stretcher was also his. Undoubtedly, he had been starting for some foreign country, where he could sell the ring, but on seeing Ivar through the mist he had thought he saw the General's ghost. Yes, that is what must have happened. Ivarsson was dressed in an old uniform and had the brim of his hat turned up in the Carolinian manner. The distance, the mist, and his evil conscience were enough to account for the mistake.

In spite, however, of this explanation, the Captain's displeasure grew; he worked himself up to a fury of bloodthirstiness. He would have liked to squeeze Ingilbert to death in his own strong arms. He craved for an outlet for his vengeance, but could find none. At the same time, he realized his own unreasonableness, and controlled himself sufficiently to explain to the Ivarssons why he and his men had come at that early hour to the forest; and added that he would like to search the dead man to see if the ring was in his possession.

His mood was such that he wished that the men would refuse to permit the search, so that he would have to fight for his rights. But they found his desire quite natural, and withdrew to one side while a couple of the Captain's own men searched the dead man's pockets, his shoes, his knapsack, even the seams in his clothing.

At first the Captain watched the examination with the greatest attention, but once he looked toward the farmers, and he thought they seemed to exchange spiteful glances with each other, as though expecting him to find nothing.

And indeed this was the case. The search had to be abandoned, for no ring could be found. The Captain's suspicions now fell on the three men, as did that of his followers. What had become of the ring? Ingilbert must certainly have had it on him when he fled. Where was it now? No one saw the General, but they left him standing in the middle of the group, pointing to the three Olsby men. They had it. It was more than probable that they had searched the dead man already and had found the ring. It was also probable that the story they had just heard was not true, and that the whole thing had happened quite differently. These men, who were from the same district as Bardsson, had probably known that he possessed the ring. They probably knew that Bardsson was dead, and on meeting his son in the forest, they understood that he intended to fly with the ring, and had therefore overpowered and killed him, in order to get possession of the treasure.

There was no wound upon him, except a contusion on his forehead. The Ivarssons had said that he struck his head against a stone as he fell; but might that contusion not also have been caused by the thick, knotted stick that Paul Eliasson was carrying in his hand?

The Captain stood staring on the ground. A great struggle was taking place in his mind. He had never heard anything but good spoken of these three men, and it went against him to think that they had robbed and murdered.

His men closed up round him. Some of them were already fingering their weapons; they never expected to leave that place without a fight.

But Eric Ivarsson stepped forward and said:

"Captain Löwensköld, my brother and I, as well as Paul Eliasson—who is our adopted son and is soon to be my son-in-law—know very well what you and your people are thinking about us. We consider that we ought not to part until you have searched our pockets and garments, also."

On hearing this offer, a ray of light stole into the blackness of the Captain's soul. He objected. Both the Ivarssons and Paul Eliasson were persons upon whom no suspicion could fall.

But the farmers wanted to put an end to the affair, and they began to take off their shoes and to turn out their pockets; so the Captain made a sign to his men to let them have their way.

No ring was to be seen; but in the wallet that Ivar Ivarsson carried on his back there was found a little goatskin bag.

"Does this bag belong to you?" asked the Captain, after searching it and finding it empty.

Now had Ivar answered "yes," the matter would have ended, but, instead, he gave utterance to the most frightful lie.

"No, it was lying on the path, not far from the place where Ingilbert fell. I picked it up and threw it into my wallet, because it looked new and unused."

"But it was in just such a bag that the ring lay when the rector threw it to Ingilbert," said the Captain; and the anger reappeared, both in his face and in his voice.

"Now there is nothing for it but you three must come with me to the sheriff, unless you prefer to hand the ring over to me voluntarily."

But the patience of the Olsby men was exhausted.

"You, Captain Löwensköld, have no right to get us arrested," said Eric Ivarsson; whereupon, seizing the very spear which lay on the bier beside Ingilbert, he proceeded to force his way through the men, accompanied by his brother and his adopted son.

In their first astonishment, the Hedeby men fell back—all except the Captain, who laughed aloud with satisfaction at the chance of letting loose his wrath. Drawing his sword, he thrust aside the spear.

But that was the only feat of arms in the battle. The Captain felt himself suddenly pulled back by his own men and the weapon snatched from his hand. It happened that Carelius, the sheriff, had seen fit to walk into the forest that morning, accompanied by a constable, and he now appeared in the centre of the path in the very nick of time.

Then began fresh searchings and questionings, with the result that Eric Ivarsson, his brother Ivar, and Paul Eliasson were all arrested and led off to prison on the charge of having robbed and murdered.

VII

It cannot be denied that in Varmland, in those olden days, our forests were vast and our fields narrow; our farms were large, but our houses were small. Our roads, too, were narrow, and our hillsides steep; the doors of our houses were not wide, but the doorposts were tall; our churches were small, but our services long! Added to this, the years of our life were few, but our difficulties were beyond reckoning. Yet, in spite of all, we folk in Varmland were neither grumblers nor commonplace individuals.

It is true that the frost spoiled our crops, and that wild beasts took our cattle, and that illness bereft us of our children—yet we had the spirit to bear up to the end. How, indeed, could we have carried on otherwise?

But one comforter was always to be found in every home, and this may have been the secret of our courage. This comforter was to be found near the poor as well as the rich, and it was one that never failed and never wearied.

But you must not imagine that it was anything solemn, or magnificent, such as the Bible, or peace of mind, or even happy love! Neither was it anything base or evil, such as drink or gambling! It was a perfectly harmless and everyday thing—in fact, it was nothing other than a fire which burned cheerily on the hearth on a winter's evening!

Dear me! how snug and homely it made the tiniest cottage; it would joke with the inhabitants for an entire evening! It crackled and hissed as if trying to laugh; it spat and fizzed as if imitating some cross or angry being. Sometimes nothing would persuade it to consume some old, gnarled log; it filled the whole room with smoke and damp, as if protesting that it had not enough to eat. Then, perhaps, it would burn away quickly and sink down into a glowing heap, just when work was in full swing, and folks must sit with folded hands in lap until it chose to burn up again.

It was most roguish, though, when the mistress of the household came with her three-legged cooking pot and tried to coax it to cook the dinner! Sometimes it would be good and docile and do its work well and quickly; but oftener it would flit round and round—anywhere except under the pot! How it gladdened the eyes of the master when he came in wet and frozen out of the snow, filling him with a sense of warmth and comfort. How pleasant to think of the watching light, streaming out into the winter's night, a guiding star to the wanderer and a warning to the prowling fox or lynx.

But there were other things the fire could do, besides give light and warmth and cook the food. It awakened a thirst for pleasure in the soul of man. For what is man's soul but a flame? It flickers in and around the body of a man as does the flame around the rough log.

Now, one winter's night, when the folk who sat round the fire had been silently gazing into the flames for a time, the fire began to speak to one and all, in their own language.

"Brother soul," it would say to one, "are you not a log, too? Why are you so sad and heavy?"

"Sister flame," would answer the human soul, "I have been chopping wood and minding the housework all day. I want nothing better than to sit still and watch you."

"I know," said the fire. "But, now it is evening, do as I do, shine and sparkle! Fun and warmth!"

And the souls obeyed the fire and began to play. They told stories, guessed riddles, they tuned the fiddles, and hung garlands on the tools and implements. Then they sang songs, played forfeits, and recalled old proverbs, thus thawing the ice out of their limbs, the peevishness out of their minds. They waked up and were merry, for the fire renewed in their hearts the wish to live out their humble and difficult lives.

One of the chief joys connected with the fire, however, was to sit round the hearth and tell stories of daring and adventure that pleased both young and old and seemed never to be exhausted, for, thank God, there have always been plenty of brave deeds to talk about.

The best-loved stories were those told about King Charles's days; he was a warrior among warriors, and there was wealth of legend about him and his men. Instead of disappearing with him into the grave, the tales lived on and were his best legacy. The most popular were, of course, those about the King himself; but next best were those about old General Löwensköld of Hedeby, whom many of them had seen and could describe from head to foot.

The General was so strong that he could bend iron as others broke chips. It was related how there dwelt a blacksmith at Smedsby in Svartsjö who made the best horseshoes in all the district. One day, the General rode to Smedsby and told Michael to shoe his horse. Soon Michael came out of the smithy with a finished shoe, and the General took it in his hand to test it. The shoe was strong and well made, but the General laughed out loud and said, "Do you call this iron?" whereupon he bent the shoe till it broke in half.

The smith grew nervous; he thought his work must be bad.

"There must have been a flaw in the iron," he said, and hurried into the smithy to get another shoe.

But the same thing happened again, only that this time the shoe was doubled up like a pair of scissors before it broke.

Then Michael grew alarmed. "You must either be King Charles himself, or else you are Strong Bengt from Hedeby."

"That wasn't such a bad guess, Michael," said the General, and then he paid the smith for shoeing his horse and for the two shoes he had broken.

Many and many were the stories told of the General, and there was not a man in the countryside who had not heard of him and who did not respect and admire him. They knew all about his ring too, and how it had been buried in his grave but had been stolen, owing to the avarice of man.

These things being so, we can understand that, if there was one thing that could excite the interest and curiosity of the people more than another, it was the news that the ring had been found and lost again; that Ingilbert Bardsson had met his death in the forest, and that the farmers at Olsby had been imprisoned on suspicion of appropriating the ring.

When the people returned from church on Sunday they hardly gave themselves time to take off their Sunday clothes and eat a mouthful of dinner, but began immediately to relate everything that had been seen and heard, and to discuss what punishment the accused would receive.

They could talk of nothing else. Every evening meetings were held around the hearth of every house, both great and small, and were attended by gentry as well as peasant.

It was a strange and dreadful case, and very difficult to get to the bottom of and to judge fairly; for it was hard, indeed almost impossible, to believe that the Ivarssons and their adopted son could have murdered a man, in order to get a ring, however valuable it might be.

To begin with, there was Eric Ivarsson. He was a rich man owning much land and several houses. If he had a fault, it was a certain arrogance and jealousy of his own honour, which made it hard to conceive that any jewel in the world could tempt him to a dishonourable action.

Even less could suspicion fall on his brother, Ivar. He was poor, it is true, but he lived with his brother and had everything he could possibly desire. He was so generous that he had given away nearly all he owned. Was it likely that such a man would steal and murder?

As for Paul Eliasson, it was well known that the brothers had the highest regard for him, and he was shortly to be married to Marit, Eric's daughter and heiress. He was the sole person of the three on whom suspicion might fall, for he was a Russian by birth; and, after all, people knew that Russians did not think it a sin to steal. Ivar had brought him back with him from Russia, where he found him in a prison. He was only three years old at that time, without father or mother, and had Ivar not rescued him, he would have starved to death there. He had been brought up honestly and uprightly, and had always been well behaved. Marit and he had grown up side by side, they had always loved each other, and it was hardly likely that a man with happiness and riches waiting for him in his future life would risk everything for the sake of a ring.

But, on the other hand, there was the General to be considered; the General, about whom they had heard so many legends, ever since their childhood; the General, whom they knew as well as their own father; he was so big and reliable—he who was dead and had been bereft of his dearest possession.

The General knew that Ingilbert Bardsson had taken the ring with him when he fled; otherwise Ingilbert would have gone on his way in peace and would not have been killed. The General must also have known that the three Olsby men had taken the ring; otherwise they would not have met the Captain in the forest or have been arrested and sent to prison.

It was very difficult to get at the truth in such a case; but the people relied on the General almost more than on King Charles himself, and therefore the self-appointed courts of justice, sitting in the cottages, pronounced judgment.

Much astonishment, however, was aroused when they learned that the district judge of the real Court, which held its sittings in Broby Town

Hall, had announced that, after the strictest examination, no proof of guilt could be found, nor could the accused be made to confess; he therefore felt himself compelled to acquit them of murder and robbery. They were not, however, set at liberty, for the decision of the District Court had to be revised by the Court of Appeal, and this latter decided that the Olsby men were guilty and would be hanged.

This sentence could not be carried out at once, since the decision of the Court of Appeal must first be ratified by the King.

But when the King's decison was pronounced and made public, the churchgoers willingly postponed their dinners in order to relate the wonderful news to their home-keeping brethren.

To put it shortly. The King had decided that it was quite evident that one of the three accused men must be guilty; but that, as none of them would confess, the Judgment of God must decide between them. Therefore, at the next sitting of the Court, the three men were to cast lots in the presence of the judge, the jury, and the whole community. He who threw the lowest number would be considered guilty, and would be hanged for his crime; the other two would immediately be set at liberty and allowed to return to their daily life.

It was a wise decision and a just one. Everyone in Varmland was satisfied with it. Was it not splendid of the old King, who, instead of thinking himself wiser than everyone else, had appealed to the All-Knowing to decide. Now at last could they be certain that the truth would come to light.

There was certainly something very unusual in this trial. It was not a case of man against man, but a dead man was a party in the case—a dead man who desired to recover his own property. In any other case, one might have hesitated to resort to dice, but not in this. The General knew perfectly well who was withholding the ring; and the best thing about the King's decision was that it would give the old dead General an opportunity to show his knowledge. It seemed almost as though King Charles wished to leave the decision to the General. He had probably known him in the old war days, and knew that he was to be relied on. Perhaps that was the idea—it was difficult to know.

In any case, everyone was determined to be present at the meeting of the Court on the day when judgment was to be pronounced. Every person not too old to walk or too young to crawl set out for the Town Hall; for it was many years since anything so wonderful as this trial had taken place. No one was content to hear the news bit by bit—no! Each one must be present in person.

The farms lay at long distances apart, in many cases, and, as a rule, one might walk for miles without meeting a soul; but when all the inhabitants of the district had gathered together in one place, it was surprising how many there were. They stood closely packed in lines outside the Courthouse. They resembled a swarm of bees clinging to a beehive on a summer's day; they resembled the bees, also, in any other way, for they were not in their usual good humour. They were not silent and reverent, as when in church, nor cheerful and talkative, as when at market; they were excited and irritable and possessed by hatred and revenge.

Can anyone wonder at it? They had imbibed a dread of malefactors with their mothers' milk; they had been rocked to sleep with cradle songs of wandering outlaws. They regarded all thieves and murderers as abominations and changelings, they no longer considered them human. They did not think it necessary to show them any pity. And now, to-day, one of these horrible creatures was to be brought to judgment, one of these bloodthirsty devils was to die, and they rejoiced at the thought; he would no longer have a chance of doing any harm!

The Ordeal, as was fitting, was to take place, not in the Courthouse, but in the open air. The crowd resented the fact that a cordon of soldiers was formed round the open space in front of the Town Hall, so that no one could get close to the prisoners; and many angry glances, you can believe, were cast at those soldiers for blocking their view. Ordinarily, such a procedure would have raised no resentment, but now everyone had grown daring and pushing.

The work people had all received permission to leave home early, so as to get good places; they had, therefore, many dreary hours to wait pressed as near to the cordon as they could get, and there was little to divert their attention. Once an official brought out a great drum and placed it in the centre of the open space; this pleased the crowd, for it showed that those inside the Courthouse proposed to start business before nightfall. Presently the official appeared again, this time carrying a table, a chair, an inkstand, and a pen, and, finally, he brought out the dice box, in which the dice rolled about. He then proceeded to throw the dice several times on to the drum, in order to test whether they were correct, whether they fell this way and that, as dice should.

This finished, he hurried back to the Courthouse again, and this was hardly to be wondered at, for each time he appeared the crowd shouted jests and sarcasms at him. They would never have behaved thus at other times, but to-day they had lost their wits.

The judge and the jurymen slipped through the cordon, having ridden, or walked, up to the Town Hall; and as soon as they appeared the crowd woke up and called out greetings and remarks in loud tones. Nothing could be done to prevent this; it was a big crowd, and in the worst of humours. The gentry present now began to slip inside the cordon; there was Löwensköld from Hedeby, the rector of Bro, the owner of the works at Ekeby, the naval Captain from Helgesäter, besides many others. These fresh arrivals were promptly informed of their good fortune in not having to stand in the crowd, fighting for places—with many more remarks of a like nature!

When there were no more left to jeer at, the crowd turned its attention to a young girl who stood pressed as close to the soldiers as possible. She was short and slight, and time after time the young men tried to force her back and take her place; but on seeing this, some of those standing near shouted that she was Marit, the daughter of Eric Ivarsson, and then she would be left in peace for a time.

Then it would begin again, but, instead of pushing her, they showered down insulting questions. She was asked which she would prefer to see hanged, her father or her betrothed. They wondered why she, the daughter of a thief, should have the best place.

People at home far away in the forest had wondered how she had had courage to stand where she was, but they knew, oh, yes, they knew very well. She was no timid girl, she had been present all through the examination of the accused and had neither spoken nor wept. She had nodded to the prisoners as if she expected them to be released the next day. Her presence had inspired them with fresh courage. They knew that there was one, at least, who believed in their innocence, who knew that no gold ring could tempt them to crime.

Beautiful, gentle, patient, she had sat the whole time in Court, disturbing nobody; indeed, she had made friends of the judge, the jury, and the sheriff. They would not absolutely assert it, but it was believed that the district judge would not have pronounced the accused innocent, had Marit not been in Court. It was impossible to believe that anyone beloved by her, could be guilty of crime.

Now here she stood, so that the prisoners might see her, might gain confidence and strength from her presence. She would pray that God's Will might be fulfilled in them, throughout the Ordeal.

It was difficult to know the truth; yet, they say that the apple never falls far from the tree, and she certainly looked good and innocent. Besides she must surely have a loving heart, to be able to remain where she now stood.

She heard all the unkind things hurled at her, but she neither wept nor answered, nor did she try to escape. She knew that the unfortunate prisoners would be glad to see her. She was the only one, in that great crowd, who had a human heart to be touched by their sorrow.

She did not, however, stand there entirely in vain. Here and there was a man who had daughters of his own, equally innocent and sweet; and each one thought to himself, he would not wish a girl of his to stand where Marit stood now. And here and there a voice would be raised to defend her, or at least to try to silence the cruel, biting remarks thrown at her.

And so, at last, when the doors of the Town Hall were thrown open, and the Ordeal was about to commence, people rejoiced, not only because the long hours of waiting were ended, but also for Marit's sake. Walking in solemn procession, came first the constable, the sheriff, and the prisoners, the latter unfettered but with a soldier on either side. Next came the sexton, the rector, the jurymen, the clerk, and the judge. Last of all followed the gentry and several farmers, whose position entitled them to a seat within the cordon.

The sheriff and the prisoners took up their position to the left of the Courthouse, the judge and jury withdrew to the right, while the gentry were placed in the centre. The clerk seated himself at the table with his roll of papers. The great drum stood entirely alone in the centre of the open space, where everyone could see it.

As soon as the procession appeared, the people began to struggle and push; several big, strong youth tried to force their way into the first row, their object being to hustle Marit. But, terrified lest she should be prevented from seeing, she ducked down and, being small and slim, managed to creep through the legs of the soldiers and get within the cordon. This was, however, contrary to all discipline, and the sheriff made a sign to the constable to remove her. The constable went up to Marit and, putting his hand on her shoulder as though to arrest her, led her in the direction of the Courthouse. But, as soon as they reached the thick crowd standing there, he let her go. He had seen enough of her to know that, if only she were allowed to stay in the vicinity of the prisoners, she would never think of trying to escape, and if, later, the sheriff wanted her, he would easily find her.

But who had time now to think of Marit? The rector and the sexton had stepped forward and taken up a position in the centre of the circle. They took off their hats, and the sexton started a hymn. As soon as the crowd heard this, they realized that something greater and more solemn than they had ever known was about to take place. An appeal was being made to the Almighty to make His Will known to them.

They grew even more serious when the rector began to speak. He prayed to Christ, the Son of God, beseeching Him who had Himself once stood at Pilate's judgment seat to watch over the accused, that they might not be wrongly judged. He prayed Him to guide the judge that he might not condemn an innocent man to death. Lastly, he prayed Him to protect the crowd, in order that they might not be witnesses to so great an injustice as had been the Jews on Golgotha.

The crowd listened with bowed heads as the rector prayed; their earthly thoughts fell away from them; their mood changed. It was as though God Himself had been called down into their very midst.

It was a lovely autumn day; the blue sky flecked with little white clouds, the trees covered with yellow leaves. The birds flew high above, starting for their winter quarters in the south; it was unusual to see such numbers as appeared that day. It surely betokened something strange. Could it be a sign from God that He approved of what was taking place?

As soon as the rector had finished, the judge stood forth and read the King's decree. It was long, with many turns of phrase that made it hard to follow. But they understood that the earthly power had laid aside its sword and sceptre, its wisdom and knowledge, for the nonce, and now desired to be guided by God. And they prayed, all and earnestly, that God would guide and help them.

Next, the sheriff took up the dice and begged the judge and several persons standing near to test them and see if they were true. The people listened, as they fell on to the parchment, with a strange shudder. Were those little objects, which had been the ruin of so many, now reckoned worthy to point out the Will of God?

When the dice had been tested, the prisoners were led forward, and the dice box handed to Eric Ivarsson, as being the eldest. The sheriff explained to him that this was not the final throw; it was only to decide which of the three should begin. The result was that Paul Eliasson threw the highest and Ivar Ivarsson the lowest. The latter, therefore, had to start.

The three accused men still wore the clothes in which they were arrested after meeting Captain Löwensköld in the forest, on their way home from their little farm, and they presented an untidy, worn appearance. Of the three, Ivar looked the least tired; having been a soldier, he was hardened by his sufferings and imprisonment during the wars. He held himself upright, and appeared courageous and unafraid.

As he stepped forward to the drum and received the dice box from the sheriff, the latter proceeded to show him what to do, but the old man replied, with a little smile:

"It isn't the first time, Mr. Sheriff, that I have thrown the dice." He spoke loudly so that the crowd could hear him. "Strong Bengt of Hedeby and I have often amused ourselves with them, on the long winter evenings away on the Steppes; but I never thought I should have to throw against him once more."

The sheriff tried to hurry him, but the people wanted to listen to him; he was a brave man to be able to joke in such a position. He placed his hands together over the dice box, and they saw that he was praying, and when he had finished the Lord's Prayer, he said in a loud voice:

"Now I pray Thee, Lord Christ, Thou Who knowest my innocence, be gracious and let me throw low, for I have neither child nor lover to weep for me." So saying, he dashed the dice down on to the drum, so that they resounded.

At that moment, there was not a man in the crowd who did not wish that Ivar Ivarsson might go free. They knew now that he was brave and upright; they wondered how they had ever supposed him to be a criminal.

It was unbearable to be so far away and unable to know what number was thrown. The judge and the sheriff bent eagerly forward, even the jury and the gentry went nearer to see the cast. There was general astonishment. Many nodded to Ivar, some shook hands with him, but great numbers knew nothing. They grumbled and growled. Then the judge made a sign to the sheriff, who mounted the steps leading to the Courthouse, so as to be better seen and heard.

"Ivar Ivarsson has thrown double sixes! The highest throw of all!"

They knew now that Ivar was acquitted. They were delighted; many shouted, "Good luck to you, Ivar Ivarsson!"

But then something happened which filled everyone with amazement. Paul Eliasson burst out in a wild hurrah, pulled off his woollen cap, and threw it into the air. It was so unexpected that his guards had not time to prevent him. Everyone wondered at him. It was true that Ivar had been like a father to him, but this was a question of his own life. Could he really be so glad that another man was acquitted?

Order was, however, quickly restored; the officials returned to their places on the right-hand side, the prisoners and their guard going, as before, to the left, the other spectators retiring toward the Courthouse, leaving the drum again exposed to view, in the centre of the ring.

It was now Eric Ivarsson's turn to undergo the Ordeal. People could scarcely recognize the broken, stumbling old man who now came forward. Could that possibly be Eric Ivarsson, he who had always been so steady and powerful? His sight was dim, and many persons thought that he seemed hardly conscious of what he was doing. But as he took the dice box into his hand he made an effort to straighten himself up and to say a few words.

"I thank God that my brother is acquitted," said he, "for though in this matter I am as innocent as he is, still he has always been the better man of us two. And now, I pray Our Lord Christ that He will give me a low throw, so that my daughter may marry the man she loves and live happily with him to her life's end."

As is the case with so many old people, all Eric's vanished strength seemed now to be concentrated in his voice. What he said could be heard by everyone, and it waked strong feeling. It was so unlike him to admit that anyone was better than himself and to wish for death in order to make another happy. No one could ever again think of him as a thief and a murderer. Tears came to the eyes of many standing around, and they prayed that God might send him a high throw. He barely shook the dice in the box, but just threw them out after moving it up and down once. His eyes were too dim for him to distinguish the black spots on the dice; indeed, he did not notice them, but stood staring out into the distance.

The judge and the others hurried forward. The same look of astonishment came over their faces as on the former occasion. The crowd seemed to understand what had happened, before the sheriff had had time to make his announcement, for a woman cried in a high voice: "God bless you, Eric Ivarsson!" and a man's voice added quickly: "God be blessed and praised for helping you, Ivarsson!"

Again Paul Eliasson's cap flew into the air, and again men wondered. Couldn't he understand what this second throw meant for himself?

Eric stood listless and indifferent; there was no light in his eyes; it seemed as though he were waiting for the sheriff to announce the result. But even after it was made known that he too, like his brother, had thrown double sixes, he remained unmoved. He made an effort to stagger back to his former place, but was so weak that the constable had to put his arm round him to support him.

Now came Paul Eliasson's turn to try his fortune at the drum, and every eye was turned toward him. They had now made up their minds that he alone could be the culprit, and his doom was a foregone conclusion, for there was no higher throw than double sixes.

They were not displeased, so far, with the result, but now they saw that Marit Ivarsson had crept close to Paul. He did not hold her in his arms, nor did any kiss or caress pass between them; she only stood close pressed to him, and he put his arm about her waist. No one knew how long they had stood thus together, for every eye had been riveted on the drum.

There, at all events, they stood now, pressed close together in an inscrutable manner, in spite of the guard, in spite of the menacing authorities and the crowd of spectators, in spite, above all, of the frightful game of life and death in which they were involved. It was love—a more than earthly love—which united them. Thus they might have stood at the garden gate on an early summer's morning, after having danced the whole night together and first agreed to take each other for man and wife. Thus might they have stood after their First Communion, with souls free from all taint of sin. And assuredly thus might they have stood when, the horror of death behind them, they had met to part no more, for all eternity.

She stood gazing at him with ineffable love, and there was something in their souls that made the people sorry for Paul. He was like a young tree that would never blossom and bear fruit; like a cornfield, to be trampled down before it had had a chance to yield its rich crop.

He took his arm gently from Marit's waist, and went with the sheriff toward the drum. There was no sign of anxiety about him as he took the dice box in his hand. He did not pray, as had the others, but turning toward Marit he said:

"Don't be afraid! God knows I am as innocent as the others are." Thereupon he shook the dice playfully and sent them spinning round the drum as they fell.

He stood eagerly watching them, as they rolled, but when, at last, they stopped there was no need to wait for the sheriff to announce the number. Paul Eliasson himself cried out in a loud voice:

"I have thrown double sixes, Marit! I have thrown double sixes, like the others!"

It never occurred to him that he would not be acquitted at once, and he could hardly stand still for joy. He jumped, he threw his cap into the air, he even seized the soldier who guarded him in his arms and kissed him!

"That shows he is a Russian," thought the people, "had he been a Swede, he would never have rejoiced so soon!"

The judge, the sheriff, the jurymen, and the gentry all went quietly and leisurely to the drum and looked at the dice. But there was no look of joy this time; they shook their heads, and no one congratulated Paul Eliasson on his throw.

For the third time the sheriff stood on the steps and announced:

"Paul Eliasson has thrown double sixes, which is the highest throw!"

Then arose a great commotion among the crowd, but no rejoicing. No one believed that there had been any fraud about the matter—that was impossible—but everyone was uneasy, for the judgment of God had not been clearly made manifest.

Were all the three prisoners equally innocent, or were they all equally guilty? Captain Löwensköld was seen to hurry excitedly toward the judge. He was trying to explain that nothing had been decided; but the judge turned brusquely away from him.

The judge and the jury retired within the Courthouse, to deliberate over the matter, and while they were absent there was not a movement in the crowd—scarcely even a whisper. Paul Eliasson stood perfectly still. He seemed to understand that the decision might be interpreted in more ways than one.

After a short deliberation, the officials returned, and the judge announced that the District Court felt bound to interpret the decision to mean that all three men should be acquitted. Once again Paul Eliasson shook himself free of his guard and cast his cap high into the air, with a great cheer. But his joy was premature, for the judge continued:

"The decision of the District Court must, however, be referred to the King by means of a courier, who will start for Stockholm to-day; the accused will, therefore, remain in custody until His Majesty's confirmation of the District Court's decision arrives."

VIII

On a fine autumn day, thirty years after the wonderful Ordeal by dice that took place in front of the Courthouse at Bro, Marit, daughter of Eric Ivarsson, sat on the steps outside the cottage, on the Big Farm at Olsby, where she lived. She was knitting a child's glove. She wanted to knit the gloves in a specially pretty pattern of diamonds and stripes, in order to please the child for whom she intended them, but she could not recall the pattern.

After sitting for a few minutes, trying patterns on the steps with the point of her knitting needle, she rose, went into the cottage, and opened a clothes chest to hunt for a good pattern. Near the bottom of the chest she came upon a woollen cap, artistically knitted in rows of various widths, and a good border; after hesitating for a few moments, she took it with her and went out again on to the steps.

While twisting it this way and that in her hand to study the pattern, Marit noticed that the moths had eaten little holes here and there in the cap. "Dear God," she said to herself, "it is hardly to be wondered at. For it is thirty years at least since it was in daily use. It is fortunate that I saw it in the chest that I may do something with it."

The cap was ornamented with a fine, big tassel made of many colours, and here the moths seemed to have enjoyed themselves most for, as Marit shook the cap, they flew out in every direction, and finally the tassel itself fell off into her lap.

She took it up to see whether there was an end of wool left by which she could sew it on to the cap again, and, as she looked, she fancied she saw something bright shining amid the strands. Hastily parting them, she found a great gold signet ring with a red stone in the centre, firmly sewn with coarse linen thread into the very middle of the tassel.

Tassel and ring fell from her hands! She had never seen the ring, but there was no need for her to stare at the royal signature on the stone, or to read the inscription on the inner side, for her to recognize it and to guess to whom it had belonged. She leaned against the railing and, shutting her eyes, sat back white and still as a dying woman. She felt her heart must break.

For the sake of that ring her father Eric, her uncle Ivar, her betrothed Paul, had yielded up their lives, and now she had found it here, sewn into Paul's woollen cap!

How had it come there? When had it come there? Had Paul known it was there? Never! she said immediately. It was impossible that he could have known it. She remembered how joyfully he had thrown this very cap into the air the day that he and the old Ivarssons had been acquitted.

It all came back to her as if it had happened yesterday! Again she saw the crowd, who had at first been so spiteful and unfriendly to her and her dearest ones, but who, later, had come to believe in their innocence. She recalled the lovely blue sky, the migrating birds flying round and round and hovering over the Courthouse. Paul had seen them too, and as she had leaned against him he had whispered that soon his soul would be flying up into the heights like a poor little lost bird. And he had asked whether he should come back to her and dwell under the eaves at Olsby.

Impossible that Paul could have known that that cap, which he threw so joyfully up into the lovely autumn sky, could contain a stolen thing.

Then there came another day. Her heart shrank within her whenever she remembered it, but now she must think of it. Message had come from Stockholm saying that God's judgment was to be interpreted to mean that the three men were equally guilty, and were, therefore, to be hanged.

She herself had been present when the sentence was carried out, so that the men whom she loved should know that there was at least one human being who believed in them, and grieved for them. But there was no longer then any need for her to have gone to the gallows. The people had all lately changed their point of view. The crowd standing outside the Courthouse even had been good to her; they had argued and debated among themselves, and they had come to the conclusion that the judgment ought to have been interpreted to mean that the three men were all innocent. The old General had allowed them each to have the highest throw—surely that could mean nothing but that none of them had taken the ring.

There had been universal lamentation when the three men were brought out. Women cried, the men stood with clenched fists and set teeth. They said that the parish of Bro would be destroyed as the city of Jerusalem had been, for putting innocent men to death. The crowd called out comforting words to the doomed men, and threatened the hangmen. Many curses were called down on Captain Löwensköld; they said that he was in Stockholm at the time, and that it was his fault that the judgment had been interpreted to the detriment of the accused.

However that may have been, it was a fact that all the people shared her belief and confidence; and that knowledge had helped her over that day—indeed, not only that day, but even up to the present time. Had the people among whom she lived considered her to be the daughter of a murderer, she could never have borne to go on living.

Paul Eliasson was the first to ascend the small platform under the gallows. He fell on his knees and prayed to God, he then turned to the priest, who stood beside him, and said something to him. Marit noticed that the priest immediately removed the woollen cap from Paul's head. When all was over he gave the cap to Marit with a message from Paul, saying that he sent it to her as a sign that she was in his thoughts during his last hour on earth.

Was it possible to believe that Paul would ever have done that had he known that the ring was hidden in the cap? Never! If there was one thing absolutely certain in this world, it was that Paul had no idea that the ring that had been on the finger of the dead man was hidden in the cap.

Marit suddenly bent down and, holding the cap close to her eyes, studied it attentively. "Where can Paul have got that from?" she thought. "He was rather fond of finery, and never liked us to weave him gray clothes; he always wanted a colour in the frieze. He liked a red cap with a big tassel. He must have been very fond of this one." . . .

She put the cap down, and leant back again against the railings, her mind going back into the past.

She remembered being in the forest the day that Ingilbert had been scared to his death. She saw how Paul, together with her father and her uncle, had stooped over the body. The two elder men had settled that Ingilbert must be carried down to the village and had gone to cut branches to make a bier. Paul had remained a moment to look at Ingilbert's cap, and had been so seized with a longing to possess it—for it was knitted in red, white, and blue wool in many patterns—that, unperceived by anyone, he had exchanged it for his own cap. He had meant no harm; probably he had intended to keep it only a little while. His own was quite as good a cap as Ingilbert's, only not composed of so many colours or so well knitted.

Ingilbert had sewed the ring into his cap before leaving his home; he probably expected to be pursued, and had thus tried to conceal it. Since his death, no one had ever thought of searching in his cap—Paul least of anyone.

She felt she could swear to it that that was what had happened, and yet one could never be entirely certain. She put the ring back in her chest and, taking the cap in her hand, she went out to the byre to speak to the milkmaid.

"Come out into the sunshine, Martha," she called into the dark cow-house, "and help me with a pattern I can't make out."

When the girl appeared, she held the cap out toward her. "I know you are good at knitting, Martha," she said. "I want to work this edge, but I can't understand it. You look at it, you are more at home with this sort of thing than I am."

The milkmaid took the cap and glanced at it. She seemed surprised, and came out of the shadow of the byre to look at it more closely.

"Where did you get this?" she asked.

"It has lain in my clothes chest for many years," said Marit. "Why do you ask?"

"Because I knitted this cap for my brother, Ingilbert, in the last summer of his life," said Martha. "I have never seen it since the morning he went away from home. How can it have come here?"

"It probably came off when he fell," said Marit. "Perhaps one of our farm hands found it in the forest and brought it here. But if it has such sad memories for you, perhaps you would rather not copy the pattern for me?"

"Leave it with me, you shall have the pattern tomorrow," said the girl.

She took the cap and went back to the cowhouse, but Marit had heard the tears in her voice.

"No! You sha'n't do it if it hurts you," she said.

"Nothing that I can do for you, Marit, ever hurts me."

It was Marit herself who had remembered Martha, Bard's daughter, sitting alone in the forest after the death of her father and her brother, and she had asked her to come and be the dairymaid at the Big Farm at Olsby. Martha had come, and had never failed to show her gratitude for being received back into the company of her fellow creatures again.

Marit returned to the steps in front of her cottage and took up her knitting, but she was too restless to work, so she leaned her head against the railings and tried to think what ought to be her next move.

If anyone on the farm at Olsby had understood the life lived by women who had left everything in the world to dwell in the cloister, he would certainly have said that Marit was one of these women. Her face was sallow and without a wrinkle. It was almost impossible for a stranger to say whether she was old or young. She had a gentle, peaceful expression, as of one who had laid aside all desires for herself. She never appeared to be very happy nor, on the other hand, to be deeply grieved about anything.

After the heavy blow she had received in her youth, she knew that life for her was ended. She had inherited the Big Farm from her father, but she knew that it was her duty to marry in order to carry on the farm and give it a master. To escape this, she had made over the whole property to one of her cousins, without any payment, on condition that she should have a cottage on the farm, and a pension for life.

She had been content and had never regretted her action. There was no chance for time to hang heavy on her hands for lack of work. Everyone relied on her wisdom and goodness; as soon as there was illness she was sent for; the children loved her—her cottage was constantly filled with young things—for they knew she always had time to adjust their little troubles.

As Marit sat wondering what she ought to do about the ring, a great wrath rose suddenly in her heart. She thought how easily it might have been found, how easily the old General might have arranged for its discovery; she understood now that he must have known where it was the whole time. Why had he not made them search Ingilbert's cap? Instead of this, he had allowed three innocent men to die on account of the ring. He had had power to allow that, but not to bring the ring out into the light of day.

At first, Marit thought she would go to the rector, tell him the whole story, and give him the ring; but finally she decided not to do so. Wherever she appeared, in church or at a party, she was always treated with respect; the contempt usually felt for the children of criminals had never attached to her. The people were firmly convinced that a great injustice had been done to her, and they wished to atone for it. The gentry in the neighbourhood also would go to meet her when they saw her leaving the church, and would exchange a few words with her. Even the family at Hedeby—not the Captain, it is true—but his wife and daughter-in-law, had made several attempts to approach Marit, but she had always evaded them. Since the trial, she had never spoken a word to anyone from Hedeby.

Was she to come forward now and confess that the Hedeby folk had been right? The ring had been found in the possession of the men of Olsby. Perhaps people would say that they had known where it was, and that they had borne imprisonment and examination in hopes of being acquitted, and of so having a chance to sell the ring.

In any case, Marit realized that it would be regarded as a justification of Captain Löwensköld—and even of his father—if she were to show the ring now and say where it had been found—and Marit was determined that she would do nothing advantageous or good for the Löwenskölds.

The Captain was now eighty years old, rich and powerful, honoured and respected. The King had made him a Baron; no misfortune had ever touched him; he had sons who also were rich and well married. And this was the man who had bereft Marit of everything—everything—everything. She lived alone, without possessions, without husband, without children, entirely through his fault. She had expected, all through the long years, that punishment would strike him, but nothing had ever happened.

Marit woke out of her deep meditation. She had heard the sound of little feet running toward her, and she knew that she was wanted. She saw two boys—one of ten, the other of eleven—approaching. One was Nils, the son of her cousin; the other, she did not know; they had probably come to ask her to help them.

"Marit," said Nils, "this is Adrian, from Hedeby; we were rolling our hoops on the road when we quarrelled and I tore Adrian's cap."

Marit looked at Adrian, a handsome boy with a gentle, friendly expression. Her heart began to beat—she always felt hurt and frightened when she saw a Löwensköld.

"We have made friends again," said Nils, "and now I want you to mend Adrian's cap for him before he goes home."

"Yes," said Marit. "I will mend it."

She took the torn cap and went into the cottage.

"This must be a sign from God," she murmured. "Play out there for a little," she called out to the boys. "It will soon be ready."

She closed the door of her cottage and sat alone inside while she mended Adrian Löwensköld's woollen cap.

IX

Several more years had passed since the ring had last been heard of. Now it happened that Miss Malvina Spaak, in the year 1788, went to Hedeby as lady-housekeeper to the Löwenskölds. She was the daughter of a poor clergyman in Södermanland who had never before set foot over the border into Varmland. She had, therefore, no idea of the customs of the house where she was going to work.

On the day of her arrival at Hedeby, Baroness Löwensköld sent for her and gave her a remarkable proof of her confidence in her.

"I think it is only fair," said the lady, "that I should tell you at once that we have reason to believe that Hedeby is haunted. It is not unusual for us to meet on the stairs, in the passages—sometimes even in the rooms—a tall, strong man, dressed in long jack boots and a blue uniform resembling that of a Carolinian. He will appear suddenly in front of you, if you come out of a room or stop on the stairs; and, before you can detain him, he disappears. He does no harm—in fact, we think he likes us—but I must beg you, Miss Spaak, not to be frightened if you meet him."

Malvina Spaak was only twenty-one, slim and neat, yet extraordinarily clever at all kinds of household and domestic matters; she was also active and industrious, so that, wherever she went, the house was run with the regularity of clockwork. But she was terrified of ghosts, and had she known beforehand that Hedeby was haunted she would never have taken the situation. But now she was here, and beggars cannot afford to be choosers! She therefore thanked the Baroness for her warning, with a little bow, and said she did not intend to let herself be frightened.

"We have no idea why he haunts us," continued the Baroness. "My daughters think he resembles my husband's grandfather, old General Löwensköld, whose picture you can see over there; they always refer to him as the old General. You can understand, however, that does not mean that the old man himself—who was really an excellent person—walks here. So, if the servants come to you with any foolish tales, I am sure you will be wise enough not to listen to them."

Again Miss Spaak bowed slightly and assured her employer that she never listened to servants' gossip about their masters and mistresses and so the audience ended.

The girl was by no means an ordinary housekeeper, for she came of gentlefolk, and, consequently, she took her meals with the family, as did also the house steward and the girls' governess. As she was a spick and span little figure with fair hair and blooming cheeks, she made a pleasing addition to the family board. Everyone found her obliging and pleasant, and useful in many ways, so she soon became very popular.

It did not take her long to discover that the ghost spoken of by the Baroness was an ordinary topic of conversation at the dinner table. Either the governess or one of the young people was sure to remark, "I saw the General to-day," as though it were something to boast of. Hardly a day passed that she was not asked whether she had seen a ghost, but she had always to reply that she had not; and her answer seemed to cause a certain misgiving. It seemed to make her inferior to the steward and the governess, who had both frequently seen the General.

Malvina Spaak had never before come in contact with so jaunty a manner of treating a ghost, and from the very first she determined to try and conquer her terror. She told herself that if it was really a being from the other world who appeared, he must be unhappy and in need of help from the living, to enable him to rest in peace in his grave. She was one of those resolute characters who felt that, had she the power, she would make serious investigation and get to the bottom of the matter; she would not allow it to become a subject of conversation at meals.

But she recognized her own position and would never allow a word of blame to pass her lips concerning the behaviour of her employers; and she herself was careful never to joke on the subject of the ghost, but kept her own forebodings to herself.

Malvina had been a whole month at Hedeby before she saw the ghost. One forenoon she had been up to the attic to count the laundry; while on the stairs, she met an unknown man, who drew aside quickly to let her pass. It was bright daylight, and she was not thinking about ghosts, so she only wondered what a strange man could be doing up near the attics, and turned to ask him his business. There was no one there. She ran upstairs quickly, went into the attic, searched every dark corner in the box room—quite prepared to take the thief by the scruff of the neck. But at last, when no human being appeared, she suddenly realized what it must have been.

"What an idiot I am!" she exclaimed. "Of course, that could be no one but the General!"

Yes, of course! The man was dressed in the very same blue coat and enormous jack boots that the General wore in his portrait. She could not quite recognize the face, for there was a gray, misty appearance over the features.

She stood for some time in the attic trying to recover herself. Her teeth chattered and her knees shook under her. Had there been no dinner to think of, she would never have got down those stairs again. She determined, however, to keep what she had seen to herself, and not to let the others joke about it.

Meanwhile, she could not get the General out of her thoughts, and she must have looked unlike her usual self, for as soon as she sat down to dinner, the son of the house, a youth of about nineteen, home from Upsala for Christmas, turned toward her.

"You have seen the General to-day, Miss Spaak," he said.

She could not deny this abrupt announcement, and immediately found herself the most important person present. Unfortunately, she could not deny, either, that she had been a little frightened, and that made them very merry! Frightened of the General! Surely nobody could possibly be frightened of him!

Malvina had often remarked that neither the Baron nor his wife ever joked about the General themselves, though they did not restrain the others from doing so. She now noticed that their son took the matter far more seriously than the others did.

"Personally," he said, "I envy all you people who see the General. I want to help him, but he never appears to me."

He spoke feelingly and in so kind a tone that Malvina prayed in her heart to God that his wish might soon be fulfilled. The young Baron would certainly be merciful to the poor ghost, and would send him to rest eternally in his grave.

During the next few days, the ghost seemed to turn his attention more particularly to Miss Spaak than to any of the others. She saw him so often as almost to become accustomed to him. He would appear on the stairs, in the passages, or in some dark corner of the kitchen.

No reason could ever be discovered for these appearances. Malvina sometimes wondered whether the General might possibly be searching for something in the house; but as he vanished the moment he met the glance of a human eye, it was impossible to gain any clear idea of his intention.

Miss Spaak noticed, in confirmation of what the Baroness told her, that the young people were firmly persuaded that it was the General who haunted Hedeby.

"He is uncomfortable in his grave," said the girls, "and it interests him to see what we are doing here at Hedeby. We mustn't deny him that little pleasure!"

Each time she met the General, the housekeeper, who was obliged to retire to the pantry to hide her chattering teeth from the raillery of the girls, wished that he would interest himself a little less in the affairs of Hedeby. But, at the same time, she realized that the whole family would frankly miss him were he to stay away.

On the long winter evenings, for instance, they would sit with their needlework; one would spin, another, perhaps, would doze. At length, both reading and conversation would stop. Then, suddenly, one of the girls would give a little shriek—she had seen a face, perhaps only two rows of glistening teeth, pressed against a windowpane. Someone would hurry out to light a lantern, the door would be opened, and all the women, the Baron at their head, would rush out to find the peacebreaker. Naturally, there would be no one. Then they would all come back again, bolt the windows, shrug their shoulders, and say it must have been the General!

But by this time everyone would be wide awake, and there was something interesting to think about; so the spinning wheel flew round with renewed vigour, and conversation began again.

It was the belief of the entire family that, as soon as they left the dining room at night, the General occupied it himself, and had anyone gone in they would have found him there. Malvina even believed that they found satisfaction in the thought that their restless ancestor was in a comfortable, warm room.

It was a peculiarity of the General that he should find the dining room tidied and arranged when he arrived. Every evening, the housekeeper noticed that the Baroness and her daughters gathered up their work and took it with them; even the spinning wheel and the embroidery frames were put into another room, not so much as an end of cotton was left on the floor.

One night Miss Spaak, who slept in a chamber near the dining room, was awakened by a loud thump on the wall near her bed, which caused her to roll out on to the floor. She had scarcely picked herself up before a fresh bang was heard, and again she rolled out. The same thing happened twice more.

"Good gracious! What is he doing in there?" she groaned, for she knew whence the noise proceeded. It was certainly not a pleasant neighbourhood. She lay the whole night sweating with terror lest the General should come in and give her a ghostly embrace.

Next morning, taking both the cook and the housemaid with her, she went into the dining room to see what had happened. Nothing was disturbed, everything was tidy, except that four apples lay in the centre of the floor. Dear, dear! They had sat eating apples in front of the fire the previous evening, and four apples had lain unperceived on the mantelshelf. But this had not pleased the General! Miss Spaak had had to pay for her carelessness with a sleepless night!

On the other hand, she had had a true proof of friendship to place to his credit.

There had been festivity at Hedeby—a big dinner party and many visitors. Malvina had been up to her eyes in work: joints on every spit, puff pastry and pies in the oven, soup kettles and saucepans on the fire and on the hearth. But this was not all. She had to see to the arrangement of the dining-room table, to receive the silver from the Baroness, who herself counted it over with her. There had been the beer and wine to be got up from the cellar, and the candles to be put into the chandeliers. When you consider that the kitchen at Hedeby was situated in a distant wing of the building, so that you had to cross the yard to reach it, and that, on these great occasions, the house was full of strange and inexperienced servants, you can understand that it needed a capable person at the head of affairs.

But all went well and as it should. No thumb marks on the tumblers, no soggy lumps in the pastry; the beer had frothed high, and the soup was flavoured to a turn, and, needless to say, the coffee was perfect. Miss Spaak had risen to the occasion, displaying her true worth, and the Baroness herself had complimented her, saying that nothing could have been better.

But there came a terrible reverse! When the moment arrived for handing the silver back to the Baroness, two spoons—one teaspoon and one tablespoon—were missing!

There was an uproar! In those days there could be no greater upset in a house than for any of the silver to be lost. There were fever and unrest at Hedeby. People did nothing but search and search; they remembered that an old beggar woman had been in the kitchen on the very day of the party, and they were prepared to go right away up to Finmark to catch her. People grew suspicious and unreasonable. The mistress mistrusted the housekeeper, the housekeeper mistrusted the servants, the servants mistrusted each other and all the rest of the world! First one and then another appeared with eyes red from weeping, because she thought that the others thought that she had taken the spoons to bed with her!

This went on for days; no spoons were found, and Miss Spaak was almost in despair. She had been to the pigsty and had hunted in the pigs' feeding trough to see if the spoons might have got there. She had crept up to the servants' clothes cupboard, and had surreptitiously searched in their little trunks, but all in vain, and she was completely at a loss where next to hunt. She could see that the Baroness, as well as the rest of the household, suspected her, for she was a stranger. She would be given notice to leave, she knew, unless she gave notice first herself.

She stood bending over the kitchen fire, weeping, so that her tears fell sizzling on to the hot iron of the grate, when she had a feeling that she must turn round. She did so, and there stood the General, by the kitchen wall, pointing to a shelf that was so high up and so inconveniently placed that nothing was ever kept on it.

As usual, the General vanished the instant she saw him, but Miss Spaak obeyed his gesture. She fetched the stepladder from the pantry, placed it under the shelf, and, stretching up her hand, took hold of a dirty old dishcloth, in the middle of which lay the two silver spoons rolled up.

How had they come there? It must certainly have been done without the knowledge or consent of anyone. During the hurry and endless work of a big party, anything might happen. The cloth had been thrown aside because it was in the way, and the spoons had gone too, without being noticed.

But now they were found, and Miss Spaak took them to the Baroness beaming with joy, and immediately became again everyone's helper and right hand.

It is an ill wind that blows nobody good. When young Baron Adrian came home in the spring, he heard how the General had shown Miss Spaak an unwonted favour, and forthwith he began to regard her in an entirely new light. As often as he could, he would go and talk to her in the dining room or out in the kitchen. He would make the excuse that he wanted a new line for his fishing rod; sometimes he said it was the delicious smell of newly baked buns that attracted him. On these occasions he always brought the conversation round to the subject of the supernatural. He led her to talk of the ghosts in the big houses in Södermanland—such as Julita and Eriksberg—and asked her what she thought of them.

But oftenest he wanted to talk about the General. He said he could not argue the matter with the others, for they only saw the amusing side of it. He himself felt only pity for the poor ghost, and wished to help him to rest. If only he could find out how it was to be done!

Miss Spaak said that, in her humble opinion, there was something in the house for which he was seeking.

The young Baron grew rather pale. He looked searchingly at the girl. "*Ma foi!* That is an idea, Miss Spaak! But I can assure you that, if we possessed anything here, in Hedeby, which he wanted, we should not hesitate a moment to give it to him."

Malvina knew that he came after her simply and solely on account of the ghost, but all the same he was a charming young man, and so handsome! Yes, but she really meant that he was something more than handsome. He carried his head slightly bent forward; he had a thoughtful expression—indeed, many people thought him too serious. But that was only because they did not know him. Sometimes he would throw back his head and laugh, and play more roguish tricks than any of them. But whatever he did, there was an indescribable charm in his gestures, his voice, his smile.

On Sunday, Malvina had been to church and was walking home by a little short cut which ran through the rectory garden. Several members of the congregation were also walking along this path, when Malvina, being in a hurry, had to pass a woman who was going very slowly. Soon afterward, she came to a high and difficult stile. With her usual thoughtful consideration for others, she remembered the woman whom she had passed walking so slowly, and determined to stop and help her over the stile. When she put out her hand to help the woman, she noticed that she was not so old as she had thought her to be from the first glance. She was extraordinarily slight and pale, but the girl did not think she could be more than fifty. Apparently only a country woman, yet she had a certain dignity about her, as if she had undergone some experience that had raised her above her station.

After helping her over the stile, Malvina and she walked side by side along the narrow path.

"You are helping with the housekeeping at Hedeby, I think," said the woman.

"Yes, I am," said the girl.

"I wonder if you get on there?"

"Why should I not get on in so good a situation?" asked the girl, with a certain reserve.

"People say the place is haunted."

"We need not believe folks' gossip," said Malvina in a tone of reproof.

"No, certainly, we should not—I know—we should not," said the other.

They went on in silence for a little. She could see the woman knew something, and, as a matter of fact, she herself was burning with a desire to question her companion, but it was not right and fitting for her to do so. It was the woman who resumed the conversation.

"I think you look good," she said, "and I will therefore give you a piece of good advice. Do not stay too long at Hedeby, for he who walks there is not good to deal with. He never goes until he has got what he wants."

When the woman began to speak, Malvina determined to thank her haughtily for her warning; but her final words aroused her curiosity.

"What does he want? Do you know what he wants?"

"Have you no idea?" asked the woman. "Then I shall say no more. Perhaps it is best that you should not know."

Thereupon, giving her hand to Malvina, she stooped and, turning into another small path, soon disappeared out of sight.

At dinner, Malvina was careful not to refer to what had happened, but when Adrian joined her in the dairy, during the afternoon, she told him what the stranger had said to her. He was very much surprised.

"It must have been Marit Ivarsson from Olsby," he said. "Do you know, that is the first friendly word she has spoken to anyone from Hedeby for the last thirty years. Once she mended my woollen cap, which was torn by one of the Olsby boys, but she looked at me then as if she would have liked to tear out my eyes."

"But does she know what the General is looking for?"

"She knows better than anyone else, Miss Spaak, and I know too. My father has often told me the story, but my parents do not want my sisters to know it, for they might be frightened then, perhaps, we should not be able to continue living in this house. I ought not to tell you the story either."

"God forbid!" said Malvina. "If the Baron has forbidden . . ."

"It hurts me not to," said Adrian, "because I believe you could help me."

"Ah! How I wish I could!"

"I repeat," said Adrian, "I want to help the poor ghost to rest. I am not afraid of him. I will follow him as soon as he calls me. Why should he show himself to everyone but me?"

X

Adrian Löwensköld was lying asleep in a gable room at the top of the house, when he was awakened by a slight noise. He opened his eyes, and, as the shutters were not fastened up and it was a light summer night, he could plainly see the door open slowly. He thought it was the draught causing the movement until he caught sight of a dark form filling up the doorway and bending down as if searching for something inside the room.

Adrian plainly discerned an elderly man dressed in an old-fashioned cavalry uniform: a buff waistcoat of elks skin showed under his partially unbuttoned coat, the boots came above his knee, and he held up his long sword, as if to prevent its rattling.

"That is certainly the General," thought the young Baron. "What a good thing! Now he shall see that I am not afraid of him!"

All the others who had seen the General maintained that he vanished as soon as they fixed their eyes on him; but this did not happen now. The General remained standing in the doorway for some time after Adrian first saw him, and, after a few moments, when he had apparently satisfied himself that Adrian could endure his scrutiny, he held up one hand and signed to him.

Adrian immediately sat up in bed. "Now or never!" thought he. "At last he wants my help, and I shall go with him."

He seemed to have been expecting this moment for years; he had prepared himself for it, had tried to fortify his courage by thinking of it. He always knew he would have to undergo some ordeal. . . .

He would not keep the General waiting, but got straight out of bed and followed him just as he was, with only a sheet wrapped round him. For a moment, as he stood in the middle of the room, it occurred to him that it might be a dangerous experiment to trust himself to a being from the other world, and he recoiled from it. But he noticed that the General now stretched out both his hands toward him, as if in despairing supplication.

"What folly is this?" he thought. "Am I frightened already, before I am even out of the room?"

He went toward the door; the General slipped out in front of him and went in the direction of the attics, walking backward, as if to make sure that the young man was following him. As Adrian was about to cross the threshold of his room to follow the ghost toward the attics, a wave of fear again passed over him. Something told him to shut the door and hurry back to his bed. He began to discover that he had miscalculated his strength. He was not one of those who could pry into the secrets of the other world without danger to himself.

Still his courage did not entirely fail him. He tried to reason with himself that the General certainly would not want to lead him into any danger. He only wanted him to show him where the ring was. If he could only hold on for a few minutes more, he would accomplish that for which he had striven so long—he would send the tired wanderer back to his eternal rest.

The General was standing outside the room, waiting for him. It was darker there, but Adrian could yet see the dark form with the hands outstretched in supplication. Controlling himself, he stepped over the threshold, and the journey began again. The Ghost turned toward the stairs, and when he saw that Adrian was following, he began to descend them. Still going backward, he seemed to stop on every step, as if to force the shrinking youth along by the power of his will.

It was a slow journey with many pauses, but continued relentlessly. Adrian tried to fortify himself with the thought of the many times he had boasted to his sisters that, whenever the General called, he would follow him. He also reminded himself how, from his very childhood, he had burned with a longing to investigate the unknown world and to get through to the other side. And now the great moment had arrived, now he was to follow a ghost out into the unknown. Was his wretched cowardice to prevent him from learning something at last?

Thus he forced himself to keep on, but he was careful not to approach too near the ghost. They walked about a couple of yards apart; when Adrian was halfway down the stairs the General had reached the bottom, and, as Adrian's foot touched the last step, the General stood in the hall.

But here Adrian stopped again. On his right, near the staircase, stood the door opening into his parents' bedroom, and he laid his fingers on the handle, not to turn it, but just to caress it lovingly. Imagine if his parents had known that he was just there, and in that company! He longed to throw himself into his mother's arms. He felt that the moment he let go the handle of the door, he would be completely in the General's power.

While he stood, still holding the handle, he saw the front door burst open and the General about to step out over the threshold.

The light had been very dim, both in Adrian's room and on the staircase; but now a bright light streamed through the open door, and, for the first time, the young Baron saw the General's features. It was the face of an old man—he recognized it at once from the portrait in the drawing room. But there was none of the peacefulness of death there—a furious greed shone in the eyes, and on the lips trembled an uncanny smile of triumph and of certainty of victory.

To see these earthly passions depicted on a dead man's face was terrifying. We like to picture our dead friends at rest, far removed and free from human lusts and sufferings. We would have them removed from earthly desires, rejoicing only in heavenly things. Adrian could see nothing in this being, fast bound by earthly passions, but a seducer—an evil spirit, dragging him to his destruction.

He was overwhelmed with terror. In unreflecting anguish, he dashed open the door of his parents' room and, stumbling over the threshold, cried out:

"Father! Mother! The General!" and fell on the floor in a dead swoon.

* * *

The pen drops from my fingers. Is it not bootless to try and write these things? This story was told me in the twilight sitting by the fire. I can still hear the compelling voice, I can feel the appropriate shiver running down my spine—that little tremor not so much of fear, as of expectation.

How breathlessly we listened to the story, for it seemed to lift a tiny corner of the veil hiding the unknown. What a strange sensation remained with us, as if a door had been opened, and now, at last, something would appear from out that great obscurity!

How much truth is there in it? Each narrator has inherited the story from his predecessor; one has added a little, another has taken away a little. But does it not contain, at least, a little germ of truth? Does it not give the impression of describing something that really happened?

Who and what was the ghost that wandered about in Hedeby, who was seen in broad daylight, who interfered in household affairs, who found lost possessions? Who was he? What was he?

Was there not something unusually clear and solid in his appearance? Can he be distinguished by any special peculiarity, from other family ghosts? Does it not seem as though Miss Spaak might really have heard him throw apples at the dining-room wall, and that the young Baron Adrian might really have followed him out of his own room and down the stairs?

Well, well! Anyhow, perhaps some of those who even here and now can see the reality that lies behind the reality in which we now live, may be able to solve the riddle.

XI

Young Baron Adrian lay in his parents' great bed, white and motionless. On laying a finger on his wrist, one could just feel the blood pulsing, but with difficulty. He had never regained consciousness after his deep swoon, but life was not extinct.

There was no doctor in the parish of Bro, but a servant had ridden at four o'clock that morning to Karlstad to fetch one. It was a very long ride, and even should the doctor be at home and willing to come so far, he could not be expected for at least twelve hours. One must even be prepared to wait a whole day or even two, if he was detained over a case.

Baroness Löwensköld sat beside the bed and never took her eyes from her son's face. She seemed to think that the faint glimmer of life could not fade so long as she sat watching and waiting.

Occasionally, the Baron sat on the other side of the bed, but he could not keep still. He would take one of the limp hands between his own and feel the pulse, then he would go to the window and look out toward the road. Again he would take a little turn to consult the dining-room clock. He shook his head in answer to the eager questions that he could read in the anxious eyes of his daughters and their governess. And then he would return to the sick room.

Except the parents, no one was allowed in that room except Malvina Spaak; neither the daughters nor the servants—only the housekeeper. She had just the right step, the gentle voice—she suited a sick room.

Adrian's scream had waked Malvina in the middle of the night. On hearing the heavy fall, she had immediately jumped up and thrown on her clothes—she could never say how—but it was one of her unfailing maxims never to leave your room undressed, for then you could be of no possible use to anyone. She had met the Baroness coming from her room to call for help, and had helped the parents to get Adrian into bed. At first they thought he was dead, but Malvina noticed a frail movement of the pulse.

They used every effort to restore him, but the little spark of life was so frail, that it seemed to grow weaker in spite of all their efforts. After a time, they lost heart, and could do no more, but only sit and wait.

The Baroness liked to have the girl in the room, for she was so calm and so convinced that Adrian would soon wake up. She allowed Malvina to arrange her hair and put on her shoes; and, though she had to move to put on her clothes, she allowed the girl to fasten the buttons, so that she need not take her eyes from her son's face.

Presently she fetched a cup of coffee, and persuaded the Baroness, with friendly solicitation, to drink a little; and though her mistress had the impression that the girl was with her the whole time, as a matter of fact, Malvina went back and forth to the kitchen to see that the meals were prepared as usual. She forgot nothing. Her face was deadly pale but she went on with her work; breakfast was on the table at the proper time, and the boys who drove the cattle to pasture found their lunch packed in their knapsacks as usual.

The maids in the kitchen wanted to know what had happened to the young Baron; she told them that all that was known was, that he had burst into his parents' room, calling out something about the General, and had then fallen into a dead faint, from which it was impossible to rouse him.

"The General must certainly have appeared to him," said the cook.

"Isn't it funny he should be so unkind to his own people?" said the housemaid.

"Oh, he has lost patience with them. They do nothing but laugh at him. He wants his ring back."

"You don't suppose the ring is here in Hedeby," said the housemaid. "He would burn the house over our heads to get it, if it was here."

"It must be here in some corner," said the cook, "or else he wouldn't be wandering all over the place as he is."

That day Miss Spaak made an exception to her good rule of never listening to servants' tales about their employers.

"What is that you are saying about a ring?" she asked.

"Don't you know, miss, that the General wanders about here looking for his signet ring?" The cook was delighted to be asked the question. She and the housemaid lost no time in telling Miss Spaak the complete history of the robbery of the ring from the grave, and all about the Ordeal of the dice; and when they had finished their tale, not a shadow of doubt remained in her mind. The ring somehow must have got to Hedeby, and was hidden in the house.

Now she was overtaken by a great trembling, such as she had experienced during her first encounter with the General on the attic stairs. She had gone in fear of him, the whole time; now she knew how cruel and merciless these ghosts could be. She saw one fact standing out clear and direct before her—unless the ring could be restored to the General, Baron Adrian would die.

Hardly had she reached this conclusion, however, before she knew precisely what she had to do, for she was a very resolute creature. If that horrible ring was really in Hedeby, it had got to be found.

She went back to the house and peeped into the sick room, where there was no change; she then ran upstairs and made Adrian's bed, so that it might be ready in case he got better and could be carried up to it. She finally went to find the governess and the girls, who were sitting about frightened and unhappy and not able to settle to anything, and told them what she had just heard from the servants about the ring. She impressed on them how important it was to find it, and begged them to help her look for it. They grew interested at once, and undertook to search inside the house—in all the rooms and in the box attics.

Malvina herself undertook the kitchen department, so she started all the women servants on the search there.

"The General appears in the kitchen as well as in the rest of the house," she thought to herself. "Something tells me the ring is about here somewhere."

They hunted everywhere. They turned out everything in the pantry, the kitchen, the bakehouse, the brewery. They searched in the cracks in the walls and in the fireplaces; they emptied all the spice boxes—they even tried the rat holes!

In spite of all her preoccupation, Malvina never omitted to run across and peep into the sick room, from time to time. On one of her visits she found the Baroness crying.

"He is worse," she said. "I think he is dying."

Malvina went up to Adrian, took his powerless hand in hers, and felt his pulse.

"Not worse, Baroness, surely a little better?"

She succeeded in reassuring the poor lady, but was very doubtful herself. Think, if he should die before she found the ring!

In her anxiety, she forgot to be as careful as usual; and in laying Adrian's hand back upon the bed, she gave it a little caress. She was scarcely aware of her own gesture, but the Baroness noticed it.

"*Mon Dieu!*" she thought. "Poor child, is that what ails her? Perhaps

I ought to tell her. . . . But if we are to lose him, it doesn't matter. The General is angry with him, and those who anger the General have got to die."

When Miss Spaak returned to the kitchen, she asked the servants whether there was anybody in the countryside who could be of use in this great trouble, or whether it was necessary to go on waiting till the doctor could come?

Yes, there was a woman called Marit Ivarsson, at Olsby, whom people always sent for when they were hurt. She could staunch the flow of blood and set bones; she might even be able to wake Baron Adrian from his death sleep—but she would certainly never come to Hedeby.

While the housemaid was telling Malvina about Marit Ivarsson, the cook had got up on to the stepladder and was feeling along the high shelf where the lost silver spoons had been found after the big dinner party.

"Ah!" she called out. "I have found something I've been looking for ever so long. Here it is! Baron Adrian's old woollen cap!"

The housekeeper was shocked! What possible kind of method could there have been in the housekeeping at Hedeby before she came? How could Baron Adrian's old cap have got there?

"It isn't so curious, after all," said the cook. "He had grown out of it, so he gave it to me to use as a dish cloth. I *am* glad I have come upon it again!"

Miss Spaak took the cap quickly out of her hand.

"It is a shame to cut it up," she said. "We can give it to some poor person."

Taking it with her, she went out into the yard, and began to beat the dust out of it. While thus employed, the Baroness came out toward her.

"We fear that Adrian is worse," she said.

"Is there no one about here who understands doctoring?" asked Malvina innocently. "The servants mentioned a woman named Marit Ivarsson."

The Baroness Löwensköld drew herself up stiffly.

"Of course, if it was a case of Adrian's life, I should not hesitate to send for my worst enemy. But it would be quite useless. Marit Ivarsson will never enter Hedeby."

Malvina dared not oppose her mistress after such a statement. She returned to her search for the ring; then she busied herself about the dinner and succeeded in persuading even the Baroness to eat something. But there was no sign of the ring, and Malvina repeated over and over again to herself: "We must find the ring. The General will let Adrian die if he doesn't get his ring back."

That afternoon she started off to Olsby. She went on her own responsibility, for the last time she had seen Adrian his pulse had grown slower and weaker, and she could no longer wait for the doctor from Karlstad. It was more than likely that this woman, Marit, would refuse, but Malvina would leave no stone unturned.

Marit was sitting in her usual place on the cottage steps when Miss Spaak arrived. She had no work in her hands, but sat leaning back with her eyes closed. She was not, however, asleep, and looked up as the other approached. She recognized her at once.

"Well?" she said. "So they have sent for me from Hedeby?"

"Have you heard of our great misfortune?" asked Malvina.

"Yes, I have heard of it," said Marit, "and I will not come."

The girl answered not a word. A great hopelessness fell upon her. Everything seemed to go against her, but this was surely the worst of all. She could see and hear that Marit was glad. She had been sitting there, on those steps, rejoicing at their misfortunes, rejoicing that Adrian Löwensköld was dying.

Hitherto, the girl had succeeded in keeping up her courage; she had neither cried out nor wept when Adrian lay helpless on the floor that night. Her one thought had been to help him and the others. But Marit's cruel opposition broke down her strength at last, and she began to weep violently and uncontrollably. Stumbling forward, she leant her forehead against the gray stone wall, and sobbed and cried.

Marit leant forward a little and sat for some time gazing at the unhappy girl. "Ah, so that is what ails her," she said.

But as Marit sat watching this young creature, weeping tears of love over her beloved, something happened in her own soul. She had heard, a few hours before, how the General had appeared to Adrian and had frightened him almost to death, and she had said that now, at last, her hour of revenge had come. She had waited for it so many years, and all in vain. Captain Löwensköld had gone down to his grave untouched by punishment. It was true that the General had haunted Hedeby ever since she had sent the ring there; but apparently he had pursued his own family with his usual cruelty.

But now that misfortune had come upon them, they immediately sent to her for help! Why did they not go rather to the dead upon the gallows?

It did her good to say, "I will not." That was her method of revenge. But when Marit saw that young girl weeping with her head pressed against the wall, a memory rose within her.

"I, too, have leant against a hard wall and have wept with no one to comfort me or support me."

Thinking thus, the full tide of her girlhood's love welled up in the woman's heart and filled her with its warmth. She sat amazed, and said to herself, "That was how I too felt then; that is what it means to love someone—so strong and sweet a feeling."

The sight of Paul Eliasson rose within her mind; she could see him as he used to look—young, bright and happy, and handsome. She could recall his look, his voice, his every gesture—her whole heart was filled with him.

She thought that she had loved him always, and so indeed she had; but now, alas, her feeling had cooled during the long years! But now, again, it rose and flooded her soul with light! Yet with her awakened love came the memory of her awful suffering, caused by the tragic death of her beloved.

Marit looked once more at Malvina Spaak, who still stood weeping by the wall; she understood now what the girl was suffering. Gradually, during the long years, her love had weakened, she had forgotten how the fire could burn. But now she remembered, and she determined she would never be the cause of suffering to another such as she herself had undergone. She rose from the steps and went to Malvina.

"Come," she said curtly, "I will go with you."

They walked back to Hedeby together. Marit uttered not a word during the journey. Malvina found, later, that she had been considering what means she should take to find the ring.

They entered the house together by the front door and went straight to the sick room. There was no change. Adrian lay there white and beautiful but still as death, and the Baroness sat motionless beside him, watching. Only when Marit came up to the bed did she look up.

The moment she recognized the figure who stood gazing at her son, she sank on her knees in front of her and laid her cheek against the woman's skirt.

"Marit! Marit!" she said. "Forget all the harm the Löwenskölds have done you! Save him, Marit, oh, save him!"

The countrywoman drew back a little, but the distracted mother crept after her on her knees.

"You don't know how terrified I have been since the General began to haunt us here again. I have been fearing and expecting something the whole time. I knew he would turn his anger against us."

Marit stood still. She shut her eyes and seemed to be pondering deeply within herself. Miss Spaak was certain that it pleased her to hear the Baroness speak of her suffering.

"I wanted to go to you, Marit, and kneel at your feet, as I am doing now, and entreat you to forgive the Löwenskölds. But I dared not, I thought it would be impossible for you to pardon us."

"It is no use your asking me, Baroness Löwensköld. I cannot forgive."

"But yet you have come here?"

"I have come for the young lady's sake, because she begged me to do so."

Marit then went round to the other side of the bed. Laying her hand on the sick man's breast, she murmured some words, at the same time knitting her brows over her half-closed eyes and pursing her lips. She reminded the girl of a fortune teller.

"He will certainly live," said Marit, "but you must remember, my lady, that I am here entirely for the girl's sake."

"Yes, Marit," answered the Baroness. "I shall never forget it."

It seemed to Miss Spaak as though her mistress had intended to add something, but she broke off suddenly, biting her lip.

"And now you must let me arrange everything."

"You must do whatever you wish, Marit. The Baron is away—I begged him to ride and meet the doctor and ask him to hasten."

Miss Spaak had expected that Marit Ivarsson would take some steps to wake the young Baron from his stupor, but to her great surprise, she did nothing of the sort. She ordered that a collection should be made of all Baron Adrian's clothes—both those in use and those set aside as worn out. She wished to see everything that had ever touched his body, socks and shirts—even his woollen gloves and caps.

The entire day was spent in searching at Hedeby. Although Malvina sighed at the thought that Marit was nothing better than an ordinary "wise woman," with the ordinary fortune teller's tricks, yet she hastened to get together everything from cupboards, drawers, chests in the attics, that had been worn by the sick man. His sisters, who remembered what Adrian had been in the habit of wearing, helped her; and soon she had collected a whole bundle, which she took to Marit.

The latter proceeded to lay them out on the kitchen table and went carefully through each article. She laid an old pair of shoes on one side, together with some little woollen gloves and a shirt, while she murmured incessantly, in a low voice, "A pair for the feet, a pair for the hands, one for the body, one for the head."

Suddenly she said, in her ordinary voice, "I must have something for the head, I must have something that is warm and soft."

The housekeeper pointed to the hats and a helmet which she had found.

"No, it must be something warm and soft," said Marit. "Hadn't Baron Adrian any woollen cap like other boys?"

The girl was on the point of saying that she had not seen one when the cook forestalled her.

"I did find his old woollen cap on the shelf up there, this morning, but Miss Spaak took it from me."

Miss Spaak was therefore obliged to produce the cap, which she had intended never to part with, but to treasure as a loved memento for the rest of her life.

As soon as Marit took the cap in her hands, she began again to murmur her incantation; but now there was a different tone in her voice—the tone of a cat purring with satisfaction.

After turning and twisting the cap and murmuring over it for a long time, she said at last: "Now, nothing more is necessary. All these things must be laid in the General's grave."

But Malvina was perfectly astounded at these words.

"How do you suppose that the Baron will ever allow the grave to be opened to receive this old rubbish?" she asked.

Marit regarded her with a little smile; then, taking her by the hand, she led her toward a window, where they could stand with their back turned toward the others in the kitchen. There, holding Adrian's cap near to Malvina's eyes, she parted the strands of the woollen tassel. Neither of the women spoke a word, but the housekeeper's face was deathly white, and her hands shook as she turned back into the room.

Marit tied the clothes into a little bundle, and gave it to Miss Spaak.

"I have done my share," she said. "Now it is for others to do theirs and to see that these things are put into the grave."

And with that she went out.

* * *

Soon after ten o'clock that same evening Malvina Spaak walked up to the churchyard. She carried Marit's little bundle in her hand; otherwise, she had only gone for a random stroll. She had not the faintest idea how she was to get the things into the General's grave.

Baron Löwensköld had come riding in accompanied by the doctor soon after Marit had left; and Miss Spaak had hoped that Adrian would be restored to consciousness without her having to do anything further in the matter. But the doctor had immediately pronounced that he could do nothing. He said that the young man had but a few hours more to live.

Then, taking the bundle under her arm, the girl had started on her walk. She knew that there was no earthly possibility of persuading Baron Löwensköld to open the grave merely to lay Adrian's old garments in it. If she could tell him what the bundle really contained, she was certain that he would immediately return the ring to its rightful owner; but then she would betray Marit Ivarsson, for she was convinced that Marit must, at some time, have conveyed the ring to Hedeby.

Adrian had told her that Marit had once mended his cap for him. No, she could not possibly let the Baron know the truth of the matter.

Later on, it occurred to Malvina to wonder why she had felt no fear that night; but she simply stepped over the low wall of the churchyard and went straight to the Löwensköld's grave, without a thought of anything but getting the ring into the vault.

She sat down on the gravestone and joined her hands together in prayer.

"If God does not help me," she thought, "the grave will be opened, not for the ring, but for one for whom I shall always grieve."

While praying, she noticed a slight movement in the grass clothing the mound on which the gravestone rested. A tiny head peeped out and disappeared the moment Malvina moved—she feared the rat as much as the rat feared her! The sight of the creature, however, gave her a swift inspiration. Running to a large lilac bush, she broke off a long dry branch. This she pushed down the rat hole. First, she tried pushing directly down, but immediately encountered an obstacle. Then she tried pushing it on the slant and succeeded in getting it in a good way toward the grave. She was surprised how far it penetrated—the whole twig disappeared—but she drew it out quickly and measured it with her arm. It was three feet long and had gone the whole length into the earth. It must have reached to the vault!

Malvina had never felt so clear-headed and collected in her whole life. She realized that the rats must have made a way into the vault—perhaps they had found a drain, or a brick might have crumbled away.

She lay down on the ground, dug up a sod, and, scattering the loose earth under it, inserted her arm. She encountered no obstacle, but did not touch the wall. Her arm was too short! She could not reach the vault!

Then, hastily untying the bundle, she took out the cap. Thrusting the branch through it, she tried slowly to push it into the hole, and soon it had disappeared. She continued to guide the branch, slowly and carefully, farther and farther in; then, suddenly, when almost the whole twig had disappeared in the ground, she felt it strongly jerked out of her hand. It fell into the hole and vanished.

It was possible that it had only fallen by its own weight, but she felt absolutely certain that it had been snatched from her.

Now, at last, she began to be frightened. Taking the contents of the bundle, she thrust them all into the hole; put back the sods and the earth as well as she could, and hurried away. She ran the whole distance back to Hedeby without stopping for a moment.

When she reached home, the Baron and Baroness were standing together on the steps. They came eagerly down to meet her.

"Where have you been?" they asked. "We have been waiting here for you."

"Is Baron Adrian dead?" she asked.

"No, he is not dead," said the Baron, "but tell us first where you have been."

Malvina was so breathless she could hardly speak; but she managed to tell them of the task put upon her by Marit, and of how she had managed to get at least one of the things into the vault by means of the rat hole.

"This is most extraordinary, Miss Spaak," said the Baron, "for Adrian is really better. He wakened up a little while ago, and his first words were: 'The General has got his ring now!' "

"His heart is beating quite normally," said the Baroness, "and he wants to speak to you. He says you are the person who has saved him."

They allowed Miss Spaak to go alone to see Adrian. As soon as he saw her, he sat up in bed and stretched out his arms toward her.

"I know it, I know it already!" he cried. "The General has got back his ring, and entirely through you!"

Malvina laughed and cried as she lay in his arms, and he kissed her on the forehead.

"I thank you for my life," he said. "Had it not been for you, I should now be a corpse. I can never be grateful enough to you."

The rapture with which Adrian greeted her had possibly caused poor Malvina to linger too long in his arms, for he hastened to add: "And not only I am grateful, but there is also another."

He showed her a locket, hanging on his breast. Miss Spaak could faintly distinguish the miniature of a young girl.

"You are the first person, besides my parents, who knows of this," he said. "When she comes to Hedeby in a few weeks' time, she will be able to thank you much better than I can."

The housekeeper, Miss Spaak, bowed to the young Baron Adrian Löwensköld and thanked him for his confidence. She longed to say that she did not intend to stay at Hedeby to meet his betrothed, but she remembered herself in time. And besides, beggars cannot be choosers!

MOWGLI'S BROTHERS

RUDYARD KIPLING

Now Chil the Kite brings home the night
  That Mang the Bat sets free—
The herds are shut in byre and hut
  For loosed till dawn are we.
This is the hour of pride and power,
  Talon and tush and claw.
Oh hear the call!—Good hunting all
  That keep the Jungle Law!

Night-Song in the Jungle.

IT was seven o'clock of a very warm evening in the Seeonee hills when Father Wolf woke up from his day's rest, scratched himself, yawned, and spread out his paws one after the other to get rid of the sleepy feeling in their tips. Mother Wolf lay with her big gray nose dropped across her four tumbling, squealing cubs, and the moon shone into the mouth of the cave where they all lived. 'Augrh!' said Father Wolf, 'it is time to hunt again'; and he was going to spring down hill when a little shadow with a bushy tail crossed the threshold and whined: 'Good luck go with you, O Chief of the Wolves; and good luck and strong white teeth go with the noble children, that they may never forget the hungry in this world.'

It was the jackal—Tabaqui, the Dish-licker—and the wolves of India despise Tabaqui because he runs about making mischief, and telling tales, and eating rags and pieces of leather from the village rubbish-heaps. But they are afraid of him too, because Tabaqui, more than any one else in the jungle, is apt to go mad, and then he forgets that he was ever afraid of any one, and runs through the forest biting everything in his way. Even the tiger runs and hides when little Tabaqui goes mad, for madness is the most disgraceful thing that can overtake a wild creature. We call it hydrophobia, but they call it *dewanee*—the madness—and run.

'Enter, then, and look,' said Father Wolf, stiffly; 'but there is no food here.'

'For a wolf, no,' said Tabaqui; 'but for so mean a person as myself a dry bone is a good feast. Who are we, the Gidur-log [the jackal people], to pick and choose?' He scuttled to the back of the cave, where he found the bone of a buck with some meat on it, and sat cracking the end merrily.

'All thanks for this good meal,' he said, licking his lips. 'How beautiful are the noble children! How large are their eyes! And so young too! Indeed, indeed, I might have remembered that the children of kings are men from the beginning.'

Now, Tabaqui knew as well as any one else that there is nothing so unlucky as to compliment children to their faces; and it pleased him to see Mother and Father Wolf look uncomfortable.

Tabaqui sat still, rejoicing in the mischief that he had made, and then he said spitefully:—

'Shere Khan, the Big One, has shifted his hunting-grounds. He will hunt among these hills for the next moon, so he has told me.'

Shere Khan was the tiger who lived near the Waingunga River, twenty miles away.

'He has no right!' Father Wolf began angrily—'By the Law of the Jungle he has no right to change his quarters without due warning. He will frighten every head of game within ten miles, and I—I have to kill for two, these days.'

'His mother did not call him Lungri [the Lame One] for nothing,' said Mother Wolf, quietly. 'He has been lame in one foot from his birth. That is why he has only killed cattle. Now the villagers of the Waingunga are angry with him, and he has come here to make *our* villagers angry. They will scour the jungle for him when he is far away, and we and our children must run when the grass is set alight. Indeed, we are very grateful to Shere Khan!'

'Shall I tell him of your gratitude?' said Tabaqui.

'Out!' snapped Father Wolf. 'Out and hunt with thy master. Thou hast done harm enough for one night.'

'I go,' said Tabaqui, quietly. 'Ye can hear Shere Khan below in the thickets. I might have saved myself the message.'

Father Wolf listened, and below in the valley that ran down to a little river, he heard the dry, angry, snarly, singsong whine of a tiger who has caught nothing and does not care if all the jungle knows it.

'The fool!' said Father Wolf. 'To begin a night's work with that noise! Does he think that our buck are like his fat Waingunga bullocks?'

'H'sh. It is neither bullock nor buck he hunts to-night,' said Mother Wolf. 'It is Man.' The whine had changed to a sort of humming purr that seemed to come from every quarter of the compass. It was the noise that

bewilders woodcutters and gipsies sleeping in the open, and makes them run sometimes into the very mouth of the tiger.

'Man!' said Father Wolf, showing all his white teeth. 'Faugh! Are there not enough beetles and frogs in the tanks that he must eat Man, and on our ground too!'

The Law of the Jungle, which never orders anything without a reason, forbids every beast to eat Man except when he is killing to show his children how to kill, and then he must hunt outside the hunting-grounds of his pack or tribe. The real reason for this is that man-killing means, sooner or later, the arrival of white men on elephants, with guns, and hundreds of brown men with gongs and rockets and torches. Then everybody in the jungle suffers. The reason the beasts give among themselves is that Man is the weakest and most defenceless of all living things, and it is unsportsmanlike to touch him. They say too—and it is true—that man-eaters become mangy, and lose their teeth.

The purr grew louder, and ended in the full-throated 'Aaarh!' of the tiger's charge.

Then there was a howl—an untigerish howl—from Shere Khan. 'He has missed,' said Mother Wolf. 'What is it?'

Father Wolf ran out a few paces and heard Shere Khan muttering and mumbling savagely, as he tumbled about in the scrub.

'The fool has had no more sense than to jump at a woodcutters' campfire, and has burned his feet,' said Father Wolf, with a grunt. 'Tabaqui is with him.'

'Something is coming up hill,' said Mother Wolf, twitching one ear. 'Get ready.'

The bushes rustled a little in the thicket, and Father Wolf dropped with his haunches under him, ready for his leap. Then, if you had been watching, you would have seen the most wonderful thing in the world—the wolf checked in mid-spring. He made his bound before he saw what it was he was jumping at, and then he tried to stop himself. The result was that he shot up straight into the air for four or five feet, landing almost where he left ground.

'Man!' he snapped. 'A man's cub. Look!'

Directly in front of him, holding on by a low branch, stood a naked brown baby who could just walk—as soft and as dimpled a little atom as ever came to a wolf's cave at night. He looked up into Father Wolf's face, and laughed.

'Is that a man's cub?' said Mother Wolf. 'I have never seen one. Bring it here.'

A wolf accustomed to moving his own cubs can, if necessary, mouth an egg without breaking it, and though Father Wolf's jaws closed right on the child's back not a tooth even scratched the skin, as he laid it down among the cubs.

'How little! How naked, and—how bold!' said Mother Wolf, softly. The baby was pushing his way between the cubs to get close to the warm hide. 'Ahai! He is taking his meal with the others. And so this is a man's cub. Now, was there ever a wolf that could boast of a man's cub among her children?'

'I have heard now and again of such a thing, but never in our Pack or in my time,' said Father Wolf. 'He is altogether without hair, and I could kill him with a touch of my foot. But see, he looks up and is not afraid.'

The moonlight was blocked out of the mouth of the cave, for Shere Khan's great square head and shoulders were thrust into the entrance. Tabaqui, behind him, was squeaking: 'My lord, my lord, it went in here!'

'Shere Khan does us great honour,' said Father Wolf, but his eyes were very angry. 'What does Shere Khan need?'

'My quarry. A man's cub went this way,' said Shere Khan. 'Its parents have run off. Give it to me.'

Shere Khan had jumped at a woodcutters' camp-fire, as Father Wolf had said, and was furious from the pain of his burned feet. But Father Wolf knew that the mouth of the cave was too narrow for a tiger to come in by. Even where he was, Shere Khan's shoulders and fore paws were cramped for want of room, as a man's would be if he tried to fight in a barrel.

'The Wolves are a free people,' said Father Wolf. 'They take orders from the Head of the Pack, and not from any striped cattle-killer. The man's cub is ours—to kill if we choose.'

'Ye choose and ye do not choose! What talk is this of choosing? By the bull that I killed, am I to stand nosing into your dog's den for my fair dues? It is I, Shere Khan, who speak!'

The tiger's roar filled the cave with thunder. Mother Wolf shook herself clear of the cubs and sprang forward, her eyes, like two green moons in the darkness, facing the blazing eyes of Shere Khan.

'And it is I, Raksha [The Demon], who answer. The man's cub is mine, Lungri—mine to me! He shall not be killed. He shall live to run with the Pack and to hunt with the Pack; and in the end, look you, hunter of little naked cubs—frog-eater—fish-killer—he shall hunt *thee!* Now get hence, or by the Sambhur that I killed (*I* eat no starved cattle), back thou goest to thy mother, burned beast of the jungle, lamer than ever thou camest into the world! Go!'

Father Wolf looked on amazed. He had almost forgotten the days when he won Mother Wolf in fair fight from five other wolves, when she ran in the Pack and was not called The Demon for compliment's sake. Shere Khan might have faced Father Wolf, but he could not stand up against

Mother Wolf, for he knew that where he was she had all the advantage of the ground, and would fight to the death. So he backed out of the cave-mouth growling, and when he was clear he shouted:—

'Each dog barks in his own yard! We will see what the Pack will say to this fostering of man-cubs. The cub is mine, and to my teeth he will come in the end, O bush-tailed thieves!'

Mother Wolf threw herself down panting among the cubs, and Father Wolf said to her gravely:—

'Shere Khan speaks this much truth. The cub must be shown to the Pack. Wilt thou still keep him, Mother?'

'Keep him!' she gasped. 'He came naked, by night, alone and very hungry; yet he was not afraid! Look, he has pushed one of my babes to one side already. And that lame butcher would have killed him and would have run off to the Waingunga while the villagers here hunted through all our lairs in revenge! Keep him? Assuredly I will keep him. Lie still, little frog. O thou Mowgli—for Mowgli the Frog I will call thee—the time will come when thou wilt hunt Shere Khan as he has hunted thee.'

'But what will our Pack say?' said Father Wolf.

The Law of the Jungle lays down very clearly that any wolf may, when he marries, withdraw from the Pack he belongs to; but as soon as his cubs are old enough to stand on their feet he must bring them to the Pack Council, which is generally held once a month at full moon, in order that the other wolves may identify them. After that inspection the cubs are free to run where they please, and until they have killed their first buck no excuse is accepted if a grown wolf of the Pack kills one of them. The punishment is death where the murderer can be found; and if you think for a minute you will see that this must be so.

Father Wolf waited till his cubs could run a little, and then on the night of the Pack Meeting took them and Mowgli and Mother Wolf to the Council Rock—a hilltop covered with stones and boulders where a hundred wolves could hide. Akela, the great gray Lone Wolf, who led all the Pack by strength and cunning, lay out at full length on his rock, and below him sat forty or more wolves of every size and colour, from badger-coloured veterans who could handle a buck alone, to young black three-year-olds who thought they could. The Lone Wolf had led them for a year now. He had fallen twice into a wolf-trap in his youth, and once he had been beaten and left for dead; so he knew the manners and customs of men. There was very little talking at the rock. The cubs tumbled over each other in the centre of the circle where their mothers and fathers sat, and now and again a senior wolf would go quietly up to a cub, look at him carefully, and return to his place on noiseless feet. Sometimes a mother would push her cub far out into the moonlight, to be sure that he had not been overlooked. Akela from his rock would cry: 'Ye know the Law—ye know the Law. Look well, O Wolves!' and the anxious mothers would take up the call: 'Look–look well, O Wolves!'

At last–and Mother Wolf's neck-bristles lifted as the time came–Father Wolf pushed 'Mowgli the Frog,' as they called him, into the centre, where he sat laughing and playing with some pebbles that glistened in the moonlight.

Akela never raised his head from his paws, but went on with the monotonous cry: 'Look well!' A muffled roar came up from behind the rocks –the voice of Shere Khan crying: 'The cub is mine. Give him to me. What have the Free People to do with a man's cub?' Akela never even twitched his ears: all he said was: 'Look well, O Wolves! What have the Free People to do with the orders of any save the Free People? Look well!'

There was a chorus of deep growls, and a young wolf in his fourth year flung back Shere Khan's question to Akela: 'What have the Free People to do with a man's cub?' Now the Law of the Jungle lays down that if there is any dispute as to the right of a cub to be accepted by the Pack, he must be spoken for by at least two members of the Pack who are not his father and mother.

'Who speaks for this cub?' said Akela. 'Among the Free People who speaks?' There was no answer, and Mother Wolf got ready for what she knew would be her last fight, if things came to fighting.

Then the only other creature who is allowed at the Pack Council–Baloo, the sleepy brown bear who teaches the wolf cubs the Law of the Jungle: old Baloo, who can come and go where he pleases because he eats only nuts and roots and honey–rose up on his hind quarters and grunted.

'The man's cub–the man's cub?' he said. '*I* speak for the man's cub. There is no harm in a man's cub. I have no gift of words, but I speak the truth. Let him run with the Pack, and be entered with the others. I myself will teach him.'

'We need yet another,' said Akela. 'Baloo has spoken, and he is our teacher for the young cubs. Who speaks beside Baloo?'

A black shadow dropped down into the circle. It was Bagheera the Black Panther, inky black all over, but with the panther markings showing up in certain lights like the pattern of watered silk. Everybody knew Bagheera, and nobody cared to cross his path; for he was as cunning as Tabaqui, as bold as the wild buffalo, and as reckless as the wounded elephant. But he had a voice as soft as wild honey dripping from a tree, and a skin softer than down.

'O Akela, and ye the Free People,' he purred, 'I have no right in your assembly; but the Law of the Jungle says that if there is a doubt which is not a killing matter in regard to a new cub, the life of that cub may be bought at a price. And the Law does not say who may or may not pay that price. Am I right?'

'Good! good!' said the young wolves, who are always hungry. 'Listen to Bagheera. The cub can be bought for a price. It is the Law.'

'Knowing that I have no right to speak here, I ask your leave.'

'Speak then,' cried twenty voices.

'To kill a naked cub is shame. Besides, he may make better sport for you when he is grown. Baloo has spoken in his behalf. Now to Baloo's word I will add one bull, and a fat one, newly killed, not half a mile from here, if ye will accept the man's cub according to the Law. Is it difficult?'

There was a clamour of scores of voices, saying: 'What matter? He will die in the winter rains. He will scorch in the sun. What harm can a naked frog do us? Let him run with the Pack. Where is the bull, Bagheera? Let him be accepted.' And then came Akela's deep bay, crying: 'Look well—look well, O Wolves!'

Mowgli was still deeply interested in the pebbles, and he did not notice when the wolves came and looked at him one by one. At last they all went down the hill for the dead bull, and only Akela, Bagheera, Baloo, and Mowgli's own wolves were left. Shere Khan roared still in the night, for he was very angry that Mowgli had not been handed over to him.

'Ay, roar well,' said Bagheera, under his whiskers; 'for the time comes when this naked thing will make thee roar to another tune, or I know nothing of man.'

'It was well done,' said Akela. 'Men and their cubs are very wise. He may be a help in time.'

'Truly, a help in time of need; for none can hope to lead the Pack for ever,' said Bagheera.

Akela said nothing. He was thinking of the time that comes to every leader of every pack when his strength goes from him and he gets feebler and feebler, till at last he is killed by the wolves and a new leader comes up—to be killed in his turn.

'Take him away,' he said to Father Wolf, 'and train him as befits one of the Free People.'

And that is how Mowgli was entered into the Seeonee wolf-pack for the price of a bull and on Baloo's good word.

* * *

Now you must be content to skip ten or eleven whole years, and only guess at all the wonderful life that Mowgli led among the wolves, because if it were written out it would fill ever so many books. He grew up with the cubs, though they, of course, were grown wolves almost before he was a child, and Father Wolf taught him his business, and the meaning of things in the jungle, till every rustle in the grass, every breath of the warm night air, every note of the owls above his head, every scratch of a bat's claws as it roosted for a while in a tree, and every splash of every little fish jumping in a pool, meant just as much to him as the work of his office means to a business man. When he was not learning he sat out in the sun and slept, and ate and went to sleep again; when he felt dirty or hot he swam in the forest pools; and when he wanted honey (Baloo told him that honey and nuts were just as pleasant to eat as raw meat) he climbed up for it, and that Bagheera showed him how to do. Bagheera would lie out on a branch and call, 'Come along, Little Brother,' and at first Mowgli would cling like the sloth, but afterward he would fling himself through the branches almost as boldly as the gray ape. He took his place at the Council Rock, too, when the Pack met, and there he discovered that if he stared hard at any wolf, the wolf would be forced to drop his eyes, and so he used to stare for fun. At other times he would pick the long thorns out of the pads of his friends, for wolves suffer terribly from thorns and burs in their coats. He would go down the hillside into the cultivated lands by night, and look very curiously at the villagers in their huts, but he had a mistrust of men because Bagheera showed him a square box with a drop-gate so cunningly hidden in the jungle that he nearly walked into it, and told him that it was a trap. He loved better than anything else to go with Bagheera into the dark warm heart of the forest, to sleep all through the drowsy day, and at night see how Bagheera did his killing. Bagheera killed right and left as he felt hungry, and so did Mowgli—with one exception. As soon as he was old enough to understand things, Bagheera told him that he must never touch cattle because he had been bought into the Pack at the price of a bull's life. 'All the jungle is thine,' said Bagheera, 'and thou canst kill everything that thou art strong enough to kill; but for the sake of the bull that bought thee thou must never kill or eat any cattle young or old. That is the Law of the Jungle.' Mowgli obeyed faithfully.

And he grew and grew strong as a boy must grow who does not know that he is learning any lessons, and who has nothing in the world to think of except things to eat.

Mother Wolf told him once or twice that Shere Khan was not a creature to be trusted, and that some day he must kill Shere Khan; but though a young wolf would have remembered that advice every hour, Mowgli forgot it because he was only a boy—though he would have called himself a wolf if he had been able to speak in any human tongue.

Shere Khan was always crossing his path in the jungle, for as Akela grew older and feebler the lame tiger had come to be great friends with the younger wolves of the Pack, who followed him for scraps, a thing Akela would never have allowed if he had dared to push his authority to the proper bounds. Then Shere Khan would flatter them and wonder that such fine young hunters were content to be led by a dying wolf and a man's cub. 'They tell me,' Shere Khan would say, 'that at Council ye dare not look him between the eyes'; and the young wolves would growl and bristle.

Bagheera, who had eyes and ears everywhere, knew something of this, and once or twice he told Mowgli in so many words that Shere Khan would kill him some day; and Mowgli would laugh and answer: 'I have the Pack and I have thee; and Baloo, though he is so lazy, might strike a blow or two for my sake. Why should I be afraid?'

It was one very warm day that a new notion came to Bagheera—born of something that he had heard. Perhaps Sahi the Porcupine had told him; but he said to Mowgli when they were deep in the jungle, as the boy lay with his head on Bagheera's beautiful black skin: 'Little Brother, how often have I told thee that Shere Khan is thy enemy?'

'As many times as there are nuts on that palm,' said Mowgli, who, naturally, could not count. 'What of it? I am sleepy, Bagheera, and Shere Khan is all long tail and loud talk—like Mor the Peacock.'

'But this is no time for sleeping. Baloo knows it; I know it; the Pack know it; and even the foolish, foolish deer know. Tabaqui has told thee, too.'

'Ho! ho!' said Mowgli. 'Tabaqui came to me not long ago with some rude talk that I was a naked man's cub and not fit to dig pig-nuts; but I caught Tabaqui by the tail and swung him twice against a palm-tree to teach him better manners.'

'That was foolishness; for though Tabaqui is a mischief-maker, he would have told thee of something that concerned thee closely. Open those eyes, Little Brother. Shere Khan dare not kill thee in the jungle; but remember, Akela is very old, and soon the day comes when he cannot kill his buck, and then he will be leader no more. Many of the wolves that looked thee over when thou wast brought to the Council first are old too, and the young wolves believe, as Shere Khan has taught them, that a man-cub has no place with the Pack. In a little time thou wilt be a man.'

'And what is a man that he should not run with his brothers?' said Mowgli. 'I was born in the jungle. I have obeyed the Law of the Jungle, and there is no wolf of ours from whose paws I have not pulled a thorn. Surely they are my brothers!'

Bagheera stretched himself at full length and half shut his eyes. 'Little Brother,' said he, 'feel under my jaw.'

Mowgli put up his strong brown hand, and just under Bagheera's silky chin, where the giant rolling muscles were all hid by the glossy hair, he came upon a little bald spot.

'There is no one in the jungle that knows that I, Bagheera, carry that mark—the mark of the collar; and yet, Little Brother, I was born among men, and it was among men that my mother died—in the cages of the King's Palace at Oodeypore. It was because of this that I paid the price for thee at the Council when thou wast a little naked cub. Yes, I too was born among men. I had never seen the jungle. They fed me behind bars from an iron pan till one night I felt that I was Bagheera—the Panther —and no man's plaything, and I broke the silly lock with one blow of my paw and came away; and because I had learned the ways of men, I became more terrible in the jungle than Shere Khan. Is it not so?'

'Yes,' said Mowgli; 'all the jungle fear Bagheera—all except Mowgli.'

'Oh, *thou* art a man's cub,' said the Black Panther, very tenderly; 'and even as I returned to my jungle, so thou must go back to men at last, —to the men who are thy brothers,—if thou art not killed in the Council.'

'But why—but why should any wish to kill me?' said Mowgli.

'Look at me,' said Bagheera; and Mowgli looked at him steadily between the eyes. The big panther turned his head away in half a minute. '*That* is why,' he said, shifting his paw on the leaves. 'Not even I can look thee between the eyes, and I was born among men, and I love thee, Little Brother. The others they hate thee because their eyes cannot meet thine; because thou art wise; because thou hast pulled out thorns from their feet—because thou art a man.'

'I did not know these things,' said Mowgli, sullenly; and he frowned under his heavy black eyebrows.

'What is the Law of the Jungle? Strike first and then give tongue. By thy very carelessness they know that thou art a man. But be wise. It is in my heart that when Akela misses his next kill,—and at each hunt it costs him more to pin the buck,—the Pack will turn against him and against thee. They will hold a jungle Council at the Rock, and then—and then—I have it!' said Bagheera, leaping up. 'Go thou down quickly to the men's huts in the valley, and take some of the Red Flower which they grow there, so that when the time comes thou mayest have even a stronger friend than I or Baloo or those of the Pack that love thee. Get the Red Flower.'

By Red Flower Bagheera meant fire, only no creature in the jungle will call fire by its proper name. Every beast lives in deadly fear of it, and invents a hundred ways of describing it.

'The Red Flower?' said Mowgli. 'That grows outside their huts in the twilight. I will get some.'

'There speaks the man's cub,' said Bagheera, proudly. 'Remember that it grows in little pots. Get one swiftly, and keep it by thee for time of need.'

'Good!' said Mowgli. 'I go. But art thou sure, O my Bagheera'—he slipped his arm round the splendid neck, and looked deep into the big eyes—'art thou sure that all this is Shere Khan's doing?'

'By the Broken Lock that freed me, I am sure, Little Brother.'

'Then, by the Bull that bought me, I will pay Shere Khan full tale for this, and it may be a little over,' said Mowgli; and he bounded away.

'That is a man. That is all a man,' said Bagheera to himself, lying down again. 'Oh, Shere Khan, never was a blacker hunting than that frog-hunt of thine ten years ago!'

Mowgli was far and far through the forest, running hard, and his heart was hot in him. He came to the cave as the evening mist rose, and drew breath, and looked down the valley. The cubs were out, but Mother Wolf, at the back of the cave, knew by his breathing that something was troubling her frog.

'What is it, Son?' she said.

'Some bat's chatter of Shere Khan,' he called back. 'I hunt among the ploughed fields to-night'; and he plunged downward through the bushes, to the stream at the bottom of the valley. There he checked, for he heard the yell of the Pack hunting, heard the bellow of a hunted Sambhur, and the snort as the buck turned at bay. Then there were wicked, bitter howls from the young wolves: 'Akela! Akela! Let the Lone Wolf show his strength. Room for the leader of the Pack! Spring, Akela!'

The Lone Wolf must have sprung and missed his hold, for Mowgli heard the snap of his teeth and then a yelp as the Sambhur knocked him over with his fore foot.

He did not wait for anything more, but dashed on; and the yells grew fainter behind him as he ran into the crop-lands where the villagers lived.

'Bagheera spoke truth,' he panted, as he nestled down in some cattle-fodder by the window of a hut. 'To-morrow is one day both for Akela and for me.'

Then he pressed his face close to the window and watched the fire on the hearth. He saw the husbandman's wife get up and feed it in the night with black lumps; and when the morning came and the mists were all white and cold, he saw the man's child pick up a wicker pot plastered inside with earth, fill it with lumps of red-hot charcoal, put it under his blanket, and go out to tend the cows in the byre.

'Is that all?' said Mowgli. 'If a cub can do it, there is nothing to fear'; so he strode round the corner and met the boy, took the pot from his hand, and disappeared into the mist while the boy howled with fear.

'They are very like me,' said Mowgli, blowing into the pot, as he had seen the woman do. 'This thing will die if I do not give it things to eat'; and he dropped twigs and dried bark on the red stuff. Half-way up the hill he met Bagheera with the morning dew shining like moonstones on his coat.

'Akela has missed,' said the Panther. 'They would have killed him last night, but they needed thee also. They were looking for thee on the hill.'

'I was among the ploughed lands. I am ready. See!' Mowgli held up the fire-pot.

'Good! Now, I have seen men thrust a dry branch into that stuff, and presently the Red Flower blossomed at the end of it. Art thou not afraid?'

'No. Why should I fear? I remember now—if it is not a dream—how, before I was a Wolf, I lay beside the Red Flower, and it was warm and pleasant.'

All that day Mowgli sat in the cave tending his fire-pot and dipping dry branches into it to see how they looked. He found a branch that satisfied him, and in the evening when Tabaqui came to the cave and told him rudely enough that he was wanted at the Council Rock, he laughed till Tabaqui ran away. Then Mowgli went to the Council, still laughing.

Akela the Lone Wolf lay by the side of his rock as a sign that the leadership of the Pack was open, and Shere Khan with his following of scrap-fed wolves walked to and fro openly being flattered. Bagheera lay close to Mowgli, and the fire-pot was between Mowgli's knees. When they were all gathered together, Shere Khan began to speak—a thing he would never have dared to do when Akela was in his prime.

'He has no right,' whispered Bagheera. 'Say so. He is a dog's son. He will be frightened.'

Mowgli sprang to his feet. 'Free People,' he cried, 'does Shere Khan lead the Pack? What has a tiger to do with our leadership?'

'Seeing that the leadership is yet open, and being asked to speak—' Shere Khan began.

'By whom?' said Mowgli. 'Are we *all* jackals, to fawn on this cattle-butcher? The leadership of the Pack is with the Pack alone.'

There were yells of 'Silence, thou man's cub!' 'Let him speak. He has kept our Law'; and at last the seniors of the Pack thundered: 'Let the Dead Wolf speak.' When a leader of the Pack has missed his kill, he is called the Dead Wolf as long as he lives, which is not long.

Akela raised his old head wearily:—

'Free People, and ye too, jackals of Shere Khan, for twelve seasons I have led ye to and from the kill, and in all that time not one has been trapped or maimed. Now I have missed my kill. Ye know how that plot was made. Ye know how ye brought me up to an untried buck to make my weakness known. It was cleverly done. Your right is to kill me here on the Council Rock, now. Therefore, I ask, who comes to make an end of the Lone Wolf? For it is my right, by the Law of the Jungle, that ye come one by one.'

There was a long hush, for no single wolf cared to fight Akela to the death. Then Shere Khan roared: 'Bah! what have we to do with this toothless fool? He is doomed to die! It is the man-cub who has lived too long.

Free People, he was my meat from the first. Give him to me. I am weary of this man-wolf folly. He has troubled the jungle for ten seasons. Give me the man-cub, or I will hunt here always, and not give you one bone. He is a man, a man's child, and from the marrow of my bones I hate him!'

Then more than half the Pack yelled: 'A man! a man! What has a man to do with us? Let him go to his own place.'

'And turn all the people of the villages against us?' clamoured Shere Khan. 'No; give him to me. He is a man, and none of us can look him between the eyes.'

Akela lifted his head again, and said: 'He has eaten our food. He has slept with us. He has driven game for us. He has broken no word of the Law of the Jungle.'

'Also, I paid for him with a bull when he was accepted. The worth of a bull is little, but Bagheera's honour is something that he will perhaps fight for,' said Bagheera, in his gentlest voice.

'A bull paid ten years ago!' the Pack snarled. 'What do we care for bones ten years old?'

'Or for a pledge?' said Bagheera, his white teeth bared under his lip. 'Well are ye called the Free People!'

'No man's cub can run with the people of the jungle,' howled Shere Khan. 'Give him to me!'

'He is our brother in all but blood,' Akela went on; 'and ye would kill him here! In truth, I have lived too long. Some of ye are eaters of cattle, and of others I have heard that, under Shere Khan's teaching, ye go by dark night and snatch children from the villager's door-step. Therefore I know ye to be cowards, and it is to cowards I speak. It is certain that I must die, and my life is of no worth, or I would offer that in the man-cub's place. But for the sake of the Honour of the Pack,—a little matter that by being without a leader ye have forgotten,—I promise that if ye let the man-cub go to his own place, I will not, when my time comes to die, bare one tooth against ye. I will die without fighting. That will at least save the Pack three lives. More I cannot do; but if ye will, I can save ye the shame that comes of killing a brother against whom there is no fault,—a brother spoken for and bought into the Pack according to the Law of the Jungle.'

'He is a man—a man—a man!' snarled the Pack; and most of the wolves began to gather round Shere Khan, whose tail was beginning to switch.

'Now the business is in thy hands,' said Bagheera to Mowgli. '*We* can do no more except fight.'

Mowgli stood upright—the fire-pot in his hands. Then he stretched out his arms, and yawned in the face of the Council; but he was furious with rage and sorrow, for, wolf-like, the wolves had never told him how they hated him. 'Listen you!' he cried. 'There is no need for this dog's jabber. Ye have told me so often to-night that I am a man (and indeed I would have been a wolf with you to my life's end), that I feel your words are true. So I do not call ye my brothers any more, but *sag* [dogs], as a man should. What ye will do, and what ye will not do, is not yours to say. That matter is with *me*; and that we may see the matter more plainly, I, the man, have brought here a little of the Red Flower which ye, dogs, fear.'

He flung the fire-pot on the ground, and some of the red coals lit a tuft of dried moss that flared up, as all the Council drew back in terror before the leaping flames.

Mowgli thrust his dead branch into the fire till the twigs lit and crackled, and whirled it above his head among the cowering wolves.

'Thou art the master,' said Bagheera, in an undertone. 'Save Akela from the death. He was ever thy friend.'

Akela, the grim old wolf who had never asked for mercy in his life, gave one piteous look at Mowgli as the boy stood all naked, his long black hair tossing over his shoulders in the light of the blazing branch that made the shadows jump and quiver.

'Good!' said Mowgli, staring round slowly. 'I see that ye are dogs. I go from you to my own people—if they be my own people. The Jungle is shut to me, and I must forget your talk and your companionship; but I will be more merciful than ye are. Because I was all but your brother in blood, I promise that when I am a man among men I will not betray ye to men as ye have betrayed me.' He kicked the fire with his foot, and the sparks flew up. 'There shall be no war between any of us in the Pack. But here is a debt to pay before I go.' He strode forward to where Shere Khan sat blinking stupidly at the flames, and caught him by the tuft on his chin. Bagheera followed in case of accidents. 'Up, dog!' Mowgli cried. 'Up, when a man speaks, or I will set that coat ablaze!'

Shere Khan's ears lay flat back on his head, and he shut his eyes, for the blazing branch was very near.

'This cattle-killer said he would kill me in the Council because he had not killed me when I was a cub. Thus and thus, then, do we beat dogs when we are men. Stir a whisker, Lungri, and I ram the Red Flower down thy gullet!' He beat Shere Khan over the head with the branch, and the tiger whimpered and whined in an agony of fear.

'Pah! Singed jungle-cat—go now! But remember when next I come to the Council Rock, as a man should come, it will be with Shere Khan's hide on my head. For the rest, Akela goes free to live as he pleases. Ye will *not* kill him, because that is not my will. Nor do I think that ye will sit here any longer, lolling out your tongues as though ye were somebodies, instead of dogs whom I drive out—thus! Go!' The fire was burning furiously at the end of the branch, and Mowgli struck right and left round the circle, and the wolves ran howling with the sparks burning their fur. At last there were only Akela, Bagheera, and perhaps ten wolves that had taken Mowgli's part. Then something began to hurt Mowgli inside him, as he had never been hurt in his life before, and he caught his breath and sobbed, and the tears ran down his face.

'What is it? What is it?' he said. 'I do not wish to leave the jungle, and I do not know what this is. Am I dying, Bagheera?'

'No, Little Brother. That is only tears such as men use,' said Bagheera. 'Now I know thou art a man, and a man's cub no longer. The Jungle is shut indeed to thee henceforward. Let them fall, Mowgli. They are only tears.' So Mowgli sat and cried as though his heart would break; and he had never cried in all his life before.

'Now,' he said, 'I will go to men. But first I must say farewell to my mother'; and he went to the cave where she lived with Father Wolf, and he cried on her coat, while the four cubs howled miserably.

'Ye will not forget me?' said Mowgli.

'Never while we can follow a trail,' said the cubs. 'Come to the foot of the hill when thou art a man, and we will talk to thee; and we will come into the crop-lands to play with thee by night.'

'Come soon!' said Father Wolf. 'Oh, wise little frog, come again soon; for we be old, thy mother and I.'

'Come soon,' said Mother Wolf, 'little naked son of mine; for, listen, child of man, I loved thee more than ever I loved my cubs.'

'I will surely come,' said Mowgli; 'and when I come it will be to lay out Shere Khan's hide upon the Council Rock. Do not forget me! Tell them in the jungle never to forget me!'

The dawn was beginning to break when Mowgli went down the hillside alone, to meet those mysterious things that are called men.

THE GIFT OF THE MAGI

O. HENRY

ONE DOLLAR and eighty-seven cents. That was all. And sixty cents of it was in pennies. Pennies saved one and two at a time by bulldozing the grocer and the vegetable man and the butcher until one's cheeks burned with the silent imputation of parsimony that such close dealing implied. Three times Della counted it. One dollar and eighty-seven cents. And the next day would be Christmas.

There was clearly nothing to do but flop down on the shabby little couch and howl. So Della did it. Which instigates the moral reflection that life is made up of sobs, sniffles, and smiles, with sniffles predominating.

While the mistress of the home is gradually subsiding from the first stage to the second, take a look at the home. A furnished flat at $8 per week. It did not exactly beggar description, but it certainly had that word on the lookout for the mendicancy squad.

In the vestibule below was a letter-box into which no letter would go, and an electric button from which no mortal finger could coax a ring. Also appertaining thereunto was a card bearing the name "Mr. James Dillingham Young."

The "Dillingham" had been flung to the breeze during a former period of prosperity when its possessor was being paid $30 per week. Now, when the income was shrunk to $20, the letters of "Dillingham" looked blurred, as though they were thinking seriously of contracting to a modest and unassuming D. But whenever Mr. James Dillingham Young came home and reached his flat above he was called "Jim" and greatly hugged by Mrs. James Dillingham Young, already introduced to you as Della. Which is all very good.

Della finished her cry and attended to her cheeks with the powder rag.

She stood by the window and looked out dully at a gray cat walking a gray fence in a gray backyard. Tomorrow would be Christmas Day and she had only $1.87 with which to buy Jim a present. She had been saving every penny she could for months, with this result. Twenty dollars a week doesn't go far. Expenses had been greater than she had calculated. They always are. Only $1.87 to buy a present for Jim. Her Jim. Many a happy hour she had spent planning for something nice for him. Something fine and rare and sterling—something just a little bit near to being worthy of the honor of being owned by Jim.

There was a pier-glass between the windows of the room. Perhaps you have seen a pier-glass in an $8 flat. A very thin and very agile person may, by observing his reflection in a rapid sequence of longitudinal strips, obtain a fairly accurate conception of his looks. Della, being slender, had mastered the art.

Suddenly she whirled from the window and stood before the glass. Her eyes were shining brilliantly, but her face had lost its color within twenty seconds. Rapidly she pulled down her hair and let it fall to its full length.

Now, there were two possessions of the James Dillingham Youngs in which they both took a mighty pride. One was Jim's gold watch that had been his father's and his grandfather's. The other was Della's hair. Had the Queen of Sheba lived in the flat across the airshaft, Della would have let her hair hang out the window some day to dry just to depreciate Her Majesty's jewels and gifts. Had King Solomon been the janitor, with all his treasures piled up in the basement, Jim would have pulled out his watch every time he passed, just to see him pluck at his beard from envy.

So now Della's beautiful hair fell about her rippling and shining like a cascade of brown waters. It reached below her knee and made itself almost a garment for her. And then she did it up again nervously and quickly. Once she faltered for a minute and stood still while a tear or two splashed on the worn red carpet.

On went her old brown jacket; on went her old brown hat. With a whirl of skirts and with the brilliant sparkle still in her eyes, she fluttered out the door and down the stairs to the street.

Where she stopped the sign read: "Mme. Sofronie. Hair Goods of All Kinds." One flight up Della ran, and collected herself, panting. Madame, large, too white, chilly, hardly looked the "Sofronie."

"Will you buy my hair?" asked Della.

"I buy hair," said Madame. "Take yer hat off and let's have a sight at the looks of it."

Down rippled the brown cascade.

"Twenty dollars," said Madame, lifting the mass with a practised hand.

"Give it to me quick," said Della.

Oh, and the next two hours tripped by on rosy wings. Forget the hashed metaphor. She was ransacking the stores for Jim's present.

She found it at last. It surely had been made for Jim and no one else. There was no other like it in any of the stores, and she had turned all of them inside out. It was a platinum fob chain simple and chaste in design, properly proclaiming its value by substance alone and not by meretricious ornamentation—as all good things should do. It was even worthy of The Watch. As soon as she saw it she knew that it must be Jim's. It was like him. Quietness and value—the description applied to both. Twenty-one dollars they took from her for it, and she hurried home with the 87 cents. With that chain on his watch Jim might be properly anxious about the time in any company. Grand as the watch was, he sometimes looked at it on the sly on account of the old leather strap that he used in place of a chain.

When Della reached home her intoxication gave way a little to prudence and reason. She got out her curling irons and lighted the gas and went to work repairing the ravages made by generosity added to love. Which is always a tremendous task, dear friends—a mammoth task.

Within forty minutes her head was covered with tiny, close-lying curls that made her look wonderfully like a truant schoolboy. She looked at her reflection in the mirror long, carefully, and critically.

"If Jim doesn't kill me," she said to herself, "before he takes a second look at me, he'll say I look like a Coney Island chorus girl. But what could I do—oh! what could I do with a dollar and eighty-seven cents?"

At 7 o'clock the coffee was made and the frying-pan was on the back of the stove hot and ready to cook the chops.

Jim was never late. Della doubled the fob chain in her hand and sat on the corner of the table near the door that he always entered. Then she heard his step on the stair away down on the first flight, and she turned white for just a moment. She had a habit of saying little silent prayers about the simplest everyday things, and now she whispered: "Please God, make him think I am still pretty."

The door opened and Jim stepped in and closed it. He looked thin and very serious. Poor fellow, he was only twenty-two—and to be burdened with a family! He needed a new overcoat and he was without gloves.

Jim stepped inside the door, as immovable as a setter at the scent of quail. His eyes were fixed upon Della, and there was an expression in them that she could not read, and it terrified her. It was not anger, nor surprise, nor disapproval, nor horror, nor any of the sentiments that she had been prepared for. He simply stared at her fixedly with that peculiar expression on his face.

Della wriggled off the table and went for him.

"Jim, darling," she cried, "don't look at me that way. I had my hair cut off and sold it because I couldn't have lived through Christmas without giving you a present. It'll grow out again—you won't mind, will you? I just had to do it. My hair grows awfully fast. Say 'Merry Christmas!'

Jim, and let's be happy. You don't know what a nice—what a beautiful, nice gift I've got for you."

"You've cut off your hair?" asked Jim, laboriously, as if he had not arrived at that patent fact yet even after the hardest mental labor.

"Cut it off and sold it," said Della. "Don't you like me just as well, anyhow? I'm me without my hair, ain't I?"

Jim looked about the room curiously.

"You say your hair is gone?" he said, with an air almost of idiocy.

"You needn't look for it," said Della. "It's sold, I tell you—sold and gone, too. It's Christmas Eve, boy. Be good to me, for it went for you. Maybe the hairs of my head were numbered," she went on with a sudden serious sweetness, "but nobody could ever count my love for you. Shall I put the chops on, Jim?"

Out of his trance Jim seemed quickly to wake. He enfolded his Della. For ten seconds let us regard with discreet scrutiny some inconsequential object in the other direction. Eight dollars a week or a million a year—what is the difference? A mathematician or a wit would give you the wrong answer. The magi brought valuable gifts, but that was not among them. This dark assertion will be illuminated later on.

Jim drew a package from his overcoat pocket and threw it upon the table.

"Don't make any mistake, Dell," he said, "about me. I don't think there's anything in the way of a haircut or a shave or a shampoo that could make me like my girl any less. But if you'll unwrap that package you may see why you had me going a while at first."

White fingers and nimble tore at the string and paper. And then an ecstatic scream of joy; and then, alas! a quick feminine change to hysterical tears and wails, necessitating the immediate employment of all the comforting powers of the lord of the flat.

For there lay The Combs—the set of combs, side and back, that Della had worshipped for long in a Broadway window. Beautiful combs, pure tortoise shell, with jewelled rims—just the shade to wear in the beautiful vanished hair. They were expensive combs, she knew, and her heart had simply craved and yearned over them without the least hope of possession. And now, they were hers, but the tresses that should have adorned the coveted adornments were gone.

But she hugged them to her bosom, and at length she was able to look up with dim eyes and a smile and say: "My hair grows so fast, Jim!"

And then Della leaped up like a little singed cat and cried, "Oh, oh!"

Jim had not yet seen his beautiful present. She held it out to him eagerly upon her open palm. The dull precious metal seemed to flash with a reflection of her bright and ardent spirit.

"Isn't it a dandy, Jim? I hunted all over town to find it. You'll have to look at the time a hundred times a day now. Give me your watch. I want to see how it looks on it."

Instead of obeying, Jim tumbled down on the couch and put his hands under the back of his head and smiled.

"Dell," said he, "let's put our Christmas presents away and keep 'em a while. They're too nice to use just at present. I sold the watch to get the money to buy your combs. And now suppose you put the chops on."

The magi, as you know, were wise men—wonderfully wise men—who brought gifts to the Babe in the manger. They invented the art of giving Christmas presents. Being wise, their gifts were no doubt wise ones, possibly bearing the privilege of exchange in case of duplication. And here I have lamely related to you the uneventful chronicle of two foolish children in a flat who most unwisely sacrificed for each other the greatest treasures of their house. But in a last word to the wise of these days let it be said that of all who give gifts these two were the wisest. Of all who give and receive gifts, such as they are wisest. Everywhere they are wisest. They are the magi.

LORD MOUNTDRAGO

W. SOMERSET MAUGHAM

DR. AUDLIN looked at the clock on his desk. It was twenty minutes to six. He was surprised that his patient was late, for Lord Mountdrago prided himself on his punctuality; he had a sententious way of expressing himself which gave the air of an epigram to a commonplace remark, and he was in the habit of saying that punctuality is a compliment you pay to the intelligent and a rebuke you administer to the stupid. Lord Mountdrago's appointment was for five-thirty.

There was in Dr. Audlin's appearance nothing to attract attention. He was tall and spare, with narrow shoulders and something of a stoop; his hair was grey and thin; his long, sallow face deeply lined. He was not more than fifty, but he looked older. His eyes, pale blue and rather large, were weary. When you had been with him for a while you noticed that they moved very little; they remained fixed on your face, but so empty of expression were they that it was no discomfort. They seldom lit up. They gave no clue to his thoughts nor changed with the words he spoke. If you were of an observant turn it might have struck you that he blinked much less often than most of us. His hands were on the large side, with long, tapering fingers; they were soft but firm, cool but not clammy. You could never have said what Dr. Audlin wore unless you had made a point of looking. His clothes were dark. His tie was black. His dress made his sallow lined face paler and his pale eyes more wan. He gave you the impression of a very sick man.

Dr. Audlin was a psychoanalyst. He had adopted the profession by accident and practised it with misgiving. When the war broke out he had not been long qualified and was getting experience at various hospitals; he offered his services to the authorities, and after a time was sent out to France. It was then that he discovered his singular gift. He could allay certain pains by the touch of his cool, firm hands, and by talking to them often induce sleep in men who were suffering from sleeplessness. He spoke slowly. His voice had no particular colour, and its tone did not alter with the words he uttered, but it was musical, soft and lulling. He told the men that they must rest, that they mustn't worry, that they must sleep; and rest stole into their jaded bones, tranquillity pushed their anxieties away, like a man finding a place for himself on a crowded bench, and slumber fell on their tired eyelids like the light rain of spring upon the fresh-turned earth. Dr. Audlin found that by speaking to men with that low, monotonous voice of his, by looking at them with his pale, quiet eyes, by stroking their weary foreheads with his long firm hands, he could soothe their perturbations, resolve the conflicts that distracted them and banish the phobias that made their lives a torment. Sometimes he effected cures that seemed miraculous. He restored speech to a man who, after being buried under the earth by a bursting shell, had been struck dumb, and he gave back the use of his limbs to another who had been paralyzed after a crash in a plane. He could not understand his powers; he was of a sceptical turn, and though they say that in circumstances of this kind the first thing is to believe in yourself, he never quite succeeded in doing that; and it was only the outcome of his activities, patent to the most incredulous observer, that obliged him to admit that he had some faculty, coming from he knew not where, obscure and uncertain, that enabled him to do things for which he could offer no explanation. When the war was over he went to Vienna and studied there, and afterwards to Zurich; and then settled down in London to practise the art he had so strangely acquired. He had been practising now for fifteen years, and had attained, in the speciality he followed, a distinguished reputation. People told one another of the amazing things he had done, and though his fees were high, he had as many patients as he had time to see. Dr. Audlin knew that he had achieved some very extraordinary results; he had saved men from suicide, others from the lunatic asylum, he had assuaged griefs that embittered useful lives, he had turned unhappy marriages into happy ones, he had eradicated abnormal instincts and thus delivered not a few from a hateful bondage, he had given health to the sick in spirit; he had done all this, and yet at the back of his mind remained the suspicion that he was little more than a quack.

It went against his grain to exercise a power that he could not understand, and it offended his honesty to trade on the faith of the people he treated when he had no faith in himself. He was rich enough now to live without working, and the work exhausted him; a dozen times he had been on the point of giving up practice. He knew all that Freud and Jung and the rest of them had written. He was not satisfied; he had an intimate conviction that all their theory was hocus-pocus, and yet there the results were, incomprehensible, but manifest. And what had he not seen of human nature during the fifteen years that patients had been coming to his dingy back room in Wimpole Street? The revelations that had been poured into his ears, sometimes only too willingly, sometimes with shame, with reservations, with anger, had long ceased to surprise him. Nothing could shock him any longer. He knew by now that men were liars, he knew how extravagant was their vanity; he knew far worse than that about them; but he knew that it was not for him to judge or to condemn. But year by year as these terrible confidences were imparted to him his face grew a little greyer, its lines a little more marked and his pale eyes more weary. He seldom laughed, but now and again when for relaxation he read a novel he smiled. Did their authors really think the men and women they wrote of were like that? If they only knew how much more complicated they were, how much more unexpected, what irreconcilable elements coexisted within their souls and what dark and sinister contentions afflicted them!

It was a quarter to six. Of all the strange cases he had been called upon to deal with, Dr. Audlin could remember none stranger than that of Lord Mountdrago. For one thing the personality of his patient made it singular. Lord Mountdrago was an able and a distinguished man. Appointed Secretary for Foreign Affairs when still under forty, now after three years in office he had seen his policy prevail. It was generally acknowledged that he was the ablest politician in the Conservative Party, and only the fact that his father was a peer, on whose death he would no longer be able to sit in the House of Commons, made it impossible for him to aim at the premiership. But if in these democratic times it is out of the question for a Prime Minister of England to be in the House of Lords, there was nothing to prevent Lord Mountdrago from continuing to be Secretary for Foreign Affairs in successive Conservative administrations and so for long directing the foreign policy of his country.

Lord Mountdrago had many good qualities. He had intelligence and industry. He was widely travelled and spoke several languages fluently. From early youth he had specialized in foreign affairs and had conscientiously made himself acquainted with the political and economic circumstances of other countries. He had courage, insight and determination. He was a good speaker, both on the platform and in the House, clear, precise and often witty. He was a brilliant debater and his gift of repartee was celebrated. He had a fine presence: he was a tall, handsome man, rather bald and somewhat too stout, but this gave him solidity and an air of maturity that were of service to him. As a young man he had been something of an athlete and had rowed in the Oxford boat, and he was known to be one of the best shots in England. At twenty-four he had married a girl of eighteen whose father was a duke and her mother a great American heiress, so that she had both position and wealth, and by her he had two sons. For several years they had lived privately apart, but in public united, so that appearances were saved, and no other attachment on either side had given the gossips occasion to whisper. Lord Mountdrago indeed was too ambitious, too hard-working, and it must be added too patriotic, to be tempted by any pleasures that might interfere with his career. He had in short a great deal to make him a popular and successful figure. He had unfortunately great defects.

He was a fearful snob. You would not have been surprised at this if his father had been the first holder of the title. That the son of an ennobled lawyer, manufacturer or distiller should attach an inordinate importance to his rank is understandable. The earldom held by Lord Mountdrago's father was created by Charles II, and the barony held by the first earl dated from the Wars of the Roses. For three hundred years the successive holders of the title had allied themselves with the noblest families of England. But Lord Mountdrago was as conscious of his birth as a *nouveau riche* is conscious of his money. He never missed an opportunity of impressing it upon others. He had beautiful manners when he chose to display them, but this he did only with people whom he regarded as his equals. He was coldly insolent to those whom he looked upon as his social inferiors. He was rude to his servants and insulting to his secretaries. The subordinate officials in the government offices to which he had been successively attached feared and hated him. His arrogance was horrible. He knew that he was a great deal cleverer than most of the persons he had to do with, and never hesitated to apprise them of the fact. He had no patience with the infirmities of human nature. He felt himself born to command and was irritated with people who expected him to listen to their arguments or wished to hear the reasons for his decisions. He was immeasurably selfish. He looked upon any service that was rendered him as a right due to his rank and intelligence and therefore deserving of no gratitude. It never entered his head that he was called upon to do anything for others. He had many enemies: he despised them. He knew no one who merited his assistance, his sympathy or his compassion. He had no friends. He was distrusted by his chiefs, because they doubted his loyalty; he was unpopular with his party, because he was overbearing and discourteous; and yet his merit was so great, his patriotism so evident, his intelligence so solid and his management of affairs so brilliant, that they had to put up with him. And what made it possible to do this was that on occasion he could be enchanting: when he was with persons whom he considered his equals, or whom he wished to captivate, in the company of foreign dignitaries or women of distinction, he could be gay, witty and debonair; his manners then reminded you that in his veins ran the same blood as had run in the veins of Lord Chesterfield; he could tell a story with point, he could be natural, sensible and even profound. You were surprised at the extent of his knowledge and the sensitiveness of his taste. You thought him the best company in the world; you forgot that he had insulted you the day before and was quite capable of cutting you dead the next.

Lord Mountdrago almost failed to become Dr. Audlin's patient. A secretary rang up the doctor and told him that his lordship, wishing to consult him, would be glad if he would come to his house at ten o'clock on the following morning. Dr. Audlin answered that he was unable to go to Lord Mountdrago's house, but would be pleased to give him an appointment at his consulting room at five o'clock on the next day but one. The secretary took the message and presently rang back to say that Lord Mountdrago insisted on seeing Dr. Audlin in his own house and the doctor could fix his own fee. Dr. Audlin replied that he saw patients only in his consulting room and expressed his regret that unless Lord Mountdrago was prepared to come to him he could not give him his attention. In a quarter of an hour a brief message was delivered to him that his lordship would come not next day but one, but next day, at five.

When Lord Mountdrago was then shown in he did not come forward, but stood at the door and insolently looked the doctor up and down. Dr. Audlin perceived that he was in a rage; he gazed at him, silently, with still eyes. He saw a big heavy man, with greying hair, receding on the forehead so that it gave nobility to his brow, a puffy face with bold regular features and an expression of haughtiness. He had somewhat the look of one of the Bourbon sovereigns of the eighteenth century.

"It seems that it is as difficult to see you as a Prime Minister, Dr. Audlin. I'm an extremely busy man."

"Won't you sit down?" said the doctor.

His face showed no sign that Lord Mountdrago's speech in any way affected him. Dr. Audlin sat in his chair at the desk. Lord Mountdrago still stood, and his frown darkened.

"I think I should tell you that I am His Majesty's Secretary for Foreign Affairs," he said acidly.

"Won't you sit down?" the doctor repeated.

Lord Mountdrago made a gesture, which might have suggested that he was about to turn on his heel and stalk out of the room; but if that was his intention he apparently thought better of it. He seated himself. Dr. Audlin opened a large book and took up his pen. He wrote without looking at his patient.

"How old are you?"

"Forty-two."

"Are you married?"

"Yes."

"How long have you been married?"

"Eighteen years."

"Have you any children?"

"I have two sons."

Dr. Audlin noted down the facts as Lord Mountdrago abruptly answered his questions. Then he leaned back in his chair and looked at him. He did not speak; he just looked, gravely, with pale eyes that did not move.

"Why have you come to see me?" he asked at length.

"I've heard about you. Lady Canute is a patient of yours, I understand. She tells me you've done her a certain amount of good."

Dr. Audlin did not reply. His eyes remained fixed on the other's face, but they were so empty of expression that you might have thought he did not even see him.

"I can't do miracles," he said at length. Not a smile, but the shadow of a smile flickered in his eyes. "The Royal College of Physicians would not approve of it if I did."

Lord Mountdrago gave a brief chuckle. It seemed to lessen his hostility. He spoke more amiably.

"You have a very remarkable reputation. People seem to believe in you."

"Why have you come to me?" repeated Dr. Audlin.

Now it was Lord Mountdrago's turn to be silent. It looked as though he found it hard to answer. Dr. Audlin waited. At last Lord Mountdrago seemed to make an effort. He spoke.

"I'm in perfect health. Just as a matter of routine I had myself examined by my own doctor the other day, Sir Augustus Fitzherbert, I daresay you've heard of him, and he tells me I have the physique of a man of thirty. I work hard, but I'm never tired, and I enjoy my work. I smoke very little and I'm an extremely moderate drinker. I take a sufficiency of exercise and I lead a regular life. I am a perfectly sound, normal, healthy man. I quite expect you to think it very silly and childish of me to consult you."

Dr. Audlin saw that he must help him.

"I don't know if I can do anything to help you. I'll try. You're distressed?"

Lord Mountdrago frowned.

"The work that I'm engaged in is important. The decisions I am called upon to make can easily affect the welfare of the country and even the peace of the world. It is essential that my judgment should be balanced and my brain clear. I look upon it as my duty to eliminate any cause of worry that may interfere with my usefulness."

Dr. Audlin had never taken his eyes off him. He saw a great deal. He saw behind his patient's pompous manner and arrogant pride an anxiety that he could not dispel.

"I asked you to be good enough to come here because I know by experience that it's easier for someone to speak openly in the dingy surroundings of a doctor's consulting room than in his accustomed environment."

"They're certainly dingy," said Lord Mountdrago acidly. He paused. It was evident that this man who had so much self-assurance, so quick and decided a mind that he was never at a loss, at this moment was embarrassed. He smiled in order to show the doctor that he was at his ease, but his eyes betrayed his disquiet. When he spoke again it was with unnatural heartiness.

"The whole thing's so trivial that I can hardly bring myself to bother you with it. I'm afraid you'll just tell me not to be a fool and waste your valuable time."

"Even things that seem very trivial may have their importance. They can be a symptom of a deep-seated derangement. And my time is entirely at your disposal."

Dr. Audlin's voice was low and grave. The monotone in which he spoke was strangely soothing. Lord Mountdrago at length made up his mind to be frank.

"The fact is I've been having some very tiresome dreams lately. I know it's silly to pay any attention to them, but—well, the honest truth is that I'm afraid they've got on my nerves."

"Can you describe any of them to me?"

Lord Mountdrago smiled, but the smile that tried to be careless was only rueful.

"They're so idiotic, I can hardly bring myself to narrate them."

"Never mind."

"Well, the first I had was about a month ago. I dreamt that I was at a party at Connemara House. It was an official party. The King and Queen were to be there, and of course decorations were worn. I was wearing my ribbon and my star. I went into a sort of cloakroom they have to take off my coat. There was a little man there called Owen Griffiths, who's a Welsh member of Parliament, and to tell you the truth, I was surprised to see him. He's very common, and I said to myself: 'Really, Lydia Connemara is going too far, whom will she ask next?' I thought he looked at me rather curiously, but I didn't take any notice of him; in fact I cut the little bounder and walked upstairs. I suppose you've never been there?"

"Never."

"No, it's not the sort of house you'd ever be likely to go to. It's a rather vulgar house, but it's got a very fine marble staircase, and the Connemaras were at the top receiving their guests. Lady Connemara gave me a look of surprise when I shook hands with her, and began to giggle; I didn't pay much attention—she's a very silly, ill-bred woman, and her manners are no better than those of her ancestress whom King Charles II made a duchess I must say the reception rooms at Connemara House are stately. I walked through, nodding to a number of people and shaking hands; then I saw the German Ambassador talking with one of the Austrian archdukes.

I particularly wanted to have a word with him, so I went up and held out my hand. The moment the Archduke saw me he burst into a roar of laughter. I was deeply affronted. I looked him up and down sternly, but he only laughed the more. I was about to speak to him rather sharply, when there was a sudden hush, and I realized that the King and Queen had come. Turning my back on the Archduke, I stepped forward, and then, quite suddenly, I noticed that I hadn't got any trousers on. I was in short silk drawers, and I wore scarlet sock suspenders. No wonder Lady Connemara had giggled; no wonder the Archduke had laughed! I can't tell you what that moment was. An agony of shame. I awoke in a cold sweat. Oh, you don't know the relief I felt to find it was only a dream."

"It's the kind of dream that's not so very uncommon," said Dr. Audlin.

"I daresay not. But an odd thing happened next day. I was in the lobby of the House of Commons, when that fellow Griffiths walked slowly past me. He deliberately looked down at my legs, and then he looked me full in the face, and I was almost certain he winked. A ridiculous thought came to me. He'd been there the night before and seen me make that ghastly exhibition of myself and was enjoying the joke. But of course I knew that was impossible because it was only a dream. I gave him an icy glare, and he walked on. But he was grinning his head off."

Lord Mountdrago took his handkerchief out of his pocket and wiped the palms of his hands. He was making no attempt now to conceal his perturbation. Dr. Audlin never took his eyes off him.

"Tell me another dream."

"It was the night after, and it was even more absurd than the first one. I dreamt that I was in the House. There was a debate on foreign affairs which not only the country, but the world, had been looking forward to with the gravest concern. The government had decided on a change in their policy which vitally affected the future of the Empire. The occasion was historic. Of course the House was crowded. All the ambassadors were there. The galleries were packed. It fell to me to make the important speech of the evening. I had prepared it carefully. A man like me has enemies—there are a lot of people who resent my having achieved the position I have at an age when even the cleverest men are content with situations of relative obscurity—and I was determined that my speech should not only be worthy of the occasion, but should silence my detractors. It excited me to think that the whole world was hanging on my lips. I rose to my feet. If you've ever been in the House you'll know how members chat to one another during a debate, rustle papers and turn over reports. The silence was the silence of the grave when I began to speak. Suddenly I caught sight of that odious little bounder on one of the benches opposite, Griffiths, the Welsh member; he put out his tongue at me. I don't know if you've ever heard a vulgar music-hall song called 'A Bicycle Made for Two.' It was very popular a great many years ago. To show Griffiths how completely I despised him I began to sing it. I sang the first verse right through. There was a moment's surprise, and when I finished they cried, 'Hear, hear,' on the opposite benches. I put up my hand to silence them and sang the second verse. The House listened to me in stony silence and I felt the song wasn't going down very well. I was vexed, for I have a good baritone voice, and I was determined that they should do me justice. When I started the third verse the members began to laugh; in an instant the laughter spread; the ambassadors, the strangers in the Distinguished Strangers' Gallery, the ladies in the Ladies' Gallery, the reporters, they shook, they bellowed, they held their sides, they rolled in their seats; everyone was overcome with laughter except the ministers on the Front Bench immediately behind me. In that incredible, in that unprecedented, uproar they sat petrified. I gave them a glance, and suddenly the enormity of what I had done fell upon me. I had made myself the laughing-stock of the whole world. With misery I realized that I should have to resign. I woke and knew it was only a dream."

Lord Mountdrago's grand manner had deserted him as he narrated this, and now having finished he was pale and trembling. But with an effort he pulled himself together. He forced a laugh to his shaking lips.

"The whole thing was so fantastic that I couldn't help being amused. I didn't give it another thought, and when I went into the House on the following afternoon I was feeling in very good form. The debate was dull, but I had to be there, and I read some documents that required my attention. For some reason I chanced to look up, and I saw that Griffiths was speaking. He had an unpleasant Welsh accent and an unprepossessing appearance. I couldn't imagine that he had anything to say that it was worth my while to listen to, and I was about to return to my papers when he quoted two lines from 'A Bicycle Made for Two.' I couldn't help glancing at him, and I saw that his eyes were fixed on me with a grin of bitter mockery. I faintly shrugged my shoulders. It was comic that a scrubby little Welsh member should look at me like that. It was an odd coincidence that he should quote two lines from that disastrous song that I'd sung all through in my dream. I began to read my papers again, but I don't mind telling you that I found it difficult to concentrate on them. I was a little puzzled. Owen Griffiths had been in my first dream, the one at Connemara House, and I'd received a very definite impression afterwards that he knew the sorry figure I'd cut. Was it a mere coincidence that he had just quoted those two lines? I asked myself if it was possible that he was dreaming the same dreams as I was. But of course the idea was preposterous, and I determined not to give it a second thought."

There was a silence. Dr. Audlin looked at Lord Mountdrago and Lord Mountdrago looked at Dr. Audlin.

"Other people's dreams are very boring. My wife used to dream occasionally and insist on telling me her dreams next day with circumstantial detail. I found it maddening."

Dr. Audlin faintly smiled.

"You're not boring me."

"I'll tell you one more dream I had a few days later. I dreamt that I went into a public house at Limehouse. I've never been to Limehouse in my life and I don't think I've ever been in a public house since I was at Oxford, and yet I saw the street and the place I went into as exactly as if I were at home there. I went into a room—I don't know whether they call it the saloon bar or the private bar; there was a fireplace and a large leather armchair on one side of it, and on the other a small sofa; a bar ran the whole length of the room, and over it you could see into the public bar. Near the door was a round marble-topped table and two armchairs beside it. It was a Saturday night, and the place was packed. It was brightly lit, but the smoke was so thick that it made my eyes smart. I was dressed like a rough, with a cap on my head and a handkerchief round my neck. It seemed to me that most of the people there were drunk. I thought it rather amusing. There was a gramophone going, or the radio, I don't know which, and in front of the fireplace two women were doing a grotesque dance. There was a little crowd round them, laughing, cheering and singing. I went up to have a look, and some man said to me: ''Ave a drink, Bill.' There were glasses on the table full of a dark liquid which I understand is called brown ale. He gave me a glass, and not wishing to be conspicuous, I drank it. One of the women who were dancing broke away from the other and took hold of the glass. ''Ere, what's the idea?' she said. 'That's my beer you're putting away.' 'Oh, I'm so sorry,' I said, 'this gentleman offered it to me, and I very naturally thought it was his to offer.' 'All right, mate,' she said, 'I don't mind. You come an' 'ave a dance with me.' Before I could protest she'd caught hold of me and we were dancing together. And then I found myself sitting in the armchair with the woman on my lap and we were sharing a glass of beer. I should tell you that sex has never played any great part in my life. I married young because in my position it was desirable that I should marry, but also in order to settle once for all the question of sex. I had the two sons I had made up my mind to have, and then I put the whole matter on one side. I've always been too busy to give much thought to that kind of thing, and living so much in the public eye as I do, it would have been madness to do anything that might give rise to scandal. The greatest asset a politician can have is a blameless record as far as women are concerned. I have no patience with the men who smash up their careers for women. I only despise them. The woman I had on my knees was drunk; she wasn't pretty and she wasn't young: in fact, she was just a blowsy old prostitute. She filled me with disgust, and yet when she put her mouth to mine and kissed me, though her breath stank of beer and her teeth were decayed, though I loathed myself, I wanted her—I wanted her with all my soul. Suddenly I heard a voice: 'That's right, old boy, have a good time.' I looked up, and there was Owen Griffiths. I tried to spring out of the chair, but that horrible woman wouldn't let me. 'Don't pay no attention to 'im,' she said, ''e's only one of them nosy parkers.' 'You go to it,' he said. 'I know Moll. She'll give you your money's worth all right.' You know, I wasn't so much annoyed at his seeing me in that absurd situation as angry that he should address me as old boy. I pushed the woman aside and stood up and faced him. 'I don't know you, and I don't want to know you,' I said. 'I know you all right,' he said. 'And my advice to you, Molly, is, see that you get your money, he'll bilk you if he can.' There was a bottle of beer standing on the table close by. Without a word I seized it by the neck and hit him over the head with it as hard as I could. I made such a violent gesture that it woke me up."

"A dream of that sort is not incomprehensible," said Dr. Audlin. "It is the revenge nature takes on persons of unimpeachable character."

"The story's idiotic. I haven't told it you for its own sake. I've told it you for what happened next day. I wanted to look up something in a hurry, and I went into the library of the House. I got the book and began reading. I hadn't noticed when I sat down that Griffiths was sitting in a chair close by me. Another of the Labour Members came in and went up to him. 'Hullo, Owen,' he said to him, 'you're looking pretty dicky today.' 'I've got an awful headache,' he answered, 'I feel as if I'd been cracked over the head with a bottle.'"

Now Lord Mountdrago's face was grey with anguish.

"I knew then that the idea I'd had and dismissed as preposterous was true. I knew that Griffiths was dreaming my dreams and that he remembered them as well as I did."

"It may also have been a coincidence."

"When he spoke he didn't speak to his friend, he deliberately spoke to me. He looked at me with sullen resentment."

"Can you offer any suggestion why this same man should come into your dreams?"

"None."

Dr. Audlin's eyes had not left his patient's face and he saw that he lied. He had a pencil in his hand, and he drew a straggling line or two on his blotting paper. It often took a long time to get people to tell the truth, and yet they knew that unless they told it he could do nothing for them.

"The dream you've just described to me took place just over three weeks ago. Have you had any since?"

"Every night."

"And does this man Griffiths come into them all?"

"Yes."

The doctor drew more lines on his blotting paper. He wanted the silence, the drabness, the dull light of that little room to have its effect on Lord Mountdrago's sensibility. Lord Mountdrago threw himself back in his chair and turned his head away so that he should not see the other's grave eyes.

"Dr. Audlin, you must do something for me. I'm at the end of my tether. I shall go mad if this goes on. I'm afraid to go to sleep. Two or three nights I haven't. I've sat up reading and when I felt drowsy put on my coat and walked till I was exhausted. But I must have sleep. With all the work I have to do I must be at concert pitch; I must be in complete control of all my faculties. I need rest; sleep brings me none. I no sooner fall asleep than my dreams begin, and he's always there, that vulgar little cad, grinning at me, mocking me, despising me. It's a monstrous persecution. I tell you, Doctor, I'm not the man of my dreams; it's not fair to judge me by them. Ask anyone you like. I'm an honest, upright, decent man. No one can say anything against my moral character either private or public. My whole ambition is to serve my country and maintain its greatness. I have money, I have rank, I'm not exposed to many of the temptations of lesser men, so that it's no credit to me to be incorruptible; but this I can claim, that no honour, no personal advantage, no thought of self would induce me to swerve by a hair's breadth from my duty. I've sacrificed everything to become the man I am. Greatness is my aim. Greatness is within my reach, and I'm losing my nerve. I'm not that mean, despicable, cowardly, lewd creature that horrible little man sees. I've told you three of my dreams; they're nothing; that man has seen me do things that are so beastly, so horrible, so shameful, that even if my life depended on it I wouldn't tell them. And he remembers them. I can hardly meet the derision and disgust I see in his eyes, and I even hesitate to speak because I know my words can seem to him nothing but utter humbug. He's seen me do things that no man with any self-respect would do, things for which men are driven out of the society of their fellows and sentenced to long terms of imprisonment; he's heard the foulness of my speech; he's seen me not only ridiculous, but revolting. He despises me and he no longer pretends to conceal it. I tell you that if you can't do something to help me I shall either kill myself or kill him."

"I wouldn't kill him if I were you," said Dr. Audlin coolly, in that soothing voice of his. "In this country the consequences of killing a fellow creature are awkward."

"I shouldn't be hanged for it, if that's what you mean. Who would know that I'd killed him? That dream of mine has shown me how. I told you, the day after I'd hit him over the head with a beer bottle he had such a headache that he couldn't see straight. He said so himself. That shows that he can feel with his waking body what happens to his body asleep. It's not with a bottle I shall hit him next time. One night, when I'm dreaming, I shall find myself with a knife in my hand or a revolver in my pocket—I must because I want to so intensely—and then I shall seize my opportunity. I'll stick him like a pig; I'll shoot him like a dog. In the heart. And then I shall be free of this fiendish persecution."

Some people might have thought that Lord Mountdrago was mad; after all the years during which Dr. Audlin had been treating the diseased souls of men he knew how thin a line divides those whom we call sane from those whom we call insane. He knew how often in men who to all appearance were healthy and normal, who were seemingly devoid of imagination, and who fulfilled the duties of common life with credit to themselves and with benefit to their fellows, when you gained their confidence, when you tore away the mask they wore to the world, you found not only hideous abnormality, but kinks so strange, mental extravagances so fantastic, that in that respect you could only call them lunatic. If you put them in an asylum, not all the asylums in the world would be large enough. Anyhow, a man was not certifiable because he had strange dreams and they had shattered his nerve. The case was singular, but it was only an exaggeration of others that had come under Dr. Audlin's observation; he was doubtful, however, whether the methods of treatment that he had so often found efficacious would here avail.

"Have you consulted any other member of my profession?" he asked.

"Only Sir Augustus. I merely told him that I suffered from nightmares. He said I was overworked and recommended me to go for a cruise. That's absurd. I can't leave the Foreign Office just now when the international situation needs constant attention. I'm indispensable, and I know it. On my conduct at the present juncture my whole future depends. He gave me sedatives. They had no effect. He gave me tonics. They were worse than useless. He's an old fool."

"Can you give any reason why it should be this particular man who persists in coming into your dreams?"

"You asked me that question before. I answered it."

That was true. But Dr. Audlin had not been satisfied with the answer.

"Just now you talked of persecution. Why should Owen Griffiths want to persecute you?"

"I don't know."

Lord Mountdrago's eyes shifted a little. Dr. Audlin was sure that he was not speaking the truth.

"Have you ever done him an injury?"

"Never."

Lord Mountdrago made no movement, but Dr. Audlin had a queer feeling that he shrank into his skin. He saw before him a large, proud man who gave the impression that the questions put to him were an insolence, and yet for all that, behind that façade, was something shifting and startled that made you think of a frightened animal in a trap. Dr. Audlin leaned forward and by the power of his eyes forced Lord Mountdrago to meet them.

"Are you quite sure?"

"Quite sure. You don't seem to understand that our ways lead along different paths. I don't wish to harp on it, but I must remind you that I am a Minister of the Crown and Griffiths is an obscure member of the Labour Party. Naturally there's no social connection between us; he's a man of very humble origin, he's not the sort of person I should be likely to meet at any of the houses I go to; and politically our respective stations are so far separated that we could not possibly have anything in common."

"I can do nothing for you unless you tell me the complete truth."

Lord Mountdrago raised his eyebrows. His voice was rasping.

"I'm not accustomed to having my word doubted, Dr. Audlin. If you're going to do that, I think to take up any more of your time can only be a waste of mine. If you will kindly let my secretary know what your fee is, he will see that a cheque is sent to you."

For all the expression that was to be seen on Dr. Audlin's face you might have thought that he simply had not heard what Lord Mountdrago said. He continued to look steadily into his eyes, and his voice was grave and low.

"Have you done anything to this man that *he* might look upon as an injury?"

Lord Mountdrago hesitated. He looked away, and then, as though there were in Dr. Audlin's eyes a compelling force that he could not resist, looked back. He answered sulkily:

"Only if he was a dirty, second-rate little cad."

"But that is exactly what you've described him to be."

Lord Mountdrago sighed. He was beaten. Dr. Audlin knew that the sigh meant he was going at last to say what he had till then held back. Now he had no longer to insist. He dropped his eyes and began again drawing vague geometrical figures on his blotting paper. The silence lasted two or three minutes.

"I'm anxious to tell you everything that can be of any use to you. If I didn't mention this before, it's only because it was so unimportant that I didn't see how it could possibly have anything to do with the case. Griffiths won a seat at the last election, and he began to make a nuisance of himself almost at once. His father's a miner, and he worked in a mine himself when he was a boy; he's been a schoolmaster in the board schools and a journalist. He's that half-baked, conceited intellectual, with inadequate knowledge, ill-considered ideas and impractical plans, that compulsory education has brought forth from the working classes. He's a scrawny, grey-faced man who looks half starved, and he's always very slovenly in appearance; heaven knows members nowadays don't bother much about their dress, but his clothes are an outrage to the dignity of the House. They're ostentatiously shabby, his collar's never clean, and his tie's never tied properly; he looks as if he hadn't had a bath for a month, and his hands are filthy. The Labour Party have two or three fellows on the Front Bench who've got a certain ability, but the rest of them don't amount to much. In the kingdom of the blind the one-eyed man is king: because Griffiths is glib and has a lot of superficial information on a number of subjects, the Whips on his side began to put him up to speak whenever there was a chance. It appeared that he fancied himself on foreign affairs, and he was continually asking me silly, tiresome questions. I don't mind telling you that I made a point of snubbing him as soundly as I thought he deserved. From the beginning I hated the way he talked, his whining voice and his vulgar accent; he had nervous mannerisms that intensely irritated me. He talked rather shyly, hesitatingly, as though it were torture for him to speak and yet he was forced to by some inner passion, and often he used to say some very disconcerting things. I'll admit that now and again he had a sort of tub-thumping eloquence. It had a certain influence over the ill-regulated minds of the members of his party. They were impressed by his earnestness, and they weren't, as I was, nauseated by his sentimentality. A certain sentimentality is the common coin of political debate. Nations are governed by self-interest, but they prefer to believe that their aims are altruistic, and the politician is justified if with fair words and fine phrases he can persuade the electorate that the hard bargain he is driving for his country's advantage tends to the good of humanity. The mistake people like Griffiths make is to take these fair words and fine phrases at their face value. He's a crank, and a noxious crank. He calls himself an idealist. He has at his tongue's end all the tedious blather that the intelligentsia have been boring us with for years. Nonresistance. The brotherhood of man. You know the hopeless rubbish. The worst of it was that it impressed not only his own party, it even shook some of the sillier, more sloppy-minded members of ours. I heard rumours that Griffiths was likely to get office when a Labour Government came in; I even heard it suggested that he might get the Foreign Office. The notion was grotesque but not impossible. One day I had occasion to wind up a debate on foreign affairs which Griffiths had opened. He'd spoken for an hour. I thought it a very good opportunity to cook his goose, and by God, sir, I cooked it. I tore his speech to pieces. I pointed out the faultiness of his reasoning and emphasized the deficiency of his knowledge. In the House of Commons the most devastating weapon is ridicule: I mocked him; I bantered him; I was in good form that day and the House rocked with laughter. Their laughter excited me, and I excelled myself. The Opposition sat glum and silent, but even some of them couldn't help laughing once or twice; it's not intolerable, you know, to see a colleague, perhaps a rival, made a fool of. And if ever a man was made a fool of, I made a fool of Griffiths. He shrank down in his seat; I saw his face go white, and presently he buried it in his hands. When I sat down I'd killed him. I'd destroyed his prestige for ever; he had no more chance of getting office when a Labour Government came in than the policeman at the door. I heard afterwards that his father, the old miner, and his mother had come up from Wales, with various supporters of his in the constituency, to watch the triumph they expected him to have. They had seen only his utter humiliation. He'd won the constituency by the narrowest margin. An incident like that might very easily lose him his seat. But that was no business of mine."

"Should I be putting it too strongly if I said you had ruined his career?" asked Dr. Audlin.

"I don't suppose you would."

"That is a very serious injury you've done him."

"He brought it on himself."

"Have you never felt any qualms about it?"

"I think perhaps if I'd known that his father and mother were there I might have let him down a little more gently."

There was nothing further for Dr. Audlin to say, and he set about treating his patient in such a manner as he thought might avail. He sought by suggestion to make him forget his dreams when he awoke; he sought to make him sleep so deeply that he would not dream. He found Lord Mountdrago's resistance impossible to break down. At the end of an hour he dismissed him.

Since then he had seen Lord Mountdrago half a dozen times. He had done him no good. The frightful dreams continued every night to harass the unfortunate man, and it was clear that his general condition was growing rapidly worse. He was worn out. His irritability was uncontrollable. Lord Mountdrago was angry because he received no benefit from his treatment, and yet continued it, not only because it seemed his only hope, but because it was a relief to him to have someone with whom he could talk openly. Dr. Audlin came to the conclusion at last that there was only one way in which Lord Mountdrago could achieve deliverance, but he knew him well enough to be assured that of his own free will he would never, never take it. If Lord Mountdrago was to be saved from the breakdown that was threatening, he must be induced to take a step that must be abhorrent to his pride of birth and his self-complacency. Dr. Audlin was convinced that to delay was impossible. He was treating his patient by suggestion, and after several visits found him more suspectible to it. At length he managed to get him into a condition of somnolence. With his low, soft, monotonous voice he soothed his tortured nerves. He repeated the same words over and over again. Lord Mountdrago lay quite still, his eyes closed; his breathing was regular, and his limbs were relaxed. Then Dr. Audlin in the same quiet tone spoke the words he had prepared.

"You will go to Owen Griffiths and say that you are sorry that you caused him that great injury. You will say that you will do whatever lies in your power to undo the harm that you have done him."

The words acted on Lord Mountdrago like the blow of a whip across his face. He shook himself out of his hypnotic state and sprang to his feet. His eyes blazed with passion, and he poured forth upon Dr. Audlin a stream of angry vituperation such as even he had never heard. He swore at him. He cursed him. He used language of such obscenity that Dr. Audlin, who had heard every sort of foul word, sometimes from the lips of chaste and distinguished women, was surprised that he knew it.

"Apologize to that filthy little Welshman? I'd rather kill myself."

"I believe it to be the only way in which you can regain your balance."

Dr. Audlin had not often seen a man presumably sane in such a condition of uncontrollable fury. Lord Mountdrago grew red in the face, and his eyes bulged out of his head. He did really foam at the mouth. Dr. Audlin watched him coolly, waiting for the storm to wear itself out, and presently he saw that Lord Mountdrago, weakened by the strain to which he had been subjected for so many weeks, was exhausted.

"Sit down," he said then, sharply.

Lord Mountdrago crumpled up into a chair.

"Christ, I feel all in. I must rest a minute and then I'll go."

For five minutes perhaps they sat in complete silence. Lord Mountdrago was a gross, blustering bully, but he was also a gentleman. When he broke the silence he had recovered his self-control.

"I'm afraid I've been very rude to you. I'm ashamed of the things I've said to you, and I can only say you'd be justified if you refused to have anything more to do with me. I hope you won't do that. I feel that my visits to you do help me. I think you're my only chance."

"You mustn't give another thought to what you said. It was of no consequence."

"But there's one thing you mustn't ask me to do, and that is to make excuses to Griffiths."

"I've thought a great deal about your case. I don't pretend to understand it, but I believe that your only chance of release is to do what I proposed. I have a notion that we're none of us one self, but many, and one of the selves in you has risen up against the injury you did Griffiths and has taken on the form of Griffiths in your mind and is punishing you for what you cruelly did. If I were a priest I should tell you that it is your conscience that has adopted the shape and lineaments of this man to scourge you to repentance and persuade you to reparation."

"My conscience is clear. It's not my fault if I smashed the man's career. I crushed him like a slug in my garden. I regret nothing."

It was on these words that Lord Mountdrago had left him. Reading through his notes, while he waited, Dr. Audlin considered how best he could bring his patient to the state of mind that, now that his usual methods of treatment had failed, he thought alone could help him. He glanced at his clock. It was six. It was strange that Lord Mountdrago did not come. He knew he had intended to because a secretary had rung up that morning to say that he would be with him at the usual hour. He must have been detained by pressing work. This notion gave Dr. Audlin something else to think of: Lord Mountdrago was quite unfit to work and in no condition to deal with important matters of state. Dr. Audlin wondered whether it behooved him to get in touch with someone in authority, the Prime Minister or the Permanent Under Secretary for Foreign Affairs, and impart to him his conviction that Lord Mountdrago's mind was so unbalanced that it was dangerous to leave affairs of moment in his hands. It was a ticklish thing to do. He might cause needless trouble and get roundly snubbed for his pains. He shrugged his shoulders.

"After all," he reflected, "the politicians have made such a mess of the world during the last five-and-twenty years, I don't suppose it makes much odds if they're mad or sane."

He rang the bell.

"If Lord Mountdrago comes now, will you tell him that I have another appointment at six-fifteen and so I'm afraid I can't see him."

"Very good, sir."

"Has the evening paper come yet?"

"I'll go and see."

In a moment the servant brought it in. A huge headline ran across the front page: Tragic Death of Foreign Minister.

"My God!" cried Dr. Audlin.

For once he was wrenched out of his wonted calm. He was shocked, horribly shocked, and yet he was not altogether surprised. The possibility that Lord Mountdrago might commit suicide had occurred to him several times, for that it was suicide he could not doubt. The paper said that Lord Mountdrago had been waiting in a tube station, standing on the edge of the platform, and as the train came in was seen to fall on the rail. It was supposed that he had had a sudden attack of faintness. The paper went on to say that Lord Mountdrago had been suffering for some weeks from the effects of overwork, but had felt it impossible to absent himself while the foreign situation demanded his unremitting attention. Lord Mountdrago was another victim of the strain that modern politics placed upon those who played the more important parts in it. There was a neat little piece about the talents and industry, the patriotism and vision, of the deceased statesman, followed by various surmises upon the Prime Minister's choice of his successor. Dr. Audlin read all this. He had not liked Lord Mountdrago. The chief emotion that his death caused in him was dissatisfaction with himself because he had been able to do nothing for him.

Perhaps he had done wrong in not getting into touch with Lord Mountdrago's doctor. He was discouraged, as always when failure frustrated his conscientious efforts, and repulsion seized him for the theory and practice of this empiric doctrine by which he earned his living. He was dealing with dark and mysterious forces that it was perhaps beyond the powers of the human mind to understand. He was like a man blindfold trying to feel his way to he knew not whither. Listlessly he turned the pages of the paper. Suddenly he gave a great start, and an exclamation once more was forced from his lips. His eyes had fallen on a small paragraph near the bottom of a column. Sudden Death of an M.P., he read. Mr. Owen Griffiths, member for so-and-so, had been taken ill in Fleet Street that afternoon and when he was brought to Charing Cross Hospital life was found to be extinct. It was supposed that death was due to natural causes, but an inquest would be held. Dr. Audlin could hardly believe his eyes. Was it possible that the night before Lord Mountdrago had at last in his dream found himself possessed of the weapon, knife or gun, that he had wanted, and had killed his tormentor, and had that ghostly murder, in the same way as the blow with the bottle had given him a racking headache on the following day, taken effect a certain number of hours later on the waking man? Or was it, more mysterious and more frightful, that when Lord Mountdrago sought relief in death, the enemy he had so cruelly wronged, unappeased, escaping from his own mortality, had pursued him to some other sphere, there to torment him still? It was strange. The sensible thing was to look upon it merely as an odd coincidence. Dr. Audlin rang the bell.

"Tell Mrs. Milton that I'm sorry I can't see her this evening, I'm not well."

It was true; he shivered as though of an ague. With some kind of spiritual sense he seemed to envisage a bleak, a horrible void. The dark night of the soul engulfed him, and he felt a strange, primeval terror of he knew not what.

MUSIC ON THE MUSCATATUCK

from *The Friendly Persuasion*

JESSAMYN WEST

NEAR the banks of the Muscatatuck where once the woods had stretched, dark row on row, and where the fox grapes and wild mint still flourished, Jess Birdwell, an Irish Quaker, built his white clapboard house. Here he lacked for very little. On a peg by the front door hung a starling in a wooden cage and at the back door stood a spring-house, the cold spring water running between crocks of yellow-skinned milk. At the front gate a moss-rose said welcome and on a trellis over the parlor window a Prairie Queen nodded at the roses in the parlor carpet—blooms no nurseryman's catalogue had ever carried and gay company for the sober Quaker volumes: Fox's life, Penn's "Fruits of Solitude," Woolman's "Journal," which stood in the parlor secretary.

Jess had a good wife, a Quaker minister, Eliza Cope before she was wed, and a houseful of children. Eliza was a fine woman, pious and work-brickel and good-looking as female preachers are apt to be: a little, black-haired, glossy woman with a mind of her own.

He had a good business, too. He was a nurseryman with the best stock of berries and fruits west of Philadelphia; in the apple line: Rambo, Maiden Blush, Early Harvest, Northern Spy, a half dozen others; May Duke cherries; Stump the World, a white-fleshed peach; the Lucretia dewberry, a wonder for pies and cobblers. Pears, currant bushes, gooseberries, whatever the land could support or fancy demand in the way of fruits, Jess had them.

There were extras to be had, too, there on the banks of the Muscatatuck: black bass; catfish that weren't choosy, that would come out of the water with their jaws clamped about a piece of cotton batting. Pawpaws smooth and sweet as nectar, persimmons with an October flavor, sarvice berries tart as spring.

In spring, meadow and roadside breathed flowers; in summer there was a shimmer of sunlight onto the great trees whose shadows still dappled the farmland: sycamore, oak, tulip, shagbark hickory. When fall came a haze lay across the cornfields, across the stands of goldenrod and farewell summer, until heaven and earth seemed bound together—and Jess, standing on a little rise at the back of the house, looking across the scope of land which fell away to the river, would have, in pure content, to wipe his eyes and blow his nose before he'd be in a fit state to descend to the house.

Yet, in spite of this content, Jess wasn't completely happy, and for no reason anyone could have hit upon at first guess. It certainly wasn't having Eliza ride every First Day morning to the Grove Meeting House, there to sit on the elevated minister's bench and speak when the spirit moved her. Jess knew Eliza had had a call to the ministry and was proud to hear her preach in her gentle way of loving-kindness and the brotherhood of man.

No, it wasn't Eliza's preaching nor any outward lack the eye could see that troubled Jess. It was music. Jess pined for music, though it would be hard to say how he'd come by any such longing. To the Quakers music was a popish dido, a sop to the senses, a hurdle waiting to trip man in his upward struggle. They kept it out of their Meeting Houses and out of their homes, too. Oh, there were a few women who'd hum a little while polishing their lamp chimneys, and a few men with an inclination to whistle while dropping corn, but as to real music, sung or played, Jess had no more chance to hear it than a woodchuck.

What chances there were, though, he took. He'd often manage to be around the Methodist Church when they had their midweek services and he felt a kind of glory in his soul that wasn't entirely religious when the enthusiastic Methodists hit into "Old Hundred." And when on the Fourth of July, Amanda Prentis soared upwards on the high notes of "The Star-Spangled Banner" only Eliza's determined nudgings could bring Jess back to earth.

This seemed for some time about the best Jess would be able to do in the way of music without having Eliza and her whole congregation buzzing about his ears, the best he could do anyway until he took that trip to Philadelphia and met Waldo Quigley; though of course he had no way of knowing when he was planning the trip that it would turn out as it did.

Jess had been hearing for some time about a new early cherry and he'd made up his mind to go to Philadelphia, and if they were all he'd heard, order some for the Maple Grove Nursery. There wasn't, perhaps, any real need of his going as far as Philadelphia, but to a Quaker, Philadelphia was the place to go if nothing more than a pocket handkerchief was needed. So Eliza packed his valise for him, drove him to Vernon herself and saw him on the train.

The first word Eliza had from Jess was a letter mailed a couple of days after he left. He didn't mention Waldo Quigley in that letter, though as a matter of fact he was already hand in glove with him as Eliza discovered later. The letter was short: health good, scenery pleasant, that was about the whole of it with the exception of a postscript saying, "Thank thee, dear Eliza, for the little packet thee put in my nightshirt pocket."

The "little packet" contained peppermints, and it was through offering one of these to Waldo Quigley that Jess made his acquaintance. Jess was always sociable when he traveled. He used to say that sun, moon and stars were the same everywhere and only the people different and if you didn't get to know them you'd as well have stayed home and milked the cows.

After Waldo Quigley put the peppermint in his mouth he settled his big, portly, black-suited frame onto the seat opposite Jess.

"Well, sir," he said, "you a Hoosier?"

Jess said he was and the big man went on, "Got a president shaping up out your way. Got an up-and-comer there on your prairies, a man who can out-talk a trumpet and out-see a telescope. He's a little giant. Man to elevate somewhat and he'll set our country on its feet. He's the man we need."

Jess sniffed. He was a fiery Republican, as fiery at least as a Quaker's apt to be. "Friend," said he, "the man we need is no little giant, but a big one. Not a man busy rousing up the countryside, setting state against state, but a man with the interest of all at heart, little farmer as well as plantation owner, black as well as white."

Jess could see, "That's Stephen A. Douglas," work up Waldo Quigley's gullet as far as his back teeth but there he stopped the words, said, "Them's my sentiments precisely, Brother Birdwell, them's my very thoughts, only better said."

Jess wrinkled up his big nose. "I see thee's a man of harmony, friend."

"Brother," replied the big man, "you put your tongue to the right word. Harmony's what I preach and harmony's what I practice."

Jess listened to these words, took another look at the big man's black suit and decided that he was a preacher of some sort.

"Is thee, perhaps," he asked mildly, "a minister of the gospel? Though thy habit for a man of the cloth is perhaps a mite unorthodox."

Mr. Quigley cleared his throat, swallowing the last of his first peppermint. "I can't say as I've ever been ordained," he admitted, "but my work's been so much with them that has that I've fallen into a sedate manner of dressing. It strikes me as being a more seemly thing to do. Helps business, too," he added.

"Business?" asked Jess.

"You named it yourself, Mr. Birdwell. Harmony is my business. Do-re-mi. Also la-ti-do. Not forgetting fa-sol. Harmony. The music of the spheres. God's way of speaking to his children. The power that soothes the savage beast, the song that quiets newborn babes and eases the pangs of the dying man. In a word, music."

"In several words in fact," ruminated Jess. "Is thee then, Brother Quigley, a musician?" he asked.

"Musician? Yes. But I," said he frankly, "am that rather unusual combination, a musical businessman, or perhaps more truly a businesslike musician. There's plenty of men can keep a double entry set of books and there's a number more, though fewer, can tell a grace note from a glissando, but I," handing Jess a card, "can do both."

Jess took the card and read aloud, "Professor Waldo Quigley, Traveling Representative, Payson and Clarke. The World's Finest Organs. Also Sheet Music and Song Books."

Brother Quigley reached out, took the card from Jess and wrote "Personal Compliments" on it.

"I note from your speech you're a Quaker, and knowing the way that sect—not that it ain't the finest in the world," he said politely—"feels about music I wouldn't want you to think I was trying to work against your prejudices—convictions rather. So," he said, handing the card back to Jess, "I write 'Personal Compliments,' to show I'm free of any profit-making motives; that we meet man to man. Pays to be delicate-like where religion is concerned. Pays every time," he said, nodding to Jess.

Jess tried Payson and Clarke over once or twice on his tongue. "Payson and Clarke," he said. "So thee sells Payson and Clarke's. They've got one unless I disremember in the Methodist meeting house at Rush Branch."

"Sure they have," said Brother Quigley. "Sure they have." He took a little red book from an inner pocket and flipped a few pages. "Yes, sir. I sold them that organ three years ago April 19. One more strawberry festival and they'll have it paid for."

"Thee sells a good instrument then. I've heard that organ now and again in passing."

"Good? Mr. Birdwell, it's better than good. Three years ago after them Methodists at Rush Branch heard my concert and song recital, they said to me, 'Professor Quigley, we don't ever calculate to hear the voice of God any more plain while here on earth.'"

Jess said, "That's carrying it a little far, mebbe," but he was really burning to hear more about the Payson and Clarke.

"Well, of course," Brother Quigley reminded him, "you got to remember they's Methodists. Tending toward the shouting order. But this organ, Methodists aside, is pure gumbo, absolutely pure gumbo."

"Gumbo," Jess repeated.

"Rich. Satisfying. Deep. Gumbo, pure gumbo."

Jess knew a thing or two about organs though it would be hard to say how: perhaps from reading Chalmer's "Universal Encyclopedia," perhaps from an inspection of the Methodist organ. Perhaps in neither way. Knowledge of what you love somehow comes to you; you don't have to read nor analyze nor study. If you love a thing enough, knowledge of it seeps into you, with particulars more real than any chart can furnish. Maybe it was that way with Jess and organs.

So he asked, "How many reeds in a Payson and Clarke?"

"Forty-eight, Brother Birdwell, not counting the tuba mirabalis. But in the Payson and Clarke, number ain't what counts—it's the quality. Those reeds duplicate the human throat. They got timbre." And he landed on the French word the way a hen lands on the water, skeptical, but hoping for the best.

"How many stops?" Jess asked.

"Eight. And that vox humana! The throat of an angel. It cries, it sighs, it sings. You can hear the voice of your lost child in it. Did you ever lose a child, Brother Birdwell?"

"No," said Jess shortly.

"You can hear the voice of your old mother calling to you from the further shore."

"Ma lives in Germantown," said Jess.

If the conversation had followed in this direction, Jess would never have come home with a Payson and Clarke; but in every nerve Brother Quigley could feel a prospect retreating and he changed his tack.

"The Payson and Clarke comes in four different finishes," he said. "Oak, maple, walnut and mahogany. Got a cabinet that's purely elegant. Most organ's got two swinging brackets. This one's got four. Two for lamps, two for vases. Has a plate mirror over the console. There's not a square inch of unornamented wood in the whole cabinet. No, sir, there's not an inch of dingy, unembellished wood the length and breadth of the cabinet. But, Brother Birdwell, you're a musician yourself. You're not interested in cabinets. You're interested in tone. Tone's what the artist looks for. Tone's what Payson and Clarke's got."

He began to hum under his breath. Low at first, then louder, with occasional words. "Tum-te-tum—the riverside—tum-te-tum—upon its tide."

"That's a likely tune," Jess said.

"Can't do justice to it singing."

But he stopped humming, launched into the words. He had a fine baritone. Flatted a little, Jess thought, but not bad. When he exhaled heavily on a high note, Jess was sorry to find he'd had a nip or two, but before the piece was finished Jess was beating time with his forefinger on the red plush arm of the seat, completely forgetful of the spirits Brother Quigley had surely had.

"What's the piece called?" Jess asked.

" 'The Old Musician and His Harp.' It was written to be played on an organ. Mortifies me that you have to hear it first time sung, merely."

"Thee's a good voice," Jess said.

"Fair to middling. Fair to middling, only."

He sank a fat hand in one of his big black pockets and brought up a leather-covered flask. He wiped the mouth carefully on his coat-tail and held it toward Jess.

"Wet your whistle and we'll sing it through together."

Jess shook his head.

"Well, I didn't suppose you would, but it's a pity. Cleans your pipes. Extends your range. Gives you gumbo." He took a long swig himself.

"Try it with me, Brother Birdwell."

Jess said afterward he didn't have the slightest intention of making a show of himself in a B. & O. parlor car singing "The Old Musician and His Harp," or any other song, for that matter. But that tune was a hard thing to give the go-by; the mind said the words and the toe tapped the time; with the whole body already singing it, that way, opening the mouth to let the words out seemed a mighty small matter and before Jess knew it he was taking the high notes in his fine, clear tenor. Jess had the nose for a really first-class tenor—there never was a first-class tenor with a button nose, and Jess, with his, high-bridged, more Yankee than Quaker, had just the nose for it. Before he and Brother Quigley had finished a couple of verses half the parlor car was joining in the chorus.

Bring my harp to me again,
Let me hear its gentle strain;
Let me hear its chords once more
Ere I pass to yon bright shore.

When they finished Brother Quigley had another nip. "Got to cool the pipes," he said. "Now, Brother Birdwell, when you get to Philly, when you get them cherries located, you stop in at Payson and Clarke's and hear that the way it was meant to be heard. Hear it on the organ. No obligation whatever. Privilege to play for a fellow artist."

Jess hadn't a notion in the world of buying an organ when he went into Payson and Clarke's. He'd got the cherry stock he'd come after, had had a nice visit with his mother, and was ready to start homeward when he thought he'd as well hear "The Old Musician and His Harp," on a Payson and Clarke. Brother Quigley had been clever to him and it was no more than humanly decent to let the man show him what the organ could do.

That was the way he had it figured out to himself before he went in, anyway.

When he'd walked out, the organ was his. He didn't know what he'd do with it; he didn't think Eliza would hear to keeping it; he thought he'd like as not slipped clean away from grace, but he had the papers for the organ in his pocket. He'd paid half cash, the rest to be in nursery stock. Clarke of Payson and Clarke was an orchardist.

As soon as Jess heard Waldo Quigley run his fingers over that organ's keys with a sound as liquid as the Muscatatuck after a thaw he'd known he was sunk. And when he'd found he could chord "The Old Musician" himself, when Waldo Quigley said, "Never knew a man with a better tremolo," when he pumped the air into the organ with his feet and drew it out with his fingers, sounding like an echo of eternity, he began casting up his bank balance in his mind. He was past figuring out the right and wrong of the matter; all he was interested in was getting it, having that organ where he could lay his hands across it, hear whenever he liked those caressing tones.

He managed to get home a few days before the organ arrived. He didn't say a word to Eliza about what he'd done. He figured it was a thing which would profit by being led up to gradually. He talked a good deal in those few days about music; how God must like it or He wouldn't have put songbirds in the world, and how the angels were always pictured with harp and zithern.

Eliza was not receptive. "Thee's neither bird nor angel, Jess Birdwell, and had the Lord wanted thee, either singing or plucking a harp, thee would be feathered now one way or another."

There'd been an early snow the day the organ arrived; a foot or two on the level, much more in the drifts. Jess himself brought the organ home from Vernon on the sled.

Eliza knew what it was the minute she laid eyes on the box, for all Jess' care in covering it over with an old rag carpet. Jess' talk about birds and angels had made her fearful of something of the kind, only she hadn't thought it'd be as bad as an organ; a flute, or maybe a French harp he could go down cellar and play had been the worst her imaginings had pictured for her. But she knew it was an organ before Jess had got the covering off the crate, and was out in the snow by the time Enoch had the horses out of the traces.

"What's this thee's bringing home, Jess Birdwell?"

Though she knew well enough. She just wanted to hear him put his tongue to it.

"It's a Payson and Clarke," Jess said, still trying to be gradual.

But it was no use. "It's an organ," Eliza said. "Jess, Jess, what's thee thinking of? Bringing this thing here? Me, a recorded minister and the house full of growing children. What's the neighbors to think? What's the Grove Meeting to think?"

If she'd kept on in this sorrowful strain Jess would like as not have got shut of the organ, but Eliza didn't stop there.

"Jess Birdwell," she said, "if thee takes that organ in the house, I stay out. Thee can make thy choice. Thee can have thy wife or thee can have that instrument; but both, thee cannot have."

Jess had a heart as soft as pudding, and if Eliza'd said Please, if she'd let a tear slide out of her soft black eye, that organ would have been done for; but commands, threats, that was a different matter entirely.

Jess called to the hired man who'd taken the horses to the barn, "Come and give me a hand with this organ, Enoch."

A heart soft as pudding, till someone took it on himself to tell Jess which way to turn, then the pudding froze, and if you weren't careful you'd find yourself cut to the bone on an ice splinter. A mild man until pushed, but Jess solidified fast with pushing.

Eliza saw the granite coming, but she was of martyr stock herself and felt the time had come to suffer for the right. She sat flat down in the snow, or as flat as petticoats and skirts would let her. There in the snow she sat and said, "Jess Birdwell, here I stay until that organ is taken away."

Jess said, "We'll uncrate it where it stands, Enoch, then carry it up to the house. No use having the weight of the crate to move, too."

So they went to work on it, got it out of its case and the excelsior packing. Enoch kept his eye on Eliza sitting there in the snow. She made him feel uncomfortable, as if the least he could do would be to give her his coat to sit on.

"Well, let's not dally here, Enoch," Jess said, seeming not to even see Eliza. "Let's get it up to the house."

As they went up the path to the house, straining and puffing through the snow, Enoch said, "Ain't she liable to catch her death of cold there?"

"I figure," said Jess, "that when the snow melts through the last petticoat she'll move."

He was wrong about that. Eliza was wet to the skin before she came up to the house. She had sat there casting up the matter in her mind, but she knew that when Jess was set he was a problem for the Lord. And she had enough respect for both to leave them to each other. There was nothing ever to be gained, she thought, by dissension. Peace, she could at least have. Jess had just finished dusting the organ when Eliza came in, went to the stove and stood there steaming.

"Jess," she asked, "is thee set on having this organ? Remembering thy children and my ministry, is thee still set?"

"Yes, Eliza," Jess said, "I'm set."

"Well," she said, "that's settled;" and being on the whole a reasonable as well as a pious woman, she added, "It will have to go in the attic."

"I'd thought of that," Jess said, "and I'm willing."

So that's the way it was done. The organ was put in the attic and from there it could be heard downstairs, but not in any full-bodied way. It took the gumbo out of it—having it in the attic—and besides Jess was careful not to play it when anyone was in the house. He was careful, that is, until the day the Ministry and Oversight Committee called. He was careful that day, too; it was Mattie who wasn't careful, though unlucky's more the word for it.

Jess had noted right off that Mattie had a musical turn. She'd learned to pick out "The Old Musician" by herself, with one hand, and when Jess discovered this, he taught her the bass chords so that she could play for him to sing. That was a bitter pill for Eliza to swallow, and just what she'd feared: the children becoming infected with Jess' weakness for music. Still, she couldn't keep herself from listening when the deep organ notes with Jess' sweet tenor flying above them came seeping down through the ceiling into the sitting-room below.

But in spite of Jess' being careful, in spite of Eliza's being twice as strict as usual, and speaking at the Hopewell Meeting House with increased gravity, the matter got noised about. Not that there was an organ at

Birdwells': there wasn't anything definite known, anything you could put your finger on. It was just a feeling that Friend Birdwell wasn't standing as squarely in the light as he'd done at one time. Perhaps someone had heard a strain of organ music coming out of an attic window some spring evening, but more than likely it was just the guilty look Eliza had.

However that may be, the Ministry and Oversight Committee came one night to call. It was nearing seven; supper had been over for some time, the dishes were washed and the table was set for breakfast. Jess and Eliza were in the sitting-room resting after the heat and work of the day and listening to the children who were playing duck-on-rock down by the branch.

The Committee drove up in Amos Pease's surrey, but by the back way, leaving the rig at the carriage-house, so that the first sign Jess and Eliza had of visitors was the smell of trodden mint. Amos Pease wasn't a man to note where he put his feet down when duty called.

Eliza smelled it first and stepped over to the west window to see who was coming. She saw, and in a flash she knew why. "It's the Ministry and Oversight," she said, and her voice shook, but when Amos Pease knocked at the door she was sitting in her rocker, her feet on a footstool, one hand lying loose and easy in the other.

Jess answered the knock. "Good evening, Amos. Good evening, Ezra. Good evening, Friend Hooper."

The Committee said its good evenings to Jess and Eliza, found chairs, adjusted First Day coat-tails—it wasn't First Day, but they'd put on their best since what they had to do was serious. But before they could even ease into their questions with some remark upon the weather or how the corn was shaping up—Jess heard it—the faint kind of leathery sigh the organ made when the foot first touched the bellows. That sound was like a pain hitting him in the heart and he thought, I've sold my birthright for a mess of pottage. For Jess was a Quaker through and through, no misdoubting that. For two hundred years his people had been Quakers, sometimes suffering for that right, and now he thought, I've gone and lost it all for a wheezing organ.

It was Mattie at the organ and Jess knew her habits there: they were like his own. She never began to play a piece at once, but touched the organ here and there, slowly pumped in the air, then lovingly laid her fingers across upon keys. After that the music. Jess looked across at Eliza and he saw by the way her hands had tightened round each other that she'd heard, too. I'm a far worse man than Esau, he thought, for he sold only his own birthright, and I've sold my wife's as well as my own.

Jess remembered how Eliza loved to bring the Lord's message to the Lord's people and how his own love for pushing air through a set of reeds was going to lose her all this. And before his lips moved his heart began to pray, "Lord, deliver thy servant from the snare of his own iniquity."

By the time Mattie was ready to touch the first key he was on his feet saying, "Friends, let us lift our hearts to God in prayer." This was nothing startling to a gathering of Quakers. They'd any of them take to praying at the drop of a hat. So some knelt and others didn't, but all bowed their heads and shut their eyes.

All except Jess. He stood with face uplifted to the ceiling, facing his God and his sin. By the time Mattie had got into "The Old Musician," and a few faint wisps of music were floating into the room, Jess was talking to God in a voice that shook the studding. He was talking to Him in the voice of a man whose sins have come home to roost. He was reminding Him of all the other sinners to whom His mercy had nevertheless been granted.

He went through the Bible book by book and sinner by sinner. He prayed in the name of Adam, who had sinned and fallen short of grace; of Moses, who had lost the Promised Land; of David, who had looked with desire on another man's wife. He prayed in the name of Solomon, his follies, of Abraham and his jealousies, and Jephthah, who kept his word in cruelty; he made a music of his own out of his contrition; his revulsion mounted up in melody.

He left the Old Testament and prayed for them all, sinners alike, in the name of Paul, who what he would not, he did; and of Peter, who said he knew the Man not, and of Thomas who doubted and Judas who betrayed and of that Mary who repented.

He stood with his red head lifted up while his long Irish lip wrapped itself around the good Bible names. He prayed until the light had left the room and his hair in the dark had become as colorless as Amos Pease's dun thatch. He prayed until all the mint smell had left the room and the only smell left was that of a penitent man seeking forgiveness.

Now Jess was no hypocrite and if his prayer swelled a little, if it boomed out a little stronger when Mattie pulled the fortissimo stop, it was through none of his planning; it was the Lord's doing entirely. And if his prayer wasn't finished until Mattie'd finished playing after going five times through "The Old Musician," that was the Lord's hand, too, and nothing of Jess' contriving.

Finally, when he'd made an end, and the visiting men had taken their faces out from behind their hands and looked around the dark room with dazed eyes, Jess dropped down into his chair and rubbed his forefinger across his lips, the way a man will when he's been speaking. Eliza lit them a candle, then went out to bring in the lamps.

Amos Pease picked up the candle and held it so the light fell on to Jess' face. "Friend," he said, "thee's been an instrument of the Lord this night. Thee's risen to the throne of grace and carried us all upwards on thy pinions. Thy prayer carried us so near to heaven's gates that now and again I thought I could hear angels' voices choiring and the sound of heavenly harps."

And with that he set the candle back down, put his hat on his head and said, "Praise God." Friend Griffith and Friend Hooper said, "Amen, brother. Amen to that," and with great gravity followed Amos Pease out of the door.

When Eliza came back in with the lamp, Jess was sitting there alone in the candlelight. There was a smell of trod-on mint again in the room and the children had stopped playing duck-on-rock and were whooping after lightning-bugs to put in bottles. Jess was huddled over, his eyes shut, like a man who has felt the weight of the Lord's hand between his shoulder blades. But before Eliza could clear her throat to say "Amen" to the edifying sight he made, down from the attic floated "The Old Musician" once again, and Jess' foot began to tap:

Tap, tap—the riverside,
Tap, tap—upon its tide.

THE PACING GOOSE

from *The Friendly Persuasion*

JESSAMYN WEST

JESS sat in the kitchen at the long table by the west window where in winter he kept his grafting tools: the thin-bladed knife, the paper sweet with the smell of beeswax and the resin, the boxes of roots and scions. Jess was a nurseryman and spring meant for him not only spirits flowering —but the earth's. A week more of moderating weather and he'd be out, still in gum boots, but touching an earth that had thawed, whose riches were once again fluid enough to be sucked upward, toward those burgeonings which by summer would have swelled into Early Harvests, Permains and Sweet Bows.

Spring's a various season, Jess thought, no two years the same: comes in with rains, mud deep enough to swallow horse and rider; comes in cold, snow falling so fast it weaves a web; comes in with a warm wind blowing about thy ears and bringing a smell of something flowering, not here, but southaways, across the Ohio, maybe, in Kentucky. Nothing here now but a smell of melting snow—which is no smell at all, but a kind of prickle in the nose, like a bygone sneeze. Comes in so various, winter put by and always so welcome.

"And us each spring so much the same."

"Thee speaking to me, Jess?"

"Nothing thee'd understand, Eliza."

Spring made Jess discontented with the human race—and with women, if anything more than men. It looked as if spring put them all in the shade: the season so resourceful and they each year meeting it with nothing changed from last year; digging up roots from the same sassafras thicket, licking sulphur and molasses from the same big-bowled spoon.

Behind him the table was set for supper, plates neatly turned to cover the bone-handled knives and forks, spoon vase aglitter with steel well burnished by brick dust, dishes of jam with more light to them than the sun, which was dwindling away, peaked and overcast, outside his window.

"Spring opening up," he said, "and nobody in this house so much as putting down a line of poetry."

Eliza, who was lifting dried-peach pies from a hot oven, said nothing. She set the four of them in a neat row on the edge of her kitchen cabinet to cool, and slid her pans of cornbread into the oven. Then she turned to Jess, her cheeks red with heat, and her black eyes warm with what she had to say. "Thee'd maybe relish a nice little rhyme for thy supper, Jess Birdwell."

Jess sighed, then sniffed the pies, so rich with ripe peach flavor that the kitchen smelled like a summer orchard, nothing lacking but the sound of bees. "Now, Eliza," he said, "thee knows I wouldn't have thee anyways altered. Thee . . ."

"Thee," Eliza interrupted him, "is like all men. Thee wants to have thy poetry and eat it too."

Jess wondered how what he'd felt about spring, a season with the Lord's thumbprint fresh on it, could've led to anything so unspringlike as an argument about a batch of dried-peach pies.

"Eliza," he said firmly, "I didn't mean thee. Though it's crossed my mind sometimes as strange that none of the boys have ever turned, this time of year, to rhyming."

"Josh writes poems," Eliza said.

"Thee ever read what Josh writes, Eliza?"

Eliza nodded.

Ah, well, Jess thought, no use at this late date to tell her what's the difference.

Eliza looked her husband over carefully. "Jess Birdwell," she said, "thee's full of humors. Thy blood needs thinning. I'll boil thee up a good cup of sassafras tea."

Jess turned away from the green and gold sunset and the patches of snow it was gilding and fairly faced the dried-peach pies and Eliza, who was dropping dumplings into a pot of beans.

"That's just it, Eliza," he said. "That's just the rub."

Eliza gave him no encouragement, but he went on anyway. "Earth alters, season to season, spring comes in never two times the same, only us pounding on steady as pump bolts and not freshened by so much as a grass blade."

"Jess, thee's got spring fever."

"I could reckon time and temperature, each spring, by the way thee starts honing for geese. 'Jess, don't thee think we might have a few geese?' It's a tardy spring," Jess said. "Snow still on the ground and not a word yet from thee about geese."

Eliza pulled a chair out from the table and sat. "Jess, why's thee always been so set against geese?"

"I'm not set against geese. It's geese that's set against farming. They can mow down a half acre of sprouting corn while thee's trying to head them off—and in two minutes they'll level a row of pie plant it's taken two years to get started. No, Eliza, it's the geese that's against me."

"If thee had tight fences . . ." Eliza said.

"Eliza, I got tight fences, but the goose's never been hatched that'll admit fences exist. And an old gander'd just as soon go through a fence as hiss—and if he can't find a hole or crack in a fence he'll lift the latch."

"Jess," said Eliza flatly, "thee don't like geese."

"Well," said Jess, "I wouldn't go so far's to say I didn't like them, but I will say that if there's any meaner, dirtier animal, or one that glories in it more, I don't know it. And a thing I've never been able to understand about thee, Eliza, is what thee sees in the shifty-eyed birds."

"Geese," said Eliza, with a dreaminess unusual to her, "march along so lordly like . . . they're pretty as swans floating down a branch . . . in fall they stretch out their necks and honk to geese passing overhead as if they's wild. My father never had any trouble raising geese and I've heard him say many a time that there's no better food for a brisk morning than a fried goose egg."

Jess knew, with spring his topic, he'd ought to pass over Eliza's father and his fried goose egg but he couldn't help saying, "A fried goose egg always had a kind of bloated look to me, Eliza"—but then he went on fast. "The season's shaping up," he said. "I can see thee's all primed to say, 'Jess, let's get a setting of goose eggs.'"

Eliza went over to the bean kettle and began to lift out dumplings. "It's a forwarder season than thee thinks, Jess," she said. "I got a setting under a hen now."

Jess looked at his wife. He didn't know what had made him want spring's variety in a human being—nor Eliza's substituting doing for asking. And speaking of it just now, as he had, made opposition kind of ticklish.

"When'd thee set them?" he asked finally.

"Yesterday," said Eliza.

"Where'd thee get the eggs?"

"Overbys'," said Eliza. The Overbys were their neighbors to the south.

"Well, they got enough for a surety," Jess said, "to give a few away."

"The Overbys don't give anything away, as thee knows. I paid for them. With my own money," Eliza added.

"How many?" Jess asked.

"Eight," Eliza said.

Jess turned back to his window. The sun had set, leaving a sad green sky and desolate black and white earth. "Five acres of corn gone," he calculated.

"Thee said," Eliza reminded him, "that what thee wanted was a little variety in me. 'Steady as a pump bolt,' were thy words."

"I know I did," Jess admitted glumly. "I talk too much."

"Draw up thy chair," Eliza said placidly, not contradicting him; "here's Enoch and the boys."

Next morning after breakfast Jess and Enoch left the kitchen together. The sun was the warmest the year had yet produced and the farm roofs were steaming; south branch, swollen by melting snow, was running so full the soft lap of its eddies could be heard in the barnyard; a rooster tossed his voice into the bright air, loud and clear as if aiming to be heard by every fowl in Jennings County.

"Enoch," said Jess to his hired man, "what's thy feeling about geese?"

Enoch was instantly equipped, for the most part, with feelings on every subject. Geese was a homelier topic than he'd choose himself to enlarge upon, not one that could be much embellished nor one on which Mr. Emerson, so far's he could recall, had ever expressed an opinion. "In the fall of the year," he said, "long about November or December, there's nothing tastier on the table than roast goose."

"Goose on the table's not what I mean," Jess said. "I was speaking of goose on the hoof. Goose nipping off a stand of corn, Enoch, goose roistering round, honking and hissing so's thee can't hear thyself think, goose eyeing thee like a snake on stilts."

Enoch gazed at his employer for a few seconds. "Mr. Birdwell," he said, "I think that if they's an ornery bird, it's a goose. Ornery and undependable."

"I'm glad we's so like minded about them," Jess said. "Otherwise, I'd not like to ask thee to do this little job." He pulled a long darning needle from beneath the lapel of his coat.

Enoch eyed it with some mistrust. "I can't say's I've ever been handy with a needle, Mr. Birdwell."

"Thee'll be handy enough for this," Jess said with hearty conviction. "To come to it, Enoch, Eliza's set eight goose eggs. Next year with any luck she'd have two dozen. And so on. More and more. Feeling the way thee does, Enoch, about geese it's no more'n fair to give thee a chance to put a stop to this before it goes too far. One little puncture in each egg with this and the goose project's nipped in the bud and Eliza none the wiser."

"I'm mighty awkward with my hands," said Enoch, "doing fine work. Ticklish job like this I might drop an egg and break it."

"Enoch," said Jess, "thee's not developing a weakness for geese, is thee?"

"It ain't the geese," said Enoch frankly, "it's your wife. She's been mighty clever to me and if she's got her heart set on geese, it'd go against the grain to disappoint her. Whyn't you do it, Mr. Birdwell?"

"Same reason," said Jess, "only more of them—and if Eliza ever asks if I tampered with that setting of eggs I figure on being able to say No." Jess held the needle nearer Enoch, who looked at it but still made no motion to take it.

"Likely no need to do a thing," Enoch said. "Two to one those eggs'll never hatch anyways. Overbys' such a fox-eared tribe they more'n likely sold her bad eggs to begin with."

"Thee's knowed about this," Jess asked, "all along?"

"Yes," Enoch said.

"Here's the needle," Jess said.

"You look at this," Enoch inquired, "not so much as a favor asked as a part of the day's work with orders from you?"

"Yes," Jess said, "that's about the way I look at it."

Enoch took the needle, held it somewhat gingerly, and with the sun glinting across its length, walked slowly toward the chicken-house.

It takes thirty days for a goose egg to hatch, and the time, with spring work to be done, went fast. The hen Eliza had picked was a good one and kept her mind strictly on her setting. Eliza kept her mind on the hen, and Jess and Enoch found their minds oftener than they liked on Eliza and her hoped-for geese.

At breakfast on the day the geese were due to break their shells Jess said, "If I's thee, Eliza, I wouldn't bank too much on them geese. I heard Enoch say a while back he wouldn't be surprised if not an egg hatched. Thought the eggs were likely no good."

Enoch was busy pouring coffee into a saucer, then busy cooling it, but Eliza waited until he was through. "Did thee say that, Enoch?"

Enoch looked at Jess. "Yes," he said, "I kind of recollect something of the sort."

"What made thee think so, Enoch?"

"Why," said Jess, for Enoch was busy with his coffee again, "it was the Overbys. Enoch's got a feeling they's kind of unreliable. Fox-eared, I think thee said, Enoch, didn't thee?"

Enoch's work took him outside almost at once and Jess himself said, "If thee'll just give me a little packet of food, Eliza, I won't trouble thee for anything at noon. I'm going to be over'n the south forty and it'll save time coming and going."

Eliza was surprised for Jess'd usually come twice as far for a hot dinner at midday, but she made him fried ham sandwiches and put them and some cold apple-turnovers in a bag.

"It's a pity thee has to miss thy dinner," she told him, but Jess only said, "Press of work, press of work," and hurriedly departed.

Jess came home that evening through the spring twilight, somewhat late, and found a number of things to do at the barn before he went up to the house. When he entered the kitchen nothing seemed amiss—lamps ruddy, table set, stove humming, and beside the stove a small box over which Eliza was bending. Jess stopped to look—and listen; from inside the box was coming a kind of birdlike peeping, soft and not unpleasant. Reluctantly he walked to Eliza's side. There, eating minced boiled egg, and between bites lifting its beak to Eliza, it seemed, and making those chirping sounds he'd heard was a gray-gold gosling.

Eliza looked up pleasantly. "Enoch was right," she said. "The eggs were bad. Only one hatched. I plan to call it Samantha," she told Jess. "It's a name I've always been partial to."

"Samantha," said Jess without any enthusiasm whatever for either name or gosling. "How's thee know it's a she?"

"I don't," said Eliza, "but if it's a gander it's a name easily changed to Sam."

Enoch came in just then with a load of wood for the kitchen woodbox. "Enoch," asked Jess, "has thee seen Samantha—or Sam?"

Enoch mumbled but Jess understood him to say he had.

"It was my understanding, Enoch, that thy opinion was that all those eggs were bad."

"Well, Mr. Birdwell," said Enoch, "a man could make a mistake. He could count wrong."

"A man ought to be able to count to eight without going astray," Jess said.

Eliza was paying no attention to either of them; she was making little tweeting sounds herself, bending over the chirping gosling. "Does thee know," she asked Jess, "that this is the first pet I ever had in my life?"

"Thee's got Ebony," Jess said.

"I don't mean a caged pet," Eliza said, "but one to walk beside thee. I'm reconciled the others didn't hatch. With eight I'd've had to raise geese for the table. With one only I can make Samantha a pure pet."

A pure pet was what she made of her: Samantha ate what the family ate, with the exception of articles which Eliza thought might be indigestible and would risk on humans but not on her goose. Cake, pie, corn-on-the-cob, there was nothing too good for Samantha. From a big-footed, gold-downed gosling she swelled, almost at once, like a slack sail which gets a sudden breeze, into a full-rounded convexity.

"Emphasis on the vexity," Jess said when he thought of this. Samantha was everything he'd disliked in the general run of geese, with added traits peculiar to herself, which vexed him. Because she was fed at the doorstep, she was always underfoot. No shout, however loud, would move her before she's ready to move. If she's talked to too strong she'd flail you with her wings and pinch the calf of your leg until for some days if would look to be mortifying. She'd take food out of children's hands and the pansies Jess had planted in a circle at the base of the Juneberry tree she sheared so close that there was not a naked stem left to show for all his work. And when not being crossed in any way, Jess simply looking at her and meditating, trying to fathom Samantha's fascination for Eliza, the goose would suddenly extend her snakelike neck, and almost touching Jess, hiss with such a hint of icy disapprobation that Jess would involuntarily recoil.

But she was Eliza's pure pet, no two ways about that, and would lift her head for Eliza to scratch, and walk beside her with the lordly roll of the known elect.

"There was some goddess," Enoch remembered, "who always had a big bird with her." Jess supposed Enoch was thinking of Juno and her peacock, but the reference didn't convince him that a goose was a suitable companion for any goddess—let alone Eliza, and he couldn't honestly feel much regret when one evening toward the end of November Eliza told him Samantha was missing. "She'll turn up," Jess said. "That bird's too ornery to die young."

Eliza said nothing, but next evening she proved Jess was right. "Samantha's over at Overbys'," she said.

"Well, did thee fetch her home?" Jess asked.

"No," said Eliza with righteous indignation, "they wouldn't let me. They said they had forty geese—and forty's what they got now, and they don't think Samantha's there. They provoked me so, Jess, I told them they'd sold me seven bad eggs and now they try to take the eighth away from me."

Jess felt a little abashed at this, but he asked, "How can thee be so sure Samantha's there? She might've been carried off by a varmint."

Eliza was scornful. "Thee forgets I hand-raised Samantha from a gosling. I'd know her among four hundred—let alone forty."

"Whyn't thee buy her back then," Jess asked, "if that's the only way?"

"After what I said about their eggs," Eliza answered sadly, "the Overbys say they don't want any more dealings with me."

Eliza mourned so for the lost Samantha that first Enoch and then Jess went over to the Overbys' but no one there would admit the presence of a visiting goose—forty they had, and forty you could see by counting was what they had now. Short of force there didn't seem any way of getting Samantha home again.

When Eliza heard the Overbys were going to sell geese for Christmas eating she was frantic. "Jess," she said, "I just can't bear to think of Samantha, plucked naked and resting on a table waiting to be carved. She used to sing as sweet as any bird when she was little, and she'd walk by my side taking the air. She's the only goose I ever heard of," Eliza remembered mournfully, "who'd drink tea."

In Jess' opinion a goose'd eat anything at either end of the scale, but he didn't suppose this was a suitable time to mention it to Eliza. "Eliza," he said, "short of me and Enoch's going over there and using force on old man Overby—or sneaking over at night and breaking into their chicken pen, I don't know how in the world we're going to get Samantha back for thee."

"We could sue," said Eliza.

"Thee mean go to law?" Jess asked, astounded. Quakers stayed out of courts, believing in amicable settlements without recourse to law.

"Yes," said Eliza. "I'd do it for Samantha. I'd think it my duty. Going to law'd be a misery for us . . . but not so lasting a misery as being roasted would be for Samantha."

Jess couldn't deny this, but he said, "I'd have to think it over. I've never been to law yet in my life and suing for a gone goose don't seem to me a very likely place to start."

Next morning Eliza served a good but silent breakfast, not sitting herself to eat with the rest of her family.

"Thee feeling dauncy, Eliza?" Jess asked.

"I just can't eat," she said, "for thinking of Samantha."

Labe and Mattie had tears in their eyes. Little Jess was mournfully bellowing. Enoch looked mighty glum. Jess felt ashamed to be swallowing victuals in the midst of so much sorrow. Eliza stood at the end of the stove where the gosling's box had rested for the first few weeks of its life, looking down, as if remembering how it had sung and lifted its beak to her.

Jess couldn't stand it. "Eliza," he said, "if thee wants to go through with it I'll go to Vernon and fee a lawyer for thee. Thee'll have to go to court, be on the witness stand—and even then I misdoubt thee'll ever get thy goose back. Does thee still want me to do it?"

Eliza came to the table and stood with her hand on Jess' shoulder. "Yes, Jess," she said, "I want thee to do it."

Jess went to Vernon, fee'd a lawyer, had a restraining order put on the Overbys so they couldn't sell or kill the goose Eliza said was Samantha, and awaited with misgivings the day of the trial. It came in mid-December.

Eliza, Jess and Enoch rode to the trial through a fall of light, fresh snow. Brilliant sunlight, crisp air, glittering snow, and Rome's spirited stepping made the occasion, in spite of its purpose, seem festive. Eliza made it seem festive. Jess, who did not forget its purpose, regarded her with some wonder. He couldn't say what it was about her—dress and bonnet appeared to be simply her First Day best—but she had a holiday air.

He considered it his duty to warn her. "Eliza," he said, "thee understands thee's not going to Meeting? They're not going to sit silent while thee tells them how much thee loves Samantha and how she sang when young and drank tea. Old man Overby'll have his say and he's got a lawyer hired for no other purpose than to trip thee up."

Eliza was unimpressed. "What's our lawyer fee'd for, Jess?" she asked.

Jess took another tack. "Eliza," he told her, "I don't figger thee's got a chance in a thousand to get Samantha back."

"This is a court of justice, isn't it?" Eliza asked.

"Yes," Jess said.

"Then there's no need for thee to fash thyself, Jess Birdwell. I'll get Samantha back."

Not getting Samantha back wasn't what fashed Jess—he reckoned he could bear up under that mighty well. What fashed him was the whole shooting match. . . . In some few cases, matters of life and death, going to court might be necessary, and he could imagine such. But a suit over a goose named Samantha wasn't one of them. And poor Eliza. Law to her was all Greek and turkey tracks . . . and here she was bound for court as chipper as if she was Chief Justice Taney himself. Jess sighed and shook his head. Getting shut of Samantha would be no hardship for him, but he was downcast for Eliza's sake and the way she'd have to turn homeward empty-handed.

In the courtroom hard, clear light reflected upward from the snow fell onto what Jess thought were hard faces: courthouse hangers on; farmers whose slackening work made the diversion of a trial an inviting possibility; lovers of oddity who figured a tilt between a Quaker female, preacher, to boot, and an old sinner like Milt Overby over the ownership of a goose ought to produce some enlivening quirks. They stared at Eliza, exchanged salutes with Milt Overby and inspected Samantha who in her crate awaited the court's decision.

The two lawyers, Jess considered to be on a par. Nothing fancy, either one . . . old roadsters both, gone gray in service and with a knowledge of their business. The circuit judge was something else, unaccountably young, jug-eared and dressed more sprightly than a groom for his own wedding. A city whipper-snapper, born and trained north of the Missisinewa, and now, in Jess' opinion, setting a squeamish foot in backwoods provinces, and irked to find himself trying so trifling a case. Didn't know a goose from a guinea hen, like as not, and would consider tossing a coin a more suitable manner of settling such a matter—just as near right in the end—and his valuable time saved.

Eliza, Jess saw, was of no such opinion. She, too, was scanning the young judge, and Jess, who knew her, saw from the look on her face that she was taken by him. A neat, thin, pious boy—far from home—he looked, no doubt to her; a young man who could do with better cooking and more regular eating.

The young man rapped the court to order. Spitting and shuffling slackened and in a high, precise voice he read, "Birdwell versus Overby. Charge, petty larceny. Appropriation and willful withholding of goose named Samantha." The name Samantha seemed to somewhat choke him, but he got it out.

"Ready for Birdwell," said Mr. Abel Samp, Eliza's lawyer.

"Ready for Overby," said the defendant's lawyer.

Eliza was the first witness on the stand. Jess sometimes forgot what a good-looking woman Eliza was, but the interest shown on lifted faces all about him refreshed his memory.

"Swear the plaintiff in," the judge said.

Eliza, in her sweet voice, spoke directly to the judge. "I don't swear," she said.

The judge explained that profanity was not asked for. "I understood," said Eliza, "that thee wasn't asking for profanity. No one would think that of thee. But we Quakers do not take oaths in court. We affirm."

"Permit Mrs. Birdwell to affirm," said the judge. Eliza affirmed.

Mr. Samp then proceeded to question Eliza as to Samantha's birth and habits.

"Judge," Eliza began.

"Address the judge," Mr. Samp said, "as Your Honor."

"We Quakers," Eliza told the judge, gently, "do not make use of such titles. What is thy name? I think thee'll go far in our state and thy name's one I'd like to know."

The judge appeared somewhat distraught, undecided as to whether to make the tone of the court brisk and legal (if possible) or to follow Eliza's lead of urbane sociability.

"Pomeroy," he said and made a slight bow in Eliza's direction.

Eliza returned the bow, deeper and with more grace. "Friend Pomeroy," she said, "it is indeed a pleasure to know thee."

Samantha's story as Eliza told it to Friend Pomeroy was surprisingly terse. Affecting, and losing nothing by Eliza's telling, but to the point.

"Mrs. Birdwell," said Samp, "how long have you had an acquaintanceship with geese and their habits?"

"Since I was a child," Eliza said. "My father was a great fancier of geese."

"And you think you could identify this goose Samantha, which you admit in looks was similar to the defendant's?"

"I could," Eliza said with much authority.

Mr. Samp, to Jess' surprise, left the matter there. "Take the witness," he said to Overby's lawyer—but the counsel for the defendant was in no hurry to cross-examine Eliza. Instead he put his client on the stand.

"Farewell, Samantha," Jess said to Enoch.

"You relieved?" Enoch asked.

"Putting Eliza first," Jess said, "as I do, no."

Milt Overby, whose natural truculence was somewhat stimulated by a nip he'd had to offset snappy weather, bellowed his way through his testimony. At one juncture he set the judge aright when he asked some elementary questions concerning the habits and configurations of geese. "Where in tarnation you from?" he snorted. "What they mean sending us judges down here who don't know Toulouse from Wyandotte, or goose from gander?"

The young judge used voice and gavel to quiet the guffawing which filled the courtroom and the trial proceeded. A number of witnesses for both sides were brought to the stand and while it was shown that Overbys had maybe eaten a goose or two and neglected out of pure fondness for the creatures to count them as among the departed, still nobody had been able to positively identify Samantha.

Mr. Overby's lawyer seemed somewhat loath to cross-examine Eliza, but he put her on the stand. She'd said she knew geese and her testimony had been direct and positive. "Mrs. Birdwell," he said, "how can you be so sure your goose was with my client's geese?"

Eliza's black eyes rested confidingly upon the judge. "Friend Pomeroy," she said, "I raised Samantha from a gosling."

Jess sighed. "Here it comes," he said, "how that goose could sing and drink tea."

Eliza continued, "And there's one thing about her that always set her apart from every other goose."

"Yes, Mrs. Birdwell," said Judge Pomeroy, who was inclined to forget, with Eliza on the stand, that he was in a courtroom.

"Samantha," said Eliza, with much earnestness, "from the day she was born had a gait unlike any other goose I ever saw and one that set her apart from all her Overby connections. I picked her out at once when I went over there, because of it. Thee couldn't've missed it, Friend Pomeroy."

"Yes, Mrs. Birdwell," said the judge with interest in his voice.

"Samantha," said Eliza, "was a born pacer. Thee knows what a pacer is?"

"Certainly," said Judge Pomeroy. "A pacer," he repeated with no surprise—and with obvious pleasure that Eliza'd hit upon so clear and differentiating an aspect of her goose and one that made identification possible.

A titter was mounting through the courtroom—Judge Pomeroy lifted his head. He had no desire to be further instructed as to the history, habits and breeds of geese, and he liked to see a trial settled by some such little and too often overlooked subtlety. Judge Pomeroy brought down his gavel. "The court awards decision in favor of the plaintiff. Case dismissed." While the silence that followed on his words still prevailed Judge Pomeroy stepped briskly and with obvious pleasure out through the rear door.

Jess was also brisk about departure. No use lingering until friend Pomeroy had been more thoroughly informed as to gaits in general and geese in particular. Mid-afternoon's a quiet time in any season. In winter with snow on the ground, no leaves to rustle and bare limbs rigid as rock against a cloudless sky, the hush is deepest of all. Nothing broke that hush in the surrey, except the squeak of leather and snow, the muffled footfalls of Rome Beauty. Jess and Eliza, on the front seat, rode without speaking. Enoch, in the back, seemed to meditate. Even Samantha in her crate at Enoch's feet was silent.

Maple Grove Nursery was in sight before Jess spoke. "Eliza," he said, "would thee mind telling me—did thee ever see a trotting goose?"

Enoch ceased to meditate and listened. He had been wondering about this himself.

"Certainly not," said Eliza. "Thee knows as well as I, Jess Birdwell, an animal can't trot without hind feet and forefeet."

"So far, Eliza," Jess said, "we see eye to eye. Now maybe thee'd tell me —did thee ever see a goose that didn't pace?"

Eliza was truly amazed, it seemed. "Why, Jess," she said, "an ordinary goose just walks—but Samantha paces."

Jess was silent for a spell. "What'd thee say the difference is?"

"It's the swing, Jess Birdwell," said Eliza, "same as in a horse that nature's formed for a pacer . . . it's the natural bent, the way the spirit leads the beast to set his feet down. Samantha's a natural pacer."

That seemed as far as they'd likely get on the subject and Jess joined Enoch in meditation. In the barnyard, before she went up to the house, Eliza said, like an old hand at the business, "Attending court whettens the appetite. It's a little early but I thought if thee'd relish it"—and she looked at Jess and Enoch, never sparing a glance for Samantha, as if her menfolk's welfare was her sole concern—"I'd stir us up a bite to eat. Hot tea and fresh sweetcakes, say. Might fry a little sausage and open some cherry preserves. If thee'd relish it," she repeated.

Jess wasn't taken in, but he'd relish it, and so would Enoch, and they

both said so. They hustled with the unhitching so they could uncrate Samantha and note her progress with eyes newly instructed as to what made a pacer. Jess dumped her in the snow, and Enoch tapped her with his hat. Samantha made for the back door.

"By sugar," said Jess, "Eliza's right. She paces." Samantha had the smooth roll of a racker—there were no two ways about it. At heart she was a pacer, and what two legs could do in that line, Samantha accomplished.

"With four legs," Enoch said, "you could enter her in any county fair—rack on," he cried with enthusiasm. As they followed Samantha to the house, Enoch, for whom any event existed chiefly in its after aspects as a cud for rumination, asked, "How you feel in respect of court trials, now, Mr. Birdwell?"

"I'm still against them," Jess said, "though they's three things this trial's taught me I might never otherwise have learned. Two's about women."

Enoch revered all knowledge and he had a notion that information on this subject might have a more than transcendental value. "What's the two things you learned about women, Mr. Birdwell?"

"Well, Enoch, I learned first, dependability's woman's greatest virtue. Steady as a pump bolt, day in, day out. When thee finds a woman like that, Enoch, don't try to change her. Not even in spring."

"No, sir," said Enoch, "I won't."

"Second, when it's a case of woman and the law—thee don't need to waste any worry on the woman."

"No, sir," said Enoch again.

When they reached the back steps, Enoch asked, "I understood you to say you'd learned three things, Mr. Birdwell. What's the third about?"

"Hired men," said Jess.

Enoch was taken aback, but he'd asked for it. "Yes, Mr. Birdwell," he said.

"Never hire one," Jess told him, "till thee finds out first if he can count to eight. Save thyself a lot of trouble that way, Enoch."

"How's I to know the eighth'd turn out to be Samantha?" Enoch asked.

Samantha herself, who was waiting at the doorstep for an expected tidbit, reached out and unhampered by either boots or work pants nipped Enoch firmly through his thin Sunday best.

"Thee say something, Enoch?" Jess asked.

Enoch had but he didn't repeat it. Instead he said, "Pacer or no pacer, that's Samantha," and the two of them stepped out of the snow into the warm kitchen, scented with baking sweetcakes and frying sausage.

THE BIRDS

DAPHNE DU MAURIER

ON December the third the wind changed overnight and it was winter. Until then the autumn had been mellow, soft. The leaves had lingered on the trees, golden-red, and the hedgerows were still green. The earth was rich where the plough had turned it.

Nat Hocken, because of a war-time disability, had a pension and did not work full-time at the farm. He worked three days a week, and they gave him the lighter jobs: hedging, thatching, repairs to the farm buildings.

Although he was married, with children, his was a solitary disposition; he liked best to work alone. It pleased him when he was given a bank to build up, or a gate to mend at the far end of the peninsula, where the sea surrounded the farmland on either side. Then, at midday, he would pause and eat the pasty that his wife had baked for him, and, sitting on the cliff's edge, would watch the birds. Autumn was best for this, better than spring. In spring the birds flew inland, purposeful, intent; they knew where they were bound, the rhythm and ritual of their life brooked no delay. In autumn those that had not migrated overseas but remained to pass the winter were caught up in the same driving urge, but because migration was denied them followed a pattern of their own. Great flocks of them came to the peninsula, restless, uneasy, spending themselves in motion; now wheeling, circling in the sky, now settling to feed on the rich new-turned soil, but even when they fed it was as though they did so without hunger, without desire. Restlessness drove them to the skies again.

Black and white, jackdaw and gull, mingled in strange partnership, seeking some sort of liberation, never satisfied, never still. Flocks of starlings, rustling like silk, flew to fresh pasture, driven by the same necessity of movement, and the smaller birds, the finches and the larks, scattered from tree to hedge as if compelled.

Nat watched them, and he watched the sea birds too. Down in the bay they waited for the tide. They had more patience. Oyster catchers, redshank, sanderling, and curlew watched by the water's edge; as the slow sea sucked at the shore and then withdrew, leaving the strip of seaweed bare and the shingle churned, the sea birds raced and ran upon the beaches. Then that same impulse to flight seized upon them too. Crying, whistling, calling, they skimmed the placid sea and left the shore. Make haste, make speed, hurry and begone; yet where, and to what purpose? The restless urge of autumn, unsatisfying, sad, had put a spell upon them and they must flock, and wheel, and cry; they must spill themselves of motion before winter came.

"Perhaps," thought Nat, munching his pasty by the cliff's edge, "a message comes to the birds in autumn, like a warning. Winter is coming. Many of them perish. And like people who, apprehensive of death before their time, drive themselves to work or folly, the birds do likewise."

The birds had been more restless than ever this fall of the year, the agitation more marked because the days were still. As the tractor traced its path up and down the western hills, the figure of the farmer silhouetted on the driving seat, the whole machine and the man upon it would be lost momentarily in the great cloud of wheeling, crying birds. There were many more than usual, Nat was sure of this. Always, in autumn, they followed the plough, but not in great flocks like these, nor with such clamour.

Nat remarked upon it when hedging was finished for the day. "Yes," said the farmer, "there are more birds about than usual; I've noticed it too. And daring, some of them, taking no notice of the tractor. One or two gulls came so close to my head this afternoon I thought they'd knock my cap off! As it was, I could scarcely see what I was doing, when they were overhead and I had the sun in my eyes. I have a notion the weather will change. It will be a hard winter. That's why the birds are restless."

Nat, tramping home across the fields and down the lane to his cottage, saw the birds still flocking over the western hills, in the last glow of the sun. No wind, and the grey sea calm and full. Campion in bloom yet in the hedges, and the air mild. The farmer was right, though, and it was that night the weather turned. Nat's bedroom faced east. He woke just after two and heard the wind in the chimney. Not the storm and bluster of a sou'westerly gale, bringing the rain, but east wind, cold and dry. It sounded hollow in the chimney, and a loose slate rattled on the roof. Nat listened, and he could hear the sea roaring in the bay. Even the air in the small bedroom had turned chill: a draught came under the skirting of the door, blowing upon the bed. Nat drew the blanket round him, leant closer to the back of his sleeping wife, and stayed wakeful, watchful, aware of misgiving without cause.

Then he heard the tapping on the window. There was no creeper on the cottage walls to break loose and scratch upon the pane. He listened, and the tapping continued until, irritated by the sound, Nat got out of bed and went to the window. He opened it, and as he did so something brushed his hand, jabbing at his knuckles, grazing the skin. Then he saw the flutter of the wings and it was gone, over the roof, behind the cottage.

It was a bird; what kind of bird he could not tell. The wind must have driven it to shelter on the sill.

He shut the window and went back to bed, but, feeling his knuckles wet, put his mouth to the scratch. The bird had drawn blood. Frightened, he supposed, and bewildered, the bird, seeking shelter, had stabbed at him in the darkness. Once more he settled himself to sleep.

Presently the tapping came again, this time more forceful, more insistent, and now his wife woke at the sound and, turning in the bed, said to him, "See to the window, Nat, it's rattling."

"I've already seen to it," he told her; "there's some bird there trying to get in. Can't you hear the wind? It's blowing from the east, driving the birds to shelter."

"Send them away," she said, "I can't sleep with that noise."

He went to the window for the second time, and now when he opened it there was not one bird upon the sill but half a dozen; they flew straight into his face, attacking him.

He shouted, striking out at them with his arms, scattering them; like the first one, they flew over the roof and disappeared. Quickly he let the window fall and latched it.

"Did you hear that?" he said. "They went for me. Tried to peck my eyes." He stood by the window, peering into the darkness, and could see nothing. His wife, heavy with sleep, murmured from the bed.

"I'm not making it up," he said, angry at her suggestion. "I tell you the birds were on the sill, trying to get into the room."

Suddenly a frightened cry came from the room across the passage where the children slept.

"It's Jill," said his wife, roused at the sound, sitting up in bed. "Go to her, see what's the matter."

Nat lit the candle, but when he opened the bedroom door to cross the passage the draught blew out the flame.

There came a second cry of terror, this time from both children, and stumbling into their room, he felt the beating of wings about him in the darkness. The window was wide open. Through it came the birds, hitting first the ceiling and the walls, then swerving in mid-flight, turning to the children in their beds.

"It's all right, I'm here," shouted Nat, and the children flung themselves, screaming, upon him, while in the darkness the birds rose and dived and came for him again.

"What is it, Nat, what's happened?" his wife called from the further bedroom, and swiftly he pushed the children through the door to the passage and shut it upon them, so that he was alone now in their bedroom with the birds.

He seized a blanket from the nearest bed and, using it as a weapon, flung it to right and left about him in the air. He felt the thud of bodies, heard the fluttering of wings, but they were not yet defeated, for again and again they returned to the assault, jabbing his hands, his head, the little stabbing beaks sharp as pointed forks. The blanket became a weapon of defence; he wound it about his head, and then in greater darkness beat at the birds with his bare hands. He dared not stumble to the door and open it, lest in doing so the birds should follow him.

How long he fought with them in the darkness he could not tell, but at last the beating of the wings about him lessened and then withdrew, and through the density of the blanket he was aware of light. He waited, listened; there was no sound except the fretful crying of one of the children from the bedroom beyond. The fluttering, the whirring of the wings had ceased.

He took the blanket from his head and stared about him. The cold grey morning light exposed the room. Dawn and the open window had called the living birds; the dead lay on the floor. Nat gazed at the little corpses, shocked and horrified. They were all small birds, none of any size; there must have been fifty of them lying there upon the floor. There were robins, finches, sparrows, blue tits, larks, and bramblings, birds that by nature's law kept to their own flock and their own territory, and now, joining one with another in their urge for battle, had destroyed themselves against the bedroom walls, or in the strife had been destroyed by him. Some had lost feathers in the fight; others had blood, his blood, upon their beaks.

Sickened, Nat went to the window and stared out across his patch of garden to the fields.

It was bitter cold, and the ground had all the hard black look of frost. Not white frost, to shine in the morning sun, but the black frost that the east wind brings. The sea, fiercer now with the turning tide, white-capped and steep, broke harshly in the bay. Of the birds there was no sign. Not a sparrow chattered in the hedge beyond the garden gate, no early missel-thrush or blackbird pecked on the grass for worms. There was no sound at all but the east wind and the sea.

Nat shut the window and the door of the small bedroom, and went back across the passage to his own. His wife sat up in bed, one child asleep beside her, the smaller in her arms, his face bandaged. The curtains were tightly drawn across the window, the candles lit. Her face looked garish in the yellow light. She shook her head for silence.

"He's sleeping now," she whispered, "but only just. Something must have cut him, there was blood at the corner of his eyes. Jill said it was the birds. She said she woke up, and the birds were in the room."

His wife looked up at Nat, searching his face for confirmation. She looked terrified, bewildered, and he did not want her to know that he was also shaken, dazed almost, by the events of the past few hours.

"There are birds in there," he said, "dead birds, nearly fifty of them. Robins, wrens, all the little birds from hereabouts. It's as though a madness seized them, with the east wind." He sat down on the bed beside his wife, and held her hand. "It's the weather," he said, "it must be that, it's the hard weather. They aren't the birds, maybe, from here around. They've been driven down from upcountry."

"But, Nat," whispered his wife, "it's only this night that the weather turned. There's been no snow to drive them. And they can't be hungry yet. There's food for them out there in the fields."

"It's the weather," repeated Nat. "I tell you, it's the weather."

His face, too, was drawn and tired, like hers. They stared at one another for a while without speaking.

"I'll go downstairs and make a cup of tea," he said.

The sight of the kitchen reassured him. The cups and saucers, neatly stacked upon the dresser, the table and chairs, his wife's roll of knitting on her basket chair, the children's toys in a corner cupboard.

He knelt down, raked out the old embers, and relit the fire. The glowing sticks brought normality, the steaming kettle and the brown teapot comfort and security. He drank his tea, carried a cup up to his wife. Then he washed in the scullery, and, putting on his boots, opened the back door.

The sky was hard and leaden, and the brown hills that had gleamed in the sun the day before looked dark and bare. The east wind, like a razor, stripped the trees, and the leaves, crackling and dry, shivered and scattered with the wind's blast. Nat stubbed the earth with his boot. It was frozen hard. He had never known a change so swift and sudden. Black winter had descended in a single night.

The children were awake now. Jill was chattering upstairs and young Johnny crying once again. Nat heard his wife's voice, soothing, comforting. Presently they came down. He had breakfast ready for them, and the routine of the day began.

"Did you drive away the birds?" asked Jill, restored to calm because of the kitchen fire, because of day, because of breakfast.

"Yes, they've all gone now," said Nat. "It was the east wind brought them in. They were frightened and lost, they wanted shelter."

"They tried to peck us," said Jill. "They went for Johnny's eyes."

"Fright made them do that," said Nat. "They didn't know where they were in the dark bedroom."

"I hope they won't come again," said Jill. "Perhaps if we put bread for them outside the window they will eat that and fly away."

She finished her breakfast and then went for her coat and hood, her schoolbooks and her satchel. Nat said nothing, but his wife looked at him across the table. A silent message passed between them.

"I'll walk with her to the bus," he said. "I don't go to the farm today."

And while the child was washing in the scullery he said to his wife, "Keep all the windows closed, and the doors too. Just to be on the safe side. I'll go to the farm. Find out if they heard anything in the night." Then he walked with his small daughter up the lane. She seemed to have forgotten her experience of the night before. She danced ahead of him, chasing the leaves, her face whipped with the cold and rosy under the pixie hood.

"Is it going to snow, Dad?" she said. "It's cold enough."

He glanced up at the bleak sky, felt the wind tear at his shoulders. "No," he said, "it's not going to snow. This is a black winter, not a white one."

All the while he searched the hedgerows for the birds, glanced over the top of them to the fields beyond, looked to the small wood above the farm where the rooks and jackdaws gathered. He saw none.

The other children waited by the bus stop, muffled, hooded like Jill, the faces white and pinched with cold.

Jill ran to them, waving. "My Dad says it won't snow," she called, "it's going to be a black winter."

She said nothing of the birds. She began to push and struggle with another little girl. The bus came ambling up the hill. Nat saw her on to it, then turned and walked back towards the farm. It was not his day for work, but he wanted to satisfy himself that all was well. Jim, the cowman, was clattering in the yard.

"Boss around?" asked Nat.

"Gone to market," said Jim. "It's Tuesday, isn't it?"

He clumped off round the corner of a shed. He had no time for Nat. Nat was said to be superior. Read books, and the like. Nat had forgotten it was Tuesday. This showed how the events of the preceding night had shaken him. He went to the back door of the farmhouse and heard Mrs. Trigg singing in the kitchen, the wireless making a background to her song.

"Are you there, missus?" called out Nat.

She came to the door, beaming, broad, a good-tempered woman.

"Hullo, Mr. Hocken," she said. "Can you tell me where this cold is coming from? Is it Russia? I've never seen such a change. And it's going on, the wireless says. Something to do with the Arctic Circle."

"We didn't turn on the wireless this morning," said Nat. "Fact is, we had trouble in the night."

"Kiddies poorly?"

"No . . ." He hardly knew how to explain it. Now, in daylight, the battle of the birds would sound absurd.

He tried to tell Mrs. Trigg what had happened, but he could see from her eyes that she thought his story was the result of a nightmare.

"Sure they were real birds," she said, smiling, "with proper feathers and all? Not the funny-shaped kind that the men see after closing hours on a Saturday night?"

"Mrs. Trigg," he said, "there are fifty dead birds, robins, wrens, and such, lying low on the floor of the children's bedroom. They went for me; they tried to go for young Johnny's eyes."

Mrs. Trigg stared at him doubtfully.

"Well there, now," she answered, "I suppose the weather brought them. Once in the bedroom, they wouldn't know where they were to. Foreign birds maybe, from that Arctic Circle."

"No," said Nat, "they were the birds you see about here every day."

"Funny thing," said Mrs. Trigg, "no explaining it, really. You ought to write up and ask the *Guardian*. They'd have some answer for it. Well, I must be getting on."

She nodded, smiled, and went back into the kitchen.

Nat, dissatisfied, turned to the farm gate. Had it not been for those corpses on the bedroom floor, which he must now collect and bury somewhere, he would have considered the tale exaggeration too.

Jim was standing by the gate.

"Had any trouble with the birds?" asked Nat.

"Birds? What birds?"

"We got them up our place last night. Scores of them, came in the children's bedroom. Quite savage they were."

"Oh?" It took time for anything to penetrate Jim's head. "Never heard of birds acting savage," he said at length. "They get tame, like, sometimes. I've seen them come to the windows for crumbs."

"These birds last night weren't tame."

"No? Cold, maybe. Hungry. You put out some crumbs."

Jim was no more interested than Mrs. Trigg had been. It was, Nat thought, like air raids in the war. No one down this end of the country knew what the Plymouth folk had seen and suffered. You had to endure something yourself before it touched you. He walked back along the lane and crossed the stile to his cottage. He found his wife in the kitchen with young Johnny.

"See anyone?" she asked.

"Mrs. Trigg and Jim," he answered. "I don't think they believed me. Anyway, nothing wrong up there."

"You might take the birds away," she said. "I daren't go into the room to make the beds until you do. I'm scared."

"Nothing to scare you now," said Nat. "They're dead, aren't they?"

He went up with a sack and dropped the stiff bodies into it, one by one. Yes, there were fifty of them, all told. Just the ordinary common birds of the hedgerow, nothing as large even as a thrush. It must have been fright that made them act the way they did. Blue tits, wrens—it was incredible to think of the power of their small beaks jabbing at his face and hands the night before. He took the sack out into the garden and was faced now with a fresh problem. The ground was too hard to dig. It was frozen solid, yet no snow had fallen, nothing had happened in the past hours but the coming of the east wind. It was unnatural, queer. The weather prophets must be right. The change was something connected with the Arctic Circle.

The wind seemed to cut him to the bone as he stood there uncertainly, holding the sack. He could see the white-capped seas breaking down under in the bay. He decided to take the birds to the shore and bury them.

When he reached the beach below the headland he could scarcely stand, the force of the east wind was so strong. It hurt to draw breath, and his bare hands were blue. Never had he known such cold, not in all the bad winters he could remember. It was low tide. He crunched his way over the shingle to the softer sand and then, his back to the wind, ground a pit in the sand with his heel. He meant to drop the birds into it, but as he opened up the sack the force of the wind carried them, lifted them, as though in flight again, and they were blown away from him along the beach, tossed like feathers, spread and scattered, the bodies of the fifty frozen birds. There was something ugly in the sight. He did not like it. The dead birds were swept away from him by the wind.

"The tide will take them when it turns," he said to himself.

He looked out to sea and watched the crested breakers, combing green. They rose stiffly, curled, and broke again, and because it was ebb tide the roar was distant, more remote, lacking the sound and thunder of the flood.

Then he saw them. The gulls. Out there, riding the seas.

What he had thought at first to be the whitecaps of the waves were gulls. Hundreds, thousands, tens of thousands . . . They rose and fell in the trough of the seas, heads to the wind, like a mighty fleet at anchor, waiting on the tide. To eastward, and to the west, the gulls were there. They stretched as far as his eye could reach, in close formation, line upon line. Had the sea been still they would have covered the bay like a white cloud, head to head, body packed to body. Only the east wind, whipping the sea to breakers, hid them from the shore.

Nat turned and, leaving the beach, climbed the steep path home. Someone should know of this. Someone should be told. Something was happening, because of the east wind and the weather, that he did not understand. He wondered if he should go to the call box by the bus stop and ring up the police. Yet what could they do? What could anyone do? Tens and thousands of gulls riding the sea there in the bay because of storm, because of hunger. The police would think him mad, or drunk, or take the statement from him with great calm. "Thank you. Yes, the matter has already been reported. The hard weather is driving the birds inland in great numbers." Nat looked about him. Still no sign of any other bird. Perhaps the cold had sent them all from upcountry? As he drew near to the cottage his wife came to meet him at the door. She called to him, excited. "Nat," she said, "it's on the wireless. They've just read out a special news bulletin. I've written it down."

"What's on the wireless?" he said.

"About the birds," she said. "It's not only here, it's everywhere. In London, all over the country. Something has happened to the birds."

Together they went into the kitchen. He read the piece of paper lying on the table.

"Statement from the Home Office at 11 A.M. today. Reports from all over the country are coming in hourly about the vast quantity of birds flocking above towns, villages, and outlying districts, causing obstruction and damage and even attacking individuals. It is thought that the Arctic air stream, at present covering the British Isles, is causing birds to migrate south in immense numbers, and that intense hunger may drive these birds to attack human beings. Householders are warned to see to their windows, doors, and chimneys, and to take reasonable precautions for the safety of their children. A further statement will be issued later."

A kind of excitement seized Nat; he looked at his wife in triumph. "There you are," he said. "Let's hope they'll hear that at the farm. Mrs. Trigg will know it wasn't any story. It's true. All over the country. I've been telling myself all morning there's something wrong. And just now, down on the beach, I looked out to sea and there are gulls, thousands of them, tens of thousands—you couldn't put a pin between their heads—and they're all out there, riding on the sea, waiting."

"What are they waiting for, Nat?" she asked.

He stared at her, then looked down again at the piece of paper.

"I don't know," he said slowly. "It says here the birds are hungry."

He went over to the drawer where he kept his hammer and tools.

"What are you going to do, Nat?"

"See to the windows and the chimneys too, like they tell you."

"You think they would break in, with the windows shut? Those sparrows and robins and such? Why, how could they?"

He did not answer. He was not thinking of the robins and the sparrows. He was thinking of the gulls. . . .

He went upstairs and worked there the rest of the morning, boarding the windows of the bedrooms, filling up the chimney bases. Good job it was his free day and he was not working at the farm. It reminded him of the old days, at the beginning of the war. He was not married then, and he had made all the black-out boards for his mother's house in Plymouth. Made the shelter too. Not that it had been of any use when the moment came. He wondered if they would take these precautions up at the farm. He doubted it. Too easygoing, Harry Trigg and his missus. Maybe they'd laugh at the whole thing. Go off to a dance or a whist drive.

"Dinner's ready." She called him, from the kitchen.

"All right. Coming down."

He was pleased with his handiwork. The frames fitted nicely over the little panes and at the bases of the chimneys.

When dinner was over and his wife was washing up, Nat switched on the one o'clock news. The same announcement was repeated, the one which she had taken down during the morning, but the news bulletin enlarged upon it. "The flocks of birds have caused dislocation in all areas," read the announcer, "and in London the sky was so dense at ten o'clock this morning that it seemed as if the city was covered by a vast black cloud.

"The birds settled on roof tops, on window ledges, and on chimneys. The species included blackbird, thrush, the common house sparrow, and, as might be expected in the metropolis, a vast quantity of pigeons and starlings, and that frequenter of the London river, the black-headed gull. The sight has been so unusual that traffic came to a standstill in many thoroughfares, work was abandoned in shops and offices, and the streets and pavements were crowded with people standing about to watch the birds."

Various incidents were recounted, the suspected reason of cold and hunger stated again, and warnings to householders repeated. The announcer's voice was smooth and suave. Nat had the impression that this man, in particular, treated the whole business as he would an elaborate joke. There would be others like him, hundreds of them, who did not know what it was to struggle in darkness with a flock of birds. There would be parties tonight in London, like the ones they gave on election nights. People standing about, shouting and laughing, getting drunk. "Come and watch the birds!"

Nat switched off the wireless. He got up and started work on the kitchen windows. His wife watched him, young Johnny at her heels.

"What, boards for down here too?" she said. "Why, I'll have to light up before three o'clock. I see no call for boards down here."

"Better be sure than sorry," answered Nat. "I'm not going to take any chances."

"What they ought to do," she said, "is to call the Army out and shoot the birds. That would soon scare them off."

"Let them try," said Nat. "How'd they set about it?"

"They have the Army to the docks," she answered, "when the dockers strike. The soldiers go down and unload the ships."

"Yes," said Nat, "and the population of London is eight million or more. Think of all the buildings, all the flats and houses. Do you think they've enough soldiers to go round shooting birds from every roof?"

"I don't know. But something should be done. They ought to do something."

Nat thought to himself that "they" were no doubt considering the problem at that very moment, but whatever "they" decided to do in London and the big cities would not help the people here, three hundred miles away. Each householder must look after his own.

"How are we off for food?" he said.

"Now, Nat, whatever next?"

"Never mind. What have you got in the larder?"

"It's shopping day tomorrow, you know that. I don't keep uncooked food hanging about, it goes off. Butcher doesn't call till the day after. But I can bring back something when I go in tomorrow."

Nat did not want to scare her. He thought it possible that she might not go to town tomorrow. He looked in the larder for himself, and in the cupboard where she kept her tins. They would do for a couple of days. Bread was low.

"What about the baker?"

"He comes tomorrow too."

He saw she had flour. If the baker did not call she had enough to bake one loaf.

"We'd be better off in old days," he said, "when the women baked twice a week, and had pilchards salted, and there was food for a family to last a siege, if need be."

"I've tried the children with tinned fish, they don't like it," she said.

Nat went on hammering the boards across the kitchen windows. Candles. They were low in candles too. That must be another thing she meant to buy tomorrow. Well, it could not be helped. They must go early to bed tonight. That was, if . . .

He got up and went out of the back door and stood in the garden, looking down towards the sea. There had been no sun all day, and now, at barely three o'clock, a kind of darkness had already come, the sky sullen, heavy, colourless like salt. He could hear the vicious sea drumming on the rocks. He walked down the path, halfway to the beach. And then he stopped. He could see the tide had turned. The rock that had shown in midmorning was now covered, but it was not the sea that held his eyes. The gulls had risen. They were circling, hundreds of them, thousands of them, lifting their wings against the wind. It was the gulls that made the darkening of the sky. And they were silent. They made not a sound. They just went on soaring and circling, rising, falling, trying their strength against the wind.

Nat turned. He ran up the path, back to the cottage.

"I'm going for Jill," he said. "I'll wait for her at the bus stop."

"What's the matter?" asked his wife. "You've gone quite white."

"Keep Johnny inside," he said. "Keep the door shut. Light up now, and draw the curtains."

"It's only just gone three," she said.

"Never mind. Do what I tell you."

He looked inside the tool shed outside the back door. Nothing there of much use. A spade was too heavy, and a fork no good. He took the hoe. It was the only possible tool, and light enough to carry.

He started walking up the lane to the bus stop, and now and again glanced back over his shoulder.

The gulls had risen higher now, their circles were broader, wider, they were spreading out in huge formation across the sky.

He hurried on; although he knew the bus would not come to the top of the hill before four o'clock he had to hurry. He passed no one on the way. He was glad of this. No time to stop and chatter.

At the top of the hill he waited. He was much too soon. There was half an hour still to go. The east wind came whipping across the fields from the higher ground. He stamped his feet and blew upon his hands. In the distance he could see the clay hills, white and clean, against the heavy pallor of the sky. Something black rose from behind them, like a smudge at first, then widening, becoming deeper, and the smudge became a cloud, and the cloud divided again into five other clouds, spreading north, east, south, and west, and they were not clouds at all; they were birds. He watched them travel across the sky, and as one section passed overhead, within two or three hundred feet of him, he knew, from their speed, they were bound inland, upcountry; they had no business with the people here on the peninsula. They were rooks, crows, jackdaws, magpies, jays, all birds that usually preyed upon the smaller species; but this afternoon they were bound on some other mission.

"They've been given the towns," thought Nat; "they know what they have to do. We don't matter so much here. The gulls will serve for us. The others go to the towns."

He went to the call box, stepped inside, and lifted the receiver. The exchange would do. They would pass the message on.

"I'm speaking from Highway," he said, "by the bus stop. I want to report large formations of birds travelling upcountry. The gulls are also forming in the bay."

"All right," answered the voice, laconic, weary.

"You'll be sure and pass this message on to the proper quarter?"

"Yes . . . yes . . . ." Impatient now, fed-up. The buzzing note resumed.

"She's another," thought Nat, "she doesn't care. Maybe she's had to answer calls all day. She hopes to go to the pictures tonight. She'll squeeze some fellow's hand, and point up at the sky, and 'Look at all them birds!' She doesn't care."

The bus came lumbering up the hill. Jill climbed out, and three or four other children. The bus went on towards the town.

"What's the hoe for, Dad?"

They crowded around him, laughing, pointing.

"I just brought it along," he said. "Come on now, let's get home. It's cold, no hanging about. Here, you. I'll watch you across the fields, see how fast you can run."

He was speaking to Jill's companions, who came from different families, living in the council houses. A short cut would take them to the cottages.

"We want to play a bit in the lane," said one of them.

"No, you don't. You go off home or I'll tell your Mammy."

They whispered to one another, round-eyed, then scuttled off across the fields. Jill stared at her father, her mouth sullen.

"We always play in the lane," she said.

"Not tonight, you don't," he said. "Come on now, no dawdling."

He could see the gulls now, circling the fields, coming in towards the land. Still silent. Still no sound.

"Look, Dad, look over there, look at all the gulls."

"Yes. Hurry, now."

"Where are they flying to? Where are they going?"

"Upcountry, I dare say. Where it's warmer."

He seized her hand and dragged her after him along the lane.

"Don't go so fast. I can't keep up."

The gulls were copying the rooks and crows. They were spreading out in formation across the sky. They headed, in bands of thousands, to the four compass points.

"Dad, what is it? What are the gulls doing?"

They were not intent upon their flight, as the crows, as the jackdaws had been. They still circled overhead. Nor did they fly so high. It was as though they waited upon some signal. As though some decision had yet to be given. The order was not clear.

"Do you want me to carry you, Jill? Here, come pick-a-back."

This way he might put on speed; but he was wrong. Jill was heavy. She kept slipping. And she was crying too. His sense of urgency, of fear, had communicated itself to the child.

"I wish the gulls would go away. I don't like them. They're coming closer to the lane."

He put her down again. He started running, swinging Jill after him. As they went past the farm turning he saw the farmer backing his car out of the garage. Nat called to him.

"Can you give us a lift?" he said.

"What's that?"

Mr. Trigg turned in the driving seat and stared at them. Then a smile came to his cheerful, rubicund face.

"It looks as though we're in for some fun," he said. "Have you seen the gulls? Jim and I are going to take a crack at them. Everyone's gone bird-crazy, talking of nothing else. I hear you were troubled in the night. Want a gun?"

Nat shook his head.

The small car was packed. There was just room for Jill, if she crouched on top of petrol tins on the back seat.

"I don't want a gun," said Nat, "but I'd be obliged if you'd run Jill home. She's scared of the birds."

He spoke briefly. He did not want to talk in front of Jill.

"O.K.," said the farmer, "I'll take her home. Why don't you stop behind and join the shooting match? We'll make the feathers fly."

Jill climbed in, and, turning the car, the driver sped up the lane. Nat followed after. Trigg must be crazy. What use was a gun against a sky of birds?

Now Nat was not responsible for Jill, he had time to look about him. The birds were circling still above the fields. Mostly herring gull, but the black-backed gull amongst them. Usually they kept apart. Now they were united. Some bond had brought them together. It was the black-backed gull that attacked the smaller birds, and even newborn lambs, so he'd heard. He'd never seen it done. He remembered this now, though, looking above him in the sky. They were coming in towards the farm. They were circling lower in the sky, and the black-backed gulls were to the front, the black-backed gulls were leading. The farm, then, was their target. They were making for the farm.

Nat increased his pace towards his own cottage. He saw the farmer's car turn and come back along the lane. It drew up beside him with a jerk.

"The kid has run inside," said the farmer. "Your wife was watching for her. Well, what do you make of it? They're saying in town the Russians have done it. The Russians have poisoned the birds."

"How could they do that?" asked Nat.

"Don't ask me. You know how stories get around. Will you join my shooting match?"

"No, I'll get along home. The wife will be worried else."

"My missus says if you could eat gull there'd be some sense in it," said Trigg, "we'd have roast gull, baked gull, and pickle 'em into the bargain. You wait until I let off a few barrels into the brutes. That'll scare 'em."

"Have you boarded your windows?" asked Nat.

"No. Lot of nonsense. They like to scare you on the wireless. I've had more to do today than to go round boarding up my windows."

"I'd board them now, if I were you."

"Garn. You're windy. Like to come to our place to sleep?"

"No, thanks all the same."

"All right. See you in the morning. Give you a gull breakfast."

The farmer grinned and turned his car to the farm entrance.

Nat hurried on. Past the little wood, past the old barn, and then across the stile to the remaining field.

As he jumped the stile he heard the whir of wings. A black-backed gull dived down at him from the sky, missed, swerved in flight, and rose to

dive again. In a moment it was joined by others, six, seven, a dozen, black-backed and herring mixed. Nat dropped his hoe. The hoe was useless. Covering his head with his arms, he ran towards the cottage. They kept coming at him from the air, silent save for the beating wings. The terrible, fluttering wings. He would feel the blood on his hands, his wrists, his neck. Each stab of a swooping beak tore his flesh. If only he could keep them from his eyes. Nothing else mattered. He must keep them from his eyes. They had not learnt yet how to cling to a shoulder, how to rip clothing, how to dive in mass upon the head, upon the body. But with each dive, with each attack, they became bolder. And they had no thought for themselves. When they dived low and missed, they crashed, bruised and broken, on the ground. As Nat ran he stumbled, kicking their spent bodies in front of him.

He found the door; he hammered upon it with his bleeding hands. Because of the boarded windows no light shone. Everything was dark.

"Let me in," he shouted, "it's Nat. Let me in."

He shouted loud to make himself heard above the whir of the gulls' wings.

Then he saw the gannet, poised for the dive, above him in the sky. The gulls circled, retired, soared, one after another, against the wind. Only the gannet remained. One single gannet above him in the sky. The wings folded suddenly to its body. It dropped like a stone. Nat screamed, and the door opened. He stumbled across the threshold, and his wife threw her weight against the door.

They heard the thud of the gannet as it fell.

His wife dressed his wounds. They were not deep. The backs of his hands had suffered most, and his wrists. Had he not worn a cap they would have reached his head. As to the gannet . . . the gannet could have split his skull.

The children were crying, of course. They had seen the blood on their father's hands.

"It's all right now," he told them. "I'm not hurt. Just a few scratches. You play with Johnny, Jill. Mammy will wash these cuts."

He half shut the door to the scullery so that they could not see. His wife was ashen. She began running water from the sink.

"I saw them overhead," she whispered. "They began collecting just as Jill ran in with Mr. Trigg. I shut the door fast, and it jammed. That's why I couldn't open it at once when you came."

"Thank God they waited for me," he said. "Jill would have fallen at once. One bird alone would have done it."

Furtively, so as not to alarm the children, they whispered together as she bandaged his hands and the back of his neck.

"They're flying inland," he said, "thousands of them. Rooks, crows, all the bigger birds. I saw them from the bus stop. They're making for the towns."

"But what can they do, Nat?"

"They'll attack. Go for everyone out in the streets. Then they'll try the windows, the chimneys."

"Why don't the authorities do something? Why don't they get the Army, get machine guns, anything?"

"There's been no time. Nobody's prepared. We'll hear what they have to say on the six o'clock news."

Nat went back into the kitchen, followed by his wife. Johnny was playing quietly on the floor. Only Jill looked anxious.

"I can hear the birds," she said. "Listen, Dad."

Nat listened. Muffled sounds came from the windows, from the door. Wings brushing the surface, sliding, scraping, seeking a way of entry. The sound of many bodies, pressed together, shuffling on the sills. Now and again came a thud, a crash, as some bird dived and fell. "Some of them will kill themselves that way," he thought, "but not enough. Never enough."

"All right," he said aloud, "I've got boards over the windows, Jill. The birds can't get in."

He went and examined all the windows. His work had been thorough. Every gap was closed. He would make extra certain, however. He found wedges, pieces of old tin, strips of wood and metal, and fastened them at the sides to reinforce the boards. His hammering helped to deafen the sound of the birds, the shuffling, the tapping, and more ominous—he did not want his wife or the children to hear it—the splinter of cracked glass.

"Turn on the wireless," he said, "let's have the wireless."

This would drown the sound also. He went upstairs to the bedrooms and reinforced the windows there. Now he could hear the birds on the roof, the scraping of claws, a sliding, jostling sound.

He decided they must sleep in the kitchen, keep up the fire, bring down the mattresses, and lay them out on the floor. He was afraid of the bedroom chimneys. The boards he had placed at the chimney bases might give way. In the kitchen they would be safe because of the fire. He would have to make a joke of it. Pretend to the children they were playing at camp. If the worst happened, and the birds forced an entry down the bedroom chimneys, it would be hours, days perhaps, before they could break down the doors. The birds would be imprisoned in the bedrooms. They could do no harm there. Crowded together, they would stifle and die.

He began to bring the mattresses downstairs. At sight of them his wife's eyes widened in apprehension. She thought the birds had already broken in upstairs.

"All right," he said cheerfully, "we'll all sleep together in the kitchen tonight. More cosy here by the fire. Then we shan't be worried by those silly old birds tapping at the windows."

He made the children help him rearrange the furniture, and he took the precaution of moving the dresser, with his wife's help, across the window. It fitted well. It was an added safeguard. The mattresses could now be lain, one beside the other, against the wall where the dresser had stood.

"We're safe enough now," he thought. "We're snug and tight, like an air-raid shelter. We can hold out. It's just the food that worries me. Food, and coal for the fire. We've enough for two or three days, not more. By that time . . ."

No use thinking ahead as far as that. And they'd be giving directions on the wireless. People would be told what to do. And now, in the midst of many problems, he realised that it was dance music only coming over the air. Not Children's Hour, as it should have been. He glanced at the dial. Yes, they were on the Home Service all right. Dance records. He switched to the Light programme. He knew the reason. The usual programmes had been abandoned. This only happened at exceptional times. Elections and such. He tried to remember if it had happened in the war, during the heavy raids on London. But of course. The B.B.C. was not stationed in London during the war. The programmes were broadcast from other, temporary quarters. "We're better off here," he thought; "we're better off here in the kitchen, with the windows and the doors boarded, than they are up in the towns. Thank God we're not in the towns."

At six o'clock the records ceased. The time signal was given. No matter if it scared the children, he must hear the news. There was a pause after the pips. Then the announcer spoke. His voice was solemn, grave. Quite different from midday.

"This is London," he said. "A National Emergency was proclaimed at four o'clock this afternoon. Measures are being taken to safeguard the lives and property of the population, but it must be understood that these are not easy to effect immediately, owing to the unforeseen and unparalleled nature of the present crisis. Every householder must take precautions to his own building, and where several people live together, as in flats and apartments, they must unite to do the utmost they can to prevent entry. It is absolutely imperative that every individual stay indoors tonight and that no one at all remain on the streets, or roads, or anywhere without-doors. The birds, in vast numbers, are attacking anyone on sight, and have already begun an assault upon buildings; but these, with due care, should be impenetrable. The population is asked to remain calm and not to panic. Owing to the exceptional nature of the emergency, there will be no further transmission from any broadcasting station until 7 A.M. tomorrow."

They played the National Anthem. Nothing more happened. Nat switched off the set. He looked at his wife. She stared back at him.

"What's it mean?" said Jill. "What did the news say?"

"There won't be any more programmes tonight," said Nat. "There's been a breakdown at the B.B.C."

"Is it the birds?" asked Jill. "Have the birds done it?"

"No," said Nat, "it's just that everyone's very busy, and then of course they have to get rid of the birds, messing everything up, in the towns. Well, we can manage without the wireless for one evening."

"I wish we had a gramophone," said Jill, "that would be better than nothing."

She had her face turned to the dresser backed against the windows. Try as they did to ignore it, they were all aware of the shuffling, the stabbing, the persistent beating and sweeping of wings.

"We'll have supper early," suggested Nat, "something for a treat. Ask Mammy. Toasted cheese, eh? Something we all like?"

He winked and nodded at his wife. He wanted the look of dread, of apprehension, to go from Jill's face.

He helped with the supper, whistling, singing, making as much clatter as he could, and it seemed to him that the shuffling and the tapping were not so intense as they had been at first. Presently he went up to the bedrooms and listened, and he no longer heard the jostling for place upon the roof.

"They've got reasoning powers," he thought; "they know it's hard to break in here. They'll try elsewhere. They won't waste their time with us."

Supper passed without incident, and then, when they were clearing away, they heard a new sound, droning, familiar, a sound they all knew and understood.

His wife looked up at him, her face alight. "It's planes," she said; "they're sending out planes after the birds. That's what I said they ought to do all along. That will get them. Isn't that gunfire? Can't you hear guns?"

It might be gunfire out at sea. Nat could not tell. Big naval guns might have an effect upon the gulls out at sea, but the gulls were inland now. The guns couldn't shell the shore because of the population.

"It's good, isn't it," said his wife, "to hear the planes?" And Jill, catching her enthusiasm, jumped up and down with Johnny. "The planes will get the birds. The planes will shoot them."

Just then they heard a crash about two miles distant, followed by a second, then a third. The droning became more distant, passed away out to sea.

"What was that?" asked his wife. "Were they dropping bombs on the birds?"

"I don't know," answered Nat. "I don't think so."

He did not want to tell her that the sound they had heard was the crashing of aircraft. It was, he had no doubt, a venture on the part of the authorities to send out reconnaissance forces, but they might have known the venture was suicidal. What could aircraft do against birds that flung themselves to death against propeller and fuselage, but hurtle to the ground themselves? This was being tried now, he supposed, over the whole country. And at a cost. Someone high up had lost his head.

"Where have the planes gone, Dad?" asked Jill.

"Back to base," he said. "Come on, now, time to tuck down for bed."

It kept his wife occupied, undressing the children before the fire, seeing to the bedding, one thing and another, while he went round the cottage again, making sure that nothing had worked loose. There was no further drone of aircraft, and the naval guns had ceased. "Waste of life and effort," Nat said to himself. "We can't destroy enough of them that way. Cost too heavy. There's always gas. Maybe they'll try spraying with gas, mustard gas. We'll be warned first, of course, if they do. There's one thing, the best brains of the country will be on to it tonight."

Somehow the thought reassured him. He had a picture of scientists, naturalists, technicians, and all those chaps they called the back-room boys, summoned to a council; they'd be working on the problem now. This was not a job for the government, for the chiefs of staff—they would merely carry out the orders of the scientists.

"They'll have to be ruthless," he thought. "Where the trouble's worst they'll have to risk more lives, if they use gas. All the livestock, too, and the soil—all contaminated. As long as everyone doesn't panic. That's the trouble. People panicking, losing their heads. The B.B.C. was right to warn us of that."

Upstairs in the bedrooms all was quiet. No further scraping and stabbing at the windows. A lull in battle. Forces regrouping. Wasn't that what they called it in the old wartime bulletins? The wind hadn't dropped, though. He could still hear it roaring in the chimneys. And the sea breaking down on the shore. Then he remembered the tide. The tide would be on the turn. Maybe the lull in battle was because of the tide. There was some law the birds obeyed, and it was all to do with the east wind and the tide.

He glanced at his watch. Nearly eight o'clock. It must have gone high water an hour ago. That explained the lull: the birds attacked with the flood tide. It might not work that way inland, upcountry, but it seemed as if it was so this way on the coast. He reckoned the time limit in his head. They had six hours to go without attack. When the tide turned again, around one-twenty in the morning, the birds would come back. . . .

There were two things he could do. The first to rest, with his wife and the children, and all of them snatch what sleep they could, until the small hours. The second to go out, see how they were faring at the farm, see if the telephone was still working there, so that they might get news from the exchange.

He called softly to his wife, who had just settled the children. She came halfway up the stairs and he whispered to her.

"You're not to go," she said at once, "you're not to go and leave me alone with the children. I can't stand it."

Her voice rose hysterically. He hushed her, calmed her.

"All right," he said, "all right. I'll wait till morning. And we'll get the wireless bulletin then too, at seven. But in the morning, when the tide ebbs again, I'll try for the farm, and they may let us have bread and potatoes, and milk too."

His mind was busy again, planning against emergency. They would not have milked, of course, this evening. The cows would be standing by the gate, waiting in the yard, with the household inside, battened behind boards, as they were here at the cottage. That is, if they had time to take precautions. He thought of the farmer, Trigg, smiling at him from the car. There would have been no shooting party, not tonight.

The children were asleep. His wife, still clothed, was sitting on her mattress. She watched him, her eyes nervous.

"What are you going to do?" she whispered.

He shook his head for silence. Softly, stealthily, he opened the back door and looked outside.

It was pitch dark. The wind was blowing harder than ever, coming in steady gusts, icy, from the sea. He kicked at the step outside the door. It was heaped with birds. There were dead birds everywhere. Under the windows, against the walls. These were the suicides, the divers, the ones with broken necks. Wherever he looked he saw dead birds. No trace of the living. The living had flown seaward with the turn of the tide. The gulls would be riding the seas now, as they had done in the forenoon.

In the far distance, on the hill where the tractor had been two days before, something was burning. One of the aircraft that had crashed; the fire, fanned by the wind, had set light to a stack.

He looked at the bodies of the birds, and he had a notion that if he heaped them, one upon the other, on the window sills they would make added protection for the next attack. Not much, perhaps, but something. The bodies would have to be clawed at, pecked, and dragged aside before the living birds could gain purchase on the sills and attack the panes. He set to work in the darkness. It was queer; he hated touching them. The bodies were still warm and bloody. The blood matted their feathers. He felt his stomach turn, but he went on with his work. He noticed grimly that every windowpane was shattered. Only the boards had kept the birds from breaking in. He stuffed the cracked panes with the bleeding bodies of the birds.

When he had finished he went back into the cottage. He barricaded the kitchen door, made it doubly secure. He took off his bandages, sticky with the birds' blood, not with his own cuts, and put on fresh plaster.

His wife had made him cocoa and he drank it thirstily. He was very tired.

"All right," he said, smiling, "don't worry. We'll get through."

He lay down on his mattress and closed his eyes. He slept at once. He dreamt uneasily, because through his dreams there ran a thread of something forgotten. Some piece of work, neglected, that he should have done. Some precaution that he had known well but had not taken, and he could not put a name to it in his dreams. It was connected in some way with the burning aircraft and the stack upon the hill. He went on sleeping, though; he did not awake. It was his wife shaking his shoulder that awoke him finally.

"They've begun," she sobbed, "they've started this last hour. I can't listen to it any longer alone. There's something smelling bad too, something burning."

Then he remembered. He had forgotten to make up the fire. It was smouldering, nearly out. He got up swiftly and lit the lamp. The hammering had started at the windows and the doors, but it was not that he minded now. It was the smell of singed feathers. The smell filled the kitchen. He knew at once what it was. The birds were coming down the chimney, squeezing their way down to the kitchen range.

He got sticks and paper and put them on the embers, then reached for the can of paraffin.

"Stand back," he shouted to his wife. "We've got to risk this."

He threw the paraffin on to the fire. The flame roared up the pipe, and down upon the fire fell the scorched, blackened bodies of the birds.

The children woke, crying. "What is it?" said Jill. "What's happened?"

Nat had no time to answer. He was raking the bodies from the chimney, clawing them out on to the floor. The flames still roared, and the danger of the chimney catching fire was one he had to take. The flames would send away the living birds from the chimney top. The lower joint was the difficulty, though. This was choked with the smouldering, helpless bodies of the birds caught by fire. He scarcely heeded the attack on the windows and the door: let them beat their wings, break their beaks, lose their lives, in the attempt to force an entry into his home. They would not break in. He thanked God he had one of the old cottages, with small windows, stout walls. Not like the new council houses. Heaven help them up the lane in the new council houses.

"Stop crying," he called to the children. "There's nothing to be afraid of, stop crying."

He went on raking at the burning, smouldering bodies as they fell into the fire.

"This'll fetch them," he said to himself, "the draught and the flames together. We're all right, as long as the chimney doesn't catch. I ought to be shot for this. It's all my fault. Last thing, I should have made up the fire. I knew there was something."

Amid the scratching and tearing at the window boards came the sudden homely striking of the kitchen clock. Three A.M. A little more than four hours yet to go. He could not be sure of the exact time of high water. He reckoned it would not turn much before half-past seven, twenty to eight.

"Light up the Primus," he said to his wife. "Make us some tea, and the kids some cocoa. No use sitting around doing nothing."

That was the line. Keep her busy, and the children too. Move about, eat, drink; always best to be on the go.

He waited by the range. The flames were dying. But no more blackened bodies fell from the chimney. He thrust his poker up as far as it could go and found nothing. It was clear. The chimney was clear. He wiped the sweat from his forehead.

"Come on now, Jill," he said, "bring me some more sticks. We'll have a good fire going directly." She wouldn't come near him, though. She was staring at the heaped singed bodies of the birds.

"Never mind them," he said, "we'll put those in the passage when I've got the fire steady."

The danger of the chimney was over. It could not happen again, not if the fire was kept burning day and night.

"I'll have to get more fuel from the farm tomorrow," he thought. "This will never last. I'll manage, though. I can do all that with the ebb tide. It can be worked, fetching what we need, when the tide's turned. We've just got to adapt ourselves, that's all."

They drank tea and cocoa and ate slices of bread and Bovril. Only half a loaf left, Nat noticed. Never mind though, they'd get by.

"Stop it," said young Johnny, pointing to the windows with his spoon, "stop it, you old birds."

"That's right," said Nat, smiling, "we don't want the old beggars, do we? Had enough of 'em."

They began to cheer when they heard the thud of the suicide birds.

"There's another, Dad," cried Jill, "he's done for."

"He's had it," said Nat. "There he goes, the blighter."

This was the way to face up to it. This was the spirit. If they could keep this up, hang on like this until seven, when the first news bulletin came through, they would not have done too badly.

"Give us a fag," he said to his wife. "A bit of a smoke will clear away the smell of the scorched feathers."

"There's only two left in the packet," she said. "I was going to buy you some from the Co-op."

"I'll have one," he said, "t'other will keep for a rainy day."

No sense trying to make the children rest. There was no rest to be got while the tapping and the scratching went on at the windows. He sat with one arm round his wife and the other round Jill, with Johnny on his mother's lap and the blankets heaped about them on the mattress.

"You can't help admiring the beggars," he said; "they've got persistence. You'd think they'd tire of the game, but not a bit of it."

Admiration was hard to sustain. The tapping went on and on and a new rasping note struck Nat's ear, as though a sharper beak than any hitherto had come to take over from its fellows. He tried to remember the names of birds; he tried to think which species would go for this particular job. It was not the tap of the woodpecker. That would be light and frequent. This was more serious, because if it continued long the wood would splinter as the glass had done. Then he remembered the hawks. Could the hawks have taken over from the gulls? Were there buzzards now upon the sills, using talons as well as beaks? Hawks, buzzards, kestrels, falcons—he had forgotten the birds of prey. He had forgotten the gripping power of the birds of prey. Three hours to go, and while they waited, the sound of the splintering wood, the talons tearing at the wood.

Nat looked about him, seeing what furniture he could destroy to fortify the door. The windows were safe because of the dresser. He was not certain of the door. He went upstairs, but when he reached the landing he paused and listened. There was a soft patter on the floor of the children's bedroom. The birds had broken through. . . . He put his ear to the door. No mistake. He could hear the rustle of wings and the light patter as they searched the floor. The other bedroom was still clear. He went into it and began bringing out the furniture, to pile at the head of the stairs should the door of the children's bedroom go. It was preparation. It might never be needed. He could not stack the furniture against the door, because it opened inward. The only possible thing was to have it at the top of the stairs.

"Come down, Nat, what are you doing?" called his wife.

"I won't be long," he shouted. "Just making everything shipshape up here."

He did not want her to come; he did not want her to hear the pattering of the feet in the children's bedroom, the brushing of those wings against the door.

At five-thirty he suggested breakfast, bacon and fried bread, if only to stop the growing look of panic in his wife's eyes and to calm the fretful children. She did not know about the birds upstairs. The bedroom, luckily, was not over the kitchen. Had it been so, she could not have failed to hear the sound of them up there, tapping the boards. And the silly, senseless thud of the suicide birds, the death and glory boys, who flew into the bedroom, smashing their heads against the walls. He knew them of old, the herring gulls. They had no brains. The black-backs were different; they knew what they were doing. So did the buzzards, the hawks . . .

He found himself watching the clock, gazing at the hands that went so slowly round the dial. If his theory was not correct, if the attack did not cease with the turn of the tide, he knew they were beaten. They could not continue through the long day without air, without rest, without more fuel, without . . . His mind raced. He knew there were so many things they needed to withstand siege. They were not fully prepared. They were not ready. It might be that it would be safer in the towns after all. If he could get a message through on the farm telephone to his cousin, only a short journey by train upcountry, they might be able to hire a car. That would be quicker—hire a car between tides . . .

His wife's voice, calling his name, drove away the sudden, desperate desire for sleep.

"What is it? What now?" he said sharply.

"The wireless," said his wife. "I've been watching the clock. It's nearly seven."

"Don't twist the knob," he said, impatient for the first time. "It's on the Home where it is. They'll speak from the Home."

They waited. The kitchen clock struck seven. There was no sound. No chimes, no music. They waited until a quarter past, switching to the Light. The result was the same. No news bulletin came through.

"We've heard wrong," he said. "They won't be broadcasting until eight o'clock."

They left it switched on, and Nat thought of the battery, wondered how much power was left in it. It was generally recharged when his wife went shopping in the town. If the battery failed they would not hear the instructions.

"It's getting light," whispered his wife. "I can't see it, but I can feel it. And the birds aren't hammering so loud."

She was right. The rasping, tearing sound grew fainter every moment. So did the shuffling, the jostling for place upon the step, upon the sills. The tide was on the turn. By eight there was no sound at all. Only the wind. The children, lulled at last by the stillness, fell asleep. At half-past eight Nat switched the wireless off.

"What are you doing? We'll miss the news," said his wife.

"There isn't going to be any news," said Nat. "We've got to depend upon ourselves."

He went to the door and slowly pulled away the barricades. He drew the bolts and, kicking the bodies from the step outside the door, breathed the cold air. He had six working hours before him, and he knew he must reserve his strength for the right things, not waste it in any way. Food, and light, and fuel; these were the necessary things. If he could get them in sufficiency, they could endure another night.

He stepped into the garden, and as he did so he saw the living birds. The gulls had gone to ride the sea, as they had done before; they sought sea food, and the buoyancy of the tide, before they returned to the attack. Not so the land birds. They waited and watched. Nat saw them, on the hedgerows, on the soil, crowded in the trees, outside in the field, line upon line of birds, all still, doing nothing.

He went to the end of his small garden. The birds did not move. They went on watching him.

"I've got to get food," said Nat to himself. "I've got to go to the farm to find food."

He went back to the cottage. He saw to the windows and the doors. He went upstairs and opened the children's bedroom. It was empty, except for the dead birds on the floor. The living were out there, in the garden, in the fields. He went downstairs.

"I'm going to the farm," he said.

His wife clung to him. She had seen the living birds from the open door.

"Take us with you," she begged. "We can't stay here alone. I'd rather die than stay here alone."

He considered the matter. He nodded.

"Come on, then," he said. "Bring baskets, and Johnny's pram. We can load up the pram."

They dressed against the biting wind, wore gloves and scarves. His wife put Johnny in the pram. Nat took Jill's hand.

"The birds," she whimpered, "they're all out there in the fields."

"They won't hurt us," he said, "not in the light."

They started walking across the field towards the stile, and the birds did not move. They waited, their heads turned to the wind.

When they reached the turning to the farm, Nat stopped and told his wife to wait in the shelter of the hedge with the two children.

"But I want to see Mrs. Trigg," she protested. "There are lots of things we can borrow if they went to market yesterday; not only bread, and . . ."

"Wait here," Nat interrupted. "I'll be back in a moment."

The cows were lowing, moving restlessly in the yard, and he could see a gap in the fence where the sheep had knocked their way through, to roam unchecked in the front garden before the farmhouse. No smoke came from the chimneys. He was filled with misgiving. He did not want his wife or the children to go down to the farm.

"Don't gib now," said Nat, harshly, "do what I say."

She withdrew with the pram into the hedge, screening herself and the children from the wind.

He went down alone to the farm. He pushed his way through the herd of bellowing cows, which turned this way and that, distressed, their udders full. He saw the car standing by the gate, not put away in the garage. The windows of the farmhouse were smashed. There were many dead gulls lying in the yard and around the house. The living birds perched on the group of trees behind the farm and on the roof of the house. They were quite still. They watched him.

Jim's body lay in the yard . . . what was left of it. When the birds had finished, the cows had trampled him. His gun was beside him. The door of the house was shut and bolted, but as the windows were smashed it was easy to lift them and climb through. Trigg's body was close to the telephone. He must have been trying to get through to the exchange when the birds came for him. The receiver was hanging loose, the instrument torn from the wall. No sign of Mrs. Trigg. She would be upstairs. Was it any use going up? Sickened, Nat knew what he would find.

"Thank God," he said to himself, "there were no children."

He forced himself to climb the stairs, but halfway he turned and descended again. He could see her legs protruding from the open bedroom door. Beside her were the bodies of the black-backed gulls, and an umbrella, broken.

"It's no use," thought Nat, "doing anything. I've only got five hours, less than that. The Triggs would understand. I must load up with what I can find."

He tramped back to his wife and children.

"I'm going to fill up the car with stuff," he said. "I'll put coal in it, and paraffin for the Primus. We'll take it home and return for a fresh load."

"What about the Triggs?" asked his wife.

"They must have gone to friends," he said.

"Shall I come and help you, then?"

"No; there's a mess down there. Cows and sheep all over the place. Wait, I'll get the car. You can sit in it."

Clumsily he backed the car out of the yard and into the lane. His wife and the children could not see Jim's body from there.

"Stay here," he said, "never mind the pram. The pram can be fetched later. I'm going to load the car."

Her eyes watched his all the time. He believed she understood, otherwise she would have suggested helping him to find the bread and groceries.

They made three journeys altogether, backwards and forwards between their cottage and the farm, before he was satisfied they had everything they needed. It was surprising, once he started thinking, how many things were necessary. Almost the most important of all was planking for the windows. He had to go round searching for timber. He wanted to renew the boards on all the windows at the cottage. Candles, paraffin, nails, tinned stuff; the list was endless. Besides all that, he milked three of the cows. The rest, poor brutes, would have to go on bellowing.

On the final journey he drove the car to the bus stop, got out, and went to the telephone box. He waited a few minutes, jangling the receiver. No good, though. The line was dead. He climbed on to a bank and looked over the countryside, but there was no sign of life at all, nothing in the fields but the waiting, watching birds. Some of them slept—he could see the beaks tucked into the feathers.

"You'd think they'd be feeding," he said to himself, "not just standing in that way."

Then he remembered. They were gorged with food. They had eaten their fill during the night. That was why they did not move this morning. . . .

No smoke came from the chimneys of the council houses. He thought of the children who had run across the fields the night before.

"I should have known," he thought; "I ought to have taken them home with me."

He lifted his face to the sky. It was colourless and grey. The bare trees on the landscape looked bent and blackened by the east wind. The cold did not affect the living birds waiting out there in the fields.

"This is the time they ought to get them," said Nat; "they're a sitting target now. They must be doing this all over the country. Why don't our aircraft take off now and spray them with mustard gas? What are all our chaps doing? They must know, they must see for themselves."

He went back to the car and got into the driver's seat.

"Go quickly past that second gate," whispered his wife. "The postman's lying there. I don't want Jill to see."

He accelerated. The little Morris bumped and rattled along the lane. The children shrieked with laughter.

"Up-a-down, up-a-down," shouted young Johnny.

It was a quarter to one by the time they reached the cottage. Only an hour to go.

"Better have cold dinner," said Nat. "Hot up something for yourself and the children, some of that soup. I've no time to eat now. I've got to unload all this stuff."

He got everything inside the cottage. It could be sorted later. Give them all something to do during the long hours ahead. First he must see to the windows and the doors.

He went round the cottage methodically, testing every window, every door. He climbed on to the roof also, and fixed boards across every chimney, except the kitchen. The cold was so intense he could hardly bear it, but the job had to be done. Now and again he would look up, searching the sky for aircraft. None came. As he worked he cursed the inefficiency of the authorities.

"It's always the same," he muttered, "they always let us down. Muddle, muddle, from the start. No plan, no real organisation. And we don't matter down here. That's what it is. The people upcountry have priority. They're using gas up there, no doubt, and all the aircraft. We've got to wait and take what comes."

He paused, his work on the bedroom chimney finished, and looked out to sea. Something was moving out there. Something grey and white amongst the breakers.

"Good old Navy," he said, "they never let us down. They're coming down-channel, they're turning in the bay."

He waited, straining his eyes, watering in the wind, towards the sea. He was wrong, though. It was not ships. The Navy was not there. The gulls were rising from the sea. The massed flocks in the fields, with ruffled feathers, rose in formation from the ground and, wing to wing, soared upwards to the sky.

The tide had turned again.

Nat climbed down the ladder and went inside the kitchen. The family were at dinner. It was a little after two. He bolted the door, put up the barricade, and lit the lamp.

"It's nighttime," said young Johnny.

His wife had switched on the wireless once again, but no sound came from it.

"I've been all round the dial," she said, "foreign stations, and that lot. I can't get anything."

"Maybe they have the same trouble," he said, "maybe it's the same right through Europe."

She poured out a plateful of the Triggs' soup, cut him a large slice of the Triggs' bread, and spread their dripping upon it.

They ate in silence. A piece of the dripping ran down young Johnny's chin and fell on to the table.

"Manners, Johnny," said Jill, "you should learn to wipe your mouth."

The tapping began at the windows, at the door. The rustling, the jostling, the pushing for position on the sills. The first thud of the suicide gulls upon the step.

"Won't America do something?" said his wife. "They've always been our allies, haven't they? Surely America will do something?"

Nat did not answer. The boards were strong against the windows, and on the chimneys too. The cottage was filled with stores, with fuel, with all they needed for the next few days. When he had finished dinner he would put the stuff away, stack it neatly, get everything shipshape, handy-like. His wife could help him, and the children too. They'd tire themselves out, between now and a quarter to nine, when the tide would ebb; then he'd tuck them down on their mattresses, see that they slept good and sound until three in the morning.

He had a new scheme for the windows, which was to fix barbed wire in front of the boards. He had brought a great roll of it from the farm. The nuisance was, he'd have to work at this in the dark, when the lull came between nine and three. Pity he had not thought of it before. Still, as long as the wife slept, and the kids, that was the main thing.

The smaller birds were at the window now. He recognised the light tap-tapping of their beaks and the soft brush of their wings. The hawks ignored the windows. They concentrated their attack upon the door. Nat listened to the tearing sound of splintering wood, and wondered how many million years of memory were stored in those little brains, behind the stabbing beaks, the piercing eyes, now giving them this instinct to destroy mankind with all the deft precision of machines.

"I'll smoke that last fag," he said to his wife. "Stupid of me, it was the one thing I forgot to bring back from the farm."

He reached for it, switched on the silent wireless. He threw the empty packet on the fire, and watched it burn.

THE MAN WHO LIVED FOUR THOUSAND YEARS

from the novel *The Queen's Necklace*

ALEXANDRE DUMAS

PROLOGUE

ON one of the early days in April, 1784, at about quarter past three in the afternoon, our old acquaintance Maréchal de Richelieu, having with his own hands colored his eyebrows with a perfumed dye, pushed away the mirror held before him by his valet,—the successor, but not the equal, of his faithful Rafté,—and shaking his head in the manner peculiar to himself, said: "Ah, that will do very well!"

He arose from his armchair, brushing from his blue-velvet small-clothes, with a movement of the finger almost juvenile, the atoms of white powder which had floated down from his wig. Then, after taking two or three turns up and down the room, stretching his instep, and straightening his knee, "My major-domo!" said he.

In five minutes the major-domo presented himself, in full dress.

The marshal assumed a grave air, befitting the occasion. "Monsieur," said he, "I suppose you have prepared me a good dinner."

"Most certainly, Monseigneur."

"I have sent you the list of my guests, have I not?"

"And I have carefully noted their number,—a dinner for nine, is it not?"

"There are dinners and dinners, Monsieur."

"Yes, Monseigneur, but—"

The marshal interrupted him with a slightly impatient movement, though tempered with dignity. "'But'—that is not an answer, Monsieur. Every time I hear the word 'but,' and I have heard it many times in eighty-eight years,—well, Monsieur, every time I have heard that word, I am sorry to say, Monsieur, it has preceded some folly."

"Monseigneur!"

"In the first place, at what hour are we to dine?"

"Monseigneur, the common people dine at two, the bar at three, the nobility at four–"

"And I, Monsieur?"

"Monseigneur will dine to-day at five."

"Oh, oh, at five!"

"Yes, Monseigneur, like the king."

"And why like the king?"

"Because on the list Monseigneur has done me the honor to send me, is the name of a king."

"Not at all, Monsieur, you are mistaken; among my guests to-day are none but simple gentlemen."

"Monseigneur doubtless is inclined to jest with his humble servant, and I thank him for the honor he does me; but Monsieur le Comte de Haga, who is among the guests–"

"Well, Monsieur?"

"Well, the Comte de Haga is a king."

"I know no king of that name."

"Monseigneur must pardon me, then," said the major-domo, bowing; "but I had believed, I had supposed–"

"Your business is not to believe, Monsieur; your duty is not to suppose. What you have to do is to read the orders which I give you, without adding to them any comments. When I wish a thing to be known I tell it; when I do not tell it I wish it unknown."

The major-domo bowed again, and this time more respectfully, perhaps, than he would have bowed in talking with a reigning monarch.

"Therefore, Monsieur," continued the old marshal, "since I have only gentlemen to dinner, you will let us dine at my usual hour, four o'clock."

At this order the major-domo's face darkened as if he had heard his death-warrant. He grew pale, and bent under the blow. Then arousing himself, with the courage of despair he said: "Let come what God wills; but Monseigneur will not dine till five o'clock."

"Why, and what does that mean?" said the marshal, straightening himself up.

"Because it is a material impossibility that Monseigneur should dine earlier."

"Monsieur," said the old marshal, shaking his head haughtily, like one still young and vigorous, "it is now, I believe, twenty years since you entered my service?"

"Twenty-one years, one month, and two weeks."

"Well, Monsieur, to these twenty-one years, one month, and two weeks, you will not add a day,–not an hour. You understand me, Monsieur," he continued, biting his thin lips and knitting his dyed eyebrows; "this evening you seek a new master. I will not have the word 'impossible' pronounced in my house. I have no wish, at my age, to begin an apprenticeship to that word. I have no time to waste."

The major-domo bowed a third time. "This evening," he said, "I shall take leave of Monseigneur. But at any rate, up to the last moment my service will be performed as it ought to be;" and he made two steps toward the door.

"What do you mean by 'as it ought to be'?" cried the marshal. "Understand, Monsieur, that things must be done here according to my will; that is the only 'ought.' Now, it is my will to dine at four, and it is against my will that you make me wait till five."

"Monseigneur," replied the major-domo, gravely, "I have served as butler to his Highness the Prince de Soubise, and as steward to his Eminence the Cardinal de Rohan. With the former his Majesty the late king of France dined once a year; with the latter his Majesty the emperor of Austria dined once a month. I know, therefore, how sovereigns should be treated, Monseigneur. King Louis XV, when he visited the Prince de Soubise, vainly called himself the Baron de Gonesse; he was always a king. In the house of Monsieur de Rohan the Emperor Joseph was vainly called the Comte de Packenstein; he was always the emperor. To-day, Monsieur le Maréchal receives a guest who vainly calls himself the Comte de Haga. The Comte de Haga is none the less the king of Sweden. I will leave the hôtel of Monsieur le Maréchal this evening; but meantime Monsieur le Comte de Haga will have been treated like a king."

"But that is the very thing that I kill myself with trying to prevent, you obstinate fellow. The Comte de Haga wishes to keep himself strictly, absolutely, unknown. *Pardieu!* I understand your absurd vanities, gentlemen of the napkin. It is not that you would honor the crown; you would magnify yourselves with our crowns."

"I do not imagine," said the major-domo, gloomily, "that Monseigneur speaks to me seriously of money."

"Eh, no, Monsieur!" said the marshal, almost ashamed. "No! Money! —who the devil said anything to you about money? Don't evade the question, if you please. I repeat, I want nothing said about the presence here of a king."

"Why, Monsieur le Maréchal, for whom do you take me? Do you think I am blind? Why, there will not be the slightest mention of a king."

"Then do not be obstinate; let us dine at four."

"But at four o'clock, Monseigneur, what I am expecting will not have arrived."

"What are you expecting?—a fish, like Monsieur Vatel?"

"Monsieur Vatel, Monsieur Vatel," murmured the major-domo.

"Well, are you shocked by the comparison?"

"No; but for a miserable sword-thrust which Monsieur Vatel gave himself through the body, Monsieur Vatel is immortalized."

"Ah, ah, and you think, Monsieur, that your brother artist obtained glory at too cheap a price?"

"No, Monseigneur; but how many others in our profession suffer more than he did, devouring griefs and humiliations a hundred times worse than a sword-thrust, who nevertheless are not immortalized!"

"Eh, Monsieur! do you not know that to be immortalized one must be a member of the Academy or must be dead?"

"Monseigneur, if that is so it is much better for one to be alive, and do his duty. I will not die and my service will be performed as that of Monsieur Vatel would have been if Monsieur le Prince de Condé had had the patience to wait half an hour."

"Oh, now you are promising me wonders; it is adroit."

"No, Monseigneur; nothing wonderful."

"But what, then, are you expecting?"

"Monseigneur wishes me to tell him?"

"Faith, yes; I am curious."

"Then, Monseigneur, I am expecting a bottle of wine."

"A bottle of wine! explain yourself, Monsieur; the thing begins to interest me."

"Listen then, Monseigneur; his Majesty the king of Sweden—I beg pardon, the Comte de Haga I should have said—drinks nothing but Tokay."

"Well, am I so poor as to have no Tokay in my cellar? If so, I must dismiss my butler."

"Not so, Monseigneur; on the contrary, you have about sixty bottles."

"Well, do you think the Comte de Haga will drink sixty-one bottles with his dinner?"

"Patience, Monseigneur; when the Comte de Haga first visited France, while he was only Prince Royal, he dined with the late king, who had received twelve bottles of Tokay from the emperor of Austria. You are aware that the Tokay of the finest vintages is reserved exclusively for the cellar of the emperor, and that kings themselves can drink it only when he pleases to send it to them."

"I know it."

"Well, Monseigneur, of these twelve bottles, from one of which the Prince Royal drank with much satisfaction, only two remain."

"Oh! oh!"

"One is still in the cellar of his Majesty Louis XVI."

"And the other?"

"Ah, Monseigneur," said the major-domo, with a triumphant smile,—

for he felt that, after the long battle he had been fighting, the moment of victory was at hand,—"the other was stolen."

"By whom?"

"By one of my friends, the late king's butler, who was under great obligations to me."

"Oh, and so he gave it to you?"

"Certainly, Monseigneur," said the major-domo, with pride.

"And what did you do with it?"

"I placed it carefully in my master's cellar, Monseigneur."

"Your master; and who was your master at that time, Monsieur?"

"His Eminence the Cardinal de Rohan."

"Ah, *mon Dieu!* at Strasburg?"

"At Saverne."

"And you have sent to seek this bottle for me!" cried the old marshal.

"For you, Monseigneur," replied the major-domo, in a tone which plainly said, "ungrateful as you are."

The Duc de Richelieu seized the hand of the old servant and cried, "I beg your pardon, Monsieur; you are the king of major-domos."

"And you would have dismissed me!" he replied, with an indescribable shrug of his shoulders.

"Oh, I will pay you one hundred pistoles for that bottle of wine!"

"And the expense of bringing it here will be another hundred, that will make two hundred pistoles; but Monseigneur will admit that it is a trifle."

"I will admit anything you please, Monsieur; and meantime, from today I double your salary."

"But, Monseigneur, there is no occasion for that; I have but done my duty."

"And when will your hundred-pistole courier arrive?"

"Monseigneur may judge if I have lost time; on what day did I have my orders for the dinner?"

"Why, three days ago, I believe."

"It takes a courier, at his utmost speed, twenty-four hours to go, and the same to return."

"There still remained to you twenty-four hours. Prince of major-domos, what have you done with those twenty-four hours?"

"Alas, Monseigneur, I lost them! The idea came to me only the day after I received the list of your guests. Now calculate the time necessary for the negotiation, and you will perceive that in asking you to wait till five, I am asking only for the time that is absolutely necessary."

"What! the bottle is not yet here?"

"No, Monseigneur."

"Ah, Monsieur, if your colleague at Saverne is as devoted to the Prince de Rohan as you are to me, and refuses the bottle, as you would do in his place—"

"I, Monseigneur?"

"Yes; you would not, I suppose, give away such a bottle if it were in my cellar?"

"I humbly beg Monseigneur's pardon; but should a friend, having a king to provide for, ask me for your best bottle of wine, I would give it to him immediately."

"Oh!" said the marshal, with a grimace.

"It is only through helping others that we can expect help in our own need, Monseigneur."

"Then I may feel somewhat reassured," said the marshal, with a sigh; "but there is still another risk,—if the bottle should be broken?"

"Oh, Monseigneur, no man ever broke a bottle of wine worth two thousand francs!"

"I was wrong; let us say no more about it. At what time, then, do you expect your courier?"

"At four o'clock, precisely."

"Then why not dine at four?" replied the marshal, with the obstinacy of a Castilian mule.

"Monseigneur, the wine must rest for an hour; and but for an invention of my own, it would need three days."

Beaten at all points, the marshal saluted his major-domo in token of surrender.

"Besides," continued the old servant, "Monseigneur's guests, knowing that they will have the honor of dining with the Comte de Haga, will not arrive until half-past four."

"Here is still another reason!"

"Certainly, Monseigneur; the guests are the Comte de Launay, the Comtesse Dubarry, Monsieur de Lapeyrouse, Monsieur de Favras, Monsieur de Condorcet, Monsieur de Cagliostro, and Monsieur de Taverney."

"Very well?"

"Well, Monseigneur, let us take them in their order. Monsieur de Launay comes from the Bastille, and with the ice at present covering the roads he will be three hours coming from Paris."

"Yes; but he will leave immediately after the prisoners' dinner, at twelve o'clock."

"Pardon, Monseigneur, but the dinner hour at the Bastille has been changed since Monseigneur was there; it is now one."

"Monsieur, one learns something every day, and I thank you! Go on."

"Madame Dubarry comes from Luciennes, one continued descent, and in this frost—"

"That would not prevent her being punctual. Since she is now only a duke's favorite, she plays the queen only among barons. But let me tell you, Monsieur, that I desired to have dinner early on account of Monsieur de Lapeyrouse, who sets off to-night, and will not wish to be late."

"Monseigneur, Monsieur de Lapeyrouse is with the king, discussing geography and cosmography; he will not get away too early."

"It is possible."

"It is certain, Monseigneur; and it will be the same with Monsieur de Favras, who is with the Comte de Provence, talking, no doubt, of the new play, by Monsieur Caron de Beaumarchais."

"You mean the 'Mariage de Figaro'?"

"Yes, Monseigneur."

"Why, you are quite literary also, it seems, Monsieur."

"In my leisure moments I read, Monseigneur."

"We have, however, Monsieur de Condorcet, who, being a geometrician, should at least be punctual."

"Yes; but he will be deep in some calculation, from which when he rouses himself, he will find that he is half an hour too late. As for the Comte de Cagliostro, as he is a stranger, and not well acquainted with the customs of Versailles, he will, in all probability, make us wait for him."

"Well," said the marshal, "you have disposed of all my guests, except Monsieur de Taverney, in a manner worthy of Homer, or of my poor Rafté."

The major-domo bowed. "I have not," said he, "named Monsieur de Taverney; because being an old friend, he will probably be punctual. I believe, Monseigneur, these eight are all the guests, are they not?"

"Precisely. Where will you have us dine, Monsieur?"

"In the great dining-room, Monseigneur."

"But we shall freeze there."

"It has been warmed for three days, Monseigneur; and I believe you will find it perfectly comfortable."

"Very well, but there is a clock striking. Why, it is half-past four!" cried the marshal.

"Yes, Monseigneur, and there is the courier entering the court-yard, with my bottle of Tokay."

"May I continue for another twenty years to be served in this manner," said the marshal, turning again to his looking-glass, while the major-domo ran downstairs.

"Twenty years!" said a laughing voice, interrupting the marshal in his survey of himself,—"twenty years, my dear Duke! I hope you may have them; but then I shall be sixty,—I shall be very old."

"You, Countess!" cried the marshal. "You are the first, and *mon Dieu!* you look as young and charming as ever."

"Duke, I am frozen."

"Come into the boudoir, then."

"Oh, *tête-à-tête*, Marshal?"

"Not so," replied a somewhat broken voice.

"Ah, Taverney," said the marshal; and then whispering to the countess, "Plague take him for disturbing us."

Madame Dubarry laughed, and they all entered the adjoining room.

At the same moment the noise of carriages in the street warned the marshal that his guests were arriving; and soon after, thanks to the punctuality of his major-domo, nine persons were seated round the oval table in the dining-room. Nine lackeys, silent as shadows, quick without bustle, and attentive without importunity, glided over the carpet, and moved among the guests, without ever touching their chairs, placed in the midst of furs, which covered to their knees the legs of those who occupied them. These furs, with the heat from the stoves, and the odors from the wine and the dinner, diffused a degree of comfort which manifested itself in the gayety of the guests, who had just finished their soup.

No sound was heard from without and none within, save that made by the guests themselves; for the plates were changed, and the silver-ware was brought to the table without the slightest noise. Nor from the major-domo could a whisper be heard; he seemed to give his orders with his eyes. The guests, therefore, began to feel as though they were alone. It seemed to them that servants so silent must also be deaf.

Monsieur de Richelieu broke the silence by saying to the guest on his right hand, "Monsieur le Comte, you do not drink."

This was addressed to a man about thirty-eight years of age, short, fair-haired, and with high shoulders; his eye, a clear blue, was sometimes bright, but oftener melancholy. Nobility was stamped unmistakably on his open and manly forehead.

"I drink only water, Marshal," he replied.

"Excepting with Louis XV," returned the marshal; "I had the honor of dining at his table with you, and you deigned that day to drink wine."

"Ah, you recall a pleasing remembrance, Marshal. That was in 1771; it was Tokay, from the imperial cellar."

"It was like that with which my major-domo will now have the honor to fill your glass, Monsieur le Comte," replied Richelieu, bowing.

The Comte de Haga raised his glass, and looked through it. The wine sparkled in the light like liquid rubies. "It is true, Monsieur le Maréchal," said he; "I thank you."

These words were uttered in a manner so noble that the guests, as if by a common impulse, rose, and cried, "Long live his Majesty!"

"Yes," said the Comte de Haga, "long live his Majesty the king of France. What say you, Monsieur de Lapeyrouse?"

"Monsieur le Comte," replied the captain, with the tone, at once flattering and respectful, common to those accustomed to address crowned heads, "I have just left the king, and his Majesty has shown me so much kindness that no one will more willingly cry, 'Long live the king,' than I. But as in one hour I shall be travelling post to the seashore, to join the two ships which the king has placed at my disposal, I will ask your permission, as soon as I have left this house, to cry, 'Long life to another king,' whom I should be proud to serve, had I not already so good a master;" and raising his glass, Monsieur de Lapeyrouse bowed humbly to the Comte de Haga.

"This health that you propose," said Madame Dubarry, who sat at the marshal's left hand, "we are all ready to drink; but the oldest of us should take the lead as in parliament."

"Is it to you that this remark applies or to me, Taverney?" said the marshal, laughing.

"I do not believe—" said a new speaker, sitting opposite the marshal.

"What is it that you do not believe, Monsieur de Cagliostro?" asked the Comte de Haga, fixing his piercing look on the speaker.

"I do not believe, Monsieur le Comte," said Cagliostro, bowing, "that Monsieur de Richelieu is the senior of our party."

"Oh, that is good," said the marshal; "apparently it is you, Taverney."

"Come, now; I am eight years younger than you. I was born in 1704," returned the old nobleman.

"How rude," said the marshal, "to expose my eighty-eight years!"

"Really! Monsieur le Duc; you are eighty-eight years old!" said Monsieur de Condorcet.

"Oh, *mon Dieu!* yes. It is a calculation easy to make, and therefore unworthy of an algebraist like you, Marquis. I am of the last century,—the great century, as we call it. My date is 1696."

"Impossible!" cried De Launay.

"Oh, if your father were here, he would not say impossible,—he who when governor of the Bastille had me for a lodger in 1714."

"The senior in age, here, however," said Monsieur de Favras, "is the wine which the Comte de Haga is at this moment pouring into his glass."

"You are right, Monsieur de Favras; this wine is a hundred and twenty years old. To the wine then belongs the honor of proposing the health of the king."

"One moment, gentlemen," said Cagliostro, raising his eyes, beaming with intelligence and vivacity; "I claim the precedence."

"You claim precedence over the Tokay!" exclaimed all the guests in chorus.

"Assuredly," returned Cagliostro, calmly; "since it was I who bottled it."

"You?"

"Yes, I; on the day of the victory won by Montecuculli over the Turks in 1664."

A burst of laughter followed these words, which Cagliostro had pronounced with quiet gravity.

"By this calculation, you would be something like one hundred and thirty years old," said Madame Dubarry; "for you must have been at least ten years old when you bottled the wine."

"I was more than ten when I performed that operation, Madame; as on the following day I had the honor of being deputed by his Majesty the emperor of Austria to congratulate Montecuculli, who by the victory of Saint Gothard had avenged the day at Especk in Sclavonia,—a day on which the infidels treated the imperialists so roughly, who were my friends and companions in arms in 1536."

"Oh," said the Comte de Haga, as coldly as Cagliostro himself, "you must have been at least ten years old when you were at that memorable battle."

"A terrible defeat, Monsieur le Comte," returned Cagliostro, bowing.

"Less terrible than Cressy, however," said Condorcet, smiling.

"True, Monsieur, for at the battle of Cressy, it was not only an army, but all France, that was beaten. But then this defeat was scarcely a fair victory to the English; for King Edward had cannon, a circumstance of which Philippe de Valois was ignorant, or rather which he would not believe, although I warned him that I had with my own eyes seen four pieces of artillery, which Edward had bought from the Venetians."

"Ah," said Madame Dubarry, "you knew Philippe de Valois?"

"Madame, I had the honor to be one of the five noblemen who escorted him off the field of battle," replied Cagliostro; "I came to France with the poor old king of Bohemia, who was blind, and who threw away his life when he heard that the battle was lost."

"Ah, Monsieur," said Monsieur de Lapeyrouse, "how much I regret that instead of the battle of Cressy, it was not that of Actium at which you assisted."

"Why so, Monsieur?"

"Oh, because you might have given me some nautical details, which, in spite of Plutarch's fine narration, have ever been obscure to me."

"Which, Monsieur? I should be happy to be of service to you."

"You were there, then?"

"No, Monsieur; I was then in Egypt. I had been employed by Queen Cleopatra to restore the library at Alexandria,—an office for which I was better qualified than any one else, from having personally known the best authors of antiquity."

"And you have seen Queen Cleopatra, Monsieur de Cagliostro?" said Madame Dubarry.

"As I now see you, Madame."

"Was she as pretty as they say?"

"Madame, you know beauty is only comparative; a charming queen in Egypt, in Paris she would have been only a pretty grisette."

"Say no harm of grisettes, Monsieur le Comte."

"God forbid!"

"Then Cleopatra was—"

"Little, slender, lively, and intelligent; with large almond-shaped eyes, a Grecian nose, teeth like pearls, and a hand like your own, Madame,—a fit hand to hold a sceptre. See, here is a diamond which she gave me, and which she had from her brother Ptolemy; she wore it on her thumb."

"On her thumb?" cried Madame Dubarry.

"Yes. It was an Egyptian fashion, and I, you see, can hardly put it on my little finger;" and taking off the ring, he handed it to Madame Dubarry.

It was a magnificent diamond of such fine water, and so beautifully cut, as to be worth thirty thousand or forty thousand francs.

The diamond was passed round the table and returned to Cagliostro, who, putting it quietly on his finger again, said, "Ah, I see well you are all incredulous; this fatal incredulity I have had to contend against all my life. Philippe de Valois would not listen to me when I told him to leave open a retreat to Edward; Cleopatra would not believe me when I warned her that Antony would be beaten; the Trojans would not credit me when I said to them, with reference to the wooden horse, 'Cassandra is inspired; listen to Cassandra.'"

"Oh, but this is marvellous!" said Madame Dubarry, shaking with laughter; "I have never met a man at once so serious and so diverting."

"I assure you," replied Cagliostro, bowing, "that Jonathan was much more so. Oh, he was a charming companion; until he was killed by Saul he nearly drove me crazy with laughing."

"Do you know, Count," said the Duc de Richelieu, "if you go on in this way you will drive poor Taverney crazy; he is so afraid of death that he is staring at you with all his eyes, thinking you to be immortal. Come, frankly, are you immortal,—yes, or no?"

"Immortal?"

"Immortal."

"I cannot say, but one thing I can affirm—"

"What?" cried Taverney, who was the most eager listener.

"That I have seen all the people and events of which I have been speaking to you."

"You have known Montecuculli?"

"As well as I know you, Monsieur de Favras; and, indeed, much better; for this is but the second or third time I have had the honor of seeing you, while I lived nearly a year under the same tent with the skilful strategist of whom you speak."

"You knew Philippe de Valois?"

"As I have already had the honor of telling you, Monsieur de Condorcet; but when he returned to Paris, I left France and returned to Bohemia."

"And Cleopatra?"

"Yes, Madame la Comtesse; Cleopatra, I can tell you, had eyes as black as yours, and shoulders almost as beautiful."

"But what do you know of my shoulders?"

"They are like what Cassandra's once were; and there is still a further resemblance,—she had like you, or rather you have like her, a little black spot on your left side, just above the sixth rib."

"Oh, Count, now you really are a sorcerer."

"No, no," cried the marshal, laughing; "it was I who told him."

"And pray how do you know?"

The marshal bit his lips, and replied, "Oh, it is a family secret."

"Well, really, Marshal," said the countess, "one should put on a double coat of rouge before visiting you;" and turning again to Cagliostro, "then, Monsieur, you have the art of renewing your youth; for although you say you are three or four thousand years old you scarcely look forty."

"Yes, Madame, I do possess that secret."

"Oh, then, Monsieur, impart it to me."

"To you, Madame? It is useless,—your youth is already renewed; your age is only what it appears to be, and you do not look thirty."

"Ah! you flatter."

"No, Madame, I speak only the truth, but it is easily explained; you have already tried my receipt."

"How so?"

"You have taken my elixir."

"I?"

"You, Countess. Oh, you cannot have forgotten it. Do you not remember a certain house in the Rue Saint Claude, and coming there on some business respecting Monsieur de Sartines? You remember rendering a service to one of my friends, called Joseph Balsamo; and that this Joseph Balsamo gave you a bottle of elixir, recommending you to take three drops every morning? Do you not remember having done this regularly until the last year, when the bottle became exhausted? If you do not remember all this, Countess, it is more than forgetfulness,—it is ingratitude."

"Oh! Monsieur de Cagliostro, you are telling me things—"

"Which were only known to yourself, I am aware; but what would be the use of being a sorcerer if one did not know one's neighbor's secrets?"

"Then, Joseph Balsamo has, like you, the secret of this famous elixir?"

"No, Madame; but he was one of my best friends, and I gave him three or four bottles."

"And has he any left?"

"Oh, I know nothing of that; for the last two or three years, poor Balsamo has disappeared. I saw him for the last time in America, on the banks of the Ohio; he was setting off on an expedition to the Rocky Mountains, and since then I have heard that he is dead."

"Come, come, Count," said the marshal, "a truce to compliments, for pity's sake! The secret, Count, the secret!"

"Are you speaking seriously, Monsieur?" asked the Comte de Haga.

"Very seriously, Sire,—I beg pardon; I mean Monsieur le Comte," and Cagliostro bowed in such a way as to indicate that his error was a voluntary one.

"Then," said the marshal, "Madame Dubarry is not old enough to be made young again?"

"No, on my conscience."

"Well, then, I will give you another subject. Here is my friend Taverney,—what do you say to him? Does he not look like a contemporary of Pontius Pilate? But perhaps he, on the contrary, is too old."

Cagliostro looked at the baron. "No," said he.

"Ah, my dear Count," exclaimed Richelieu; "if you will renew his youth, I will proclaim you a pupil of Medea."

"You wish it?" asked Cagliostro, of the host, and looking round at the same time on all assembled.

All present signified their assent.

"And you also, Monsieur de Taverney?"

"I more than any one, *morbleu!*" said the baron.

"Well, it is easy," said Cagliostro; and he drew from his pocket a small bottle, and poured into a glass a few drops of the liquid it contained. Then mixing these drops with half a glass of iced-champagne, he passed it to the baron. All eyes followed his movements eagerly.

The baron took the glass, but as he was about to drink he hesitated. Every one, on observing his hesitation, began to laugh,—so noisily that Cagliostro became impatient, and said, "Make haste, Baron, or you will waste a cordial of which each drop is worth a hundred louis d'or."

"The devil!" cried Richelieu, trying to jest; "that is even better than Tokay."

"I must, then, drink?" said the baron, almost trembling.

"Or pass the glass to another, Monsieur, that some one at least may profit by the elixir."

"Pass it to me," said Richelieu, holding out his hand.

The baron raised the glass, and decided doubtless by the delicious smell and the beautiful rose color which those few drops had given to the champagne, he swallowed the magic cordial. In an instant a kind of shiver ran through him; he seemed to feel all the old and sluggish blood stagnant in his veins flowing toward the surface of his body; his wrinkled skin became smooth; his eyes, half-covered by their lids, opened without his will; the pupils became larger and brighter; the trembling of his hands was arrested; his voice strengthened; and his limbs recovered their former youthful elasticity. In fact it seemed as if the liquid in its descent had regenerated his whole body.

A cry of surprise, stupefaction, and admiration rang through the room. Taverney, who had been slowly chewing with his gums, began to feel famished; he seized a plate, knife, and fork, and helped himself largely to a ragoût, and then demolished a partridge, bones and all, calling out that his teeth were coming back to him. He ate, laughed, and cried for joy for about half an hour, while the others remained gazing at him in stupefied wonder; then little by little he failed again, like a lamp whose oil is burning out. First, his forehead, from which the wrinkles had disappeared, became wrinkled anew; his eyes were veiled and darkened; he lost his sense of taste; his back was bent again; his appetite departed; his knees began again to tremble.

"Oh!" he groaned, "once more, adieu to my youth!" and he gave utterance to a deep sigh, while two tears rolled over his cheeks.

Instinctively, at this mournful spectacle of the old man first made young again, and then, by contrast, seeming to become yet older than before, the sigh breathed by the old man was echoed around the table.

"It is easy to explain, gentlemen," said Cagliostro; "I gave the baron but thirty-five drops of the elixir, and he became young for only thirty-five minutes."

"Oh, more, more, Count!" cried the old man, eagerly.

"No, Monsieur; for perhaps the second trial would kill you."

Of all the guests, Madame Dubarry, who had already tested the virtue of the elixir, seemed most deeply interested while old Taverney's youth seemed thus to renew itself. As by degrees youth and life flowed through the arteries of the old man, the eyes of the countess eagerly followed the changes in his appearance. She laughed and applauded, and appeared regenerated simply by watching him.

When the success of the elixir was at its height the countess was about to seize the hand of Cagliostro, for the purpose of snatching from him the precious bottle. But at the moment when Taverney became old again, so much more suddenly than he had become young, "Alas! I see plainly," said she, sorrowfully, "all is vanity and deception; the effect of this marvellous secret lasts thirty-five minutes."

"That is to say," said the Comte de Haga, "in order to resume your youth for two years, you would have to drink a river."

Every one laughed.

"No," said Condorcet, "the calculation is simple; as thirty-five drops last thirty-five minutes, it would require only a mere nothing of three million one hundred and fifty-three thousand drops for one year's youth."

"An inundation," said Lapeyrouse.

"However, Monsieur," continued Madame Dubarry, "according to you, I have not needed so much; as a small bottle of about four times the size of that you hold, given me by your friend Joseph Balsamo, has been sufficient to arrest the march of time for ten years."

"Precisely, Madame, and you alone approach this mysterious truth. The man who has already grown old needs this large quantity to produce an immediate and powerful effect; but a woman of thirty years, like you, Madame, or a man of forty years,—which was my age when I began to drink this elixir,—still full of life and youth, needs but ten drops at each period of decay; and with these ten drops may eternally continue life and youth at the same point of attractiveness and force."

"What do you call the periods of decay?" asked the Comte de Haga.

"The natural periods, Monsieur le Comte. In a state of nature man's strength increases until he is thirty-five years of age. It then remains stationary until forty; and from that time forward it begins to diminish, but almost imperceptibly until fifty; then the process becomes quicker and quicker to the day of his death. In our state of civilization, when the body is weakened by excess, cares, and maladies, increase of strength is arrested at thirty years; the failure begins at thirty-five. The time, then, to take Nature is when she is stationary, so as to combat the tendency to decay at the very moment when it begins to operate. He, who, possessing as I do the secret of this elixir, knows how to seize the happy moment, will live as I live,—always young, or at least always young enough for what he has to do in the world."

"Oh, Monsieur Cagliostro!" cried the countess, "why, if you could choose your own age, did you not stop at twenty years instead of at forty?"

"Because, Madame," said Cagliostro, smiling, "it suits me better to be a man forty years old, healthy and vigorous, than a raw youth of twenty."

"Oh!" said the countess.

"Doubtless, Madame," continued Cagliostro, "at twenty years of age one pleases women of thirty years; at forty years we govern women of twenty and men of sixty."

"I yield, Monsieur," said the countess, "for you are a living proof of the truth of your own words."

"Then I," said Taverney, piteously, "am condemned; it is too late for me!"

"Monsieur de Richelieu has been more skilful than you," said Lapeyrouse, naïvely, with the frankness of a sailor; "and I have always heard that he had a certain receipt—"

"It is a report that the women have spread," laughed the Comte de Haga.

"Is that a reason for disbelieving it, Count?" asked Madame Dubarry.

The old marshal colored,—a rare thing for him,—but replied, "Do you wish, gentlemen, to have my receipt?"

"Oh, by all means!"

"Well, then, it is simply to take care of yourself."

"Oh, oh!" cried all.

"I would contest the receipt," continued the countess, "if I had not seen the effect of that of Monsieur de Cagliostro. So be on your guard, Monsieur the Sorcerer; I am not yet through with my questions."

"Well, Madame."

"You said that when you used your elixir of life for the first time, you were forty years old?"

"Yes, Madame."

"And that since that time,—that is, since the siege of Troy—"

"A little before, Madame."

"You have always remained forty years old?"

"You see me now."

"But, then, Monsieur," said Condorcet, "you prove to us more than your theorem requires."

"What do I prove to you, Monsieur le Marquis?"

"You prove, not only the perpetuation of youth, but the preservation of life; for if since the siege of Troy you have been always forty years old, you have never died."

"True, Marquis; I humbly admit it. I have never died."

"Yet you are not invulnerable, like Achilles; and even Achilles was not invulnerable, for Paris killed him by wounding his heel with an arrow."

"No, I am not invulnerable, and that is my great regret," said Cagliostro.

"Then, Monsieur, you may be killed; you may die a violent death?"

"Alas! yes."

"How, then, have you escaped all accidents for three thousand five hundred years?"

"It is chance, Monsieur le Comte; but will you follow my reasoning?"

"Yes, yes!" cried all, with eagerness; and with these expressions of unusual interest, every one leaned on the table and prepared to listen.

Cagliostro continued: "What is the first requisite to life?" he asked, spreading out his white and beautiful hands, covered with rings, among which Cleopatra's shone conspicuously. "Is it not health?"

"Certainly."

"And the way to preserve health is—"

"Proper diet," said the Comte de Haga.

"You are right, Monsieur le Comte. It is proper diet that produces good health. Well, then, why should not these drops of my elixir constitute the best possible diet?"

"Who knows that?"

"You, Count."

"Yes, without doubt; but—"

"But no others," said Madame Dubarry.

"That, Madame, is a question which we will not discuss now. Well, then, I have always followed the regimen of my drops; and since they fulfil the dream of men of all times, since they are that which the ancients searched for under the name of the 'Water of Youth,' and which the moderns have sought to discover under the name of the 'Elixir of Life,' I have constantly preserved my youth, and consequently my health, and consequently my life. That is clear enough."

"But all things get worn out, Count,—the most excellent body as well as everything else."

"That of Paris, like that of Vulcan," said the countess. "You knew Paris, doubtless, Monsieur de Cagliostro?"

"Perfectly, Madame; he was a fine young man, but really did not deserve all that Homer said of him, and that women think of him. In the first place, he had red hair."

"Red hair? Horrible!"

"Unluckily, Madame, Helen was not of your opinion. But let us return to our elixir."

"Yes, yes!" all exclaimed.

"You say, Monsieur de Taverney, that all things get worn out; but you also know that everything recovers again, is regenerated, or replaced, whichever you please to call it. The famous knife of Saint Hubert, which so often changed both blade and handle, is an example; for through every change it still remained the knife of Saint Hubert. The wine which the monks of Heidelberg preserve so carefully in their cellars still remains the same wine, although each year they pour into it a fresh supply. Therefore, this wine always remains clear, bright, and delicious; while the wine which Opimus and I hid in the earthen jars was, when I tried it a hundred years after, only a thick mud, which might, indeed, have been eaten, but certainly could not have been drunk. Well, I follow the example of the monks of Heidelberg, and preserve my body by introducing into it every year new elements, which regenerate the old. Every morning a new and fresh atom replaces in my blood, my flesh, and my bones, a worn-out, inert molecule. I stay that ruin which most men allow insensibly to invade their whole being, and I force into action all those powers which God has given to the human constitution as a defence against destruction,—powers which commonly are misdirected, or abandoned to the paralysis of inactivity; those powers I have compelled to continuous labor, which has facilitated, has caused even, the introduction of a stimulant always new. In consequence of that assiduous study of life, my thought, my movements, my nerves, my heart, my soul, have never failed in their operation; and as all things are bound together in this world,—as those succeed best in anything who are always doing that thing,—I have naturally become more skilful than any one else by avoiding the dangers of an existence of three thousand years; and that because I have succeeded in acquiring from everything such an experience that I foresee misfortunes,—I feel the dangers of any situation, be it what it may. Thus, you would not get me to enter a house which is in danger of falling. Oh, no! I have seen too many houses not to tell at a glance the safe from the unsafe. You would not see me go out hunting with a man who managed his gun badly. From Cephalus, who killed his wife Procris, down to the regent who shot the prince in the eye, I have seen too many unskilful people. You could not make me accept, in battle, the post which many a man would take without thinking, because I should have calculated in a moment all the chances of danger at that point. You will tell me that one cannot foresee a stray bullet; but the man who has escaped a million gunshots is inexcusable if he allows himself to be killed by a stray bullet. Ah, you look incredulous! but am I not a living proof? I do not tell you that I am immortal, only that I know better than others how to avoid danger. For instance, I would not remain here now alone with Monsieur de Launay, who is thinking that if he had me in the Bastille he would put my immortality to the test of starvation. Neither would I remain with Monsieur de Condorcet; for he is thinking that he might just empty into my glass the contents of that ring which he wears on his left hand, and which is full of poison,—not with any evil intent, but only as a scientific experiment, to see if I should die."

The two people named made a movement.

"Confess, Monsieur de Launay! We are not in a court of justice; besides, thoughts are not punished. Did you not think what I said? And you, Monsieur de Condorcet, would you not have liked to let me taste the poison in your ring, in the name of your beloved mistress, science?"

"Indeed," said Monsieur de Launay, laughing and blushing, "I confess you are right; it was folly, but that folly did pass through my mind at the very moment when you accused me."

"And I," said Monsieur de Condorcet, "will not be less candid; I did think that if you tasted the contents of my ring, I would not give a farthing for your immortality."

A cry of admiration burst from the rest of the party; these avowals confirming not the immortality, but the penetration of the Comte de Cagliostro.

"You see," said Cagliostro, quietly, "that I divined these dangers; well, it is the same with other things. The experience of a long life reveals to me, at a glance, the past and the future of those whom I meet. My infallibility on this point is such that it extends even to animals and inanimate objects. If I get into a carriage, I can tell from the look of the horses that they are likely to run away; and from that of the coachman that he will overturn me. If I go on board ship, I can see that the captain is ignorant or obstinate, and consequently cannot, or will not, navigate his vessel skilfully. Thereupon I avoid the coachman and the captain, and leave those horses or that ship. I do not deny chance, I only lessen it, and instead of incurring a hundred chances, like the rest of the world, I prevent ninety-nine of them, and endeavor to guard against the hundredth. This is the advantage of having lived three thousand years."

"Then," said Lapeyrouse, laughing, amid the wonder and enthusiasm created by Cagliostro's words, "my dear prophet, you should come with me when I embark to make the tour of the world; you would render me a signal service."

Cagliostro did not reply.

"Monsieur de Richelieu," continued Lapeyrouse, "since the Comte de Cagliostro,—and I understand that,—does not wish to leave so good company, you must permit me to go without him. Excuse me, Comte de Haga, and you, Madame, but it is seven o'clock, and I have promised his Majesty to start at a quarter past. But since Comte de Cagliostro will not be tempted to come with me and see my ships, perhaps he can tell me what will happen to me between Versailles and Brest. From Brest to the Pole, I ask nothing,—that is my own business. But, *pardieu!* he ought to give me an opinion on what may happen on the way to Brest."

Cagliostro looked at Lapeyrouse with such a melancholy air, so full both of pity and kindness, that the others were struck by it. The navigator himself, however, did not remark it. He took leave of the company; his valet threw over his shoulders a large fur riding-coat, and Madame Dubarry slipped into his pocket some of those exquisite cordials which are so pleasing to the traveller, but which he rarely thinks of providing for himself, and which recall to him his absent friends during the long nights of a journey under wintry skies.

Lapeyrouse, still full of gayety, bowed respectfully to the Comte de Haga, and held out his hand to the old marshal.

"Adieu, dear Lapeyrouse," said the latter.

"No, Monsieur le Duc, au revoir," replied Lapeyrouse. "One would think I was departing for eternity; now I have but to circumnavigate the globe,—five or six years' absence only; it is scarcely worth while to say 'adieu' for that."

"Five or six years," said the marshal; "you might almost as well say five or six centuries; days are years at my age,—therefore I say adieu."

"Bah! ask the sorcerer," returned Lapeyrouse, still laughing, "he will promise you twenty years more life. Will you not, Monsieur de Cagliostro? Oh, Count, why did I not hear sooner of those precious drops of yours? Whatever the price, I should have shipped a tun of them on the 'Astrolabe.' Madame, another kiss of that beautiful hand; I shall certainly not see such another till I return; au revoir," and he left the room.

Cagliostro still preserved the same mournful silence. They heard the steps of the captain as he left the house, his gay voice in the court-yard, and his farewells to the persons assembled there to see him depart. Then the horses shook their heads covered with bells, the door of the carriage shut with some noise, and the wheels were heard rolling along the street.

Lapeyrouse had started on that voyage from which he was destined never to return.

When the last sound had died away all eyes were directed, as if controlled by a superior power, toward Cagliostro. At that moment there was a pythonic illumination in his face which startled all the company. A strange silence lasted some moments. The Comte de Haga was the first to speak. "And why," said he, "did you not reply to him, Monsieur?"

Cagliostro started, as if the question had roused him from a revery. "Because," said he, "I must either have told a falsehood or a sad truth."

"How so?"

"I must have said to him, Monsieur de Lapeyrouse, the duke is right in saying to you 'adieu' and not 'au revoir.'"

"Eh! but," said Richelieu, turning pale, "what the devil, Monsieur Cagliostro, are you saying, then, about Lapeyrouse?"

"Oh, reassure yourself, Monsieur le Maréchal," replied Cagliostro, quickly, "it is not as regards you that the prediction is ominous."

"What!" cried Madame Dubarry, "is poor Lapeyrouse, who has just kissed my hand—"

"Not only, Madame, will never kiss it again, but he will never again see those he has just left," said Cagliostro, looking attentively at his glass full of water, which, from the position in which it was placed, exhibited a luminous surface of an opal tint, crossed by the shadows of surrounding objects.

A cry of astonishment burst from all. The interest of the conversation deepened every moment, and it might have been thought, from the solemn and anxious air with which all regarded Cagliostro, that they were awaiting the infallible predictions of an ancient oracle.

In the midst of this preoccupation, Monsieur de Favras, representing the general feeling, rose, made a sign, and went on tiptoe to listen in the antechamber, and ascertain whether any of the servants were within hearing. But, as we have said, the house of Monsieur le Maréchal de Richelieu was well regulated, and Monsieur de Favras found in the antechamber only an old intendant, who, implacable as a sentinel at an exposed post, defended the approaches to the dining-room at the solemn hour of dessert. He therefore returned to his seat, making a sign to the guests that they were alone.

"In that case," said Madame Dubarry, replying to the assurance of Monsieur de Favras as if it had been uttered aloud, "tell us what is to happen to that poor Lapeyrouse."

Cagliostro still maintained the same ominous silence.

"Oh, yes; let us hear," cried all the rest.

"Well, then, Monsieur de Lapeyrouse intends, as you know, to make the tour of the globe, and continue the researches of poor Captain Cook, who was killed in the Sandwich Islands."

"Yes, yes, we know," said all the company, by signs, rather than in words.

"Everything should foretell a happy termination to this voyage; Monsieur de Lapeyrouse is a good seaman, and his route has been most skilfully traced by the king."

"Yes," interrupted Comte de Haga, "the king of France is a clever geographer; is he not, Monsieur de Condorcet?"

"More skilful than is needful for a king," replied the marquis. "Kings ought to know things only slightly; then they will let themselves be guided by those who know them thoroughly."

"Is this a lesson, Marquis?" said the Comte de Haga, smiling.

Condorcet blushed. "Oh, no, Monsieur le Comte," said he; "only a simple reflection, a general truth."

"Well, he has set out?" said Madame Dubarry, anxious to bring the conversation back to Lapeyrouse.

"Yes, he has set out," replied Cagliostro; "but don't believe, in spite of his haste, that he will soon embark. I foresee much time lost at Brest."

"That would be a pity," said Condorcet; "this is the proper time for sailing; it is even now rather late,—February or March would have been better."

"Oh, do not grudge him these two or three months, Monsieur de Condorcet; he lives, at least, during that time,—he lives and hopes."

"He has good officers, I suppose," said Richelieu.

"Yes, he who commands the second ship is a distinguished officer. I see him—young, adventurous, and too brave, unhappily."

"Why unhappily?"

"A year later I look for him, and see him no more," said Cagliostro, anxiously consulting his glass. "No one here is related to Monsieur de Langle?"

"No."

"No one knows him?"

"No."

"Well, death will begin with him; I see him no longer."

A murmur of affright escaped from all the guests.

"But he, Lapeyrouse?" cried several voices, eagerly.

"He sails, he lands, he re-embarks; I see one, two years of successful navigation. We hear news of him,[1] and then—"

"Then?"

"Years pass—"

"But at last?"

"The sea is vast, the heavens are clouded. Here and there appear unknown lands, and figures hideous as the monsters of the Grecian Archipelago. They watch the ship, which in a fog is drifting among the rocks, at the mercy of the currents. At last the tempest, the tempest more hospitable than the land, and then—ominous flames. Oh, Lapeyrouse! Lapeyrouse! if you could hear me, I would cry to you. You set out, like Columbus, to discover a world; Lapeyrouse, beware of unknown isles." He ceased, and an icy shiver ran through the assembly.

"But why did you not warn him?" asked the Comte de Haga, submitting like the others to the influence of this extraordinary man, who moved all hearts at his will.

"Yes," cried Madame Dubarry, "why not send after him and bring him back? The life of a man like Lapeyrouse is surely worth the journey of a courier, my dear Marshal."

The marshal understood, and rose to ring the bell. Cagliostro extended his arm to stop him. The marshal returned to his chair.

"Alas!" said Cagliostro, "all advice would be useless. The man who can foresee destiny cannot change it. Monsieur de Lapeyrouse would laugh if he heard my words, as the son of Priam laughed when Cassandra prophesied; and see, you begin to laugh yourself, Monsieur le Comte de Haga, and laughing is contagious,—your companions are catching it. Oh, do not restrain yourself, Monsieur de Favras; I have never yet found a hearer who believed."

"Oh, we believe," said Madame Dubarry and the old Duc de Richelieu.

"I believe," murmured Taverney.

"I, also," said the Comte de Haga, politely.

"Yes," replied Cagliostro, "you believe, because it concerns Lapeyrouse; but if I spoke of you, you would not believe."

[1] The officer who brought the last news received from Lapeyrouse was Monsieur de Lesseps,—the only man on the expedition who returned to France.

"Oh!"

"I am sure of it."

"I confess that what would have made me believe," returned the Comte de Haga, "would have been that you should say to him, 'Beware of unknown isles;' then he would, at least, have had the chance of avoiding them."

"I assure you, no, Monsieur le Comte; and if he had believed me, consider the horrible effect of that revelation. Then in presence of danger, at sight of those unknown isles which were to be fatal to him, the unhappy man, believing in my prediction, would have felt the mysterious approach of death without being able to flee from it. And so he would have suffered not one death but a thousand; for it is suffering a thousand deaths to wander in gloom with despair at one's side. That hope which I should take from him—think of it!—is the last consolation to which the wretched victim still clings under the executioner's knife, when even the knife has touched him, when he feels its sharp edge, when his blood begins to flow. Life is extinguished while still the man is hoping."

"That is true!" said several of the guests, in a suppressed whisper.

"Yes," said Condorcet; "the veil which hides from us our future is the only real good which God has vouchsafed to man."

"Nevertheless," said the Comte de Haga, "did a man like you tell me to shun a certain man, or a certain thing, I would beware, and I would thank you for the counsel."

Cagliostro gently shook his head, with a serious smile.

"I mean it, Monsieur de Cagliostro," continued the Comte de Haga, "warn me, and I will thank you."

"You wish me to tell you what I would not tell Lapeyrouse?"

"Yes; I wish it."

Cagliostro made a movement as if to begin, and then stopped, and said, "Oh no, Monsieur le Comte, no!"

"I beg you."

Monsieur de Cagliostro turned away his head, "Never!" he murmured.

"Take care," said the count, smiling; "you are making me incredulous."

"Incredulity is better than misery."

"Monsieur de Cagliostro," said the count, gravely, "you forget one thing."

"And what is that?" asked the prophet, respectfully.

"It is that though there are men who had better remain ignorant of their destiny, there are others who should know it, as it concerns not themselves alone, but millions of others."

"I must have an order, then. Without an order I will do nothing."

"What do you mean?"

"That if your Majesty commands," said Cagliostro, in a low voice, "I will obey."

"I command you to reveal to me my destiny, Monsieur de Cagliostro," said the king, with an air at once courteous and dignified.

At this moment, as the Comte de Haga had dropped his incognito in giving that order, Monsieur de Richelieu advanced toward him, and humbly saluting the prince, said, "Thanks, Sire, for the honor which the king of Sweden has done my house; will your Majesty assume the place of honor? From this moment it belongs to you alone."

"Let us remain as we are, Marshal; I wish to hear what Monsieur de Cagliostro is about to say."

"One does not speak the truth to kings, Sire."

"Bah! I am not in my kingdom; take your place again, Monsieur le Duc. Proceed, Monsieur de Cagliostro, I beg."

Cagliostro looked again in his glass. Globules like those seen in champagne rose from the bottom to the surface. The water seemed to be attracted by his powerful gaze, and to become agitated at his will. "Sire," said he, "tell me what you wish to know; I am ready to answer."

"Tell me by what death I shall die."

"By a gunshot, Sire."

The eyes of Gustavus grew bright. "Ah, in a battle," said he; "the death of a soldier! Thanks, Monsieur de Cagliostro, a hundred times I thank you. Oh, I foresee battles! and Gustavus Adolphus and Charles XII have shown me how a king of Sweden should die."

Cagliostro drooped his head, without replying.

The Comte de Haga frowned. "Oh, oh!" said he, "is it not in battle that the gunshot will be discharged?"

"No, Sire."

"In a sedition? Yes, that is possible."

"No, not in a sedition, Sire."

"But where, then?"

"At a ball, Sire."

The king remained silent, and Cagliostro buried his head in his hands.

Every one looked pale and frightened; and all watched the author of the prophecy and him whom it chiefly concerned. Then Monsieur de Condorcet took the glass of water, in which the fatal augury had been read, and raising it to his eye, examined carefully the glittering facets of the glass and its mysterious contents. His look seemed to be inquiring of both the solid and liquid crystal the solution of the problem, which his reason reduced to the import of a purely physical speculation.

In fact, the scientist was trying to compute the water's depth, luminous refractions, and microscopic play. He was asking himself the cause and explanation of this jugglery, practised upon men so enlightened as those who surrounded the table, by a man to whom he could not deny the possession of extraordinary power. Doubtless he found no solution of his problem, for he ceased his examination of the glass, returned it to the table, and amid the stupefaction caused by the prediction of Cagliostro, "Well, I also," he said, "will beg our illustrious prophet to consult for me his magic mirror. Unfortunately, I am not a powerful lord; I cannot command, and my obscure life concerns no millions of people."

"Monsieur," said the Comte de Haga, "you command in the name of science, and your life belongs not only to a nation, but to all mankind."

"I thank you, Monsieur le Comte!" said Condorcet; "but perhaps your opinion on this subject is not shared by Monsieur de Cagliostro."

Cagliostro quickly raised his head. "Yes, Marquis," said he, with a beginning of nervous irritability, which in ancient times would have been attributed to the presence of the god that inspired him, "you are indeed a powerful lord in the kingdom of intelligence; look me, then, in the face, and tell me seriously if you also wish that I should prophesy to you."

"Seriously, Monsieur le Comte,—upon my honor."

"Well, Marquis," said Cagliostro, in a hollow voice, and closing his eyelids, "you will die of that poison which you carry in your ring; you will die—"

"Oh! but if I throw it away?"

"Throw it away."

"You allow that it is very easy?"

"Then throw it away, I tell you."

"Oh, yes, Marquis!" cried Madame Dubarry; "throw away that horrid poison,—throw it away, if it be only to falsify this prophet of evil who threatens us all with his prophecies. For if you throw it away you cannot die by it, as Monsieur de Cagliostro predicts; so there, at least, he will have been wrong."

"Madame la Comtesse is right," said the Comte de Haga.

"Bravo, Countess!" said Richelieu. "Come, Marquis, throw away that poison, for now that I know you carry it, I shall tremble every time we drink together; the ring might open of itself, and—"

"And two glasses touched together come very close," said Taverney. "Throw it away, Marquis,—throw it away!"

"It is useless," said Cagliostro, quietly; "Monsieur de Condorcet will not throw it away."

"No," returned Condorcet, "I will not throw it away,—not that I wish to aid my destiny, but because this is a unique poison, prepared by Cabanis, which chance has completely hardened, and that chance might never occur again; therefore I will not throw it away. Triumph if you will, Monsieur de Cagliostro!"

"Destiny," replied Cagliostro, "ever finds faithful agents to aid in the execution of her decrees."

"Then I shall die by poison!" said the marquis. "Well, so be it. It is an admirable death, I think,—a little poison on the tip of the tongue, and I am gone. That is not death; it is only minus life, as we say in algebra."

"It is no wish of mine that you should suffer, Monsieur," said Cagliostro, coldly; and he made a sign indicating that he desired to say no more regarding Monsieur de Condorcet.

"Then, Monsieur," said Monsieur de Favras, "we have a shipwreck, a gunshot, and a poisoning; they make my mouth water. Will you not do me the favor to predict to me, also, some little catastrophe of the same kind?"

"Oh, Marquis!" replied Cagliostro, beginning to grow warm under this irony, "it would be wrong in you to envy these gentlemen, for I assure you that you will have still better."

"Better!" said Monsieur de Favras, laughing; "that is pledging yourself to a great deal. Better than the sea, fire, poison,—that is difficult."

"There remains the rope, Monsieur le Marquis," said Cagliostro, bowing.

"The rope! Oh, oh! what are you telling me?"

"I am telling you that you will be hanged!" replied Cagliostro, with a sort of prophetic rage, which he could no longer control.

"Hanged! The devil!" cried the guests.

"Monsieur forgets that I am a nobleman," said Monsieur de Favras, coldly; "or if he means to speak of a suicide, I warn him that I shall respect myself sufficiently, even in my last moments, not to use a rope while I have a sword."

"I do not speak of a suicide, Monsieur."

"Then you speak of a punishment?"

"Yes."

"You are a foreigner, Monsieur, and therefore I pardon you."

"For what?"

"Your ignorance, Monsieur. In France we decapitate noblemen."

"You will arrange that matter with the executioner," replied Cagliostro, crushing his interlocutor with that rough answer.

There was a moment's hesitation among those present.

"Do you know that I begin to tremble?" said Monsieur de Launay; "my predecessors have had so bad luck that I am afraid I shall find only evil if I plunge my hand into the same bag."

"Then you are more reasonable than they, and do not seek to know the future. You are right. Be it good or bad, let us respect the secret of God."

"Oh, Monsieur de Launay!" said Madame Dubarry, "I hope you will not be less courageous than the others have been."

"I hope so too, Madame," said the governor, bowing. Then turning to Cagliostro, "Monsieur," he said, "favor me in my turn with my horoscope, if you please."

"It is easy," replied Cagliostro; "a blow on the head with a hatchet, and all will be over."

A cry of terror sounded through the hall. Richelieu and Taverney begged Cagliostro to say no more, but feminine curiosity prevailed.

"To hear you talk, Count," said Madame Dubarry, "one would think the whole universe must die by violence. Here we are, eight of us, and five are already condemned by you."

"Oh, you understand that it is all a prearranged affair, and that we laugh at it, Madame," said Monsieur de Favras, trying to laugh in fact.

"Certainly we will laugh at it," said the Comte de Haga, "be it true or false."

"Oh, I will laugh too, then," said Madame Dubarry; "I will not dishonor the assembly by my cowardice; but alas! I am only a woman, and shall not have the honor to be ranked with you by a tragical death; a woman dies in her bed. Alas, my death, that of a sorrowful old woman abandoned by every one, will be the worst of all. Will it not, Monsieur de Cagliostro?"

She stopped and seemed to wait for the prophet to reassure her. Cagliostro did not speak; so, her curiosity obtaining the mastery over her fears, she went on, "Well, Monsieur de Cagliostro, will you not answer me?"

"How can I answer you, Madame, when you ask me no questions?"

"But–" said she.

"Decide," said Cagliostro; "do you question me,–yes, or no?"

The countess made an effort, and drawing courage from the smiles of the company, "Yes," she cried, "I will run the risk. Tell me the fate of Jeanne de Vaubernier, Comtesse Dubarry."

"On the scaffold, Madame," replied the prophet of evil.

"A jest, Monsieur, is it not?" stammered she, looking at him with a supplicating air.

Cagliostro did not observe that look. "Why do you think I jest?" said he.

"Oh, because to die on the scaffold one must have committed some crime,–stolen, or committed murder, or done something dreadful; and it is not likely I shall do that. It was a jest, was it not?"

"Oh, my God! yes," said Cagliostro; "all I have said is but a jest."

The countess laughed, but a skilled observer would have thought her laugh too noisy to be quite natural. "Come, Monsieur de Favras," said she, "let us order our funeral coaches."

"Oh, that will be needless for you, Madame," said Cagliostro.

"Why so, Monsieur?"

"Because you will go to the scaffold in a cart."

"Oh, how horrible! oh, the dreadful man! Marshal, for Heaven's sake choose more cheerful guests next time, or I will never visit you again."

"Excuse me, Madame," said Cagliostro; "but you, like all the rest, would have me speak."

"I, like all the rest. At least, you will grant me time to choose my confessor?"

"It will be superfluous, Countess."

"Why?"

"The last one to mount the scaffold with a confessor will be—"

"Will be?" asked all the company.

"Will be the king of France;" and Cagliostro said these words in a voice so hollow and melancholy that it was to the company like a blast of death, and it chilled them to the bottom of their hearts.

Then ensued a silence which lasted several minutes. Meantime, Cagliostro raised to his lips the glass of water in which he had read these fearful prophecies; but scarcely had it touched his mouth when he set it down, and pushed it from him with a movement of disgust. He turned his eyes to Monsieur de Taverney.

"Oh," cried the latter in terror, "do not tell me anything, I do not wish to know."

"Well, then, I will ask in his place," said Richelieu.

"You, Marshal, be happy; you are the only one of us all who will die in his bed."

"Coffee, gentleman, coffee!" cried the marshal, enchanted with the prediction.

Every one rose.

But before passing into the salon, the Comte de Haga, approaching Cagliostro, said: "Monsieur, I have no idea of trying to escape my destiny; but tell me what I ought to distrust."

"A muff, Sire," replied Cagliostro.

Monsieur de Haga withdrew.

"And I?" said Condorcet.

"An omelette."

"Good, I renounce eggs;" and he followed the count.

"And I?" said Monsieur de Favras,—"what must I fear?"

"A letter."

"Very good; I thank you."

"And I?" asked De Launay.

"The taking of the Bastille."

"Oh, you quite reassure me;" and he went away, laughing.

"Now for me, Monsieur," said the countess, with anxiety.

"You, beautiful Countess, beware of the Place Louis XV."

"Alas!" said the countess, "one day already, I lost myself there; that day I suffered much; I nearly lost my head."

"Well, Countess, this time it will be lost never to be regained."

Madame Dubarry uttered a cry, and fled to the salon to join the other guests. Cagliostro was about to follow her, when Richelieu stopped him. "One moment," said he. "There remain only Taverney and I, to whom you have predicted nothing, my dear sorcerer."

"Monsieur de Taverney begged me to say nothing, and you, Monsieur le Maréchal, have asked me nothing."

"Oh, I still entreat you to tell me nothing," said Taverney, clasping his hands.

"But come, to prove your power, tell us something that only Taverney and I know," said Richelieu.

"What?" asked Cagliostro, smiling.

"Tell us what makes Taverney come to Versailles, instead of living quietly in his beautiful house at Maison-Rouge, which the king repurchased for him three years ago."

"Nothing more simple, Marshal," said Cagliostro. "Ten years ago, Monsieur de Taverney wished to give his daughter, Mademoiselle Andrée, to the King Louis XV; but he did not succeed."

"Oh! oh!" groaned Taverney.

"Now Monsieur wishes to give his son, Philippe de Taverney, to the Queen Marie Antoinette; ask him if I speak the truth."

"On my word," said Taverney, trembling, "this man is a sorcerer; devil take me if he is not."

"Oh, oh! do not speak so cavalierly of the Devil, my old comrade," said the marshal.

"Frightful! frightful!" murmured Taverney; and he turned to implore Cagliostro to be discreet, but he had disappeared.

"Come, Taverney, to the salon," said the marshal; "or they will drink their coffee without us." But when they arrived there the room was empty; not one of the guests had courage to face again the author of these terrible predictions.

The wax lights burned in the candelabra, the coffee was smoking in the urn, the fire burned on the hearth,—but all for nothing.

"Faith, old friend, it seems we must take our coffee *tête-à-tête*. Why, what the devil has become of you?" Richelieu looked all round him, but Taverney had vanished like the rest. "Never mind," said the marshal, chuckling as Voltaire might have done, and rubbing his withered though still white hands; "I shall be the only one to die in my bed. Eh, eh! in my bed. Well, Comte de Cagliostro, at least I believe. In my bed, that was it; I shall die in my bed, and I trust not for a long time. Hola! my valet and my drops."

The valet entered with the bottle, and the marshal went with him into the bed-room.

THE POPE'S MULE

ALPHONSE DAUDET

Of all the pretty sayings, proverbs, or adages with which our Provençal peasants interlard their discourse, I know of none more picturesque or more singular than this. For leagues around my mill it is the custom to say, in speaking of a rancorous, vindictive man, "Beware of that man; he is like the pope's mule, he keeps his kick seven years."

I tried for a long time to ascertain the origin of this proverb—what was meant by this papal mule, and this kick kept seven years. But no one could throw any light on the question, not even Francet Mamaï, my fifer, though he has his Provençal legendary lore at his fingers' ends. Francet thinks with me that it must have reference to some ancient chronicle of Avignon. "You will find that only in the library of the cicadas," he said to me, with a laugh. The idea struck me as a good one, and the cicada's library being right at my door, I shut myself up in it for a week.

It is a beautiful library, admirably well stocked, open to the poets day and night, and served by little librarians with cymbals that make music for you all the time. I passed several delicious days there; and after a week's research—on my back—I found at last what I wanted—that is, the story of my mule and the kick kept seven years. It is a pretty story, albeit a trifle *naïf*, and I will try to tell it you as I read it yesterday morning in a time-colored manuscript, with a delicious scent of dry lavender, and with large cobwebs for clasps.

Whoever did not see Avignon in the days of the popes has seen nothing. For gayety, life, animation, feasting, never was there such a city. From morning till night there were processions and pilgrimages, streets strewn with flowers, high-warp tapestry, cardinals arriving by the Rhone, banners flying, galleys streaming, the pope's soldiers chanting their Latin on the squares, mendicant friars with their rattles; and from top to bottom of the houses that swarmed about the papal palace like bees about their hive, there was the tic-tac of lace-makers, the flying of shuttles weaving the gold of the chasubles, the little hammers of cruet-carvers, the tuning of sounding-boards, the songs of warping-women; and above all this, the ringing of bells, and always a few drums rolling on the bridge. For with us, when the people are happy they must dance, and the streets being too narrow for the farandole, fifes and drums were posted on the Avignon bridge, and day and night they danced in the fresh air from the Rhone. Ah, happy days! happy city! days of halberds that did not cut, and prisons used for storing wine! No famine! no war! This is how the Avignon popes understood governing their people. This is why their people so sorely regretted them.

There was one in particular, a good old pope named Boniface. What rivers of tears flowed in Avignon when he died! He was so amiable, so handsome a prince! He smiled to you so benignly from the back of his mule, and whether you were the poor madder dyer or the great *"viguier"* of the town, gave you his blessing so civilly as he passed! A real Pope of Yvetot, but a Provençal Yvetot, with something sly in his laugh, a bunch of marjoram in his berretta, and not the least Jenny. The only Jenny this good father had ever known was his vine—a little vine which he had planted himself three leagues from Avignon, among the myrtles of Chateauneuf.

Every Sunday after vespers the worthy man would go to pay his court to her; and when there, seated in the bright sun, his mule at his side

and his cardinals all around, he would uncork a bottle of his own wine, the beautiful red wine since known as Chateauneuf-des-papes, and sip it slowly while he gazed lovingly at his vine. Then, when the bottle was emptied and the sun gone down, he returned gayly to the town, followed by his whole chapter; and when he passed the drums on the bridge, his mule, intoxicated by the music, would set off in a little canter, the pope himself keeping time with his berretta, to the scandal of the cardinals, but which made all the people say, "Ah! the good prince, the dear pope!"

Next to his Chateauneuf vine, what the pope loved best in the world was his mule. In fact the good man doted on his beast. Every night before retiring to rest he went himself to see if the stabledoor was shut close, the crib well filled; and he never rose from table without seeing prepared under his own eyes a large bowl of French wine with plenty of sugar and spices, which he carried her himself, regardless of the strictures of his cardinals.

It is proper to add that the animal was not unworthy of the trouble. She was a beautiful black mule, speckled red, with a shining skin and large, full croup, sure of foot, carrying proudly her little head all bedizened with knots and bows and silver bells; withal gentle as a lamb, with an artless eye and two long ears always shaking, which gave her an easy, good-natured air. All Avignon respected her, and when she passed along the streets there was no sort of civility they did not show her. For in truth everybody knew this to be the surest way of winning favor at court, and that with all her innocent air the pope's mule had helped many a one on the road to fortune, as witness Tistet Védène and his wonderful career.

This Tistet Védène was an impudent, worthless varlet, whom his father, the gold-carver, had turned out-of-doors because he could not be made to work and demoralized his apprentices. For six months he might have been seen dragging his jacket in the Avignon gutters, but generally in the neighborhood of the papal mansion; for the scamp entertained ideas of his own with regard to the pope's mule, and very designing ones they were as will be seen.

One day when his Holiness was walking alone under his walls with his beast, Tistet Védène approached, and clasping his hands in an ecstasy, exclaimed,

"Oh, *mon Dieu!* great Holy Father, what a beautiful mule! Stop a moment while I look at her! Oh, Pope! what a mule! The Emperor of Germany hasn't such an animal!" And he caressed her and spoke softly to her, as if she had been a girl. "Come, my darling, my treasure, my sweet love!" And the good pope, all melted, said to himself, "What a nice little boy! what pretty ways he has with my mule!" And do you know what happened? The next day Tistet Védène exchanged his yellow jacket for a beautiful lace alb, a crimson silk camail, and buckled shoes, and entered the pope's household, which had never before received any but sons of nobles and nephews of cardinals. So much for diplomacy. But Tistet did not stop here.

Once established in the pope's service the rascal continued the game which had succeeded so well. Insolent to the rest of the world, he was all thoughtfulness and attention to the mule. He was constantly to be met in the palace court with a handful of oats or bundle of sainfoin, shaking the red clusters as he looked towards the Holy Father's balcony, as much as to say, "Who is this for?" Till at last the good pope ended by intrusting to him the entire care of the stable and the office of carrying the mule her bowl of French wine—which didn't make the cardinals laugh.

Neither did it make the mule laugh. Now, when the hour for her wine came, she always saw approaching five or six little boys attached to the household, with their camials and lace. Another moment and the stable was filled with a warm scent of caramels and spices, and Tistet Védène would appear, carefully carrying a bowl of French wine. Then the poor beast's martyrdom would begin.

This perfumed wine which she loved so, which kept her warm, which lent her wings, they had the cruelty to bring to her crib, to make her smell it, and then, when her nostrils were filled with the aroma of the beautiful ruby liquor, it would all be poured down the throats of these varlets. And as if to steal her wine were not enough, after they had been drinking they became like so many little devils. One would pull her ears, another her tail. Quiquet would mount on her back, Béloquet would try his berretta on her, and not one of the rascals once reflected that the good creature, if she pleased, could launch a kick at them that would send them to the North Star, if not farther. But no! it is not for nothing that one is a papal mule, the mule of benedictions and indulgences. Do what they might she would not lose her temper with the boys; it was only Tistet Védène that she had hard thoughts of; she felt an itching in her hoofs when he was behind her. And indeed she had good cause—this scamp of a Tistet played her such ugly tricks. There was no end to his cruel inventiveness after he had drunk her wine.

One day he took into his head to make her climb with him into the bell-tower on the top of the palace. This is no fable that I am about to relate. Two hundred thousand Provençals saw it. Picture to yourself the unlucky mule, when, after turning and turning in a spiral staircase and climbing I don't know how many steps, she suddenly found herself on a platform sparkling with light, and saw, a thousand feet below her, a whole fantastic Avignon—market, shops no bigger than nuts, the pope's soldiers looking like red ants before their barracks; on a silver thread a microscopic bridge where they danced. Ah! how terrified the poor beast was! She raised a cry that made all the windows in the palace rattle.

"What is the matter? what are they doing to her?" exclaimed the good pope, rushing out on the balcony.

Tistet Védène was already on the balcony, weeping and wringing his hands.

"Ah! great Holy Father, the matter is that your mule—*mon Dieu!* what is to become of us?—your mule has climbed into the bell-tower."

"All alone???"

"Yes, great Holy Father, all alone. Look up yonder. Don't you see her ears passing? you might think they were two swallows."

"*Miséricorde!*" exclaimed the pope, rolling his eyes, "she has gone mad! she will kill herself! Will you come down, wretched beast?"

Come down! She would have asked nothing better, but how? The stairs were not to be thought of; they might be climbed, but as for coming down, that would be to run a hundred risks of breaking her neck. And as the poor mule, in deep distress, walked round and round the platform, her large eyes full of vertigo, she thought of Tistet Védène.

"Ah! rascal! if I catch you again! what a kick I shall have for you to-morrow!"

This idea of the kick put a little heart in her, and gave her strength to stand on her feet; otherwise she would have dropped.

At last they came to take her down, and it was no trifling matter. She had to be lowered with a screwjack, ropes, and a litter. And fancy what a humiliation for the poor mule to see herself suspended from such a height, her feet dangling like a June bug at the end of a string! And all Avignon looking on!

The poor beast never slept a wink that night. She seemed to be still turning, turning, around that accursed platform, with all the town below laughing. Then she thought of the infamous Tistet Védène, and of the kick she would send him next morning. They should see the smoke of it all the way to Pampelune.

But while this handsome reception was being prepared for him, what, think you, was Tistet Védène doing? Sailing down the Rhone, singing, on his way to the Court of Naples, with a troop of young nobles who were sent every year to practise themselves in diplomacy and fine manners. Tistet Védène was not a noble, but the pope felt that he owed him something for his attentions to his mule, especially for the activity he had displayed on the day of the rescue.

What a disappointed mule that was the next morning! "The rascal! he suspected something!" thought she, shaking her bells with fury. "But no matter, you shall have it yet. I will keep it for you!" And she kept it for him.

After Tistet's departure the pope's mule resumed the old even tenor of her ways. There was no more Quiquet nor Béloquet. The good old days of

French wine returned, and with them good humor, long siestas, and her little amble as she passed the bridge. Since her adventure, however, she could not but remark that the towns-people treated her a trifle coolly. There were whisperings as she passed, the old people would shake their heads, the children would laugh and point to the bell-tower. Even the good pope seemed to have lost a little of his old confidence in his friend, and when he would fall into a doze on her back was never without an uneasy after-thought: "What if I should awake to find myself on the bell-tower!" The mule saw all this, and suffered in silence. Only when the name of Tistet Védène was mentioned in her hearing, her long ears would quiver, and with a little chuckle she would sharpen her iron hoofs on the pavement.

Matters went on thus for seven years, and then Tistet Védène returned from the Court of Naples. His time there had not expired, but he had learned that the pope's premier moutardier had just died suddenly, and the place being a good one, had returned in haste to enter the lists.

When this intriguer of a Védène entered the hall of the palace the Holy Father scarcely recognized him, he was grown so much taller and stouter. It must be added that the old pope himself had aged, and could no longer see without his glasses. But Tistet was nothing daunted.

"What! great Holy Father! you do not recognize me? It is I, Tistet Védène."

"Védène?"

"Yes; don't you know?—that used to carry the French wine to your mule."

"Ah! yes, yes, I remember; an excellent little fellow, Tistet Védène. And what is it you want of us?"

"Oh, not much, great Holy Father. I came to ask you—by-the-way, have you your mule still? And is she well? Ah! I am glad!—I came to ask you for the place of the premier moutardier who has just died."

"Premier moutardier! You! But you are too young. What is your age?"

"Twenty years and two months, illustrious pontiff—just five years older than your mule. Ah! *palme de Dieu!* the dear, good creature; if you knew how I loved that mule, how I pined for her in Italy! Will you not let me see her?"

"Yes, my child, you shall see her; and since you love the dear beast so I will not suffer you to live apart. From this day I attach you to my person in the capacity of premier moutardier. My cardinals will cry out, but I am used to that. Come to us tomorrow, and we will invest you with the insignia of your office in presence of all the chapter. After that I will take you to see the mule, and you shall accompany me to visit the vine. Ha! ha!"

Whether Tistet Védène was happy as he quitted the great hall, with what impatience he waited for the ceremony of the next day, it is needless to relate. But some one else in the palace was even happier and more impatient than he. This was the mule. From the time of Tistet's return till vespers the next day she never ceased to stuff herself with oats, and to draw close to the wall with her hind feet.

She, too, was preparing for the ceremony.

The next day, vespers being over, Tistet Védène made his entry in the court of the papal palace. All the high clergy were there—the cardinals in red robes, the devil's advocate in black velvet, the monastery abbés with their little mitres, the wardens of Saint Agrico, the pope's household in their crimson camails, the lower clergy, the pope's soldiers in full dress, the three orders of penitents, the hermits of Mount Ventour, the sacristans in their judges' robes, the little clerk heading the procession with the handbell—all, all, to the dispensers of holy water, the lighter and extinguisher—not one was missing. Ah! it was a grand ceremony—bells, petards, sunshine, music, and, as ever, the frenzied drum leading the dance on the bridge.

When Védène made his appearance, with his handsome person and fine bearing, a murmur of admiration ran through the assemblage. He was a magnificent Provençal of the blond type, with hair curling at the ends, and a wanton little beard that might have been made of the filings that fell from the graver of his father, the sculptor in gold. Rumor said that the fingers of Queen Jeanne had toyed with this golden beard, and the Sire de Védène had in truth the distrait and self-conscious air of the men whom queens have loved. To-day he had, in honor of his country, substituted for his Neapolitan vestments a red-bordered jacket *à la Provençal*, and on his chaperon there floated a large plume of the ibis of Camargue.

When he entered, the premier moutardier bowed with a knightly grace, and turned to the grand steps where the pope was waiting to invest him with the insignia of his rank—the yellow boxwood spoon and the saffron coat. The mule was at the foot of the steps, caparisoned and ready to set out for the vine. Tistet smiled as he passed close to her, and paused a moment to give her a few friendly taps on the back, glancing out of the corner of his eye to see whether the pope was observing. Now was her chance! The position was excellent. "Here, rascal! take that! I have kept it for you seven years." And she launched him a kick so terrible, so terrible, that all the way to Pampelune they saw a whirlwind of golden smoke out of which fluttered an ibis plume. It was all that remained of the unfortunate Tistet Védène.

The kicks of mules are not commonly so terrific, it is true, but this was a papal mule, and then it had been kept seven years. A better example of ecclesiastical rancor could hardly be found.

THE STORY OF THE LATE MR. ELVESHAM

H. G. WELLS

I SET this story down, not expecting it will be believed, but, if possible, to prepare a way of escape for the next victim. He, perhaps, may profit by my misfortune. My own case, I know, is hopeless, and I am now in some measure prepared to meet my fate.

My name is Edward George Eden. I was born at Trentham, in Staffordshire, my father being employed in the gardens there. I lost my mother when I was three years old, and my father when I was five, my uncle, George Eden, then adopting me as his own son. He was a single man, self-educated, and well-known in Birmingham as an enterprising journalist; he educated me generously, fired my ambition to succeed in the world, and at his death, which happened four years ago, left his entire fortune, a matter of about five hundred pounds after all outgoing charges were paid. I was then eighteen. He advised me in his will to expend the money in completing my education. I had already chosen the profession of medicine, and through his posthumous generosity and my good fortune in a scholarship competition, I became a medical student at University College, London. At the time of the beginning of my story I lodged at 11A University Street in a little upper room, very shabbily furnished and drafty, overlooking the back of Shoolbred's premises. I used this little room both to live in and sleep in, because I was anxious to eke out my means to the very last shillingsworth.

I was taking a pair of shoes to be mended at a shop in the Tottenham Court Road when I first encountered the little old man with the yellow face, with whom my life has now become so inextricably entangled. He was standing on the curb, and staring at the number on the door in a doubtful way, as I opened it. His eyes—they were dull gray eyes, and reddish under the rims—fell to my face, and his countenance immediately assumed an expression of corrugated amiability.

"You come," he said, "apt to the moment. I had forgotten the number of your house. How do you do, Mr. Eden?"

I was a little astonished at his familiar address, for I had never set eyes on the man before. I was a little annoyed, too, at his catching me with my boots under my arm. He noticed my lack of cordiality.

"Wonder who the deuce I am, eh? A friend, let me assure you. I have seen you before, though you haven't seen me. Is there anywhere where I can talk to you?"

I hesitated. The shabbiness of my room upstairs was not a matter for every stranger. "Perhaps," said I, "we might walk down the street. I'm unfortunately prevented——" My gesture explained the sentence before I had spoken it.

"The very thing," he said, and faced this way, and then that. "The street? Which way shall we go?" I slipped my boots down in the passage. "Look here!" he said abruptly; "this business of mine is a rigmarole. Come and lunch with me, Mr. Eden. I'm an old man, a very old man, and not good at explanations, and what with my piping voice and the clatter of the traffic——"

He laid a persuasive skinny hand that trembled a little upon my arm.

I was not so old that an old man might not treat me to a lunch. Yet at the same time I was not altogether pleased by this abrupt invitation. "I had rather——" I began. "But I had rather," he said, catching me up, "and a certain civility is surely due to my gray hairs."

And so I consented, and went with him.

He took me to Blavitiski's; I had to walk slowly to accommodate myself to his paces; and over such a lunch as I had never tasted before, he fended off my leading questions, and I took a better note of his appearance. His clean-shaven face was lean and wrinkled, his shriveled lips fell over a set of false teeth, and his white hair was thin and rather long; he seemed small to me—though, indeed, most people seemed small to me—and his shoulders were rounded and bent. And watching him, I could not help but observe that he too was taking note of me, running his eyes, with a curious touch of greed in them, over me, from my broad shoulders to my sun-tanned hands, and up to my freckled face again. "And now," said he, as we lit our cigarettes, "I must tell you of the business in hand.

"I must tell you, then, that I am an old man, a very old man." He paused momentarily. "And it happens that I have money that I must presently be leaving, and never a child have I to leave it to." I thought of the confidence trick, and resolved I would be on the alert for the vestiges of my five hundred pounds. He proceeded to enlarge on his loneliness, and the trouble he had to find a proper disposition of his money. "I have weighed this plan and that plan, charities, institutions, and scholarships, and libraries, and I have come to this conclusion at last"—he fixed his eyes on my face—"that I will find some young fellow, ambitious, pure-minded, and poor, healthy in body and healthy in mind, and, in short, make him my heir, give him all that I have." He repeated, "Give him all that I have. So that he will suddenly be lifted out of all the trouble and struggle in which his sympathies have been educated, to freedom and influence."

I tried to seem disinterested. With a transparent hypocrisy I said, "And you want my help, my professional services maybe, to find that person."

He smiled, and looked at me over his cigarette, and I laughed at his quiet exposure of my modest pretense.

"What a career such a man might have!" he said. "It fills me with envy to think how I have accumulated that another man may spend——

"But there are conditions, of course, burdens to be imposed. He must, for instance, take my name. You cannot expect everything without some return. And I must go into all the circumstances of his life before I can accept him. He *must* be sound. I must know his heredity, how his parents and grandparents died, have the strictest inquiries made into his private morals."

This modified my secret congratulations a little.

"And do I understand," said I, "that I——"

"Yes," he said, almost fiercely. "You. *You.*"

I answered never a word. My imagination was dancing wildly, my innate skepticism was useless to modify its transports. There was not a particle of gratitude in my mind—I did not know what to say nor how to say it. "But why me in particular?" I said at last.

He had chanced to hear of me from Professor Haslar, he said, as a typically sound and sane young man, and he wished, as far as possible, to leave his money where health and integrity were assured.

That was my first meeting with the little old man. He was mysterious about himself; he would not give his name yet, he said, and after I had answered some questions of his, he left me at the Blavitiski portal. I noticed that he drew a handful of gold coins from his pocket when it came to paying for the lunch. His insistence upon bodily health was curious. In accordance with an arrangement we had made I applied that day for a life policy in the Loyal Insurance Company for a large sum, and I was exhaustively overhauled by the medical advisers of that company in the subsequent week. Even that did not satisfy him, and he insisted I must be re-examined by the great Doctor Henderson.

It was Friday in Whitsun week before he came to a decision. He called me down, quite late in the evening—nearly nine it was—from cramming chemical equations for my Preliminary Scientific examination. He was standing in the passage under the feeble gas lamp, and his face was a grotesque interplay of shadows. He seemed more bowed than when I had first seen him, and his cheeks had sunk in a little.

His voice shook with emotion. "Everything is satisfactory, Mr. Eden," he said. "Everything is quite, quite satisfactory. And this night of all nights, you must dine with me and celebrate your—accession." He was interrupted by a cough. "You won't have long to wait, either," he said, wiping his handkerchief across his lips, and gripping my hand with his long bony claw that was disengaged. "Certainly not very long to wait."

We went into the street and called a cab. I remember every incident of that drive vividly, the swift, easy motion, the vivid contrast of gas and oil and electric light, the crowds of people in the streets, the place in Regent Street to which we went, and the sumptuous dinner we were served with there. I was disconcerted at first by the well-dressed waiter's glances at my rough clothes, bothered by the stones of the olives, but as the champagne warmed my blood, my confidence revived. At first the old man talked of himself. He had already told me his name in the cab; he was Egbert Elvesham, the great philosopher, whose name I had known since I was a lad at school. It seemed incredible to me that this man, whose intelligence had so early dominated mine, this great abstraction, should suddenly realize itself as this decrepit, familiar figure. I dare say every young fellow who has suddenly fallen among celebrities has felt

something of my disappointment. He told me now of the future that the feeble streams of his life would presently leave dry for me, houses, copyrights, investments; I had never suspected that philosophers were so rich. He watched me drink and eat with a touch of envy. "What a capacity for living you have!" he said; and then with a sigh, a sigh of relief I could have thought it, "it will not be long."

"Ay," said I, my head swimming now with champagne; "I have a future perhaps—of a passing agreeable sort, thanks to you. I shall now have the honor of your name. But you have a past. Such a past as is worth all my future."

He shook his head and smiled, as I thought, with half sad appreciation of my flattering admiration. "That future," he said, "would you in truth change it?" The waiter came with liqueurs. "You will not perhaps mind taking my name, taking my position, but would you indeed—willingly—take my years?"

"With your achievements," said I gallantly.

He smiled again. "Kümmel—both," he said to the waiter, and turned his attention to a little paper packet he had taken from his pocket. "This hour," said he, "this after-dinner hour is the hour of small things. Here is a scrap of my unpublished wisdom." He opened the packet with his shaking yellow fingers, and showed a little pinkish powder on the paper. "This," said he—"well, you must guess what it is. But Kümmel—put but a dash of this powder in it—is Himmel."

His large grayish eyes watched mine with an inscrutable expression.

It was a bit of a shock to me to find this great teacher gave his mind to the flavor of liqueurs. However, I feigned an interest in his weakness, for I was drunk enough for such small sycophancy.

He parted the powder between the little glasses, and, rising suddenly, with a strange unexpected dignity, held out his hand towards me. I imitated his action, and the glasses rang. "To a quick succession," said he, and raised his glass towards his lips."

"Not that," I said hastily. "Not that."

He paused with the liqueur at the level of his chin, and his eyes blazing into mine.

"To a long life," said I.

He hesitated. "To a long life," said he, with a sudden bark of laughter, and with eyes fixed on one another we tilted the little glasses. His eyes looked straight into mine, and as I drained the stuff off, I felt a curiously intense sensation. The first touch of it set my brain in a furious tumult; I seemed to feel an actual physical stirring in my skull, and a seething humming filled my ears. I did not notice the flavor in my mouth, the aroma that filled my throat; I saw only the gray intensity of his gaze that burnt into mine. The draft, the mental confusion, the noise and stirring in my head, seemed to last an interminable time. Curious vague impressions of half-forgotten things danced and vanished on the edge of my consciousness. At last he broke the spell. With a sudden explosive sigh he put down his glass.

"Well?" he said.

"It's glorious," said I, though I had not tasted the stuff.

My head was spinning. I sat down. My brain was chaos. Then my perception grew clear and minute as though I saw things in a concave mirror. His manner seemed to have changed into something nervous and hasty. He pulled out his watch and grimaced at it. "Eleven-seven! And to-night I must— Seven-twenty-five. Waterloo! I must go at once." He called for the bill, and struggled with his coat. Officious waiters came to our assistance. In another moment I was wishing him good-by, over the apron of a cab, and still with an absurd feeling of minute distinctness, as though—how can I express it?—I not only saw but *felt* through an inverted opera-glass.

"That stuff," he said. He put his hand to his forehead. "I ought not to have given it to you. It will make your head split to-morrow. Wait a minute. Here." He handed me out a little flat thing like a seidlitz powder. "Take that in water as you are going to bed. The other thing was a drug. Not till you're ready to go to bed, mind. It will clear your head. That's all. One more shake—Futurus!"

I gripped his shriveled claw. "Good-by," he said, and by the droop of his eyelids I judged he too was a little under the influence of that brain-twisting cordial.

He recollected something else with a start, felt in his breastpocket, and produced another packet, this time a cylinder the size and shape of a shaving-stick. "Here," said he. "I'd almost forgotten. Don't open this until I come to-morrow—but take it now."

It was so heavy that I well-nigh dropped it. "All ri'!" said I, and he grinned at me through the cab window as the cabman flicked his horse into wakefulness. It was a white packet he had given me, with red seals at either end and along its edge. "If this isn't money," said I, "it's platinum or lead."

I stuck it with elaborate care into my pocket, and with a whirling brain walked home through the Regent Street loiterers and the dark back streets beyond Portland Road. I remember the sensations of that walk very vividly, strange as they were, I was still so far myself that I could notice my strange mental state, and wonder whether this stuff I had had was opium —a drug beyond my experience. It is hard now to describe the peculiarity of my mental strangeness—mental doubling vaguely expresses it. As I was walking up Regent Street I found in my mind a queer persuasion that it was Waterloo Station, and had an odd impulse to get into the Polytechnic as a man might get into a train. I put a knuckle in my eye, and it was

Regent Street. How can I express it? You see a skillful actor looking quietly at you, he pulls a grimace, and lo!—another person. Is it too extravagant if I tell you that it seemed to me as if Regent Street had, for the moment, done that? Then, being persuaded it was Regent Street again, I was oddly muddled about some fantastic reminiscences that cropped up. "Thirty years ago," thought I, "it was here that I quarreled with my brother." Then I burst out laughing, to the astonishment and encouragement of a group of night prowlers. Thirty years ago I did not exist, and never in my life had I boasted a brother. The stuff was surely liquid folly, for the poignant regret for that lost brother still clung to me. Along Portland Road the madness took another turn. I began to recall vanished shops, and to compare the street with what it used to be. Confused, troubled thinking is comprehensible enough after the drink I had taken, but what puzzled me were these curiously vivid phantasm memories that had crept into my mind, and not only the memories that had crept in, but also the memories that had slipped out. I stopped opposite Stevens's, the natural history dealer's, and cudgeled my brains to think what he had to do with me. A 'bus went by, and sounded exactly like the rumbling of a train. I seemed to be dipping into some dark, remote pit for the recollection. "Of course," said I, at last, "he has promised me three frogs to-morrow. Odd I should have forgotten."

Do they still show children dissolving views? In those I remember one view would begin like a faint ghost, and grow and oust another. In just that way it seemed to me that a ghostly set of new sensations was struggling with those of my ordinary self.

I went on through Euston Road to Tottenham Court Road, puzzled, and a little frightened, and scarcely noticed the unusual way I was taking, for commonly I used to cut through the intervening network of back streets. I turned into University Street, to discover that I had forgotten my number. Only by a strong effort did I recall 11A, and even then it seemed to me that it was a thing some forgotten person had told me. I tried to steady my mind by recalling the incidents of the dinner, and for the life of me I could conjure up no picture of my host's face; I saw him only as a shadowy outline, as one might see oneself reflected in a window through which one was looking. In his place, however, I had a curious exterior vision of myself, sitting at a table, flushed, bright-eyed, and talkative.

"I must take this other powder," said I. "This is getting impossible."

I tried the wrong side of the hall for my candle and the matches, and had a doubt of which landing my room might be on. "I'm drunk," I said, "that's certain," and blundered needlessly on the staircase to sustain the proposition.

At the first glance my room seemed unfamiliar. "What rot!" I said, and stared about me. I seemed to bring myself back by the effort, and the odd phantasmal quality passed into the concrete familiar. There was the old glass still, with my notes on the albumens stuck in the corner of the frame, my old everyday suit of clothes pitched about the floor. And yet it was not so real after all. I felt an idiotic persuasion trying to creep into my mind, as it were, that I was in a railway carriage in a train just stopping, that I was peering out of the window at some unknown station. I gripped the bed-rail firmly to reassure myself. "It's clairvoyance, perhaps," I said. "I must write to the Psychical Research Society."

I put the rouleau on my dressing-table, sat on my bed, and began to take off my boots. It was as if the picture of my present sensations was painted over some other picture that was trying to show through. "Curse it!" said I; "my wits are going, or am I in two places at once?" Half-undressed, I tossed the powder into a glass and drank it off. It effervesced, and became a fluorescent amber color. Before I was in bed my mind was already tranquillized. I felt the pillow at my cheek, and thereupon I must have fallen asleep.

I awoke abruptly out of a dream of strange beasts, and found myself lying on my back. Probably everyone knows that dismal, emotional dream from which one escapes, awake indeed, but strangely cowed. There was a curious taste in my mouth, a tired feeling in my limbs, a sense of cutaneous discomfort. I lay with my head motionless on my pillow, expecting that my feeling of strangeness and terror would pass away, and that I should then doze off again to sleep. But instead of that, my uncanny sensations increased. At first I could perceive nothing wrong about me. There was a faint light in the room, so faint that it was the very next thing to darkness, and the furniture stood out in it as vague blots of absolute darkness. I stared with my eyes just over the bedclothes.

It came into my mind that someone had entered the room to rob me of my rouleau of money, but after lying for some moments, breathing regularly to stimulate sleep, I realized this was mere fancy. Nevertheless, the uneasy assurance of something wrong kept fast hold of me. With an effort I raised my head from the pillow, and peered about me at the dark. What it was I could not conceive. I looked at the dim shapes around me, the greater and lesser darknesses that indicated curtains, table, fireplace, bookshelves, and so forth. Then I began to perceive something unfamiliar in the forms of the darkness. Had the bed turned round? Yonder should be the bookshelves, and something shrouded and pallid rose there, something that would not answer to the bookshelves, however I looked at it. It was far too big to be my shirt thrown on a chair.

Overcoming a childish terror, I threw back the bedclothes and thrust my leg out of bed. Instead of coming out of my truckle-bed upon the floor, I found my foot scarcely reached the edge of the mattress. I made another step, as it were, and sat up on the edge of the bed. By the side of my bed should be the candle, and the matches upon the broken chair. I put out my hand and touched—nothing. I waved my hand in the darkness, and it came against some heavy hanging, soft and thick in texture, which gave a rustling noise at my touch. I grasped this and pulled it; it appeared to be a curtain suspended over the head of my bed.

I was now thoroughly awake, and beginning to realize that I was in a strange room. I was puzzled. I tried to recall the overnight circumstances, and I found them now, curiously enough, vivid in my memory; the supper, my reception of the little packages, my wonder whether I was intoxicated, my slow undressing, the coolness to my flushed face of my pillow. I felt a sudden distrust. Was that last night, or the night before? At any rate, this room was strange to me, and I could not imagine how I had got into it. The dim, pallid outline was growing paler, and I perceived it was a window, with the dark shape of an oval toilet-glass against the weak intimation of the dawn that filtered through the blind. I stood up, and was surprised by a curious feeling of weakness and unsteadiness. With trembling hands outstretched, I walked slowly towards the window, getting, nevertheless, a bruise on the knee from a chair by the way. I fumbled round the glass, which was large, with handsome brass sconces, to find the blind-cord. I could not find any. By chance I took hold of the tassel, and with the click of a spring the blind ran up.

I found myself looking out upon a scene that was altogether strange to me. The night was overcast, and through the flocculent gray of the heaped clouds there filtered a faint half-light of dawn. Just at the edge of the sky the cloud-canopy had a blood-red rim. Below, everything was dark and indistinct, dim hills in the distance, a vague mass of buildings running up into pinnacles, trees like spilt ink, and below the window a tracery of black bushes and pale gray paths. It was so unfamiliar that for the moment I thought myself still dreaming. I felt the toilet-table; it appeared to be made of some polished wood, and was rather elaborately furnished—there were little cut-glass bottles and a brush upon it. There was also a queer little object, horseshoe shape it felt, with smooth, hard projections, lying in a saucer. I could find no matches nor candle-stick.

I turned my eyes to the room again. Now the blind was up, faint specters of its furnishing came out of the darkness. There was a huge curtained bed, and the fireplace at its foot had a large white mantel with something of the shimmer of marble.

I leant against the toilet-table, shut my eyes and opened them again, and tried to think. The whole thing was far too real for dreaming. I was inclined to imagine there was still some hiatus in my memory, as a consequence of my draft of that strange liqueur; that I had come into my inheritance perhaps, and suddenly lost my recollection of everything since my good fortune had been announced. Perhaps, if I waited a little, things would be clearer to me again. Yet my dinner with old Elvesham was now singularly vivid and recent. The champagne, the observant waiters, the powder, and the liqueurs—I could have staked my soul it all happened a few hours ago.

And then occurred a thing so trivial and yet so terrible to me that I shiver now to think of that moment. I spoke aloud. I said, "How the devil did I get here?" . . . *And the voice was not my own.*

It was not my own, it was thin, the articulation was slurred, the resonance of my facial bones was different. Then, to reassure myself, I ran one hand over the other, and felt loose folds of skin, the bony laxity of age. "Surely," I said, in that horrible voice that had somehow established itself in my throat, "surely this thing is a dream!" Almost as quickly as if I did it involuntarily, I thrust my fingers into my mouth. My teeth had gone. My finger-tips ran on the flaccid surface of an even row of shriveled gums. I was sick with dismay and disgust.

I felt then a passionate desire to see myself, to realize at once in its full horror the ghastly change that had come upon me. I tottered to the mantel, and felt along it for matches. As I did so, a barking cough sprang up in my throat, and I clutched the thick flannel nightdress I found about me. There were no matches there, and I suddenly realized that my extremities were cold. Sniffing and coughing, whimpering a little, perhaps, I fumbled back to bed. "It is surely a dream," I whispered to myself as I clambered back, "surely a dream." It was a senile repetition. I pulled the bedclothes over my shoulders, over my ears, I thrust my withered hand under the pillow, and determined to compose myself to sleep. Of course it was a dream. In the morning the dream would be over, and I should wake up strong and vigorous again to my youth and studies. I shut my eyes, breathed regularly, and, finding myself wakeful, began to count slowly through the powers of three.

But the thing I desired would not come. I could not get to sleep. And the persuasion of the inexorable reality of the change that had happened to me grew steadily. Presently I found myself with my eyes wide open, the powers of three forgotten, and my skinny fingers upon my shriveled gums. I was, indeed, suddenly and abruptly, an old man. I had in some unaccountable manner fallen through my life and come to old age, in some way I had been cheated of all the best of my life, of love, of struggle, of strength, and hope. I groveled into the pillow and tried to persuade myself that such hallucination was possible. Imperceptibly, steadily, the dawn grew clearer.

At last, despairing of further sleep, I sat up in bed and looked about me. A chill twilight rendered the whole chamber visible. It was spacious and well-furnished, better furnished than any room I had ever slept in before. A candle and matches became dimly visible upon a little pedestal in a recess. I threw back the bedclothes, and, shivering with the rawness of the early morning, albeit it was summer-time, I got out and lit the candle. Then, trembling horribly, so that the extinguisher rattled on its spike—I tottered to the glass and saw—*Elvesham's face!* It was nonetheless horrible because I had already dimly feared as much. He had already seemed physically weak and pitiful to me, but seen now, dressed only in a coarse flannel nightdress, that fell apart and showed the stringy neck, seen now as my own body, I cannot describe its desolate decrepitude. The hollow cheeks, the straggling tail of dirty gray hair, the rheumy bleared eyes, the quivering, shriveled lips, the lower displaying a gleam of the pink interior lining, and those horrible dark gums showing. You who are mind and body together, at your natural years, cannot imagine what this fiendish imprisonment meant to me. To be young and full of the desire and energy of youth, and to be caught, and presently to be crushed in this tottering ruin of a body. . . .

But I wander from the course of my story. For some time I must have been stunned at this change that had come upon me. It was daylight when I did so far gather myself together as to think. In some inexplicable way I had been changed, though how, short of magic, the thing had been done, I could not say. And as I thought, the diabolical ingenuity of Elvesham came home to me. It seemed plain to me that as I found myself in his, so he must be in possession of *my* body, of my strength, that is, and my future. But how to prove it? Then, as I thought, the thing became so incredible, even to me, that my mind reeled, and I had to pinch myself, to feel my toothless gums, to see myself in the glass, and touch the things about me, before I could steady myself to face the facts again. Was all life hallucination? Was I indeed Elvesham, and he me? Had I been dreaming of Eden overnight? Was there any Eden? But if I was Elvesham, I should remember where I was on the previous morning, the name of the town in which I lived, what happened before the dream began. I struggled with my thoughts. I recalled the queer doubleness of my memories overnight. But now my mind was clear. Not the ghost of any memories but those proper to Eden could I raise.

"This way lies insanity!" I cried in my piping voice. I staggered to my feet, dragged my feeble, heavy limbs to the washhand-stand, and plunged my gray head into a basin of cold water. Then, toweling myself, I tried again. It was no good. I felt beyond all question that I was indeed Eden, not Elvesham. But Eden in Elvesham's body!

Had I been a man of any other age, I might have given myself up to my fate as one enchanted. But in these skeptical days miracles do not pass current. Here was some trick of psychology. What a drug and a steady stare could do, a drug and a steady stare, or some similar treatment, could surely undo. Men have lost their memories before. But to exchange memories as one does umbrellas! I laughed. Alas! not a healthy laugh, but a wheezing, senile titter. I could have fancied old Elvesham laughing at my plight, and a gust of petulant anger, unusual to me, swept across my feelings. I began dressing eagerly in the clothes I found lying about on the floor, and only realized when I was dressed that it was an evening suit I had assumed. I opened the wardrobe and found some more ordinary clothes, a pair of plaid trousers, and an old-fashioned dressing-gown. I put a venerable smoking-cap on my venerable head, and, coughing a little from my exertions, tottered out upon the landing.

It was then, perhaps, a quarter to six, and the blinds were closely drawn and the house quite silent. The landing was a spacious one, a broad, richly carpeted staircase went down into the darkness of the hall below, and before me a door ajar showed me a writing-desk, a revolving bookcase, the back of a study chair, and a fine array of bound books, shelf upon shelf.

"My study," I mumbled, and walked across the landing. Then at the sound of my voice a thought struck me, and I went back to the bedroom and put in the set of false teeth. They slipped in with the ease of old habit. "That's better," said I, gnashing them, and so returned to the study.

The drawers of the writing-desk were locked. Its revolving top was also locked. I could see no indications of the keys and there were none in the pocket of my trousers. I shuffled back at once to the bedroom, and went through the dress-suit, and afterwards the pockets of all the garments I could find. I was very eager, and one might have imagined that burglars had been at work, to see my room when I had done. Not only were there no keys to be found, but not a coin, nor a scrap of paper—save only the receipted bill of the overnight dinner.

A curious weariness asserted itself. I sat down and stared at the garments flung here and there, their pockets turned inside out. My first frenzy had already flickered out. Every moment I was beginning to realize the immense intelligence of the plans of my enemy, to see more and more clearly the hopelessness of my position. With an effort I rose and hurried hobbling into the study again. On the staircase was a housemaid pulling up the blinds. She stared, I think, at the expression of my face. I shut the door of the study behind me, and, seizing a poker, began an attack upon the desk. That is how they found me. The cover of the desk was split, the lock smashed, the letters torn out of the pigeon-holes and tossed about the room. In my senile rage I had flung about the pens and other such light stationery, and overturned the ink. Moreover, a large vase upon the mantel had got broken—I do not know how. I could find no check-book, no money, no indications of the slightest use for the recovery of my body.

I was battering madly at the drawers, when the butler, backed by two women-servants, intruded upon me.

That simply is the story of my change. No one will believe my frantic assertions. I am treated as one demented, and even at this moment I am under restraint. But I am sane, absolutely sane, and to prove it I have sat down to write this story minutely as the things happened to me. I appeal to the reader, whether there is any trace of insanity in the style or method of the story he has been reading. I am a young man locked away in an old man's body. But the clear fact is incredible to everyone. Naturally I appear demented to those who will not believe this, naturally I do not know the names of my secretaries, of the doctors who come to see me, of my servants and neighbors, of this town (wherever it is) where I find myself. Naturally I lose myself in my own house, and suffer inconveniences of every sort. Naturally I ask the oddest questions. Naturally I weep and cry out, and have paroxysms of despair. I have no money and no check-book. The bank will not recognize my signature, for I suppose that, allowing for the feeble muscles I now have, my handwriting is still Eden's. These people about me will not let me go to the bank personally. It seems, indeed, that there is no bank in this town, and that I have an account in some part of London. It seems that Elvesham kept the name of his solicitor secret from all his household. I can ascertain nothing. Elvesham was, of course, a profound student of mental science, and all my declarations of the facts of the case merely confirm the theory that my insanity is the outcome of overmuch brooding upon psychology. Dreams of the personal identity indeed! Two days ago I was a healthy youngster, with all life before me; now I am a furious old man, unkempt, and desperate, and miserable, prowling about a great, luxurious, strange house, watched, feared, and avoided as a lunatic by everyone about me. And in London is Elvesham beginning life again in a vigorous body, and with all the accumulated knowledge and wisdom of threescore and ten. He has stolen my life.

What has happened I do not clearly know. In the study are volumes of manuscript notes referring chiefly to the psychology of memory, and parts of what may be either calculations or ciphers in symbols absolutely strange to me. In some passages there are indications that he was also occupied with the philosophy of mathematics. I take it he has transferred the whole of his memories, the accumulation that makes up his personality, from this old withered brain of his to mine, and, similarly, that he has transferred mine to his discarded tenement. Practically, that is, he has changed bodies. But how such a change may be possible is without the range of my philosophy. I have been a materialist for all my thinking life, but here, suddenly, is a clear case of man's detachability from matter.

One desperate experiment I am about to try. I sit writing here before putting the matter to issue. This morning, with the help of a table-knife that I had secreted at breakfast, I succeeded in breaking open a fairly obvious secret drawer in this wrecked writing-desk. I discovered nothing save a little green glass phial containing a white powder. Round the neck of the phial was a label, and thereon was written this one word, "*Release.*" This may be—is most probably—poison. I can understand Elvesham placing poison in my way, and I should be sure that it was his intention so to get rid of the only living witness against him, were it not for this careful concealment. The man has practically solved the problem of immortality. Save for the spite of chance, he will live in my body until it has aged, and then, again, throwing aside, he will assume some other victim's youth and strength. When one remembers his heartlessness, it is terrible to think of the ever-growing experience that . . . How long has he been leaping from body to body? . . . But I tire of writing. The powder appears to be soluble in water. The taste is not unpleasant.

There the narrative found upon Mr. Elvesham's desk ends. His dead body lay between the desk and the chair. The latter had been pushed back, probably by his last convulsions. The story was written in pencil, and in a crazy hand, quite unlike his usual minute characters. There remain only two curious facts to record. Indisputably there was some connection between Eden and Elvesham, since the whole of Elvesham's property was bequeathed to the young man. But he never inherited. When Elvesham committed suicide, Eden was, strangely enough, already dead. Twenty-four hours before, he had been knocked down by a cab and killed instantly, at the crowded crossing at the intersection of Gower Street and Euston Road. So that the only human being who could have thrown light upon this fantastic narrative is beyond the reach of questions. Without further comment, I leave this extraordinary matter to the reader's individual judgment.

THE BLUE CROSS

G. K. CHESTERTON

BETWEEN the silver ribbon of morning and the green glittering ribbon of sea, the boat touched Harwich and let loose a swarm of folk like flies, among whom the man we must follow was by no means conspicuous—nor wished to be. There was nothing notable about him, except a slight contrast between the holiday gaiety of his clothes and the official gravity of his face. His clothes included a slight, pale grey jacket, a white waistcoat, and a silver straw hat with a grey-blue ribbon. His lean face was dark by contrast, and ended in a curt black beard that looked Spanish and suggested an Elizabethan ruff. He was smoking a cigarette with the seriousness of an idler. There was nothing about him to indicate the fact that the grey jacket covered a loaded revolver, that the white waistcoat covered a police card, or that the straw hat covered one of the most powerful intellects in Europe. For this was Valentin himself, the head of the Paris police and the most famous investigator of the world; and he was coming from Brussels to London to make the greatest arrest of the century.

Flambeau was in England. The police of three countries had tracked the great criminal at last from Ghent to Brussels, from Brussels to the Hook of Holland; and it was conjectured that he would take some advantage of the unfamiliarity and confusion of the Eucharistic Congress, then taking place in London. Probably he would travel as some minor clerk or secretary connected with it; but, of course, Valentin could not be certain; nobody could be certain about Flambeau.

It is many years now since this colossus of crime suddenly ceased keeping the world in a turmoil; and when he ceased, as they said after the death of Roland, there was a great quiet upon the earth. But in his best days (I mean, of course, his worst) Flambeau was a figure as statuesque and international as the Kaiser. Almost every morning the daily paper announced that he had escaped the consequences of one extraordinary crime by committing another. He was a Gascon of gigantic stature and bodily daring; and the wildest tales were told of his outbursts of athletic humour; how he turned the *juge d'instruction* upside down and stood him on his head, "to clear his mind"; how he ran down the Rue de Rivoli with a policeman under each arm. It is due to him to say that his fantastic physical strength was generally employed in such bloodless though undignified scenes; his real crimes were chiefly those of ingenious and wholesale robbery. But each of his thefts was almost a new sin, and would make a story by itself. It was he who ran the great Tyrolean Dairy Company in London, with no dairies, no cows, no carts, no milk, but with some thousand subscribers. These he served by the simple operation of moving the little milk cans outside people's doors to the doors of his own customers. It was he who had kept up an unaccountable and close correspondence with a young lady whose whole letter-bag was intercepted, by the extraordinary trick of photographing his messages infinitesimally small upon the slides of a microscope. A sweeping simplicity, however, marked many of his experiments. It is said that he once repainted all the numbers in a street in the dead of night merely to divert one traveller into a trap. It is quite certain that he invented a portable pillar-box, which he put up at corners in quiet suburbs on the chance of strangers dropping postal orders into it. Lastly, he was known to be a startling acrobat; despite his huge figure, he could leap like a grasshopper and melt into the tree-tops like a monkey. Hence the great Valentin, when he set out to find Flambeau, was perfectly aware that his adventures would not end when he had found him.

But how was he to find him? On this the great Valentin's ideas were still in process of settlement.

There was one thing which Flambeau, with all his dexterity of disguise, could not cover, and that was his singular height. If Valentin's quick eye had caught a tall apple-woman, a tall grenadier, or even a tolerably tall duchess, he might have arrested them on the spot. But all along his train there was nobody that could be a disguised Flambeau, any more than a cat could be a disguised giraffe. About the people on the boat he had already satisfied himself; and the people picked up at Harwich or on the journey limited themselves with certainty to six. There was a short railway official travelling up to the terminus, three fairly short market gardeners picked up two stations afterwards, one very short widow lady going up from a small Essex town, and a very short Roman Catholic priest going up from a small Essex village. When it came to the last case, Valentin gave it up and almost laughed. The little priest was so much the essence of those Eastern flats; he had a face as round and dull as a Norfolk dumpling; he had eyes as empty as the North Sea; he had several brown paper parcels, which he was quite incapable of collecting. The Eucharistic Congress had doubtless sucked out of their local stagnation many such creatures, blind and helpless, like moles disinterred. Valentin was a sceptic in the severe style of France, and could have no love for priests. But he could have pity for them, and this one might have provoked pity in anybody. He had a large, shabby umbrella, which constantly fell on the floor. He did not seem to know which was the right end of his return ticket. He explained with a moon-calf simplicity to everybody in the carriage that he had to be careful, because he had something made of real silver "with blue stones" in one of his brown-paper parcels. His quaint blending of Essex flatness with saintly simplicity continuously amused the Frenchman till the priest arrived (somehow) at Tottenham with all his parcels, and came back for his umbrella. When he did the last, Valentin even had the good nature to warn him not to take care of the silver by telling everybody about it. But to whomever he talked, Valentin kept his eye open for someone else; he looked out steadily for anyone, rich or poor, male or female, who was well up to six feet; for Flambeau was four inches above it.

He alighted at Liverpool Street, however, quite conscientiously secure that he had not missed the criminal so far. He then went to Scotland Yard to regularise his position and arrange for help in case of need; he then lit another cigarette and went for a long stroll in the streets of London. As he was walking in the streets and squares beyond Victoria, he paused suddenly and stood. It was a quaint, quiet square, very typical of London, full of an accidental stillness. The tall, flat houses round looked at once prosperous and uninhabited; the square of shrubbery in the centre looked as deserted as a green Pacific islet. One of the four sides was much higher than the rest, like a dais; and the line of this side was broken by one of London's admirable accidents—a restaurant that looked as if it had strayed from Soho. It was an unreasonably attractive object, with dwarf plants in pots and long, striped blinds of lemon yellow and white. It stood specially high above the street, and in the usual patchwork way of London, a flight of steps from the street ran up to meet the front door almost as a fire-escape might run up to a first-floor window. Valentin stood and smoked in front of the yellow-white blinds and considered them long.

The most incredible thing about miracles is that they happen. A few clouds in heaven do come together into the staring shape of one human eye. A tree does stand up in the landscape of a doubtful journey in the exact and elaborate shape of a note of interrogation. I have seen both these things myself within the last few days. Nelson does die in the instant of victory; and a man named Williams does quite accidentally murder a man named Williamson; it sounds like a sort of infanticide. In short, there is in life an element of elfin coincidence which people reckoning on the prosaic may perpetually miss. As it has been well expressed in the paradox of Poe, wisdom should reckon on the unforeseen.

Aristide Valentin was unfathomably French; and the French intelligence is intelligence specially and solely. He was not "a thinking machine"; for that is a brainless phrase of modern fatalism and materialism. A machine only *is* a machine because it cannot think. But he was a thinking man, and a plain man at the same time. All his wonderful successes, that looked like conjuring, had been gained by plodding logic, by clear and commonplace French thought. The French electrify the world not by starting any paradox, they electrify it by carrying out a truism. They carry a truism so far—as in the French Revolution. But exactly because Valentin understood reason, he understood the limits of reason. Only a man who knows nothing of motors talks of motoring without petrol; only a man who knows nothing of reason talks of reasoning without strong, undisputed first principles. Here he had no strong first principles. Flambeau had been missed at Harwich; and if he was in London at all, he might be anything from a tall tramp on Wimbledon Common to a tall toast-master at the Hôtel Métropole. In such a naked state of nescience, Valentin had a view and a method of his own.

In such cases he reckoned on the unforeseen. In such cases, when he could not follow the train of the reasonable, he coldly and carefully followed the train of the unreasonable. Instead of going to the right places—banks, police stations, rendezvous—he systematically went to the wrong places; knocked at every empty house, turned down every *cul de sac*, went up every lane blocked with rubbish, went round every crescent that led him uselessly out of the way. He defended this crazy course quite logically. He said that if one had a clue this was the worst way; but if one had no clue at all it was the best, because there was just the chance that any oddity that caught the eye of the pursuer might be the same that had caught the eye of the pursued. Somewhere a man must begin, and it had better be just where another man might stop. Something about that flight of steps up to the shop, something about the quietude and quaintness of the restaurant, roused all the detective's rare romantic fancy and made him resolve to strike at random. He went up the steps, and sitting down at a table by the window, asked for a cup of black coffee.

It was half-way through the morning, and he had not breakfasted; the slight litter of other breakfasts stood about on the table to remind him of his hunger; and adding a poached egg to his order, he proceeded musingly to shake some white sugar into his coffee, thinking all the time about Flambeau. He remembered how Flambeau had escaped, once by a pair of nail scissors, and once by a house on fire; once by having to pay for an unstamped letter, and once by getting people to look through a telescope at a comet that might destroy the world. He thought his detective brain as good as the criminal's, which was true. But he fully realised the disadvantage. "The criminal is the creative artist; the detective only the critic," he said with a sour smile, and lifted his coffee cup to his lips slowly, and put it down very quickly. He had put salt in it.

He looked at the vessel from which the silvery powder had come; it was certainly a sugar-basin; as unmistakably meant for sugar as a champagne-bottle for champagne. He wondered why they should keep salt in it. He looked to see if there were any more orthodox vessels. Yes; there were two salt-cellars quite full. Perhaps there was some speciality in the condiment in the salt-cellars. He tasted it; it was sugar. Then he looked round at the restaurant with a refreshed air of interest, to see if there were any other traces of that singular artistic taste which puts the sugar in the salt-cellars and the salt in the sugar-basin. Except for an odd splash of some dark fluid on one of the white-papered walls, the whole place appeared neat, cheerful and ordinary. He rang the bell for the waiter.

When that official hurried up, fuzzy-haired and somewhat blear-eyed at that early hour, the detective (who was not without an appreciation of the simpler forms of humour) asked him to taste the sugar and see if it was up to the high reputation of the hotel. The result was that the waiter yawned suddenly and woke up.

"Do you play this delicate joke on your customers every morning?" inquired Valentin. "Does changing the salt and sugar never pall on you as a jest?"

The waiter, when this irony grew clearer, stammeringly assured him that the establishment had certainly no such intention; it must be a most curious mistake. He picked up the sugar-basin and looked at it; he picked up the salt-cellar and looked at that, his face growing more and more bewildered. At last he abruptly excused himself, and hurrying away, returned in a few seconds with the proprietor. The proprietor also examined the sugar-basin and then the salt-cellar; the proprietor also looked bewildered.

Suddenly the waiter seemed to grow inarticulate with a rush of words. "I zink," he stuttered eagerly, "I zink it is those two clergymen."

"What two clergymen?"

"The two clergymen," said the waiter, "that threw soup at the wall."

"Threw soup at the wall?" repeated Valentin, feeling sure this must be some singular Italian metaphor.

"Yes, yes," said the attendant excitedly, and pointed at the dark splash on the white paper; "threw it over there on the wall."

Valentin looked his query at the proprietor, who came to his rescue with fuller reports.

"Yes, sir," he said, "it's quite true, though I don't suppose it has anything to do with the sugar and salt. Two clergymen came in and drank soup here very early, as soon as the shutters were taken down. They were both very quiet, respectable people; one of them paid the bill and went out; the other, who seemed a slower coach altogether, was some minutes longer getting his things together. But he went at last. Only, the instant before he stepped into the street he deliberately picked up his cup, which he had only half emptied, and threw the soup slap on the wall. I was in the back room myself, and so was the waiter; so I could only rush out in time to find the wall splashed and the shop empty. It don't do any particular damage, but it was confounded cheek; and I tried to catch the men in the street. They were too far off though; I only noticed they went round the next corner into Carstairs Street."

The detective was on his feet, hat settled and stick in hand. He had already decided that in the universal darkness of his mind he could only follow the first odd finger that pointed; and this finger was odd enough. Paying his bill and clashing the glass doors behind him, he was soon swinging round into the other street.

It was fortunate that even in such fevered moments his eye was cool and quick. Something in a shop-front went by him like a mere flash; yet he went back to look at it. The shop was a popular greengrocer and fruiterer's, an array of goods set out in the open air and plainly ticketed with their names and prices. In the two most prominent compartments were two heaps, of oranges and of nuts respectively. On the heap of nuts lay a scrap of cardboard, on which was written in bold, blue chalk, "Best tangerine oranges, two a penny." On the oranges was the equally clear and exact description, "Finest Brazil nuts, 4d. a lb." M. Valentin looked at these two placards and fancied he had met this highly subtle from of humour before, and that somewhat recently. He drew the attention of the red-faced fruiterer, who was looking rather sullenly up and down the street, to this inaccuracy in his advertisements. The fruiterer said nothing, but sharply put each card into its proper place. The detective, leaning elegantly on his walking-cane, continued to scrutinise the shop. At last he said, "Pray excuse my apparent irrelevance, my good sir, but I should like to ask you a question in experimental psychology and the association of ideas."

The red-faced shopman regarded him with an eye of menace; but he continued gaily, swinging his cane, "Why," he pursued, "why are two tickets wrongly placed in a greengrocer's shop like a shovel hat that has come to London for a holiday? Or, in case I do not make myself clear, what is the mystical association which connects the idea of nuts marked as oranges with the idea of two clergymen, one tall and the other short?"

The eyes of the tradesman stood out of his head like a snail's; he really seemed for an instant likely to fling himself upon the stranger. At last he stammered angrily: "I don't know what you 'ave to do with it, but if you're one of their friends, you can tell 'em from me that I'll knock their silly 'eads off, parsons or no parsons, if they upset my apples again."

"Indeed?" asked the detective, with great sympathy. "Did they upset your apples?"

"One of 'em did," said the heated shopman; "rolled 'em all over the street. I'd 'ave caught the fool but for havin' to pick 'em up."

"Which way did these parsons go?" asked Valentin.

"Up that second road on the left-hand side, and then across the square," said the other promptly.

"Thanks," replied Valentin, and vanished like a fairy. On the other side of the second square he found a policeman, and said: "This is urgent, constable; have you seen two clergymen in shovel hats?"

The policeman began to chuckle heavily. "I 'ave, sir; and if you arst me, one of 'em was drunk. He stood in the middle of the road that bewildered that–"

"Which way did they go?" snapped Valentin.

"They took one of them yellow buses over there," answered the man; "them that go to Hampstead."

Valentin produced his official card and said very rapidly: "Call up two of your men to come with me in pursuit," and crossed the road with such contagious energy that the ponderous policeman was moved to almost agile obedience. In a minute and a half the French detective was joined on the opposite pavement by an inspector and a man in plain clothes.

"Well, sir," began the former, with smiling importance, "and what may–?"

Valentin pointed suddenly with his cane. "I'll tell you on the top of that omnibus," he said, and was darting and dodging across the tangle of the traffic. When all three sank panting on the top seats of the yellow vehicle, the inspector said: "We could go four times as quick in a taxi."

"Quite true," replied their leader placidly, "if we only had an idea of where we were going."

"Well, where *are* you going?" asked the other, staring.

Valentin smoked frowningly for a few seconds; then, removing his cigarette, he said: "If you *know* what a man's doing, get in front of him; but if you want to guess what he's doing, keep behind him. Stray when he strays; stop when he stops; travel as slowly as he. Then you may see what he saw and may act as he acted. All we can do is to keep our eyes skinned for a queer thing."

"What sort of queer thing do you mean?" asked the inspector.

"Any sort of queer thing," answered Valentin, and relapsed into obstinate silence.

The yellow omnibus crawled up the northern roads for what seemed like hours on end; the great detective would not explain further, and perhaps his assistants felt a silent and growing doubt of his errand. Perhaps, also, they felt a silent and growing desire for lunch, for the hours crept long past the normal luncheon hour, and the long roads of the North London suburbs seemed to shoot out into length after length like an infernal telescope. It was one of those journeys on which a man perpetually feels that now at last he must have come to the end of the universe, and then finds he has only come to the beginning of Tufnell Park. London died away in draggled taverns and dreary scrubs, and then was unaccountably born again in blazing high streets and blatant hotels. It was like passing through thirteen separate vulgar cities all just touching each other. But though the winter twilight was already threatening the road ahead of them, the Parisian detective still sat silent and watchful, eyeing the frontage of the streets that slid by on either side. By the time they had left Camden Town behind, the policemen were nearly asleep; at least, they gave something like a jump as Valentin leapt erect, struck a hand on each man's shoulder, and shouted to the driver to stop.

They tumbled down the steps into the road without realising why they had been dislodged; when they looked round for enlightenment they found Valentin triumphantly pointing his finger towards a window on the left side of the road. It was a large window, forming part of the long façade of a gilt and palatial public-house; it was the part reserved for respectable dining, and labelled "Restaurant." This window, like all the rest along the frontage of the hotel, was of frosted and figured glass; but in the middle of it was a big, black smash, like a star in the ice.

"Our cue at last," cried Valentin, waving his stick; "the place with the broken window."

"What window? What cue?" asked his principal assistant. "Why, what proof is there that this has anything to do with them?"

Valentin almost broke his bamboo stick with rage.

"Proof!" he cried. "Good God! the man is looking for proof! Why, of course, the chances are twenty to one that it has *nothing* to do with them. But what else can we do? Don't you see we must either follow one wild possibility or else go home to bed?" He banged his way into the restaurant, followed by his companions, and they were soon seated at a late luncheon at a little table, and looked at the star of smashed glass from the inside. Not that it was very informative to them even then.

"Got your window broken, I see," said Valentin to the waiter as he paid the bill.

"Yes, sir," answered the attendant, bending busily over the change, to which Valentin silently added an enormous tip. The waiter straightened himself with mild but unmistakable animation.

"Ah, yes, sir," he said. "Very odd thing, that, sir."

"Indeed? Tell us about it," said the detective with careless curiosity.

"Well, two gents in black came in," said the waiter; "two of those foreign parsons that are running about. They had a cheap and quiet little lunch, and one of them paid for it and went out. The other was just going out to join him when I looked at my change again and found he'd paid me more than three times too much. 'Here,' I says to the chap who was nearly out of the door, 'you've paid too much.' 'Oh,' he says, very cool, 'have we?' 'Yes,' I says, and picks up the bill to show him. Well, that was a knock-out."

"What do you mean?" asked his interlocutor.

"Well, I'd have sworn on seven Bibles that I'd put 4s. on that bill. But now I saw I'd put 14s., as plain as paint."

"Well?" cried Valentin, moving slowly, but with burning eyes, "and then?"

"The parson at the door he says all serene, 'Sorry to confuse your accounts, but it'll pay for the window.' 'What window?' I says. 'The one I'm going to break,' he says, and smashed that blessed pane with his umbrella."

All three inquirers made an exclamation; and the inspector said under his breath, "Are we after escaped lunatics?" The waiter went on with some relish for the ridiculous story:

"I was so knocked silly for a second, I couldn't do anything. The man marched out of the place and joined his friend just round the corner. Then they went so quick up Bullock Street that I couldn't catch them, though I ran round the bars to do it."

"Bullock Street," said the detective, and shot up that thoroughfare as quickly as the strange couple he pursued.

Their journey now took them through bare brick ways like tunnels; streets with few lights and even with few windows; streets that seemed built out of the blank backs of everything and everywhere. Dusk was deepening, and it was not easy even for the London policemen to guess in what exact direction they were treading. The inspector, however, was pretty certain that they would eventually strike some part of Hampstead Heath. Abruptly one bulging gas-lit window broke the blue twilight like a bull's-eye lantern; and Valentin stopped an instant before a little garish sweetstuff shop. After an instant's hesitation he went in; he stood amid the gaudy colours of the confectionery with entire gravity and bought thirteen chocolate cigars with a certain care. He was clearly preparing an opening; but he did not need one.

An angular, elderly young woman in the shop had regarded his elegant appearance with a merely automatic inquiry; but when she saw the door behind him blocked with the blue uniform of the inspector, her eyes seemed to wake up.

"Oh," she said, "if you've come about that parcel, I've sent it off already."

"Parcel!" repeated Valentin; and it was his turn to look inquiring.

"I mean the parcel the gentleman left—the clergyman gentleman."

"For goodness' sake," said Valentin, leaning forward with his first real confession of eagerness, "for Heaven's sake tell us what happened exactly."

"Well," said the woman a little doubtfully, "the clergymen came in about half an hour ago and bought some peppermints and talked a bit, and then went off towards the Heath. But a second after, one of them runs back into the shop and says, 'Have I left a parcel?' Well, I looked everywhere and couldn't see one; so he says, 'Never mind; but if it should turn up, please post it to this address,' and he left me the address and a shilling for my trouble. And sure enough, though I thought I'd looked everywhere, I found he'd left a brown paper parcel, so I posted it to the place he said. I can't remember the address now; it was somewhere in Westminster. But as the thing seemed so important, I thought perhaps the police had come about it."

"So they have," said Valentin shortly. "Is Hampstead Heath near here?"

"Straight on for fifteen minutes," said the woman, "and you'll come right out on the open." Valentin sprang out of the shop and began to run. The other detectives followed him at a reluctant trot.

The street they threaded was so narrow and shut in by shadows that when they came out unexpectedly into the void common and vast sky they were startled to find the evening still so light and clear. A perfect dome of peacock-green sank into gold amid the blackening trees and the dark violet distances. The glowing green tint was just deep enough to pick out in points of crystal one or two stars. All that was left of the daylight lay in a golden glitter across the edge of Hampstead and that popular hollow which is called the Vale of Health. The holiday makers who roam this region had not wholly dispersed; a few couples sat shapelessly on benches; and here and there a distant girl still shrieked in one of the swings. The glory of heaven deepened and darkened around the sublime vulgarity of man; and standing on the slope and looking across the valley, Valentin beheld the thing which he sought.

Among the black and breaking groups in that distance was one especially black which did not break—a group of two figures clerically clad. Though they seemed as small as insects, Valentin could see that one of them was much smaller than the other. Though the other had a student's stoop and an inconspicuous manner, he could see that the man was well over six feet high. He shut his teeth and went forward, whirling his stick impatiently. By the time he had substantially diminished the distance and magnified the two black figures as in a vast microscope, he had perceived something else; something which startled him, and yet which he had somehow expected. Whoever was the tall priest, there could be no doubt about the identity of the short one. It was his friend of the Harwich train, the stumpy little *curé* of Essex whom he had warned about his brown paper parcels.

Now, so far as this went, everything fitted in finally and rationally enough. Valentin had learned by his inquiries that morning that a Father Brown from Essex was bringing up a silver cross with sapphires, a relic of considerable value, to show some of the foreign priests at the congress. This undoubtedly was the "silver with blue stones"; and Father Brown undoubtedly was the little greenhorn in the train. Now there was nothing wonderful about the fact that what Valentin had found out Flambeau had also found out; Flambeau found out everything. Also there was nothing wonderful in the fact that when Flambeau heard of a sapphire cross he should try to steal it; that was the most natural thing in all natural history. And most certainly there was nothing wonderful about the fact that Flambeau should have it all his own way with such a silly sheep as the man with the umbrella and the parcels. He was the sort of man whom anybody could lead on a string to the North Pole; it was not surprising that an actor like Flambeau, dressed as another priest, could lead him to Hampstead Heath. So far the crime seemed clear enough; and while the detective pitied the priest for his helplessness, he almost despised Flambeau for condescending to so gullible a victim. But when Valentin thought of all that had happened in between, of all that had led him to his triumph, he racked his brains for the smallest rhyme or reason in it. What had the stealing of a blue-and-silver cross from a priest from Essex to do with chucking soup at wall paper? What had it to do with calling nuts oranges, or with paying for windows first and breaking them afterwards? He had come to the end of his chase; yet somehow he had missed the middle of it. When he failed (which was seldom), he had usually grasped the clue, but nevertheless missed the criminal. Here he had grasped the criminal, but still he could not grasp the clue.

The two figures that they followed were crawling like black flies across the huge green contour of a hill. They were evidently sunk in conversation, and perhaps did not notice where they were going; but they were certainly going to the wilder and more silent heights of the Heath. As their pursuers gained on them, the latter had to use the undignified attitudes of the deer-stalker, to crouch behind clumps of trees and even to crawl prostrate in deep grass. By these ungainly ingenuities the hunters even came close enough to the quarry to hear the murmur of the discussion, but no word could be distinguished except the word "reason" recurring frequently in a high and almost childish voice. Once over an abrupt dip of land and a dense tangle of thickets, the detectives actually lost the two figures they were following. They did not find the trail again for an agonising ten minutes, and then it led round the brow of a great dome of hill overlooking an amphitheatre of rich and desolate sunset scenery.

Under a tree in this commanding yet neglected spot was an old ramshackle wooden seat. On this seat sat the two priests still in serious speech together. The gorgeous green and gold still clung to the darkening horizon; but the dome above was turning slowly from peacock-green to peacock-blue, and the stars detached themselves more and more like solid jewels. Mutely motioning to his followers, Valentin contrived to creep up behind the big branching tree, and, standing there in deathly silence, heard the words of the strange priests for the first time.

After he had listened for a minute and a half, he was gripped by a devilish doubt. Perhaps he had dragged the two English policemen to the wastes of a nocturnal heath on an errand no saner than seeking figs on its thistles. For the two priests were talking exactly like priests, piously, with learning and leisure, about the most aerial enigmas of theology. The little Essex priest spoke the more simply, with his round face turned to the strengthening stars; the other talked with his head bowed, as if he were not even worthy to look at them. But no more innocently clerical conversation could have been heard in any white Italian cloister or black Spanish cathedral.

The first he heard was the tail of one of Father Brown's sentences, which ended: ". . . what they really meant in the Middle Ages by the heavens being incorruptible."

The taller priest nodded his bowed head and said:

"Ah, yes, these modern infidels appeal to their reason; but who can look at those millions of worlds and not feel that there may well be wonderful universes above us where reason is utterly unreasonable?"

"No," said the other priest; "reason is always reasonable, even in the last limbo, in the lost borderland of things. I know that people charge the Church with lowering reason, but it is just the other way. Alone on earth, the Church makes reason really supreme. Alone on earth, the Church affirms that God himself is bound by reason."

The other priest raised his austere face to the spangled sky and said:

"Yet who knows if in that infinite universe—?"

"Only infinite physically," said the little priest, turning sharply in his seat, "not infinite in the sense of escaping from the laws of truth."

Valentin behind his tree was tearing his fingernails with silent fury. He seemed almost to hear the sniggers of the English detectives whom he had brought so far on a fantastic guess only to listen to the metaphysical gossip of two mild old parsons. In his impatience he lost the equally elaborate answer of the tall cleric, and when he listened again it was again Father Brown who was speaking:

"Reason and justice grip the remotest and the loneliest star. Look at those stars. Don't they look as if they were single diamonds and sapphires? Well, you can imagine any mad botany or geology you please.

Think of forests of adamant with leaves of brilliants. Think the moon is a blue moon, a single elephantine sapphire. But don't fancy that all that frantic astronomy would make the smallest difference to the reason and justice of conduct. On plains of opal, under cliffs cut out of pearl, you would still find a notice-board, 'Thou shalt not steal.'"

Valentin was just in the act of rising from his rigid and crouching attitude and creeping away as softly as might be, felled by the one great folly of his life. But something in the very silence of the tall priest made him stop until the latter spoke. When at last he did speak, he said simply, his head bowed and his hands on his knees:

"Well, I think that other worlds may perhaps rise higher than our reason. The mystery of heaven is unfathomable, and I for one can only bow my head."

Then, with brow yet bent and without changing by the faintest shade his attitude or voice, he added:

"Just hand over that sapphire cross of yours, will you? We're all alone here, and I could pull you to pieces like a straw doll."

The utterly unaltered voice and attitude added a strange violence to that shocking change of speech. But the guarder of the relic only seemed to turn his head by the smallest section of the compass. He seemed still to have a somewhat foolish face turned to the stars. Perhaps he had not understood. Or, perhaps, he had understood and sat rigid with terror.

"Yes," said the tall priest, in the same low voice and in the same still posture, "yes, I am Flambeau."

Then, after a pause, he said:

"Come, will you give me that cross?"

"No," said the other, and the monosyllable had an odd sound.

Flambeau suddenly flung off all his pontifical pretensions. The great robber leaned back in his seat and laughed low but long.

"No," he cried, "you won't give it me, you proud prelate. You won't give it me, you little celibate simpleton. Shall I tell you why you won't give it me? Because I've got it already in my own breast-pocket."

The small man from Essex turned what seemed to be a dazed face in the dusk, and said, with the timid eagerness of "The Private Secretary":

"Are—are you sure?"

Flambeau yelled with delight.

"Really, you're as good as a three-act farce," he cried. "Yes, you turnip, I am quite sure. I had the sense to make a duplicate of the right parcel, and now, my friend, you've got the duplicate and I've got the jewels. An old dodge, Father Brown—a very old dodge."

"Yes," said Father Brown, and passed his hand through his hair with the same strange vagueness of manner. "Yes, I've heard of it before."

The colossus of crime leaned over to the little rustic priest with a sort of sudden interest.

"*You* have heard of it?" he asked. "Where have *you* heard of it?"

"Well, I mustn't tell you his name, of course," said the little man simply. "He was a penitent, you know. He had lived prosperously for about twenty years entirely on duplicate brown paper parcels. And so, you see, when I began to suspect you, I thought of this poor chap's way of doing it at once."

"Began to suspect me?" repeated the outlaw with increased intensity. "Did you really have the gumption to suspect me just because I brought you up to this bare part of the heath?"

"No, no," said Brown with an air of apology. "You see, I suspected you when we first met. It's that little bulge up the sleeve where you people have the spiked bracelet."

"How in Tartarus," cried Flambeau, "did you ever hear of the spiked bracelet?"

"Oh, one's little flock, you know!" said Father Brown, arching his eyebrows rather blankly. "When I was a curate in Hartlepool, there were three of them with spiked bracelets. So, as I suspected you from the first, don't you see, I made sure that the cross should go safe, anyhow. I'm afraid I watched you, you know. So at last I saw you change the parcels. Then, don't you see, I changed them back again. And then I left the right one behind."

"Left it behind?" repeated Flambeau, and for the first time there was another note in his voice beside his triumph.

"Well, it was like this," said the little priest, speaking in the same unaffected way. "I went back to that sweet-shop and asked if I'd left a parcel, and gave them a particular address if it turned up. Well, I knew I hadn't; but when I went away again I did. So, instead of running after me with that valuable parcel, they have sent it flying to a friend of mine in Westminster." Then he added rather sadly: "I learnt that, too, from a poor fellow in Hartlepool. He used to do it with handbags he stole at railway stations, but he's in a monastery now. Oh, one gets to know, you know," he added, rubbing his head again with the same sort of desperate apology. "We can't help being priests. People come and tell us these things."

Flambeau tore a brown-paper parcel out of his inner pocket and rent it in pieces. There was nothing but paper and sticks of lead inside it. He sprang to his feet with a gigantic gesture, and cried:

"I don't believe you. I don't believe a bumpkin like you could manage all that. I believe you've still got the stuff on you, and if you don't give it up—why, we're all alone, and I'll take it by force!"

"No," said Father Brown simply, and stood up also, "you won't take it by force. First, because I really haven't still got it. And, second, because we are not alone."

Flambeau stopped in his stride forward.

"Behind that tree," said Father Brown, pointing, "are two strong policemen and the greatest detective alive. How did they come here, do you ask? Why, I brought them, of course! How did I do it? Why, I'll tell you if you like! Lord bless you, we have to know twenty such things when we work among the criminal classes! Well, I wasn't sure you were a thief, and it would never do to make a scandal against one of our own clergy. So I just tested you to see if anything would make you show yourself. A man generally makes a small scene if he finds salt in his coffee; if he doesn't, he has some reason for keeping quiet. I changed the salt and sugar, and *you* kept quiet. A man generally objects if his bill is three times too big. If he pays it, he has some motive for passing unnoticed. I altered your bill, and *you* paid it."

The world seemed waiting for Flambeau to leap like a tiger. But he was held back as by a spell; he was stunned with the utmost curiosity.

"Well," went on Father Brown, with lumbering lucidity, "as you wouldn't leave any tracks for the police, of course somebody had to. At every place we went to, I took care to do something that would get us talked about for the rest of the day. I didn't do much harm—a splashed wall, spilt apples, a broken window; but I saved the cross, as the cross will always be saved. It is at Westminster by now. I rather wonder you didn't stop it with the Donkey's Whistle."

"With the what?" asked Flambeau.

"I'm glad you've never heard of it," said the priest, making a face. "It's a foul thing. I'm sure you're too good a man for a Whistler. I couldn't have countered it even with the Spots myself; I'm not strong enough in the legs."

"What on earth are you talking about?" asked the other.

"Well, I did think you'd know the Spots," said Father Brown, agreeably surprised. "Oh, you can't have gone so very wrong yet!"

"How in blazes do you know all these horrors?" cried Flambeau.

The shadow of a smile crossed the round, simple face of his clerical opponent.

"Oh, by being a celibate simpleton, I suppose," he said. "Has it never struck you that a man who does next to nothing but hear men's real sins is not likely to be wholly unaware of human evil? But, as a matter of fact, another part of my trade, too, made me sure you weren't a priest."

"What?" asked the thief, almost gaping.

"You attacked reason," said Father Brown. "It's bad theology."

And even as he turned away to collect his property, the three policemen came out from under the twilight trees. Flambeau was an artist and a sportsman. He stepped back and swept Valentin a great bow.

"Do not bow to me, *mon ami*," said Valentin with silver clearness. "Let us both bow to our master."

And they both stood an instant uncovered while the little Essex priest blinked about for his umbrella.

A Novel
PORTRAIT OF JENNIE

ROBERT NATHAN

PORTRAIT OF JENNIE

ROBERT NATHAN

CHAPTER I

THERE is such a thing as hunger for more than food, and that was the hunger I fed on. I was poor, my work unknown; often without meals; cold, too, in winter in my little studio on the West Side. But that was the least of it.

When I talk about trouble, I am not talking about cold and hunger. There is another kind of suffering for the artist which is worse than anything a winter, or poverty, can do; it is more like a winter of the mind, in which the life of his genius, the living sap of his work, seems frozen and motionless, caught—perhaps forever—in a season of death; and who knows if spring will ever come again to set it free?

It was not only that I could not sell my work—that has happened to good men, even to great men, before—but that I couldn't seem to get through, myself, to the things that were bottled up inside me. No matter what I did, figure, landscape, still-life, it all seemed different from what I meant—from what I knew, as surely as my name was Eben Adams, was the thing I really wanted to say in the world; to tell people about, somehow, through my painting.

I cannot tell you what that period was like; because the worst part of it was an anxiety it is very hard to describe. I suppose most artists go through something of the sort; sooner or later it is no longer enough for them just to live—to paint, and have enough, or nearly enough, to eat. Sooner or later God asks His question: are you for me, or against me? And the artist must have some answer, or feel his heart break for what he cannot say.

One evening in the winter of 1938 I was walking home through the Park. I was a good deal younger then; I carried a portfolio of drawings under my arm, and I walked slowly because I was tired. The damp mist of the winter evening drifted around me; it drifted down across the sheep meadow, and through the Mall which was empty and quiet at that hour. The children who usually played there had gone home, leaving the bare, dark trees and the long rows of benches wet and spidery with mist. I kept shifting the portfolio from one arm to the other; it was heavy and clumsy, but I had no money to ride.

I had been trying all day to sell some of my pictures. There is a sort of desperation which takes hold of a man after a while, a dreadful feeling of the world's indifference, not only to his hunger or his pain, but to the very life which is in him. Each day the courage with which I started out was a little less; by now it had all run out, like sand from a glass.

That night I was at the bottom, without money or friends, cold, hungry, and tired, without hope, not knowing where to turn. I think I was a little lightheaded, from not having had enough to eat. I crossed the Drive, and started down the long, deserted corridor of the Mall.

In front of me, the spaced, even rows of lights shone yellow in the shadowy air; I heard the crisp sound of my own footsteps on the pavement; and behind me the hiss and whisper of traffic turned homeward at the end of day. The city sounds were muted and far away, they seemed to come from another time, from somewhere in the past, like the sound of summer, like bees in a meadow long ago. I walked on, as though through the quiet arches of a dream. My body seemed light, without weight, made up of evening air.

The little girl playing by herself in the middle of the Mall made no sound either. She was playing hopscotch; she went up in the air with her legs apart, and came down again as silent as dandelion seed.

I stopped and watched her, for I was surprised to see her there, all alone. No other little children were in sight, only the mist and the long, even rows of lights stretching away to the terrace and the lake. I looked around for her nurse, but the benches were empty. "It's getting pretty dark," I said. "Oughtn't you to go home?"

I don't believe it sounded unfriendly. The child marked her next jump, and got ready; but first she looked at me sideways over her shoulder. "Is it late?" she asked. "I don't know time very well."

"Yes," I said; "it's late."

"Well," she said, "I don't have to go home yet." And she added in a matter of fact tone,

"Nobody's ready for me."

I turned away; after all, I thought, what business is it of mine? She straightened up, and pushed the dark hair back from her face, under the brim of her bonnet. Her arms were thin, they made the sharp, bird-like motions of a child. "I'll walk a ways with you, if you don't mind," she said. "I guess it's a little lonesome here all by myself."

I said I didn't mind, and we went up the Mall together, between the

empty benches. I kept looking around for someone she might belong to, but there was nobody. "Are you all alone?" I asked after a while. "Isn't anybody with you?"

She came to some chalk marks left there by another child, and stopped to jump over them. "No," she said. "Who would there be?

"Anyway," she added a moment later, "you're with me."

And for some reason that seemed to her quite enough. She wanted to know what I had in the portfolio. When I told her, she nodded her head in a satisfied way. "I knew they were pictures," she said. I asked her how she knew.

"Oh, I just knew," she said.

The damp mist drifted along beside us, cold, with the smell of winter in it. It was my not having eaten all day that made everything seem so queer, I thought, walking up the Mall with a little girl no higher than my elbow. I wondered if I could be arrested for what I was doing; I don't even know her name, I thought, in case they ask me.

She said nothing for a while; she seemed to be counting the benches. But she must have known what I was thinking, for as we passed the fifth bench, she told me her name without my asking. "It's Jennie," she said; "just so's you'll know."

"Jennie," I repeated, a little stupidly. "Jennie what?"

"Jennie Appleton," she said. She went on to say that she lived with her parents in a hotel, but that she didn't see them very often. "Father and mother are actors and actresses," she declared. "They're at the Hammerstein Music Hall. They do juggling on a rope."

She gave a sort of skip; and then she came over to me, and put her hand in mine. "They're not home very much," she said; "on account of being in the profession."

But something has begun to worry me. Wait a minute, I said to myself, there's something wrong here. Wait, I thought . . . wait a minute . . . and then I remembered. Of course—that was it: the Hammerstein Music Hall had been torn down years ago, when I was a boy.

"Well," I said; "well . . ."

Her hand in mine was real enough, firm and warm; she wasn't a ghost, and I wasn't dreaming. "I go to school," she said, "but only in the mornings. I'm too little to go all day yet."

I heard her give a child's sigh, full of a child's trouble, light as air. "I don't have very exciting lessons," she remarked. "They're mostly two and two is four, and things like that. When I'm bigger, I'm going to learn geography and history, and about the Kaiser. He's the King of Germany."

"He was," I said gravely. "But that was long ago."

"I think you're wrong," said Jennie. She walked a little away from me, smiling to herself about something. "Cecily Jones is in my class," she said. "I can fight her. I'm stronger than she is, and I can fight her good.

"She's just a little girl."

She gave a skip. "It's fun having somebody to play with," she said.

I looked down at her: a child dressed in old fashioned clothes, a coat and gaiters and a bonnet. Who was it painted children like that? Henri? Brush? One of the old fellows. . . . There was a picture in the Museum, somebody's daughter, it hung over the stairs as you went up. But children always dressed the same. She didn't look to me as though she played with other children very often.

I said yes, I supposed it was fun.

"Don't you have anyone to play with?" she asked.

"No," I said.

I had an idea that she was sorry for me, and at the same time glad that I had nobody else but her to play with. It made me smile; a child's games are so real, I thought, for children believe everything. We came to an interesting crack, and she hopped along on one foot until she got to the end of it. "I know a song," she said. "Would you like to hear it?"

And without waiting for me to answer, looking up at me from under the brim of her bonnet, she sang in a clear, tuneless voice:

> Where I come from
> Nobody knows;
> And where I'm going
> Everything goes.

The wind blows,
The sea flows—
And nobody knows.

The song caught me off my guard, it was so unlike what I had expected. I don't know what I had been waiting for—some nursery rhyme, perhaps, or a popular tune of the day; little girls whose parents were actors and actresses sometimes sang about love. "Who taught you that?" I asked in surprise.

But she only shook her head, and stood there looking at me. "Nobody taught me," she said. "It's just a song."

We had come to the great circle at the end of the Mall, and my path led away to the left, across the Drive again, and out the west gate. The winter evening wrapped us round in mist, in solitude and silence, the wet trees stood up dark and bare around us, and the distant city sounded its notes, falling and fading in the air. "Well, goodbye," I said; "I have to go now."

I held out my hand to her, and she took it gravely. "Do you know the game I like to play best?" she asked. "No," I said.

"It's a wishing game."

I asked her what she wished for most.

"I wish you'd wait for me to grow up," she said. "But you won't, I guess."

A moment later she had turned and was walking quietly back down the Mall. I stood there looking after her; after a while I couldn't see her any more.

When I got home I heated a can of soup on the gas burner, and cut myself a slice of bread, and some cheese. It was heavy in my stomach, but it made me feel better. Then I took my paintings out of the portfolio, and set them up on the floor, against the wall, and looked at them. They were all New England scenes: Cape Cod, churches, boats, old houses . . . water colors, mostly, with a few drawings among them. But none of the city . . . funny that I had never thought of that before . . .

I went over to the window, and looked out. There wasn't much to see, a line of roofs and chimneys, dark and indistinct, a few lighted windows, and in the north some taller buildings dim against the sky. And over all, the damp, cold air of winter, the raw, heavy air of the coast. A tug boat hooted in the bay; the sad, mysterious sound passed over the roofs, and floated above the city's restless grumble like a sea bird over a river. I wondered why I had never wanted to do any pictures of the city . . . I could do some pastels of the river, I thought, if I could get the cold tone of the sky. And that line of buildings south of the park, in the evening —if I could get that dim blue mountain look they have. But all the time, in the back of my mind, I was thinking about the child I had met in the Mall. Where I am going, nobody knows; The wind blows, And nobody knows. It was a strange little song, its very tunelessness made it hard to forget, the tunelessness was so much a part of it.

I thought of the last thing she had said to me, before she turned and walked away. But people couldn't wait for other people to grow up; they grew up together, side by side, and pace by pace, one as much as the other; they were children together, and old folks together; and they went off together into that something that was waiting—sleep, or heaven, I didn't know which.

I shivered; the big gray dusty radiator in front of the window was only luke-warm. I should have to talk to Mrs. Jekes again, I thought. But I felt suddenly sad, as though someone had just told me an old story about grief. There was no use trying to work any more that night; I went to bed, to keep my courage up.

CHAPTER II

I was behind in my rent again. I think Mrs. Jekes would have asked me to leave, if she could have found anyone to take my place; but nobody wanted a studio like mine, with the furniture falling to pieces, and the ceiling dusty with age. Just the same, she took what I had to say about the heat in very bad part. "This isn't a hotel," she said. "Not for what you pay, it isn't.

"That is," she added grimly, "when you pay it."

I used to dread my meetings with her. She would stand there in front of me, her mouth tight, her thin hands folded across her stomach, and a look in her eyes as though she were seeing through me into the future, and finding it as hopeless as the past. You may wonder that I didn't leave and go somewhere else; but the truth is, I had nowhere else to go. Cheap studios were hard to find; and besides, I was almost always in arrears, and so much without hope myself, those days, that I stayed on because I didn't believe that anything else would be any better.

It was a time of depression everywhere. Hatreds clashed and fought in the air above our heads, like the heavenly battles of angels and demons in the dawn of creation. What a world for a painter; a world for a Blake, or a Goya. But not for me. I was neither—neither mystic nor revolutionary; there was too much of my mid-western father in me for the one, and too much of my New England grandmother for the other. Yet their heaven had been bright with faith.

I believe that Mrs. Jekes admired my paintings, although she never said so. She used to stand and look at them, with her tight mouth and folded hands; and once she accepted a sketch of the town landing on the Pamet River in Truro, in place of a week's rent. It would fetch a much bigger price today, I suppose, but I doubt if she knows it. Nor do I know what she saw in it—some memory, perhaps, of sunnier days. I had tried to put the stillness of summer into it, the peace of the ever-moving river, the quiet of old boats deserted in the grass. Perhaps she saw it there, too—or only guessed; I don't know.

She didn't care for my pictures of the city. Now that I look back at it, I can see that they were only an old story to her—only the city, in which she was caught like a fly in molasses. What did she care for the cold sky above the river, or the mountain blue of the windy, shadowy streets? She knew them only too well; she had to live her life with them.

But I was full of hope; it lasted for three days. By the end of that time, I had found out that I could not sell my city sketches, either.

It was late in the afternoon of the fourth day that the turn came. I didn't think of it then as a turn; it seemed to me just a piece of luck, and no more.

I was on my way home from tramping about the streets, my drawings under my arm, when I found myself in front of the Mathews Gallery. I had never been there before; it was a small gallery in those days, on one of the side streets off Sixth Avenue. There was a show going on, of some young painter's work—mostly figures and flower pieces; and I went in more or less out of curiosity. I was looking around when Mr. Mathews came up to me, and asked me what I wanted.

I know Henry Mathews very well by now, I know all about him. In fact, it was he who sold my *Girl In A Black Dress* to the Metropolitan six years ago. I know him to be both timid and kind; he must have hated to see me come in, for he knew at once that I wasn't there to buy anything. But it was getting late, and he wanted to close up; and so he had to get rid of me. Miss Spinney ran the office for him in those days, too; she had gone home, otherwise he would have sent her out to talk to me. She knew how to deal with people who wanted to sell him something.

He came out of his little office at the rear of the gallery, and smiled at me uncertainly. "Yes sir," he said; "what can I do for you?"

I looked at him, and I looked down at the portfolio under my arm. Oh well, I thought, what's the difference? "I don't know," I said; "you could buy one of my pictures, perhaps."

Mr. Mathews coughed gently behind his hand. "Landscapes?" he asked.

"Yes," I said; "mostly."

Mr. Mathews coughed again; I know that he wanted to say to me, My dear young man, there's not a chance. But he could not bring himself to say it; for he dreaded the look in people's eyes when he had to say No. If only Miss Spinney had not gone home—she would have sent me about my business in short order.

"Well," he said doubtfully, "I don't know. Of course, we buy very little . . . almost nothing . . . and the times being what they are . . . However, let me see what you have. Landscapes. Hmm . . . yes; too bad."

I undid the strings of my portfolio, and propped it up on a table. I had no hope of anything, but even to be allowed to show my work, was something. It was warm in the gallery, and I was cold and tired. "Those are some studies from down on Cape Cod," I told him. "That one is the fisheries at North Truro. That's Cornhill. That's the church at Mashpee."

"Landscapes," said Mr. Mathews sadly.

All the tiredness, the hunger, the cold, the long waiting and disappointment, caught me by the throat, and for a moment I couldn't speak. I wanted to take my pictures, and go away. Instead, "Here are one or two sketches of the city," I said. "There's the bridge—"

"What bridge?"

"The new one," I said.

Mr. Mathews sighed. "I was afraid of it," he said.

"And here's a view from the Park, looking south . . ."

"That's better," said Mr. Mathews wanly. He was trying not to look too discouraging; but I could see that he was unhappy. He seemed to be wondering what on earth to say to me. Well, go on, I thought to myself, why don't you say it? Tell me to get out. You don't want any of these . . .

"There's the lake, with ducks feeding . . ."

All of a sudden his eyes lighted up, and he reached out for the portfolio. "Here," he cried; "what's that?"

I looked, myself, with curiosity at the drawing he had in his hand. "Why," I said uncertainly, "that's not anything. That's only a sketch—it's just a little girl I met in the Park. I was trying to remember something . . . I didn't know I'd brought it along with me."

"Ah," said Mr. Mathews happily; "but still—this is different. It's good; it's very good. Do you know why I like it? I can see the past in it. Yes, sir—I've seen that little girl before, somewhere; and yet I couldn't tell you where."

He held it out in front of him; then he put it down, walked away, and came back to it again. He seemed a lot more cheerful; I had an idea that he was glad because he wouldn't have to send me away without buying anything. My heart began to beat, and I felt my hands trembling.

"Yes," he said, "there is something about the child that reminds me of something. Could it be that child of Brush's up at the Museum?"

I drew in my breath sharply; for a moment I felt again the dream-like quality of that misty walk through the Mall with Jennie. "Not that it's a copy," he said hastily, "or even the same child; and the style is very much your own. There's just something in each that reminds me of the other."

He straightened up briskly. "I'll buy it," he said. But all at once his face fell, and I could see that he was wondering what to pay me for it. I knew that it wasn't worth much, just a sketch done with a little wash . . . if he paid me what it was worth, I should hardly have enough for one decent meal. I am sure now, as I look back on it, that he was thinking so too.

"Look here, young man," he said . . . "What's your name?"

I told him.

"Well, then, Mr. Adams, I tell you what I'll do. I'll take the girl—and that park scene—and give you twenty-five dollars for the pair."

My hands were trembling in good earnest now. Twenty-five dollars . . . that was a lot of money to me then. But I didn't want to seem too eager. What trouble we go to, trying to fool people who see right through us anyhow.

"All right," I said; "it's a deal."

Before he went back to his office to get me the money, he took a little pad out of his pocket, and wrote something down on it. I happened to glance at it where he had left it lying open on the table. It must have been the Gallery expense account, for there were two columns of figures, marked Sales and Expenses. Under Sales he had written: 1 small etching, water scene, Marin, 2nd impression, $35; 1 colored print, blue flower piece, Cézanne, $7.50; 1 litho, Le Parc, Sawyer, pear wood frame, $45.

Under Expenses he had written:

lunch, with beer	$ .80
cigar	.10
hat check	.10
bus (both ways)	.20
stamps	.39
Spinney	5.00
flag from man in veteran's hat	.10
2 water colors, Adams	15.00

For a moment my heart sank, for I had thought he had said twenty-five. But before I had time to feel too badly about it, he came out again with the full amount, two tens and a five. I tried to thank him, but he stopped me. "No," he said, "don't thank me; who knows, in the end I may have to thank you."

He gave me a timid smile. "The trouble is," he said, "that nobody paints our times. Nobody paints the age we live in."

I murmured something about Benton, and John Stuart Curry. "No," he said, "we'll never find out what the age is like, by peering in a landscape."

I must have looked startled, for he coughed in a deprecating way. "Let me tell you something, Mr. Adams," he said. "Let me give you some advice. The world is full of landscapes; they come in every day by the dozens. Do me a portrait of the little girl in the Park. I'll buy it; I'll buy them all. Never mind bridges; the world is full of bridges. Do a great portrait, and I'll make you famous."

Clapping me timidly on the shoulder, he ushered me out into the cold winter air, blue with twilight. But I no longer knew whether it was winter or not. Twenty-five dollars . . .

It was not until long after that I found out the truth about that fifteen dollars in the expense account. It was all he thought they were worth, and he was afraid of what Miss Spinney would say in the morning. He meant to make up the difference out of his own pocket.

CHAPTER III

So swift is the hot heart of youth, that I thought I had already made a success, and wanted all the world to share it with me. That night I had supper at Moore's Alhambra, on Amsterdam Avenue; for all my glory, that was the best I could do for myself. As I came in, Gus Meyer, who owned the taxicab that used to stand at the corner of our street, waved to me from a table. "Hi, Mack," he exclaimed; "park yourself." He called everybody Mack; it was his way of telling people that they meant nothing to him personally; or else that he liked them.

"Well," he said, after I was seated, "how are you doing?" He had a big plate of pigsknuckles in front of him, and a glass of beer. "The specialty today," he said; "you'd ought to have some."

Fred, the smaller of the two waiters, came over and I gave him my order. "I'm doing all right," I said to Gus. "I just sold two pictures to an art gallery."

His fork stopped half way to his mouth; and he gaped at me. "You mean you got money?" he asked.

He put his fork down, and shook his head in wonder. "I guess you probably had it coming to you," he said. "But don't lose it, now. Put it in a bank, like you read about in the advertisements."

I told him that most of it would have to go to my landlady, and he looked sorry for me. "An artist don't make so much," he remarked, to comfort me. "It's the same as me. You don't get a chance to lay nothing aside."

For a moment or two he gazed with a peaceful look at his plate. "I had six hundred dollars once," he remarked. "But I spent it."

Almost as an afterthought, he added, "I gave some of it to my mother."

And he returned to his eating, with an air of having finished off the matter.

"This is elegant pigsknuckles," he declared.

For a while we ate in silence. When he was finished, he pushed his empty plate away, and taking a wooden toothpick from a glass on the table, leaned back to remember, and to reflect.

"Some day," he said thoughtfully, "there'll be no more pigsknuckles, and no more beer. When that time comes, I don't want to be here, neither."

"I don't want to be here now," I said; "but I am."

"Well," he said, "you can't do nothing about that. Here you are, and here you stay. So what's it all about? I ask myself."

He gave his toothpick a long, careful look. "But I don't answer," he declared. "You're born poor, and you die poor; and if you got anything, they try to take it off you."

I made the obvious answer, that some men though born poor died rich.

"Then they got other troubles," said Gus. "I don't envy them. All I want is a new coil for the cab. She stalls on me."

"I want more than that," I said.

"You got the wrong idea," he said. "I had six hundred dollars once, and I spent it."

I reminded him that he had given some of it away to his mother.

"So what?" he said. "A feller's got a mother, he's got to look after her, don't he?"

"I don't know," I said. "I haven't got one."

"I'm sorry, Mack," said Gus. He remained downcast, and silent. "Maybe you're married," he said presently. I told him no.

"Well, you're young yet," he said. "Some day you'll meet up with the right one, and you'll be all set." He leaned forward, and looked at me earnestly. "You're a nice kid, Mack," he said. "Put your money in a bank, so when you meet up with the right one, you'll be all set."

I didn't want to talk about things like that. "Listen," I said; "I haven't any money. I never have had any. I just go along, and trust to God."

"Sure," he agreed; "sure. But that don't signify. What you want to ask yourself is, what does God think about it?"

It brought me up short, and made me feel a little uncomfortable. "I don't know, Gus," I said. "What do you think He thinks?"

The toothpick was well chewed out by now; he wrapped his legs around the rungs of his chair, and leaned back. "I wish I could tell you, Mack," he said; "I do indeed. Sometimes you'd almost think He don't know we're here at all. And then when it looks worst, you get a break; along comes a fare for Jersey City, or some drunk tips you what's left of a five dollar bill. That don't make you believe in God, but it shows which way the land lies."

"The pillar of fire," I said, "which went before the chosen people."

But Gus shook his head gloomily. "That was the toughest break we ever got," he said. He brought his chair down, and leaned forward across the table. "Listen, Mack," he said, "did you ever ask yourself what for were we chosen? How I see it is, we weren't chosen for no favors. We were chosen because we were tough; and He needed us like that, so we could tell the world about Him. Well, the world don't want to listen; they want it their way. So they kick us around. God don't care; He says, just keep on telling them."

"And Jesus?" I asked.

"He was a Jew, wasn't He?" said Gus. "He told them; and what did it get Him? If you did what Jesus said today, you'd be kicked around so fast you wouldn't know your tail from a hole in the ground."

He sat up and looked at me, a dark look, like one of the old prophets. "That's where we got a tough break," he said; "being chosen."

"Have another beer," I said; "on me."

"Okay," he said. "I don't mind if I do."

Mr. Moore brought over our beer himself. He was a big man, stout and anxious. "How are you, Gus?" he said. "You look fine. Was everything all right?"

"Elegant," said Gus. "Meet my friend. What's your name, Mack?"

Mr. Moore and I shook hands, and he sat down at our table. "Mind if I sit with you for a minute?" he asked. "Not at all," I said.

"Mack here is a artist," said Gus. "A painter. He just made a lot of money."

The proprietor of the Alhambra beamed at me. "Well now," he said, "that's fine. You satisfied with everything?"

I said yes, that everything was fine.

"We got a nice little place here," said Mr. Moore, looking around slowly, as if he were seeing it all for the first time. "We try to have everybody satisfied."

I felt warm and happy; it was good to be with people, to talk about things without thinking all the time, What am I going to do now?

"You're in a good business, Mr. Moore," I said. "But I guess you know it."

He looked at me, suddenly cautious. "Well, now," he declared, "I don't know. We have a lot of trouble in this business, what with the unions and all. And food costs a lot. We don't make out any too good in this business. At night we don't fill half our tables. It's a lunch business mostly."

"You'd ought to brighten up the place," said Gus. "You take my cab; I give the old bus a going over once a week. Make it shine. That attracts the customers; they like things to look good."

"Sure," said Mr. Moore. "Only I can't afford it."

Gus broke his toothpick in half, and reached for another. "Mack here is a painter," he said. "Leave him paint you something."

Mr. Moore looked from Gus to me; he took up a bowl of sugar, and set it down again. "Well, now," he said, "that's an idea." But I could see that he was waiting to hear what I might have to say.

I thought it was a good idea, too, although it surprised me; it wasn't the sort of thing I would have thought of myself. "Of course," said Mr. Moore. "I couldn't pay much."

"All right," said Gus; "you can feed him, can't you?"

"Yes," said Mr. Moore thoughtfully; "I can feed him."

"Well, Mack," said Gus; "there's your meal ticket."

"It's a good idea," I said.

Mr. Moore gave me a sideways look. "Maybe you could paint me a little something over the bar," he said. "Something tasty, like you'd enjoy standing and looking at."

"He means something with dames in it," explained Gus. "You know—sitting in the grass without nothing on."

The restaurant owner moved uncomfortably; and his fat face grew pink. "It ought to be ladies," he said, "on account of people being a little particular."

"A sort of modern Picnic in the Park," I said, nodding my head. "Yes."

He looked more uncomfortable than ever. "It has to be clean," he said. "Something that wouldn't get me into trouble."

I told him that I thought I knew what he wanted, and he looked grateful. "All right," he said; "go ahead. You can eat here while you're doing it, and afterwards, if it's all right, we can come to an agreement."

It was not a very business-like arrangement, but we shook hands, and he beckoned to the waiter. "Your little dinner was on me," he said, taking our bill and scribbling across it.

When we got outside, Gus patted me on the shoulder. "You're in the money now, Mack," he said. I tried to thank him, but he waved it aside. "Listen," he said; "I got my own dinner out of it, didn't I?"

And as he climbed into his cab, he added with a chuckle,

"Keep it clean, Mack."

I went home thinking what a good world it was. That night I gave Mrs. Jekes the money for two weeks' rent I owed her, and a week's rent in advance. "What's the matter," she inquired; "you been robbing a bank?"

It didn't even spoil things any, to have her say that. "No," I said. "I'm doing some murals."

CHAPTER IV

It was on a Sunday morning that I saw Jennie again. There had been two or three weeks of clear, cold weather, and the big lake in the Park at Seventy-second Street was frozen, and good for skating. I took out my old pair of Lunns, and went over. The ice was crowded with skaters; I sat down on a bench by the shore to put on my skates, and strapped my shoes to my belt. I stepped off the edge in a wide glide, drew up in a turn that made the snow fly, and set off with the sun in my face.

It was one of those days of beautiful weather such as we get in New York in winter, with a blue-white sky, and light, high, white-grey clouds going slowly over from west to east. The city shone in the sun, roof-tops gleamed, and the buildings looked as though they were made of water and air. I struck out in a long stride, taking deep breaths, feeling young and strong, feeling the blood run warm in my veins, and the air cold and fresh on my face. Couples crossed me, going by with linked hands and red cheeks; schoolboys fled past, like schools of minnows, bent over, on racing skates, cutting ice and wind. An old gentleman was doing fancy figures by himself; dressed in brown, with a red woolen scarf, he swung forward, turned, jumped, and circled backward, his skates together in a straight line, knees bent, and arms akimbo, intent and proud. I stopped and watched him for a moment, and then went on again, into the sun. All around me was the quiet flow of skaters moving and gliding, the creaking sound of steel on ice, the cold air, the bright colors.

I found Jennie near the bridge between the two ponds. She was all in black velvet, with a short, wide skirt, and white boots attached to her round, old-fashioned skates. She was doing a figure eight; and none too well, I thought. But she seemed to me to be taller than I had remembered her—older, too; I wasn't even sure that it was she, until she looked up and saw me. "Hello, Mr. Adams," she said.

She coasted over to me, and put out her hands to stop herself. "I didn't know it was you," I told her. "You look older than last time." She smiled, and pressed the toe of one skate down into the ice, to hold herself. "Oh well," she said; "maybe you didn't see me very good."

I don't know how long we stood there, smiling at each other. In a little while, Jennie put her arm in mine. "Come along," she said. "Let's skate."

We started off together arm in arm; and once again the world around me grew misty and unreal. Skaters flowing like a river around us, the little flash of steel in the sun, the sound of that river moving, forms seen for a moment and then gone—our own quiet and gentle motion—all served to bring back to me a feeling I had had once before . . . that feeling of being in a dream, and yet awake. How strange, I thought. I looked down at the slender figure at my side; there was no question about it, she was taller than I had remembered.

"It seems to me," I said, "that you've grown a lot since I saw you."

"I know," she answered.

And as I said nothing, but only smiled uncertainly, she added seriously, "I'm hurrying."

She seemed as light as a feather beside me, but I could feel her arm in mine as we skated. I could see the wide black ripple of her skirt flare out as we swung along; and I wondered if we looked like something in an old print. "How are your parents?" I asked her. "Are they having a good season?"

"Yes," she answered. "They're in Boston now."

I thought: and they left you here all alone. But I suppose that's better than taking you everywhere with them . . .

"I did a little sketch of you," I told her, "and I sold it. It brought me luck."

"I'm glad," she said. "I wish I could see it."

"I'll do one some day just for you," I said.

She wanted to know more about the sketch I had made. I told her about Mr. Mathews, and the portrait he had asked me to do; and about Gus, and the picture I was painting over Mr. Moore's bar. She wanted to see that, too; but it was the portrait for Mr. Mathews that interested her most. "Who will it be of?" she asked; I thought that her voice sounded almost too casual. "I don't know," I answered. "I haven't found out yet."

She skated along a moment or two without saying anything. Then, "Perhaps, . . ." she said. And all at once, in a breathless rush—"Will you let it be me?"

Of course, I thought . . . who else? I realized suddenly that there was no one else, that there never could be anyone else for the picture that Mr. Mathews wanted. If only she were a little older . . .

"I don't know," I said. "Perhaps."

She gave my arm another squeeze, and made a wild swoop to the right. "Hooray," she cried; "I'm going to have my picture painted.

"Won't Emily be mad."

"Emily?" I asked.

"Emily is my best friend," she explained. "She had her picture painted by Mr. Fromkes, and I said you were going to do mine, and she said she'd never heard of you, and so I slapped her, and we quarreled."

"Well," I said. "But I thought it was Cecily you always fought with."

She looked away suddenly, and I felt her hand tremble on my arm. "Cecily died," she said in a whisper. "She had scarlet fever. Now my best friend is Emily. I thought you'd know."

"How would I know?" I asked.

She stumbled suddenly. "My shoe is untied," she said. "I've got to stop."

We coasted to the bank, and I knelt down to tie her shoe lace. Kneeling there, I looked up at her, the flushed face of the child, framed in its dark hair, the brown eyes tenderly dreaming, lost in some other time, some other where and when . . . I thought: she is playing at being Cinderella, or perhaps Snow White, so proud to have me kneeling in front of her, tieing her shoe lace.

We had come to shore near the little refreshment booth which they build each year for the skaters, and I asked Jennie if she would care to go in and rest, and if she would like a cup of hot chocolate. She came out of her dream with a long sigh; then her whole body began to quiver, and she clapped her hands gleefully. "Oh yes," she cried. "I love hot chocolate."

Sitting at the counter together, while the hot, watery brew steamed under our noses, we talked about the weather and the world. She wanted to hear, all over again, about how I had sold the sketch of her to Mr. Mathews; and I for my part wanted to know how she was getting along in school. "It's all right," she said, but without much enthusiasm. "I'm having French."

"French?" I asked; startled, because the last time she had been just beginning her sums. "Yes," she said. "I can say colors, and I can count to ten. Un, deux, trois, quatre . . .

"I can say the war, in French. C'est la guerre."

I couldn't make out what she was talking about. "The war?" I asked. "What war?"

But she only shook her head. "I don't know," she said. "It's just the war."

But then her eyes grew wide, and she looked at me in fright. "They won't hurt children like me," she asked; "will they?"

"No," I said. "No."

She took a deep breath. "That's good," she said. "I don't like being hurt."

And she dipped her little nose happily into the chocolate again.

I was happy too, sitting there, with the air smelling of ice and damp wool, peppermint, and wet wood and leather; and Jennie next to me, drinking her chocolate. Perhaps there was something strange about it; but just the same, it felt altogether right, as though we belonged just there, where we were, together. Our eyes met in a glance of understanding; we looked at each other and smiled, as though we had both had the same thought.

"This is lots of fun," she said.

The chocolate was finished at last; we climbed down from our stools, and clumped our way to the door. "Come along," I said; "we've time for one more round." She took my arm, going down the steps to the ice. "I hate it to stop," she said, "because when will we ever have it again?"

We set off together hand in hand, and made a grand tour of the lake; after that it was time for me to be getting back to work at the Alhambra. I said goodbye to her at the bridge between the two ponds, where we had met. But before I left, I wanted to get one thing straight in my mind.

"Jennie," I said, "tell me—when did Cecily die?"

She looked away; it seemed to me that her eyes grew clouded, and that her small face grew dim.

"Two years ago," she said.

CHAPTER V

"She has a look," I said, "of not altogether belonging to today."

I was showing Mr. Mathews some sketches I had made of Jennie in her skating costume, little pictures of the child in motion, doing an inner edge, or poised on her toes as though to run—the same sketches, as a matter of fact, which were shown last year at the Corcoran, as part of the Blumenthal collection. Miss Spinney was there, too, looking over his shoulder; it was my first meeting with her. I liked her dry voice, her sharp, frosty eyes, and her rough way of talking; for her part, she liked my sketches. When it came to painting and painters, there was no getting around Miss Spinney; she judged a man by his work, and nothing else; she wanted it, or she didn't want it.

Mr. Mathews held the sketches out at arm's length, with his head tilted back, looking at them down his nose. "This girl looks older to me than the first one," he said. "But I rather like it, on the whole. She was, perhaps, a little young, before . . .

"Yes," he said; "they aren't bad—are they, Spinney?"

"Is that all you can say?" remarked Miss Spinney. "That they aren't bad?"

Mr. Mathews tilted his head a little to one side, like a bird. "The thing I like about them," he said, "is the way you've managed to catch that look of not belonging—how was it you said?—not altogether belonging to today. There ought to be something timeless about a woman. Not about a man—we've always been more present-minded."

"You can have the present," said Miss Spinney. "And you know what you can do with it."

Mr. Mathews, who was used to Miss Spinney, went right on. "I don't know what the matter is with women today," he said, sighing. "In my opinion, they lack some quality which they used to have—some quality of timelessness which made them seem to belong to all ages at once. Something eternal—you can see it in all the great paintings from Leonardo to Sargent. Did you ever stop to think how much more real and alive those long-dead women seem to us than the men? The men are done for—finished; there's not a one of them, except perhaps some of the Holbeins, that you'd ever expect to see in the world again. But the women—why, you could meet them anywhere. Mona Lisa, or Madame X . . . on the street, anywhere."

He looked at me accusingly. "The portrait of today," he said, as though it were all my fault, "is planted in the present as firmly as a potato."

"Have you seen Tasker's new portrait of Mrs. Potterly?" asked Miss Spinney.

Mr. Mathews coughed grimly behind his hand. "I understand he received three thousand dollars for it," he remarked.

"One thousand five hundred," said Miss Spinney, "and his trip to Florida."

"One cannot make a living at that rate," said Mr. Mathews.

At my hoarse croak, half envy and half derision, Miss Spinney turned to me and laid a warning hand on my arm. "Now, now, Adams," she said; "control yourself.

"You'll be getting that, too, some day."

It seemed fantastic to me then, fifteen hundred dollars for a portrait; I thought that Tasker must be either a genius or a scoundrel. A man changes his mind about such things as he grows older; but it made me feel bold, and—as I look back at it now—probably a little reckless, too.

"All right," I said; "in that case, what do I get for my sketches?"

"Spinney," murmured Mr. Mathews, "you talk too much."

And Miss Spinney replied almost at the same moment,

"They are hardly worth anything at all."

It was a cruel way to take me down, though I dare say I deserved it. I picked up my sketches, and started to put them away.

"My dear young man," began Mr. Mathews unhappily . . .

"Look here . . ."

But I meant to carry it off with a high hand. "Goodbye," I said; and to Miss Spinney, "I'm very glad to have met you."

She looked at me for a moment with eyes like black frost. I thought she was going to help me to the door, but all at once, to my surprise, her face grew warm and rosy, and she burst out laughing. "I like you, Adams," she said, and fetched me a terrific clip on the back. "You're proud, aren't you?

"Come along—take them out again, and let's have a look at them."

She went over them a lot more carefully than Mr. Mathews had done; for one thing, she seemed less interested in Jennie, and more interested in my drawing. Mr. Mathews watched her in a timid sort of way; he wanted her to like them, because that would help him to feel right about me. He kept drumming with his fingers on the table, and clearing his throat.

"I suppose it could be the clothes," he said, "that make her look a little older."

I didn't think so, but I didn't know how to say what I thought; I stood there feeling uneasy, feeling my heart beating a little fast, and wondering what Miss Spinney would say. She put the sketches down at last, and gave me a clear, hard look. "All right, Adams," she said; "we'll give you twenty-five dollars for the lot."

I suppose I might have taken it, if I had been able to forget her remark about the sketches not being worth anything. I was still a little angry, and I wanted to stand up to her. I was young; and I didn't know very much about art dealers. "It isn't enough," I said; and I got ready to go.

I thought to myself that I didn't care, that I'd sell them to somebody else. But I did care, and I had no way of hiding it. "Look, Adams," she said; "you're a nice boy, but you don't know the art business. I know you can paint; but we aren't collectors, we don't buy things we like just for the fun of sitting around and looking at them the rest of our lives. If we buy these sketches, we've got to sell them too. We can give you thirty dollars. What do you say?"

"Yes," said Mr. Mathews eagerly; "what do you say, young man?"

I took a deep breath, and said "Fifty dollars."

Miss Spinney turned slowly away; I thought that she was angry, and I thought what a fool I was being. I was stubborn, but I was unhappy; I looked at Mr. Mathews, but he was looking at Miss Spinney, and drumming on the table. I started to say, "All right, take them," but she didn't wait for me. "The hell with it," she said. "Give him the fifty."

Mr. Mathews jumped with relief. "That's right, Spinney," he exclaimed. "That's right; I'm glad you see it my way."

She shrugged her shoulders. "I'm just a potato, Henry," she said, "with nothing eternal about me. You'll have to sell them yourself."

"Yes," he said. He took up the sketches, looked at them, put them down, and then picked them up again. "Yes," he said; "yes, of course. I'll sell them—never fret; I'll find a customer for them. Not right away, perhaps . . ."

They gave me fifty. It doesn't seem important now, but it did then. I was getting my meals at Moore's Alhambra, and so it seemed like a fortune to me, almost as much as Tasker's fifteen hundred. I suppose it seemed like such a lot because it was my own. It was real, and I could spend it.

Before I left, Mr. Mathews spoke to me again about doing a portrait for him, but this time he said in so many words that he wanted it to be of Jennie. "There's something in the girl," he declared, "reminds me of something . . . I haven't placed it yet, but I can tell you what it feels like. It feels like when I was young."

He looked up at me apologetically. "I don't know if I can express it any other way," he said. "I shouldn't think you'd understand."

But I thought I understood. "Do you mean that she's old fashioned?" I asked.

"No," he said, "that isn't what I mean. Not altogether."

"Well, I do," I replied. "I think she's old fashioned."

Miss Spinney saw me to the door. "Goodbye," she said; "come in again. And if you have any nice flower-pieces, about two or two and a half by four . . ." She looked around for Mr. Mathews, and seeing him behind her with his back turned, lowered her voice to a whisper. "I like flower-pieces," she said.

I went over to Fifth Avenue, because that was the avenue I wanted to walk on. For the first time I felt that it was my world, my city, that it belonged to me, to my youth and to my hopes; there was a taste of exultation in my mouth, and my heart, filled with joy, lifted like a sail and carried me along with it. The windy, high walls over my head, the wide and gleaming shop windows strung out before me with their mingled colors, the women's bright, hard faces, and the sun over everything—the sun and the wind—

I thought of Jennie's song. And then I thought to myself that I didn't know where she lived, or even how to find her; and the light went out of everything.

CHAPTER VI

"So what you want," said Gus, "is I should find a girl whose name is Jennie. You don't know where she lives, nor nothing about her. So you've got what I would call a good start."

"Her parents are jugglers," I told him. "On a tight rope."

"That makes it easier," he said. "Are they on the circuit?"

I didn't know. I told him that their name was Appleton.

"Appleton," he grumbled; "Appleton." He set himself to think for a moment. "There used to be an act called by that name," he declared. "Down at the old Hammerstein."

"That's right," I said eagerly. "That's where they were."

Gus looked at me strangely. "Well, then, Mack," he said, "they'd be in the old folks' home by now. This must be some other people.

"You sure you seen this girl?"

"Yes," I said. "I made some sketches of her."

He shook his head uncertainly. "That don't signify," he remarked. "I was thinking maybe you made her up."

"No," I said. "I didn't make her up."

We were standing in front of his cab, on the corner, in the grey, raw, morning air. There was snow coming. I could smell it back of the wind, and I shivered a little. But Gus, in his two tattered sweaters, one over the other, didn't seem to feel it; he was used to cold, as he was to heat; he made me think of some old fisherman at Truro, whipped by years of weather, blackened and toughened by the sea. But there was no clear salt for Gus; his tides and channels were the streets, and his face was a city face, pale, quick to anger, quick to rejoice, alert, sly, and confident. None of the slow brooding of the ocean there, the patient, sea-way thought . . .

"I'll take a look around if you want," he said, "and ask some people I know. But listen, Mack–" his voice sank to a low and urgent level– "don't go getting into any trouble with the police. A girl as young as that–

"I don't want no trouble myself, neither," he added as an afterthought.

"All I want to do," I said, "is to paint her picture."

And I thought that was all; I would have sworn that was all I wanted.

Back in my studio again, I tried to work. I was doing a fair-sized canvas of the lake with the skaters on it, from memory and from some sketches, but it was hard to get on with. My heart wasn't in it; my mind flew off in a dozen directions at once. I kept wondering whether I oughtn't to start a flower-piece for Miss Spinney, and whether Gus would be able to find out anything about the Appletons; and I kept thinking about the Alhambra, about my picture over the bar; there was still a lot of work to be done on it. I was restless and uneasy, my brush was uncertain, and the light was poor. I was glad when it was lunch time, and I could put my things away, and go out.

Gus wasn't at the restaurant when I got there. I ate by myself, and then put up my step-ladder back of the bar, and went to work. He came in after I had been working about an hour, and sat down at a table where he could watch me. I looked down at him anxiously, but he shook his head.

"No luck, Mack," he said. "I'm sorry."

"Didn't you find out anything at all?" I asked. He looked back at me with a strange expression on his face. "There were some Appletons did a tight wire act, like I thought," he said, "back in 1914. They had a sort of accident; it seems the wire broke on them one day, back in '22."

We stared at each other for a moment, and then the waiter came with his beer. Gus took a long drink, and, leaning back, gazed solemnly up at my picture. "It's coming along fine," he said.

I had painted a picnic by the shore of a lake not unlike the lake in the Park; and there, by the side of the water, under the trees, my women were gathered to tease and gossip on the grass. They were innocent figures, and I knew that Gus thought that they could do with some men. To that extent he was a realist; but he did not go to extremes. What he asked of a picture was simply this: that it should remind him with the clearest force of what he already knew, along with some further suggestion of a better and a happier world.

"Yes, sir," he declared; "when I see things like that, I think I've been wasting my time."

All at once he sat up in his chair, and pointed to the figure of a young woman lying on her side, her face half turned away, at the edge of the water. "What's the matter with that one?" he demanded. "She don't look so good to me."

"Why?" I asked carelessly, without looking up. "What's the matter with her?"

"She looks drowned," said Gus.

I turned quickly back to the picture. "What do you mean?" I said. But even as I spoke, I saw what he meant; there was something about the way I had placed her under the trees which made her face seem dim, and green with leaf-shadow; her dark hair gave the impression of being wet, and her whole body seemed shadowy with water . . . I felt an indefinable anguish as I looked at it, which I attributed to anger at my own lack of skill; and reached hurriedly for my tube of raw umber.

But even after I had brought her out into the sun again, I felt a depression which I could not account for. It was that figure, half seen, half hidden, which I had imagined secretly in my heart to be Jennie—as she would some day be—and I could not bear to think that brush and heart had so failed each other.

However, Mr. Moore was well satisfied with the picture. "Well, now," he said, coming over and looking up at me where I sat on my stepladder, "that's just about what I wanted. Yes sir, that's what I had in mind. I'd call it entertaining, but it don't offend. I've got a spot over the service door I've been thinking about; we could maybe do a little something there."

"What's the matter," said Gus; "you want a museum?"

"I like to have it nice here," said Mr. Moore. "A picture brightens things up for the customers."

"All right," said Gus; "tell him to do one of me and my cab. That'll be nice for you, and nice for me, too.

"Only make it look good," he added. "Don't drown me."

The first snow was falling as I went home, small flakes coming down slowly, twisting down through the grey levels of air, on the north east wind. The whole city was grey under the heavy sky which seemed to press against me as I walked. I thought of the Cape, of how this storm must be already singing across the dunes, driving its wet snow in from the sea over the little houses huddled in their hollows, the foam breaking below the cliff at High Land, the thunder of surf filling the long nooks and valleys like the sound of trains rolling and rumbling behind the hills—the storm and the snow driving south, out of the black, empty, wrinkled ocean, out of Labrador, out of Greenland waters dark with winter and night. How little we have, I thought, between us and the waiting cold, the mystery, death—a strip of beach, a hill, a few walls of wood or stone, a little fire—and tomorrow's sun, rising and warming us, tomorrow's hope of peace and better weather . . . What if tomorrow vanished in the storm? What if time stood still? And yesterday—if once we lost our way, blundered in the storm—would we find yesterday again ahead of us, where we had thought tomorrow's sun would rise?

I let myself into the house, shaking the snow from my shoulders on the door sill. As I stood there in the hall, which was as cold and somber as myself, Mrs. Jekes came out of her parlor and looked at me with eyes in which there was suspicion, resentment, and a curious excitement. It was apparent that she had been waiting for me. "Well," she said; "there you are. Hah."

And she folded her hands virtuously in front of her.

I looked back at her without speaking. My rent was paid, and I couldn't think of any reason to be anxious. I had an idea that she disliked me, and that she was glad to have some bad news for me; but what she said next, wasn't what I expected at all.

"You have a visitor," she said. "A young lady."

And as I only stared at her with my mouth open, she added harshly, "Fine doings, I must say."

With a sniff of disdain, she turned to go back into her parlor again. "The young lady is waiting for you upstairs," she said, and closed the door, as though to say "I wash my hands of all of it."

I went up slowly, puzzled and concerned, my heart beating fast. I had no friends, there was no one it could be. It seemed impossible that anyone should be waiting for me.

But I was wrong. I knew it even before I opened my door; some inner sense told me.

It was Jennie. She was sitting in the old chair near the easel, prim and upright, her hands tucked away in a little muff in her lap, her toes just touching the floor, a round fur bonnet like a little cake on the top of her head. I came in slowly, and leaned for a moment against the side of the door, looking at her. I felt almost weak with happiness.

"I thought maybe you wanted me to come, Eben," she said.

CHAPTER VII

She sat quietly in the big chair while I put away my brushes and went to look for something with which to make tea. Her gaze, moving slowly about, lingered on everything, the shabby furniture, the dusty walls, the stacked canvases on the floor, the closet bursting with odds and ends of clothing, sketches, paints, cans, and broken boxes, the tumbled cot with its dilapidated blankets—all that I myself had never thought to look at very carefully, or even notice, before she came. But now I saw it all, and for the first time, as she did. Her eyes widened, and she took a long breath. "I've never been in a studio before," she said. "It's lovely."

The tin kettle still had some water in it left over from the morning, so I lit the gas ring under it, and went to search in the closet for a box of crackers. "It's an awful place, Jennie," I said. "It's pretty dirty."

"Yes," she agreed, "it is. I didn't want to say it . . . but I guess as long as you said it first . . ."

She got up, and took off her bonnet and laid it with her coat and her muff very neatly on the chair. "I don't suppose you have an apron?" she asked. "And something to dust with?"

I looked at her in consternation. "You're not going to try to clean it?" I cried.

"Yes," she said. "While the water's boiling . . ."

All I could find was a towel and a clean handkerchief. She tied the handkerchief over her hair and under her chin, the way they do on the

Cape, and took up the towel with an air of determination. Then, with her slender legs planted wide apart, she looked around once more like a general before a battle, and her face fell. "Oh goodness," she cried; "I don't know where to begin."

I found the crackers, and some lumps of sugar for the tea, and I went down the hall to rinse the cups in the basin. I peered over the bannisters as I went by, to see what I could see; sure enough, there was Mrs. Jekes standing very still in the hall below, listening with all her might. I wondered what she expected to hear, and let out a shrill whistle, to show her what I was doing. She looked up, startled, and then scuttled back into her room again.

When I returned to the studio, Jennie was seated on the floor, the dust-rag towel beside her, and my sketches of the city spread out around her. Smiling, she looked up at me as I entered, a dark smudge across her chin, and another along her arm between her wrist and elbow. "I was looking at these," she said. "Do you mind?"

I told her no, of course I didn't mind.

"They're beautiful," she said. "I think you're a very good artist. Only, some of them . . ." she held a small canvas up to the light . . . "I don't know where they are. I've never seen those places."

I glanced over her shoulder as she sat there on the floor. She was looking at a little picture I had done in tempera of the skyscrapers at Radio City. "Yes," I said; "well . . . they're new, I guess. They haven't been built very long."

"I guess that's it," she agreed.

She looked for a long time at the picture, holding it out toward the window, toward the last grey light of afternoon. "It's funny," she said at last, "how sometimes you've never seen things, and still, you know them. As though you were going to see them some time, and because you were going to see them you could remember what they looked like . . . That doesn't sound right, does it?"

"I don't know," I replied. "It sounds pretty mixed up."

"I guess so," she said. "I guess it does. You couldn't remember what you hadn't ever seen."

She sat with the picture on her lap, staring in front of her. It was almost dark by now in the room, the snow outside, falling more heavily, making a grey light in the window, and everything in shadow. She seemed to be gazing through the shadows themselves into some other where, somewhere far off and strange, for her bosom rose and fell, her lips parted, and a long sigh escaped her. The snow, caught in a sudden rift of wind, made a soft, spitting sound on the window pane, and in the river somewhere a boat sounded its lonely hoot. She stirred uneasily; her hand crept up and touched mine. "No," she said in a whisper; "you couldn't possibly."

I went over and snapped on the lights, and the bare, untidy room sprang out of the gloom at us, harsh and real, its four stained walls holding the present in a cube of unmoving light. Jennie gave a sort of cry, and rose to her feet. "What a silly," she said; "here I haven't dusted hardly at all."

"Never mind," I told her; "the water's boiling. Let's have our tea."

She was all gayety after that, sitting up in the chair again, with her toes barely touching the floor, pouring water out of the rusty kettle, passing the crackers, and talking happily about a thousand things. I had to tell her all about Miss Spinney, who had such a hard heart and liked flower-pieces, and how we had fought over the sketches, and I had won; and she clapped her hands with excitement. "Oh Eben," she cried, "you are a good one." She wanted to hear about Gus and his taxicab; she thought he must be very rich to have a cab of his own. "Do you think some time he'd let me ride in it?" she asked. "I've never ridden in a taxicab.

"But I've been in a hansom, once, with mother in the Park; the driver sat up on top, and had a high hat."

She told me that her friend Emily was going away to boarding school. "I think perhaps I'll go with her," she said. "It's a convent, really, called St. Mary's, but it isn't Catholic. It's on a hill, and you see the river; and Emily says they go out every Easter and bless the pigs. I don't want to go very much, but mother says I have to, and anyway, Emily's going . . . I'll miss you, Eben."

"I'll miss you, too, Jennie," I said. "Will you pose for me, before you go?"

"I was hoping you'd say that," she answered. "Yes, I will."

"Will you come tomorrow, then?"

But she looked away, and her face took on a puzzled expression. "I don't know," she said. "I don't know if I can."

"The day after?"

She shook her head. "I'll come as soon as I can," she answered; and that was all she would say.

I told her about Tasker's portrait of Mrs. Potterly, and the great price—as it seemed to me—he had got for it. Her face lit up, and she gave a little laugh. "Will you be glad to be so rich?" she asked. "You mustn't forget me."

"Forget you?" I cried incredulously.

"Oh well," she said; "when you're rich and famous.

"But I guess you won't," she added contentedly. "Because maybe I'll be rich and famous too, and we can be it together."

I said: "I don't think I care very much about being rich, Jennie. I just want to paint—and to know what I'm painting. That's what's so hard—to know what you're painting; to reach to something beyond these little, bitter times. . . ."

"Are these bitter times, Eben?" she asked in surprise.

I stared at her, thinking: of course, how would she know about bitterness, how would she know about the artist at all? caught in a mystery for which he must find some answer, both for himself and for his fellow men, a mystery of good and evil, of blossom and rot—the mystery of a world which learns too late, always too late, which is the mold, and which the bloom . . .

She had been watching my face, and now she held out the box of crackers to me. "Here," she said, "take one. Then you won't feel so bad." I burst out laughing at myself, at both of us; and she laughed, too.

But presently she grew serious again. "You're not sad any more, are you, Eben?" she asked. "I mean—you were so sad the first time I saw you."

"No," I said, "I'm fine now. I was scared that night I met you. I felt as though I were lost. . . ."

She cowered down in her chair, and put her hands up as though I were about to strike her. "No," she cried out, "Oh no—don't ever say that, not ever again. And besides, you weren't lost—you were here, and here isn't lost. It can't be; it mustn't be. I couldn't bear it."

And turning to me almost piteously, she added,

"We can't both of us be lost."

It lasted only a moment, and then it was gone—and we were back again, in my room, with the yellow-lighted walls, and the grey snow outside, and my pictures spread out on the floor about me, the world I knew, the world I saw every day real and around me. "No," I said, "I'm not lost. Why should I be?

"What a foolish way to talk."

She smiled up at me in a forlorn sort of way. "Yes," she said; "it's foolish. Don't let's talk like that any more."

"Because," I said, "with little girls like you . . ."

"Yes," she agreed gravely; "little girls like me." She got up, and gave me her cup, and the tea pot. "Here," she said. "You go and wash them out, before you forget."

"All right," I said. "Wait for me; I'll be right back."

"Yes," she said. "I'll wait for you."

I went down the hall; it was dark on the stairs; the door of Mrs. Jekes' parlor was tight shut. I could hear the snow pitting down on the skylight in the roof. I rinsed the cups out, and hurried back. "Jennie," I said.

But she was gone; and the room was empty. I hadn't heard her go; I hadn't heard the hall door close. But she was gone.

It wasn't until later that I remembered that I hadn't even asked her where she lived.

CHAPTER VIII

After the storm, the city sparkled for a little while; then the snow was gone, upgathered in hard white hills and carted off in trucks to the river. For a day the air was full of winter sounds, the sounds a child remembers from his youth—the wooden tock of shovels on the ice, the clink of picks, the whine and whirr of motors, and the little musical note of chains over the snow. I did a sketch of the river, with its swift and leaden current, and a little oil painting of the Park, with children coasting. But mostly I was content to do nothing, to wander in the city, and to let my mind drift where it pleased. I kept thinking about the portrait I wanted to do of Jennie, and wondering when I would see her again. I no longer thought of her as a child. She seemed to me at that time to be of no particular age, or at that age between ages when it is impossible to say that the child is a young lady, or that the young lady is still a child. From the mystery which surrounded her, my mind hung back, my thoughts turned themselves away. It was enough for me to believe that wherever in this world she actually belonged, in some way, for some reason, she belonged with me.

Even if I had known, it could have made no difference; I can see that now. It was not in my hands, nothing was in my hands; I could not bring the spring nearer before its time, I could not keep the winter from vanishing behind me.

Sometimes in late summer or in early fall there is a day lovelier than all the others, a day of such pure weather that the heart is entranced, lost in a sort of dream, caught in an enchantment beyond time and change. Earth, sky, and sea are in their deepest colors, still, windless, and shining; the eye travels like a bird out across the distance, over the motionless air. All is fixed and clear, never to end, never to change. But in the evening the mist rises; and from the sea comes the grey warning.

In Truro they call it a weather breeder. So it was with me; it seemed to me that the entire world was bathed in a pure and peaceful light. Death had been arrested, and evil was far away; man's cries, the madness, the anguish, were stilled, and in the stillness, like far off surf, I heard the sound of yet more distant things. Far beyond the close horizon of death, there is something else; beyond evil, some spirit untouched, untroubled, and remote.

Once upon a time, not so very long ago, men thought that the earth was flat, and that where earth and heaven met, the world ended. Yet when they finally set sail for that tremendous place, they sailed right through it, and found themselves back again where they had started from. It taught them only that the earth was round.

It might have taught them more.

This short and happy season was made even happier for me, by the visit of my friend Arne Kunstler, from Provincetown. He arrived one morning in his sheepskin jacket, big, red-faced, and bearded like an artist of the 'eighties. But the resemblance stopped with his beard; there was nothing else of the 'eighties about him. He brought a bundle of canvases down with him from the Cape, and set them up on stretchers in my room. The wild and violent pictures flamed at me from the walls and from the floor, like scenes from an inferno. Next to them, my own paintings seemed restrained and mild, colorless and discreet.

He was not pleased with me. "What is this work you are doing, Eben?" he cried. "Portraits—flower-pieces—what has come over you? Not," he added, "that you ever were on the way to being an important painter; but I always thought there was hope for you, at least."

His voice, like that of an old sea-captain, was always pitched at half a gale. Poor Arne, I never took him very seriously, for all his roaring; and as for his painting, I had long ago given up trying to understand it. But I was fond of him, for we had been students together; and I was delighted to see him. His mind was a cave of winds, blowing from all corners at once, a tempest of ideas; he was in love with color, he was like a Viking gone berserk in a rainbow. He lived on next to nothing: I doubt if he sold more than a canvas a year. But he was a happy man, for he never doubted his own genius. His wants were few; and his sorrows were vast, and without pain.

His favorite remark was this: "Art should belong to the masses." But when I declared that the masses would never understand his paintings, he stared at me in astonishment. "Understand?" he thundered; "understand? Who asked them to understand?

"Art can have meaning only to the creative spirit itself.

"Besides," he added, "the masses aren't as stupid as you think. Look how they took to Homer."

"Not to his water colors," I replied. "And anyhow, what in the name of heaven have you and Homer in common?"

He couldn't answer that, of course. "Oh, well," he mumbled, half in his beard, "I was only trying to show you . . . But you'll see," he bellowed, "just the same."

He brought the past back with him, the old, free, careless days in the wind and sun of New England, the winter at the Atelier Dufoix in the Rue St. Jacques—the great cold shadowy room with its charcoal stove, and the shivering students, the evenings in the little bistro on the Boule Miche' —the early lessons here at the Academy, under Hawthorne and Olinsky—

days of work, and nights of argument, when it was enough to settle forever such things as the eternal verities, and never stop to think of what was to become of the artist and his pictures. I took him to the Modern, to see the Modiglianis, and to the Ferargil, to see the single Brockhurst, my own favorite; but he was as contemptuous of the one as of the other, he had no use for any work except his own.

It was the city he admired most, and coming from the flat, windy winter on the Cape, he helped me to see with fresh eyes the soaring stone, the sun-drenched skylines, the brawling shadows all around me. And my heart, in which the old brew of doubt and anxiety had already begun to clear, stirred by hope, by the bright weather, and by something else which I did not know how to name, opened itself in a thrust of joy to the future.

Needless to say, Mrs. Jekes took an instant dislike to him. The very first night, she came hurrying up the stairs, pale and grim, to ask us to make less noise—though she did not so much ask us, as tell us, standing there in the doorway with her hands folded across her stomach, and her eyes steeped in bitterness. "I don't know what sort of a house you think this is," she said, "or what you think you're doing in it; but there's others want to sleep if you don't, and I can always call the police if I have to."

I can hardly blame her, for we were young, and happy, and we must have been making a lot of noise. I was afraid that Arne would throw something at her, but after one long, startled look, he only mumbled, "Yes ma'am," and went off into a corner. After she had left, marching down the stairs with a tread like an army, I saw that he was pale, and actually uneasy. I started to laugh at him, but he stopped me. "No, Eben," he said, "you're wrong to laugh. That's a dreadful woman. She comes in here like black ice, and my pictures freeze over. Oh no, Oh no, I am going to whisper from now on."

But although I laughed at him, I remembered what he said.

For a week or so, I roamed about the city with Arne, delighting in the fine weather, and in the companionship of my friend. I took him to the Alhambra where, I need hardly add, he thundered at my mural like Dufoix himself in the old days in Paris. In his opinion, I had painted a stupid and vulgar scene; nevertheless, with a plate of sauerbraten in front of him, he went so far as to consider the possibility of doing a panel himself, perhaps the one over the service door, in return for a week's good eating. Mr. Moore thought it over for a while, but after he had seen an example of Arne's work, he shook his head regretfully. "It's not that I don't think Mr. Kunstler is a fine artist," he said, "but I've got to think of the customers. I want everybody to be satisfied around here."

"Never mind," said Arne. "Forget it."

"Yes," said Mr. Moore. "Well, thanks for the offer."

It was Gus who did his best to console him. "Never mind, Mack," he said; "some people don't have no eye for anything but their food. Now you take me; I like to look at something pretty when I got the time. But you take most people, they don't feel that way. What they say is, bring in the soup, and get on with it."

"Forget it," said Arne. He waved his arm in a dignified way. "The artist ought not to have to paint for a living," he declared. "Eben, let us all have another glass of beer, and I will repay you some day when I am able."

"Ho," said Gus; "there's a man for you."

His big, red-knuckled hand wrapped around his glass, Arne beamed at us all. "Here's to art," he said.

"And to friends," I added.

"Any friend of Mack's here is a friend of mine," said Gus.

We dipped our noses into the yellow foam. "Just the same," said Arne in a mild bellow, coming up for air, "art can only mean something to the artist who creates it."

CHAPTER IX

Arne went back to Provincetown by boat and bus, leaving behind him by way of a gift, or to repay me for his bed and board, a picture of what he said was a sunset, all in such tones of light as had never been seen on earth before, at least not since the age of reptiles—and which, once his back was turned, I lost no time in hiding under the bed.

During the fortnight which followed, I was busy both at home and at the Alhambra. Among other things, I finished a flower-piece for Miss Spinney, and took it down to the gallery to give to her. As I had feared, Mr. Mathews groaned when he saw it. "Look here," he exclaimed; "whatever put that into your head? A flower-piece . . . and gladiolas, of all things. What do you expect me to do with it, young man?"

I replied that Miss Spinney had asked for it, and that gladiolas were all that I could get at the florist. "It's winter now," I reminded him. "There aren't any summer flowers."

"Spinney," said Mr. Mathews, "you will be my death."

And he gave a cry of indignation.

"Never mind," said Miss Spinney calmly; "I like it. Give Adams thirty dollars, and I'll sell it myself before the week is up."

But for once Mr. Mathews refused to be bullied. Faced with a flower-piece, he put his foot down. "Twenty-five," he said, like a mouse at bay, "and not a penny more."

Miss Spinney looked at him carefully; she knew when to insist, and when to give in. "All right," she said; "twenty-five, then. Is that enough, Adams?"

As a matter of fact, I would have let her have it for less than that, or for nothing. "It isn't enough," I said, "but I'll take it."

"You're hard as nails, aren't you?" she said with her wintry smile. "So am I. That's why I like you.

"Just the same," she added grimly, "we've lost money on you so far. So don't go getting ideas."

Mr. Mathews scratched his chin in an unhappy way. "Well now," he said uncomfortably, "that isn't strictly true, Mr. Adams. I mean to say, we've only sold one sketch, but of course we still have the others."

"Forget it," said Miss Spinney. "Adams here is all right. He understands me."

Nevertheless, as I went out, she drew me aside and pressed a five dollar bill into my hand. "When I say thirty," she declared, "I mean thirty." I tried to give it back to her, but she pushed me out of the door. "On your way, Adams," she said; "on your way. Don't irritate me."

The next day I prepared a five foot canvas; I stretched and mounted it, wet one side of it with water, and worked in a light surface of white lead with my palette knife. Then I set it out to dry. It was a trick Jerry Farnsworth had taught me up on the Cape.

After that there was nothing to do but wait.

Jennie came at the end of the week. I heard her light step on the stairs, and ran to open the door. She looked pale, I thought, and she was dressed in some kind of mourning. She stood in the doorway, and looked at me in a pitiable way.

"It's father and mother," she said. "They had an accident." She tried to smile, but her eyes filled, and she had to wink hard to keep the tears back. "They're dead," she said, almost in surprise.

"I know," I answered, without thinking; and then bit my lip. I took her hand, and led her into the room. I thought that I ought to say something, that I ought to explain how I knew . . . "I read about it," I told her. "In the paper."

"Oh," she said vaguely. "Yes." But she wasn't thinking about me.

I made her sit down, and took her hat and coat and laid them on the bed. "I'm sorry, Jennie," I said.

She drew a deep breath. "They were sweet to me," she said in a voice which trembled a little. "I didn't use to see them very much. But . . . the way they died . . ."

"I know," I said.

"Oh Eben," she cried; and hid her face, and wept.

I wanted to comfort her; but I thought it would be better if I let her cry herself out. Turning my back, I walked over to the window, and stared at the deep blue sky. "Look," I said after a while; "you don't want to pose, do you? I mean—after this?"

I wasn't looking at her, but I could hear her sit up, and blow her nose. "I wanted to come," she said unevenly. "I wanted to see you. Just to be here." She gave a little hiccup, after crying; and then a shaky sigh. "I might as well pose," she concluded. "I don't look very pretty, though."

I thought that if anything, she looked prettier than before. The tears had left no mark on her young face, but they had washed her eyes and left them dark and dreaming. I placed her in the chair, and put a piece of old, yellow silk behind her, something I had bought years before in Paris. It took a long while to get the light to fall just as I wanted it, and to set my easel at the right angle; and all that time she just sat there quietly, staring in front of her, without saying anything. When I was satisfied that I had everything the way I wanted it, I set my canvas up, and began to work.

The picture I started that day needs no description, for most of you have seen it in the Metropolitan Museum, in New York. It is the picture of a girl somewhere in her early 'teens, seated in front of a golden screen. The Museum calls it *Girl In A Black Dress*, but to me it has always been simply Jennie.

I worked in silence, almost in a dream, filled with a strange excitement. So lost was I in what I was doing, that I failed to keep track of the time; I must have been painting well over two hours, when I suddenly saw Jennie droop forward in her chair, and start to slip to the floor. I dropped my brush and ran to her, with my heart in my mouth. But when I lifted her in my arms, she opened her eyes, and smiled timidly up at me. "I'm tired, Eben," was all she said.

She seemed to me to weigh almost nothing. I laid her down on the bed, with her coat over her; and put some water on the stove to heat for tea. When it was ready I made her drink it, and a little color came back into her cheeks. "I'm better now," she said. "I'm not so cold. I can sit there again, if you want me to."

But of course I didn't want her to. "No," I declared, "it's time for you to rest. You've been the best kind of model; we've done very well, we've got a good start. There's lots of time."

She gave another little sigh, almost like a whisper. "No," she said, "there isn't. But I'll do as you say; I'll rest, if you say so."

Shivering a little, she lay back beneath her coat, with closed eyes, her night-dark hair spread out on my pillow, her hand cold as earth in mine. I stood looking down at her, the narrow curve of the young brow, the long lashes which rested so gently on the cheek beneath them; and I felt my heart contract with a sort of fear, and yet at the same time with delight. Who are you? I thought; and what has brought you here to me? . . . child and stranger, lost and lonely, out of some story in the past? . . .

My hands must have trembled a little, for she opened her eyes and looked gravely up at me. "You're all I have now, Eben," she said.

At my start, half surprise, and half dismay, she let go of my hand, and sat up, huddled under her coat, her thin arms wrapped around her knees. "Except for my aunt," she said, to reassure me. "Only I don't know her very well. She's going to take care of me from now on."

"Well," I said uncomfortably, "that's all right, then, isn't it."

She looked at me beseechingly; it was her turn to ask for reassurance. "You do want me to come," she asked uncertainly, "don't you? To pose, I mean?

"You don't want me never to come again?"

I couldn't speak, but she must have seen in my face the answer to her doubts, for she smiled, and brushed the hair back from her face with the same gesture I had seen her use that first evening—how many years ago?—in the Mall. "I'll come as soon as I can," she said.

"Jennie—" I began hoarsely.

"Yes, Eben?"

I looked away; after all, what was there to say? Nothing; I did not even know what I had been thinking. "Where does your aunt live?" I asked. At least, I thought, I shall know where she is, and then if I must, I can find her. But she shook her head. "What does it matter where I live?" she said. "You can't come to me.

"I can only come to you."

She spoke sadly, with exquisite gentleness, but with infinite finality. For a moment we looked at each other across a gulf of more than air—a gulf over which no soul had ever passed before, either to go or to return. . . . She made a little, helpless gesture, as though to reach out to me. And then the moment was gone, and she withdrew once more into herself, a stranger, dreaming of something I could not see.

But I knew then that we both knew.

After a while she got up and put on her hat and coat. "Goodbye, Eben," she said. "I'll come back as soon as I can. I'll hurry—truly."

She looked up at me with eyes wide and dark and earnest. "I didn't want you to know," she said.

She turned once, in the doorway. "Try to wait," she whispered.

"Try to wait for me."

CHAPTER X

One must sometimes believe what one cannot understand. That is the method of the scientist as well as the mystic: faced with a universe which must be endless and infinite, he accepts it, although he cannot really imagine it. For there is no picture in our minds of infinity; somewhere, at the furthermost limits of thought, we never fail to plot its end. Yet—if there is no end? Or if, at the end, we are only back at the beginning again? . . .

When Jennie returned, a fortnight later, I realized how much taller she had grown in the last few meetings. She was dressed in a uniform such as young ladies wear at a convent boarding school—a middy blouse, and a skirt which hung almost to her ankles. She came bounding up the stairs, and threw her hat on the bed. "Eben," she cried, "what fun."

For a moment I was thoroughly taken aback, for if I had expected anything at all, it was certainly not that. There was nothing to remind me of the last time I had seen her; in fact, there was nothing of the child about her at all, as far as I could see. On the contrary, she seemed to stand almost within the shadow of vigorous young womanhood. I thought: I must finish my portrait quickly, before it's too late . . .

I couldn't avoid saying, "You've grown, Jennie. And those clothes . . ."

She looked down at herself, and laughed ruefully. "I know," she said. "Aren't they awful? They make us wear them at the convent."

Breaking off suddenly, she looked at me in a startled way. "Oh," she cried; "of course . . . you didn't know . . .

"I'm at St. Mary's now, with Emily. My aunt sent me."

"I suppose I guessed as much," I answered. "Well—I've been waiting for you. We'd better begin."

She took her place in the chair, and I brought out an old black coat of my own to put over the middy blouse. "I can do the dress some other time," I told her. "I won't need you for that."

She sat up very stiff and straight in the chair. "Well," she said with a pout, "aren't you glad to see me?"

It was a very different sitting from the one before, and harder, too. Jenny was restless, and in high spirits; she wanted to stop every few minutes, to talk or to walk around. She was full of her life at school, enchanted with the friendships, the comings and goings, the daily incidents of the convent society—happy at having friends, at having secrets—at being, for the first time in her life, part of a little community. There was the plainsong she had to tell me about; the daily walks to the little green-house, where the girls were allowed to buy fruit from one of the sisters; the little bunches of flowers they gave one another, which they called "bunching"; the convent-school itself, high on its hill above the shining river; and Sister Therese, who taught her mathematics and history, and whose calm, untroubled face had already roused in Jennie's breast the first sharp, sweet experience of love. And then there was Emily, of course, whose secrets and whose room she shared, who exchanged stockings and blouses with her, and on whose dresser there was a picture—but only when nobody would be likely to come in—of a young man in a high collar, with dark eyes and wavy hair, and the printed name beneath it, Mr. John Gilbert.

Yes—Jennie had changed; I even noticed that she had filled out a little. On the whole, I thought it a change for the better. I let her talk on and on, barely listening, my fingers racing in tiny spurts over the canvas, trying at their best speed to follow my eyes; and my eyes, in turn, searching for what they could not see—not only what was there, but what had been, and what would some day be. I felt that I was truly working against time, and felt myself carried forward on a wave of exultation as the picture bloomed under the brush, as I saw, each time I stepped away from it, its growing strength, its gathering beauty.

We stopped at noon for a bite of lunch, although I would gladly have gone on without any. But that would never do for Jennie. It turned out that she had been planning all along to cook lunch for me, on my little gas stove; and that she had even taken lessons in cooking in school. Unfortunately, there was nothing in the studio, as far as I could see, for her to cook.

"I have some sardines," I said, "and some cheese, and crackers, and milk. I'm sorry, Jennie. You see, I didn't know you were coming."

She laughed happily. "That's all I can cook, anyhow," she said. "I could cook an egg, but it doesn't matter. I'll cook the cheese."

And she did, actually, get the cheese to melt, though not without some scorching, and a smell of burning that I was afraid would bring up Mrs. Jekes. After it was melted, she dropped it on the crackers, and there it lay, altogether inedible, and more and more like rubber. I ate a few sardines, and after a while, she did, too. "Isn't this fun?" she said.

And of course, to her, it was. For if Emily had Mr. Gilbert, Jennie had me—her own exciting secret, to be shared in whispers if she felt like it, or held close and inviolable to her breast. Everyone has a secret at that age; a special secret, a private secret—for everything between earth and sky is part of the one great, general secret which young hearts whisper to one another. New sights—new sounds—new meanings—new joys and fears—her heart, which through her childhood was all one color, has turned into a kaleidoscope, made up of shining fragments which fall at each turn of the glass into ever newer, more breath-taking patterns. Emily . . . Sister Therese . . . plain-song and flowers . . . and finally, myself—all her own, her own private secret, which no one else can know, until she tells.

"The girls keep asking me about you," she confessed. "But I won't tell them anything. Except . . ." she considered a moment . . . "that you're very handsome . . ." And she began to count off on her fingers.

"Jennie," I said; "don't be silly."

". . . and that you're a great artist; and that you nearly starved to death . . ."

She smiled at me shyly. "They loved that part of it," she declared. "They thought it was very romantic."

"Good God," I said.

"Well, they did," she insisted. "And they think it's romantic my coming to see you like this, too."

Her voice was still full of laughter, but her cheeks were pink, and she kept her head bent. "Perhaps it is," I replied a little grimly. "But we've got work to do, and if you've finished with that last bit of milk, we might begin."

Her eyes flew to my face in dismay. "You're not angry, are you, Eben?" she faltered. "I was only joking."

"Of course I'm not angry," I said a little too gruffly, and stood up. "Let's get back to work—shall we?"

She took her place again in a somewhat chastened mood; but she couldn't stay quiet for long. "Eben," she said.

"Mmm?"

"I didn't really say you were handsome."

But that didn't comfort me much.

"I wish I had nicer clothes to wear," she said after a while. "We have a blue dress with a guimpe, for Sundays, and we have to wear long white veils in church. Emily's fell off, the last time; she didn't pin it on right, she was in such a hurry, and she got a whole day's silence."

Receiving no reply to this bit of information, she went on to other things. "I like some of my lessons," she said. "I like things like science, and math. But I don't like history. It makes me feel too sad.

"I have a funny mind, I guess."

I was holding one brush in my teeth while I worked with another, and I mumbled something in reply.

"You have a funny mind, too," she said.

"Perhaps I have," I agreed absently. "Perhaps I have. Just turn your head a little to the right—"

"Eben," she began presently in a queer, breathless voice, "do you think sometimes people can know what lies ahead? I mean—what's going to happen to them?"

But I was working, and thinking only of what I was doing. Otherwise I would have stopped—and thought—and perhaps have been too much troubled by the question to make any answer at all. As it was, I only half heard it; and I answered without thinking.

"Nonsense," I said.

Jennie was silent for a moment; then, "I don't know," she said slowly. "I'm not so sure. You know how you feel sad about things sometimes—

things that haven't happened. Perhaps they're things that are going to happen. Perhaps we know it, and are just afraid to admit it to ourselves. Why couldn't you, Eben—if you could see ahead—feel sorry for what was coming? Only you wouldn't know it was coming, you'd call it worry, or something."

I heard it, but I wasn't really paying attention. "You sound like the White Queen," I said.

"The White Queen?"

"The one in Alice," I told her. "She hollered first, and stuck herself afterwards."

"Oh," said Jennie in a small voice. Even with the little mind I had to attend to anything but my painting, I could tell that I had hurt her.

"All right," she said. "I won't talk any more."

And for the remainder of the sitting, she sat there silent and unsmiling, drawn back once more into herself, dreaming and distant. But I was too busy to try to explain; and besides, it did the picture good. When the light began to fail, I put down my brush, and took a deep breath.

"I think I've got it, Jennie," I said.

There was no answer; she seemed to be half asleep. I went quietly down the hall to the wash room, to freshen up; I doubt if I was away for more than a minute or so. But when I got back, Jennie was gone.

She left a note for me, on the bed. "Eben dear," it said; "I'll be back again some day. But not soon. In the spring, I think.

Jennie."

CHAPTER XI

Even before I telephoned out to the school, I knew what the answer would be. "I'm sorry; there is no one here by that name." I didn't ask them to go back over their files; I knew what the answer would be to that, too.

So there it was.

I must try to describe, if I can, my state of mind in the weeks which followed. I knew that what I had been asked to believe, was impossible; yet I believed it. And at the same time, I was afraid. The fact that my fears were formless, that I did not know what I feared, made it all the worse; for waking or sleeping, nothing frightens us more than the unknown.

I do not know which was harder to bear—the feeling of being afraid, or the sudden sense of desolation which swept down upon me after Jennie had left. She was gone beyond the farthest sea; and there was nowhere I could even look for her.

It made the world around me seem curiously empty—silent, and empty, like the wooden belly of a violin on which nothing is being played. One note would bring it all to life; one note would make an instrument of it. But the note is not played; no one touches it. It remains an empty box.

At first, I was absorbed in my own helplessness; and at the same time, baffled by it. Never before had it occurred to me to ask myself why the sun should rise each morning on a new day instead of upon the old day over again; or to wonder how much of what I did was really my own to do. It may be that here on this earth we are not grateful enough for our ignorance, and our innocence. We think that there is only one road, one direction—forward; and we accept it, and press on. We think of God, we think of the mystery of the universe, but we do not think about it very much, and we do not really believe that it is a mystery, or that we could not understand it if it were explained to us. Perhaps that is because when all is said and done, we do not really believe in God. In our hearts, we are convinced that it is our world, not His.

How stupid of us. Yet we are created stupid—innocent and ignorant; and it is this ignorance alone which makes it possible for us to live on this earth, in comfort, among the mysteries. Since we do not know, and cannot guess, we need not bother our heads too much to understand. It is innocence which wakes us each morning to a new day, a fresh day, another day in a long chain of days; it is ignorance which makes each of our acts appear to be a new one, and the result of an exercise of will. Without such ignorance, we should perish of terror, frozen and immobile; or, like the old saints who learned the true name of God, go up in a blaze of unbearable vision.

I went back to work; and there, before my easel again, I got back a little of my peace of mind. I realized that I was still anchored to earth, and that no matter what God was about, if I was to live, it would have to be by my own efforts. Little by little the sense of being helpless, the fog of fear, burned itself out of my heart, and left me clear, and grateful —and lonely.

It was this loneliness, which I had not expected, and to which I was unused, which kept me from taking the finished portrait to Mr. Mathews at once. It was all I had of Jennie, all I had to remind me that she was really there in the world; and I could not bring myself to part with it. I found that I kept waiting for her to come back; some part of me which had always been whole and satisfied, was suddenly so no longer; something was missing.

Mrs. Jekes found me talking to the portrait one day. I don't know what I was saying—probably something I had said before, to the real Jennie. She came quietly up behind me, with a duster in her hand, and stood looking over my shoulder. "Well," she said; "well."

It startled me; and disturbed me, too. I moved away, trying to look as though I hadn't been talking out loud to myself, as though it were all a mistake, as though it was something quite natural. But Mrs. Jekes wasn't fooled. "That's the girl who's been visiting you," she said, and her voice was full of malice.

"That's your sweetheart."

I whirled on her in a rage. "You're a fool," I shouted. I wanted to strike her, to push her out of the room. But she stood her ground, and gave me back look for look. "It isn't me is the fool," she said bitterly.

She moved to the door with a sort of bleak dignity. "You can always leave this house if you've a mind to," she said. "There's others will be glad to take your place."

And she added, as she went out,

"You're not a gentleman."

I wanted to run after her and tell her that I was leaving, that I was leaving at once . . . but before I had taken two steps, I halted in dismay. For I realized that I couldn't leave. This was Jennie's room: this was where she had sat, where we had had lunch together, this was what she loved to come back to—how could I leave it? It was full of memories of her.

And besides—if I moved—how would she ever find me again?

I closed the door gently, and turned slowly back into the room again. I'd have to stay; I'd have to tell Mrs. Jekes that I was sorry for what I had said. It put a bitter taste in my mouth. I took Jennie's picture, and turned it to the wall. I didn't want to think about her for a while.

Just the same, I thought about very little else. That was early in March; it was early in April before I saw her again. At least, I know now that I saw her; though I wasn't sure at the time. It was only for a moment; and I had no chance to talk to her.

It was at the gallery, at an exhibition of some of Jerry Farnsworth's things, with one or two of Helen Sawyer's landscapes hanging with them—scenes of the Cape, the crossing at North Truro, an old house, and a painting of the Pamet where it flows past the town landing at Truro. There had been a good crowd in to see them, quite a lot of people; and I had gone back into Mr. Mathews' little office in the rear of the gallery, to talk to Miss Spinney. She had sold the flower-piece at a profit; and she was feeling friendly, and pleased with herself.

"Adams," she said, after she had greeted me, "tell me something: what is it makes a painter? A man will starve all his life, go around with holes in his pants and his toes sticking out of his boots, and still all he wants to do is slap some paint on a yard of canvas. Who's crazy—him or us? What did you do with the twenty-five dollars you got off us the last time?"

"I spent it," I said.

"Sure," she agreed; "I didn't think you'd bought a bond with it. Only, why not a new coat, or a pair of shoes?"

I looked down at my scuffed and broken shoes, and shrugged my shoulders. I didn't see what business it was of hers. "Oh well," I said, "I could get them shined, and they'd look all right. That is, if I ever thought about it."

"Have they got any soles left on them at all?" she asked.

I grinned at her, but I kept my feet planted firmly on the floor, for I knew it would be like her to pick one of them up the way a blacksmith does when he wants to shoe a horse. "I didn't know you cared," I murmured.

"Don't be an ass," she said. But a slow blush ran up her neck, up over the clean, strong lines of her jaw.

"All right," I said, feeling a little silly, "next time throw in a pair of shoes with the price."

She swore at me like a truck driver; and I went out to look for Mr. Mathews.

I didn't see him at first, for he was at the door saying goodbye to one of the customers. The gallery was nearly empty by this time; a few people were still standing in front of Farnsworth's "Rest After Work," but otherwise the big room was deserted. The Sawyers were over in a far corner, near the door; and I started toward them.

Like all galleries, the room itself was only dimly lighted; the pictures on the wall seemed to have their own light, to give out reflections of sun and sea, or morning sky and noonday earth, which made the air of the room itself seem shadowy and vague. I thought I heard Miss Spinney come out of the office behind me, and turned back for a moment. But there was no one there. When I turned around again, it seemed to me that my heart stopped beating.

There was somebody in front of the Sawyers—a young girl, dressed in a middy blouse, and a skirt which hung almost to her ankles. She was standing directly in front of the picture of the Pamet; that much I could see across the room, in the shadowy light; but no more. She had her hands to her face; and I thought that she was weeping.

"Jennie," I said; or perhaps I only thought I said it. I tried to move, to get across to her, but my legs were like lead. It was all I could do to put one foot before the other. I could feel the slow, heavy surge of my heart, as I kept trying to breathe, catching at my breath, the way you do in a gale.

She lifted her head, and for a moment I had a glimpse of her face, wet and shiny with tears. And then—she was gone. It was just as simple as that. Perhaps she went out through the door—I don't know. Mr. Mathews, coming in at that moment, bent aside as though to let someone pass. Perhaps it was Jennie.

He came across the floor to me, smiling; but when he saw my face, his expression changed. "Good heavens, Mr. Adams," he cried, "is anything the matter? You look sick, man."

I shook my head; I couldn't say anything. I passed him without speaking, and stumbled out of the door. He looked after me in bewilderment. I left him there wondering what had happened to me.

There were only the usual passers-by in the street. I hadn't expected there would be anyone else.

CHAPTER XII

Spring was early that year; the rainy winds blew themselves out before the end of April. One day the grass in the Park smelt sweet and fresh, and a robin sang on the lawn below the Mall. From then on, the sky seemed made of another blue, and the clouds, too, were a different white, with tones of yellow in them. Yellow is the true color of spring, not green; the new grass, the clouds, the misty, sunny air, the sticky buds like little feathers on the trees, all are mixed with yellow tone, with the haze of sun and earth and water. Green is for summer; blue, for fall.

The city comes up dreaming from the winter, its high roofs seem to melt in the air. The wind blows from the south, across Jersey; it smells sweet, it brings the smell of earth with it. People move more slowly, there is a gentleness about them, the cold is not yet out of their bones, they warm themselves in the sun. The days are longer, and the shadows are not as deep; evenings come down almost imperceptibly, there are long twilights, the dusk is peaceful, and the sounds of evening are tranquil and comforting. Summer lies ahead, the summer of the heart; it is coming, it has been caught sight of, it is on the way, bringing flowers and sea-bathing.

Summer is the worst time of all to be alone. Then earth is warm and lovely, free to go about in; and always somewhere in the distance there is a place where two people might be happy if only they were together. It is in the spring that one dreams of such places; one thinks of the summer which is coming, and the heart dreams of its friend.

Now in the Park I began to see people walking together, slowly, arm in arm, not hurrying as they did in winter, but taking time to talk to each other, stopping a moment to laugh at the children, or to watch the swans on the lake. When summer came, they would be together still; they could enjoy the spring. But for me, it was different. I had no way of knowing when I should see Jennie again. And as the days passed, I missed her more and more.

There is one thing about distance: that no matter how far away it is, it can be reached. It is over there, beyond the Jersey hills—one can drive to it—it is north, among the pines, or eastward to the sea. It is never yesterday, or tomorrow. That is another, and a crueller distance; there is no way to get there.

Yet, though I missed her, though I could not reach her, I was not altogether without her. For I found that my memory had grown sharper; or else it was beginning to play tricks on me. It was not so much that I began to live in the past, as that the past began to take on more and more the clarity, the actual form of the present, and to intrude itself into my daytime thoughts. The present, on the contrary, seemed to grow a little hazy, to begin to slip away from me . . . so many things reminded me of her. And then I would be seized by memory so urgent that what I remembered seemed almost more real to me than what was before me.

Where others dreamed ahead that spring, toward the summer, I dreamed backward into the past. Sights, sounds, and smells, all served that journey well—the smell of scorching, the sound of wood—perhaps a shovel?—scraped along the pavement; the hoot of a tugboat in the river. At nightfall the shrill, sad voices of children, floating in through my window, brought back to me another evening, in the mist, in the Park, and a child walking beside me down the long avenue of empty benches, skipping along on one foot, hopping over the chalk marks . . . *"Do you know the game I like to play best? It's a wishing game."* Or on a sunny morning, beside the lake on which the boats were lazily drifting, I'd suddenly find myself entranced and motionless, seeing in front of me not the blue, dancing water, but the white, shining ice and the skaters, feeling the cold wind on my cheeks again, and Jennie's arm in mine, so firm and light. . . . Or coming home in the afternoon, I'd hurry up the stairs with a beating heart, because she might be there—remembering so clearly the first time she had come to see me, in her little velvet dress with the muff. *"I thought maybe you wanted me to come,"* she had said.

Such was my state of mind those early days of spring—neither happy nor unhappy; dreaming, and waiting. I didn't want very much, or hope for very much—just to see her again, and to be with her once more. I tried not to think about the summer, or, indeed, about the future at all; —how could I? I left that to her, just as I had left the past to her. Why we had met, or how it had come about, I did not know. I still do not know. I only know that we were meant to be together, that the strands of her life were woven in with mine; and that even time and the world could not part us altogether. Not then. Not ever.

What is it which makes a man and a woman know that they, of all other men and women in the world, belong to each other? Is it no more than chance and meeting? no more than being alive together in the world at the same time? Is it only a curve of the throat, a line of the chin, the way the eyes are set, a way of speaking? Or is it something deeper and stranger, something beyond meeting, something beyond chance and fortune? Are there others, in other times of the world, whom we would have loved, who would have loved us? Is there, perhaps, one soul among all others—among all who have lived, the endless generations, from world's end to world's end—who must love us or die? And whom we must love, in turn—whom we must seek all our lives long—headlong and homesick—until the end?

By May I had no money left at all, and so I took the portrait down to Mr. Mathews. I hated to give it up, but there was no help for it; I needed money for rent, and for more paints, and canvas. I was still getting some of my meals at the Alhambra, although I had finished my work there; the picnic over the bar seemed to please the customers, and Mr. Moore didn't mind my having one free meal a day, as long as I didn't eat too much. As a matter of fact, he was thinking of getting up a fancy menu with an illustrated cover—possibly a picture of the restaurant, with himself standing in the doorway. Gus wanted me to get his cab into it, too. I didn't mind; an artist works for his meals one way or another.

Gus helped me bring the picture downtown in his cab, and went along with me to see that I wasn't cheated. We carried it into the gallery together, and set it up on the table in the office in the rear. Then we stepped aside, and let Mr. Mathews look at it.

He didn't say anything for a long while. At first I thought that he was disappointed, and my heart sank; but then I saw that he was really very much moved. He had grown a little pale; his eyes first widened, and then narrowed; and he kept stroking the palm of one hand with the fingers of the other. "Well," he said. "Well.

"Yes."

I began to feel excited, too. Up till then, I doubt if I had really looked at the picture myself with any sort of critical eye. There, in my room, it had been so much a part of me; I could still feel the brush strokes in my fingers . . . and besides, it was Jennie, it was all I had of her. . . . But here, in the gallery, seeing it as Mr. Mathews was seeing it, I could realize for the first time what I had done. It made me feel proud, and at the same time humble.

After a while Miss Spinney came in and joined us. She didn't say anything for a minute; and then she took a long breath. "Well, Adams," she said in a strangely gentle voice, "that's it, all right."

Mr. Mathews cleared his throat. "Yes," he said, "that's it. That's what

I meant. It's . . . it's . . ." He seemed unable to continue. It was Gus who spoke up for him.

"She's a honey, Mack," he said. "I don't noways blame you."

And turning to Miss Spinney, he added in an easy tone,

"Treat him right, ma'am, on account of he's a friend of mine."

"I'll keep it in mind," said Miss Spinney.

She and Mr. Mathews went outside, to talk it over; and Gus edged up to me and gave me a nudge with his elbow. "I think they like it, Mack," he whispered.

"Yes," I said; "I think they do."

"Well, don't be too easy on them," he said. "Ask for fifty, right off."

"It's worth twice that," I said.

Gus' jaw dropped. "No," he croaked. "Go on. I wouldn't of believed it."

Mr. Mathews and Miss Spinney came back again, looking solemn; and Mr. Mathews settled down to business. "Mr. Adams," he began–

"Why so formal?" said Miss Spinney. "He's in the family."

"Well, then–Eben," said Mr. Mathews, swallowing, "I won't try to disguise my feelings from you. You have given me a great surprise. I am powerfully moved. This picture . . . well . . . I don't like to use the word masterpiece, but just the same . . ."

"Get on with it, Henry," said Miss Spinney.

"Yes," said Mr. Mathews hurriedly. "Quite. The point is, that we don't want to buy it. No," he said, holding up his hand as he saw my face fall–"it's not for the reason you think. The reason is, that I honestly don't know what it's worth."

"Well," I said, "what do you think it's worth?"

"That depends," he answered, "on who buys it. The market isn't very good just at the moment, for individual collectors. But if the museum were to take it–"

"Yes?" I said.

"It might bring more than a thousand dollars," he said.

I heard Gus give a gulp beside me. "What I want to do," continued Mr. Mathews–"what we want to do–is to take it on consignment, and then do the very best we can for it. And as an advance–" he cleared his throat nervously–"as an advance, I can let you have two hundred dollars . . ."

"Henry," said Miss Spinney ominously.

"Three hundred," amended Mr. Mathews unhappily.

Then Gus found his voice again. "Take it, Mack," he said hoarsely; and gave me a shove.

I went home in his cab, leaning back on the cushion, and looking out proudly at my city, which seemed to me to return my look with joy.

Through the open window in front, I could see the back of Gus' head; I noticed that he had turned the flag down on his meter, and that the meter was ticking. Well, why not? I was a rich man. But just the same, I was surprised; and it surprised me that Gus wasn't saying anything. His silence wasn't natural; it wasn't like him.

He left me at my house, and took my fare without a word. When I tried to thank him for helping me, he looked away. "Forget it," he said. "It don't signify."

He took his hands off the wheel, and stared at them helplessly, as though in some way or other they had disappointed him. Then he let them drop again.

"I couldn't do nothing for you, Mack," he said. "And that's the truth."

CHAPTER XIII

Early next morning, in the bright spring sunshine, Jennie came back to me. I heard her voice in the hall, and had only time to slip into my coat, before she was up the stairs and in at the door. She had a little suitcase in her hand; she dropped it just inside the doorway, and came flying across the room, and kissed me.

It was the most natural thing in the world. We held each other out at arm's length and looked at each other, smiling, and not saying anything. We couldn't have spoken . . . The whole sunny, sweet-smelling spring morning had come in with her.

She was older—I saw that at once; a young lady now, dressed in a travelling suit; she even had gloves on. She was breathless, but only from running up the stairs, or from happiness; her brown eyes never faltered as they searched my face. I took a deep breath. "Jennie," I said; "I've missed you."

"I know," she answered. "I've missed you, too. And it's been longer for me." She drew her hands away from mine with sudden gravity. "I'm not in school any more," she said.

"I know," I said. "I can see."

She turned slowly on her heel, and looked around the room with simple joy. "How I've dreamed of this, Eben," she said; "I can't tell you. The nights I've lain awake, thinking of this room . . ."

"I know," I said.

"Do you?" she answered gently. "No, I don't think so."

She stood there, looking around her, and slowly taking off her gloves; and I looked around, too, and wished the room were more in order. I went over to smooth the bed a little, but she stopped me. "No," she said; "don't touch it. Do you remember how I wanted to tidy up for you once, when I was little? Let me do it now. And show me where the coffee is . . . Poor Eben—I did get you up so early. Go and dress yourself, and then we'll have breakfast, and I'll tell you all that's happened."

"But Jennie," I said, "if we have so little time . . ."

"We have a whole long day," she answered breathlessly. "And—and a little more."

I went along down the hall to the washroom, and left Jennie to tidy up, as she wanted. I thought I saw Mrs. Jekes on the landing below, but I didn't pay much attention to her; I was too happy, the day was too lovely . . . a whole long day, and a little more. What did that mean—a little more? I cut myself twice, shaving.

Jennie had learned how to make a bed, and how to make coffee. I hardly knew my room when I got back to it: my work-table was laid with a clean towel, and my two cups, one of them with a broken handle, and the coffee pot, stood side by side, along with a pat of butter I'd had out on the window sill, and some bread she had toasted on a fork over the gas burner. There was a good smell in the air. We sat down together, hand in hand, to our breakfast.

I told her about the picture; and her fingers tightened on mine. "Oh, but that's grand," she cried. "That's wonderful, Eben. Aren't you happy?"

She was silent for a moment, thinking about something. "Eben," she said at last, "let's do something special—shall we? To celebrate? Because I haven't really very long to stay with you. You see . . . I'm being sent abroad—to France—to a finishing school—for two years."

"Jennie," I cried.

"I know," she said quickly. "I don't want to go; but I guess I have to. And anyhow—it won't seem very long. And then . . ."

"And then?" I asked.

"I'm going to hurry," she said earnestly. "And then some day I'll be as old as you."

"I'm twenty-eight, Jennie," I said gravely. She nodded her head.

"I know it," she replied. "And so will I be . . . then."

"But not when you come back from France," I said.

"No," she agreed. "There'll be a long time still, after that."

She held my hand tight. "I'm going to hurry, though," she said. "I've got to."

For a moment she seemed to be lost in thought, her head bent, her eyes hidden under their long lashes. Then she roused herself, and sat up with a smile. "Let's go on a picnic, Eben," she said. "Somewhere in the country—for the whole day—

"It's something we've never done before."

Something we'd never done before—as though we'd ever done very much of anything. But she didn't have to urge me. A whole day in the country, in the warm spring weather, together . . . "Yes," I said, "yes. That's what we'll do." She could hardly wait for me to finish my coffee; we hurried down the stairs and out into the street, hand in hand; and the bright sunny morning fell on us like an armful of flowers.

Gus was in his cab, at the corner. When he saw me with Jennie, he took his hat off, and looked frightened. I don't believe he had ever thought she was real, or ever expected to see her. I went up to the cab, and opened the door. "Gus," I said, "we're going on a picnic. We're going out into the country for the day . . . somewhere . . . anywhere. I want you to take us. How much will it cost?"

He twisted his hat in his hands, and tried to smile; he seemed to be having some trouble in swallowing. "Now listen, Mack," he said; "now listen . . ."

"It doesn't matter what it costs," I said, and helped Jennie into the cab.

What was the good of being rich, if I couldn't do what I liked?

Gus looked back once or twice, as though to make sure that we were really there. "So it's a fact," he said finally, more to himself than to me; and in a kind of awe. "Well—

"Where do you want to go, Mack?"

I waved him forward. "Wherever it's green," I said. "Wherever it's country."

I don't know where we went, but it was green and lovely. It was somewhere north of the city—perhaps in Westchester. It took us about an hour to get there. We left the cab by the roadside, and climbed a fence, and ran across a field with a cow in it. The cow didn't notice us. We climbed a little hill, among some trees. Jennie was flushed and breathless, and full of laughter; she and I ran ahead, and Gus came after us.

At noon we sat together on a warm stone wall in the sun at the edge of a meadow, and near a little wood. There were yellow dandelions in the grass, and the air was sweet as honey. We had some sandwiches along—lettuce and bread for Jennie, sausage for Gus and me. We ate our sandwiches, and drank some beer out of cans. It was the first beer Jennie had ever tasted; she didn't like it, she said it tasted bitter.

Gus and Jennie did most of the talking. He told her how he had tried to find her once; and how he had helped me sell the picture; and she told him please to take good care of me, and not to let anything happen. I didn't talk very much; I felt drowsy in the sun, I kept wishing Arne were there, too; I kept thinking about what it would be like some day when we were all together.

Jennie sat on the wall beside me, her head against my shoulder. She had twined a yellow dandelion in her hair; it gave out a fresh, weedy fragrance. The sky was robin's egg blue; I heard a bird singing in the woods. I was happy—happier than I had ever been before, happier than I've ever been since.

Gus left us after lunch, and went back to the cab, to take a nap. Then Jennie too grew silent, resting against me, dreamy and content. After a while, I felt her stir, and draw a long, uneven breath. "What are you thinking, Jennie?" I asked.

She answered slowly and gently, "I'm thinking how beautiful the world is, Eben; and how it keeps on being beautiful—no matter what happens to us. The spring comes year after year, for us, or Egypt; the sun goes down in the same green, lovely sky; the birds sing . . . for us, or yesterday . . . or for tomorrow. It was never made for anything but beauty, Eben—whether we lived now, or long ago."

"Tomorrow," I said. "But when is tomorrow, Jennie?"

"Does it matter?" she asked. "It's always. This was tomorrow—once.

"Promise me you'll never forget."

I quoted softly:

> "Where I come from
> Nobody knows;
> And where I'm going
> Everything goes."

She took it up with a little cry of surprise:

> "The wind blows,
> The sea flows—
> And God knows.

"I think He knows, Eben," she said.

And she lifted her lips, trusting and innocent, to mine.

Later we walked in the faint green of the woods, through the shadow of branches, over the ferns and the moss. We found a little brook, and violets hidden among their leaves. Jennie stopped to pick them; she made a tiny bunch, to carry home. "It's to remember today," she said.

The sun began to sink in the west; the shadows fell around us. It grew chilly; we turned, and started home.

CHAPTER XIV

I had one clear day of happiness, and I shall never forget it. Even the miserable ending to it cannot change its quality in my memory; for everything that Jennie and I did was good, and unhappiness came only from the outside. Not many—lovers or friends—can say as much. For friends and lovers are quick to wound, quicker than strangers, even; the heart that opens itself to the world, opens itself to sorrow.

I don't think that we spoke of the question of where Jennie was to stay that night. She was sailing in the morning (on the Mauretania, I remember she told me—how strange it was to hear the old name again) and we both seemed to take it for granted that we'd stay together until then.

We had supper at the Alhambra, at a little table near the bar, where she could see my mural, and then we walked home together in the quiet evening. It was cool, the air was still, and in the green west the evening star hung like a lantern over the city.

Those are the scenes, the memories, with which I comfort myself. The spring comes year after year, she had said, and tomorrow is always. When at last there was no tomorrow any more, I remembered yesterday. Yesterday is always, too.

She told me that she had been at the gallery that day of the exhibition, when I thought I had seen her; and that she had been crying. "I don't know why," she said. "It was a picture of a river, and some little hills across on the other side—the Pamet, it was called. And all of a sudden I felt that I knew it, and that it was a sad place—and I found myself crying. I wanted to come to you, but I couldn't; I had to go back. I was unhappy for a while, and then I forgot it."

She put her hand in mine; it was trembling a little. "I'm sorry that you asked me," she said. "I didn't want to remember it."

I turned her hand over, and patted it. "It's a funny little river, Jennie," I said, "and not sad at all. It comes in from the bay, and it's not very deep. The children play there, and the bitterns croak in the reeds at night. And at low tide, everybody goes out and digs for clams."

She smiled uncertainly. "I know," she said. "I'm being silly. Don't let's talk about it any more. Tell me about Paris, instead—you were there, weren't you? Is it very lovely? My school is in Passy—is that near where you were? Tell me what to see, and what to do—so that some day we'll have done it all together. . . ."

We sat on the edge of the bed, and talked for a long time. I told her about Arne, about the Atelier Dufoix, about the Clos des Lilas, where we used to go sometimes when we had money, and the little bistro on the Rue du Bac where we went when we didn't. She listened to me hungrily, seeing it all ahead of her. "Oh Eben," she said; "it's going to be such fun."

We even planned what we'd do together. I remembered a room on the Île St. Louis, where a friend of mine had lived—a room like the prow of a ship, butting its way up the Seine, and the river pouring by on both sides, under the windows. I promised to take her to the Luxembourg, to the Quai des Marinières, and to the Fair at Neuilly—I promised to dance with her in the Place Pigalle on Bastille Day—and to take her out into the Forest of St. Cloud in the spring, to drink new wine under the trees. "It's going to be such fun," she said.

It was late when Mrs. Jekes knocked on the door. I think I shall remember the sound of it all my life. When death comes at last, I expect he'll sound like that, too.

Even before the door opened, I think I had an idea of what was coming. She stood in the doorway, a still, wintry figure, her hands folded, as always, across her stomach. "Oh no," she said; "oh no. Not in my house, not at night, you won't. There's a limit to everything, my friends. I've run a decent place all my life, and I mean to keep it so."

And pointing a white, shaking finger at Jennie, she cried suddenly,

"Get out."

I was too startled even to speak. I seemed to freeze up inside; perhaps it was just as well, for otherwise there's no telling what I might have done. Jennie got up from the bed, slowly, as though in a dream; she turned her frightened face away from me, so that I shouldn't see how ashamed she was. She went quietly over to the chair where she had laid her hat and coat.

"I'm sorry, Eben," she faltered. "I didn't think . . ."

"Get out," said Mrs. Jekes.

I found my voice then. "Be still," I cried to her; and to Jennie: "Don't listen . . . don't listen to her."

But Jennie shook her head. "No," she said; "no—it's too late now: it's been said. It couldn't ever not be said again."

She took up her hat and coat, and stooped to pick up the little suitcase which lay by the door where she had dropped it that morning. Mrs. Jekes moved aside to let her pass. She went by her without a glance, but she turned in the doorway, and looked back at me—a look so full of longing, of love, and of trust, that it was like a hand laid for a moment against my cheek. It was that look, more than anything else, which kept me from rushing after her.

"Goodbye, Eben," she said clearly. "I'll be back again some day—But not like this. Not ever again like this. Not until we can be together always."

Mrs. Jekes watched her go. She followed her down the stairs; I heard her footsteps grow fainter and fainter down the stairs.

CHAPTER XV

I moved out of Mrs. Jekes' house after that; and since summer was not far off, I decided to join Arne on the Cape at once. Mr. Mathews and Miss Spinney said goodbye to me like old friends; Mr. Mathews gave me a little folding easel which had belonged to Fromkes, and Miss Spinney gave me a bottle of brandy—to keep, as she put it, the fog out of my fingers. "I want another flower-piece," she declared; "a two-and-a-half by four; and a church. I'm sort of fond of churches, the little white ones, with the big steeples. Goodbye, and God bless you. Don't drown yourself in the sea."

"What would I want to drown myself in the sea for?" I asked.

"I don't know," she answered. "Men are fools enough to do anything. Personally, I don't trust the sea. I wouldn't go within fifty miles of it."

"You're tough," I said. "The sea would never get you."

She looked at me with a strange expression; I saw the red start to creep up over her chin. "It's the tough ones drown easy," she said, and turned away.

Mr. Mathews walked to the door with me; he kept reaching up every now and then to pat me on the back. "Goodbye, my boy," he said, "goodbye. I'm glad you came to me; we'll do big things together. You've earned a rest; now enjoy it. But remember—no landscapes. Leave the dunes to Eastwood."

"I want to do the fishermen," I said.

"Fishermen," he echoed doubtfully; "well . . ."

"In the traps," I said, "in the early morning, with the fish churning in the nets."

Mr. Mathews looked at me gloomily. "Listen," he said. "There are enough fish in the world."

He sighed heavily. "But not enough women," he added.

Gus took me to my train. "Take care of yourself, Mack," he said. "Don't do anything I wouldn't do." I had Jennie's violets in a paper bag in my pocket; they were withered by now, but they still retained a little of their fragrance. My paints and canvases and my easel were in one bundle, and my clothes were in another. The train went at midnight, the great office buildings were dark as we drove down to the station. I kept thinking of how Jennie had been there in the cab with me only the day before.

I knew that I'd see her again, and I told Gus so. "Sure," he said; "sure. Why not? You don't want to be too wise in this world, Mack, because there's always something happens you don't expect. You take my own people, now—they thought they weren't going to get out of Egypt. But they got out all right. And why? So they could write the Bible.

"They couldn't have guessed that."

"They didn't have to guess it," I said.

"I know," said Gus; "you mean Somebody told them. Well—what did He tell them? That's what I want to know."

"I thought He made it clear," I said.

"Not to me," said Gus. "I'm still trying to figure it out. And the way I figure it, is like this: whatever it was, it was good news, on account of the only bad news would be that what we knew was all there was."

I started to pull out some money to pay him for the ride, but he waved it away. "Forget it," he said. "The flag wasn't down. You've done plenty for me."

"Goodbye, Gus," I said. "I'll see you in the fall."

"Sure," he agreed. "Drop me a postal."

I hesitated a moment before picking up my bags. "You think God is trying to tell me something?" I asked, half in earnest.

"I wouldn't put it past Him," said Gus.

"But what?" I cried.

He shook his head. "I wouldn't know," he said.

I came down into Provincetown the next afternoon. The moment we crossed the bridge at Bourne, and I breathed the warm, sunny fragrance of scrub pine and broom, I felt the old peace of summer flow into me. Lilac was out in the Yarmouth yards and doorways, and in Brewster the juice-pear and the wild plum had opened their blossoms, white as snow. The marshes at Wellfleet were all a silvery green; and beyond Truro, there was the bay, still and shining, bluer than a bluebird's wing, with Plymouth clear, dark, and distant on the horizon.

Arne was waiting for me; he had a room in the west end of town, down near Furtado's boat yard, and he took me there to wash up and get settled. I went to the window, and drew in a deep breath of the past. How well I remembered it. The old weedy, fishy smell rose from the tide; the gulls were circling and crying, out in the harbor; and on the sand below, Manuel was hammering at the white hull of a lobsterman. The schooner *Mary P. Goulart* was in harbor, along with most of the fisheries' fleet; and I saw John Worthington's tunaman, the *Bocage*, come chugging in across the blue water from the North Truro nets, kicking up a little foam at her bows. Slowly and peacefully sky and water deepened; the sun went down over Peaked Hill Bars, and the ruby light came on at Wood End, and the white light at the Point.

We walked down to the fish wharf, past Dyer's hardware store and Page's Garage, past the post office, and the little square with its great elms. The summer visitors hadn't begun to arrive yet, and the town was quiet, with only its own people in the streets. Dark faced fishermen lounged in the doorways, talking together in their own language, half argot and half Portuguese; and the girls went by, two by two in the dusk, hatless and laughing. We stopped in at Taylor's for supper, and I ordered a chowder, the way they make it down there. I wanted to hear the Provincetown news:—who was teaching that year, and how the classes were shaping up, whether Jerry Farnsworth had his old studio, and whether Tom Blakeman was going to take a class in etching again. And then, of course, Arne had to hear about the portrait. When I told him that Mr. Mathews hoped to sell it to a museum some day, he flung out his hands in horror.

"Don't have it, Eben," he thundered. "Never allow it. A museum? The death of the soul."

"Sure," I said. "Like Innes, or Chase."

"They're dead," he answered. "That's all past and done with."

"Is it?" I asked. "I'm not so sure."

"Good God," he bellowed earnestly; "the past is behind us. What?"

"There's still Rembrandt," I said, "and Van Gogh. We're not quite done with them yet. . . . The past isn't behind us, Arne—it's all around us. And down here, on the Cape, is where one ought to feel it most—where the years follow each other like tides in the Pamet, and the boats come in each day with the same fish they had before."

I smiled at him across the table. "I'm only beginning to think about things like that," I said.

"Well," he said unhappily, "I wish you wouldn't. The artist ought not to think so much, it's bad for his color sense."

And with that, we plunged into the old debate, and for the rest of the meal the talk was all of color and line, symbol, form, and mass. "I tell you," cried Arne, pulling at his beard, "we must be like little children again. We must bring back color into the world. That is what color is for, to look at. Do not think: paint. Like children."

He pounded the table, clutched his beard, and roared like a bull. He was perfectly happy. I asked him whether he expected the children to understand his paintings, and he gave me a look of scorn. "Only an artist," he declared, "can hope to understand what another artist is trying to do. That is why there is so little understanding of art among the masses.

"Just the same," he added inconsequentially, "the museums are always full of children."

It was always like that with Arne.

As we went out into the street again after supper, on our way home, he said to me in a hopeful way,

"Is this model of yours coming to the Cape this summer, Eben?"

I answered almost without thinking. "Yes," I said. "Some day." He nodded his great head thoughtfully. "Good," he said. "I shall do a portrait of her, myself."

It amused me, as I laughed quietly in the darkness. That would be something to see, that picture.

But it made me feel lonely all of a sudden. I wondered where Jennie was, and what she was doing—in what far off place over which this velvet blue and soft spring evening of ours had long since passed like a wind. Was she still at sea? Night was on the sea, the dark sweep of earth's shadow; but tomorrow's sun was already rising above the eastern slopes of the Urals. And yesterday's sun? did it still shine on the low stone wall at the meadow's edge, near the little wood? It was still today, still noon on the Pacific, on the long, blue swells which washed Hawaii. Yesterday . . . tomorrow . . . where were they?

It would be a long time until Jennie came back to me. Not until we could be together always, she had said. A long summer . . . Hurry, I said to her, in my heart.

I knew that I could never explain it to Arne. I didn't try.

The damp sea air, salty and fresh from the flats, or suddenly pierced with spice from the flowering gardens of Provincetown, flowed around us as we wandered home under the white street lamps. In the harbor the riding lights of the *Mary P. Goulart* rocked gently in the gloom; the beams of the lighthouses at Long Point and Wood End, blinked at the bay; and the great white cross of High Land Light at North Truro swept like the spokes of a wheel through the heavens. The stars burned calmly overhead . . . how many years ago had those metallic rays first leaped out across the empty spaces between their home and ours? Long, long ago; from beyond our furthest yesterday.

The gulls were sleeping out on the water, in the blue dark, silent and forgetful, ranged in rows along the decks of the empty fishing boats. The streets were quiet and deserted; we heard our footsteps following us home.

CHAPTER XVI

But I didn't want to stay in Provincetown for the summer. I still had more than two hundred dollars left of the money I had received for the portrait, and I decided to take a small house in Truro, on the Pamet. It was little more than a shack, really, up on the bluff above the water; the pines stood close, making a brown carpet of needles all around the house, and you looked down at the river through their branches. I could hear the waters of the bay endlessly sounding, and the wind in the pines, not unlike the sound of the sea. The air was warm and sweet with the odor of earth and sun, and there was shelter from the easterly rains, and from the northwest wind, which soared up strong and cold over Cornhill behind me. I was right in the path of a southeast blow, or a smoky sou'wester, but that was an advantage; the winds from the south were fair weather winds, and came in warm and soft.

At low tide the Pamet is no more than a trickle of water among the reeds; but at full moon, and with a full course tide, it overflows the marshes, and one can imagine it as it once was, before the sand piled up at the harbor mouth—a wide, deep river on which as many as thirty whalers could ride to their moorings. But that was long ago. Today the little river pours in and out of a narrow channel to the bay, and wanders crookedly across the Cape between the bay and the ocean. Perhaps a hundred yards from where the Pamet rises among its springs, the low dunes begin; and just across them is the beach and the sea. It's not a long trip from ocean to bay; the Cape is narrow at that end, less than three miles wide.

The little houses nestle in the hollows, safe from the northwest winds which blow so hard in winter. There is pine, and scrub oak, locust, aspen, and elm, bearberry, gorse, wintergreen, beach plum, and cherry. Everything is on a small scale; the tiny hills and hollows, seen in perspective, have the appearance of mountains and valleys. The spires of the two old churches and the meeting house dominate everything; they rise on the highest ridge, and brood serene and lovely over the valleys.

Families still live in Truro from the old days: the Snows, the Dyers, the Atwoods, Atkinses, Cobbs, Paines, Riches. Old names, old families of Cape Cod. . . . It is their country, their home, it belongs to them. They are quiet and kind, hard-working people.

I settled down to work, too. But for a week or so, the colors of the Cape made all my senses drowsy—the pale sand-yellow, the light green, and the faded blue of water and sky deepening off to violet in the distance. Birds on their way north were stopping off to visit; robins searched the lawns, finches darted like minnows in and out of the trees, a pair of orioles had built a nest in the elm tree back of my house.

By June the gorse was yellow, and the bearberries pink and white on the downs; bob-whites called to each other in the grass. I went down to swim in the river; it was swift and fresh, and the little green crabs fled away from me in the shallows. Some children were there already, playing in an old hulk drawn up on the shore. One, with hair the color of hay, was playing that he was a pirate. He had his crew ready for battle; they consisted of a cap pistol, and his sister. He could not find an enemy.

All summer the children play on the beaches. They are happy and friendly; as each wave sweeps in across the sand, the smaller ones turn their backs to the sea, and run sensibly away. When the water, edged with foam, draws back again, they go running after it, with an air of driving the ocean before them. But at the next wave, they flee as before, with shrill alarm, and fresh surprise. The sun warms their small brown legs, and they collect with enthusiasm bits of clam shell, sand dollars, and colored stones worn by the tide. The larger children plunge into the waves like little dolphins. The water is clear and cold.

Time stands still in Truro; the weeks slip by, one after another. In June there was a nor'easter, the wind came whistling in from the sea, driving the rain almost level before it; it blew for three days, doors swelled and stuck, bureau drawers wouldn't open, and a green mold appeared on some of my canvases. Even the pine logs which burned all day in the fireplace couldn't keep my little house warm or dry. Then the wind swung around to the west, the sun came out, and there was the summer again, the pale sand-yellow, the light green, and the faded blue.

I did a good deal of painting: I did a canvas of the South Truro church for Miss Spinney, the old building, lonely and empty on the downs above the bay; and a watercolor of the sea from the end of Long Nook valley. It was a breezy day, with the wind northeast, the sea was dark, the wine-dark of the Greeks, with bands of green in it, darkening out to the horizon; and the sky was like the inside of a blue porcelain bowl with the light shining through it. I sent them both to Mr. Mathews. But the best thing I did was a painting of the men out in the traps in the early morning. I had to do it mostly from memory: the boats go out to the nets before it's light.

Everything is quiet and dark, the water comes in in long swells out of the darkness. The boats head out into the swells . . . in the east the sky turns grey, and then pink, the dawn comes up slowly. The stars pale out, tones of blue begin to show in the sky. Far out from shore, one boat slips into the traps, drawing the nets up as it goes. The fish are down there, they pass backwards and forwards under the boat like shadows. The nets come higher; suddenly they break water in a rush of silver, and the fishermen begin scooping them in over the sides. The sun rises, the bay sparkles in the light, the fish are silver underfoot. Slowly and heavily one of the boats crosses the bay to Provincetown, while the other heads back again to the shore.

I wanted Arne to go with me, but he said there wasn't enough color in it for him. He was painting the Provincetown Electric Light and Power Plant; he said that it represented industry, and that industry represented the real world of today, and that it was this real world in which an artist should look for a subject worthy of him.

"Let us not fool ourselves, Eben," he exclaimed. "Beauty is only noble when it is useful. The symbol of the world today is a power plant; and if it appears ugly to us, that is only because we do not look at it in the right way."

But he came to Truro for the beach picnics in July. We lay on the sand at Cornhill, while the sun set, and the moon rose over the hill behind us, and men in corduroys and women with kerchiefs around their hair tended the fire of driftwood gathered on the beach. The sunset paled away into rose and green; the old blue night came down dim and hazy over the shore, and across the bay the lanterns of Provincetown twinkled in the dusk. Within the leaping yellow light of our fire the figures of our friends moved about; more wood was gathered, baskets unpacked, rugs laid down. As the flames burned lower toward the coals, steaks and sausages were broiled; a great bean pot was set beside the fire, a pail of mussels, a kettle of coffee. Afterwards we sang, sitting around the fire, while the moon sailed gently overhead, and the tide sent little ripples to break against the sand . . . "*I dream of Jeannie with the light brown hair* . . ."

Or in the still, warm afternoons of August, we swam together in the sea, as the long rollers came lifting in, green and clear, to break in a bounce of foam, and slide hissing and dying up the beach. Far out, beyond the line of the horizon, beyond sight, over the world's rim, lay Europe, torn with her wars; but here all was peace, the empty shore curved away endlessly to the south under the summer sun, the light breeze stirred the grasses on the dunes, and only the shouts of children rose against the rolling thunder of the sea.

It was then that I longed for Jennie, at such times as these, when the world's beauty fell most upon my heart. And yet, in a way which I found hard to explain, I was not lonely; for I had a sense—as I have had ever since—of not being alone—a feeling that the world and Jennie and I were one, joined together in a unity for which there was no name, an inexpressible one-ness. Her very absence, not only from my sight, but from the slow-wheeling days around me, made them seem less real and solid to me; she was nowhere in the weather, the rains which fell across the Cape were not the rains which fell upon her little figure hurrying along somewhere—in what city, in what year?—yet for that reason all weathers seemed one weather to me, and the seasons of the past mingled in my dreams with the summer all around me. For she was somewhere in the world; and wherever she was, there, too, was something of me.

She had said: "How beautiful the world is, Eben. It was never made for anything but beauty—whether we lived now, or long ago."

We had that beauty together. We never lost it.

CHAPTER XVII

Summer drained away into fall, but Jennie did not return. By September the bearberries were red, and people were picking beach plums in the fields along the roads, to make into jelly. The reeds in the river were silver-brown; and in the afternoons the sun slanted lower through the pines around my house. The birds which had been gone most of the summer, began to appear again, on their way south: red-headed woodpeckers, bluebirds, warblers, and grackles. Swallows swept nervously through the air, and sometimes at evening I saw a wedge of wild duck wavering southward against the sky.

I had received a good-sized check from Mr. Mathews, and decided to use some of it to rent a little sailboat from John Worthington's brother, Bill, who lived near the railroad bridge, close to where the Pamet emptied into the bay. I knew something about sailing, though not a great deal; but

I didn't think I could get into much trouble. The boat, an eighteen-foot center-board knock-about, was kept moored near the mouth of the river, in a small backwater to one side of the swiftly moving stream. It took a good bit of navigating to get out into the bay, through the narrow channel; tide and wind both had to be right, but the wind seemed almost always easterly that month, streaming back from the Bermuda high which stood like a formidable but invisible cloud somewhere out at sea; and with a stiff breeze behind me, I could usually manage to make out, even against the tide. Coming back, I had to wait for the current, and then come in close-hauled. Arne constituted himself my crew; he sat forward, ducked the boom when we came about, and handled the jib sheets with a sort of wild solemnity. It was exciting to lean against the wind, and feel the boat fight back against it; to watch the green water slide by, and hear the current chuckle against the planking. It was good exercise, too; it made my arms ache, and put blisters on my hands.

We used to sail out into the bay, sometimes as far as the traps, once or twice as far as Provincetown. It was a world by itself, out there on the water, in the shine and sun-dazzle, a world of never-ending blue, of steady wind, of clear and arrowy distance; and I was happy there.

Late in September a hurricane was reported in the Caribbean. We thought little about it, it was the time of year for hurricanes, they either hit the Florida Keys, or blew themselves out in the Atlantic. This one apparently was headed for Florida.

On the Cape we had a period of unusually clear weather—a weather-breeder, Arne said. We made the most of it, for the season was drawing to an end, the line storm would be along soon, and after that it would be too cold and rough for sailing. We went out every day. The weather was warm—unnaturally so for that time of year—and the wind southeast. We waited for it to swing around into the north.

On Monday the report was that the storm had missed Florida, and was heading for the Carolinas. That meant rain and a southwest blow; but on Tuesday we heard that it had turned east again, and would lose itself out at sea. So we figured we still had a few days' good sailing weather left to us, and decided to make a long trip up the coast, camp over night on Great Island off Wellfleet, and come home the next day. We left a little before noon on Tuesday; there was a steady breeze from the southeast, and we made a fair reach of it all the way.

We camped that night on the island, and built a fire at the sand's edge. We talked for a long time in the firelight; the shadows danced in the scrub behind us, the pale sky, sown with its stars, lay like a great lake above us, and the little boat rocked quietly at its anchor, on the tide. I tried to tell Arne something of what was in my mind, about myself, and about the world. "We know so little," I said, "and there's so much to know. We live by taste and touch; we see only what is under our noses. There are solar systems up there above us, greater than our own; and whole universes in a drop of water. And time stretches out endlessly on every side. This earth, this ocean, this little moment of living, has no meaning by itself . . . Yesterday is just as true as today; only we forget."

Arne yawned. "Yes," he said. "So it is. Go to sleep."

"And love," I said, "is endless, too; and today's little happiness is only part of it."

"Go to sleep," said Arne. "Tomorrow is another day."

That night, for the first time in my life, I dreamed of Jennie: I dreamed of our meeting, long ago, I dreamed it over again as it had happened; I saw her as the child, walking down the long empty row of benches in the Mall, and I heard her say as she had said then, "I wish you'd wait for me to grow up, but you won't, I guess." And in my dream, I remembered the words of her little tuneless song—

"The wind blows, the sea flows . . ."

I woke with a sense of alarm, with a feeling that something was wrong. The wind was still blowing, warm and steadily southeast, but I thought a little stronger. There was a faint haze in the air, and a few strange looking clouds passed by overhead. They seemed to be travelling fast. I leaned over and shook Arne by the shoulder. "Get up, Arne," I said. "We've got to get home."

We put the sail up and headed north for Truro. We didn't waste any time. Out on the water, the wind seemed even stronger; it was a little aft of us, and I let the sail take all it would. It was something of a job to hold the tiller, for a fair sea was running, and the boat yawed a good deal. Arne said nothing; he kept watching the sky.

The haze deepened very slowly, but the clouds increased; they were at different levels, moving rapidly, and of a shape I'd never seen before—long cylinders, fog-like tentacles, smoky fingers. They were a different tone of white, too, like cotton gone a little dusty. I had made the main sheet fast, but I wondered if the sail would hold. "Arne," I called to him, "hadn't we better reef?"

He nodded without speaking, and I managed to bring the boat up into the wind. I noticed that my fingers were trembling, and I thought that Arne looked a little pale. There was a curious urgency in the wind. "We'd better get out of here," I said.

The boat went off with a rush under a single reef, and I tried to head up a little to windward, to get some shelter from the shore. The waves were running a good deal higher now, and breaking at the crests; I had to put all my weight on the tiller to hold her steady. I was feeling decidedly uneasy, and I wondered whether I oughtn't to try to make for shore directly, but there was nowhere except the Pamet at Truro where I could have found shelter for the boat. I had no idea how hard the wind was blowing, but I knew it was blowing hard. And there was a strange sound to it, from somewhere far away.

A little before noon I saw Arne point behind us, and followed his glance back over the stern. The horizon to the south had disappeared behind a grey haze. It wasn't altogether grey, but grey-yellow, like mud. I thought perhaps it was rain, but it didn't look like it. We've got to get out of this, I thought.

My arms and hands were aching from holding the tiller, and my legs were tired from bracing myself against the sides. I beckoned Arne to come aft and take over, while I went forward to bail some of the water that had come in, mostly over the stern. Down in the cockpit, the waves seemed higher than ever; we would tilt up at the stern, hang for a moment on a crest, and then rush down the slope after it, and slew around in the hollow till Arne straightened us out. Each time the tip of the boom hit the water, I thought we'd go over. My throat was dry, but I didn't feel frightened, I didn't have time. I kept listening to the wind; it wasn't like anything I'd ever heard before.

A little after that we started to work in toward the Pamet. I went back to the tiller, and told Arne to take the sheet, and let it out whenever we got over too far. He snubbed it around a cleat as well as he could, but it took all his great strength to hold it. We lay out to windward on the deck, with our legs braced against the centerboard scabbard; the huge seas broke behind us, and then foamed up over the counter, and the dark green water poured along the leeward deck up to the coaming. It seemed to me that we looked right down at the sea under our feet; it rose sometimes in a slice of wave and curled up over the cockpit; then I kicked the tiller, and we came up. We seemed half in and half out of the water most of the time, I couldn't tell which. "I think we'll make it, though," I said. Arne shook his head. "Maybe," he answered.

About two hundred yards from shore, the mainsail went out, torn loose near the peak; and a moment later, the jib. I thought we were done for then; but both sails caught in the rigging and snagged, and the boat eased. I saw that as long as they held, we had a sort of double reef; and we hadn't much further to go. "I think we'll make it, Arne," I said.

I could barely see the river mouth for the waves, which gave me an idea of how high the tide was running; but I set a course for the railroad bridge, and trusted to luck. We hit it right, and went in through a white fury of foam, on a roaring breaker which picked us up and ran us up the channel like a chip of wood, and flung us out on the sand a hundred yards from the bay. Arne was out first, but before he could get the mainsail down, the wind tore it out of his hands, and sent it ballooning across the river, with half the rigging attached to it. We got the anchor out, but I knew it wouldn't hold. The waves were booming in through the river mouth, six feet high, and coming up the channel like wild horses. "It's no good, Arne," I said. "The tide's coming in; she'll drag right down to the bridge, and lose her mast." There was nothing we could do. I hadn't figured on such a high tide.

Bill Worthington had seen us come in. He was waiting for us as we climbed up onto the road from what was left of the beach. "Well, by God," he said, "you boys were out in something."

I grinned back at him, but I felt pretty shaky. My legs were trembling, and I couldn't keep my teeth together. "I'm sorry about the boat, Bill," I said. "I didn't figure the storm would be so bad."

Bill looked at me, and shook his head. "Storm, hell," he said. "This one's a hurricane."

CHAPTER XVIII

Bill told us that hurricane signals were flying at High Land Light; he said it made him feel queer in the pit of his stomach. But it was still only the beginning; we all knew that.

We made the boat fast as well as we could, and then Bill drove us home to the north side of the river. We could hear the sand pit against the car whenever we crossed an exposed place in the road, and once or twice the car swerved sharply in a sudden gust. Bill left us at the house, and went back to watch the tide. His own house wasn't any too far above high water.

It was only then, as we started down the path to the shack, that I began to have an idea of what the wind was really like. Out there, on the water, I'd been too busy; and besides, in a sort of way, we had been part of it, moving with it, running before it. But here, facing the open sweep from the southeast, I caught it full and fair, and it hit me like a blow.

The wind was coming across the Pamet in a steady flow, almost like a river of air in flood. There was no let up to it, it came flowing over heavy and solid and fast; it had pushed the marsh grass down flat, and bent the pines over in a quarter circle. There was something unnatural about it; it seemed to be coming from far away, but all the time it was coming nearer, and I had a feeling that it was darkness itself coming, and a force that didn't belong on this earth. My heart was beating fast; I felt cold and excited. I could hear that strange sound I had heard out on the bay, a sort of roaring hum, high up and far off; and the yellow-grey wall was still down there to the south. Or had it come closer? I couldn't tell. I looked down the slope at the river; it was up over the marsh, and the water was brown, and streaked with yellow foam. "I'm glad we're here,"

I said to Arne, shouting against the wind. He smiled then, for the first time. "If the house holds," he said.

A branch from a locust down at the water's edge suddenly snapped, and sailed a few yards up the slope toward us. "Come on," I said; "let's go in."

We went around the back way, to get out of the direct force of the wind. While we'd been gone the grocer had left a box of eggs on the little back porch; they were all over the floor. I thought, that'll be a mess to clean up tomorrow, but I didn't stop. The wind picked us up, and swept us in through the door, and we had to lean back against it to close it. It was cold and still in the house, but I could hear the roaring in my ears, from those hours out on the bay. After a while the noise in my ears went away, and then I could hear the storm itself, and that high, far off, humming sound.

Arne made a fire, and I got out the whiskey. I took a big drink; I could feel it warm me all the way down. We stood in front of the fire, and looked at each other. I could feel the house shake every now and then, and I heard the windows rattle; I wondered if I ought to try to put up the shutters, I tried to remember what I'd read about hurricanes. But then I remembered that the house had no shutters. There didn't seem to be anything to do.

"I wonder if the boat will hold," I said.

"I wouldn't think so," said Arne.

"We were lucky, at that," I said.

I took another drink. "I wonder how they're making out in Provincetown," I said.

Arne shook his head gloomily. "It'll be bad, all right," he remarked.

The rain began about then. It wasn't much of a downpour, but it came in almost level. In ten minutes there was a fair-sized puddle just inside the door. I laid a towel along the lintel, to keep the water out.

The wind seemed to be getting stronger all the time; once or twice it shook the house so hard I thought the walls would go. There was nothing to do but just sit there and wait for something to happen; and after a while, Arne said he thought we ought to go out and have a look around. He said he wanted to see what a hurricane looked like. We went out the back way, and it took all our strength to get the door closed after us. But when we got around to the front of the house, we couldn't breathe; the wind tore the air right out of our mouths. "Boy," said Arne, holding his hands in front of his face, "I'm glad I'm not out on the bay now."

I tried to see the bay, but it was lost in weather, a grey smother of rain and spray and blowing sand. I saw that the telegraph poles beyond Cat Island were down, and I pointed at them. And then the big elm behind the house went.

It went over slowly, with a sort of sigh, taking a lot of ground with it. Arne didn't say anything, but his eyes had a wild look in them. He grabbed my arm, and pointed across the river. A moment later we saw Bill Worthington's old barn sag over on its side, and watched the wind worry it along toward the river. "Maybe we ought to go over and help him," I shouted, with my mouth close to Arne's ear. He made a gesture of helplessness. "How are we going to get there?" he shouted back.

We were still watching Bill's house, crouched together with our arms wrapped around one of the straining pines, when the coastguard truck came by. It stopped on the road behind us, and a guardsman came clumping over in boots and oilskins. "Jeez," he said, "what do you guys think you're doing?" We told him that we were watching Bill's barn being blown into the river. "Well," he said, "there'll be more than that in the river soon. The ocean's breaking through at Dune Hollow." He walked back to the truck, and they went on, toward Cat Island, and John Rule's house out at the edge of the marsh.

We were pretty high above the water where we were, and I didn't think even the ocean would reach that far. At any rate, we didn't have long to wait; in about ten minutes we saw the wave coming down the valley toward us, from the sea. It didn't look very high—just a line of brown foam, with branches and sand in it, but it was scary. It passed under us, and then there wasn't any marsh left, just water, moving fast.

And a moment later, I saw her.

She was below me, and a little to the east, near the town landing, trying to get up the slope from the river. She seemed tired; and the wind was worrying her like a dog. While I watched, she lost her balance, and half fell; and then she began to slip backward toward the water again. Another wave was coming down the valley from the east; I could see it coming.

I don't know how I got down the hill to her, against the wind, but I did. I got my arm around her just in time, and pulled her up out of the way; the crest went by almost a foot below us. She lay back against me, white and spent, with closed eyes. "I was afraid I wouldn't get here, darling," she said.

I held her close. Even then, with that mad flood below us, I thought we'd make it all right. I put my face down against hers; her cheeks were deathly cold. She lifted her hands slowly, as though they were a great weight, and put her arms around my neck. "I had to get back to you, Eben," she said.

"We'll have to hurry, Jennie," I told her. I tried to pull her along, up the slope, but she was like a dead weight, she seemed to have no strength left at all. She smiled at me piteously, and shook her head. "You go, Eben," she said; "I can't make it."

I tried to lift her, then, but she was too heavy for me; I couldn't find a foothold on the slippery ground. The water was higher, now, almost at our feet; a dark ripple washed in over my ankles. "Jennie," I cried, "for God's sake . . ."

"Let me look at you," she whispered. I couldn't hear her, but I knew what she was saying. She held my face in her hands, and looked at me for a moment with wide, dark eyes. "It's been a long time, darling," she said.

I didn't want to talk, I wanted to get out of there, I wanted to get her up the slope away from the water. "Look," I said, "if I could lift you up on my back . . ."

But she didn't seem to hear me. "Yes," she said, almost to herself; "I wasn't wrong."

"Jennie," I cried; "please . . ."

Her arms tightened around me for a moment. "Hold me close, Eben," she said. "We're together, now."

I held her close, but my mind was in a panic. I couldn't lift her, I couldn't get her away, and the ground where we were standing was beginning to give. "Arne," I shouted as loudly as I could; "Arne."

It was then I saw it coming.

It came in from the bay, a great brown wave, sweeping back up the valley toward the sea. There was no escape from it; we could never have climbed above it; it came in steady and very fast, with a strange sucking noise. Well, I thought, we'll go together, anyhow.

Bending over, I kissed her full on the lips. "Yes, Jennie," I said; "we're together now."

She knew what was coming. "Eben," she whispered, pressed against my cheek, "there's only one love . . . nothing can change it. It's still all right, darling, whatever happens, because we'll always be together . . . somewhere . . ."

"I know," I said.

And then the wave hit us. I tried to hold on to her, to go out with her, but it tore us apart. I felt her whirled out of my arms; the water drew me under, and rolled me over and over; I felt myself flung upwards, sucked down, and then flung upwards again. Then something crashed into me, and that was all I knew.

Arne found me sprawled in a tree half in and half out of the water, and dragged me back to safety. How he managed to carry me up the slope and back to the house in that wind, I don't know. He put me to bed, and made me drink almost a pint of whiskey; and he sat beside me all that night. He told me later that he had to hold me down in bed, that I kept trying to get back to the river. I don't remember much about it, it was all dark for me, all I remember is the dark.

It was a week before I could travel, but it made no difference, because the roads were out, and we couldn't have gotten through, anyway. I lay in bed, and ate what Arne gave me, and tried not to think about what had happened. Arne brought back the news from outside; he told me that there hadn't been as much damage in Truro as we'd thought; a lot of trees had gone over in Provincetown, and a fishing boat had been flung up on the rocks; John Worthington's nets were gone at North Truro, but except for the ocean breaking through into the Pamet, it hadn't been so bad. Even Bill's home had escaped, though the water had come up as high as the windows. The beach at Dune Hollow had started to build up again; pretty soon everything would be the same as before.

I came back to the city on a bright autumn day, deep blue and sun-yellow in the streets, and the great buildings rising clear and sharp in the keen, high air. Mr. Mathews was waiting for me at the gallery. "We worried about you, Eben," he said. "Miss Spinney and I . . . we couldn't get any news for a long while."

He patted me awkwardly on the shoulder. "I'm glad to see you, my boy," he said. "I—I'm very glad . . ."

Miss Spinney didn't say anything. She looked to me as though she had been crying.

It was Gus who gave me the little clipping from the newspaper. "I thought maybe you hadn't seen it, Mack," he said.

It was from the Times, of September 22nd. "The steamship Latania," it read, "has reported by wireless today the loss of one of its passengers in the storm, a hundred miles off the Nantucket Lightship. Miss Jennie Appleton, who was returning to America after a stay of eight years abroad, was swept overboard by a wave which smashed a part of the bridge, and injured several of the passengers. Officials of the line are endeavoring to discover the whereabouts of Miss Appleton's relatives in this country."

Gus hesitated; he looked at me, and then he looked away. "I thought maybe you didn't know," he said. "I'm sorry, Mack."

I gave the clipping back to him. "No," I said, "I knew.

"It's still all right," I said. "It's all right."

Truro,
1949

LA GRANDE BRETÊCHE

HONORÉ DE BALZAC

AH! MADAME," replied the doctor, "I have some appalling stories in my collection. But each one has its proper hour in a conversation—you know the pretty jest recorded by Chamfort, and said to the Duc de Fronsac: 'Between your sally and the present moment lie ten bottles of champagne.'"

"But it is two in the morning, and the story of Rosina has prepared us," said the mistress of the house.

"Tell us, Monsieur Bianchon!" was the cry on every side.

The obliging doctor bowed, and silence reigned.

"At about a hundred paces from Vendôme, on the banks of the Loire," said he, "stands an old brown house, crowned with very high roofs, and so completely isolated that there is nothing near it, not even a fetid tannery or a squalid tavern, such as are commonly seen outside small towns. In front of this house is a garden down to the river, where the box shrubs, formerly clipped close to edge the walks, now straggle at their own will. A few willows, rooted in the stream, have grown up quickly like an enclosing fence, and half hide the house. The wild plants we call weeds have clothed the bank with their beautiful luxuriance. The fruit-trees, neglected for these ten years past, no longer bear a crop, and their suckers have formed a thicket. The espaliers are like a copse. The paths, once gravelled, are overgrown with purslane; but, to be accurate, there is no trace of a path.

"Looking down from the hill-top, to which cling the ruins of the old castle of the Dukes of Vendôme, the only spot whence the eye can see into this enclosure, we think that at a time, difficult now to determine, this spot of earth must have been the joy of some country gentleman devoted to roses and tulips, in a word, to horticulture, but above all a lover of choice fruit. An arbour is visible, or rather the wreck of an arbour, and under it a table still stands, not entirely destroyed by time. From the aspect of this garden that is no more, the negative joys of the peaceful life of the provinces may be divined as we divine the history of a worthy tradesman when we read the epitaph on his tomb. To complete the mournful and tender impressions which seize the soul, on one of the walls there is a sundial graced with this homely Christian motto, '*Ultimam cogita.*'

"The roof of this house is dreadfully dilapidated; the outside shutters are always closed; the balconies are hung with swallows' nests; the doors are for ever shut. Straggling grasses have outlined the flagstones of the steps with green; the ironwork is rusty. Moon and sun, winter, summer, and snow have eaten into the wood, warped the boards, peeled off the paint. The dreary silence is broken only by birds and cats, pole-cats, rats, and mice, free to scamper round, and fight, and eat each other. An invisible hand has written over it all: 'Mystery.'

"If, prompted by curiosity, you go to look at this house from the street, you will see a large gate, with a round-arched top; the children have made many holes in it. I learned later that this door had been blocked for ten years. Through these irregular breaches you will see that the side towards the courtyard is in perfect harmony with the side towards the garden. The same ruin prevails. Tufts of weeds outline the paving stones; the walls are scored by enormous cracks, and the blackened coping is laced with a thousand festoons of pellitory. The stone steps are disjointed; the bell-cord is rotten; the gutter-spouts broken. What fire from heaven can have fallen there? By what decree has salt been sown on this dwelling? Has God been mocked here? Or was France betrayed? These are the questions we ask ourselves. Reptiles crawl over it, but give no reply. This empty and deserted house is a vast enigma of which the answer is known to none.

"It was formerly a little domain, held in fief, and is known as La Grande Bretêche. During my stay at Vendôme, where Despleins had left me in charge of a rich patient, the sight of this strange dwelling became one of my keenest pleasures. Was it not far better than a ruin? Certain memories of indisputable authenticity attach themselves to a ruin; but this house, still standing, though being slowly destroyed by an avenging hand, contained a secret, an unrevealed thought. At the very least it testified to a caprice. More than once in the evening I attacked the hedge, run wild, which surrounded the enclosure. I braved scratches, I got into this ownerless garden, this plot which was no longer public or private; I lingered there for hours gazing at the disorder. I would not, as the price of the story to which this strange scene no doubt was due, have asked a single question of any gossiping native. On that spot I wove delightful romances, and abandoned myself to little debauches of melancholy which enchanted me. If I had known the reason—perhaps quite commonplace—of this neglect, I should have lost the unwritten poetry which intoxicated me. To me this refuge represented the most various phases of human life, shadowed by misfortune; sometimes the calm of a cloister without the monks; sometimes the peace of the graveyard without the dead, who speak in the language of epitaphs; one day I saw in it the home of lepers; another, the house of the Atridæ; but above all, I found there provincial life, with its contemplative ideas, its hour-glass existence. I often wept there, I never laughed.

"More than once I felt involuntary terrors as I heard overhead the dull hum of the wings of some hurrying wood-pigeon. The earth is dank; you must be on the watch for lizards, vipers, and frogs, wandering about with the wild freedom of nature; above all, you must have no fear of cold, for in a few minutes you feel an icy cloak settle on your shoulders, like the Commendatore's hand on Don Giovanni's neck.

"One evening I felt a shudder; the wind had turned an old rusty weathercock, and the creaking sounded like a cry from the house, at the very moment when I was finishing a gloomy drama to account for this monumental embodiment of woe. I returned to my inn, lost in gloomy thoughts. When I had supped, the hostess came into my room with an air of mystery, and said, 'Monsieur, here is Monsieur Regnault.'

" 'Who is Monsieur Regnault?'

" 'What, sir, don't you know Monsieur Regnault?—Well, that's odd,' said she, leaving the room.

"Suddenly I saw a man appear, tall, slim, dressed in black, hat in hand, who came in like a ram ready to butt his opponent, showing a receding forehead, a small pointed head, and a colourless face of the hue of a glass of dirty water. You would have taken him for an usher. The stranger wore an old coat, much worn at the seams; but he had a diamond in his shirt frill, and gold rings in his ears.

" 'Monsieur,' said I, 'whom have I the honour of addressing?'—He took a chair, placed himself in front of my fire, put his hat on my table, and answered while he rubbed his hands: 'Dear me, it is very cold.—Monsieur, I am Monsieur Regnault.'

"I was encouraging myself by saying to myself, '*Il bondo cani!* Seek!'

" 'I am,' he went on, 'the notary at Vendôme.'

" 'I am delighted to hear it, Monsieur,' I exclaimed. 'But I am not in a position to make a will for reasons best known to myself.'

" 'One moment!' said he, holding up his hand as though to gain silence. 'Allow me, Monsieur, allow me! I am informed that you sometimes go to walk in the garden of la Grande Bretêche.'

" 'Yes, Monsieur.'

" 'One moment!' said he, repeating his gesture. 'That constitutes a misdemeanour. Monsieur, as executor under the will of the late Comtesse de Merret, I come in her name to beg you to discontinue the practice. One moment! I am not a Turk, and do not wish to make a crime of it. And besides, you are probably ignorant of the circumstances which compel me to leave the finest mansion in Vendôme to fall into ruin. Nevertheless, Monsieur, you must be a man of education, and you should know that the laws forbid, under heavy penalties, any trespass on enclosed property. A hedge is the same as a wall. But, the state in which the place is left may be an excuse for your curiosity. For my part, I should be quite content to make you free to come and go in the house; but being bound to respect the will of the testatrix, I have the honour, Monsieur, to beg that you will go into the garden no more. I myself, Monsieur, since the will was read, have never set foot in the house, which, as I had the honour of informing you, is part of the estate of the late Madame de Merret. We have done nothing there but verify the number of doors and windows to assess the taxes I have to pay annually out of the funds left for that purpose by the late Madame de Merret. Ah! my dear sir, her will made a great commotion in the town.'

"The good man paused to blow his nose. I respected his volubility, perfectly understanding that the administration of Madame de Merret's estate had been the most important event of his life, his reputation, his glory, his Restoration. As I was forced to bid farewell to my beautiful reveries and romances, I now hoped to learn the truth on official authority.

"'Monsieur,' said I, 'would it be indiscreet if I were to ask you the reasons for such eccentricity?'

"At these words an expression, which revealed all the pleasure which men feel who are accustomed to ride a hobby, overspread the lawyer's countenance. He pulled up the collar of his shirt with an air, took out his snuffbox, opened it, and offered me a pinch; on my refusing, he took a large one. He was happy! A man who has no hobby does not know all the good to be got out of life. A hobby is the happy medium between a passion and a monomania. At this moment I understood the whole bearing of Sterne's charming passion, and had a perfect idea of the delight with which my Uncle Toby, encouraged by Trim, bestrode his hobby-horse.

"'Monsieur,' said Monsieur Regnault, 'I was head clerk in Monsieur Roguin's office, in Paris. A first-rate house, which you may have heard mentioned? No! An unfortunate bankruptcy made it famous.—Not having money enough to purchase a practice in Paris at the price to which they were run up in 1816, I came here and bought my predecessor's business. I had relations in Vendôme; among others, a wealthy aunt, who allowed me to marry her daughter.—Monsieur,' he went on after a little pause, 'three months after being licensed by the Keeper of the Seals, one evening, as I was going to bed—it was before my marriage—I was sent for by Madame la Comtesse de Merret, to her Château of Merret. Her maid, a good girl, who is now a servant in this inn, was waiting at my door with the Countess's own carriage. Ah! one moment! I ought to tell you that Monsieur le Comte de Merret had gone to Paris to die two months before I came here. He came to a miserable end, flinging himself into every kind of dissipation. You understand?

" 'On the day he left, Madame la Comtesse had quitted la Grande Bretêche, having dismantled it. Some people even say that she had burnt all the furniture, the hangings—in short, all the chattels and furniture whatever used in furnishing the premises now let by the said M.—(Dear! what am I saying? I beg your pardon, I thought I was dictating a lease.)—in short, that she burnt everything in the meadow at Merret. Have you been to Merret, Monsieur?—No,' said he, answering himself. 'Ah, it is a very fine place.'

" 'For about three months previously,' he went on, with a jerk of his head, 'the Count and Countess had lived in a very eccentric way; they admitted no visitors; Madame lived on the ground floor, and Monsieur on the first floor. When the Countess was left alone, she was never seen except at church. Subsequently, at home, at the château, she refused to see the friends, whether gentlemen or ladies, who went to call on her. She was already very much altered when she left la Grande Bretêche to go to Merret. That dear lady—I say dear lady, for it was she who gave me this diamond, but indeed I saw her but once—that kind lady was very ill; she had, no doubt, given up all hope, for she died without choosing to send for a doctor; indeed, many of our ladies fancied she was not quite right in her head. Well, sir, my curiosity was strangely excited by hearing that Madame de Merret had need of my services. Nor was I the only person who took an interest in the affair. That very night, though it was already late, all the town knew that I was going to Merret.

" 'The waiting-woman replied but vaguely to the questions I asked her on the way; nevertheless, she told me that her mistress had received the Sacrament in the course of the day at the hands of the Curé of Merret, and seemed unlikely to live through the night. It was about eleven when I reached the château. I went up the great staircase. After crossing some large, lofty, dark rooms, diabolically cold and damp, I reached the state bedroom where the Countess lay. From the rumours that were current concerning this lady (Monsieur, I should never end if I were to repeat all the tales that were told about her), I had imagined her a coquette. Imagine, then, that I had great difficulty in seeing her in the great bed where she was lying. To be sure, to light this enormous room, with old-fashioned heavy cornices, and so thick with dust that merely to see it was enough to make you sneeze, she had only an old Argand lamp. Ah! but you have not been to Merret. Well, the bed is one of those old-world beds, with a high tester hung with flowered chintz. A small table stood by the bed, on which I saw an "Imitation of Christ," which, by the way, I bought for my wife, as well as the lamp. There were also a deep armchair for her confidential maid, and two small chairs. There was no fire. That was all the furniture; not enough to fill ten lines in an inventory.

"'My dear sir, if you had seen, as I then saw, that vast room, papered and hung with brown, you would have felt yourself transported into a scene of romance. It was icy, nay more, funereal,' and he lifted his hand with a theatrical gesture and paused.

"'By dint of seeking, as I approached the bed, at last I saw Madame de Merret, under the glimmer of the lamp, which fell on the pillows. Her face was as yellow as wax, and as narrow as two folded hands. The Countess wore a lace cap, showing abundant hair, but as white as linen thread. She was sitting up in bed, and seemed to keep upright with great difficulty. Her large black eyes, dimmed by fever, no doubt, and half-dead already, hardly moved under the bony arch of her eyebrows.—There,' he added, pointing to his own brow. 'Her forehead was clammy; her fleshless hands were like bones covered with soft skin; the veins and muscles were perfectly visible. She must have been very handsome; but at this moment I was startled into an indescribable emotion at the sight. Never, said those who wrapped her in her shroud, had any living creature been so emaciated and lived. In short, it was awful to behold! Sickness had so consumed that woman, that she was no more than a phantom. Her lips, which were pale violet, seemed to me not to move when she spoke to me.

"'Though my profession has familiarized me with such spectacles, by calling me not unfrequently to the bedside of the dying to record their

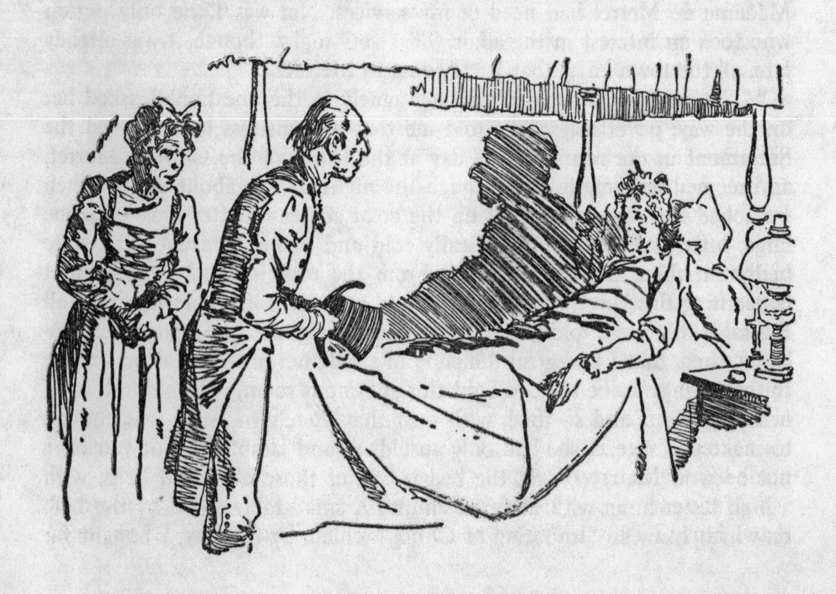

last wishes, I confess that families in tears and the agonies I have seen were as nothing in comparison with this lonely and silent woman in her vast château. I heard not the least sound, I did not perceive the movement which the sufferer's breathing ought to have given to the sheets that covered her, and I stood motionless, absorbed in looking at her in a sort of stupor. In fancy I am there still.—At last her large eyes moved; she tried to raise her right hand, but it fell back on the bed, and she uttered these words, which came like a breath, for her voice was no longer a voice: "I have waited for you with the greatest impatience." A bright flush rose to her cheeks. It was a great effort for her to speak.

" 'Madame,' I began. She signed to me to be silent. At that moment the old housekeeper rose and said in my ear, "Do not speak; Madame la Comtesse is not in a state to bear the slightest noise, and what you would say might agitate her."

" 'I sat down. A few instants after, Madame de Merret collected all her remaining strength to move her right hand, and slipped it, not without infinite difficulty, under the bolster; she then paused a moment. With a last effort she withdrew her hand; and when she brought out a sealed paper, drops of perspiration rolled from her brow. "I place my will in your hands—Oh! God! Oh!" and that was all. She clutched a crucifix that lay on the bed, lifted it hastily to her lips, and died.

" 'The expression of her eyes still makes me shudder as I think of it. She must have suffered much! There was joy in her last glance, and it remained stamped on her dead eyes.

" 'I brought away the will, and when it was opened I found that Madame de Merret had appointed me her executor. She left the whole of her property to the hospital of Vendôme, excepting a few legacies. But these were her instructions as relating to la Grande Bretêche: she ordered me to leave the place, for fifty years counting from the day of her death, in the state in which it might be at the time of her decease, forbidding anyone, whoever he might be, to enter the apartments, prohibiting any repairs whatever, and even setting a salary to pay watchmen if it were needful to secure the absolute fulfilment of her intentions. At the expiration of that term, if the will of the testatrix has been duly carried out, the house is to become the property of my heirs, for, as you know, a notary cannot take a bequest. Otherwise la Grande Bretêche reverts to the heirs-at-law, but on condition of fulfilling certain conditions set forth in a codicil to the will, which is not to be opened till the expiration of the said term of fifty years. The will has not been disputed, so—' and without finishing his sentence, the lanky notary looked at me with an air of triumph; I made him quite happy by offering him my congratulations.

" 'Monsieur,' I said in conclusion, 'you have so vividly impressed me that I fancy I see the dying woman whiter than her sheets; her glittering eyes frighten me; I shall dream of her tonight.—But you must have formed some idea as to the instructions contained in that extraordinary will.'

"'Monsieur,' said he, with comical reticence, 'I never allow myself to criticize the conduct of a person who honours me with the gift of a diamond.'

"However, I soon loosened the tongue of the discreet notary of Vendôme, who communicated to me, not without long digressions, the opinions of the deep politicians of both sexes whose judgments are law in Vendôme. But these opinions were so contradictory, so diffuse, that I was near falling asleep in spite of the interest I felt in this authentic history. The notary's ponderous voice and monotonous accent, accustomed no doubt to listen to himself and to make himself listened to by his clients or fellowtownsmen, were too much for my curiosity. Happily, he soon went away.

"'Ah, ha, Monsieur,' said he on the stairs, 'a good many persons would be glad to live five-and-forty years longer; but—one moment!' and he laid the first finger of his right hand to his nostril with a cunning look, 'Mark my words!—To last as long as that—as long as that, you must not be past sixty now.'

"I closed my door, having been roused from my apathy by this last speech, which the notary thought very funny; then I sat down in my armchair, with my feet on the fire-dogs. I had lost myself in a romance *à la* Radcliffe, constructed on the juridical base given me by Monsieur Regnault, when the door, opened by a woman's cautious hand, turned on the hinges. I saw my landlady come in, a buxom, florid dame, always good-humoured, who had missed her calling in life. She was a Fleming, who ought to have seen the light in a picture by Teniers.

"'Well, Monsieur,' said she, 'Monsieur Regnault has no doubt been giving you his history of la Grande Bretêche?'

"'Yes, Madame Lepas.'

"'And what did he tell you?'

"I repeated in a few words the creepy and sinister story of Madame de Merret. At each sentence my hostess put her head forward, looking at me with an innkeeper's keen scrutiny, a happy compromise between the instinct of a police constable, the astuteness of a spy, and the cunning of a dealer.

"'My good Madame Lepas,' said I as I ended, 'you seem to know more about it. Heh? If not, why have you come up to me?'

"'On my word, as an honest woman—'

"'Do not swear; your eyes are big with a secret. You knew Monsieur de Merret; what sort of man was he?'

"'Monsieur de Merret—well, you see he was a man you never could see the top of, he was so tall! A very good gentleman, from Picardy, and who had, as we say, his head close to his cap. He paid for everything down, so as never to have difficulties with anyone. He was hot-tempered, you see! All our ladies liked him very much.'

"'Because he was hot-tempered?' I asked her.

"'Well, maybe,' said she; 'and you may suppose, sir, that a man had to have something to show for a figure-head before he could marry Madame de Merret, who, without any reflection on others, was the handsomest and richest heiress in our parts. She had about twenty thousand francs a year. All the town was at the wedding; the bride was pretty and sweet-looking, quite a gem of a woman. Oh, they were a handsome couple in their day!'

"'And were they happy together?'

"'Hm, hm! so-so—so far as can be guessed, for, as you may suppose, we of the common sort were not hail-fellow-well-met with them.—Madame de Merret was a kind woman and very pleasant, who had no doubt sometimes to put up with her husband's tantrums. But though he was rather haughty, we were fond of him. After all, it was his place to behave so. When a man is a born nobleman, you see—'

"'Still, there must have been some catastrophe for Monsieur and Madame de Merret to part so violently?'

"'I did not say there was any catastrophe, sir. I know nothing about it.'

"'Indeed. Well, now, I am sure you know everything.'

"'Well, sir, I will tell you the whole story.—When I saw Monsieur Regnault go up to see you, it struck me that he would speak to you about Madame de Merret as having to do with la Grande Bretêche. That put it into my head to ask your advice, sir, seeming to me that you are a man of good judgment and incapable of playing a poor woman like me false—for I never did anyone a wrong, and yet I am tormented by my conscience. Up to now I have never dared to say a word to the people of these parts; they are all chatterers, with tongues like knives. And never till now, sir, have I had any traveller here who stayed so long in the inn as you have, and to whom I could tell the history of the fifteen thousand francs—'

"'My dear Madame Lepas, if there is anything in your story of a nature to compromise me,' I said, interrupting the flow of her words, 'I would not hear it for all the world.'

"'You need have no fears,' said she; 'you will see.'

"Her eagerness made me suspect that I was not the only person to whom my worthy landlady had communicated the secret of which I was to be a sole possessor, but I listened.

"'Monsieur,' said she, 'when the Emperor sent the Spaniards here, prisoners of war and others, I was required to lodge at the charge of the Government a young Spaniard sent to Vendôme on parole. Notwithstanding his parole, he had to show himself every day to the sub-prefect. He was a

Spanish grandee—neither more nor less. He had a name in *os* and *dia*, something like Bagos de Férédia. I wrote his name down in my books, and you may see it if you like. Ah! he was a handsome young fellow for a Spaniard, who are ugly they say. He was not more than five feet two or three in height, but so well made; and he had little hands that he kept so beautifully! Ah! you should have seen them. He had as many brushes for his hands as a woman has for her toilet. He had thick, black hair, a flame in his eye, a somewhat coppery complexion, but which I admired all the same. He wore the finest linen I have ever seen, though I have had princesses to lodge here, and, among others, General Bertrand, the Duc and Duchesse d'Abrantés, Monsieur Descazes, and the King of Spain. He did not eat much, but he had such polite and amiable ways that it was impossible to owe him a grudge for that. Oh! I was very fond of him, though he did not say four words to me in a day, and it was impossible to have the least bit of talk with him; if he was spoken to, he did not answer; it is a way, a mania they all have, it would seem.

"'He read his breviary like a priest, and went to Mass and all the services quite regularly. And where did he post himself?—we found this out later.—Within two yards of Madame de Merret's chapel. As he took that place the very first time he entered the church, no one imagined that there was any purpose in it. Besides, he never raised his nose above his book, poor young man! And then, Monsieur, of an evening he went for a walk on the hill among the ruins of the old castle. It was his only amusement, poor man; it reminded him of his native land. They say that Spain is all hills!

"'One evening, a few days after he was sent here, he was out very late. I was rather uneasy when he did not come in till just on the stroke of midnight; but we all got used to his whims; he took the key of the door, and we never sat up for him. He lived in a house belonging to us in the Rue des Casernes. Well, then, one of our stable-boys told us one evening that, going down to wash the horses in the river, he fancied he had seen the Spanish grandee swimming some little way off, just like a fish. When he came in, I told him to be careful of the weeds, and he seemed put out at having been seen in the water.

"'At last, Monsieur, one day, or rather one morning, we did not find him in his room; he had not come back. By hunting through his things, I found a written paper in the drawer of his table, with fifty pieces of Spanish gold of the kind they call doubloons, worth about five thousand francs; and in a little sealed box ten thousand francs' worth of diamonds. The paper said that in case he should not return, he left us this money and these diamonds in trust to found Masses to thank God for his escape and for his salvation.

"'At that time I still had my husband, who ran off in search of him.

And this is the queer part of the story: he brought back the Spaniard's clothes, which he had found under a big stone on a sort of breakwater along the river bank, nearly opposite la Grande Bretêche. My husband went so early that no one saw him. After reading the letter, he burnt the clothes, and, in obedience to Count Férédia's wish, we announced that he had escaped.

" 'The sub-prefect set all the constabulary at his heels; but, pshaw! he was never caught. Lepas believed that the Spaniard had drowned himself. I, sir, have never thought so; I believe, on the contrary, that he had something to do with the business about Madame de Merret, seeing that Rosalie told me that the crucifix her mistress was so fond of that she had it buried with her, was made of ebony and silver; now in the early days of his stay here, Monsieur Férédia had one of ebony and silver which I never saw later.—And now, Monsieur, do not you say that I need have no remorse about the Spaniard's fifteen thousand francs? Are they not really and truly mine?'

" 'Certainly.—But have you never tried to question Rosalie?' said I.

" 'Oh, to be sure I have, sir. But what is to be done? That girl is like a wall. She knows something, but it is impossible to make her talk.'

"After chatting with me for a few minutes, my hostess left me a prey to vague and sinister thoughts, to romantic curiosity, and a religious dread not unlike the deep emotion which comes upon us when we go into a dark church at night and discern a feeble light glimmering under a lofty vault—a dim figure glides across—the sweep of a gown or of a priest's cassock is audible—and we shiver! La Grande Bretêche, with its rank grasses, its shuttered windows, its rusty ironwork, its locked doors, its deserted rooms, suddenly rose before me in fantastic vividness. I tried to get into the mysterious dwelling to search out the heart of this solemn story, this drama which had killed three persons.

"Rosalie became in my eyes the most interesting being in Vendôme. As I studied her, I detected signs of an inmost thought, in spite of the blooming health that glowed in her dimpled face. There was in her soul some element of ruth or of hope; her manner suggested a secret, like the expression of devout souls who pray in excess, or of a girl who has killed her child and for ever hears its last cry. Nevertheless, she was simple and clumsy in her ways; her vacant smile had nothing criminal in it, and you would have pronounced her innocent only from seeing the large red and blue checked kerchief that covered her stalwart bust, tucked into the tight-laced square bodice of a lilac- and white-striped gown. 'No,' said I to myself, 'I will not quit Vendôme without knowing the whole history of la Grande Bretêche. To achieve this end, I will make love to Rosalie if it proves necessary.'

" 'Rosalie!' said I one evening.

" 'Your servant, sir?'

" 'You are not married?' She started a little.

" 'Oh! there is no lack of men if ever I take a fancy to be miserable!' she replied, laughing. She got over her agitation at once; for every woman, from the highest lady to the inn-servant inclusive, has a native presence of mind.

" 'Yes; you are fresh and good-looking enough never to lack lovers! But tell me, Rosalie, why did you become an inn-servant on leaving Madame de Merret? Did she not leave you some little annuity?'

" 'Oh yes, sir. But my place here is the best in all the town of Vendôme.'

"This reply was such a one as judges and attorneys call evasive. Rosalie, as it seemed to me, held in this romantic affair the place of a middle square of the chess-board; she was at the very centre of the interest and of the truth; she appeared to me to be tied into the knot of it. It was not a case for ordinary love-making; this girl contained the last chapter of a romance, and from that moment all my attentions were devoted to Rosalie. By dint of studying the girl, I observed in her, as in every woman whom we make our ruling thought, a variety of good qualities; she was clean and neat; she was handsome, I need not say; she soon was possessed of every charm that desire can lend to a woman in whatever rank of life. A fortnight after the notary's visit, one evening, or rather one morning, in the small hours, I said to Rosalie:

" 'Come, tell me all you know about Madame de Merret.'

" 'Oh!' she cried in terror, 'do not ask me that, Monsieur Horace!'

"Her handsome features clouded over, her bright colouring grew pale, and her eyes lost their artless, liquid brightness.

" 'Well,' she said, 'I will tell you; but keep the secret carefully.'

" 'All right, my child; I will keep all your secrets with a thief's honour, which is the most loyal known.'

" 'If it is all the same to you,' said she, 'I would rather it should be with your own.'

"Thereupon she set her head-kerchief straight, and settled herself to tell the tale; for there is no doubt a particular attitude of confidence and security is necessary to the telling of a narrative. The best tales are told at a certain hour—just as we are all here at table. No one ever told a story well standing up, or fasting.

"If I were to reproduce exactly Rosalie's diffuse eloquence, a whole volume would scarcely contain it. Now, as the event of which she gave me a confused account stands exactly midway between the notary's gossip and that of Madame Lepas, as precisely as the middle term of a rule-of-three sum stands between the first and third, I have only to relate it in as few words as may be. I shall therefore be brief.

"The room at la Grande Bretêche in which Madame de Merret slept was on the ground floor; a little cupboard in the wall, about four feet deep, served her to hang her dresses in. Three months before the evening of which I have to relate the events, Madame de Merret had been seriously ailing, so much so that her husband had left her to herself, and had his own bedroom on the first floor. By one of those accidents which it is impossible to foresee, he came in that evening two hours later than usual from the club, where he went to read the papers and talk politics with the residents in the neighbourhood. His wife supposed him to have come in, to be in bed and asleep. But the invasion of France had been the subject of a very animated discussion; the game of billiards had waxed vehement; he had lost forty francs, an enormous sum at Vendôme, where everybody is thrifty, and where social habits are restrained within the bounds of a simplicity worthy of all praise, and the foundation perhaps of a form of true happiness which no Parisian would care for.

"For some time past Monsieur de Merret had been satisfied to ask Rosalie whether his wife was in bed; on the girl's replying always in the affirmative, he at once went to his own room, with the good faith that comes of habit and confidence. But this evening, on coming in, he took it into his head to go to see Madame de Merret, to tell her of his ill-luck, and perhaps to find consolation. During dinner he had observed that his wife was very becomingly dressed; he reflected as he came home from the club that his wife was certainly much better, that convalescence had improved her beauty, discovering it, as husbands discover everything, a little too late. Instead of calling Rosalie, who was in the kitchen at the moment watching the cook and the coachman playing a puzzling hand at cards, Monsieur de Merret made his way to his wife's room by the light of his lantern, which he set down on the lowest step of the stairs. His step, easy to recognize, rang under the vaulted passage.

"At the instant when the gentleman turned the key to enter his wife's room, he fancied he heard the door shut of the closet of which I have spoken; but when he went in, Madame de Merret was alone, standing in front of the fireplace. The unsuspecting husband fancied that Rosalie was in the cupboard; nevertheless, a doubt, ringing in his ears like a peal of bells, put him on his guard; he looked at his wife, and read in her eyes an indescribably anxious and haunted expression.

"'You are very late,' said she.—Her voice, usually so clear and sweet, struck him as being slightly husky.

"Monsieur de Merret made no reply, for at this moment Rosalie came in. This was like a thunderclap. He walked up and down the room, going from one window to another at a regular pace, his arms folded.

"'Have you had bad news, or are you ill?' his wife asked him timidly, while Rosalie helped her to undress. He made no reply.

"'You can go, Rosalie,' said Madame de Merret to her maid; 'I can put in my curl-papers myself.'—She scented disaster at the mere aspect of her husband's face, and wished to be alone with him. As soon as Rosalie was gone, or supposed to be gone, for she lingered a few minutes in the passage, Monsieur de Merret came and stood facing his wife, and said coldly, 'Madame, there is someone in your cupboard!' She looked at her husband calmly, and replied quite simply, 'No, Monsieur.'

"This 'No' wrung Monsieur de Merret's heart; he did not believe it; and yet his wife had never appeared purer or more saintly than she seemed to be at this moment. He rose to go and open the closet door. Madame de Merret took his hand, stopped him, looked at him sadly, and said in a voice of strange emotion, 'Remember, if you should find no one there, everything must be at an end between you and me.'

"The extraordinary dignity of his wife's attitude filled him with deep esteem for her, and inspired him with one of those resolves which need only a grander stage to become immortal.

"'No, Josephine,' he said, 'I will not open it. In either event we should be parted for ever. Listen; I know all the purity of your soul, I know you lead a saintly life, and would not commit a deadly sin to save your life.'—At these words Madame de Merret looked at her husband with a haggard stare—'See, here is your crucifix,' he went on. 'Swear to me before God that there is no one in there; I will believe you—I will never open that door.'

"Madame de Merret took up the crucifix and said, 'I swear it.'

"'Louder,' said her husband; 'and repeat: "I swear before God that there is nobody in that closet."' She repeated the words without flinching.

"'That will do,' said Monsieur de Merret coldly. After a moment's silence: 'You have there a fine piece of work which I never saw before,' said he, examining the crucifix of ebony and silver, very artistically wrought.

"'I found it at Duvivier's; last year when that troop of Spanish prisoners came through Vendôme, he bought it of a Spanish monk.'

"'Indeed,' said Monsieur de Merret, hanging the crucifix on its nail; and he rang the bell.

"He had not to wait for Rosalie. Monsieur de Merret went forward quickly to meet her, led her into the bay of the window that looked on to the garden, and said to her in an undertone:

"'I know that Gorenflot wants to marry you, that poverty alone prevents your setting up house, and that you told him you would not be his wife till he found means to become a master mason.—Well, go and fetch him; tell him to come here with his trowel and tools. Contrive to wake no one in his house but himself. His reward will be beyond your wishes. Above all, go out without saying a word—or else!' and he frowned.

"Rosalie was going, and he called her back. 'Here, take my latch-key,' said he.

"'Jean!' Monsieur de Merret called in a voice of thunder down the passage. Jean, who was both coachman and confidential servant, left his cards and came.

"'Go to bed, all of you,' said his master, beckoning him to come close; and the gentleman added in a whisper, 'When they are all asleep—mind, *asleep*—you understand?—come down and tell me.'

Monsieur de Merret, who had never lost sight of his wife while giving his orders, quietly came back to her at the fireside, and began to tell her the details of the game of billiards and the discussion at the club. When Rosalie returned she found Monsieur and Madame de Merret conversing amiably.

"Not long before this Monsieur de Merret had had new ceilings made to all the reception-rooms on the ground floor. Plaster is very scarce at Vendôme; the price is enhanced by the cost of carriage; the gentleman had therefore had a considerable quantity delivered to him, knowing that he could always find purchasers for what might be left. It was this circumstance which suggested the plan he carried out.

"'Gorenflot is here, sir,' said Rosalie in a whisper.

"'Tell him to come in,' said her master aloud.

"Madame de Merret turned paler when she saw the mason.

"'Gorenflot,' said her husband, 'go and fetch some bricks from the coachhouse; bring enough to wall up the door of this cupboard; you can use the plaster that is left for cement.' Then, dragging Rosalie and the workman close to him—'Listen, Gorenflot,' said he, in a low voice, 'you are to sleep here to-night; but to-morrow morning you shall have a passport to take you abroad to a place I will tell you of. I will give you six thousand francs for your journey. You must live in that town for ten years; if you find you do not like it, you may settle in another, but it must be in the same country. Go through Paris and wait there till I join you. I will there give you an agreement for six thousand francs more, to be paid to you on your return, provided you have carried out the conditions of the bargain. For that price you are to keep perfect silence as to what you have to do this night. To you, Rosalie, I will secure ten thousand francs, which will not be paid to you till your wedding day, and on condition of your marrying Gorenflot; but, to get married, you must hold your tongue. If not, no wedding gift!'

"'Rosalie,' said Madame de Merret, 'come and brush my hair.'

"Her husband quietly walked up and down the room, keeping an eye on the door, on the mason, and on his wife, but without any insulting display of suspicion. Gorenflot could not help making some noise. Madame de Merret seized a moment when he was unloading some bricks, and when her husband was at the other end of the room, to say to Rosalie: 'My dear child, I will give you a thousand francs a year if only you will tell Gorenflot to leave a crack at the bottom.' Then she added aloud quite coolly: 'You had better help him.'

"Monsieur and Madame de Merret were silent all the time while Gorenflot was walling up the door. This silence was intentional on the husband's part; he did not wish to give his wife the opportunity of saying anything with a double meaning. On Madame de Merret's side it was pride or prudence. When the wall was half built up, the cunning mason took advantage of his master's back being turned to break one of the two panes in the top of the door with a blow of his pick. By this Madame de Merret understood that Rosalie had spoken to Gorenflot. They all three then saw the face of a dark, gloomy-looking man, with black hair and flaming eyes.

"Before her husband turned round again the poor woman had nodded to the stranger, to whom the signal was meant to convey, 'Hope.'

"At four o'clock, as day was dawning, for it was the month of September, the work was done. The mason was placed in charge of Jean, and Monsieur de Merret slept in his wife's room.

"Next morning when he got up he said with apparent carelessness, 'Oh, by the way, I must go to the Mairie for the passport.' He put on his hat, took two or three steps towards the door, paused, and took the crucifix. His wife was trembling with joy.

" 'He will go to Duvivier's,' thought she.

"As soon as he had left, Madame de Merret rang for Rosalie, and then in a terrible voice she cried: 'The pick! Bring the pick! and set to work. I saw how Gorenflot did it yesterday; we shall have time to make a gap and build it up again.'

"In an instant Rosalie had brought her mistress a sort of cleaver; she, with a vehemence of which no words can give an idea, set to work to demolish the wall. She had already got out a few bricks, when, turning to deal a stronger blow than before, she saw behind her Monsieur de Merret. She fainted away.

" 'Lay Madame on her bed,' said he coldly.

"Foreseeing what would certainly happen in his absence, he had laid this trap for his wife; he had merely written to the Mairie and sent for Duvivier. The jeweller arrived just as the disorder in the room had been repaired.

" 'Duvivier,' asked Monsieur de Merret, 'did not you buy some crucifixes of the Spaniards who passed through the town?'

" 'No, Monsieur.'

" 'Very good; thank you,' said he, flashing a tiger's glare at his wife. 'Jean,' he added, turning to his confidential valet, 'you can serve my meals here in Madame de Merret's room. She is ill, and I shall not leave her till she recovers.'

"The cruel man remained in his wife's room for twenty days. During the earlier time, when there was some little noise in the closet, and Josephine wanted to intercede for the dying man, he said, without allowing her to utter a word, 'You swore on the Cross that there was no one there.' "

After this story all the ladies rose from table, and thus the spell under which Bianchon had held them was broken. But there were some among them who had almost shivered at the last words.

LOVE'S CONUNDRUM

ANTHONY HOPE

IT was a charmingly mild and balmy day. The sun shone beyond the orchard, and the shade was cool inside. A light breeze stirred the boughs of the old apple tree under which the philosopher sat. None of these things did the philosopher notice, unless it might be when the wind blew about the leaves of the large volume on his knees, and he had to find his place again. Then he would exclaim against the wind, shuffle the leaves till he got the right page, and settle to his reading. The book was a treatise on ontology; it was written by another philosopher, a friend of this philosopher's; it bristled with fallacies, and this philosopher was discovering them all, and noting them on the fly-leaf at the end. He was not going to review the book (as some might have thought from his behaviour), or even to answer it in a work of his own. It was just that he found a pleasure in stripping any poor fallacy naked and crucifying it.

Presently a girl in a white frock came into the orchard. She picked up an apple, bit it, and found it ripe. Holding it in her hand she walked up to where the philosopher sat, and looked at him. He did not stir. She took a bite out of the apple, munched it, and swallowed it. The philosopher crucified a fallacy on the fly-leaf. The girl flung the apple away.

"Mr. Jerningham," said she, "are you very busy?"

The philosopher, pencil in hand, looked up.

"No, Miss May," said he, "not very."

"Because I want your opinion."

"In one moment," said the philosopher apologetically.

He turned back to the fly-leaf and began to nail the last fallacy a little tighter to the cross. The girl regarded him first with amused impatience, then with a vexed frown, finally with a wistful regret. He was so very old for his age, she thought; he could not be much beyond thirty; his hair was thick and full of waves, his eyes bright and clear, his complexion not yet divested of all youth's relics.

"Now, Miss May, I'm at your service," said the philosopher with a

From *Comedies of Courtship*, by Anthony Hope, reprinted by permission of the Author's Estate and Messrs. Ward Lock & Company.

lingering look at his impaled fallacy. And he closed the book, keeping it, however, on his knee.

The girl sat down just opposite to him. "It's a very important thing I want to ask you," she began, tugging at a tuft of grass, "and it's very—difficult, and you mustn't tell any one I asked you; at least, I'd rather you didn't."

"I shall not speak of it; indeed, I shall probably not remember it," said the philosopher.

"And you mustn't look at me, please, while I'm asking you."

"I don't think I was looking at you, but if I was I beg your pardon," said the philosopher apologetically.

She pulled the tuft of grass right out of the ground and flung it from her with all her force.

"Suppose a man—" she began. "No, that's not right."

"You can take any hypothesis you please," observed the philosopher, "but you must verify it afterwards, of course."

"Oh, do let us go on. Suppose a girl, Mr. Jerningham—I wish you wouldn't nod."

"It was only to show that I followed you."

"Oh, of course you 'follow me,' as you call it. Suppose a girl had two

lovers—you're nodding again!—or, I ought to say, suppose there were two men who might be in love with a girl."

"Only two?" asked the philosopher. "You see any number of men *might* be in love with—"

"Oh, we can leave the rest out," said Miss May with a sudden dimple; "they don't matter."

"Very well," said the philosopher. "If they are irrelevant we will put them aside."

"Suppose then that one of these men was, oh, *awfully* in love with the girl, and—and proposed, you know—"

"A moment!" said the philosopher, opening a note-book. "Let me take down his proposition. What was it?"

"Why, proposed to her—asked her to marry him," said the girl, with a stare.

"Dear me! How stupid of me! I forgot that special use of the word. Yes?"

"The girl likes him pretty well, and her people approve of him and all that, you know."

"That simplifies the problem," said the philosopher, nodding again.

"But she's not in—in love with him, you know. She doesn't *really* care for him—*much*. Do you understand?"

"Perfectly. It is a most natural state of mind."

"Well then, suppose that there's another man—what are you writing?"

"I only put down (B)—like that," pleaded the philosopher, meekly exhibiting his note-book.

She looked at him in a sort of helpless exasperation, with just a smile somewhere in the background of it.

"Oh, you really are—" she exclaimed. "But let me go on. The other man is a friend of the girl's; he's very clever—oh, fearfully clever; and he's rather handsome. You needn't put that down."

"It is certainly not very material," admitted the philosopher and he crossed out "handsome." "Clever" he left.

"And the girl is most awfully—she admires him tremendously; she thinks him just the greatest man that ever lived, you know. And she—she—" The girl paused.

"I'm following," said the philosopher, with pencil poised.

"She'd think it better than the whole world if—if she could be anything to him, you know."

"You mean become his wife?"

"Well, of course I do—at least I suppose I do."

"You spoke rather vaguely, you know."

The girl cast one glance at the philosopher as she replied—

"Well, yes. I did mean become his wife."

"Yes. Well?"

"But," continued the girl, starting on another tuft of grass, "he doesn't think much about those things. He likes her. I think he likes her—"

"Well, doesn't dislike her?" suggested the philosopher. "Shall we call him indifferent?"

"I don't know. Yes, rather indifferent. I don't think he thinks about it, you know. But she—she's pretty. You needn't put that down."

"I was about to do so," observed the philosopher.

"She thinks life with him would be just heaven; and—and she thinks she would make him awfully happy. She would—would be so proud of him, you see."

"I see. Yes!"

"And—I don't know how to put it, quite—she thinks that if he ever thought about it at all, he might care for her; because he doesn't care for anybody else; and she's pretty—"

"You said that before."

"Oh, dear, I dare say I did. And most men care for somebody, don't they? some girl, I mean."

"Most men, no doubt," conceded the philosopher.

"Well, then, what ought she to do? It's not a real thing, you know, Mr. Jerningham. It's in—in a novel I was reading." She said this hastily, and blushed as she spoke.

"Dear me! And it's quite an interesting case! Yes, I see. The question is, Will she act most wisely in accepting the offer of the man who loves her exceedingly, but for whom she entertains only a moderate affection."

"Yes. Just a liking. He's just a friend."

"Exactly. Or in marrying the other man whom she loves ex—"

"That's not it. How can she marry him? He hasn't—he hasn't asked her, you see."

"True. I forgot. Let us assume, though, for the moment, that he has asked her. She would then have to consider which marriage would probably be productive of the greater sum total of—"

"Oh, but you needn't consider that."

"But it seems the best logical order. We can afterwards make allowance for the element of uncertainty caused by—"

"Oh no. I don't want it like that. I know perfectly well which she'd do if he—the other man, you know—asked her."

"You apprehend that—"

"Never mind what I 'apprehend.' Take it just as I told you."

"Very good. A has asked her hand, B has not."

"Yes."

"May I take it that, but for the disturbing influence of B, A would be a satisfactory—er—candidate?"

"Ye-es. I think so."

"She therefore enjoys a certainty of considerable happiness if she marries A."

"Ye-es. Not perfect, because of—B, you know."

"Quite so, quite so; but still a fair amount of happiness. Is it not so?"

"I don't—well, perhaps."

"On the other hand, if B did ask her, we are to postulate a higher degree of happiness for her?"

"Yes, please, Mr. Jerningham—much higher."

"For both of them?"

"For her. Never mind him."

"Very well. That again simplifies the problem. But his asking her is a contingency only?"

"Yes, that's all."

The philosopher spread out his hands.

"My dear young lady," he said, "it becomes a question of degree. How probable or improbable is it?"

"I don't know. Not very probable—unless—unless—"

"Well?"

"Unless he did happen to notice, you know."

"Ah, yes. We supposed that, if he thought of it, he would probably take the desired step—at least, that he might be led to do so. Could she not—er—indicate her preference?"

"She might try—no, she couldn't do much. You see, he—he doesn't think about such things."

"I understand precisely. And it seems to me, Miss May, that in that very fact we find our solution."

"Do we?" she asked.

"I think so. He has evidently no natural inclination towards her—perhaps not towards marriage at all. Any feeling aroused in him would be necessarily shallow and in a measure artificial—and in all likelihood purely temporary. Moreover, if she took steps to arouse his attention, one of two things would be likely to happen. Are you following me?"

"Yes, Mr. Jerningham."

"Either he would be repelled by her overtures—which you must admit is not improbable—and then the position would be unpleasant, and even degrading, for her. Or, on the other hand, he might, through a misplaced feeling of gallantry—"

"Through what?"

"Through a mistaken idea of politeness or a mistaken view of what was kind, allow himself to be drawn into a connection for which he has no genuine liking. You agree with me that one or other of these things would be likely?"

"Yes, I suppose they would, unless he did come to care for her."

"Ah, you return to that hypothesis. I think it's an extremely fanciful one. No. She needn't marry A, but she must let B alone."

The philosopher closed his book, took off his glasses, wiped them, replaced them, and leaned back against the trunk of the apple tree. The girl picked a dandelion in pieces. After a long pause she asked:

"You think B's feelings wouldn't be at all likely to—to change?"

"That depends on the sort of man he is. But if he is an able man, with intellectual interests which engross him—a man to whom women's society is not a necessity—"

"He's just like that," said the girl, and she bit the head off a daisy.

"Then," said the philosopher, "I see not the least reason for supposing that his feelings will change."

"And would you advise her to marry the other—A?"

"Well, on the whole, I should. A is a good fellow (I think we made A a good fellow): he is a suitable match, his love for her is true and genuine—"

"It's tremendous!"

"Yes, and—er—extreme. She likes him. There is every reason to hope that her liking will develop into a sufficiently deep and stable affection. She will get rid of her folly about B and make A a good wife. Yes, Miss May, if I were the author of your novel, I should make her marry A, and I should call that a happy ending."

A silence followed. It was broken by the philosopher.

"Is that all you wanted my opinion about, Miss May?" he asked, with his finger between the leaves of the treatise on ontology.

"Yes, I think so. I hope I haven't bored you?"

"I've enjoyed the discussion extremely. I had no idea that novels raised points of such psychological interest. I must find time to read one."

The girl shifted her position till, instead of her full face, her profile was turned towards him. Looking away towards the paddock that lay brilliant in sunshine on the skirts of the apple orchard, she asked in low, slow tones, twisting her hands in her lap:

"Don't you think that perhaps if B found out afterwards—when she had married A, you know—that she had cared for him so very, very much, he might be a little sorry?"

"If he were a gentleman, he would regret it deeply."

"I mean—sorry on his own account; that—that he had thrown away all that, you know?"

The philosopher looked meditative.

"I think," he pronounced, "that it is very probable he would. I can well imagine it."

"He might never find anybody to love him like that again," she said, gazing on the gleaming paddock.

"He probably would not," agreed the philosopher.

"And—and most people like being loved, don't they?"

"To crave for love is an almost universal instinct, Miss May."

"Yes, almost," she said, with a dreary little smile. "You see, he'll get old and—and have no one to look after him."

"He will."

"And no home."

"Well, in a sense, none," corrected the philosopher, smiling. "But really you'll frighten me. I'm a bachelor myself, you know, Miss May."

"Yes," she whispered just audibly.

"And all your terrors are before me."

"Well, unless—"

"Oh, we needn't have that 'unless,'" laughed the philosopher, cheerfully. "There's no 'unless' about it, Miss May."

The girl jumped to her feet; for an instant she looked at the philosopher. She opened her lips as if to speak, and, at the thought of what lay at her tongue's tip, her face grew red. But the philosopher was gazing past her, and his eyes rested in calm contemplation on the gleaming paddock.

"A beautiful thing, sunshine, to be sure," said he.

Her blush faded away into paleness; her lips closed. Without speaking she turned and walked slowly away, her head drooping. The philosopher heard the rustling of her skirt in the long grass of the orchard; he watched her for a few moments.

"A pretty, graceful creature," said he with a smile.

Then he opened his book, took his pencil in his hand, and slipped in a careful forefinger to mark the fly-leaf.

The sun had passed mid-heaven, and began to decline westwards before he finished the book. Then he stretched himself and looked at his watch.

"Good gracious, two o'clock! I shall be late for lunch!" and he hurried to his feet.

He was very late for lunch.

"Everything's cold," wailed his hostess. "Where have you been, Mr. Jerningham?"

"Only in the orchard—reading."

"And you've missed May!"

"Missed Miss May? How do you mean? I had a long talk with her this morning—a most interesting talk."

"But you weren't here to say good-by. Now, you don't mean to say that you forgot that she was leaving by the two o'clock train? What a man you are!"

"Dear me! To think of my forgetting it!" said the philosopher, shamefacedly.

"She told me to say good-by to you for her."

"She's very kind. I can't forgive myself."

His hostess looked at him for a moment; then she sighed, and smiled, and sighed again.

"Have you everything you want?" she asked.

"Everything, thank you," said he, sitting down opposite the cheese, and propping his book (he thought he would just run through the last chapter again) against the loaf; "everything in the world that I want, thanks."

His hostess did not tell him that the girl had come in from the apple orchard, and run hastily upstairs, lest her friend should see what her friend did see in her eyes. So that he had no suspicion at all that he had received an offer of marriage and refused it. And he did not refer to anything of that sort when he paused once in his reading and exclaimed:

"I'm really sorry I missed Miss May. That was an interesting case of hers. But I gave the right answer. The girl ought to marry A."

And so the girl did.

THE GREAT STONE FACE

NATHANIEL HAWTHORNE

ONE afternoon, when the sun was going down, a mother and her little boy sat at the door of their cottage, talking about the Great Stone Face. They had but to lift their eyes, and there it was plainly to be seen, though miles away, with the sunshine brightening all its features.

And what was the Great Stone Face?

Embosomed amongst a family of lofty mountains, there was a valley so spacious that it contained many thousand inhabitants. Some of these good people dwelt in log-huts, with the black forest all around them, on the steep and difficult hillsides. Others had their homes in comfortable farm-houses, and cultivated the rich soil on the gentle slopes or level surfaces of the valley. Others, again, were congregated into populous villages, where some wild, highland rivulet, tumbling down from its birthplace in the upper mountain region, had been caught and tamed by human cunning, and compelled to turn the machinery of cotton-factories. The inhabitants of this valley, in short, were numerous, and of many modes of life. But all of them, grown people and children, had a kind of familiarity with the Great Stone Face, although some possessed the gift of distinguishing this grand natural phenomenon more perfectly than many of their neighbors.

The Great Stone Face, then, was a work of Nature in her mood of majestic playfulness, formed on the perpendicular side of a mountain by some immense rocks, which had been thrown together in such a position as, when viewed at a proper distance, precisely to resemble the features of the human countenance. It seemed as if an enormous giant, or a Titan, had sculptured his own likeness on the precipice. There was the broad arch of the forehead, a hundred feet in height; the nose, with its long bridge; and the vast lips, which, if they could have spoken, would have rolled their thunder accents from one end of the valley to the other. True, it is, that if the spectator approached too near, he lost the outline of the gigantic visage, and could discern only a heap of ponderous and gigantic rocks, piled in chaotic ruin one upon another. Retracing his steps, however, the wondrous features would again be seen; and the farther he withdrew from them, the more like a human face, with all its original divinity intact, did they appear; until, as it grew dim in the distance, with the clouds and glorified vapor of the mountains clustering about it, the Great Stone Face seemed positively to be alive.

It was a happy lot for children to grow up to manhood or womanhood with the Great Stone Face before their eyes, for all the features were noble, and the expression was at once grand and sweet, as if it were the glow of a vast, warm heart, that embraced all mankind in its affections, and had room for more. It was an education only to look at it. According to the belief of many people, the valley owed much of its fertility to this benign aspect that was continually beaming over it, illuminating the clouds, and infusing tenderness into the sunshine.

As we began with saying, a mother and her little boy sat at their cottage door, gazing at the Great Stone Face, and talking about it. The child's name was Ernest.

"Mother," said he, while the Titanic visage smiled on him, "I wish that it could speak, for it looks so very kindly that its voice must needs be pleasant. If I were to see a man with such a face, I should love him dearly."

"If an old prophecy should come to pass," answered his mother, "we may see a man, some time or other, with exactly such a face as that."

"What prophecy do you mean, dear mother?" eagerly inquired Ernest. "Pray tell me all about it!"

So his mother told him a story that her own mother had told to her, when she herself was younger than little Ernest; a story, not of things that were past, but of what was yet to come; a story, nevertheless, so very old, that even the Indians, who formerly inhabited this valley, had heard it from their forefathers, to whom, as they affirmed, it had been murmured by the mountain streams, and whispered by the wind among the tree-tops. The purport was, that, at some future day, a child should be born hereabouts, who was destined to become the greatest and noblest personage of his time, and whose countenance in manhood should bear an exact resemblance to the Great Stone Face. Not a few old-fashioned people, and young ones likewise, in the ardor of their hopes, still cherished an enduring faith in this old prophecy. But others, who had seen more of the world, had watched and waited till they were weary, and had beheld no man with such a face, nor any man that proved to be much greater or nobler than his neighbors, concluded it to be nothing but an idle tale. At all events, the great man of the prophecy had not yet appeared.

"O mother, dear mother!" cried Ernest, clapping his hands above his head, "I do hope that I shall live to see him!"

His mother was an affectionate and thoughtful woman, and felt that it was wisest not to discourage the generous hopes of her little boy. So she only said to him, "Perhaps you may."

And Ernest never forgot the story that his mother told him. It was always in his mind, whenever he looked upon the Great Stone Face. He spent his childhood in the log-cottage where he was born, and was dutiful to his mother, and helpful to her in many things, assisting her much with his little hands, and more with his loving heart. In this manner, from a happy yet often pensive child, he grew up to be a mild, quiet, unobtrusive boy, and sun-browned with labor in the fields, but with more intelligence brightening his aspects than is seen in many lads who have been taught at famous schools. Yet Ernest had no teacher, save only that the Great Stone Face became one to him. When the toil of the day was over, he would gaze at it for hours, until he began to imagine that those vast features recognized him, and gave him a smile of kindness and encouragement, responsive to his own look of veneration. We must not take upon us to affirm that this was a mistake, although the Face may have looked no more kindly at Ernest than at all the world besides. But the secret was, that the boy's tender and confiding simplicity discerned what other people could not see; and thus the love, which was meant for all, became his peculiar portion.

About this time, there went a rumor throughout the valley, that the great man, foretold from ages long ago, who was to bear a resemblance to the Great Stone Face, had appeared at last. It seems that, many years before, a young man had migrated from the valley and settled at a distant seaport, where, after getting together a little money, he had set up as a shopkeeper. His name—but I could never learn whether it was his real one, or a nickname that had grown out of his habits and success in life—was Gathergold. Being shrewd and active, and endowed by Providence with that inscrutable faculty which develops itself in what the world calls luck, he became an exceedingly rich merchant, and owner of a whole fleet of bulky-bottomed ships. All the countries of the globe appeared to join hands for the mere purpose of adding heap after heap to the mountainous accumulation of this man's wealth. The cold regions of the North, almost within the gloom and shadow of the Arctic Circle, sent him their tribute in the shape of furs; hot Africa sifted for him the golden sands of her rivers, and gathered up the ivory tusks of her great elephants out of the forests; the East came bringing him the rich shawls, and spices, and teas, and the effulgence of diamonds, and the gleaming purity of large pearls. The ocean, not to be behindhand with the earth, yielded up her mighty whales, that Mr. Gathergold might sell their oil, and make a profit on it. Be the original commodity what it might, it was gold within his grasp. It might be said of him, as of Midas in the fable, that whatever he touched with his finger immediately glistened, and grew yellow, and was changed at once into sterling metal, or, which suited him still better, into piles of coin. And, when Mr. Gathergold had become so very rich that it would have taken him a hundred years only to count his wealth, he bethought himself of his native valley, and resolved to go back thither, and end his days where he was born. With this purpose in view, he sent a skilful architect to build him such a palace as should be fit for a man of his vast wealth to live in.

As I have said above, it had already been rumored in the valley that Mr. Gathergold had turned out to be the prophetic personage so long and vainly looked for, and that his visage was the perfect and undeniable similitude of the Great Stone Face. People were the more ready to believe that this must needs be the fact, when they beheld the splendid edifice that rose, as if by enchantment, on the site of his father's old weather-beaten farm-house. The exterior was of marble, so dazzling white that it seemed as though the whole structure might melt away in the sunshine, like those humbler ones which Mr. Gathergold, in his young play-days, before his fingers were gifted with the touch of transmutation, had been accustomed to build of snow. It had a richly ornamented portico, supported by tall pillars, beneath which was a lofty door, studded with silver knobs, and made of a kind of variegated wood that had been brought from beyond the sea. The windows, from the floor to the ceiling of each stately apartment, were composed, respectively, of but one enormous pane of glass, so transparently pure that it was said to be a finer medium than even the vacant atmosphere. Hardly anybody had been permitted to see the interior of this palace; but it was reported, and with good semblance of truth, to be far more gorgeous than the outside, insomuch that whatever was iron or brass in other houses was silver or gold in this; and Mr. Gathergold's bed-chamber, especially, made such a glittering appearance that no ordinary man would have been able to close his eyes there. But, on the other hand, Mr. Gathergold was now so inured to wealth, that perhaps he could not have closed his eyes unless where the gleam of it was certain to find its way beneath his eyelids.

In due time the mansion was finished; next came the upholsterers, with magnificent furniture; then, a whole troop of black and white servants, the harbingers of Mr. Gathergold, who, in his own majestic person, was expected to arrive at sunset. Our friend Ernest, meanwhile, had been deeply stirred by the idea that the great man, the noble man, the man of prophecy, after so many ages of delay, was at length to be made manifest to his native valley. He knew, boy as he was, that there were a thousand ways in which Mr. Gathergold, with his vast wealth, might transform himself into an angel of beneficence, and assume a control over human affairs as wide and benignant as the smile of the Great Stone Face. Full of faith and hope, Ernest doubted not that what the people said was true, and that now he was to behold the living likeness of those wondrous features on the mountain-side. While the boy was still gazing up the valley, and fancying, as he always did, that the Great Stone Face returned his gaze and looked kindly at him, the rumbling of wheels was heard, approaching swiftly along the winding road.

"Here he comes!" cried a group of people who were assembled to witness the arrival. "Here comes the great Mr. Gathergold!"

A carriage, drawn by four horses, dashed round the turn of the road. Within it, thrust partly out of the window, appeared the physiognomy of a little old man, with a skin as yellow as if his own Midas-hand had transmuted it. He had a low forehead, small, sharp eyes, puckered about with innumerable wrinkles, and very thin lips, which he made still thinner by pressing them forcibly together.

"The very image of the Great Stone Face!" shouted the people. "Sure enough, the old prophecy is true; and here we have the great man come, at last!"

And, what greatly perplexed Ernest, they seemed actually to believe that here was the likeness which they spoke of. By the roadside there chanced to be an old beggar-woman and two little beggar-children, stragglers from some far-off region, who, as the carriage rolled onward, held out their hands and lifted up their doleful voices, most piteously beseeching charity. A yellow claw—the very same that had clawed together so much wealth—

poked itself out of the coach-window, and dropped some copper coins upon the ground; so that, though the great man's name seems to have been Gathergold, he might just as suitably have been nicknamed Scattercopper. Still, nevertheless, with an earnest shout, and evidently with as much good faith as ever, the people bellowed,—

"He is the very image of the Great Stone Face!"

But Ernest turned sadly from the wrinkled shrewdness of that sordid visage, and gazed up the valley, where, amid a gathering mist, gilded by the last sunbeams, he could still distinguish those glorious features which had impressed themselves into his soul. Their aspect cheered him. What did the benign lips seem to say?

"He will come! Fear not, Ernest; the man will come!"

The years went on, and Ernest ceased to be a boy. He had grown to be a young man now. He attracted little notice from the other inhabitants of the valley; for they saw nothing remarkable in his way of life, save that, when the labor of the day was over, he still loved to go apart and gaze and meditate upon the Great Stone Face. According to their idea of the matter, it was a folly, indeed, but pardonable, inasmuch as Ernest was industrious, kind, and neighborly, and neglected no duty for the sake of indulging this idle habit. They knew not that the Great Stone Face had become a teacher to him, and that the sentiment which was expressed in it would enlarge the young man's heart, and fill it with wider and deeper sympathies than other hearts. They knew not that thence would come a better wisdom than could be learned from books, and a better life than could be moulded on the defaced example of other human lives. Neither did Ernest know that the thoughts and affections which came to him so naturally, in the fields and at the fireside, and wherever he communed with himself, were of a higher tone than those which all men shared with him. A simple soul,—simple as when his mother first taught him the old prophecy,—he beheld the marvellous features beaming adown the valley, and still wondered that their human counterpart was so long in making his appearance.

By this time poor Mr. Gathergold was dead and buried; and the oddest part of the matter was, that his wealth, which was the body and spirit of his existence, had disappeared before his death, leaving nothing of him but a living skeleton, covered over with a wrinkled, yellow skin. Since the melting away of his gold, it had been very generally conceded that there was no such striking resemblance, after all, betwixt the ignoble features of the ruined merchant and that majestic face upon the mountain-side. So the people ceased to honor him during his lifetime, and quietly consigned him to forgetfulness after his decease. Once in a while, it is true his memory was brought up in connection with the magnificent palace which he had built, and which had long ago been turned into a hotel for the accommodation of strangers, multitudes of whom came, every summer, to visit that famous natural curiosity, the Great Stone Face. Thus, Mr. Gathergold being discredited and thrown into the shade, the man of prophecy was yet to come.

It so happened that a native-born son of the valley, many years before, had enlisted as a soldier, and, after a great deal of hard fighting, had now become an illustrious commander. Whatever he may be called in history, he was known in camps and on the battlefield under the nickname of Old Blood-and-Thunder. This war-worn veteran, being now infirm with age and wounds, and weary of the turmoil of a military life, and of the roll of the drum and the clangor of the trumpet, that had so long been ringing in his ears, had lately signified a purpose of returning to his native valley, hoping to find repose where he remembered to have left it. The inhabitants, his old neighbors and their grown-up children, were resolved to welcome the renowned warrior with a salute of cannon and a public dinner; and all the more enthusiastically, it being affirmed that now, at last, the likeness of the Great Stone Face had actually appeared. An aide-de-camp of Old Blood-and-Thunder, travelling through the valley, was said to have been struck with the resemblance. Moreover, the schoolmates and early acquaintances of the general were ready to testify, on oath, that, to the best of their recollection, the aforesaid general had been exceedingly like the majestic image, even when a boy, only that the idea had never occurred to them at that period. Great, therefore, was the excitement throughout the valley; and many people, who had never once thought of glancing at the Great Stone Face for years before, now spent their time in gazing at it, for the sake of knowing exactly how General Blood-and-Thunder looked.

On the day of the great festival, Ernest, with all the other people of the valley, left their work, and proceeded to the spot where the sylvan banquet was prepared. As he approached, the loud voice of the Reverend Doctor Battleblast was heard, beseeching a blessing on the good things set before them, and on the distinguished friend of peace in whose honor they were assembled. The tables were arranged in a cleared space of the woods, shut in by the surrounding trees, except where a vista opened eastward, and afforded a distant view of the Great Stone Face. Over the general's chair, which was a relic from the home of Washington, there was an arch of verdant boughs, with the laurel profusely intermixed, and surmounted by his country's banner, beneath which he had won his victories. Our friend Ernest raised himself on his tip-toes, in hopes to get a glimpse of the celebrated guest; but there was a mighty crowd about the tables anxious to hear the toasts and speeches, and to catch any word that might fall from the general in reply; and a volunteer company, doing duty as a guard, pricked ruthlessly with their bayonets at any particularly quiet person among the throng. So Ernest, being of an unobtrusive character, was thrust quite into the background, where he could see no more of Old Blood-and-Thunder's physiognomy than if it had been still blazing on the battlefield. To console himself, he turned towards the Great Stone Face, which, like a faithful and long-remembered friend, looked back and smiled upon him through the vista of the forest. Meantime, however, he could overhear the remarks of various individuals, who were comparing the features of the hero with the face on the distant mountain-side.

" 'T is the same face, to a hair!" cried one man, cutting a caper for joy.

"Wonderfully like, that's a fact!" responded another.

"Like! why, I call it Old Blood-and-Thunder himself, in a monstrous looking-glass!" cried a third. "And why not? He's the greatest man of this or any other age, beyond a doubt."

And then all three of the speakers gave a great shout, which communicated electricity to the crowd, and called forth a roar from a thousand voices, that went reverberating for miles among the mountains, until you might have supposed that the Great Stone Face had poured its thunder-breath into the cry. All these comments, and this vast enthusiasm, served the more to interest our friend; nor did he think of questioning that now, at length, the mountain-visage had found its human counterpart. It is true, Ernest had imagined that this long-looked-for personage would appear in the character of a man of peace, uttering wisdom, and doing good, and making people happy. But, taking an habitual breadth of view, with all his simplicity, he contended that Providence should choose its own method of blessing mankind, and could conceive that this great end might be effected even by a warrior and a bloody sword, should inscrutable wisdom see fit to order matters so.

"The general! the general!" was now the cry. "Hush! silence! Old Blood-and-Thunder's going to make a speech."

Even so; for, the cloth being removed, the general's health had been drunk amid shouts of applause, and he now stood upon his feet to thank the company. Ernest saw him. There he was, over the shoulders of the crowd, from the two glittering epaulets and embroidered collar upward, beneath the arch of green boughs with intertwined laurel, and the banner drooping as if to shade his brow! And there, too, visible in the same glance, through the vista of the forest, appeared the Great Stone Face! And was there, indeed, such a resemblance as the crowd had testified? Alas, Ernest could not recognize it! He beheld a war-worn and weather-beaten countenance, full of energy, and expressive of an iron will; but the gentle wisdom, the deep, broad, tender sympathies were altogether wanting in Old Blood-and-Thunder's visage; and even if the Great Stone Face had assumed his look of stern command, the milder traits would still have tempered it.

"This is not the man of prophecy," sighed Ernest to himself, as he made his way out of the throng. "And must the world wait longer yet?"

The mists had congregated about the distant mountain-side, and there were seen the grand and awful features of the Great Stone Face, awful but benignant, as if a mighty angel were sitting among the hills, and enrobing himself in a cloud-vesture of gold and purple. As he looked, Ernest could hardly believe but that a smile beamed over the whole visage, with a radiance still brightening, although without motion of the lips. It was probably the effect of the western sunshine, melting through the thinly diffused vapors that had swept between him and the object that he gazed at. But—as it always did—the aspect of his marvellous friend made Ernest as hopeful as if he had never hoped in vain.

"Fear not, Ernest," said his heart, even as if the Great Face were whispering him,—"fear not, Ernest; he will come."

More years sped swiftly and tranquilly away. Ernest still dwelt in his native valley, and was now a man of middle age. By imperceptible degrees, he had become known among the people. Now, as heretofore, he labored for his bread, and was the same simple-hearted man that he had always been. But he had thought and felt so much, he had given so many of the best hours of his life to unworldly hopes for some great good to mankind, that it seemed as though he had been talking with the angels, and had imbibed a portion of their wisdom unawares. It was visible in the calm and well-considered beneficence of his daily life, the quiet stream of which had made a wide green margin all along its course. Not a day passed by, that the world was not the better because this man, humble as he was, had lived. He never stepped aside from his own path, yet would always reach a blessing to his neighbor. Almost involuntarily, too, he had become a preacher. The pure and high simplicity of his thought, which, as one of its manifestations, took shape in the good deeds that dropped silently from his hand, flowed also forth in speech. He uttered truths that wrought upon and moulded the lives of those who heard him. His auditors, it may be, never suspected that Ernest, their own neighbor and familiar friend, was more than an ordinary man; least of all did Ernest himself suspect it; but, inevitably as the murmur of a rivulet, came thoughts out of his mouth that no other human lips had spoken.

When the people's minds had had a little time to cool, they were ready enough to acknowledge their mistake in imagining a similarity between General Blood-and-Thunder's truculent physiognomy and the benign visage on the mountain-side. But now, again, there were reports and many paragraphs in the newspapers, affirming that the likeness of the Great Stone Face had appeared upon the broad shoulders of a certain eminent statesman. He, like Mr. Gathergold and Old Blood-and-Thunder, was a native of the valley, but had left it in his early days, and taken up the trades of law and politics. Instead of the rich man's wealth and the warrior's sword, he had but a tongue, and it was mightier than both together. So wonderfully eloquent was he, that whatever he might choose to say, his auditors had no choice but to believe him; wrong looked like right, and right like wrong; for when it pleased him he could make a kind of illuminated fog with his mere breath, and obscure the natural daylight with it. His tongue, indeed, was a magic instrument: sometimes it rumbled like the thunder; sometimes it warbled like the sweetest music. It was the blast of war,—the song of peace; and it seemed to have a heart in it, when there was no such matter. In good truth he was a wondrous man; and when his tongue had acquired him all other imaginable success,—when it had been heard in halls of state, and in the courts of princes and potentates,—after it had made him known all over the world, even as a voice crying from shore to shore,—it finally persuaded his countrymen to select him for the presidency. Before this time,—indeed, as soon as he began to grow celebrated,—his admirers had found out the resemblance between him and the Great Stone Face; and so much were they struck by it, that throughout the country this distinguished gentleman was known by the name of Old Stony Phiz. The phrase was considered as giving a highly favorable aspect to his political prospects; for, as is likewise the case with the Popedom, nobody ever comes president without taking a name other than his own.

While his friends were doing their best to make him president, Old Stony Phiz, as he was called, set out on a visit to the valley where he was born. Of course, he had no other object than to shake hands with his fellow-citizens, and neither thought nor cared about any effect which his progress through the country might have upon the election. Magnificent preparations were made to receive the illustrious statesman; a cavalcade of horsemen set forth to meet him at the boundary line of the State, and all the people left their business and gathered along the wayside to see him pass. Among these was Ernest. Though more than once disappointed, as we have seen, he had such a hopeful and confiding nature, that he was always ready to believe in whatever seemed beautiful and good. He kept his heart continually open, and thus was sure to catch the blessing from on high, when it should come. So now again, as buoyantly as ever, he went forth to behold the likeness of the Great Stone Face.

The cavalcade came prancing along the road, with a great clattering of hoofs and a mighty cloud of dust, which rose up so dense and high that the visage of the mountain-side was completely hidden from Ernest's eyes. All the great men of the neighborhood were there on horseback: militia officers in uniform; the member of Congress; the sheriff of the county;

the editors of newspapers; and many a farmer too had mounted his patient steed, with his Sunday coat upon his back. It really was a very brilliant spectacle, especially as there were numerous banners flaunting over the cavalcade, on some which were gorgeous portraits of the illustrious statesman and the Great Stone Face, smiling familiarly at one another, like two brothers. If the pictures were to be trusted, the mutual resemblance, it must be confessed, was marvellous. We must not forget to mention that there was a band of music, which made the echoes of the mountains ring and reverberate with the loud triumph of its strains; so that airy and soul-thrilling melodies broke out among all the heights and hollows, as if every nook of his native valley had found a voice, to welcome the distinguished guest. But the grandest effect was when the far-off mountain precipice flung back the music; for then the Great Stone Face itself seemed to be swelling the triumphant chorus, in acknowledgment that, at length, the man of prophecy was come.

All this while the people were throwing up their hats and shouting, with enthusiasm so contagious that the heart of Ernest kindled up, and he likewise threw up his hat, and shouted, as loudly as the loudest, "Huzza for the great man! Huzza for Old Stony Phiz!" But as yet he had not seen him.

"Here he is, now!" cried those who stood near Ernest. "There! There! Look at Old Stony Phiz and then at the Old Man of the Mountain, and see if they are not as like as two twin-brothers!"

In the midst of all this gallant array came an open barouche, drawn by four white horses; and in the barouche, with his massive head uncovered, sat the illustrious statesman, Old Stony Phiz himself.

"Confess it," said one of Ernest's neighbors to him, "the Great Stone Face has met its match at last."

Now, it must be owned that, at his first glimpse of the countenance which was bowing and smiling from the barouche, Ernest did fancy that there was a resemblance between it and the old familiar face upon the mountain-side. The brow, with its massive depth and loftiness, and all the other features, indeed, were boldly and strongly hewn, as if in emulation of a more than heroic, of a Titanic model. But the sublimity and stateliness, the grand expression of a divine sympathy, that illuminated the mountain visage, and etherealized its ponderous granite substance into spirit, might here be sought in vain. Something had been originally left out, or had departed. And therefore the marvellously gifted statesman had always a weary gloom in the deep caverns of his eyes, as of a child that has outgrown its playthings, or a man of mighty faculties and little aims, whose life, with all its high performances, was vague and empty, because no high purpose had endowed it with reality.

Still, Ernest's neighbor was thrusting his elbow into his side, and pressing him for an answer.

"Confess! confess! Is not he the very picture of your Old Man of the Mountain?"

"No!" said Ernest, bluntly, "I see little or no likeness."

"Then so much the worse for the Great Stone Face!" answered his neighbor; and again he set up a shout for Old Stony Phiz.

But Ernest turned away, melancholy, and almost despondent; for this was the saddest of his disappointments, to behold a man who might have fulfilled the prophecy, and had not willed to do so. Meantime, the cavalcade, the banners, the music, and the barouches swept past him, with the vociferous crowd in the rear, leaving the dust to settle down, and the Great Stone Face to be revealed again, with the grandeur that it had worn for untold centuries.

"Lo, here I am, Ernest!" the benign lips seemed to say. "I have waited longer than thou, and am not yet weary. Fear not; the man will come."

The years hurried onward, treading in their haste on one another's heels. And now they began to bring white hairs, and scatter them over the head of Ernest; they made reverend wrinkles across his forehead, and furrows in his cheeks. He was an aged man. But not in vain had he grown old: more than the white hairs on his head were the sage thoughts in his mind; his wrinkles and furrows were inscriptions that Time had graved, and in which he had written legends of wisdom that had been tested by the tenor of a life. And Ernest had ceased to be obscure. Unsought for, undesired, had come the fame which so many seek, and made him known in the great world, beyond the limits of the valley in which he had dwelt so quietly. College professors, and even the active men of cities, came from far to see and converse with Ernest; for the report had gone abroad that this simple husbandman had ideas unlike those of other men, not gained from books, but of a higher tone,—a tranquil and familiar majesty, as if he had been talking with the angels as his daily friends. Whether it were sage, statesman, or philanthropist, Ernest received these visitors with the gentle sincerity that had characterized him from boyhood, and spoke freely with them of whatever came uppermost, or lay deepest in his heart or their own. While they talked together, his face would kindle, unawares, and shine upon them, as with a mild evening light. Pensive with the fulness of such discourse, his guests took leave and went their way; and, passing up the valley, paused to look at the Great Stone Face, imagining that they had seen its likeness in a human countenance, but could not remember where.

While Ernest had been growing up and growing old, a bountiful Providence had granted a new poet to this earth. He, likewise, was a native of the valley, but had spent the greater part of his life at a distance from that romantic region, pouring out his sweet music amid the bustle and din of cities. Often, however, did the mountains which had been familiar to him in his childhood lift their snowy peaks into the clear atmosphere of his poetry. Neither was the Great Stone Face forgotten, for the poet had celebrated it in an ode, which was grand enough to have been uttered by its own majestic lips. This man of genius, we may say, had come down from heaven with wonderful endowments. If he sang of a mountain, the eyes of all mankind beheld a mightier grandeur reposing on its breast, or soaring to its summit, than had before been seen there. If his theme were a lovely lake, a celestial smile had now been thrown over it, to gleam forever on its surface. If it were the vast old sea, even the deep immensity of its dread bosom seemed to swell the higher, as if moved by the emotions of the song. Thus the world assumed another and a better aspect from the hour that the poet blessed it with his happy eyes. The Creator had bestowed him, as the last, best touch to his own handiwork. Creation was not finished till the poet came to interpret, and so complete it.

The effect was no less high and beautiful, when his human brethren were the subject of his verse. The man or woman, sordid with the common dust of life, who crossed his daily path, and the little child who played in it, were glorified if he beheld them in his mood of poetic faith. He showed the golden links of the great chain that intertwined them with an angelic kindred; he brought out the hidden traits of a celestial birth that made them worthy of such kin. Some, indeed, there were, who thought to show the soundness of their judgment by affirming that all the beauty and dignity of the natural world existed only in the poet's fancy. Let such men speak for themselves, who undoubtedly appear to have been spawned forth by Nature with a contemptuous bitterness; she having plastered them up out of her refuse stuff, after all the swine were made. As respects all things else, the poet's ideal was the truest truth.

The songs of this poet found their way to Ernest. He read them, after his customary toil, seated on the bench before his cottage door, where, for such a length of time, he had filled his repose with thought, by gazing at the Great Stone Face. And now, as he read stanzas that caused the soul to thrill within him, he lifted his eyes to the vast countenance beaming on him so benignantly.

"O majestic friend," he murmured, addressing the Great Stone Face, "is not this man worthy to resemble thee?"

The Face seemed to smile, but answered not a word.

Now it happened that the poet, though he dwelt so far away, had not only heard of Ernest, but had meditated much upon his character, until he deemed nothing so desirable as to meet this man, whose untaught wisdom walked hand in hand with the noble simplicity of his life. One summer morning, therefore, he took passage by the railroad, and, in the decline of the afternoon, alighted from the cars at no great distance from Ernest's cottage. The great hotel, which had formerly been the palace of Mr. Gathergold, was close at hand, but the poet, with his carpet-bag on his arm, inquired at once where Ernest dwelt, and was resolved to be accepted as his guest.

Approaching the door, he there found the good old man, holding a volume in his hand, which alternately he read, and then, with a finger between the leaves, looked lovingly at the Great Stone Face.

"Good evening," said the poet. "Can you give a traveller a night's lodging?"

"Willingly," answered Ernest; and then he added, smiling, "Methinks I never saw the Great Stone Face look so hospitably at a stranger."

The poet sat down on the bench beside him, and he and Ernest talked together. Often had the poet held intercourse with the wittiest and the wisest, but never before with a man like Ernest, whose thoughts and feelings gushed up with such a natural freedom, and who made great truths so familiar by his simple utterance of them. Angels, as had been so often said, seemed to have wrought with him at his labor in the fields; angels seemed to have sat with him by the fireside; and, dwelling with angels as friend with friends, he had imbibed the sublimity of their ideas, and imbued it with the sweet and lowly charm of household words. So thought the poet. And Ernest, on the other hand, was moved and agitated by the living images which the poet flung out of his mind, and which peopled all the air about the cottage door with shapes of beauty, both gay and pensive. The sympathies of these two men instructed them with a profounder sense than either could have attained alone. Their minds accorded into one strain, and made delightful music which neither of them could have claimed as all his own, nor distinguished his own share from the other's. They led one another, as it were, into a high pavilion of their thoughts, so remote, and hitherto so dim, that they had never entered it before, and so beautiful that they desired to be there always.

As Ernest listened to the poet, he imagined that the Great Stone Face was bending forward to listen too. He gazed earnestly into the poet's glowing eyes.

"Who are you, my strangely gifted guest?" he said.

The poet laid his finger on the volume that Ernest had been reading.

"You have read these poems," said he. "You know me, then,—for I wrote them."

Again, and still more earnestly than before, Ernest examined the poet's features; then turned towards the Great Stone Face; then back, with an uncertain aspect, to his guest. But his countenance fell; he shook his head, and sighed.

"Wherefore are you sad?" inquired the poet.

"Because," replied Ernest, "all through life I have awaited the fulfilment of a prophecy; and, when I read these poems, I hoped that it might be fulfilled in you."

"You hoped," answered the poet, faintly smiling, "to find in me the likeness of the Great Stone Face. And you are disappointed, as formerly with Mr. Gathergold, and Old Blood-and-Thunder, and Old Stony Phiz. Yes, Ernest, it is my doom. You must add my name to the illustrious three, and record another failure of your hopes. For—in shame and sadness do I speak it, Ernest—I am not worthy to be typified by yonder benign and majestic image."

"And why?" asked Ernest. He pointed to the volume. "Are not those thoughts divine?"

"They have a strain of the Divinity," replied the poet. "You can hear in them the far-off echo of a heavenly song. But my life, dear Ernest, has not corresponded with my thought. I have had grand dreams, but they have been only dreams, because I have lived—and that, too, by my own choice—among poor and mean realities. Sometimes even—shall I dare to say it?—I lack faith in the grandeur, the beauty, and the goodness which my own works are said to have made more evident in nature and in human life. Why, then, pure seeker of the good and true, shouldst thou hope to find me in yonder image of the divine!"

The poet spoke sadly, and his eyes were dim with tears. So, likewise, were those of Ernest.

At the hour of sunset, as had long been his frequent custom, Ernest was to discourse to an assemblage of the neighboring inhabitants, in the open air. He and the poet, arm in arm, still talking together as they went along, proceeded to the spot. It was a small nook among the hills, with a gray precipice behind, the stern front of which was relieved by the pleasant foliage of many creeping plants, that made a tapestry for the naked rock, by hanging their festoons from all its rugged angles. At a small elevation above the ground, set in a rich framework of verdure, there appeared a niche, spacious enough to admit a human figure, with freedom for such gestures as spontaneously accompany earnest thought and genuine emotion. Into this natural pulpit Ernest ascended, and threw a look of familiar kindness around upon his audience. They stood, or sat, or reclined upon the grass, as seemed good to each, with the departing sunshine falling obliquely over them, and mingling its subdued cheerfulness with the solemnity of a grove of ancient trees, beneath and amid the boughs of which the golden rays were constrained to pass. In another direction was seen the Great Stone Face, with the same cheer, combined with the same solemnity, in its benignant aspect.

Ernest began to speak, giving to the people of what was in his heart and mind. His words had power, because they accorded with his thoughts;

and his thoughts had reality and depth, because they harmonized with the life which he had always lived. It was not mere breath that this preacher uttered; they were the words of life, because a life of good deeds and holy love was melted into them. Pearls, pure and rich, had been dissolved into this precious draught. The poet, as he listened, felt that the being and character of Ernest were a nobler strain of poetry than he had ever written. His eyes glistening with tears, he gazed reverentially at the venerable man, and said within himself that never was there an aspect so worthy of a prophet and a sage as that mild, sweet, thoughtful countenance, with the glory of white hair diffused about it. At a distance, but distinctly to be seen, high up in the golden light of the setting sun, appeared the Great Stone Face, with hoary mists around it, like the white hairs around the brow of Ernest. Its look of grand beneficence seemed to embrace the world.

At that moment, in sympathy with a thought which he was about to utter, the face of Ernest assumed a grandeur of expression, so imbued with benevolence, that the poet, by an irresistible impulse, threw his arms aloft, and shouted,—

"Behold! Behold! Ernest is himself the likeness of the Great Stone Face!"

Then all the people looked, and saw that what the deep-sighted poet said was true. The prophecy was fulfilled. But Ernest, having finished what he had to say, took the poet's arm, and walked slowly homeward, still hoping that some wiser and better man than himself would by and by appear, bearing a resemblance to the GREAT STONE FACE.

GERMELSHAUSEN

FRIEDRICH GERSTÄCKER

I

IN the autumn of the year 1847 a strapping young fellow, knapsack on back and stick in hand, was walking with slow and easy stride along the broad highroad that leads up from Marisfeld to Wichtelhausen. He was not one of those journeyman artizans who travel about from place to place seeking work; any one could see that at the first glance, even if the small neatly made leather portfolio which he carried strapped on his knapsack had not betrayed his calling. There was certainly no denying the fact that he was an artist.

His black, broad-brimmed hat cocked jauntily on one side, his long, fair, curly hair, his downy beard, full but youthful still—everything announced it, even the somewhat threadbare black velvet jacket, which seemed likely to be a little too warm for him on this bright, warm morning. He had unbuttoned it, and the white shirt underneath—for he wore no waistcoat—was but loosely held together round his neck by a black silk scarf.

He might have been about a mile distant from Marisfeld when the bell of the village church rang out, and he halted, leaning upon his stick and listening intently to the full tones of the bell, which sounded wondrously sweet to him across the breezes.

The sounds had long since died away, and yet he still stood there gazing dreamily out over the hill-slopes. His heart was at home with his loved ones in the dear little village among the Taunus mountains, with his mother and his sisters, and it almost seemed as if a tear was like to spring to his eye.

But his light and merry heart would not suffer the intrusion of sad and melancholy thoughts. He only took off his hat, waved a loving, smiling greeting in the direction in which he knew his home lay, and then, gripping his stout stick more firmly, he gaily stepped out along the road, continuing the journey he had already begun.

Meanwhile the sun was beating down with considerable warmth upon the broad, monotonous highway, which was covered with a thick layer of dust; and our traveller had already for some time been casting glances to right and left to see if he could anywhere discover some pleasanter footpath.

At one point, indeed, a road did branch off to the right, but it looked to him unpromising, and besides it would lead him too far out of his way; so he stuck to his original track a little longer, until he at length came to a limpid mountain stream, across which he could discern the ruins of an old stone bridge.

Away on the other side ran a grassy path, leading farther into the valley; so, with no definite purpose in view—for he was only passing through the beautiful Werra valley to enrich his portfolio—he crossed the brook dry-shod by leaping from one great stone to another, and so reached the close-cropped meadow on the other side, where he advanced rapidly on the springy turf under the shadow of the thick alder-bushes, well content with the change.

"Now I have the advantage," he said to himself with a laugh, "of not knowing whither I am bound. There is no tiresome sign-post here telling one miles beforehand what is the name of the next village, and invariably giving the wrong distance. However do people in these parts measure their miles, I should like to know!

"How wonderfully quiet it is in this valley! To be sure, on Sundays farmers have nothing to do out of doors, and since they have to walk behind their plough or by their cart the whole week, they don't care much about going for a walk when Sunday comes; they first of all make up for their arrears of sleep in church during the morning, and after dinner stretch their legs under the table in the tavern. Tavern! h'm, a glass of beer wouldn't be such a bad thing in this heat; but until I can get it this clear stream will quench my thirst just as well."

And with that he flung off knapsack and hat, knelt down at the waterside, and drank to his heart's content.

Somewhat cooled by his drink, his glance fell on an old, strangely gnarled willow tree, which he rapidly sketched with practised hand; and then, completely rested and refreshed, he took up his knapsack again and continued his way, regardless as to where it would lead him.

He had wandered on thus for perhaps an hour or so, jotting down in his sketch-book here a crag, there a peculiar clump of alder-bushes, or again a knotty oak-branch; the sun had meanwhile mounted higher and higher, and he had just made up his mind to quicken his steps in order at least not to miss his dinner in the next village, when before him in the valley, sitting close to the brook and by an old stone, on which perhaps in times gone by there had stood a sacred shrine, he caught sight of a peasant girl, who was gazing down the road along which he came.

As he was hidden by the alders, he had been able to see her before she saw him; but following the bank of the stream, he had hardly passed beyond the bushes which had hitherto concealed him from her sight when she leapt to her feet and flew toward him with a cry of pleasure.

Arnold, as the young painter was called, stood amazed, and was soon aware that a beautiful girl of hardly seventeen years, dressed in a peculiar but extremely pretty peasant's costume, was running up to him with outstretched arms.

Arnold of course saw at once that she had mistaken him for some one else, and that this joyful greeting was not meant for him; and the girl no sooner recognised him than she stood stock-still with horror, turned pale at first and then red all over, and finally said with shy embarrassment:

"Do not be offended, stranger! I—I thought—"

"That it was your sweetheart, my dear child, didn't you?" laughed the young man. "And now you are vexed that a different person, an uninteresting stranger, has met you! Don't be angry because I am not he."

"Ah, how can you say such things?" said the girl in a distressed whisper. "Why should I be angry?—oh! but if you only knew how delighted I was!"

"Then he certainly does not deserve that you should wait any longer for him," said Arnold, who now for the first time noticed the truly wonderful charm of the graceful peasant girl. "Were I in his place, you would not have had to wait for me in vain for a single moment."

"You do say such strange things," said the girl, abashed. "If he could have come he would certainly be here by now. Perhaps he is ill, or—even dead," she added slowly, and with a sigh that came from the depths of her heart.

"And has he let you have no news of himself all this time?"

"No, all this long, long time."

"Then his home is perhaps a long way from here?"

"A long way? Why, yes; quite a great distance from here," said the girl. "In Bischofsroda."

"Bischofsroda?" cried Arnold. "I spent four weeks there only recently, and I know every child in the whole village. What is his name?"

"Heinrich—Heinrich Vollgut," said the girl shyly; "the mayor's son in Bischofsroda."

"H'm," mused Arnold, "I was in and out of the mayor's house, but *his* name was Bäuerling, as far as I know, and I never heard the name of Vollgut in the whole village."

"Probably you didn't know all the people there," argued the girl, and over the sorrowful expression which clouded her sweet face there stole a soft, roguish smile, which became her as well and much better than her previous melancholy.

"Well, but from Bischofsroda," said the young man, "you can get here over the mountains easily in two hours, at most in three."

"And yet he is not here," said the girl, sighing deeply again, "though he promised me so faithfully."

"Then he'll come sure enough," Arnold assured her with hearty conviction; "for once any one has given you a promise, he must surely have a heart of stone if he went back on his word—and that I am sure your Heinrich has not got."

"No," she answered resolutely; "but now I cannot wait any longer for him, as I have to be home for dinner, or else Father will scold me."

"And where is your home?"

"Straight down there in the valley. Hark! there's the bell; they are just coming out of church."

Arnold listened, and at no great distance off he could hear the slow pealing of a bell; but the sound came to him not deep and full, but sharp and discordant, and when he turned his eyes toward the spot it seemed to him almost as if a thick mountain mist lay over that part of the valley.

"Your bell is cracked," he laughed; "it doesn't ring true."

"Yes, I know that," answered the girl calmly; "it has not a pleasant sound, and we should have had it recast long ago, but we are always short of money and time, for hereabouts there are no bell-casters. Yet, what does it matter? We know it all right, and we know what it means when it rings—so even though it is cracked it serves its purpose."

"And what is the name of your village?"

"Germelshausen."

"And can I get to Wichtelhausen from there?"

"Quite easily; by the footpath it takes hardly half an hour—perhaps, indeed, not so much, if you put your best foot forward."

"Then I'll go with you through the village, and if you have a good inn in the place I'll have my dinner there too."

"The inn is only too good," said the maiden with a sigh, as she cast a glance backward to see if her expected lover might not yet be coming.

"Can any inn be too good?"

"For the farmer, yes," said the girl gravely, as she walked slowly by his side along the valley. "Of an evening after his work he still has much to do in the house, and this he neglects if he sits in the public-house till late at night."

"But I, at any rate, have nothing more to neglect to-day."

"Yes, with townfolk it is rather different: they don't do anything, and consequently haven't got much to neglect either. Yet the farmer has to earn bread for them."

"Well, not exactly so," said Arnold with a laugh. "He has to grow it, I grant you, but we have to earn it for ourselves; and a hard job it is too, many a time; for what the farmer does he sees that he is well paid."

"But you don't work, anyhow."

"Why not, pray?"

"Your hands don't look like it."

"Then I will show you at once how I work and what I work at," laughed Arnold. "Just you sit down on that flat stone under the old lilac tree. . . ."

"And what am I to do there?"

"Just sit down," cried the young painter, who threw off his knapsack and took out his sketch-book and pencil.

"But I must go home."

"I shall be done in five minutes. I should very much like to take a reminder of you away into the world with me; even your Heinrich will have no objection to that!"

"A reminder of me? What a funny man you are!"

"I will take your portrait away with me."

"You are a painter, then?"

"Yes."

"What a lucky thing! Then you might set to work and touch up the pictures in Germelshausen church; they look so very poor and shabby."

"What is your name?" was Arnold's next question. He had meanwhile opened his portfolio and was rapidly sketching in the girl's charming features.

"Gertrud."

"And what is your father?"

"The mayor of the village. If you are a painter, you must not go to the inn either; I will take you straight home with me, and after dinner you can talk over the whole matter with Father."

"Oh, the pictures in the church?" said Arnold, laughing.

"Of course," said the girl gravely; "and then you must stay with us a long, long time until—until the pictures are finished."

"Well, we'll talk about that later, Gertrud," said the young painter, busily plying his pencil the while; "but won't your Heinrich be angry if I am often—very often with you, and if I talk with you a good deal?"

"Heinrich?" said she. "Oh, he won't come now."

"Not to-day, no; but perhaps to-morrow."

"No," said Gertrud, quite calmly; "as he wasn't there by eleven o'clock, he will stay away until our day comes again."

"Your day? What do you mean by that?"

The girl looked at him with wide-open, earnest eyes, but gave no answer to his question, and her gaze turning to the clouds floating away high over their heads fastened upon them with a peculiar expression of pain and melancholy.

Gertrud's beauty at this moment was truly the beauty of an angel, and Arnold forgot all else in the interest which he was taking in the completion of her picture. Nor had he much more time left. The girl suddenly stood up, and tossing a kerchief over her head to shield her from the sun's rays, she said:

"Go I must; the day is so short, and they are expecting me at home."

But Arnold had finished his little picture, and indicating with a few bold strokes the folds of her dress, he held out the sketch to her and said:

"Have I caught your likeness?"

"It is myself!" gasped Gertrud, almost in fright.

"Well, who else could it be?" laughed Arnold.

"And do you wish to keep the picture and take it away with you?" asked the girl shyly, almost wistfully.

"Why, certainly I do," cried the young man, "and then when I am far, far away from here I shall think of you hard, and often."

"But will my father allow that?"

"Allow me to think of you? Is he capable of forbidding me to do so?"

"No—but—to take the picture away with you—out into the world?"

"He can't hinder me, dear girl," said Arnold tenderly; "but would you yourself hate to know that it was in my possession?"

"I? No!" was the girl's answer after short reflexion; "if only—but I must ask Father about it."

"What a silly child you are!" said the young painter with a laugh; "even a princess would have no objection to an artist securing a sketch of her features for himself. No harm can come to you from it. But please don't run off like that, you wild creature; I am coming with you, you know—or do you want to leave me behind without my dinner? Have you forgotten about the church pictures?"

"Oh, yes, the pictures," said the girl, standing still and waiting for him; but Arnold, who had quickly tied up his portfolio again, was by her side in a moment, and they both continued their way toward the village far quicker than before.

The village, however, was much nearer than Arnold had supposed from the sound of the cracked bell, for what the young man from afar had taken for an alder-grove, proved to be, on their nearer approach, a row of fruit trees enclosed by a hedge. Closely hidden behind these, yet surrounded on the north and north-east by broad fields, lay the old village with its low church-tower and its smoke-blackened cottages.

Here, too, it was that the pair first struck a firm, well-laid street, planted on either side with fruit trees. But over the village lowered a thick mist which Arnold had already perceived from afar, and it dimmed the bright sunshine, which fell upon the grey, old, weather-beaten roofs with a weird and yellowish light.

But Arnold scarcely had eyes for this. Gertrud, stepping out by his side, had meekly slipped her hand in his as they came to the first houses, and clasping it in her own she turned with him into the next street.

A strange feeling thrilled the lusty youth at the touch of her warm hand, and almost involuntarily his eyes sought to meet those of the young maiden. But Gertrud did not look in his direction; with eyes fixed modestly on the ground, she conducted her guest to her father's house, and Arnold's attention, too, was at length taken up with the villagers he met, who all passed him by in silence and without a word of greeting.

He could not help noticing this at first, for in all the neighbouring villages it would have been deemed almost a crime not to offer a stranger at least a "Good day" or a "God bless you." Here no one thought of such a thing, and, just as in any large town, the people either passed by in silence and without showing any interest, or else stood here and there and looked after them; but no one spoke a word to them—not one of all the passers-by gave a greeting even to the girl.

And how strange the old houses looked, with their pointed gables ornamented with carved work, and their hard thatched roofs weather-worn and grey; and though it was Sunday no window was polished bright, and the round panes set in leaden frames looked tarnished and dim, and showed on their dull surface shimmering rainbow colours.

Here and there a window would open as they walked by, and pleasant-faced girls or elderly worthy matrons would peep out. The curious dress of the people struck him also, differing essentially as it did from that of the villages in the vicinity. And besides all this an almost soundless stillness reigned everywhere so that Arnold, to whom this silence at last became oppressive, said to his companion:

"Do you observe Sunday in your village so strictly that people when they meet one another haven't even a word of greeting to utter? If one didn't hear a dog barking now and then or a cock crowing, one might really think the whole place dumb and dead."

"It is dinner-time," said Gertrud quietly, "and people are not inclined to talk then; this evening you will find them all the noisier."

"Thank Heaven!" exclaimed Arnold, "there are at least some children yonder playing in the street. I had begun to feel quite uncanny; I can tell you they spend Sunday quite differently in Bischofsroda."

"There's my father's house," said Gertrud in a low voice.

"But I can't thrust myself in upon him thus unexpectedly at dinner-time. I might be an unwelcome intruder, and I like to have friendly faces round me at meals. So show me rather where the inn is, my child, or let me find it myself, for probably Germelshausen is no exception to the rule of other villages. Generally the public-house is quite close to the church, and if you take the church-tower to guide you you can't go far wrong."

"There you are right; that is exactly the case with us," said Gertrud quietly; "but they expect us already at home, and you need have no fear of getting an unfriendly reception."

"Expect *us*? ah, you mean yourself and your Heinrich? Yes, Gertrud, if you would take me to-day in his place, then I would stay with you—until—until you yourself should tell me to go away again."

He had spoken these last words in such feeling tones, almost against his will, the while gently pressing the hand which still held his, that Gertrud suddenly stopped, looked at him out of her big, grave eyes, and said:

"Would you really wish that?"

"A thousand times yes," cried the young painter, utterly carried away by the girl's wonderful beauty. But Gertrud made no further answer, and pursuing her way as if she was pondering over the words of her companion, she at length came to a halt in front of a tall house, which was approached by a flight of broad, stone steps protected by iron railings. Speaking in her former shy and timid manner she resumed:

"This is where I live, kind sir, and if it would please you, come in with me to my father, who will no doubt be proud to see you at his table."

II

Before Arnold could return any answer to this invitation the mayor himself appeared in the doorway at the top of the steps, and a window was thrown open, revealing the kindly face of an old lady who looked out and nodded to them.

"Why, Gertrud," exclaimed the farmer, "what a long time you have stayed out to-day, and look what a smart young fellow she has brought back with her!"

"My dear sir!"

"Please, no ceremony on the steps! The dumplings are ready; come in, or they'll get hard and cold."

"But that's not Heinrich," cried the old lady from the window. "Now, didn't I always say that he would never come back again?"

"All right, Mother, all right," said the mayor, "this one will do very well instead"; and holding out his hand to the stranger he went on: "A hearty welcome to Germelshausen, young gentleman, wherever the lass may have picked you up. And now come in to dinner and fall to to your heart's content; anything else we can talk of later."

He left the young painter no possible further chance to make any excuses, but vigorously shaking his hand, which Gertrud had released as soon as he had set foot on the stone steps, he took his arm with familiar kindness and conducted him into the spacious living-room.

Although he was well acquainted with the habits of the German farmer, who shuts himself off from every breath of fresh air in his room, and not unfrequently, even in summer, keeps up a fire so as to produce the broiling heat he so delights in, yet what was most noticeable to Arnold at once was the musty, earthy atmosphere which pervaded the house. The narrow entrance hall was likewise far from inviting. The plaster had fallen from the walls and appeared to have just been hastily swept to one side. The single dim window at the back of the hall hardly admitted the meagre light, and the stairs which led to the upper storey looked old and out of repair.

Little time, however, was given him to observe all this, for in the very next moment his hospitable host threw open the door of the parlour, and Arnold saw himself in a low but broad and spacious room, which was airy and fresh, with white sand sprinkled over the floor, and which with its large table in the centre spread with a snow-white cloth contrasted pleasantly with the rest of the rather dilapidated arrangements of the house.

Besides the old lady, who now had shut the window and moved her chair up to the table, there were also sitting in the corner a few red-cheeked children; and a buxom peasant-woman, who also was wearing a costume utterly different from that of the neighbouring villages, was just opening the door to admit the maid who came in with a large dish.

And now the dumplings were smoking on the board and every one made for the chairs to partake of the welcome meal; but no one sat down, and the children, as it seemed to Arnold, cast almost anxious eyes on their father.

The latter advanced to his chair, and leaning his arms upon it, stared dumbly, silently, even gloomily upon the ground. Was he praying? Arnold saw that he kept his lips firmly pressed while his right hand hung down clenched by his side. In his features was no sign of prayer, only an obstinate yet irresolute defiance.

Gertrud then turned quietly to him and laid her hand on his shoulder, while the old lady stood speechless opposite to him, and looked at him with earnestly pleading eyes.

"Let us eat," growled the man, "it's no use, I fear"; and pushing his chair aside, nodded to his guest, dropped into his seat, and seizing the huge ladle served out helpings all round.

To Arnold the man's whole behaviour was almost uncanny, nor could he feel comfortable amid the depression shown by the others. But the mayor was not the man to eat his dinner to the accompaniment of melancholy thoughts. In answer to his rap on the table the maid came in again bearing bottles and glasses, and with the rich old wine which he now poured out a very different and more cheerful state of mind soon prevailed among the company round the table.

The glorious beverage ran through Arnold's veins like liquid fire; never in his life had he tasted anything like it. Gertrud drank some too, and so did the old lady, who later seated herself at her spinning-wheel in the corner and in a low voice sang a little song of the merry life in Germelshausen. The mayor himself seemed a different being.

He now became as cheerful and jovial as earlier he had been morose and silent, and Arnold himself could not escape the influence of the rich wine.

He could not precisely tell how it came about, but the mayor had taken a violin in his hand and was playing a merry dance, and Arnold, with his arm about fair Gertrud's waist, whirled with her round the room so madly that he upset the spinning-wheel and the chair, bumped into the maid who was trying to carry away the dinner things, and cut all sorts of merry capers, so that the others almost died of laughter to see him.

Suddenly there was complete silence in the room, and as Arnold looked round at the magistrate in astonishment, the latter pointed with his violin-bow out of the window, and then laid the instrument back again in the wooden case from which he had taken it. And Arnold perceived that outside in the street a coffin was being carried by.

Six men dressed in white shirts were bearing it upon their shoulders, and behind them, quite alone, walked an old man leading a little, fair-haired girl by the hand.

The old man walked along the street as one crushed with grief, but the little girl, who could hardly have been four years old, and probably had no idea who was lying in that black coffin, kept gaily nodding her head wherever she saw a face she knew, and laughed shrilly when two or three dogs scampered by and one of them ran up against the steps of the mayor's house and rolled over and over.

But the silence endured only as long as the coffin was in sight, and Gertrud drew up to the young man and said:

"Now rest a little while; you have been romping quite enough; otherwise, the heavy wine will get into your head more and more. Come, take your hat and let us go for a little walk together. By the time we get back it will be time to go to the inn, for there is a dance this evening."

"A dance? That's splendid," exclaimed Arnold, delighted; "I've come just at the right time. You'll give me the first dance, I hope, Gertrud?"

"Certainly, if you wish."

Arnold had already seized his hat and sketch-book.

"What do you want with the book?" asked the mayor.

"He sketches, Father," said Gertrud, "and he has already drawn me. Just have a look at the picture."

Arnold opened the sketch-book and held out the picture to her father.

The farmer looked at it quietly for a while without speaking.

"And do you want to take that home with you?" he asked at length, "and perhaps frame it and hang it up in your room?"

"Why not, pray?"

"May he, Father?" asked Gertrud.

"If he does not stay with us," laughed the mayor, "I have no objection —but there's something wanting in the background."

"What?"

"Why, the funeral procession that passed a moment ago. Draw that on the paper, and you may take the picture with you."

"What! the funeral procession with Gertrud!"

"There's room enough," said the mayor obstinately; "you must put it in the sketch, or else I will not permit you to take away with you my lassie's portrait all by itself. In such solemn company no one can possibly think evil of it."

At this strange proposal to give the pretty maiden a funeral party as a guard of honour, Arnold laughingly shook his head. But the old man seemed to have made up his mind, and so, to humour him, he did as he wished. Later on he could quite easily rub out the dismal additional feature.

With practised hand he drew on the paper the figures that had just passed by, though only from memory, and the whole family crowded round him as he worked, and watched with evident astonishment the rapid completion of the drawing.

"There, have I been successful?" cried Arnold at length, jumping up from his chair and holding out the picture at arm's length.

"Splendidly!" nodded the mayor; "I should never have thought you could finish it so quickly. Now, that will do; out you go with the lassie and have a look at the village; it may be a long while before you have a chance of seeing it again. Be back here by five o'clock sharp—we are having high jinks to-night and you must be there."

The musty room and the wine which had mounted to his head had begun to make Arnold feel heavy and oppressed. He longed to be out of doors, and a few minutes later he was striding along the street which led through the village, with fair Gertrud by his side.

As they made their way along there was not the same absence of noise as there had been before; children were playing in the road here and there, old people were sitting at their doors looking at them, and the whole place with its quaint ancient houses might have presented quite a pleasant appearance if only the sun had been able to pierce the thick brown smoke which hung like a cloud over the roofs.

"Is the moor or forest on fire hereabouts?" he asked the girl. "This sort of smoke does not hang over any other village and cannot come from the chimneys."

"It is earth-vapour," said Gertrud quietly; "but have you never heard of Germelshausen?"

"Never."

"That is strange, and yet the village is old, oh! so old."

"The houses look like it, at any rate, and the people too have such a curious way with them, and their speech sounds quite differently from that of places near at hand. You go very little outside your own village, I expect?"

"Very little," said Gertrud, curtly.

"And not a single swallow is left. They can't surely have flown away yet?"

"Oh, a long time ago," answered the girl apathetically; "in Germelshausen they never come now to build their nests. Perhaps they can't stand the earth-vapour."

"But surely you don't have that always?"

"Yes, always."

"Then that is the reason why your fruit trees bear no fruit, and yet in Marisfeld this year they had to prop up the branches, so fruitful has the season been."

Gertrud said not a word in answer, and walked on in silence by his side straight through the village until they came to the extreme limit. On the way she gave a kindly nod to a child here and there or spoke a low word or two with one of the young girls—maybe about the evening's dance and the dresses they were to wear.

And as they talked the girls cast sympathetic glances at the young painter, so that his heart warmed and saddened—he did not quite know why—and for all that he did not dare to ask Gertrud why it should be so.

They had now at length reached the last houses, and if it had been lively in the village itself, here at any rate everything was still and lonely and death-like. The gardens looked as if they had not been walked in for years and years; grass was growing in the pathways, and it seemed especially noticeable to the young stranger that not a single fruit tree bore a single bit of fruit.

At this point some men met them, going back home from outside the village, and at once Arnold recognised them as the funeral party returning. They moved noiselessly past them into the village again, and almost involuntarily the pair turned their steps to the graveyard.

Arnold tried now to cheer up his companion, who seemed to him so very serious, by telling her about other places where he had been and what the great outer world was like. She had never seen a railway, never even heard of one, and listened with attention and astonishment to his explanations.

Nor had she any knowledge of the electric telegraph, and she knew just as little about all the other more modern inventions; so that the young artist could not understand how it was possible that there should be still living in Germany human beings so secluded, so absolutely cut off from the rest of the world and without the slightest connection with it.

Conversing thus they reached the cemetery, and here the young stranger was immediately struck by the old-world appearance of the stones and monuments, simple and plain though they were as a general rule.

"Here is an old, old stone," he said, bending down to the nearest one and with difficulty deciphering the scrollwork upon it. "Anna Maria Berthold, maiden name Stieglitz, born 16th December 1188, died 2nd December 1224."

"That is my mother," said Gertrud solemnly, and the big, crystal tears filled her eyes and slowly trickled down on to her bodice.

"Your mother, dear child?" said Arnold in astonishment; "your great-great-grandmother perhaps it might have been."

"No," said Gertrud, "my own mother. Father married again, and the one at home is my step-mother."

"But surely it says, died 1224?"

"What does the year matter?" said Gertrud mournfully; "it is sad enough to be thus parted from one's mother, and yet," she added sorrowfully under her breath, "perhaps it was well, very well that she was suffered to go to God beforehand."

Arnold bent down over the stone, shaking his head, and made a closer examination of the inscription, in case the first "2" in the date might be an "8," for in the old-time writing such a thing was not impossible, but the second "2" was exactly the same as the first, and it was as yet too soon to write 1884. Perhaps it was the stone-mason who had made the mistake, and the girl was so deep in her memories of the departed that he did not like to trouble her any further with questions that were perhaps displeasing to her.

He therefore left her by the gravestone before which she had sunk to her knees and was silently praying, and proceeded to examine some other monuments, but all of them without exception bore dates of many hundred years back, even as far back as 930 and 900 A.D. No more recent gravestone could be discovered, and yet the dead were even now laid to rest in this place, as the latest fresh grave betokened.

From the low churchyard wall there was a splendid view of the old village, and Arnold quickly availed himself of the opportunity of making a sketch of it. But over this place also lay the strange fog, though toward the wood he could see the sunlight falling bright and clear on the mountain slopes.

Then from the village came the sound of the old cracked bell again, and Gertrud quickly rising from her knees and dashing the tears from her eyes, gently beckoned to the young man to follow her.

Arnold was quickly by her side.

"Now we must sorrow no more," she said with a smile, "the church bell is ringing the end of the service, and now for the dance. Up to the present you have no doubt imagined that the people of Germelshausen are nothing but kill-joys, but to-night you will think the contrary."

"But yonder is the church door," said Arnold, "and I can see nobody coming out."

"That is perfectly natural," laughed the girl, "for no one ever goes in, not even the priest. Only the old verger allows himself no rest, and still rings the service in and out."

"And do none of your people ever go to church?"

"No, neither to Mass nor to confession," said the girl quietly. "We have quarrelled with the Pope, who lives among foreigners, and has forbidden it until we return to obedience."

"Why, I've never heard of such a thing in all my life."

"Yes, it is a long time ago," said the girl carelessly. "Look, there's the verger all alone coming out of church and shutting the door; he never goes to the inn of an evening either, but sits silent all by himself at home."

"And does the priest go?"

"I should think so, and he is the jolliest of them all. He does not take things to heart."

"And how has all this come about?" asked Arnold, who was amazed not so much at the facts he had heard as at the girl's simplicity.

"It's a long story," Gertrud said, "and the priest has written it all down in a big, thick book. If you are interested, and if you understand Latin, you may read all about it there."

"But," she added by way of warning, "don't speak of it when Father is by, for he doesn't like it. Look, here come the boys and girls out of doors already; I must hurry off home now and dress, for I should not like to be the last."

"And the first dance, Gertrud?"

"I dance it with you; you have my promise."

The two walked quickly back to the village, which was now all astir with life, very different from what it was in the morning. Laughing groups of young people were standing about on all sides; the girls were all dressed up for the festival, and the young fellows too were in their best clothes, while on the face of the inn, as they sped past, festoons of leaves were hanging from window to window, and formed a broad triumphal arch over the door.

Seeing that every one was tricked out most resplendently, Arnold was unwilling to mingle with the merry-makers dressed in his travelling garb; so he unbuckled his knapsack in the mayor's house, took out of it his smart suit, and had just completed his toilet when Gertrud knocked at the door and called him.

And what a picture of loveliness the girl looked now in her simple yet rich gown, and how cordially she asked him to escort her, saying that her father and mother would not follow on till later!

"Yearning after her Heinrich cannot be depressing her spirits to any particular extent," was the youth's uppermost thought, as he drew her arm through his and passed with her to the ballroom through the gathering dusk. But he refrained from giving utterance to such thoughts, for a strange, a wonderful feeling thrilled his breast, and his own heart throbbed violently as he felt the girl's heart beating against his arm.

"To think that to-morrow I must depart," he sighed softly to himself.

Although he had not intended it, his words reached the ears of his companion, and she said with a smile:

"Don't trouble about that; we shall be together longer—longer perhaps than you like."

"And would you be glad, Gertrud, if I stayed with you?" asked Arnold, and as he spoke he felt the blood surging in tumultuous waves over forehead and temples.

"Of course I should," said the young girl simply; "you are nice and kind, and Father likes you too, of that I'm sure, and—Heinrich hasn't come, you know," she added in an undertone and somewhat angrily.

"Suppose he came to-morrow?"

"To-morrow?" said Gertrud, looking at him gravely out of her great dark eyes; "between now and to-morrow lies a long, long night. To-morrow! You will understand to-morrow what that word means. But to-day let us not speak of it," she said abruptly, yet pleasantly; "to-day is a holiday, to which we have looked forward so long, oh! so long, and do not let us spoil it by gloomy thoughts.

"Here we are at the place; the boys will stare a good deal when they see me bringing a new partner."

Arnold was about to make some reply to her, but his words were drowned by the noisy music which rolled out from within the ballroom. Strange tunes too were the musicians playing, not one of which he recognised, and at first he was almost blinded by the flash of the many lights that sparkled before his eyes.

Gertrud led him into the centre of the hall, where a bevy of young peasant girls stood chatting together, and not till then did she leave him to himself so that, until the real business of the dance began, he might look about him a little and make the acquaintance of the other young men.

III

At the first moment Arnold felt ill at ease among these many strangers; moreover, their strange costume and their strange speech repelled him, and though the harsh, unwonted accents came sweetly from Gertrud's lips, yet they grated on his ear when pronounced by others. The young fellows were all warmly disposed toward him, however, and one of them approached him, took him by the hand, and said:

"You have done wisely, sir, in choosing to bide with us. We lead a merry life, and the interval passes quickly enough."

"What do you mean by the interval?" asked Arnold, astonished not so much at the expression as because the youth pronounced so firmly his conviction that he had chosen to make the village his home. "Do you mean that I shall come back here?"

"But do you wish to go away?" asked the young peasant sharply.

"To-morrow, yes, or the day after to-morrow; but I'll come back."

"To-morrow; oh!" laughed the youth; "then that's all right. Well, we'll talk more about it to-morrow. But now come and I'll show you how we enjoy ourselves, for if you really want to go away to-morrow, you might not after all get a chance of seeing the fun."

The others looked at each other and laughed knowingly, while the young peasant took Arnold by the hand and conducted him all over the house, which was now packed full of a crowd of merry-makers. First they passed through rooms wherein sat card-players with great heaps of money lying before them. Next they came to a bowling-alley, inlaid with shining flagstones.

In a third room ring-throwing and other games were being played, and the young girls tripped in and out laughing and singing and teasing the young men, till all of a sudden a flourish from the band, which up to now had been playing away merrily, gave the signal for the dance to commence, and Gertrud stood at Arnold's side and took his arm.

"Come, we must not be the last," said the lovely girl, "for as the mayor's daughter it is for me to open the ball."

"But what strange tune is that?" said Arnold; "I can't catch the time at all."

"Oh, you soon will," smiled Gertrud; "you'll catch the time in the first five minutes, and I'll tell you how."

With jubilant shouts the whole company, with the exception of the card-players, crowded into the ballroom, and Arnold was soon oblivious of everything else in the first blissful feeling of holding the wondrously beautiful maiden in his arms.

Again and again he danced with Gertrud, and no one else seemed to want to claim his partner from him, although the other girls often threw teasing remarks at him as they flew by.

One thing only struck him and alarmed him. Close by the inn stood the ancient church, and the shrill discordant clang of the cracked bell could be distinctly heard in the ballroom. At the first stroke of the bell it was as if a magician's wand had smitten the dancers.

The music stopped playing in the middle of a beat, the merry surging crowd stood still and motionless, as if spellbound, and everyone silently counted the slow strokes one by one.

But as soon as the last sound died away the animation and merriment broke out afresh. This was repeated at eight, at nine, at ten o'clock, and when Arnold would fain inquire what was the reason for such a strange proceeding, Gertrud laid her finger on her lips and at the same time looked so solemn and sad that he would not have troubled her further for all the world.

At ten o'clock there was a pause in the dancing, and the musicians, who must have had lungs of iron, headed the procession of young people down to the supper-room.

There were merry doings there. The wine simply ran in streams, and Arnold, who could not be behindhand among all the others, reckoned up in his own mind what sort of hole this expensive evening would make in his modest pocket.

But Gertrud was sitting by his side, drinking with him out of the same glass, and how could he give way to any such misgivings? Even though her Heinrich should come to-morrow?

The first stroke of eleven o'clock rang out. Again the loud merriment of the revellers was silenced, again the same breathless listening to the long-drawn strokes.

A peculiar horror overcame him; he could not tell why; and the thought of his mother at home smote through his heart. He slowly raised his glass and drained it in a toast to his absent dear ones.

At the eleventh stroke the company sprang up from the table; the dancing was to begin again and they all scuttled back to the ballroom.

"Who was it you drank your last toast to?" asked Gertrud, as she laid her arm again in his.

Arnold hesitated before replying. Maybe Gertrud would only laugh at him if he told her. But no; she herself had prayed so fervently on that very afternoon by her own mother's grave—and so he said in a low voice: "My mother."

Gertrud answered never a word, but walked in silence by his side up the stairs. Her laughter had ceased also, and before they took their places for the dance again she asked him:

"Do you love your mother so much?"

"More than life itself."

"And does she love you?"

"Does not a mother love her child?"

"And what if you never went back home to her?"

"Poor mother!" said Arnold, "her heart would break."

"The dance is just starting again," cried Gertrud quickly; "come along, we mustn't miss a moment more."

So wilder than ever the dance began. The young men, fired by the strong wine, shouted and hurrahed, and shrieked, and such a din arose as threatened to drown the music.

Arnold did not now feel so happy in all this uproar, and Gertrud too had become serious and silent. But with all the others the merriment seemed only to increase, and during a pause the mayor came up to them, gave the young man a hearty slap on the shoulder and said, laughing:

"That's right, Mr. Painter, shake a merry leg to-night; we shall have plenty of time to have a good long rest. Nay, then, Gertie, why pull such a solemn face? Does that fit in with the dance this day? Merry's the word —there, they're off again!

"Now I must look up my old woman and trip the last dance with her. Take your places; the bandsmen are fairly bursting their cheeks again." And with a huzzah he plunged through the crowd of revellers.

Arnold was embracing Gertrud once more for a fresh dance when the latter suddenly broke away from him, gripped his arm and whispered softly: "Come!"

Arnold had no time to ask her whither, for she slipped from his grasp and sped away toward the door.

"Whither away, Gertie?" some of her playmates called out to them.

"Coming back in a moment," came the sound of her curt answer, and a few seconds later she was standing with Arnold outside before the house in the sharp night air.

"Where do you propose to go, Gertrud?"

"Come!"

Again she caught his arm and led him through the village, past her father's house, into which she dashed and presently emerged with a small bundle.

"What is the meaning of this?" asked Arnold in alarm.

"Come!" was the only word she said in answer, and past the houses she strode with him until they left the outermost wall of the village behind them. So far they had followed the broad, firm, hard-trodden highway; now Gertrud turned off the road to the left and mounted a little low hill from the top of which could be seen the brilliantly lighted windows and doors of the inn.

Here she came to a halt, held out her hand to Arnold and said tenderly:

"My greetings to your mother; farewell!"

"Gertrud," cried Arnold, astonished, aghast, "do you wish to send me away from you thus? Has any word of mine offended you?"

"No, Arnold," said the girl, calling him by his Christian name for the first time. "Just . . . just because I love you, you must go away."

"But I cannot let you go away from me back to the village like this, all alone and in the dark," pleaded Arnold. "Girl, you don't know how much I love you, how utterly and entirely you have won my heart in these few hours. You know not . . ."

"Say no more," she interrupted him quickly, "we will not say good-bye. When the clock has struck twelve—it can hardly want ten minutes yet—return to the inn door; there I shall be expecting you."

"And until then . . . !"

"Stay just where you are. Promise me not to take one step to right or left till the clock has struck the last stroke of twelve."

"I promise, Gertrud; but then . . ."

"Then come," she said, holding out her hand in farewell, and would have left him.

"Gertrud!" cried Arnold, in a pleading, anguished voice.

Gertrud stood a moment as if in hesitation, then suddenly she turned toward him, threw her arms around his neck, and Arnold felt the icy lips of the lovely maiden pressed on his. It was but for a moment; in the next instant she had torn herself away and was flying toward the village. And Arnold in amaze at her strange behaviour, yet mindful of his promise, remained standing just where she had left him.

Now for the first time he saw how the weather had changed in these few hours. The wind was howling through the trees, the sky was overcast with heavy racing clouds, and one or two large drops of rain proclaimed the approach of a storm.

Through the darkness of the night the lights glowed bright from the inn, and when the wind came roaring across he could hear in broken waves of sound the riotous blare of the instruments—but not for long. Only for a few moments had he been standing in his place when the clock in the old church tower began to strike. In that same instant the music ceased or was drowned in the howling storm, which raged so violently over the hill-slope that Arnold was obliged to stoop down to the ground in order not to lose his balance.

Before him on the ground he felt the bundle which Gertrud had fetched out of the house—his own knapsack and sketch-book—and affrighted he stood upright again. The clock had finished striking, the hurricane roared past over his head, but nowhere in the village was there any longer a light to be seen. The dogs which but a short while ago had been barking and howling were silent, and a thick damp mist was rising up from the hollow.

"The time is up," muttered Arnold to himself, hoisting his knapsack on his back, "and I must see Gertrud once again; I cannot part from her like this. The dance is over; the dancers will now be going home, and if the mayor will not put me up for the night I can stay at the inn. Besides, in the darkness I shouldn't find my way through the forest."

He cautiously went down the gentle slope which he and Gertrud had ascended together, in order to strike the broad white road which would bring him to the village, but in vain did he grope about for it among the bushes below.

The ground was soft and swampy, and in his thin boots he sank in up to the ankles; there was everywhere a tangle of alder-bushes growing just where he had imagined the road to be. He could not possibly have crossed it in the dark; he could not have failed to feel it the moment he stepped on it; and besides, he knew that the village wall ran right across it—this at any rate he could not miss.

But it was in vain that with anguished haste he sought for it; the ground became more soft, more swampy the farther he advanced, the undergrowth became thicker and everywhere beset with thorns, which tore his clothes and scratched his hands till they bled.

Had he wandered off to the right or to the left and beyond the village? He feared lest he should lose his bearings still more completely, and came to a halt on a fairly dry spot, determined to wait there until the old clock should strike one.

But it did not strike, not a dog barked, no sound of human voice reached him, and with great difficulty, wet to the skin, and shivering with cold, he toiled back again to the higher ground of the hill-slope where Gertrud had left him.

From this spot he tried, indeed, a few more times to penetrate the thicket and find the village, but in vain. Tired to death, and a prey to a peculiar horror, he at last avoided the low, dark, weird hollow and sought the shelter of a tree, there to spend the night.

And how slowly for him did the hours pass by! For shivering as he was with cold, he was not able to steal from that long night even one moment's sleep. And he was for ever straining his ears into the darkness, as again and again he thought he heard the rasping sound of the bell, only to find again and again that he had been mistaken.

At last the first glow of light began to dawn out of the far east. The clouds had dispersed, the sky was once more clear and bright with stars, and the awakening birds twittered softly in the gloomy trees.

Brighter and lighter grew the golden horizon; already he could clearly discern the tree-tops round about him; but it was in vain that his eye sought the view of the old brown church-tower and the weather-worn roofs. Nothing but a wilderness of alder-bushes dotted here and there with a few stunted willows, stretched out before him. No road was to be seen leading to the right or to the left, no sign of human habitation in the vicinity.

The day broke clearer and clearer. The earliest sunbeams fell upon the broad green expanse that spread out before his gaze; and Arnold, who was at a loss to solve the riddle, wandered some considerable distance back into the valley. He *must*, he thought, have lost his way in the dark, without knowing it, while he was seeking for the place, and had got too far away. He was now firmly determined to find it again.

At length he came to the stone near which he had drawn Gertrud's picture. This spot he would have recognised again out of thousands, for the old lilac-tree with its stiff branches indicated it only too clearly.

He now knew exactly from what direction he had come and where Germelshausen must lie; so he paced rapidly back along the valley, keeping closely to the same track which he and Gertrud had followed yesterday. Over there also he recognised the bend in the slope over which had hung the murky fog, and only the alder-bushes still separated him from the nearest houses.

Now he had reached it; he pressed on and—found himself once more in the very same swampy morass in which he had waded about the night before.

Completely at a loss and not trusting his own senses, he was for forcing a way through at this point, but the filthy swamp-ooze at length compelled him to make for dry ground again, and there he wandered helplessly backward and forward.

The village had disappeared, and that was the end of it.

Several hours had perhaps been consumed in this fruitless search, and his weary limbs at last refused to serve him any longer. He could go no further; before anything else he must rest. What had been the use of his vain quest? At the first village he came across he could easily find a guide to conduct him to Germelshausen, and then he could not miss the road again.

Dead tired he flung himself down under a tree—and how utterly ruined was his best suit! This, however, did not trouble him now; he produced his sketch-book and out of it he took Gertrud's portrait. With bitter pain his eyes fastened on the dear, sweet features of the maiden, who, as he realised to his great alarm, had already taken too firm a hold upon his heart.

Then he heard behind him a rustling among the leaves—a dog began to bark, and quickly springing to his feet, he was aware of an old woodsman standing not far away from him and curiously observing the strange figure who was so decently dressed and yet presented such a wild appearance.

"Greeting!" exclaimed Arnold, heartily pleased to meet a human being, and quickly thrusting the picture back into the portfolio. "You could not have been more welcome if I had invited you here, Herr Forester, for I think I have lost my way."

"H'm," said the old man, "if you have been lying here in the bush all night, I should think so too, and hardly half an hour's walk over yonder to Dillstedt and a good inn. Heavens! what a sight you are, for all the world as if you had been dragged neck and crop out of thorns and mud!"

"Are you quite familiar with the forest here?" asked Arnold, who before all things wanted to know where he really was.

"I should think I was," laughed the woodsman as he struck a light and lighted his pipe again.

"What is the name of the nearest village?"

"Dillstedt—straight over there. When you get on to that little hill yonder, you can easily see it lying below you."

"And how far is it from here to Germelshausen?"

"To where?" cried the woodsman, removing his pipe in horror from his lips.

"To Germelshausen."

"God help me!" said the old man, casting a scared look about him; "the forest I know well enough, but how many fathoms deep down below the earth the 'cursed village' lies, God alone knows—nor is it any business of ours."

"The 'cursed village'?" cried Arnold in astonishment.

"Germelshausen—yes," said the woodsman. "Just there in the swamp, where now grow the old willows and alders, it is said to have stood hundreds and hundreds of years ago. Later on it sank away, no man knows why or whither; and the story goes that every hundred years on a certain day it is raised up again to the light of heaven, but I should not wish any Christian man to chance to be there then.

"But, man alive! camping out in the bush last night does not seem to have agreed with you. You look as white as a ghost. There now, just you have a sip out of this flask; it will do you good—now have a good pull!"

"Thank you."

"Tut, tut, that wasn't half enough—take a proper, first-class pull at it. That's right; that's the real stuff to take. And now make haste and get across to the inn, and into a warm bed."

"In Dillstedt?"

"Why, of course: there's none nearer."

"What about Germelshausen?"

"Be good enough not to mention the place again, especially here on the spot where we are standing. Let the dead rest, and above all those who do not even enjoy rest, but keep on rising again unexpectedly amongst us."

"But only yesterday the village was still standing here," cried Arnold, who had almost lost his trust in his own senses. "I was inside it—eating and drinking and dancing there!"

The woodsman calmly looked the young man up and down, and then said with a smile:

"But it went by some other name, didn't it? Probably you have come straight over from Dillstedt. There was a dance there yesterday evening, and it's not everybody can stand the strong beer that the landlord brews at present."

By way of answer Arnold opened his portfolio and drew out the drawing that he had made from the churchyard.

"Do you know that village?"

"No," said the woodsman shaking his head; "there's not such a flat tower as that in the whole countryside."

"That is Germelshausen," cried Arnold; "and do the peasant girls in this neighbourhood dress as this girl does here?"

"Um—no! and what's that queer-looking funeral procession you have put in the picture?"

Arnold returned no answer. He thrust the sheets back again into the portfolio, and a strange feeling of pain thrilled through him.

"You can't miss the road to Dillstedt," said the woodsman good-naturedly, for a dark suspicion now occurred to him that the stranger might perhaps not be quite right in the head. "But if you would like, I will accompany you till we come to where we can see the place; that won't take me much out of my way."

Arnold declined with many thanks. "I'll find my way over there all right. And so it is only once in every hundred years that they say the village comes up again?"

"So people say," answered the woodsman, "but who can say if it is true?"

Arnold had taken up his knapsack again.

"God be wi' you!" he said, holding out his hand to the woodsman.

"Many thanks," answered he; "where are you going now?"

"To Dillstedt."

"That's right—when you get over the slope you'll come to the broad highroad again."

Arnold turned away, and slowly proceeded on his way. Only when he had reached the top of the slope which commanded a view over the whole of the valley, did he pause once again and look back.

"Farewell, Gertrud!" he murmured softly, and as he walked over the hill, the big crystal tears were streaming from his eyes.

I AM BORN

from the novel *David Copperfield*

CHARLES DICKENS

WHETHER I shall turn out to be the hero of my own life, or whether that station will be held by anybody else, these pages must show. To begin my life with the beginning of my life, I record that I was born (as I have been informed and believe) on a Friday, at twelve o'clock at night. It was remarked that the clock began to strike, and I began to cry, simultaneously.

In consideration of the day and hour of my birth, it was declared by the nurse, and by some sage women in the neighbourhood who had taken a lively interest in me several months before there was any possibility of our becoming personally acquainted, first, that I was destined to be unlucky in life; and secondly, that I was privileged to see ghosts and spirits: both these gifts inevitably attaching, as they believed, to all unlucky infants of either gender born towards the small hours on a Friday night.

I need say nothing here on the first head, because nothing can show better than my history whether that prediction was verified or falsified by the result. On the second branch of the question, I will only remark, that unless I ran through that part of my inheritance while I was still a baby, I have not come into it yet. But I do not at all complain of having been kept out of this property; and if anybody else should be in the present enjoyment of it, he is heartily welcome to keep it.

I was born with a caul, which was advertised for sale in the newspapers at the low price of fifteen guineas. Whether seagoing people were short of money about that time, or were short of faith and preferred cork jackets, I don't know; all I know is, that there was but one solitary bidding, and that was from an attorney connected with the bill-broking business, who offered two pounds in cash, and the balance in sherry, but declined to be guaranteed from drowning on any higher bargain. Consequently the advertisement was withdrawn at a dead loss—for as to sherry, my poor dear mother's own sherry was in the market then—and ten years afterwards the caul was put up in a raffle down in our part of the country, to fifty members at half a crown a head, the winner to spend five shillings. I was present myself, and I remember to have felt quite uncomfortable and confused at a part of myself being disposed of in that way. The caul was won, I recollect, by an old lady with a hand-basket, who, very reluctantly, produced from it the stipulated five shillings, all in halfpence, and twopence halfpenny short—as it took an immense time and a great waste of arithmetic to endeavour, without any effect, to prove to her. It is a fact which will be long remembered as remarkable down there, that she was never drowned, but died triumphantly in bed at ninety-two. I have understood that it was, to the last, her proudest boast that she never had been on the water in her life, except upon a bridge; and that over her tea (to which she was extremely partial) she, to the last, expressed her indignation at the impiety of mariners and other who had the presumption to go "meandering" about the world. It was in vain to represent to her that some conveniences, tea perhaps included, resulted from this objectionable practice. She always returned, with greater emphasis and with an instinctive knowledge of the strength of her objection, "Let us have no meandering."

Not to meander myself, at present, I will go back to my birth.

I was born at Blunderstone, in Suffolk, or "thereby," as they say in Scotland. I was a posthumous child. My father's eyes had closed upon the light of this world six months when mine opened on it. There is something strange to me, even now, in the reflection that he never saw me; and something stranger yet in the shadowy remembrance that I have of my first childish associations with his white gravestone in the churchyard, and of the indefinable compassion I used to feel for it lying out alone there in the dark night, when our little parlour was warm and bright with fire and candle, and the doors of our house were—almost cruelly, it seemed to me sometimes—bolted and locked against it.

An aunt of my father's, and consequently a great-aunt of mine, of whom I shall have more to relate by-and-by, was the principal magnate of our family. Miss Trotwood, or Miss Betsey, as my poor mother always called her when she sufficiently overcame her dread of this formidable personage to mention her at all (which was seldom), had been married to a husband younger than herself, who was very handsome, except in the sense of the homely adage, "handsome is, that handsome does;" for he was strongly suspected of having beaten Miss Betsey, and even of having once, on a disputed question of supplies, made some hasty but determined arrangements to throw her out of a two-pair-of-stairs window. These evidences of an incompatibility of temper induced Miss Betsey to pay him off, and effect a separation by mutual consent. He went to India with his capital, and there, according to a wild legend in our family, he was once seen riding on an elephant, in company with a Baboon; but I think it must have been a Baboo—or a Begum. Anyhow, from India tidings of his death reached home, within ten years. How they affected my aunt, nobody knew; for immediately upon the separation she took her maiden name again, bought a cottage in a hamlet on the seacoast a long way off, established herself there as a single woman with one servant, and was understood to live secluded, ever afterwards, in an inflexible retirement.

My father had once been a favourite of hers, I believe; but she was mortally affronted by his marriage, on the ground that my mother was "a wax doll." She had never seen my mother, but she knew her to be not yet twenty. My father and Miss Betsey never met again. He was double my mother's age when he married, and of but a delicate constitution. He died a year afterwards, and, as I have said, six months before I came into the world.

This was the state of matters on the afternoon of, what *I* may be excused for calling, that eventful and important Friday. I can make no claim, therefore, to have known, at that time, how matters stood; or to have any remembrance, founded on the evidence of my own senses, of what follows.

My mother was sitting by the fire, but poorly in health, and very low in spirits, looking at it through her tears, and desponding heavily about herself and the fatherless little stranger, who was already welcomed by some grosses of prophetic pins, in a drawer upstairs, to a world not at all excited on the subject of his arrival—my mother, I say, was sitting by the fire that bright, windy March afternoon, very timid and sad, and very doubtful of ever coming alive out of the trial that was before her, when, lifting her eyes as she dried them to the window opposite, she saw a strange lady coming up the garden.

My mother had a sure foreboding at the second glance that it was Miss Betsey. The setting sun was glowing on the strange lady, over the garden fence; and she came walking up to the door with a fell rigidity of figure and composure of countenance that could have belonged to nobody else.

When she reached the house, she gave another proof of her identity. My father had often hinted that she seldom conducted herself like any ordinary Christian; and now, instead of ringing the bell, she came and looked in at that identical window, pressing the end of her nose against the glass to that extent that my poor dear mother used to say it became perfectly flat and white in a moment.

She gave my mother such a turn that I have always been convinced I am indebted to Miss Betsey for having been born on a Friday.

My mother had left her chair in her agitation, and gone behind it in the corner. Miss Betsey, looking round the room, slowly and inquiringly, began on the other side, and carried her eyes on, like a Saracen's Head in a Dutch clock, until they reached my mother. Then she made a frown and a gesture to my mother, like one who was accustomed to be obeyed, to come and open the door. My mother went.

"Mrs. David Copperfield, I *think*," said Miss Betsey; the emphasis referring, perhaps, to my mother's mourning weeds, and her condition.

"Yes," said my mother faintly.

"Miss Trotwood," said the visitor. "You have heard of her, I dare say?"

My mother answered she had had that pleasure. And she had a disagreeable consciousness of not appearing to imply that it had been an overpowering pleasure.

"Now you see her," said Miss Betsey. My mother bent her head, and begged her to walk in.

They went into the parlour my mother had come from, the fire in the best room on the other side of the passage not being lighted—not having been lighted, indeed, since my father's funeral; and when they were both seated, and Miss Betsey said nothing, my mother, after vainly trying to restrain herself, began to cry.

"Oh, tut, tut, tut!" said Miss Betsey, in a hurry. "Don't do that! Come, come."

My mother couldn't help it notwithstanding, so she cried until she had had her cry out.

"Take off your cap, child," said Miss Betsey, "and let me see you."

My mother was too much afraid of her to refuse compliance with this odd request, if she had any disposition to do so. Therefore she did as she was told, and did it with such nervous hands that her hair (which was luxuriant and beautiful) fell all about her face.

"Why, bless my heart!" exclaimed Miss Betsey, "you are a very Baby!"

My mother was, no doubt, unusually youthful in appearance even for her years. She hung her head, as if it were her fault, poor thing, and said, sobbing, that indeed she was afraid she was but a childish widow, and would be but a childish mother if she lived. In a short pause which ensued she had a fancy that she felt Miss Betsey touch her hair, and that with no ungentle hand; but, looking at her, in her timid hope, she found that lady sitting with the skirt of her dress tucked up, her hands folded on one knee, and her feet upon the fender, frowning at the fire.

"In the name of Heaven," said Miss Betsey suddenly, "why Rookery?"

"Do you mean the house, ma'am?" asked my mother.

"Why Rookery?" said Miss Betsey. "Cookery would have been more to the purpose, if you had had any practical ideas of life, either of you."

"The name was Mr. Copperfield's choice," returned my mother. "When he bought the house, he liked to think that there were rooks about it."

The evening wind made such a disturbance just now among some tall old elm trees at the bottom of the garden, that neither my mother nor Miss Betsey could forbear glancing that way. As the elms bent to one another, like giants who were whispering secrets, and after a few seconds of such repose, fell into a violent flurry, tossing their wild arms about, as if their late confidences were really too wicked for their peace of mind, some weather-beaten ragged old rooks' nests, burdening their higher branches, swung like wrecks upon a stormy sea.

"Where are the birds?" asked Miss Betsey.

"The——?" My mother had been thinking of something else.

"The rooks—what has become of them?" asked Miss Betsey.

"There have not been any since we have lived here," said my mother. "We thought—Mr. Copperfield thought—it was quite a large rookery; but the nests were very old ones, and the birds have deserted them a long while."

"David Copperfield all over!" cried Miss Betsey. "David Copperfield from head to foot! Calls a house a rookery when there's not a rook near it, and takes the birds on trust, because he sees the nests!"

"Mr. Copperfield," returned my mother, "is dead, and if you dare to speak unkindly of him to me——"

My poor dear mother, I suppose, had some momentary intention of committing an assault and battery upon my aunt, who could easily have settled her with one hand, even if my mother had been in far better training for such an encounter than she was that evening. But it passed with the action of rising from her chair, and she sat down again very meekly, and fainted.

When she came to herself, or when Miss Betsey had restored her, whichever it was, she found the latter standing at the window. The twilight was by this time shading down into darkness, and dimly as they saw each other, they could not have done that without the aid of the fire.

"Well?" said Miss Betsey, coming back to her chair, as if she had only been taking a casual look at the prospect; "and when do you expect——"

"I am all in a tremble," faltered my mother. "I don't know what's the matter. I shall die, I am sure!"

"No, no, no," said Miss Betsey. "Have some tea."

"Oh, dear me, dear me, do you think it will do me any good?" cried my mother in a helpless manner.

"Of course it will," said Miss Betsey. "It's nothing but fancy. What do you call your girl?"

"I don't know that it will be a girl, yet, ma'am," said my mother innocently.

"Bless the Baby!" exclaimed Miss Betsey, unconsciously quoting the second sentiment of the pincushion in the drawer upstairs, but applying it to my mother instead of me, "I don't mean that. I mean your servant-girl."

"Peggotty," said my mother.

"Peggotty!" repeated Miss Betsey, with some indignation. "Do you mean to say, child, that any human being has gone into a Christian church and got herself named Peggotty?"

"It's her surname," said my mother faintly. "Mr. Copperfield called her by it, because her Christian name was the same as mine."

"Here, Peggotty!" cried Miss Betsey, opening the parlour door. "Tea. Your mistress is a little unwell. Don't dawdle."

Having issued this mandate with as much potentiality as if she had been a recognized authority in the house ever since it had been a house, and having looked out to confront the amazed Peggotty coming along the passage with a candle at the sound of a strange voice, Miss Betsey shut the door again, and sat down as before, with her feet on the fender, the skirt of her dress tucked up, and her hands folded on one knee.

"You were speaking about its being a girl," said Miss Betsey. "I have no doubt it will be a girl. I have a presentiment that it must be a girl. Now, child, from the moment of the birth of this girl—"

"Perhaps boy," my mother took the liberty of putting in.

"I tell you I have a presentiment that it must be a girl," returned Miss Betsey. "Don't contradict. From the moment of this girl's birth, child, I intend to be her friend. I intend to be her godmother, and I beg you'll call her Betsey Trotwood Copperfield. There must be no mistakes in life with *this* Betsey Trotwood. There must be no trifling with *her* affections, poor dear. She must be well brought up, and well guarded from reposing any foolish confidences where they are not deserved. I must make that *my* care."

There was a twitch of Miss Betsey's head, after each of these sentences, as if her own old wrongs were working within her, and she repressed any plainer reference to them by strong constraint. So my mother suspected, at least, as she observed her by the low glimmer of the fire—too much scared by Miss Betsey, too uneasy in herself, and too subdued and bewildered altogether, to observe anything very clearly, or to know what to say.

"And was David good to you, child?" asked Miss Betsey, when she had been silent for a little while, and these motions of her head had gradually ceased. "Were you comfortable together?"

"We were very happy," said my mother. "Mr. Copperfield was only too good to me."

"What! he spoilt you, I suppose?" returned Miss Betsey.

"For being quite alone and dependent on myself in this rough world again, yes, I fear he did indeed," sobbed my mother.

"Well, don't cry!" said Miss Betsey. "You were not equally matched, child—if any two people *can* be equally matched—and so I asked the question. You were an orphan, weren't you?"

"Yes."

"And a governess?"

"I was nursery-governess in a family where Mr. Copperfield came to visit. Mr. Copperfield was very kind to me, and took a great deal of notice of me, and paid me a good deal of attention, and at last proposed to me. And I accepted him. And so we were married," said my mother simply.

"Ha! Poor baby!" mused Miss Betsey, with her frown still bent upon the fire. "Do you know anything?"

"I beg your pardon, ma'am," faltered my mother.

"About keeping house, for instance," said Miss Betsey.

"Not much, I fear," returned my mother. "Not so much as I could wish. But Mr. Copperfield was teaching me—"

"Much he knew about it himself!" said Miss Betsey in a parenthesis.

"And I hope I should have improved, being very anxious to learn, and he very patient to teach, if the great misfortune of his death"—my mother broke down again here, and could get no further.

"Well, well!" said Miss Betsey.

"I kept my housekeeping-book regularly, and balanced it with Mr. Copperfield every night," cried my mother in another burst of distress, and breaking down again.

"Well, well!" said Miss Betsey. "Don't cry any more."

"And I am sure we never had a word of difference respecting it, except when Mr. Copperfield objected to my threes and fives being too much like each other, or to my putting curly tails to my sevens and nines," resumed my mother in another burst, and breaking down again.

"You'll make yourself ill," said Miss Betsey, "and you know that will not be good either for you or for my goddaughter. Come! you mustn't do it!"

This argument had some share in quieting my mother, though her increasing indisposition perhaps had a larger one. There was an interval of silence, only broken by Miss Betsey's occasionally ejaculating "Ha!" as she sat with her feet upon the fender.

"David had bought an annuity for himself with his money, I know," said she by-and-by. "What did he do for you?"

"Mr. Copperfield," said my mother, answering with some difficulty, "was so considerate and good as to secure the reversion of a part of it to me."

"How much?" asked Miss Betsey.

"A hundred and five pounds a year," said my mother.

"He might have done worse," said my aunt.

The word was appropriate to the moment. My mother was so much worse that Peggotty, coming in with the tea-board and candles, and seeing at a glance how ill she was—as Miss Betsey might have done sooner if

there had been light enough—conveyed her upstairs to her own room with all speed; and immediately dispatched Ham Peggotty, her nephew, who had been for some days past secreted in the house, unknown to my mother, as a special messenger in case of emergency, to fetch the nurse and doctor.

Those allied powers were considerably astonished, when they arrived within a few minutes of each other, to find an unknown lady of portentous appearance sitting before the fire, with her bonnet tied over her left arm, stopping her ears with jewellers' cotton. Peggotty knowing nothing about her, and my mother saying nothing about her, she was quite a mystery in the parlour; and the fact of her having a magazine of jewellers' cotton in her pocket, and sticking the article in her ears in that way, did not detract from the solemnity of her presence.

The doctor having been upstairs and come down again, and having satisfied himself, I suppose, that there was a probability of this unknown lady and himself having to sit there, face to face, for some hours, laid himself out to be polite and social. He was the meekest of his sex, the mildest of little men. He sidled in and out of a room, to take up the less space. He walked as softly as the Ghost in Hamlet, and more slowly. He carried his head on one side, partly in modest depreciation of himself, partly in modest propitiation of everybody else. It is nothing to say that he hadn't a word to throw at a dog. He couldn't have *thrown* a word at a mad dog. He might have offered him one gently, or half a one, or a fragment of one—for he spoke as slowly as he walked; but he wouldn't have been rude to him, and he couldn't have been quick with him, for any earthly consideration.

Mr. Chillip, looking mildly at my aunt, with his head on one side, and making her a little bow, said, in allusion to the jewellers' cotton, as he softly touched his left ear,—

"Some local irritation, ma'am?"

"What?" replied my aunt, pulling the cotton out of one ear like a cork.

Mr. Chillip was so alarmed by her abruptness—as he told my mother afterwards—that it was a mercy he didn't lose his presence of mind. But he repeated sweetly,—

"Some local irritation, ma'am?"

"Nonsense!" replied my aunt, and corked herself again, at one blow.

Mr. Chillip could do nothing after this but sit and look at her feebly, as she sat and looked at the fire, until he was called upstairs again. After some quarter of an hour's absence he returned.

"Well?" said my aunt, taking the cotton out of the ear nearest to him.

"Well, ma'am," returned Mr. Chillip, "we are—we are progressing slowly, ma'am."

"Ba—a—ah!" said my aunt, with a perfect shake on the contemptuous interjection, and corked herself as before.

Really—really—as Mr. Chillip told my mother, he was almost shocked; speaking in a professional point of view alone, he was almost shocked. But he sat and looked at her, notwithstanding, for nearly two hours, as she sat looking at the fire, until he was again called out. After another absence, he again returned.

"Well?" said my aunt, taking out the cotton on that side again.

"Well, ma'am," returned Mr. Chillip, "we are—we are progressing slowly, ma'am."

"Ya—a—ah!" said my aunt, with such a snarl at him, that Mr. Chillip absolutely could not bear it. It was really calculated to break his spirit, he said afterwards. He preferred to go and sit upon the stairs, in the dark and a strong draught, until he was again sent for.

Ham Peggotty, who went to the national school, and was a very dragon at his catechism, and who may therefore be regarded as a credible witness, reported next day that, happening to peep in at the parlour door an hour after this, he was instantly descried by Miss Betsey, then walking to and fro in a state of agitation, and pounced upon before he could make his escape. That there were now occasional sounds of feet and voices overhead, which he inferred the cotton did not exclude, from the circumstance of his evidently being clutched by the lady as a victim on whom to expend her superabundant agitation when the sounds were loudest. That, marching him constantly up and down by the collar (as if he had been taking too much laudanum), she, at those times, shook him, rumpled his hair, made light of his linen, stopped *his* ears as if she confounded them with her own, and otherwise touzled and maltreated him. This was in part confirmed by his aunt, who saw him at half-past twelve o'clock, soon after his release, and affirmed that he was then as red as I was.

The mild Mr. Chillip could not possibly bear malice at such a time, if at any time. He sidled into the parlour as soon as he was at liberty, and said to my aunt in his meekest manner,—

"Well, ma'am, I am happy to congratulate you."

"What upon?" said my aunt sharply.

Mr. Chillip was fluttered again by the extreme severity of my aunt's manner; so he made her a little bow, and gave her a little smile, to mollify her.

"Mercy on the man, what's he doing!" cried my aunt impatiently. "Can't he speak?"

"Be calm, my dear ma'am," said Mr. Chillip in his softest accents. "There is no longer any occasion for uneasiness, ma'am. Be calm."

It has since been considered almost a miracle that my aunt didn't shake him, and shake what he had to say out of him. She only shook her own head at him, but in a way that made him quail.

"Well, ma'am," resumed Mr. Chillip, as soon as he had courage, "I am happy to congratulate you. All is now over, ma'am, and well over."

During the five minutes or so that Mr. Chillip devoted to the delivery of this oration my aunt eyed him narrowly.

"How is she?" said my aunt, folding her arms, with her bonnet still tied on one of them.

"Well, ma'am, she will soon be quite comfortable, I hope," returned Mr. Chillip—"quite as comfortable as we can expect a young mother to be, under these melancholy domestic circumstances. There cannot be any objection to your seeing her presently, ma'am. It may do her good."

"And *she*—how is *she?*" said my aunt sharply.

Mr. Chillip laid his head a little more on one side, and looked at my aunt like an amiable bird.

"The baby," said my aunt—"how is she?"

"Ma'am," returned Mr. Chillip, "I apprehended you had known. It's a boy."

My aunt said never a word, but took her bonnet by the strings, in the manner of a sling, aimed a blow at Mr. Chillip's head with it, put it on bent, walked out, and never came back. She vanished like a discontented fairy—or like one of those supernatural beings whom it was popularly supposed I was entitled to see—and never came back any more.

No. I lay in my basket, and my mother lay in her bed, but Betsey Trotwood Copperfield was for ever in the land of dreams and shadows, the tremendous region whence I had so lately travelled; and the light upon the window of our room shone out upon the earthly bourne of all such travellers, and the mound above the ashes and the dust that once was he, without whom I had never been.

THE LEGEND OF SLEEPY HOLLOW

(*Found among the papers of the late Diedrich Knickerbocker*)

WASHINGTON IRVING

A pleasing land of drowsy head it was,
Of dreams that wave before the half-shut eye;
And of gay castles in the clouds that pass,
For ever flushing round a summer sky.
"CASTLE OF INDOLENCE."

IN THE bosom of one of those spacious coves which indent the eastern shore of the Hudson, at that broad expansion of the river denominated by the ancient Dutch navigators the Tappan Zee, and where they always prudently shortened sail, and implored the protection of St. Nicholas when they crossed, there lies a small market-town or rural port, which by some is called Greensburgh, but which is more generally and properly known by the name of Tarry Town. This name was given, we are told, in former days, by the good housewives of the adjacent country, from the inveterate propensity of their husbands to linger about the village tavern on market days. Be that as it may, I do not vouch for the fact, but merely advert to it, for the sake of being precise and authentic. Not far from this village, perhaps about two miles, there is a little valley, or rather lap of land, among high hills, which is one of the quietest places in the whole world. A small brook glides through it, with just murmur enough to lull one to repose; and the occasional whistle of a quail or tapping of a woodpecker, is almost the only sound that ever breaks in upon the uniform tranquillity.

I recollect that, when a stripling, my first exploit in squirrel-shooting was in a grove of tall walnut-trees that shades one side of the valley. I had wandered into it at noon time, when all nature is peculiarly quiet, and was startled by the roar of my own gun, as it broke the Sabbath stillness around, and was prolonged and reverberated by the angry echoes. If ever I should wish for a retreat, whither I might steal from the world and its distractions, and dream quietly away the remnant of a troubled life, I know of none more promising than this little valley.

From the listless repose of the place, and the peculiar character of its inhabitants, who are descendants from the original Dutch settlers, this sequestered glen has long been known by the name of Sleepy Hollow, and its rustic lads are called the Sleepy Hollow Boys throughout all the neighbouring country. A drowsy dreamy influence seems to hang over the land, and to pervade the very atmosphere. Some say that the place was bewitched by a high German doctor, during the early days of the settlement; others, that an old Indian chief, the prophet or wizard of his tribe, held his powwows there before the country was discovered by Master Hendrick Hudson. Certain it is, the place still continues under the sway of some witching power, that holds a spell over the minds of the good people, causing them to walk in a continual reverie. They are given to all kinds of marvellous beliefs; are subject to trances and visions; and frequently see strange sights, and hear music and voices in the air. The whole neighbourhood abounds with local tales, haunted spots, and twilight superstitions; stars shoot and meteors glare oftener across the valley than in any other part of the country, and the nightmare, with her whole nine fold, seems to make it the favourite scene of her gambols.

The dominant spirit, however, that haunts this enchanted region, and seems to be commander-in-chief of all the powers of the air, is the apparition of a figure on horseback without a head. It is said by some to be the ghost of a Hessian trooper, whose head had been carried away by a cannon-ball, in some nameless battle during the Revolutionary War; and who is ever and anon seen by the country folk, hurrying along in the gloom of night, as if on the wings of the wind. His haunts are not confined to the valley, but extend at times to the adjacent roads, and especially to the vicinity of a church at no great distance. Indeed, certain of the most authentic historians of those parts, who have been careful in collecting and collating the floating facts concerning this spectre, allege that the body of the trooper, having been buried in the churchyard, the ghost rides forth to the scene of battle in nightly quest of his head; and that the rushing speed with which he sometimes passes along the Hollow, like a midnight blast, is owing to his being belated, and in a hurry to get back to the churchyard before daybreak.

Such is the general purport of this legendary superstition, which has furnished materials for many a wild story in that region of shadows; and the spectre is known at all the country firesides by the name of the Headless Horseman of Sleepy Hollow.

It is remarkable that the visionary propensity I have mentioned is not confined to the native inhabitants of the valley, but is unconsciously imbibed by every one who resides there for a time. However wide awake they may have been before they entered that sleepy region, they are sure, in a little time, to inhale the witching influence of the air, and begin to grow imaginative—to dream dreams, and see apparitions.

I mention this peaceful spot with all possible laud; for it is in such little retired Dutch valleys, found here and there embosomed in the great state of New York, that population, manners, and customs, remain fixed; while the great torrent of migration and improvement, which is making such incessant changes in other parts of this restless country, sweeps by them unobserved. They are like those little nooks of still water which border a rapid stream; where we may see the straw and bubble riding quietly at anchor, or slowly revolving in their mimic harbour, undisturbed by the rush of the passing current. Though many years have elapsed since I trod the drowsy shades of Sleepy Hollow, yet I question whether I should not still find the same trees and the same families vegetating in its sheltered bosom.

In this by-place of nature there abode, in a remote period of American history, that is to say, some thirty years since, a worthy wight of the name of Ichabod Crane; who sojourned, or, as he expressed it, "tarried," in Sleepy Hollow, for the purpose of instructing the children of the vicinity. He was a native of Connecticut; a state which supplies the Union with pioneers for the mind as well as for the forest, and sends forth yearly its legions of frontier woodmen and country school-masters. The cognomen of Crane was not inapplicable to his person. He was tall, but exceedingly lank, with narrow shoulders, long arms and legs, hands that dangled a mile out of his sleeves, feet that might have served for shovels, and his whole frame most loosely hung together. His head was small, and flat at top, with huge ears, large green glassy eyes, and a long snipe nose, so that it looked like a weathercock, perched upon his spindle neck, to tell which way the wind blew. To see him striding along the profile of a hill on a windy day, with his clothes bagging and fluttering about him, one might have mistaken him for the genius of famine descending upon the earth, or some scarecrow eloped from a corn-field.

His school-house was a low building of one large room, rudely constructed of logs; the windows partly glazed, and partly patched with leaves of old copy-books. It was most ingeniously secured at vacant hours, by a withe twisted in the handle of the door, and stakes set against the window-shutters; so that, though a thief might get in with perfect ease, he would find some embarrassment in getting out; an idea most probably borrowed by the architect, Yost Van Houten, from the mystery of an eel-pot. The school-house stood in a rather lonely but pleasant situation, just at the foot of a woody hill, with a brook running close by, and a formidable birch-tree growing at one end of it. From hence the low murmur of his pupils' voices, conning over their lessons, might be heard in a drowsy summer's day, like the hum of a bee-hive; interrupted now and then by the authoritative voice of the master, in the tone of menace or command; or, peradventure, by the appalling sound of the birch, as he urged some tardy loiterer along the flowery path of knowledge. Truth to say, he was a conscientious man, and ever bore in mind the golden maxim, "Spare the rod and spoil the child." Ichabod Crane's scholars certainly were not spoiled.

I would not have it imagined, however, that he was one of those cruel potentates of the school, who joy in the smart of their subjects; on the contrary, he administered justice with discrimination rather than severity; taking the burthen off the backs of the weak, and laying it on those of the strong. Your mere puny stripling, that winced at the least flourish of the rod, was passed by with indulgence; but the claims of justice were satisfied by inflicting a double portion on some little tough, wrong-headed, broad-skirted Dutch urchin, who sulked and swelled and grew dogged and sullen beneath the birch. All this he called "doing his duty by their parents"; and he never inflicted a chastisement without following it by the assurance, so consolatory to the smarting urchin, that "he would remember it and thank him for it the longest day he had to live."

When school-hours were over, he was even the companion and playmate of the larger boys; and on holiday afternoons would convoy some of the smaller ones home, who happened to have pretty sisters, or good housewives for mothers, noted for the comforts of the cupboard. Indeed, it behoved him to keep on good terms with his pupils. The revenue arising from his school was small, and would have been scarcely sufficient to furnish him with daily bread, for he was a huge feeder, and though lank, had the dilating powers of an anaconda; but to help out his maintenance, he was, according to country custom in those parts, boarded and lodged at the houses of the farmers, whose children he instructed. With these he lived successively a week at a time; thus going the rounds of the neighbourhood, with all his worldly effects tied up in a cotton handkerchief.

That all this might not be too onerous on the purses of his rustic patrons, who are apt to consider the costs of schooling a grievous burden, and school-masters as mere drones, he had various ways of rendering himself both useful and agreeable. He assisted the farmers occasionally in the lighter labours of their farms; helped to make hay; mended the fences; took the horses to water; drove the cows from pasture; and cut wood for the winter fire. He laid aside, too, all the dominant dignity and absolute sway with which he lorded it in his little empire, the school, and became wonderfully gentle and ingratiating. He found favour in the eyes of the mothers by petting the children, particularly the youngest; and like the lion bold, which whilom so magnanimously the lamb did hold, he would sit with a child on one knee, and rock a cradle with his foot for whole hours together.

In addition to his other vocations, he was the singing-master of the neighbourhood, and picked up many bright shillings by instructing the young folks in psalmody. It was a matter of no little vanity to him, on Sundays, to take his station in front of the church gallery, with a band of chosen singers; where, in his own mind, he completely carried away the palm from the parson. Certain it is, his voice resounded far above all the rest of the congregation; and there are peculiar quavers still to be heard in that church, and which may even be heard half a mile off, quite to the opposite side of the mill-pond, on a still Sunday morning, which are said to be legitimately descended from the nose of Ichabod Crane. Thus, by divers little make-shifts, in that ingenious way which is commonly denominated "by hook and by crook," the worthy pedagogue got on tolerably enough, and was thought, by all who understand nothing of the labour of head-work, to have a wonderfully easy life of it.

The school-master is generally a man of some importance in the female circle of a rural neighbourhood; being considered a kind of idle gentlemanlike personage, of vastly superior taste and accomplishments to the rough country swains, and, indeed, inferior in learning only to the parson. His appearance, therefore, is apt to occasion some little stir at the tea-table of a farm-house and the addition of a supernumerary dish of cakes or sweetmeats, or peradventure the parade of a silver tea-pot. Our man of letters, therefore, was peculiarly happy in the smiles of all the country damsels. How he would figure among them in the churchyard between services on Sundays! gathering grapes for them from the wild vines that overran the surrounding trees; reciting for their amusement all the epitaphs on the tombstones; or sauntering with a whole bevy of them along the banks of the adjacent mill-pond; while the more bashful country bumpkins hung sheepishly back, envying his superior elegance and address.

From his half itinerant life, also, he was a kind of travelling gazette, carrying the whole budget of local gossip from house to house; so that his appearance was always greeted with satisfaction. He was, moreover, esteemed by the women as a man of great erudition, for he had read several books quite through, and was a perfect master of Cotton Mather's *History of New England Witchcraft*, in which, by the way, he most firmly and potently believed.

He was, in fact, an odd mixture of small shrewdness and simple credulity. His appetite for the marvellous, and his powers of digesting it, were equally extraordinary; and both had been increased by his residence in this spellbound region. No tale was too gross or monstrous for his capacious swallow. It was often his delight, after his school was dismissed in the afternoon, to stretch himself on the rich bed of clover, bordering the little brook that whimpered by his school-house, and there con over old Mather's direful tales, until the gathering dusk of the evening made the printed page a mere mist before his eyes. Then, as he wended his way by swamp and stream and awful woodland, to the farm-house where he happened to be quartered, every sound of nature, at that witching hour, fluttered his excited imagination: the moan of the whip-poor-will[1] from the hill-side; the boding cry of the tree-toad, that harbinger of storm; the dreary hooting of the screech-owl, or the sudden rustling in the thicket of birds frightened from their roost. The fireflies, too, which sparkled most vividly in the darkest places, now and then startled him, as one of uncommon brightness would stream across his path; and if by chance a huge blackhead of a beetle came winging his blundering flight against him, the poor varlet was ready to give up the ghost, with the idea that he was struck with a witch's token. His only resource on such occasions, either to drown thought or drive away evil spirits, was to sing psalm tunes;—and the good people of Sleepy Hollow, as they sat by their doors of an evening, were often filled with awe at hearing his nasal melody, "in linked sweetness long drawn out," floating from the distant hill, or along the dusky road.

Another of his sources of fearful pleasure was, to pass long winter evenings with the old Dutch wives, as they sat spinning by the fire, with a row of apples roasting and spluttering along the hearth, and listen to their marvellous tales of ghosts and goblins, and haunted fields, and haunted brooks, and haunted bridges, and haunted houses, and particularly of the headless horseman, or Galloping Hessian of the Hollow, as they sometimes called him. He would delight them equally by his anecdotes of witchcraft, and of the direful omens and portentous sights and sounds in the air, which prevailed in the earlier times of Connecticut; and would frighten them wofully with speculations upon comets and shooting stars; and with the alarming fact that the world did absolutely turn round, and that they were half the time topsy-turvy!

But if there was a pleasure in all this, while snugly cuddling in the chimney-corner of a chamber that was all of a ruddy glow from the crackling wood fire, and where, of course, no spectre dared to show its face, it was dearly purchased by the terrors of his subsequent walk homewards. What fearful shapes and shadows beset his path amidst the dim and ghastly glare of a snowy night!—With what wistful look did he eye every trembling ray of light streaming across the waste fields from some distant window!—How often was he appalled by some shrub covered with snow,

[1] The whip-poor-will is a bird which is only heard at night. It receives its name from its note, which is thought to resemble those words.

which, like a sheeted spectre, beset his very path!—How often did he shrink with curdling awe at the sound of his own steps on the frosty crust beneath his feet! and dread to look over his shoulder, lest he should behold some uncouth being tramping close behind him!—and how often was he thrown into complete dismay by some rushing blast, howling among the trees, in the idea that it was the Galloping Hessian on one of his nightly scourings!

All these, however, were mere terrors of the night, phantoms of the mind that walk in darkness; and though he had seen many spectres in his time, and been more than once beset by Satan in divers shapes, in his lonely perambulations, yet daylight put an end to all these evils; and he would have passed a pleasant life of it, in despite of the devil and all his works, if his path had not been crossed by a being that causes more perplexity to mortal man than ghosts, goblins, and the whole race of witches put together, and that was—a woman.

Among the musical disciples who assembled one evening in each week to receive his instructions in psalmody, was Katrina Van Tassel, the daughter and only child of a substantial Dutch farmer. She was a blooming lass of fresh eighteen; plump as a partridge; ripe and melting and rosy-cheeked as one of her father's peaches, and universally famed, not merely for her beauty, but her vast expectations. She was, withal, a little of a coquette, as might be perceived even in her dress, which was a mixture of ancient and modern fashions, as most suited to set off her charms. She wore the ornaments of pure yellow gold, which her great-great-grandmother had brought over from Saardam; the tempting stomacher of the olden time; and withal a provokingly short petticoat, to display the prettiest foot and ankle in the country round.

Ichabod Crane had a soft and foolish heart towards the sex, and it is not to be wondered at that so tempting a morsel soon found favour in his eyes, more especially after he had visited her in her paternal mansion. Old Baltus Van Tassel was a perfect picture of a thriving, contented, liberal-hearted farmer. He seldom, it is true, sent either his eyes or his thoughts beyond the boundaries of his own farm; but within those, everything was snug, happy, and well-conditioned. He was satisfied with his wealth, but not proud of it; and piqued himself upon the hearty abundance, rather than the style in which he lived. His stronghold was situated on the banks of the Hudson, in one of those green, sheltered, fertile nooks, in which the Dutch farmers are so fond of nestling. A great elm-tree spread its broad branches over it, at the foot of which bubbled up a spring of the softest and sweetest water, in a little well formed of a barrel, and then stole sparkling away through the grass to a neighbouring brook that bubbled along among alders and dwarf willows. Hard by the farmhouse was a vast barn that might have served for a church, every window and crevice of which seemed bursting forth with the treasures of the farm; the flail was busily resounding within it from morning to night; swallows and martins skimmed twittering about the eaves; and rows of pigeons, some with one eye turned up, as if watching the weather, some with their heads under their wings, or buried in their bosoms, and others swelling, and cooing, and bowing about their dames, were enjoying the sunshine on the roof. Sleek unwieldy porkers were grunting in the repose and abundance of their pens, whence sallied forth now and then troops of sucking pigs, as if to snuff the air. A stately squadron of snowy geese were riding in an adjoining pond, convoying whole fleets of ducks; regiments of turkeys were gobbling through the farm-yard, and guinea-fowls fretting about it, like ill-tempered housewives, with their peevish, discontented cry. Before the barn door strutted the gallant cock, that pattern of a husband, a warrior, and a fine gentleman, clapping his burnished wings, and crowing in the pride and gladness of his heart—sometimes tearing up the earth with his feet, and then generously calling his ever-hungry family of wives and children to enjoy the rich morsel which he had discovered.

The pedagogue's mouth watered as he looked upon his sumptuous promise of luxurious winter fare. In his devouring mind's eye he pictured to himself every roasting-pig running about with a pudding in his belly, and an apple in his mouth; the pigeons were snugly put to bed in a comfortable pie, and tucked in with a coverlet of crust; the geese were swimming in their own gravy; and the ducks pairing cosily in dishes, like snug married couples, with a decent competency of onion sauce. In the porkers he saw carved out the future sleek side of bacon and juicy relishing ham; not a turkey but he beheld daintily trussed-up, with its gizzard under its wing, and, peradventure, a necklace of savoury sausages; and even bright chanticleer himself lay sprawling on his back in a side dish, with uplifted claws, as if craving that quarter which his chivalrous spirit disdained to ask while living.

As the enraptured Ichabod fancied all this, and as he rolled his great green eyes over the fat meadow-lands, the rich fields of wheat, of rye, of buckwheat, and Indian corn, and the orchards burthened with ruddy fruit, which surrounded the warm tenement of Van Tassel, his heart yearned after the damsel who was to inherit these domains, and his imagination expanded with the idea, how they might be readily turned into cash, and the money invested in immense tracts of wild land, and shingle palaces in the wilderness. Nay, his busy fancy already realised his hopes, and presented to him the blooming Katrina, with a whole family of children, mounted on the top of a waggon loaded with household trumpery, with pots and kettles dangling beneath; and he beheld himself bestriding a pacing mare, with a colt at her heels, setting out for Kentucky, Tennessee, or the Lord knows where.

When he entered the house, the conquest of his heart was complete. It was one of those spacious farm-houses, with high-ridged, but lowly-sloping roofs, built in the style handed down from the first Dutch settlers; the low projecting eaves forming a piazza along the front, capable of being closed up in bad weather. Under this were hung flails, harness, various utensils of husbandry, and nets for fishing in the neighbouring river. Benches were built along the sides for summer use; and a great spinning-wheel at one end, and a churn at the other, showed the various uses to which this important porch might be devoted. From this piazza the wondering Ichabod entered the hall, which formed the centre of the mansion and the place of usual residence. Here rows of resplendent pewter, ranged on a long dresser, dazzled his eyes. In one corner stood a huge bag of wool ready to be spun; in another, a quantity of linsey-woolsey just from the loom; ears of Indian corn, and strings of dried apples and peaches, hung in gay festoons along the wall, mingled with the gaud of red peppers; and a door left ajar gave him a peep into the best parlour, where the claw-footed chairs and dark mahogany tables shone like mirrors; and irons, with their accompanying shovel and tongs, glistened from their covert of asparagus tops; mock oranges and conch-shells decorated the mantelpiece; strings of various coloured birds' eggs were suspended above it; a great ostrich egg was hung from the centre of the room, and a corner-cupboard, knowingly left open, displayed immense treasures of old silver and well-mended china.

From the moment Ichabod laid his eyes upon these regions of delight, the peace of his mind was at an end, and his only study was how to gain the affections of the peerless daughter of Van Tassel. In this enterprise, however, he had more real difficulties than generally fell to the lot of a knight-errant of yore, who seldom had anything but giants, enchanters, fiery dragons, and such like easily conquered adversaries, to contend with; and had to make his way merely through gates of iron and brass, and walls of adamant, to the castle keep, where the lady of his heart was confined; all which he achieved as easily as a man would carve his way to the centre of a Christmas pie, and then the lady gave him her hand as a matter of course. Ichabod, on the contrary, had to win his way to the heart of a country coquette, beset with a labyrinth of whims and caprices, which were for ever presenting new difficulties and impediments; and he had to encounter a host of fearful adversaries of real flesh and blood, the numerous rustic admirers who beset every portal to her heart, keeping a watchful and angry eye upon each other, but ready to fly out in the common cause against any new competitor.

Among these the most formidable was a burly, roaring, roistering blade, of the name of Abraham, or, according to the Dutch abbreviation, Brom Van Brunt, the hero of the country round, which rang with his feats of strength and hardihood. He was broad-shouldered and double-jointed, with short curly black hair, and a bluff but not unpleasant countenance, having a mingled air of fun and arrogance. From his Herculean frame and great powers of limb, he had received the nickname of Brom Bones, by which he was universally known. He was famed for great knowledge and skill in horsemanship, being as dexterous on horseback as a Tartar. He was foremost at all races and cock-fights, and, with the ascendency which bodily strength acquires in rustic life, was the umpire in all disputes, setting his hat on one side, and giving his decisions with an air and tone admitting of no gainsay or appeal. He was always ready for either a fight or frolic, but had more mischief than ill-will in his composition; and, with all his overbearing roughness, there was a strong dash of waggish good humour at bottom. He had three or four boon companions, who regarded him as their model, and at the head of whom he scoured the country, attending every scene of feud or merriment for miles round. In cold weather he was distinguished by a fur cap, surmounted with a flaunting fox's tail; and when the folks at a country gathering descried this well-known crest at a distance, whisking about among a squad of hard riders, they always stood by for a squall. Sometimes his crew would be heard dashing along past the farm-houses at midnight, with hoop and halloo, like a troop of Don Cossacks, and the old dames, startled out of their sleep, would listen for a moment, till the hurry-scurry had clattered by, and then exclaim, "Ay, there goes Brom Bones and his gang!" The neighbours looked upon him with a mixture of awe, admiration, and good-will; and when any madcap prank or rustic brawl occurred in the vicinity, always shook their heads and warranted Brom Bones was at the bottom of it.

This rantipole hero had for some time singled out the blooming Katrina for the object of his uncouth gallantries, and though his amorous toyings were something like the gentle caresses and endearments of a bear, yet it was whispered that she did not altogether discourage his hopes. Certain it is, his advances were signals for rival candidates to retire, who felt no inclination to cross a lion in his amours; insomuch that when his horse was seen tied to Van Tassel's paling on a Sunday night, a sure sign that his master was courting, or, as it is termed, "sparking," within, all other suitors passed by in despair, and carried the war into other quarters.

Such was the formidable rival with whom Ichabod Crane had to contend, and, considering all things, a stouter man that he would have shrank from the competition, and a wiser man would have despaired. He had, however, a happy mixture of pliability and perseverance in his nature; he was in form and spirit like a supple-jack,—yielding, but tough; though he bent, he never broke; and though he bowed beneath the slightest pressure, yet, the moment it was away—jerk! he was as erect, and carried his head as high as ever.

To have taken the field openly against his rival would have been madness; for he was not a man to be thwarted in his amours, any more than that stormy lover, Achilles. Ichabod, therefore, made his advances in a quiet and gently-insinuating manner. Under cover of his character of singing-master, he made frequent visits at the farm-house; not that he had anything to apprehend from the meddlesome interference of parents, which is so often a stumbling-block in the path of lovers. Balt Van Tassel was an easy, indulgent soul; he loved his daughter better even than his pipe, and, like a reasonable man and an excellent father, let her have her way in everything. His notable little wife, too, had enough to do to attend to her housekeeping, and manage her poultry; for, as she sagely observed, ducks and geese are foolish things, and must be looked after, but girls can take care of themselves. Thus, while the busy dame bustled about the house, or plied her spinning-wheel at one end of the piazza, honest Balt would sit smoking his evening pipe at the other, watching the achievements of a little wooden warrior, who, armed with a sword in each hand, was most valiantly fighting the wind on the pinnacle of the barn. In the meantime, Ichabod would carry on his suit with the daughter by the side of the spring under the great elm, or sauntering along in the twilight, that hour so favourable to the lover's eloquence.

I profess not to know how women's hearts are wooed and won. To me they have always been matters of riddle and admiration. Some seem to have but one vulnerable point, or door of access; while others have a thousand avenues, and may be captured in a thousand different ways. It is a great triumph of skill to gain the former, but a still greater proof of generalship to maintain possession of the latter, for a man must battle for his fortress at every door and window. He who wins a thousand common hearts is therefore entitled to some renown; but he who keeps undisputed sway over the heart of a coquette, is indeed a hero. Certain it is, this was not the case with the redoubtable Brom Bones; and from the moment Ichabod Crane made his advances, the interests of the former evidently declined; his horse was no longer seen tied at the palings on Sunday nights, and a deadly feud gradually arose between him and the preceptor of Sleepy Hollow.

Brom, who had a degree of rough chivalry in his nature, would fain have carried matters to open warfare, and have settled their pretensions to the lady, according to the mode of those most concise and simple reasoners, the knights-errant of yore—by single combat; but Ichabod was too conscious of the superior might of his adversary to enter the lists against him; he had overheard a boast of Bones, that he "would double the schoolmaster up, and lay him on a shelf of his own school-house"; and he was too wary to give him an opportunity. There was something extremely provoking in this obstinately pacific system; it left Brom no alternative but to draw upon the funds of rustic waggery in his disposition, and to play off boorish practical jokes upon his rival. Ichabod became the object of whimsical persecution to Bones and his gang of rough riders. They harried his hitherto peaceful domains; smoked out his singing-school, by stopping up the chimney; broke into the school-house at night, in spite of his formidable fastenings of withe and window stakes, and turned everything topsy-turvy; so that the poor school-master began to think all the witches in the country held their meetings there. But what was still more annoying, Brom took all opportunities of turning him into ridicule in presence of his mistress, and had a scoundrel dog whom he taught to whine in the most ludicrous manner, and introduced as a rival of Ichabod's to instruct her in psalmody.

In this way matters went on for some time, without producing any material effect on the relative situation of the contending powers. On a fine autumnal afternoon, Ichabod, in pensive mood, sat enthroned on the lofty stool whence he usually watched all the concerns of his little literary realm. In his hand he swayed a ferule, that sceptre of despotic power; the birch of justice reposed on three nails behind the throne, a constant terror to evil-doers; while on the desk before him might be seen sundry contraband articles and prohibited weapons, detected upon the persons of idle urchins; such as half-munched apples, pop-guns, whirligigs, fly-cages, and whole legions of rampant little paper game-cocks. Apparently there had been some appalling act of justice recently inflicted, for his scholars were all busily intent upon their books, or slyly whispering behind them with one eye kept upon the master; and a kind of buzzing stillness reigned throughout the school-room. It was suddenly interrupted by the appearance of a negro, in tow-cloth jacket and trousers, a round-crowned fragment of a hat, like the cap of Mercury, and mounted on the back of a ragged, wild, half-broken colt, which he managed with a rope by way of halter. He came clattering up to the school door with an invitation to Ichabod to attend a merry-making, or "quilting frolic," to be held that evening at Mynheer Van Tassel's; and having delivered his message with that air of importance and effort at fine language which a negro is apt to display on petty embassies of the kind, he dashed over the brook, and was seen scampering away up the hollow, full of the importance and hurry of his mission.

All was now bustle and hubbub in the late quiet school-room. The scholars were hurried through their lessons without stopping at trifles; those who were nimble skipped over half with impunity, and those who were tardy had a smart application now and then in the rear, to quicken their speed, or help them over a tall word. Books were flung aside without being put away on the shelves; inkstands were overturned, benches thrown down, and the whole school was turned loose an hour before the usual time, bursting forth like a legion of young imps, yelping and racketing about the green in joy at their early emancipation.

The gallant Ichabod now spent at least an extra half-hour at his toilet, brushing and furbishing up his best, and indeed only suit of rusty black, and arranging his locks by a bit of broken looking-glass that hung up in the school-house. That he might make his appearance before his mistress in the true style of a cavalier, he borrowed a horse from the farmer with whom he was domiciliated, a choleric old Dutchman, of the name of Hans Van Ripper, and, thus gallantly mounted, issued forth like a knight-errant in quest of adventures. But it is meet I should, in the true spirit of romantic story, give some account of the looks and equipments of my hero and his steed. The animal he bestrode was a broken-down plough-horse that had outlived almost everything but his viciousness. He was gaunt and shagged, with a ewe neck and a head like a hammer; his rusty mane and tail were tangled and knotted with burrs; one eye had lost its pupil, and was glaring and spectral; but the other had the gleam of a genuine devil in it. Still he must have had fire and mettle in his day, if we may judge from the name he bore of Gunpowder. He had, in fact, been a favourite steed of his master's, the choleric Van Ripper, who was a furious rider, and had infused, very probably, some of his own spirit into the animal; for, old and broken-down as he looked, there was more of the lurking devil in him than in any young filly in the country.

Ichabod was a suitable figure for such a steed. He rode with short stirrups, which brought his knees nearly up to the pommel of the saddle; his sharp elbows stuck out like grasshoppers; he carried his whip perpendicularly in his hand, like a sceptre, and, as his horse jogged on, the motion of his arms was not unlike the flapping of a pair of wings. A small wool hat rested on the top of his nose, for so his scanty strip of forehead might be called; and the skirts of his black coat fluttered out almost to the horse's tail. Such was the appearance of Ichabod and his steed, as they shambled out of the gate of Hans Van Ripper, and it was altogether such an apparition as is seldom to be met with in broad daylight.

It was, as I have said, a fine autumnal day, the sky was clear and serene, and nature wore that rich and golden livery which we always associate with the idea of abundance. The forests had put on their sober brown and yellow, while some trees of the tenderer kind had been nipped by the frosts into brilliant dyes of orange, purple, and scarlet. Streaming files of wild ducks began to make their appearance high in the air; the bark of the squirrel might be heard from the groves of beech and hickory nuts, and the pensive whistle of the quail at intervals from the neighbouring stubble field.

The small birds were taking their farewell banquets. In the fulness of their revelry, they fluttered, chirping and frolicking, from bush to bush and tree to tree, capricious from the very profusion and variety around them. There was the honest cock-robin, the favourite game of stripling sportsmen, with its loud, querulous note; and the twittering blackbirds flying in sable clouds; and the golden-winged woodpecker, with his crimson crest, his broad black gorget, and splendid plumage; and the cedar-bird, with its red-tipt wings and yellow-tipt tail, and its little monteiro cap of feathers; and the blue jay, that noisy coxcomb, in his gay light-blue coat and white under-clothes; screaming and chattering, nodding and bobbing and bowing, and pretending to be on good terms with every songster of the grove.

As Ichabod jogged slowly on his way, his eye, ever open to every symptom of culinary abundance, ranged with delight over the treasures of jolly autumn. On all sides he beheld vast stores of apples; some hanging in oppressive opulence on the trees; some gathered into baskets and barrels for the market; others heaped up in rich piles for the cider-press. Further on he beheld great fields of Indian corn, with its golden ears peeping from their leafy coverts, and holding out the promise of cakes and hasty-pudding; and the yellow pumpkins lying beneath them, turning up their fair round bellies to the sun, and giving ample prospects of the most luxurious of pies; and anon he passed the fragrant buckwheat fields breathing the odour of the bee-hive, and as he beheld them, soft anticipations stole over his mind of dainty slapjacks, well buttered, and garnished with honey or treacle, by the delicate little dimpled hand of Katrina Van Tassel.

Thus feeding his mind with many sweet thoughts and "sugared suppositions," he journeyed along the sides of a range of hills which look out upon some of the goodliest scenes of the mighty Hudson. The sun gradually wheeled his broad disc down into the west. The wide bosom of the Tappan Zee lay motionless and glassy, except that here and there a gentle undulation waved and prolonged the blue shadow of the distant mountain. A few amber clouds floated in the sky, without a breath of air to move them. The horizon was of a fine golden tint, changing gradually into a pure apple-green, and from that into the deep blue of the mid-heaven. A slanting ray lingered on the woody crests of the precipices that overhung some parts of the river, giving greater depth to the dark-gray and purple of their rocky sides. A sloop was loitering in the distance, dropping slowly down with the tide, her sail hanging uselessly against the mast; and as the reflection of the sky gleamed along the still water, it seemed as if the vessel was suspended in the air.

It was toward evening that Ichabod arrived at the castle of the Heer Van Tassel, which he found thronged with the pride and flower of the adjacent country. Old farmers, a spare leathern-faced race, in homespun coats and breeches, blue stockings, huge shoes, and magnificent pewter buckles. Their brisk withered little dames, in close crimped caps, long-waisted short gowns, homespun petticoats, with scissors and pincushions, and gay calico pockets hanging on the outside. Buxom lasses, almost as antiquated as their mothers, excepting where a straw hat, a fine riband, or perhaps a white frock, gave symptoms of city innovation. The sons, in short square-skirted coats with rows of stupendous brass buttons, and their hair generally queued in the fashion of the times, especially if they could procure an eel-skin for the purpose, it being esteemed throughout the country as a potent nourisher and strengthener of the hair.

Brom Bones, however, was the hero of the scene, having come to the gathering on his favourite steed Daredevil, a creature like himself, full of mettle and mischief, and which no one but himself could manage. He was, in fact, noted for preferring vicious animals, given to all kinds of tricks, which kept the rider in constant risk of his neck, for he held a tractable, well-broken horse as unworthy of a lad of spirit.

Fain would I pause to dwell upon the world of charms that burst upon the enraptured gaze of my hero, as he entered the state parlour of Van Tassel's mansion. Not those of the bevy of buxom lasses, with their luxurious display of red and white; but the ample charms of a genuine Dutch country tea-table in the sumptuous time of autumn. Such heaped-up platters of cakes of various and almost indescribable kinds, known only to experienced Dutch housewives! There was the doughty dough-nut, the tenderer oly koek, and the crisp and crumbling cruller; sweet-cakes and short-cakes, ginger-cakes and honey-cakes, and the whole family of cakes. And then there were apple-pies and peach-pies and pumpkin-pies; besides slices of ham and smoked beef; and, moreover, delectable dishes of preserved plums, and peaches, and pears, and quinces; not to mention broiled shad and roasted chickens; together with bowls of milk and cream, all mingled higgledy-piggledy, pretty much as I have enumerated them, with the motherly tea-pot sending up its clouds of vapour from the midst—Heaven bless the mark! I want breath and time to discuss this banquet as it deserves, and am too eager to get on with my story. Happily, Ichabod Crane was not in so great a hurry as his historian, but did ample justice to every dainty.

He was a kind and thankful creature, whose heart dilated in proportion as his skin was filled with good cheer; and whose spirits rose with eating as some men's do with drink. He could not help, too, rolling his large eyes round him as he ate, and chuckling with the possibility that he might one day be lord of all this scene of almost unimaginable luxury and splendour. Then he thought, how soon he'd turn his back upon the old schoolhouse, snap his fingers in the face of Hans Van Ripper and every other niggardly patron, and kick any itinerant pedagogue out of doors that should dare to call him comrade!

Old Baltus Van Tassel moved about among his guests with a face dilated with content and good humour, round and jolly as the harvest moon. His hospitable attentions were brief, but expressive, being confined to a shake of the hand, a slap on the shoulder, a loud laugh, and a pressing invitation to "fall to, and help themselves."

And now the sound of the music from the common room or hall summoned to the dance. The musician was an old gray-headed negro, who had been the itinerant orchestra of the neighbourhood for more than half a century. His instrument was as old and battered as himself. The greater part of the time he scraped on two or three strings, accompanying every movement of the bow with a motion of the head; bowing almost to the ground, and stamping with his foot whenever a fresh couple were to start.

Ichabod prided himself upon his dancing as much as upon his vocal powers. Not a limb, not a fire about him was idle; and to have seen his loosely-hung frame in full motion, and clattering about the room, you would have thought Saint Vitus himself, that blessed patron of the dance, was figuring before you in person. He was the admiration of all the negroes; who, having gathered, of all ages and sizes, from the farm and the neighbourhood, stood forming a pyramid of shining black faces, at every door and window, gazing with delight at the scene, rolling their white eyeballs, and showing grinning rows of ivory from ear to ear. How could the flogger of urchins be otherwise than animated and joyous? The lady of his heart was his partner in the dance, and smiling graciously in reply to all his amorous oglings; while Brom Bones, sorely smitten with love and jealousy, sat brooding by himself in one corner.

When the dance was at an end, Ichabod was attracted to a knot of the sager folks, who, with old Van Tassel, sat smoking at one end of the piazza, gossiping over former times, and drawing out long stories about the war.

This neighbourhood, at the time of which I am speaking, was one of those highly-favoured places which abound with chronicle and great men. The British and American line had run near it during the war; it had, therefore, been the scene of marauding, and infested with refugees, cowboys, and all kinds of border chivalry. Just sufficient time had elapsed to enable each storyteller to dress up his tale with a little becoming fiction, and, in the indistinctness of his recollection, to make himself the hero of every exploit.

There was the story of Doffue Martling, a large blue-bearded Dutchman, who had nearly taken a British frigate with an old iron nine-pounder from a mud breastwork, only that his gun burst at the sixth discharge. And there was an old gentleman who shall be nameless, being too rich a mynheer to be lightly mentioned, who, in the battle of Whiteplains, being an excellent master of defence, parried a musket-ball with a small sword, insomuch that he absolutely felt it whiz round the blade, and glance off at the hilt; in proof of which he was ready at any time to show the sword, with the hilt a little bent. There were several more that had been equally great in the field, not one of whom but was persuaded that he had a considerable hand in bringing the war to a happy termination.

But all these were nothing to the tales of ghosts and apparitions that succeeded. The neighbourhood is rich in legendary treasures of the kind. Local tales and superstitions thrive best in these sheltered long-settled retreats; but are trampled under-foot by the shifting throng that forms the population of most of our country places. Besides, there is no encouragement for ghosts in most of our villages, for they have scarcely had time to finish their first nap, and turn themselves in their graves, before their surviving friends have travelled away from the neighbourhood; so that when they turn out at night to walk their rounds, they have no acquaintance left to call upon. This is perhaps the reason why we so seldom hear of ghosts except in our long-established Dutch communities.

The immediate cause, however, of the prevalence of supernatural stories in these parts, was doubtless owing to the vicinity of Sleepy Hollow. There was a contagion in the very air that blew from that haunted region; it breathed forth an atmosphere of dreams and fancies infecting all the land. Several of the Sleepy Hollow people were present at Van Tassel's, and, as usual, were doling out their wild and wonderful legends. Many dismal tales were told about funeral trains, and mourning cries and wailings heard and seen about the great tree where the unfortunate Major André was taken, and which stood in the neighbourhood. Some mention was made also of the woman in white, that haunted the dark glen at Raven Rock, and was often heard to shriek on winter nights before a storm, having perished there in the snow. The chief part of the stories, however, turned upon the favourite spectre of Sleepy Hollow, the headless horseman, who had been heard several times of late, patrolling the country; and, it was said, tether his horse nightly among the graves in the churchyard.

The sequestered situation of this church seems always to have made it a favourite haunt of troubled spirits. It stands on a knoll surrounded by locust-trees and lofty elms, from among which its decent whitewashed walls shine modestly forth, like Christian purity, beaming through the shades of retirement. A gentle slope descends from it to a silver sheet of water, bordered by high trees, between which peeps may be caught at the blue hills of the Hudson. To look upon its grass-grown yard, where the sunbeams seem to sleep so quietly, one would think that there at least the dead might rest in peace. On one side of the church extends a wide woody dell, along which raves a large brook among broken rocks and trunks of fallen trees. Over a deep black part of the stream, not far from the church, was formerly thrown a wooden bridge; the road that led to it, and the bridge itself, were thickly shaded by overhanging trees, which cast a gloom about it, even in the daytime; but occasioned a fearful darkness at night. Such was one of the favourite haunts of the headless horseman, and the place where he was most frequently encountered. The tale was told of old Brouwer, a most heretical disbeliever in ghosts, how he met the horseman returning from his foray into Sleepy Hollow, and was obliged to get up behind him; how they galloped over bush and brake, over hill and swamp, until they reached the bridge; when the horseman suddenly turned into a skeleton, threw old Brouwer into the brook, and sprang away over the tree-tops with a clap of thunder.

This story was immediately matched by a thrice marvellous adventure of Brom Bones, who made light of the Galloping Hessian as an arrant jockey. He affirmed that, on returning one night from the neighbouring village of Sing-Sing, he had been overtaken by this midnight trooper; that he had offered to race with him for a bowl of punch, and should have won it too, for Daredevil beat the goblin horse all hollow, but, just as they came to the church bridge, the Hessian bolted, and vanished in a flash of fire.

All these tales, told in that drowsy under-tone with which men talk in the dark, the countenances of the listeners only now and then receiving a casual gleam from the glare of a pipe, sank deep in the mind of Ichabod. He repaid them in kind, with large extracts from his invaluable author, Cotton Mather, and added many marvellous events that had taken place in his native state of Connecticut, and fearful sights which he had seen in his nightly walks about Sleepy Hollow.

The revel now gradually broke up. The old farmers gathered together their families in their waggons, and were heard for some time rattling along the hollow roads, and over the distant hills. Some of the damsels mounted on pillions behind their favourite swains, and their light-hearted laughter, mingling with the clatter of hoofs, echoed along the silent woodlands, sounding fainter and fainter until they gradually died away—and the late scene of noise and frolic was all silent and deserted. Ichabod only lingered behind, according to the custom of country lovers, to have a *tête-à-tête* with the heiress, fully convinced that he was now on the high road to success. What passed at this interview I will not pretend to say, for in fact I do not know. Something, however, I fear me, must have gone wrong, for he certainly sallied forth, after no very great interval, with an air quite desolate and chop-fallen. Oh these women! these women! Could that girl have been playing off any of her coquettish tricks?—Was her encouragement of the poor pedagogue all a mere sham to secure her conquest of his rival?—Heaven only knows, not I!—Let it suffice to say, Ichabod stole forth with the air of one who had been sacking a hen-roost, rather than a fair lady's heart. Without looking to the right or left to notice the scene of rural wealth on which he had so often gloated, he went straight to the stable, and with several hearty cuffs and kicks, roused his steed most uncourteously from the comfortable quarters in which he was soundly sleeping, dreaming of mountains of corn and oats, and whole valleys of timothy and clover.

It was the very witching time of night that Ichabod, heavy-hearted and crest-fallen, pursued his travels homewards, along the sides of the lofty hills which rise above Tarry Town, and which he had traversed so cheerily in the afternoon. The hour was as dismal as himself. Far below him the Tappan Zee spread its dusky and indistinct waste of waters, with here and there the tall mast of a sloop riding quietly at anchor under the land. In the dead hush of midnight he could even hear the barking of the watch-dog from the opposite shore of the Hudson; but it was so vague and faint as only to give an idea of his distance from this faithful companion of man. Now and then, too, the long-drawn crowing of a cock, accidentally awakened, would sound far, far off, from some farm-house away among the hills—but it was like a dreaming sound in his ear. No signs of life occurred near him, but occasionally the melancholy chirp of a cricket, or perhaps the guttural twang of a bull-frog, from a neighbouring marsh, as if sleeping uncomfortably, and turning suddenly in his bed.

All the stories of ghosts and goblins that he had heard in the afternoon now came crowding upon his recollection. The night grew darker and darker; the stars seemed to sink deeper in the sky, and driving clouds occasionally hid them from his sight. He had never felt so lonely and dismal. He was, moreover, approaching the very place where many of the scenes of the ghost-stories had been laid. In the centre of the road stood an enormous tulip-tree, which towered like a giant above all the other trees of the neighbourhood, and formed a kind of landmark. Its limbs were gnarled and fantastic, large enough to form trunks for ordinary trees, twisting down almost to the earth, and rising again into the air. It was connected with the tragical story of the unfortunate André, who had been taken prisoner hard by; and was universally known by the name of Major André's tree. The common people regarded it with a mixture of respect and superstition, partly out of sympathy for the fate of its ill-starred namesake and partly from the tales of strange sights and doleful lamentations told concerning it.

As Ichabod approached this fearful tree, he began to whistle; he thought his whistle was answered; it was but a blast sweeping sharply through the dry branches. As he approached a little nearer, he thought he saw something white hanging in the midst of the tree—he paused and ceased whistling; but on looking more narrowly, perceived that it was a place where the tree had been scathed by lightning, and the white wood laid bare. Suddenly he heard a groan—his teeth chattered, and his knees smote against the saddle; it was but the rubbing of one huge bough upon another, as they were swayed about by the breeze. He passed the tree in safety, but new perils lay before him.

About two hundred yards from the tree a small brook crossed the road, and ran into a marshy and thickly-wooded glen, known by the name of Wiley's Swamp. A few rough logs, laid side by side, served for a bridge over this stream. On that side of the road where the brook entered the wood, a group of oaks and chestnuts, matted thick with wild grape-vines, threw a cavernous gloom over it. To pass this bridge was the severest trial. It was at this identical spot that the unfortunate André was captured, and under the covert of those chestnuts and vines were the sturdy yeomen concealed who surprised him. This has ever since been considered a haunted stream, and fearful are the feelings of the schoolboy who has to pass it alone after dark.

As he approached the stream, his heart began to thump; he summoned up, however, all his resolution, gave his horse half a score of kicks in the ribs, and attempted to dash briskly across the bridge; but instead of starting forward, the perverse old animal made a lateral movement, and ran broadside against the fence. Ichabod, whose fears increased with the delay, jerked the reins on the other side, and kicked lustily with the contrary foot: it was all in vain; his steed started, it is true, but it was only to plunge to the opposite side of the road into a thicket of brambles and alder-bushes. The school-master now bestowed both whip and heel upon the starveling ribs of old Gunpowder, who dashed forward, snuffling and snorting, but came to a stand just by the bridge, with a suddenness that had nearly sent his rider sprawling over his head. Just at this moment a plashy tramp by the side of the bridge caught the sensitive ear of Ichabod. In the dark shadow of the grove, on the margin of the brook, he beheld something huge, misshapen, black and towering. It stirred not, but seemed gathered up in the gloom, like some gigantic monster ready to spring upon the traveller.

The hair of the affrighted pedagogue rose upon his head with terror. What was to be done? To turn and fly was now too late; and besides, what chance was there of escaping ghost or goblin, if such it was, which could ride upon the wings of the wind? Summoning up, therefore, a show of courage, he demanded in stammering accents—"Who are you?" He received no reply. He repeated his demand in a still more agitated voice. Still there was no answer. Once more he cudgelled the sides of the inflexible Gunpowder, and, shutting his eyes, broke forth with involuntary fervour into a psalm tune. Just then the shadowy object of alarm put itself in motion, and with a scramble and a bound, stood at once in the middle of the road. Though the night was dark and dismal, yet the form of the unknown might now in some degree be ascertained. He appeared to be a horseman of large dimensions, and mounted on a black horse of powerful frame. He made no offer of molestation or sociability, but kept aloof on one side of the road, jogging along on the blind side of old Gunpowder, who had now got over his fright and waywardness.

Ichabod, who had no relish for this strange midnight companion, and bethought himself of the adventure of Brom Bones with the Galloping Hessian, now quickened his steed, in hopes of leaving him behind. The stranger, however, quickened his horse to an equal pace. Ichabod pulled up, and fell into a walk, thinking to lag behind—the other did the same. His heart began to sink within him; he endeavoured to resume his psalm tune, but his parched tongue clove to the roof of his mouth, and he could not utter a stave. There was something in the moody and dogged silence of this pertinacious companion that was mysterious and appalling. It was soon fearfully accounted for. On mounting a rising ground, which brought the figure of his fellow-traveller in relief against the sky, gigantic in height, and muffled in a cloak, Ichabod was horror-struck on perceiving that he was headless!—but his horror was still more increased on observing that the head, which should have rested on his shoulders, was carried before him on the pommel of the saddle: his terror rose to desperation; he rained a shower of kicks and blows upon Gunpowder, hoping, by a sudden movement, to give his companion the slip—but the spectre started full jump with him. Away then they dashed, through thick and thin; stones flying and sparks flashing at every bound. Ichabod's flimsy garments fluttered in the air, as he stretched his long lank body away over his horse's head, in the eagerness of his flight.

They had now reached the road which turns off to Sleepy Hollow; but Gunpowder, who seemed possessed with a demon, instead of keeping up it, made an opposite turn, and plunged headlong down the hill to the left. This road leads through a sandy hollow, shaded by trees for about a quarter of a mile, where it crosses the bridge famous in goblin story, and just beyond swells the green knoll on which stands the whitewashed church.

As yet the panic of the steed had given his unskilful rider an apparent advantage in the chase; but just as he had got half way through the hollow, the girths of the saddle gave way, and he felt it slipping from under him. He seized it by the pommel, and endeavoured to hold it firm, but in vain; and had just time to save himself by clasping old Gunpowder round the neck, when the saddle fell to the earth, and he heard it trampled underfoot by his pursuer. For a moment the terror of Hans Van Ripper's wrath passed across his mind—for it was his Sunday saddle; but this was no time for petty fears; the goblin was hard on his haunches; and (unskilful rider

that he was!) he had much ado to maintain his seat; sometimes slipping on one side, sometimes on the other, and sometimes jolted on the high ridge of his horse's back-bone, with a violence that he verily feared would cleave him asunder.

An opening in the trees now cheered him with the hopes that the church bridge was at hand. The wavering reflection of a silver star in the bosom of the brook told him that he was not mistaken. He saw the walls of the church dimly glaring under the trees beyond. He recollected the place where Brom Bones' ghostly competitor had disappeared. "If I can but reach that bridge," thought Ichabod, "I am safe." Just then he heard the black steed panting and blowing close behind him; he even fancied that he felt his hot breath. Another convulsive kick in the ribs, and old Gunpowder sprang upon the bridge; he thundered over the resounding planks; he gained the opposite side; and now Ichabod cast a look behind to see if his pursuer should vanish, according to rule, in a flash of fire and brimstone. Just then he saw the goblin rising in his stirrups, and in the very act of hurling his head at him. Ichabod endeavoured to dodge the horrible missile, but too late. It encountered his cranium with a tremendous crash —he was tumbled headlong into the dust, and Gunpowder, the black steed, and the goblin rider passed by like a whirlwind.

The next morning the old horse was found without his saddle, and with the bridle under his feet, soberly cropping the grass at his master's gate. Ichabod did not make his appearance at breakfast—dinner-hour came, but no Ichabod. The boys assembled at the school-house, and strolled idly about the banks of the brook; but no school-master. Hans Van Ripper now began to feel some uneasiness about the fate of poor Ichabod and his saddle. An inquiry was set on foot, and after diligent investigation they came upon his traces. In one part of the road leading to the church was found the saddle trampled in the dirt; the tracks of horses' hoofs deeply dented in the road, and evidently at furious speed, were traced to the bridge, beyond which, on the bank of a broad part of the brook, where the water ran deep and black, was found the hat of the unfortunate Ichabod, and close beside it a shattered pumpkin.

The brook was searched, but the body of the school-master was not to be discovered. Hans Van Ripper, as executor of his estate, examined the bundle, which contained all his worldly effects. They consisted of two shirts and a half; two stocks for the neck; a pair or two of worsted stockings; an old pair of corduroy small-clothes; a rusty razor; a book of psalm tunes, full of dog's ears; and a broken pitch-pipe. As to the books and furniture of the school-house, they belonged to the community, excepting

Cotton Mather's *History of Witchcraft*, a New England Almanac, and a book of dreams and fortune-telling; in which last was a sheet of foolscap much scribbled and blotted in several fruitless attempts to make a copy of verses in honour of the heiress of Van Tassel. These magic books and the poetic scrawl were forthwith consigned to the flames by Hans Van Ripper; who from that time forward determined to send his children no more to school, observing, that he never knew any good come of this same reading and writing. Whatever money the school-master possessed, and he had received his quarter's pay but a day or two before, he must have had about his person at the time of his disappearance.

The mysterious event caused much speculation at the church on the following Sunday. Knots of gazers and gossips were collected in the church-yard, at the bridge, and at the spot where the hat and pumpkin had been found. The stories of Brouwer, of Bones, and a whole budget of others, were called to mind; and when they had diligently considered them all, and compared them with the symptoms of the present case, they shook their heads, and came to the conclusion that Ichabod had been carried off by the Galloping Hessian. As he was a bachelor, and in nobody's debt, nobody troubled his head any more about him: the school was removed to a different quarter of the Hollow, and another pedagogue reigned in his stead.

It is true, an old farmer, who had been down to New York on a visit several years after, and from whom this account of the ghostly adventure was received, brought home the intelligence that Ichabod Crane was still alive; that he had left the neighbourhood, partly through fear of the goblin and Hans Van Ripper, and partly in mortification at having been suddenly dismissed by the heiress; that he had changed his quarters to a distant part of the country; had kept school and studied law at the same time; had been admitted to the bar, turned politician, electioneered, written for the newspapers, and finally had been made a justice of the Ten-pound Court. Brom Bones, too, who shortly after his rival's disappearance conducted the blooming Katrina in triumph to the altar, was observed to look exceedingly knowing whenever the story of Ichabod was related, and always burst into a hearty laugh at the mention of the pumpkin; which led some to suspect that he knew more about the matter than he chose to tell.

The old country wives, however, who are the best judges of these matters, maintain to this day that Ichabod was spirited away by supernatural means; and it is a favourite story often told about the neighbourhood round the winter evening fire. The bridge became more than ever an object of superstitious awe, and that may be the reason why the road has been altered of late years, so as to approach the church by the border of the mill-pond. The school-house being deserted, soon fell to decay, and was reported to be haunted by the ghost of the unfortunate pedagogue; and the plough-boy, loitering homeward of a still summer evening, has often fancied his voice at a distance, chanting a melancholy psalm tune among the tranquil solitudes of Sleepy Hollow.

(Found in the handwriting of Mr. Knickerbocker)

POSTSCRIPT

The preceding tale is given, almost in the precise words in which I heard it related at a Corporation meeting of the ancient city of Manhattoes, at which were present many of its sagest and most illustrious burghers. The narrator was a pleasant, shabby, gentlemanly old fellow, in pepper-and-salt clothes, with a sadly humorous face; and one whom I strongly suspected of being poor,—he made such efforts to be entertaining. When his story was concluded, there was much laughter and approbation, particularly from two or three deputy aldermen, who had been asleep the greater part of the time. There was, however, one tall, dry-looking old gentleman, with beetling eyebrows, who maintained a grave and rather a severe face throughout: now and then folding his arms, inclining his head, and looking down upon the floor, as if turning a doubt over in his mind. He was one of your wary men, who never laugh, but upon good grounds—when they have reason and the law on their side. When the mirth of the rest of the company had subsided, and silence was restored, he leaned one arm on the elbow of his chair, and sticking the other a-kimbo, demanded, with a slight but exceedingly sage motion of the head, and contraction of the brow, what was the moral of the story, and what it went to prove?

The story-teller, who was just putting a glass of wine to his lips, as a refreshment after his toils, paused for a moment, looked at his inquirer with an air of infinite deference, and, lowering the glass slowly to the table, observed that the story was intended most logically to prove:—

"That there is no situation in life but has its advantages and pleasures —provided we will but take a joke as we find it:

"That, therefore, he that runs races with goblin troopers is likely to have rough riding of it.

"Ergo, for a country school-master to be refused the hand of a Dutch heiress is a certain step to high preferment in the state."

The cautious old gentleman knit his brows tenfold closer after this explanation, being sorely puzzled by the ratiocination of the syllogism: while, methought, the one in pepper-and-salt eyed him with something of a triumphant leer. At length he observed that all this was very well;

but still he thought the story a little on the extravagant—there were one or two points on which he had his doubts.

"Faith, sir," replied the story-teller, "as to that matter, I don't believe one half of it myself."

D. K.

THE AGE OF MIRACLES

MELVILLE DAVISSON POST

THE girl was standing apart from the crowd in the great avenue of poplars that led up to the house. She seemed embarrassed and uncertain what to do, a thing of April emerging into summer.

Abner and Randolph marked her as they entered along the gravel road. They had left their horses at the gate, but she had brought hers inside, as though after some habit unconsciously upon her.

But half-way to the house she had remembered and got down. And she stood now against the horse's shoulder. It was a black hunter, big and old, but age marred no beauty of his lines. He was like a horse of ebony, enchanted out of the earth by some Arabian magic, but not yet by that magic awakened into life.

The girl wore a long, dark riding-skirt, after the fashion of the time, and a coat of hunter's pink. Her dark hair was in a great wrist-thick plait. Her eyes, too, were big and dark, and her body firm and lithe from the out-of-doors.

"Ah!" cried Randolph, making his characteristic gesture, "Prospero has been piping in this grove. Here is a daughter of the immortal morning! We grow old, Abner, and it is youth that the gods love."

My uncle, his hands behind him, his eyes on the gravel road, looked up at the bewitching picture.

"Poor child," he said; "the gods that love her must be gods of the valleys and not gods of the hills."

"Ruth amid the alien corn! Is it a better figure, Abner? Well, she has a finer inheritance than these lands; she has youth!"

"She ought to have both," replied my uncle. "It was sheer robbery to take her inheritance."

"It was a proceeding at law," replied the Justice. "It was the law that did the thing, and we cannot hold the law in disrespect."

"But the man who uses the law to accomplish a wrong, we can so hold," said Abner. "He is an outlaw, as the highwayman and the pirate are."

He extended his arm toward the great house sitting at the end of the avenue.

"In spite of the sanction of the law, I hold this dead man for a robber. And I would have wrested these lands from him, if I could. But your law, Randolph, stood before him."

"Well," replied the Justice, "he takes no gain from it; he lies yonder waiting for the grave."

"But his brother takes," said Abner, "and this child loses."

The Justice, elegant in the costume of the time, turned his ebony stick in his fingers.

"One should forgive the dead," he commented in a facetious note; "it is a mandate of the Scripture."

"I am not concerned about the dead," replied Abner. "The dead are in God's hands. It is the living who concern me."

"Then," cried the Justice, "you should forgive the brother who takes."

"And I shall forgive him," replied Abner, "when he returns what he has taken."

"Returns what he has taken!" Randolph laughed. "Why, Abner, the devil could not filch coin out of the clutches of old Benton Wolf."

"The devil," said my uncle, "is not an authority that I depend on."

"A miracle of Heaven, then," said the Justice. "But, alas, it is not the age of miracles."

"Perhaps," replied Abner, his voice descending into a deeper tone, "but I am not so certain."

They had come now to where the girl stood, her back against the black shoulder of the horse. The morning air moved the yellow leaves about her feet. She darted out to meet them, her face aglow.

"Damme!" cried Randolph. "William of Avon knew only witches of the second order! How do you do, Julia? I have hardly seen you since you were no taller than my stick, and told me that your name was 'Pete-George,' and that you were a circus-horse, and offered to do tricks for me."

"I remember," she said, "it was up there on the porch!"

"Egad!" cried Randolph, embarrassed. "And so it was!"

He kissed the tips of the girl's fingers and the shadow in her face fled. For the man's heart was good, and he had the manner of a gentleman. But it was Abner that she turned to in her dilemma.

"I forgot," she said, "and almost rode into the house. Do you think I could leave the horse here? He will stand if I drop the rein."

Then she went on to make her explanation. She wanted to see the old house that had been so long her home. This was the only opportunity, to-day, when all the countryside came to the dead man's burial. She thought she might come, too, although her motive was no tribute of respect.

She put her hand through Abner's arm and he looked down upon her, grave and troubled.

"My child," he said, "leave the horse where he stands and come with me, for my motive, also, is no tribute of respect; and you go with a better right than I do."

"I suppose," the girl hesitated, "that one ought to respect the dead, but this man—these men—I cannot."

"Nor can I," replied my uncle. "If I do not respect a man when he is living, I shall not pretend to when he is dead. One does not make a claim upon my honor by going out of life."

They went up the avenue among the yellow poplar leaves and the ragweed and fennel springing up along the unkept gravel.

It was a crisp and glorious morning. The frost lay on the rail fence. The spider-webs stretched here and there across the high grasses of the meadows in intricate and bewildering lace-work. The sun was clear and bright, but it carried no oppressive heat as it drew on in its course toward noon.

The countryside had gathered to see Adam Wolf buried. It was a company of tenants, the idle and worthless mostly, drawn by curiosity. For in life the two old men who had seized upon this property by virtue of a defective acknowledgment to a deed, permitted no invasion of their boundary.

Everywhere the lands were posted; no urchin fished and no schoolboy hunted. The green perch, fattened in the deep creek that threaded the rich bottom lands, no man disturbed. But the quail, the pheasant, the robin and the meadow-lark, old Adam pursued with his fowling-piece. He trampled about with it at all seasons. One would have believed that all the birds of heaven had done the creature some unending harm and in revenge he had declared a war. And so the accident by which he met his death was a jeopardy of the old man's habits, and to be looked for when one lived with a fowling-piece in one's hands and grew careless in its use.

The two men lived alone and thus all sorts of mystery sprang up around them, elaborated by the negro fancy and gaining in grim detail at every story-teller's hand. It had the charm and thrilling interest of an adventure, then, for the countryside to get this entry.

The brothers lived in striking contrast. Adam was violent, and his cries and curses, his hard and brutal manner were the terror of the negro who passed at night that way, or the urchin overtaken by darkness on his road home. But Benton got about his affairs in silence, with a certain humility of manner, and a mild concern for the opinion of his fellows. Still, somehow, the negro and the urchin held him in a greater terror. Perhaps because he had got his coffin made and kept it in his house, together with his clothes for burial. It seemed uncanny thus to prepare against his dissolution and to bargain for the outfit, with anxiety to have his shilling's worth.

And yet, with this gruesome furniture at hand, the old man, it would seem, was in no contemplation of his death. He spoke sometimes with a marked savor and an unctuous kneading of the hands of that time when he should own the land, for he was the younger and by rule should have the expectancy of life.

There was a crowd about the door and filling the hall inside, a crowd that elbowed and jostled, taken with a quivering interest, and there to feed its maw of curiosity with every item.

The girl wished to remain on the portico, where she could see the ancient garden and the orchard and all the paths and byways that had been her wonderland of youth, but Abner asked her to go in.

Randolph turned away, but my uncle and the girl remained some time by the coffin. The rim of the dead man's forehead and his jaw were riddled with bird-shot, but his eyes and an area of his face below them, where the thin nose came down and with its lines and furrows made up the main identity of features, were not disfigured. And these preserved the hard stamp of his violent nature, untouched by the accident that had dispossessed him of his life.

He lay in the burial clothes and the coffin that Benton Wolf had provided for himself, all except the gloves upon his hands. These the old man had forgot. And now when he came to prepare his brother for a public burial, for no other had touched the man, he must needs take what he could find about the house, a pair of old, knit gloves with every rent and moth-hole carefully darned, as though the man had sat down there with pains to give his brother the best appearance that he could.

This little touch affected the girl to tears, so strange is a woman's heart. "Poor thing!" she said. And for this triviality she would forget the injury that the dead man and his brother had done to her, the loss they had inflicted, and her long distress.

She took a closer hold upon Abner's arm, and dabbed her eyes with a tiny kerchief.

"I am sorry for him," she said, "for the living brother. It is so pathetic."

And she indicated the old, coarse gloves so crudely darned and patched together.

But my uncle looked down at her, strangely, and with a cold, inexorable face.

"My child," he said, "there is a curious virtue in this thing that moves you. Perhaps it will also move the man whose handiwork it is. Let us go up and see him."

Then he called the Justice.

"Randolph," he said, "come with us."

The Justice turned about. "Where do you go?" he asked.

"Why, sir," Abner answered, "this child is weeping at the sight of the dead man's gloves, and I thought, perhaps, that old Benton might weep at them too, and in the softened mood return what he has stolen."

The Justice looked upon Abner as upon one gone mad.

"And be sorry for his sins! And pluck out his eye and give it to you for a bauble! Why, Abner, where is your common sense. This thing would take a miracle of God."

My uncle was undisturbed.

"Well," he said, "come with me, Randolph, and help me to perform that miracle."

He went out into the hall, and up the wide old stairway, with the girl, in tears, upon his arm. And the Justice followed, like one who goes upon a patent and ridiculous fool's errand.

They came into an upper chamber, where a great bulk of a man sat in a padded chair looking down upon his avenue of trees. He looked with satisfaction. He turned his head about when the three came in and then his eyes widened in among the folds of fat.

"Abner and Mr. Randolph and Miss Julia Clayborne!" he gurgled. "You come to do honor to the dead!"

"No, Wolf," replied my uncle, "we come to do justice to the living."

The room was big, and empty but for chairs and an open secretary of some English make. The pictures on the wall had been turned about as though from a lack of interest in the tenant. But there hung in a frame above the secretary—with its sheets of foolscap, its iron ink-pot and quill pens—a map in detail, and the written deed for the estate that these men had taken in their lawsuit. It was not the skill of any painter that gave pleasure to this mountain of a man; not fields or groves imagined or copied for their charm, but the fields and groves that he possessed and mastered. And he would be reminded at his ease of them and of no other.

The old man's eyelids fluttered an instant as with some indecision, then he replied, "It was kind to have this thought of me. I have been long neglected. A little justice of recognition, even now, does much to soften the sorrow at my brother's death." Randolph caught at his jaw to keep in the laughter. And the huge old man, his head crouched into his billowy shadows, his little reptilian eye shining like a crum of glass, went on with his speech.

"I am the greater moved," he said, "because you have been aloof and distant with me. You, Abner, have not visited my house, nor you, Randolph, although you live at no great distance. It is not thus that one gentleman should treat another. And especially when I and my dead brother, Adam, were from distant parts and came among you without a friend to take us by the hand and bring us to your door."

He sighed and put the fingers of his hands together.

"Ah, Abner," he went on, "it was a cruel negligence, and one from which I and my brother Adam suffered. You, who have a hand and a word at every turning, can feel no longing for this human comfort. But to the stranger, alone, and without the land of his nativity, it is a bitter lack."

He indicated the chairs about him.

"I beg you to be seated, gentlemen and Miss Clayborne. And overlook that I do not rise. I am shaken at Adam's death."

Randolph remained planted on his feet, his face now under control. But Abner put the child into a chair and stood behind it, as though he were some close and masterful familiar.

"Wolf," he said, "I am glad that your heart is softened."

"My heart—softened!" cried the man. "Why, Abner, I have the tenderest heart of any of God's creatures. I cannot endure to kill a sparrow. My brother Adam was not like that. He would be for hunting the wild creatures to their death with firearms. But I took no pleasure in it."

"Well," said Randolph, "the creatures of the air got their revenge of him. It was a foolish accident to die by."

"Randolph," replied the man, "it was the very end and extreme of carelessness. To look into a fowling-piece, a finger on the hammer, a left hand holding the barrel halfway up, to see if it was empty. It was a foolish and simple habit of my brother, and one that I abhorred and begged him to forego, again and again, when I have seen him do it.

"But he had no fear of any firearms, as though by use and habit he had got their spirit tamed—as trainers, I am told, grow careless of wild beasts, and jugglers of the fangs and poison of their reptiles. He was growing old and would forget if they were loaded."

He spoke to Randolph, but he looked at Julia Clayborne and Abner.

The girl sat straight and composed, in silence. The body of my uncle was to her a great protecting presence. He stood with his broad shoulders above her, his hands on the back of the chair, his face lifted. And he was big and dominant, as painters are accustomed to draw Michael in Satan's wars.

The pose held the old man's eye, and he moved in his chair; then he went on, speaking to the girl.

"It was kind of you, Abner, and you, Randolph, to come in to see me in my distress, but it was fine and noble in Miss Julia Clayborne. Men will understand the justice of the law and by what right it gives and takes. But a child will hardly understand that. It would be in nature for Miss Clayborne in her youth, to hold the issue of this lawsuit against me and my brother Adam, to feel that we had wronged her; had by some unfairness taken what her father bequeathed to her at his death, and always regarded as his own. A child would not see how the title had never vested, as our judges do. How possession is one thing, and the title in fee simple another and distinct. And so I am touched by this consideration."

Abner spoke then.

"Wolf," he said, "I am glad to find you in this mood, for now Randolph can write his deed, with consideration of love and affection instead of the real one I came with."

The old man's beady eye glimmered and slipped about.

"I do not understand, Abner. What deed?"

"The one Randolph came to write," replied my uncle.

"But, Abner," interrupted the Justice, "I did not come to write a deed." And he looked at my uncle in amazement.

"Oh, yes," returned Abner, "that is precisely what you came to do." He indicated the open secretary with his hand.

"And the grantor, as it happens, has got everything ready for you. Here are foolscap and quill pens and ink. And here, exhibited for your convenience, is a map of the lands with all the metes and bounds. And here," he pointed to the wall, "in a frame, as though it were a work of art with charm, is the court's deed. Sit down, Randolph, and write." And such virtue is there in a dominant command, that the Justice sat down before the secretary and began to select a goose quill.

Then he realized the absurdity of the direction and turned about.

"What do you mean, Abner?" he cried.

"I mean precisely what I say," replied my uncle. "I want you to write a deed."

"But what sort of deed," cried the astonished Justice, "and by what grantor, and to whom, and for what lands?"

"You will draw a conveyance," replied Abner, "in form, with covenants of general warranty for the manor and lands set out in the deed before you and given in the plat. The grantor will be Benton Wolf, esquire, and the grantee Julia Clayborne, infant, and mark you, Randolph, the consideration will be love and affection, with a dollar added for the form."

The old man was amazed. His head, bedded into his huge shoulders, swung about; his pudgy features worked; his expression and his manner changed; his reptilian eyes hardened; he puffed with his breath in gusts.

"Not so fast, my fine gentleman!" he gurgled. "There will be no such deed."

"Go on, Randolph," said my uncle, "let us get this business over."

"But, Abner," returned the Justice, "it is fool work, the grantor will not sign."

"He will sign," said my uncle, "when you have finished, and seal and acknowledge—go on!"

"But, Abner, Abner!" the amazed Justice protested.

"Randolph," cried my uncle, "will you write, and leave this thing to me?"

And such authority was in the man to impose his will that the bewildered Justice spread out his sheet of foolscap, dipped his quill into the ink and began to draw the instrument, in form and of the parties, as my uncle said. And while he wrote, Abner turned back to the gross old man.

"Wolf," he said, "must I persuade you to sign the deed?"

"Abner," cried the man, "do you take me for a fool?"

He had got his unwieldy body up and defiant in the chair.

"I do not," replied my uncle, "and therefore I think that you will sign."

The obese old man spat violently on the floor, his face a horror of great folds.

"Sign!" he sputtered. "Fool, idiot, madman! Why should I sign away my lands?"

"There are many reasons," replied Abner calmly. "The property is not yours. You got it by a legal trick, the Judge who heard you was bound by the technicalities of language. But you are old, Wolf, and the next Judge will go behind the record. He will be hard to face. He has expressed Himself on these affairs. 'If the widow and the orphan cry to me, I will surely hear their cry.' Sinister words, Wolf, for one who comes with a case like yours into the court of Final Equity."

"Abner," cried the old man, "begone with your little sermons!"

My uncle's big fingers tightened on the back of the chair.

"Then, Wolf," he said, "if this thing does not move you, let me urge the esteem of men and this child's sorrow, and our high regard."

The old man's jaw chattered and he snapped his fingers.

"I would not give that for the things you name," he cried, and he set off a tiny measure on his index-finger with the thumb.

"Why, sir, my whim, idle and ridiculous, is a greater power to move me than this drivel."

Abner did not move, but his voice took on depth and volume.

"Wolf," he said, "a whim is sometimes a great lever to move a man. Now, I am taken with a whim myself. I have a fancy, Wolf, that your brother Adam ought to go out of the world barehanded as he came into it."

The old man twisted his great head, as though he would get Abner wholly within the sweep of his reptilian eye.

"What?" he gurgled. "What is that?"

"Why, this," replied my uncle. "I have a whim—'idle and ridiculous,' did you say, Wolf? Well, then, idle and ridiculous, if you like, that your brother ought not to be buried in his gloves."

Abner looked hard at the man and, although he did not move, the threat and menace of his presence seemed somehow to advance him. And the effect upon the huge old man was like some work of sorcery. The whole mountain of him began to quiver and the folds of his face seemed spread over with thin oil. He sat piled up in the chair and the oily sweat gathered and thickened on him. His jaw jerked and fell into a baggy gaping and the great expanse of him shook.

Finally, out of the pudgy, undulating mass, a voice issued, thin and shaken.

"Abner," it said, "has any other man this fancy?"

"No," replied my uncle, "but I hold it, Wolf, at your decision."

"And, Abner," his thin voice trembled, "you will let my brother be buried as he is?"

"If you sign!" said my uncle.

The man reeked and grew wet in the terror on him, and one thought that his billowy body would never be again at peace. "Randolph," he quavered, "bring me the deed."

Outside, the girl sobbed in Abner's arms. She asked for no explanation. She wished to believe her fortune a miracle of God, forever—to the end of all things. But Randolph turned on my uncle when she was gone.

"Abner! Abner!" he cried. "Why in the name of the Eternal was the old creature so shaken at the gloves?"

"Because he saw the hangman behind them," replied my uncle. "Did you notice how the rim of the dead man's face was riddled by the bird-shot and the center of it clean? How could that happen, Randolph?"

"It was a curious accident of gun-fire," replied the Justice.

"It was no accident at all," said Abner. "That area of the man's face is clean because it was protected. Because the dead man put up his hands to cover his face when he saw that his brother was about to shoot him.

"The backs of old Adam's hands, hidden by the gloves, will be riddled with bird-shot like the rim of his face."

THE LONG RIFLE

from the novel of that title

STEWART EDWARD WHITE

1

IN OUR country two hundred years ago shooting was the national pastime and people shot guns as to-day they shoot golf. Popping at an Indian or a turkey or deer was part of the daily occupation of those who lived on the frontier and in the backwoods; but these men had no monopoly on either the interest or the skill. They might be considered as the "pros"; but the cities and civilized seaboards were full of amateurs who would never have occasion either to save their scalps or to fend off starvation. And they were just as zealous afield, and just as partisan in the matter of equipment, and just as jealous of their marksmanship, and just as studious of technique, and just as persistent in practice as any modern divot digger you ever saw. No village so small that it had not its measured range: and no crossroads tavern could be successful unless it offered facilities for tests of marksmanship. For rarely did any gathering of men—convivial, business, political, even religious—disperse without a shooting match. And at stated intervals, and at stated places, were what might be called the big open tournaments where men collected for the express purpose. It was here that reputations were made, so that the time had its Bobby Jones or its Walter Hagen, with a host of skilled aspirants only a stroke or so behind. Or perhaps the parallel of state or district champions would be more exact. Travel in those days was so difficult that it was impossible to hold a National Open. But each locality had one or more local champions, the names of whom would be mentioned wherever in the Colonies men talked of marksmanship.

2

It was first blackbird time, when the snow water is not all drained away but when the grass beneath the surface of its little pools waves green.

A young man was journeying steadily afoot alongside the deep wheel ruts of a crude country road. It was a mere track, winding across the country's face; turning to avoid high stark stumps, twisting away from bog hole of too great steepness of hills; innocent of flanking fence or ditch. For a mile, sometimes, it ran in the dim coolness of the old forest, where red tanagers flamed in green shadows, and the wild pigeons beat like distant surf. For another mile, perhaps, it threaded a marsh where poles had been laid in corduroy and soft-winged bitterns slanted aloft in erratic flight and trim small peoples swayed on limber reed ends with chucklings. But soon it shook free from these petty wildnesses, again to emerge into cleared stumpy uplands and wide fields, fenced in rail, and Pennsylvania farmhouses of a civilization by now over a hundred years old.

The youth was a tall young man, standing well over six feet, lean with the slenderness of whalebone, his face golden brown with sun, his somewhat aquiline features cast in that brooding yet watchful repose characteristic of the backwoodsman and the Indian. His blue-gray eyes too would, to the competent observer, have identified him with the wilderness, for while their quality was mild, peaceable, and serene, they were never still, turning from right to left and from left to right again, ceaselessly, in a tireless vigilance so habitual that it had become subliminal. The traveler knew he had nothing to apprehend in this peaceful countryside; indeed his thoughts were busied far from the actual scene: nevertheless no smallest stir of leaf or feather escaped the mechanics of his attention, which held its report of those matters only just below the surface of his consciousness. His basic sense of security was further evidenced by the fact that he bore his rifle carelessly across his shoulder, and had attached to it for convenience of carriage against his back a leather portmanteau. He was dressed in plain garments of homespun and wore on his head the stiff felt hat of the period.

Though the sun was already past mid-afternoon, and he had been afoot since its rising, he swung unweariedly along in the bent-kneed woodsman's slouch, which is apparently so deliberate but in reality is so swift that one unaccustomed can with difficulty keep pace, and that for a short distance only. No inequality of footing or steepness of hill broke the rhythm; nor did he pause for breath or contemplation until the road broke over a crest to disclose below him a scattering settlement amongst noble trees in the bend of a great river. Here he stopped for a moment, surveying the scene gravely, then plunged down the slope to the village street.

The place was of the ordinary type and kind—many frame and a few brick homes, wide scattered at first, clustering more thickly as one approached the main street where stood the hotel, or tavern, two or three shops, and a court or meeting house. Old forest trees and planted elms new-spangled with spring overspread the roadways and later would almost completely submerge the roofs of the town. To one side swept the bend in the river; and here along a canal were stone and frame buildings with sputtering mill wheels. At the time of week and the time of day, one would expect to find such a place moving in only a feeble current of external life: perhaps a horse or so dozing along the hitching rails; possibly a loafer or two chair-tilted before the tavern; mayhap a housewife picking her way on wooden clogs through the soft earth toward the one sidewalk of the shops. Such a normal condition of somnolence was evidently anticipated by our young traveler; for he paused in grave and puzzled observation of what he saw.

The street was aswarm with men of all ages and conditions in life. They sauntered back and forth; they stood in talkative groups beneath the elms; they sat in rows on the edge of the high sidewalk. But principally they milled in and out of the wide hospitable doors of the tavern, whence arose such a clatter mingled of talk, argument, song, shouts, laughter, and the clinking undertone of mugs, glasses, and dishes slammed about, that the combined noise seemed to burst forth like a palpable flood gone aleak. No women were to be seen; but numerous small boys and dogs were engaged in attaching themselves to the situation with as convincing an air as they could manage.

Our traveler was obviously puzzled and interested. His long free stride slowed to a saunter: his eyes, heretofore roving in the mechanics of an automatic vigilance, now brimmed with the keenest of intelligent observation. He moved forward with every sense awake to catch the smallest indicatives that would synthesize into an estimate of the situation; precisely as it might be imagined he would move in the shadows of an unknown forest. Indeed he made a slight instinctive shrug as though to bring forward his rifle to his hand. It was with him an integral part of alertness, but he caught back the movement with a flicker of a smile at the corners of his grave lips. It would have been a simple matter to resolve his curiosity by an appeal for information to the nearest group; but such a procedure would have written him down as no woodsman, for it is a curious fact that those who live by observation rarely ask.

Moving thus, the young man gradually drew nearer the focus of the tavern. There men jostled in a throng, and the opened doors crowded and eddied as those who went in made their way with difficulty against those who came out. Everybody talked or shouted or sang, for obviously the spirit was of a holiday. Many were more or less drunk. Across the bobbing heads one might glimpse in the dim interior the red round faces of waiters moving here and there, clusters of tankards held aloft. A swirl of many emotions caught at the poise of stabilities, swept men loose from grave accustomedness into the exhilaration of temporary irresponsibilities. A certain recklessness was in the air, a loosening inconstancy into which men plunged gratefully from the aridities of their daily lives. Though his outward appearance differed in no marked degree from the many who composed the throng, the gravity of the stranger's unbroken aloofness seemed to set him apart, an individual from the herd, and this very separateness drew to him men's notice as though he had carried some blazon of distinction. Heads turned; men exchanged inquiries; some few of the drunker or more reckless even threw in his direction good-naturedly jeering remarks. He seemed quite unaware.

Before the tavern veranda he came to a halt, his attention at last seizing upon a definite point of considered examination. This was a long poster of

coarse paper that had been tacked into the bark of an elm by means of sharpened wooden pegs. Before it the young man took his stand, unslinging his rifle from his back, resting its butt against the ground before him, clasping his palms across its muzzle, settling himself easily and gracefully to the interpretation of the message. To the task he gave all his serene concentration, his lips moving slowly, spelling out the words. So evidently unaccustomed and difficult was this task, that the men nearest hushed their noise to watch him in amusement. One young chap in the broadcloth of the cities, a youth with a weak reckless face, who had evidently been drinking heavily, lurched alongside.

"Want me to read it for you?" he asked, his derision thinly veiled by a mock politeness.

The stranger turned his eyes from the printed words to contemplate his interlocutor. For perhaps ten seconds he held silence.

"No, suh," he then replied, and returned tranquilly to his perusal. That was all; but the other stuttered and fell back, and a low chuckle of appreciation rippled among the bystanders. The proclamation announced:

> "God save the King! Hunters and others look this way. A great shooting match will take place on April 30 at the place by the Big Bend. The first prize will be a great fat ox and the second a snap haunce gun with a long barl. To the maker of the winning piece, the Gunsmith's Medal. Distance 15 rods. A charge of four shillings for each man. Only one shot for each four shillings. There will be more prizes for lesser amounts. Lead, powder and flints to be sold. Plenty to eat and drink for all that come. Bear and wolf traps to be sold.
> Tell any man to come to the match. God save the King!"

Having finished his painful deciphering of this document the young man swung his rifle into the crook of his arm, and had turned to enter the tavern, when his steps were again arrested. A little girl of eight or nine years was threading her way sedately between the lounging groups on the sidewalk. She was a personable little girl, but her mere prettiness of feature would probably not have sufficed to rivet the stranger's attention. It was her get-up, which was in the latest and daintiest style of the cities. It is to be conceived that our young backwoodsman, if such he were, had never seen anything quite like it before. His eye lighted with an intense interest, and the contained gravity of his face was broken.

The child was accompanied by a medium-sized woolly dog of a species also strange to our young man's knowledge. She was quite composed, a dainty, incongruous, unbelievable creature from a story book. So wholly did this apparition lie outside his experience that for the first time he abandoned his self-containment, turning to the man next him for enlightenment.

"Some rich man's darter, must be," he surmised.

"You'd think so, wouldn't you?" said the other, with a short laugh. "Well, she ain't. She's the granddaughter of old man Farrell—the gunsmith. But he's crazy anyhow."

"He must be right fond of that little gal," surmised the stranger, surveying her keenly. "Granddarter, you say? Just her and the old man, I reckon."

"How'd you guess that?" asked the other.

"He must be right lonesome," continued the younger man, pursuing his train of thought unheeding. Then, having come to his conclusion as to this unfamiliar phenomenon, he almost visibly abandoned it. "I am obleeged to you, suh," said he, and again lifted his rifle and portmanteau. But the other man did not so readily relinquish this opening for his own curiosity.

"You in town for the shootin' match?" he inquired as a preliminary to an inquisition.

"No, suh," replied the young man politely, but with finality, "Just travelin' through."

3

From across the earth street a large mongrel launched itself like a thunderbolt straight for the woolly dog. The latter, bowled over by the suddenness and weight of the onslaught, shrieked aloud in terror, writhing and snapping in the grip of its more powerful antagonist. The air was vociferous with growls, yelps and snarls.

"Dog fight! Dog fight!" yelled those nearest. The idlers surged forward joyously, forming a compact eager group around the center of disturbance, those on the outside crowding and shoving for a better view. The little girl, jostled unceremoniously aside, beat and pulled at the braced legs, frantic but quite unnoticed. She was beside herself, all her pretty poise shattered by the urgency of the crisis. The world had become a world of inhuman and indifferent backs. Casting about her distractedly she ran in appeal to the one face turned in her direction.

"He'll be killed!" she cried. "It's that old Tiger! He's always tried to kill him! Oh! Oh!"

The young man contemplated her gravely for a moment; then, with an air of having come to a deliberate decision, began to shove his way to the center of the close-packed ring. So sudden and so determined was his movement that he met no serious opposition. Some of those he thrust aside flared angrily, and would have laid hands upon him, but so quickly had he moved that he was beyond their reach. Before anybody had grasped clearly what he was about he had snatched the woolly dog aloft, and had delivered a very convincing kick into the short ribs of its assailant.

"You Tiger! Down!" he further admonished that canine. His low soft voice snapped like a whip. In its tone was that entire expectation of obedience which alone penetrates effectively to a dog's consciousness. Tiger hesitated, licked his lips: but he obeyed.

At once the air was rent by cries of angry expostulation.

"Hey you! What you think you're doin'!" "Who the hell you think you are?"

Men, red-faced, crowded belligerently forward. Fists were clenched; hands were raised. Had the young man stirred by a palm's breadth it is probable the mob would have fallen upon him bodily. He did not move. Holding the cowed and whimpering woolly dog in his arms, he waited. His blue eyes were calm, and a little remote, as though, pending the moment, he had withdrawn to secret, inner, and distant preoccupations of his own.

"Folks," said he pleasantly at last. He did not raise his voice: and instinctively the mob hushed to quiet that it might hear, "I like a good dawg fight same as anybody. But this here ain't no dawg fight: it's a killin'. Besides, this here thing ain't rightly a dog, according to my raisin': and besides that it belongs to the lady yander."

He tossed his head ever so slightly from the abject woolly dog toward the gulping small girl. Several responded, with a faint laugh, to the grave and sardonic gleam in his eye. But one burly and red-faced man was unreconciled and belligerent.

"By God!" cried this one. "Who are you to come pushin' yourself in where you ain't wanted? For a ha'penny I'd——"

The young man turned his head deliberately.

"Dawg fights most gen'lly turns into man fights," he remarked. "Don't seem no sense to it; but that's the way it is. I ain't aimin' for no trouble: I'm just a-travelin' through."

"Afraid be ye!" sneered the red-faced man. "Well, I'll——"

"No, I'm not afeard," interrupted the stranger placidly. "I'll fight ye, if so be ye're set upon it. But yere ain't no time nor place. For one thing I'm aimin' to take this young-un and her—" he glanced down, a gleam of humor crossing the bleak gravity of his face—"and her dawg," he drawled, "back home where she ought to be."

"Runnin' away," sneered the red-faced man.

"I ain't leavin'," stated the young man. He surveyed slowly one by one the faces of the crowd. "I reckon that's all," said he. "I'll be back yere afore sundown, and then you can suit yoreself." He turned away with a decision that parted the ring before him, picked up his rifle and leather portmanteau which he slung again across his shoulder.

"Come on, sister," said he. She raised her tear-stained face to his confidingly and took his hand. They moved away: the woolly dog snuggled in the hollow of his left arm, he shortening his long woodsman strides, she skipping valiantly to keep pace.

4

But they had not proceeded far in the direction the young lady rather vaguely indicated before they were met by her grandfather, out in anxious search for her. When he had learned, partly from the child, partly from the young stranger, an inkling of what had happened, he expressed his relief. The expedition had been her own fancy.

"She would be better housed just now," submitted the young man.

"Nobody rightly would mean to harm her; but men git rough in drink."

"She got away," agreed the gunsmith, "and I am obliged to you for your trouble. You're in town for the Shooting, I suppose," glancing with professional interest at the stranger's weapon.

"No, suh," the young man denied, "just travelin' through. I am from South Branch since sun-up and knew nought of the Shooting."

"Where are you stopping for the night?"

"Nowhere as yit; I aim to stop at the tavern."

"But man alive, you'll find no place there!" cried the old man. "Every nook and cranny is filled long since." He stopped abruptly, considered for a moment. "You must stay at my house," he decided, "nay, I insist."

But his urgency was unnecessary. The young man accepted the proffer as simply as, it might be conceived, he would have accepted the good cheer of a dry cave in the wilderness. He deposited the woolly dog on the ground.

"Which way, suh?" he inquired.

The four proceeded down the earth road toward the canal. The little girl prattled eagerly at her grandfather about the horrid Tiger and his attempt at canicide. The stranger moved in his serene silence. Shortly they arrived at a rambling sort of structure, or series of structures attached one to the other. A small mill wheel indicated that the greater group of these were used as a manufacturing plant. The old man unlocked the door of a smaller wing and led the way to a cool interior of plain old polished wood, diamond-shaped panes, a dark table, a great fireplace, two benches, and a number of easy chairs. Ornament there was none, unless a score or more of guns slung on pegs about the walls might be so considered.

"Sit, lad, sit!" urged the old man, thrusting forward one of the chairs. "South Branch is distant and even young limbs must weary."

"I am obleeged to you, suh," acknowledged the youth. He deposited his rifle and portmanteau in a corner, removed his hat; perched himself upright and a little gingerly on the edge of one of the great chairs, his eye roving in deliberate scrutiny of his surroundings.

The old man hung his own three-cornered headpiece in the corner, disclosing the fact that he wore no wig. He was a small, compact old gentleman, with a stiff, upright brush of brown hair on a bullet head; and he moved with the swift darting certainty of a bird. His speech, too, was swift and darting and as voluble as that of his visitor was spare.

"My people are all abroad," he observed. "There is no keeping them at their tasks, so perforce and with good grace I declared holiday. You must take cold cheer."

He darted here and there, in and out a door on the right side of the fireplace, opening and shutting a cupboard on the left, clattering tankards and trenchers, with a continued buzz of movement like the sustained high hum of a bee. Behind it, as a bridge across to the hushed and aloof serenity of the room, a serenity into which the stranger had slipped as naturally as into a grateful and familiar element, beat the measured slow *tick-tock, tick-tock* of a tall clock in the corner.

"There!" cried the old man at last. "Draw up, young man! 'Tis but cold fare, but will suffice. I'll warrant ye've done worse in your time! A venison pasty; good bread of rye; honest ale home-brewed, none of your raw spirits that is the drink of fools."

"I am obleeged to you, suh," said the young man, and unfolded his long frame from the great chair and took his place at the table.

"I have nought by which to name you," Farrell reminded his guest as they sat. . . . "Don, eh? A good Scotch name, I warrant. Nay, fall to, lad, and use your mouth for more grateful work than talking."

They ate; the stranger for most part in the calm silence that held no hint of awkwardness; the old man chattering as suggestively near to questioning as his notion of politeness permitted. The little girl, who had at first curled herself into another of the great chairs, at length slipped to the floor and sidled over to take her stand against the young man's shoulder.

"I hope you hurt that old Tiger—when you kicked him," said she.

"Leave her stay," the stranger interfered to her grandfather's admonition. "I like young-uns. There's been a plenty of 'em in my raisin'." A slow grave smile sketched his lips, and he reached a strong finger to touch her ringleted head. "But we ain't got no little ladies like this un," he added. Beyond that he volunteered nothing about himself.

They finished the meal. The old man produced clay pipes and tobacco. But before joining his host in the great chairs before the fireplace the guest stretched his long legs, wandering about the room, examining attentively the weapons on the walls.

The old man watched him a moment, then arose to join him.

"You are interested in guns?" he asked.

"Yes, suh," acknowledged the other. "You see,"—his manner almost implied an apology for intruding even so much of his personal intimacies—"we livin' on the border use 'em a lot, what with shootin' game and takin' keer of ourselves like, when it comes to Injins and such."

"You have fought Indians?" pounced the old man.

But the younger withdrew into vagueness.

"Injins is not bad folks in some ways," he submitted. "I got good friends among the Injins. But a man must take keer of himself."

"These guns are a sort of historical collection," explained the gunmaker after a moment's bright-eyed contemplation of his visitor. "I have tried to show how they have developed. See, here is an old match lock: and here a wheel lock. And this is a sample of the very first rifle with a straight-cut groove without a twist. And here is a bell-muzzle that shot slugs, or even stones."

"They surely are a clumsy-lookin' contraption," marveled the young man. "A man wonders how they ever hit anything."

"They didn't—much."

"Man has a hard enough time gettin' along nowadays, what with shots that go wild even with good holdin'." The visitor turned finally to the chairs and the pipes. "But it's surely interestin' to me, suh; and I am obleeged to you."

He lighted his pipe thoughtfully; and somehow it became evident that he was slowly coming to a decision.

"I'm figurin' on somethin', suh," he said at last. "You're the first man I ever saw that made guns. I wouldn't wish to ask too much of you, suh; but——"

"What is it, lad?" urged the old man.

"If it ain't no secret, suh, how kin you make a true bar'l? Many a time I've figgered on it—if it ain't no secret."

"Come with me, lad," he cried, eager with the master's enthusiasm over his craft. He remembered the little girl.

"Time for your posset, child; and then to bed. She is already a good housewife,"—he turned proudly to his visitor—"and shall manage her own supper—and mine and yours for the matter of that—as well as any woman grown. Make your curtsy to Don here, and kiss your old gran'ther, and run along."

He unlocked a door, and the two entered the long low workshop, now deserted for the holiday. Through the clutter of tools and half-finished pieces, he led the way to a rack on which were stacked broad flat bars of iron.

"Here are your barrels," said he.

The young man knit his brows.

"You can't bore no hole in such," he objected.

The old man smiled.

"Certainly not," he agreed. "Here,"—he exhibited a long slender rod. "That's what we call the core rod. First we heat the flat bar to welding heat; then we fold it around the core rod, and weld it together; then we draw out the core rod. There's your barrel with a hole in it. It is rough, of course," he added.

"How come the core rod don't stick?"

"We weld only a few inches at a heat, withdrawing the rod each time, but even then on occasion it will not come away." The old man sighed. "Then we must cut it out with a cold chisel or throw it away. Next, of course, we smooth the new barrel as much as possible. Have to do that with a hammer for the outside and a hand reamer for the inside, like a carpenter bores in wood."

"Cain't you use a lathe?" asked the young man keenly.

"Doesn't run steady enough."

"Can you get her straight that way by eye?"

"Pretty good. But look here." The gunsmith picked up a half-finished barrel from the bench and took down a long hickory bow from a nail on the wall. It was precisely like a bow used as a weapon, except that it was lighter, and its cord was but a fine silk thread. Farrell loosed one end of the thread, dropped it carefully through the barrel, and again attached it to the bow. He held the barrel to the light. "Look through it," he commanded. "Look at the shadow of the thread and you can see where it does not touch. That means a crooked place. We've got to straighten that out by tapping with a light hammer."

The young man turned his face slowly in admiration of this ingenuity.

"Always begin straightening in the middle of the barrel," chortled the old man, delighted. "Chase the rascals out at the ends!" he cried.

The stranger shook his head.

"I'd sure hate to try to do it, suh," he submitted.

"It's as easy for me to take a kink out of a barrel as it is for you to make shavings off a pine stick with a sharp knife!" the gunsmith boasted.

His visitor turned the barrel slowly over and over, examining mentally the problem rather than physically the thing he held in his hand.

"Yes, suh," he said at last.

"Here," said Farrell, leading the way to a long low bench, "is the most important part of all. Here's where we cut the grooves for the rifling."

"I do admire to see that!" cried the young man with an approach to eagerness.

He saw a long cherry wood cylinder of four or five inches in diameter in the surface of which had been cut four deep grooves that ran in a long spiral about the cylinder. They resembled the grooves in a rifle barrel, except that in this case, of course, they were on the outside. The cylinder was suspended in a framework. Midway in the framework had been fixed rigidly and immovably four projecting nubs that fitted into and engaged the four grooves. So if one were to push the cylinder forward on its carriage past the nubs, it must revolve at the rate and the pitch determined by the grooves in it.

"And that," explained Farrell, "is exactly the rate and pitch of the rifling we want in our barrel. All we've got to do is clamp our barrel in exact line, hitch our groove-cutting tool rigidly on the end of the wooden cylinder, and it is *bound* to cut grooves exactly the same as those in the cylinder. See?"

His visitor shoved the simple contrivance back and forth a number of times, noting the slow turn along the rifled guiding groove.

"Well," he sighed at last, "that is ce'tainly a smart trick. I'll remember that. How long mought it take you, now, to rifle a bar'l?"

"Takes about a hundred cuts to cut a groove—about two hours," replied Farrell. "Then she needs polishing and smoothing. We use lead plugs for that mostly."

They proceeded slowly. Excited by his guest's intelligent appreciation the old gunmaker expanded. He showed how the new barrels were plugged at one end of the tube, and how they were then browned by a mixture of aqua fortis, blue vitriol, tincture of iron, and water. In sketchy pantomime the old man demonstrated how the locks were constructed and applied. At the woodworking bench he paused for but a moment.

"Curly maple, that's the wood," he stated dogmatically, "and you want to work her by hand. And stain her by hand with good honest soot and oil. Then you've got a job."

They returned to the living room. The young man picked up his own rifle, which he examined gravely in the light of new knowledge. Farrell stood at his elbow.

"I see you have one of Martin Meylan's," he observed. "Like it?"

"She holds her own," replied the young man, noncommittally.

"What you done to the trigger guard?"

The stranger smiled his slow smile, in modest deprecation.

"I expect I'm wrong, suh," said he. "I expect they's a right good reason why all the gunsmiths do thisaway and not thataway; and I expect they must be right. But just for me, suh—in my own use, this trigger guard suits me better."

"Made it yourself, eh?"

"Yes, suh. 'Tain't much of a trigger guard f'r looks; but it suits me better."

"Humph!" grunted the gunmaker, setting the weapon into the corner again, and leading the way to the pipes and chairs.

"I mean no offense, suh," said the visitor. "It's just my own idee for myself."

"Offense!" snorted the old man. "But you're right, lad! Do you know why every gunmaker in the Colonies puts that foolish, cumbersome, fragile trigger guard on every gun he turns out? Simply because that is the kind they put on guns in Europe! No other reason! God knows why they wanted that kind there—thought 'em pretty, I suppose. Same way with a lot of other things. Gunmakers are pig-headed fools. They listen to no reason, but sit puffed in the arrogance of their self-conceit like toads; crying down those who—"

He had arisen and was waving about his long pipe; but, catching the expression of honest bewilderment on his guest's face, he broke off in a calm as startling as his excitement, and sat down again abruptly.

"Tell me, lad," said he persuasively. "You spoke but now with a lukewarm indifference of the quality of your piece. What is its fault? And why procure ye none more to your fancy, since, as you say, your life may depend on it? Is the barrel not true, then? Perhaps we might remedy that."

"You mistake me, suh," the young man assured him earnestly. "The bar'l is true and finely made."

"It should be. Meylan is a gunsmith of reputation."

"I would not have you think otherwise. I but spoke aloud an idle thought. I know nought of these things, and would not set my poor notions against the experience of my worshipful masters."

"Worshipful fiddlesticks!" exploded the old man. "Did I not tell ye, lad, that gunmakers are pig-headed fools, copying slavishly what is patterned for them in Europe and listening to no reason, but sunning themselves in arrogance? Come lad! your ideas?"

"They are without doubt impossible, suh; for I have no understanding of the craft."

"Perhaps, perhaps!" Farrell waved this aside. "But let us pretend there is no impossible. I would know your ideas, lad! Speak them freely."

"Well, suh, I would have a piece that used not so much good powder and lead, for powder and lead are hard to come at in the wilderness, and it has seemed to me that a well-placed ball will do its work——"

"Even a smaller ball," supplied the gunsmith. "There is nought of impossibility there; only common sense. Do you know the reason—the only reason—why all men contrive to use these great slugs? Because in Europe they know little of well-placed balls, and care less; because their only idea is to hit a regiment of men. And then?"

"Well, suh, a longer bar'l would suit me better, and I think most men who range the forests."

"Why?" snapped the old man.

"For better sighting. The woods are dark, and if a man would hold true in twilight, he must have his front sight far from his eye."

"That is true, too. And there is nought impossible there—save that gunmakers are a pig-headed lot. And then?"

For the first time the young man chuckled aloud.

"Yere is where we touch the impossible, suh; for as long as I'm a-dreaming I will tell the whole. I would have a piece that would place the ball truer to where I hold, so that when I drawed my bead and pressed my trigger true I would find my ball where my eye had rested."

"And you do not? You think you can hold truer than your ball can speed?"

"So can any good man," submitted the youth modestly, but with entire confidence, "for be yore bar'l never so truly made, and load yore piece never so carefully with the best of French powder and priming of the finest grain, cast you yore balls never so cunningly, nevertheless it may so hap that it strays, and no man can tell when this will befall."

"Why is this, in your opinion?"

"Nay, that I cannot guess," replied the young man good-humoredly. "It is, I must suppose, in the natur' of things and we must bear with it."

The old man hesitated, weighing a decision.

"Nevertheless even that might be compassed, in my belief," he said at last.

"Anon?" queried the other.

The old man leaned forward excitedly.

"Can you guard a secret?" he demanded.

"Yes, suh," said the young man gravely.

The gunsmith arose and left the room, to return after a moment bearing a rifle. This he withheld for a moment; then, as though finally making up his mind, he passed it into his visitor's hands and stood back in silence. It was a graceful weapon, strong without clumsiness, its octagon barrel nearly three feet and a half long, but so light that it would probably not have tipped the beam at over eight or nine pounds. Its stock of polished curly maple extended its full length and was gracefully carved; its trigger guard was small and compact. Beneath the barrel rings of brass held a long hickory ramrod. In the side of the butt-stock opened a brass-covered trap. The lock was small, compact, about half the size of that on the usual arm of the day, and the clean small flint was held in leathered jaws.

"There's your long barrel, and your spread of sights"—the old man could not keep silence long—"and your small strong trigger guard. There's your smaller bore. The balls run fifty-two to the pound instead of a score or less —you can carry three times the ammunition. The lock is as swift in action as a flash of light. See how smoothly the flint meets the frizzen! Throw it to your face, man! Held you ever so sweet a balance, or one that steadied itself so in the hand?"

The young man obeyed, and the extended muzzle of the long weapon came to the immobility of a rock.

"What say you?" urged the gunmaker, surveying his visitor's stance and handling with approval, but shifting from one foot to the other with an impatience ludicrously like that of a small boy.

"It is a sweet piece," sighed the visitor, lowering it at last. "A sweet piece, such as I never thought to hold atween my hands." He examined its details keenly. "I think, suh, if you don't mind my sayin' it, that you will have to make you another loadin' rod of iron."

"Hickory makes quieter loading."

"I know. But forcin' the ball down the bar'l is rough work, and a broken rod—"

The old man for the moment did not meet this issue.

"Is it not such a piece as you have dreamed?" he insisted. "Such as you described to me but now?"

The youth smiled a slow gleam of humor.

"All but one thing," he reminded.

It was Farrell's turn to look his inquiry.

"These things you have yere," explained the woodsman, "—and I do not deny they are a great leap ahead—all these things are but aids to a man's holdin'! But they do not place the ball."

"Aha, lad!" the old gunmaker burst forth in a triumph for which it was now evident he had waited not too patiently. "That too I have compassed." He placed his finger alongside his nose with a comical air of cunning. "Tell me, lad, what causes the ball to stray, when, as you say, the holding is good?"

"Nay, suh," replied the other, "how could I tell you that? It is, as I have said, in the natur' of things."

"Then I will e'en tell *you!* The first of these causes is a fouled and thereby roughened barrel."

The young man nodded acquiescence.

"That is true, in my own knowledge," he admitted, "so that, when time serves, I wipe out my piece very carefully after each shot."

"You can clean away thus the hard ash of burned powder," Farrell told him, "but you cannot thus remove the lead that is stripped from the ball flake by flake until the smoothness of the barrel is gone. The second reason is married with the third, and both have as parent the fit of the ball in the barrel. For if it sets not snugly in the grooves the force of the powder in great part leaps past it and is lost; and if it does fit snugly then it must be hammered home by force, and is thereby upset and malformed, no matter how shrewdly and gingerly one handles his rod. And a malformed bullet cannot fly straight."

"That is very interesting to me, suh," said the young man, "and part of it I had suspected, but not all. But I can see no cure."

"Here," proffered Farrell, "are the balls for this rifle."

The visitor took one of them in his fingers and examined it without comment.

"You see no difference from any ordinary bullet, save for the size. You are right: there is no difference. But look!" He dropped the butt of the rifle to the floor and inserted one of the bullets into its muzzle. In ordinary loading it was customary to drive the ball several inches into the barrel by means of a short metal rod and a small hammer called a "starter," after which it was forced home with the ramrod. In this instance, when the old man relinquished it, the ball dropped down the barrel freely, and as he reversed the muzzle it rolled slowly out again into his palm. He made no explanation, but looked expectantly toward his visitor. The latter knit his brows, knowing some comment was awaited.

"If you aim to hold it in with wadding atop," he submitted at last, "I have tried that, and it flies wild as a hawk."

"Every child knows that—has tried that!"

"Yes, suh," agreed the stranger, "but it was all I could think of."

"Now I am going to show you something. And this is what you must keep secret. You must not tell a soul of what you are to see. Remember!"

"I have passed you my word, suh," stated the young man with a quiet dignity.

The old gunmaker paused in his tremendous inner excitement long enough to pat the other hastily on the shoulder.

"No offense, my lad; I trust ye," said he. "Now see." He opened the brass trap in the side of the stock and from it took a piece of greased linen cloth cut in a round a little less in size than a half-dollar. This he stretched across the muzzle of the gun, covering with it the hole of the bore. Next he laid the bullet atop and pressed it into the aperture with his thumb.

"We are supposing we have charged the piece with powder," he explained. "Here," he forced the ramrod into the visitor's hands. "Push her home, lad!"

The young man, with the grace of long accustomedness, swung the butt of the weapon to the left and in front and at the same time inserted the tip of the ramrod into the bore and applied strongly the thrust of his right arm. An expression of surprise crossed his face.

"She slides slick and smooth as a greased shoat through a cornfield!" he marveled.

"And she stays there," supplemented the old man, snatching the rifle, turning it upside down, and striking the butt sharply by way of demonstration. "Is not that quicker than the old way? And quieter? And need ye fear now that the hickory rod will break? And mark you: each new loading wipes away the burnt powder of the last shot, so that the barrel is ever clean. And the ball is left true and round as it came from the mold. And no lead strips from it to the barrel. And the linen patch, filling well all space within, lets not the force of the powder by. So there are your reasons for wild flight all answered!"

But the visitor was not wholly satisfied.

"And the ball still takes the twist of the grooves when the naked lead touches them not?" he commented doubtfully. "How can that be?"

The old man paused in his task, which was of abstracting the bullet by means of a screw worm which he had attached to the end of the rod.

"Nay, lad: that I cannot tell you. I have thought much on it. It must be, as you say, in the nature of things. But it does."

The youth pondered in his slow and deliberate fashion.

"And the ball flies true?" he asked at length. "I do not doubt you, suh," he hastened to add, "but I mind me my father's sayin'; for when one showed him a piece and boasted of the hang of its stock and the prettiness of its carvings and the smooth dark brown of its bar'l, and the cunning of its make, he always said, 'Yes, she's purty, but she ain't worth a damn unless she shoots straight. Let's try her.' No offense, suh; but have you tried her?"

"I've shot her," replied the gunsmith briefly. He broke off; but was compelled to answer the other's waiting. "I can make a gun," he continued in gruff tone, "but I cannot hold one true. A slight palsy—a shaking of the hand. But," his voice rose to a vehemence almost of hysteria, "I'll stake my life that I am right, sneer and laugh these other pig-headed fools as they may! They know nought but what their fathers have told them; and their conceit is such. But they will sing a different tune. Fools! pig-headed fools!" He fumed, walking up and down with quick uneven steps. Abruptly he came to a halt before his visitor. "Would you credit it," he resumed in a quieter and more reasonable voice, "when, as a brother craftsman, I sought to share the workings of my mind; when I strove to discuss reasonably the things we have discussed so reasonably here—and you are an intelligent lad, Don, with more sense in your noodle than all of them together—when I would have spoken of the need for a rifle fitted to American rather than European hands, I was set aside as one sets aside a presumptuous urchin and rebuked for conceiting myself wiser than the masters!" He snorted, and again changed his mood.

"But to-morrow!" He chuckled, and again laid his finger alongside his nose. "You must linger to-morrow, lad; you are welcome here. To-morrow you shall see."

"You will shoot the piece in to-morrow's match?"

"Not I. But I forget: you are a stranger here, and perchance know not the significance of to-morrow. Know then that this is no ordinary shooting; but is an event to which once each year all gunmakers bring their best and truest pieces to the trial; so that he whose rifle carries away the palm is winner of the golden medal of the craft, so that all men come to him, and his business gains great increase and himself reputation."

"But, suh," suggested the young man diffidently, "you yourself but now said——"

"That I cannot hold true," agreed the other. "But it is an article of the contest that the maker of the piece may engage another to stand for him: and for that reason it is customary in the craft to bespeak skilled men to shoot for them at the butts. Few gunmakers test their own rifles. And

I—" he chuckled again, and rubbed his hands together—"I have been beforehand, and have compacted with John Gladden of whom even in the borders you may have heard."

"His name has reached my ears," acknowledged the young man. "I should greatly admire, suh, to see so notable a marksman perform."

"You shall!" cried the gunmaker. "You shall! To-morrow! And with the best shooter and the best rifle in the colonies it shall go hard if I do not thrust their sneers adown their very throats! And I'll tell you this . . ."

The tall clock in the corner clucked in its throat, hesitated, then struck solemnly. The young man glanced up startled at the level shafts of light.

"Yore pardon, suh, for interruptin' you," he cried. "But I must be excused. I have made a promise which I am tardy in fulfilling. It will not take me long, and I beg you to be patient, for I would hear more of these things on my return."

So saying, he snatched up his hat and hastened from the room.

5

Nor had he time to spare, for the last rays of the sun were lifting from atop the elm trees when he had regained the tavern square. His antagonist, slightly drunk, was parading to and fro at the appointed spot. He had evidently worked himself into a high state of braggadocio and belligerency; and ever and anon he would stop short, flap his elbows, and crow lustily like a cock. Many men surrounded him in a loose group, cheering him on, half laughing, half in earnest. Someone caught sight of the young man approaching and raised a shout, hastily opening a passage. The red-faced man stopped short, and peered evilly from beneath bushy brows.

"So you've come to take your licking after all, eh!" he growled.

"If so be you're of the same mind, which still seems to me a foolishness to fight like dawgs just because dawgs be a-fighting," replied the youth. "Is it not more befitting sensible men to share a tankard of mine host's good ale——"

The older man leaned forward and brought the flat of his palm smartly against the stranger's face.

"*Now* will ye fight!" he snarled. "Or are ye still too skeered?"

The young man's steadiness did not waver, nor did he show other sign than a slow darkening of the cheeks.

"That was not needful, suh," said he mildly. "Nor am I askeered."

Without further parley the red-faced man lowered his head and made a bull-like rush. The stranger slipped lightly aside in avoidance; at the same time glancing about in surprise.

A tall heavy-set man in a bottle-green topcoat with many small capes stepped forward authoritatively.

"What mean ye!" he cried in resonant tones. "Is this mannerly? Fair play and a proper ring, say I; and hurrah for the best man!"

His interference met with approval.

"Good for you, Squire!" "Fair play!" "We'll back ye in that!" came to him from many voices.

At this moment also the tavern's landlord bustled forth, appealing for no brawls before his door.

"The stable yard, gentlemen!" he cried. "It is at hand, and much more seemly!"

"The stable yard it is," agreed the Squire. "Come ye," he seized the combatants each by an elbow and marched them away like children, followed by the streaming and excited rabble.

"I thank you, suh," said the young man. "Methought for a moment that I saw the ruin of my only coat."

Arrived at the stable yard the Squire, still holding his charges by the elbow, looked about him high-headed, and rapidly named a dozen to form the ring. Back of these appointed provosts the crowd gathered dense; and men clambered rapidly atop wagons and walls, and even swarmed to the stable roof for a better view. When the stir had died the Squire released his charges, shoving each to an opposite side.

"Strip," he commanded them. It was evident that the Squire was enjoying himself hugely.

The challenger, who was aflame with eagerness—and whiskey—tore his shirt from his back and handed it at random among the spectators, disclosing himself as a heavy gorilla of a man, bull-necked, barrel-chested, thick-armed, with heavy strong muscle bands. The stranger methodically folded his coat, removed and folded his shirt, which he placed atop it. Holding the bundle in his arms he looked from face to face of those about him. He stepped to confront a placid kindly-faced man of middle age.

"Could I ask you to mind these for me, suh?" he asked courteously.

"Gladly," assented the burgher. He leaned to speak in a lower voice. "Beware of him, lad," he advised earnestly. "He is an ugly fighter and he will kill you if he can. I am sorry this must be," he added.

"Thank you, suh, I can but do my best," rejoined the youth, and turned to the center of the ring.

His torso, now stripped of its garments, was seen to be molded in lines of a smooth slenderness that at first glance contrasted ill with the heavy power of his antagonist. Nevertheless a connoisseur in bodies would have found somewhat to admire in the contrast of the broad spare shoulders and the narrow compact hips, and would have appreciated the whipcord quality of the long muscles and the ripple of their perfect condition beneath the skin. But its force would seem the force more of long endurance than the power necessary to contend successfully with the crushing oaken strength of the man over against him. Here and there in the crowd a few murmured in pitying deprecation of the inequality of the contest, but their protests were drowned in the general eagerness of excitement. Man shouted offers to wager, but the offers were all on one side and no takers, for none accorded the younger man a chance against a known and reputed rough-and-tumble fighter. Only after the clamor had died somewhat through lack of fuel did the Squire's loud voice speak on the other side.

"Damme," he bellowed at one of the most vociferous, who now offered four to one, "taken for a pound," but he added, "I'll not begrudge a pound for the sake of sport. Now hark ye," he addressed the antagonists, "this is all my say: if one or the other cries enough, at that moment ye cease, and if any offers blow or grip thereafter he reckons with me. Now fight it out."

He stepped back.

The big man slouched toward the youth, lowered his head, and rushed like a bull. The latter again slipped easily to one side, evading the outstretched hands. Thrice this was repeated.

"Stand and fight, you poltroon!" snarled the red-faced man.

The younger made no reply, watching his antagonist warily. Twice more the same maneuver with the same result; except that once the stranger laid hand on the other's shoulder as he passed, but snatched it away instantly when faced by a sudden turn in his direction. The crowd began to shout impatiently, for it was evident that if he so chose the visitor's superior agility could prolong indefinitely this avoidance; and they wanted a fight, not a foot race. So clamorous became their demands that the Squire at length raised his bull voice.

"Fair play!" he cried. "Give the lad a chance!"

At length the challenger wearied of futile rushing that grasped nothing, and came to a stand in the center, sneeringly awaiting a move by the other. The latter, stooping, his arms hanging, began then slowly to circle just out of reach. It was notable that neither man had offered as yet to strike the other with his fists. Blows in the fights of those days were a secondary offense, delivered to batter into submission only after an advantage had been gained. Twice the young man darted in, attempting some wrestler's hold, twice he failed, and wrenched himself away from the other man's countering grip.

The Squire watched, his head on one side.

"Methinks if Jack once grasps him firmly my pound is done," he observed to the man next him. "Aha!" he shouted.

The stranger's third attempt seemed like to have proved disastrous to him. His bear-like antagonist had caught him in a grip that could not be shaken off. For nearly half a minute they strained. Then the older man's superior strength began to tell. Beneath his smooth skin the youth's muscles strained as though they would burst, but slowly, inch by inch, he was bent back until he was securely held. And then powerfully and irresistibly the man called Jack half freed one massive arm, and his hand, inch by inch, overpowering the young man's opposition, crept upwards.

A lightning desperate upheaval, and the lad had twisted free and sprung apart. He was panting slightly and for the first time his face was aflame.

"He tried to gouge me!" he cried to the Squire. "Is that what you call fair play!"

"And why not?" rejoined the Squire coldly. "Stand and fight, or, if you will, cry quits."

The young man looked about the crowd in amazed appeal from the decision, but was answered by derisive laughter. Its blood was up, and it wanted blood. Still incredulous, he looked at his antagonist. The latter grinned at him evilly.

"I'll do worse to ye than that, my cockerel," he growled.

"And is that your habit!" cried the stranger indignantly. "It is not so on the borders when men settle honest differences."

"Stand and fight—or cry quits," repeated the Squire imperturbably.

No man was able afterwards to describe clearly what next happened, though many words were wasted in the matter. They saw the young man stoop; they saw him dart in with the speed and swiftness of a snake striking; they were confusedly aware of a tangle and swirl; even above the turmoil of excitement they distinctly heard a clear sharp snap like the cracking of a dead limb. Then the young man leaped back clear, leaving his antagonist standing, an expression of bewilderment on his face, gazing stupidly at his left arm which he held in his right hand.

"Well, suh!" the visitor challenged in a ringing voice. His head was high, and his nostrils expanded.

A dead silence fell that endured for perhaps ten seconds.

"Will you go on?" then inquired the Squire, in a voice calm only above a compressed excitement.

"Go on!" repeated Jack furiously. "How can I go on? He has broken my arm!"

The stupefaction broke. The ring was instantly overwhelmed by the surge of men, shouting, whooping. They crowded around the stranger, pounding him on the back, shrieking in his face, commending him, congratulating him, all on his side, fickle as crowds always are. He thrust them aside scornfully, elbowing his way to the burgher in whose charge he had given his garments, which he reclaimed with a brief word of thanks, and proceeded to assume. The Squire was at his side, red-faced and bellowing.

"Greatest thing I ever saw, lad!" he shouted. "You've won me four pounds! Damme you must drink with me! Come, I will not take nay."

The young man shook his head.

"You must excuse me, suh," he said firmly. "I must be on my way. I thank you, suh, for yo' kindness."

"But how did you do it? That you must tell me," persisted the big man. "Saw I never the like before."

"It was a trick," replied the stranger briefly, "a trick known to the Injins. They use it only when hard-pressed in battle," he added.

He turned away and, with an air of decision that none ventured to cross, threaded the gaping crowd and disappeared.

6

When he reëntered the low dark room the great clock in the corner was tolling the last note of another hour. The old gunmaker dozing by the fire awakened with a start. The young man slipped into a chair.

"Now, suh, if you don't mind, I've been figgerin'," said he, "on what you been tellin' me. And I'd like to talk some more about these idees of yours. You don't know how interestin' they are to me, suh."

"Surely, lad, surely," agreed the old man. He glanced incredulously at the tall clock, now dim in the twilight "You have been long," he commented.

"Yes, suh," agreed his visitor apologetically. "But I would have returned much sooner had I known the customs of yo' people yereabouts."

7

All late afternoon and early evening the contestants and spectators continued to pour into town. A few came in wagons; fewer still afoot; the great majority on horseback. The inn was full to overflowing; men bought high the privilege of making down their beds on the floor of the less frequented public apartments. Every private house willing to do so accommodated its visitors. At the Big Bend the flicker of fires reflected downward from the great river trees; and it seemed that those campers were perhaps the most in comfort of any; for what with the revelers spilling noisily from the tavern bar, the songs and disputations of others determined to make the most of the rare holiday, only those of strong nerves and placid powers of withdrawal could obtain more than fitful rest in the village. And as the last of the night owls went to roost, and the wearied turned on their pallets with a sigh of anticipation of deferred rest, the small hours became murmurous with the activities of those who must make preparation for the coming day's activities. Then it was made known to the campers at the Bend that it would have been well to have retired earlier; for they were fairly upon the scene of the day's sport, and men with lanthorns moved busily and shouted to one another as they made last preparation for the entertainment of the crowd, which must here, upon the very spot, be supplied with food and drink if mine host of the tavern were most to profit.

To this end long tables had been set up within bowers thatched with straw; and now men hurried about carrying or rolling or trundling provision of spirits and beer and ale; and others tended fires blazing beneath great iron pots from which steamed a most seductive savory of venison and beef stews. There was little more sleep for the campers, but a plenty of grumbling, until the aroma of the cooking was too much for their sharpened appetites, and they arose and kicked together the embers of their own dying fires and shivered slightly in the chill of dawn; and ate and were comforted; and so, gradually, slipped into the eager vibrant excitement of the day, and fell to discussing the leading contestants and raising their voices in dispute and laying wagers on the men of their choice. Nor was the element of personal emulation crowded aside by the presence of champions: for in the course of the day was room for many minor sweepstake events open to all; not to speak of a number of lesser rivalries privately arranged. And those of more modest skill staked happily their hopes on chance, for a ball flying wild from the muzzle not too rarely compensated for an ill aim; besides which in certain types of matches a tyro with good luck might very well outdo an expert with bad. There would be plenty of powder burned this day!

Those in the village stirred more sluggishly, groaning and stopping their ears as the clatter of newcomers half aroused them, slipping back less and less successfully to unconsciousness, until at last, with a curse, they kicked aside their blankets and quilts. But their ill nature did not outlast the moment. For some a morning draught; for some a plunge of the head into cold water; for some through opened casement a breath of coming morning, composed of coolness and a streak of rose in eastern sky and the soft mourning of doves in the trees, sufficed to bring them full into the eagerness of anticipation. The monotonous year filed before these pioneer people in a slow procession of gray days. Spangle days were rare, and they savored them with an expectancy and thrill, known nowadays only to children, not to be dimmed by smaller things. By the time the morning light was full all men were again afoot, save a few whose potations of the night before had been somewhat too deep.

8

One dwelling house in the village was, however, exempt from this premature arousement. Protected by the soft rushing silence of running water no noise could reach it to trouble its repose. The mill race took all the world of sound for its own and translated it into a lulling and grateful peace. Those within its insulation slept tranquilly, undisturbed.

Nevertheless robin-song found its inmates afoot; the young man at the call of long habit, the elder prowling about in foretaste of what he believed was to be his long-awaited triumph. They met in the oaken room below stairs, where they ate together at the board table, served by a grumpy and elderly woman who the day before had not been in evidence.

"Now, Don lad," advised the old gunmaker when they had finished, "I advise ye to take ye down to the Big Bend where, I doubt not, you will find much to see and to amuse yourself withal. The big shooting is not until afternoon, but there will be the smaller matches and many other doings worth your while to see."

"I will e'en do that, suh," agreed Don, "but come ye not also?"

"Nay, lad," replied the old man cunningly. "I have seen many such; and it is not my purpose to disclose for the common questioning my new production. I will be there when the hour strikes, but not before. And besides, I await John Gladden, who comes before the time to make trial of the new rifle and to fit his holding to its sighting."

"In that case, suh, I will follow your advice," said the young man, plucking his felt hat from the peg. "When the young-un awakens, give her my greeting."

"But Don!" Farrell halted him at the door. "Are you not taking your own piece with you?"

"For why?" the visitor smiled quaintly. "Do you expect an attack of the savages?"

"But will ye not enter in the shooting?" expostulated the gunmaker. "Not the great match; but there will be many others—block shoots and peg shoots and turkey shoots wherein many will take part."

Don shook his head.

"Perchance, if your piece is not quite true, another could be found for you in my shops," suggested Farrell. "Gladly may you have the loan of such."

"My piece is as true as any," the young man assured him. He hesitated, then went on steadily, "I had not thought to mention it, suh, but the truth is I am travelin' through on a visit, and must return, and my pockets are not so lined with shillings that I may spend them on aught else but the journey."

"Let me——"

"No, suh," Don interrupted firmly, "—but I am obleeged to you, suh."

He turned toward the door. At the stairway's foot stood the little girl, barefooted, in her night shift, her ringleted hair towsled about her head.

"If you see that old Tiger, you *kill* him!" cried she.

For the first time the grave young stranger laughed aloud.

"If I see that old Tigah, honey," he replied, "I'll be shore to info'm him *just* what you told me."

9

By the time he had reached the Big Bend the days activities were well under way. Don sauntered here and there, surveying them gravely. Mostly he passed unnoticed, though here and there he was proffered a greeting from some spectator of yesterday's fight, and twice he was invited boisterously to come up to the tables and take a drink as a stout lad! But he responded so gravely to the salutations and refused the invitations so firmly that they turned away from him without further thought.

The river grove and the meadow immediately adjacent were thronged. Many jostled about the tables in the bowers, breaking their morning's fast or fortifying themselves with ale or spirits. Smaller and shifting groups hovered about certain peddlers who had laid out their wares. Others clustered talking politics or crops or religion, as was to be expected. Only a comparatively few partisans or acquaintances had as yet gravitated to where the rifles were already whanging away, and where hung the thin acrid fog of powder. It was to this point, however, that Don at once betook himself. He arrived just as one match had come to an end and the preparations for another were about to begin.

On a stool behind a table sat the man Don had yesterday heard called the Squire. The day was yet young and cool, and he wore still his green greatcoat with the many capes. Below the table stood a large basket filled with pine blocks split to about six inches square and the surfaces blackened by charring. These the Squire was engaged in passing out to would-be contestants in the next event, selling them at the rate of sixpence apiece. As but one shot could be fired at each block, some were buying three, four, or as many as five. Others, either because of the slenderness of their purses or confidence in their luck or ability, contented themselves with but one. Each, on receiving his targets, drew apart to mark them. This was done either by scribing deep crosslines with a knife, or by tacking on a bit of paper or tin. The marks on the crosslines rarely centered the block of wood, for while the prize money would go to the man whose ball struck nearest the exact middle, each placed his point of aim at the spot where experience had taught him the sight should be held to compensate for the error of his gun.

The range for this match was one hundred yards and each assumed what position and took what time he pleased. If a man missed clean, he cursed vividly or withdrew in sullen silence, leaving the untouched target to be retrieved by an attendant Negro, for sale and use again. If, under the bullet's impact, the block spun from its position, he whooped and ran forward to reclaim it himself; and was on his return immediately surrounded, all eager to examine how near to center the ball had struck. When the last block had taken its chance, the best were submitted to the Squire's measurement, which determined the winner. The latter was immediately presented with the cash prize, which was a goodly percentage of the sum resulting from the entrance fees, the remainder constituting a "Kitty" that went to the promotion fund of the enterprise. In this match nearly half the targets were hit; and the winning bullet was officially declared to have entered within two inches of center.

"What think ye of that?" exulted a spectator at Don's elbow. "Is not that a good shooting?"

"Why, I think it very good," agreed the young man, "and these men can stand with the best in any company."

He turned away to where, from the right, came the sounds of occasional desultory firing. Here he found men engaged in shooting at a turkey loosely tethered at full two hundred yards. The entrance fee was also but a sixpence; and he who hit the turkey would take it away for his dinner; but the fact that the bird could continually move about within a short radius, combined with the additional fact that the range was beyond what approximate exactness the rifles of the day possessed, made of the investment no undue risk to the management.

That both contestants and bystanders realized fully the large part played by chance was fully evidenced by the atmosphere of hilarity. Men shouted facetious comments and advice, dissolved in yells of laughter as a sudden movement on the part of the distracted turkey avoided a lucky bullet. The rivals muttered curses or voiced humorous chagrin according to their various temperaments. One elderly man held his rifle at aim for a full two minutes, following with his sights in vain the erratic motions of the bird —at last lowering his arm tired with its long exertion.

"Consarn the pesky critter!" he shouted in exasperation. "Hold still, if you want to be killed!"

At last in desperation he loosed off anyhow, and a puff of dust far to the right elicited only a startled squawk.

The mark was attained after a deal of banging by a smooth-faced boy who raced excitedly to retrieve his prey, only to be greeted by a great shout of laughter as he returned with it.

"Hope you like dark meat!" "Never mind, bub, turkey hash is fine!"

The heavy bullet had smashed its way squarely through the middle of the breast.

Don shook his head.

"That's a waste of good eatin'," he remarked to one near him. "Whar I come from we just let the head stick out, and shoot at it—at a hundred ya'ds," he added.

Another small and amused group attracted him further. Here he found two men with rifles, seated on the ground. One, his piece held in a knee and elbow rest, was painfully and patiently squinting at a cockerel tethered a scant fifty yards distant. The other, his rifle laid alongside him on the ground, smoked a pipe and watched. The rooster was a noble and iridescent specimen of his kind, a beautiful creature except for one blemish. What should have been an abundant and sweeping tail consisted of four scattered feathers only.

For some time the young visitor watched. Still the rifleman held his fire. Don was puzzled.

"Why delays he, suh," he asked a bystander at last. "Shorely it is no great feat to kill the fowl at that range."

His interlocutor, a middle-aged man of evidently the better class, chuckled.

"That is the last thing he wants to do," he replied in a low and guarded voice.

"I do not understand, suh," submitted Don.

"Why," explained the other, "I see you are a stranger here. Know, then, that this is a private match between two very noted marksmen who are such rivals that I think they would very gladly use one another as targets in a duel. E'en last night at the tavern, and they in their cups, I think it might have come to blows, but the Squire, who is a rare wag at times, and hath ideas one would never suspect in so thick a noodle, bethought him of this. The terms are these: that each man in turn plucks with his bullet from the tail of that cockerel a feather. The one who shoots away the last feather wins the contest and the wager they have made. But he who by mischance slays the chicken not only loses the match, but must double the bet."

The young man chuckled in his throat.

"Already," continued the gentleman, "they have sat there three hours, each has fired twice, and the cockerel still unscathed. They are like to be there all day. What think you of that?"

"Why," rejoined the stranger, "I think it right good shootin'—and right good luck, suh, also."

The colloquy was interrupted by the resounding boom of the heavy rifle. The chicken squawked and leaped convulsively to the end of its tether. A tail feather whirled aloft and floated gently to the earth. The marksman laid aside his piece with the deep sigh of relief from long tension.

"Yore turn," he informed his rival curtly.

Beneath an arbor, and in charge of a young chap of about Don's age, was located the official sales place for ammunition. Here were canisters of the best French powder, both of the very fine grain for priming the pan, and of the coarser grain for the charge in the barrel; and clear, beautifully shaped English flints, each guaranteed to be good for fifty shots; and frizzen pricks, plain or ornamental; and bars of lead; and twists of unspun flax for swabbing the bore. Besides these essentials were exhibits of other things, brought either for sale or as samples by which to order. Of the former were hand-forged traps; moccasins and shot pouches sewn and decorated by the women; tomahawks fashioned by blacksmiths; knives of various shapes and hardness of blade; powder horns scraped so thin that the grains of powder could be seen through their sides. This bazaar was a sort of company affair; and the young man in charge was paid by fees from whoever had matters to advertise or things to sell. Thus he was prepared to take orders for the products of any one of the half-dozen or so gunmakers of the neighborhood; or to accept for reboring worn-down or rusted barrels, and either to ream out the old bullet mold to fit the new size or to supply a new mold. Between other activities he demonstrated over and over a new invention for the kindling of fire. This was in appearance a sort of pistol, with a very small stock, a full-sized flintlock, and a barrel not over an inch long, but with a huge bore fully as wide. The young man stuffed into this barrel a tight wad of unspun flax, poured a little gunpowder into the pan, and pulled the trigger. From the muzzle he pulled the smoldering flax and blew it to a glow. He extolled this simple contraption highly as an immense improvement over the ordinary flint and steel; but he sold few. The thing was expensive; and citizens settled in houses rarely required to make new fire, for they took good care to bank their coals. As for the backwoods farmers, they plugged the touch hole of their rifles, placed the flax in the pans, and got the same result. If the plug did not fit tightly enough the maneuver might result not only in the desired fire, but also in a badly frightened family and a bullet among the pewter; but it worked.

Since it was by now approaching noon, Don next took his way to the refreshment bower, where, after careful inquiry of prices, he purchased a half-loaf of bread, a slice of cold venison, and a chunk of cheese. With these he retired to sit with his back against a post, unsheathed his knife, and set to with a hearty appetite. For several minutes, so busy was he with his meal, he did not overhear the conversation near him. Then he could not but become aware that the four very solid men who sat at the table above him were members of the same craft as his host. He could not see their faces, but the wide broad-clothed backs presented to him were the very sign of pompous dignity. Their talk was technical and therefore interesting to the young man; and he did not scruple to listen, though rather idly, and off the surface of his attention. It had to do with the softness and the toughness of various charcoal irons as materials for barrels; and the relative merits of sugar or red maplewood for stocks; and the pros and cons as to whether it paid better to import Belgian-made locks entire—which they acknowledged to be excellent—or to make them at home, in which case a man knew what he had; and a rather sneering unanimity of opinion as to some visionary who had ideas as to the value of gain twist, which evidently had been suggested to him by specimens of early arquebuses.

"There is always a fool or so thinks he can improve upon the ripe wisdom of the craft," remarked the broadest back contemptuously. "I have seen in my time a score such who would overturn the world."

"And speaking of such, I see not Master Farrell's sour face to-day," observed another.

"I deem his absence no loss to the company," pronounced broad-back. "I doubt not he mourns in private his champion's fall."

"How is that? What mean ye?" queried a third.

"Have ye not heard? Nay, but that is the choicest morsel of all."

"I arrived but an hour since," explained the other.

"Why," began broad-back in the unctuous tones of one about to retail a cozy bit of gossip, "Master Farrell, I would have you know, had retained John Gladden to shoot for him in the great match."

"Nay," rejoined the other with asperity, "that I know but too well; for I had thought to engage him for myself."

"Good fortune, then, attended you," said broad-back: and paused relishingly for the question.

"Good fortune? How now?" it came.

"Why, that this John Gladden will not hold a piece to-day, nor yet for many days to come; and the reason is simple—that he cannot, on account that his arm is broken in two places."

Don jerked back his head, his whole attention caught.

Broad-back chuckled.

"See ye not our good-man Farrell——" He was going on, when he felt his shoulder seized; and, turning in outraged dignity at the unmannerly assault, met two blazing blue eyes within a foot of his own.

"Broken, you say? How happed that?" cried their owner.

"How now, sirrah——" But broad-back broke off his indignation with a stare of recognition. "Meseems you should know that," he chuckled. "For, if my eyes deceive me not, you are he who—"

But the young man was gone.

10

With swift strides he threaded his way through the crowd, shook himself free from the throng, and breaking into a long and easy lope hastened toward the village street. But before he had gained to the first of the houses he recognized to his left a small figure hurrying in the opposite direction, and so changed his course to encounter it.

"Have ye seen or heard aught of John Gladden?" called his host agitatedly as he neared, "for he hath not—"

"Master Farrell," the young man cut him short, "I think I have unwittingly done to you the greatest disservice man has ever done another."

So manifest was his distress that the gunmaker's own anxiety was set aside.

"Why how can that be, lad?" he asked.

Almost breathlessly Don told of the incident of the two dogs and the little girl; and of how he had been forced against his will to take up the foolish quarrel; and of the fight in the stable yard on account of it; and of how it fared. The old man listened attentively.

"But that was well done," he commented, "and I am much beholden to you."

"But that is not all, suh," insisted the young man. "So we fought, and I do not know how it would have gone with me, for he was very strong. At last he caught me in his grip, and then—then, suh, he sought to gouge my eyes! I had not thought men in fair fight would strive to maim; but he whom they called the Squire would have it so, and those standing about called it fair play. It is not thus with us on the border, suh; for when men settle disputes they wrestle fairly and fight as white men fight, not as savages do. So then I knew this was war."

"Yes, lad, and then?"

"Then, suh, I fit as a man fights in war, when his piece is empty, and he cannot come at his tomahawk or his knife. I used a trick long known to the Injins, and which I learned from them. By it I broke his arm, and so the fight ended."

"But, lad, that was well done," the old man repeated, "and you can take no blame to yourself for that."

"Nay, suh, I knew it not. I have but just now learned—" He hesitated, in obvious distress.

"What, lad?" the gunmaker had not yet guessed.

"The man was John Gladden."

A long silence fell while Farrell digested this information.

"Meseems I would gladly have lost an eye had not this happed—" The young man faltered, but Farrell stopped him with a peremptory gesture.

"Nay," he commanded. "You could do no different. I do not blame you. Nay, it was well done."

He drooped visibly nevertheless; remained for some moments in thought; bowed his head, then straightened with an assumed cheerfulness.

"We must accept what fortune brings," said he.

"Is it too late, suh, to seek out another—" began the young man anxiously.

The gunmaker cut him short with a decisive shake of the head.

"The Match is even now about to be called," said he, "and every marksman worth the name is long since bespoke. Nor would I place the piece in the hands of any less."

They stood there facing one another, the younger man almost wringing his hands in distress; the older contemplating the ground in a brown study. Suddenly he straightened.

"I have it!" he cried. "You shall take his place!"

"I, suh!" stammered the stranger, taken aback.

"Even you," stated the old man with decision. "You can do no less."

"But, suh," expostulated Don, "I am not fitten to stand with these men. I would not do ye a further disservice. I am not practised in these affairs. I care not for myself, but the new piece, suh—"

"Enough!" the old man cut him short with authority. "If I am willing, how should you draw back?"

"But you know not that my aim is true."

"I watched you last even as you handled the piece to your cheek. I marked you well, and I will stake my chances on your skill. Come, I ask it. You can do no less."

"If you are set upon it, I can but make the trial," agreed the young man, hesitating and troubled.

"I am set upon it."

"I can but do my best," then said he.

The volatile old man, his spirits popping up like a balloon, leaped into the air and cracked his heels together twice.

"That's my lad!" he cried heartily. "And now we must haste; for an we be not there to answer when the match is called, we shall lose our place."

He trotted back in the direction of his house, his very gait bouncing into a confidence evidently not shared by the troubled youth following at his heels. At the house Farrell carefully wrapped the new rifle in a blanket.

"They shall see no sight of it afore the time," he babbled, thrusting the muffled piece into the lad's hands. "And now let us see: here is the great powder horn, and the smaller with priming; and here is the stock of balls, and not one flawed one among them; and spare flints; yes, and a stout frizzen prick; and patches and grease in the butt—all is here; let us hasten back."

"But, suh," expostulated Don, "have I no chance to fire the piece first that I may test my holding?"

"No time now; no time," returned the old man testily. "Come, hasten; or even yet we may be too late!"

"That is a hard task you place on me, suh," observed the stranger, but more in comment than complaint.

"Hold a fine sight," panted the gunmaker as he trotted along, "hold fine, and dead center. Allow for no error; merely hold true."

The young man sighed resignedly.

"And the trigger pull, suh?" he suggested. "I have not even the feel of that."

"You will find it smooth as a hound's tooth," rejoined the other, "so that a baby's touch would suffice to trip the hammer. There is but one thing to watch. In your loading see that you center the ball on the patch, for if it be to one side or the other by any great span, the ball will not fly quite so true."

11

At the Bend all firing had ceased. Even the two men still patiently engaged in plucking with their bullets the cockerel's tail had been ordered to desist; and that demoralized fowl was enjoying a respite and the continued possession of two widely separated feathers. The concourse, which now numbered almost every available human being, was held back of a designated line by men whose official position was advertised by a white handkerchief bound about the left arm. The open space in front was occupied only by the table at which still sat the Squire, flanked by two assistants. But even as Farrell and his guest—the former somewhat out of breath—reached the outskirts, one of the assistants arose and cried out a name in a great bull voice that could have been heard in the village street. A man, whom Don recognized as broad-back, pushed forward; at his elbow a small unobtrusive fellow chewing tobacco nonchalantly and carrying a rifle which, even from a distance, could plainly be distinguished as brand-new and of fine workmanship. The two took their places to the left of the table.

"We are but just in time," observed Farrell, removing his hat and mopping his brow. "They call the contestants. That is Master Detrick, the gunmaker from Lancaster, and the small man with him is Mark Dall who will fire for him."

But now the announcer was calling other names; and other men were coming forward in response. Unlike the more impromptu and lesser matches of the earlier part of the day, the entries for this Great Match had been all made and paid for and closed the day previous: and there remained now but the formality of reading the entrants from the list. So it went until fourteen men had taken their places, of whom five were gunmakers standing only in the rôle of sponsors, five their hired champions, and the other four free lances competing on their own for their chance at the "great fat ox" and the snap haunce gun and the glory. Then the announcer sat down.

"How now! How now!" cried Farrell, breaking through the cordon. "Find ye not my name on your list?"

The Squire slowly turned his great bulk to survey the speaker.

"And is it you, Master Farrell!" he exclaimed in surprise. He turned his eyes toward Detrick. "But of a certain it is here, and you are welcome."

"Then why was I not called?" indignantly demanded the gunmaker.

"We were informed," said the Squire slowly, "that you had withdrawn." He continued to stare at Detrick, until the latter stirred uneasily and muttered:

"It is known to all that John Gladden lies abed and——"

"You take much upon yourself, sir!" interrupted Farrell, hotly.

"Peace, gentlemen!" commanded the Squire with authority, "your name is here, Master Farrell. You will yourself shoot your match?"

"Nay, I have a man for that."

"His name?"

"Don—nay, I know not the rest. Where is the pesky lad?" Farrell searched vainly with his eyes in the shifting crowd.

"Put him down as Master Don," the Squire told the recorder. "Time passes. Your man fires last," he instructed Farrell. "See that he is here."

The first test was at one hundred yards. The targets were the six-inch wooden blocks already described. The number of shots, five. Each man was to fire once in rotation until the tally was complete.

Detrick's champion was called upon. The little man, still chewing his tobacco, stepped calmly forward. His piece was already charged, so all he had to do by way of preparation was to shake the priming powder into the pan. Any position was allowed, so Dall disposed himself deliberately with muzzle and elbow rest, aimed carefully for what seemed a very long time, and fired. His block spun backward as the heavy bullet smashed into it. Dall arose deliberately and withdrew to the background, where he at once set about an elaborate cleaning of his piece. One by one the other contestants took their turn. The majority followed his example in selecting the muzzle and elbow rest as the most certain; though one man lay prone; and one other sat, his elbows clamped between his knees. Of the nine, seven registered hits; and a murmur of admiration swept the spectators, for this was marvelous percentage. The location of the hits would not be determined until later; which delay enhanced the dramatic suspense.

"Master Don, firing for Master Farrell," called the announcer.

Farrell slapped the young man on the back and pushed him forward. "God be with ye, lad," he muttered.

He was shifting from one foot to the other nervously, and he was breathing sharply; but Don seemed unconcerned. He walked forward to the mark carrying the long rifle at trail, woodsman fashion. A wave of excited comment rose. Men's interest was caught by the strange appearance of the new weapon.

"Look at the length of that bar'l," they murmured to one another. "What think you is in the hinged boxes in the butt?" "Flints," suggested another.

Farrell suppressed a cry of anguish, for Don, instead of disposing himself in any one of the several positions that afforded a steadying rest, had squared to his shot standing upright on his two feet. And barely, it seemed, had the muzzle reached the level when, without perceptible pause for aim, as it seemed, the piece was discharged.

The excited babel was now full-voiced, for there was much to say.

"Don't you suppose the damn fool knows he don't have to shoot offhand?" "He didn't hardly take no aim at all!" "Must have a ha'r trigger and she went off on him accidental," surmised one sagely. And everybody

commented on the salient phenomenon of the whole performance; the sharp whip-like *crack* of the discharge, in arresting contrast to the full roar of the other rifles. The fact that the block of wood had been struck was unremarked, unimportant, dismissed as a lucky accident that could not recur in the same conditions.

"Lad! Lad!" agonized Farrell, as the young man returned to his side. "Be not so hasty and so rash! Get ye a steady rest, and assure your aim better!"

Don dropped the butt of the long rifle to the ground and prepared to reload.

"Nay, suh," he returned tranquilly. "I have never la'rned these fancy tricks. I must e'en do as I may; and my schooling has been in the forests. An I dwell upon my aim or seek a spot whereon to rest my piece I am like to lose either my dinner or my scalp."

"Think you you can hit the mark again?" asked Farrell anxiously.

"That we shall see in good time," replied Don. "But this I will say." His grave face lighted for an instant with a rare enthusiasm. "Never have I held a piece so sweet to the hand; never have I pulled trigger so smooth to the touch; never have I looked across sights so clear to the eye. And if the ball speeds as true as the rifle holds, why, then, suh, without wishin' to boast, I may say that I will knock over those bits of wood as long as men will cut 'em fo' me!"

Suddenly he lapsed into an embarrassed silence.

"I babble overmuch," he muttered; and went on loading.

The second round proceeded with no more than the usual cries of encouragement and comment. But when the young stranger again methodically took his place, and with the same absence of delay proceeded to spin his second block of wood from its resting place, the noise rose to a pandemonium, and the guards found difficulty in holding back the surge of the crowd.

Farrell was hopping about with joy; and the young man himself showed symptoms of excitement. But it was the excitement of a growing interest and enthusiasm, not of nervousness, against which now his patron was frantically urging him to beware. At last Don stopped him with a good-humored laugh.

"I will do my possible, suh," he reassured the old man. "And I think you need not be afeard, for yore billets carry neither arrows nor fusees, nor are they like to run away."

The five rounds finished at last and in an excitement that constantly grew, for never had the like been seen before. Men told one another that they were present at the greatest shooting match ever known. All records had gone by the board. For of the fifty shots delivered, thirty-seven had found the mark, which in itself was enough to make history. And of the thirty-seven hits, five must be accredited to the young stranger! He had not once missed!

This alone was sufficient to set men's tongues clacking with amazement. But still remained the decision; for the award must go to him whose ball had struck closest to dead center, and all awaited the announcement from the table on which the attendant Negro had piled the basketful of billets he had gathered up. Each had been marked with the name of its owner, of course, and the Squire and his assistants sorted them out and laid them aside for examination, and the contestants and their sponsors gathered close about, awaiting his verdict. At last the Squire looked up, and his broad face was amazed.

"Gentlemen," said he, holding up one of the blocks, and it could be seen that the ball had cut almost into the cross itself, "Here is the winning shot, and a good one it is. But, gentlemen, here are the others that come nearest." He exhibited one after the other four other targets, and of them all the farthest ball had centered not over three inches from perfection. "That is good shooting; each one of these is worthy of a prize, for never in the long years of my life have I seen the like!" He slowly arose to his full height, and his rubicund face was overspread with an emotion that was close to awe. "And this I must tell you, that these balls, one and all, were delivered by the same hand!" His face broke into a broad grin as he turned to Farrell. "Methinks," said he, "fate did you a shrewd good turn that this young man stood for you in the stead of Gladden. As for you, my lad, you shoot as well as you fight—or you fight as well as you shoot, I know not how to say it."

"It is the rifle," stated Don modestly. "Never was piece made that shot so true."

"A man cannot win at cards without an ace," agreed the Squire. "And of the rifle, more anon; for I confess myself curious to examine it. Natheless the holding was better than I have seen. But to your places, gentlemen. It waxeth toward evening, and we must finish. Announcer, call the list for the peg shot."

* * *

13

The Squire's command to proceed with the next stage of the Great Match was delayed in obedience to a storm of vigorous protest on the part of Detrick, backed by his fellow craftsmen, who demanded that this new-fangled contraption be excluded from competition. The basis of the protest seemed to be a vague "unfairness." But the Squire, grinning in relish over the situation, brushed this aside.

"Nay, my masters," he observed, with fundamental common sense, "I see nought of unfairness here. This is a contest of rifles; and while this new piece of Master Farrell's is of unusual appearance, and most certainly of unusual performance—and I confess myself curious to examine it further—it is most indubitably a rifle. Continue."

In the course of the subsequent proceedings the crowd fell from its vociferous excitement to a low buzz of attention that, strangely enough, seemed to have in its elements a strong compound of something curiously like awe. Or perhaps not so strangely. Possibly they felt across the occasion the shadow of greatness; realizing dimly in the instinctive parts of themselves that they assisted at one of those significant events that turn the currents of history. As why not? For in the chronicles of their country the patched ball and the grooved barrel were to play a great part and the sharp crack of the American rifle was destined to call them into far places.

The matches that succeeded were in no true sense contests, and need not here be described in what would prove wearisome detail. In the peg match each man fired five shots at seventy-five yards. Pegs were inserted in the bullet holes, and around the outside a string was stretched. He who had the shortest string was pronounced the winner. Of the others, the man Dall turned in one of nine and five eighths inches, which was commented upon as close to a record; but Don's measured but a scant five, and one shot a trifle out.[1] And even in the loading contest, which was a matter of speed and personal dexterity, the patched ball so advantaged Farrell's arm that Don reported ready in the astounding time of twenty seconds,[1] which far outdid his nearest competitor.

It was a clean sweep, and nobody awaited the Squire's formal announcement of the winner. The instant the Match had closed, the crowd swarmed about Farrell, eager to examine the new weapon, to hear the principles of its miraculous precision. The marksman, Dall, was the first to get his hands upon it, turning it over and over, his shrewd expert's eye noting its features, his ear cocked to Farrell's explanations.

"You must e'en make me one of these, Master Farrell," said he at the last. "I bespeak one now."

"And I!" "And I!" interposed several others.

It was the little gunmaker's great moment. He was the center of all attention, speaking his piece over and over again to changing audiences who listened to him with the keen and intelligent attention that men would now bestow on the impossible him who might suddenly bring forth a club that could never fail of a three-hundred-yard drive. Detrick and his fellow artisans stood apart in a disgruntlement that tried unsuccessfully for an air of disdain. Don, also apart, received likewise his share,

[1] These figures are actual measured records.

though lesser, of the attention. Men's eagerest interest centered for the moment—and practically so—more on the possibilities of the new weapon for themselves than on the feats they had witnessed. A few praised his marksmanship; but most pressed him for his impressions of the rifle; its trigger pull, its sights, its powder charge and the weight of the ball, and the secrets of its loading. The young man replied as best he could, but always in modest repudiation of his own part.

"Nay, sirs," he insisted, "ye must award the day to Master Farrell, not to me. For these others be noted marksmen, as you well know; and with this same rifle any one of them, or indeed any other man who is skilled to hold a piece, could have done as well, or better."

But at last the concourse began to thin. The sun was low and the air was cooling. Long flights of crows crossed the redness of the skies. Negroes and other servants were collecting together the various gear that had been used for the different purposes and were piling it in a wagon. Lines of men streamed across the fields toward the tavern's cheer. Here and there in the village shone lights in windows.

Farrell, freed at last, joined his guest, and the two turned toward home. The little gunmaker was still so excited that he fairly babbled. The young man strode silently at his side, listening.

"Did ye note their glum faces, lad!" cried Farrell. "And did ye see how their own very champions left them apart to come to me! And did you remark how each of them jumped to possess one of my rifles: nay, and gave order for them on the spot! I must hasten to write down their names, so that I shall not disappoint them! And," the old man chuckled triumphantly, "the matter that warms my heart the most is that now, will they, nill they, these stiff-necked obstinate fools must themselves make arms of my pattern—unless they would sell only to farmers and the like! That will grind their haughty souls. For, lad, you shall see, all the world shall now use the long grooved barrel and the patched ball; for the old style is past and gone, and ye shall soon see them only on the walls to be viewed by the curious, as one looks upon the arquebuses of ancient days!"

Which was in the main an excellent bit of soothsaying; though Master Farrell overlooked the asinine conservatism of government officialdom, or his prophetic eye would have seen the troops of otherwise progressive nations banging away with smooth-bore slugs a hundred years after.

But soon he turned his pæan of exultation.

"And you, lad!" he cried. "You were magnificent! Never have I seen any man who held so; and I have seen many of the best. You beat all records; as well I know, for I know them all."

"Nay, suh," repeated Don. "Any man who could hold a bar'l could have done the like. If so happed I beat records, as you say, it was because never on range before was fired a bar'l that shot so true."

"That is so. Natheless I do maintain, and always shall, that none could have done as well. Some might have done its equal from a rest, but none in my knowledge could have done so offhand."

The youth flushed with a pleasure he could not conceal.

"I am obleeged to you fo' your good opinion, suh," said he steadily. "And I am rejoiced if you deem I have been of service to you."

"Richly do you deserve the prize!" cried Farrell.

"Anon?" queried Don.

"The prize, lad," repeated the gunmaker. "Did you not realize it is yours?"

"Nay, suh. I but stood in your stead."

"Mine is the gold medal of the craft. Nay, do not protest. It goes to you according to established rule."

The young man stopped in his tracks.

"And what, suh," he inquired with quiet humor, "should I do with a 'great fat ox'? Drive it afore me on my journey?"

Farrell laughed appreciatively.

"I doubt not the matter may be compounded for a sum," said he. "I will charge myself with that. And I shall insist you take the further sum I would have paid John Gladden. That is but just."

"Why, suh," said Don, "I will not gainsay you but this is a welcome surprise, for the thought had not occurred to me, and I admit my purse is but slender."

"It is nought, nought!" cried Farrell. "And were it thrice as much I should still be in your debt; for were it not for this happy chance I would even yet be suffering scorn, and now I shall prosper greatly, for all men will desire a rifle of Farrell's make, and—"

He in his turn stopped short in the illumination of a sudden idea. He thrust the rifle, which he had been carrying, into the young man's hands.

"This is yours!" said he.

"Mine?" repeated Don, incredulously.

"Whose the better right? Nay, protest not; I shall not listen."

A slow flush overspread the youth's face; then drained away, leaving it almost pale.

"Gainsay me not!" commanded the gunmaker peremptorily. "I shall make scores, nay hundreds more; and all because of you."

"I cannot refuse you, suh," replied the young man in a low voice, "for I will confess that ever since I first pulled trigger at the Shooting my heart has been eaten with the desire for one such. But I know not how to tell you—"

"No need, lad; no need!" Farrell interrupted, his face glowing with pleasure. "And with it shall go molds for balls, and a horn thin as paper and—"

"Nay, suh, you overwhelm me!" expostulated Don. His head was up, and his eyes were far away. "I shall try to do it honor, suh," said he slowly, "and I can see it is to stand me in good stead, for I shall take it with me over the mountains to the west, where even now I am preparing to go."

"Over the mountains?"

"Into the land known as Kentucky, suh, where, save for John Finley, no man has trod."

"And the work of my hands shall be carried into new and strange lands!" exulted the gunmaker. "And what could better befall, for itself is new and strange! And so shall I share in a great undertaking! And," he cried, inspired, "so shall we name it, so that men forever shall speak of the Kentucky Rifle!" He reached his hand and took the weapon from the young man's grasp. "See, right here, I shall set it down, in fair engraved letters, your name and mine together. That I shall do before you depart. But I know you only as Don. What is your surname?"

The young man looked a little embarrassed.

"No, suh, my name is not Don," he confessed. "You misheard me; and I did not trouble to set you right."

"Not Don? What is it then?" rejoined the other.

"Dan, suh," said the young man. "Dan'l Boone."

THE FALL OF THE HOUSE OF USHER

EDGAR ALLAN POE

Son cœur est un luth suspendu;
Sitôt qu'on le touche il résonne.
—De Béranger

DURING the whole of a dull, dark, and soundless day in the autumn of the year, when the clouds hung oppressively low in the heavens, I had been passing alone, on horseback, through a singularly dreary tract of country, and at length found myself, as the shades of the evening drew on, within view of the melancholy House of Usher. I know not how it was—but, with the first glimpse of the building, a sense of insufferable gloom pervaded my spirit. I say insufferable; for the feeling was unrelieved by any of that half-pleasurable, because poetic, sentiment with which the mind usually receives even the sternest natural images of the desolate or terrible. I looked upon the scene before me—upon the mere house, and the simple landscape features of the domain—upon the bleak walls—upon the vacant eye-like windows—upon a few rank sedges—and upon a few white trunks of decayed trees—with an utter depression of soul which I can compare to no earthly sensation more properly than to the after-dream of the reveller upon opium—the bitter lapse into every-day life—the hideous dropping off of the veil. There was an iciness, a sinking, a sickening of the heart—an unredeemed dreariness of thought which no goading of the imagination could torture into aught of the sublime. What was it—I paused to think—what was it that so unnerved me in the contemplation of the House of Usher? It was a mystery all insoluble; nor could I grapple with the shadowy fancies that crowded upon me as I pondered. I was forced to fall back upon the unsatisfactory conclusion, that while, beyond doubt, there *are* combinations of very simple natural objects which have the power of thus affecting us, still the analysis of this power lies among considerations beyond our depth. It was possible, I reflected, that a mere different arrangement of the particulars of the scene, of the details of the picture, would be sufficient to modify, or perhaps to annihilate its capacity for sorrowful impression; and, acting upon this idea, I reined my horse to the precipitous brink of a black and lurid tarn that lay in unruffled lustre by the dwelling, and gazed down—but with a shudder even more thrilling than before—upon the remodelled and inverted images of the gray sedge, and the ghastly tree-stems, and the vacant and eye-like windows.

Nevertheless, in this mansion of gloom I now proposed to myself a sojourn of some weeks. Its proprietor, Roderick Usher, had been one of my boon companions in boyhood; but many years had elapsed since our last meeting. A letter, however, had lately reached me in a distant part of the country—a letter from him—which, in its wildly importunate nature, had admitted of no other than a personal reply. The MS. gave evidence of nervous agitation. The writer spoke of acute bodily illness—of a mental disorder which oppressed him—and of an earnest desire to see me, as his best and indeed his only personal friend, with a view of attempting, by the cheerfulness of my society, some alleviation of his malady. It was the manner in which all this, and much more, was said—it was the apparent *heart* that went with his request—which allowed me no room for hesitation; and I accordingly obeyed forthwith what I still considered a very singular summons.

Although, as boys, we had been even intimate associates, yet I really knew little of my friend. His reserve had been always excessive and habitual. I was aware, however, that his very ancient family had been noted, time out of mind, for a peculiar sensibility of temperament, displaying itself, through long ages, in many works of exalted art, and manifested, of late, in repeated deeds of munificent yet unobtrusive charity, as well as in a passionate devotion to the intricacies, perhaps even more than to the orthodox and easily recognizable beauties, of musical science. I had learned, too, the very remarkable fact, that the stem of the Usher race, all time-honored as it was, had put forth, at no period, any enduring branch; in other words, that the entire family lay in the direct line of descent, and had always, with very trifling and very temporary variation, so lain. It was this deficiency, I considered, while running over in thought the perfect keeping of the character of the premises with the accredited character of the people, and while speculating upon the possible influence which the one, in the long lapse of centuries, might have exercised upon the other—it was this deficiency, perhaps, of collateral issue, and the consequent undeviating transmission, from sire to son, of the patrimony with the name, which had, at length, so identified the two as to merge the original title of the estate in the quaint and equivocal appellation of the "House of Usher"—an appellation which seemed to include, in the minds of the peasantry who used it, both the family and the family mansion.

I have said that the sole effect of my somewhat childish experiment—that of looking down within the tarn—had been to deepen the first singular impression. There can be no doubt that the consciousness of the rapid increase of my superstition—for why should I not so term it?—served mainly to accelerate the increase itself. Such, I have long known, is the paradoxical law of all sentiments having terror as a basis. And it might have been for this reason only, that, when I again uplifted my eyes to the house itself, from its image in the pool, there grew in my mind a strange fancy—a fancy so ridiculous, indeed, that I but mention it to show the vivid force of the sensations which oppressed me. I had so worked upon my imagination as really to believe that about the whole mansion and domain there hung an atmosphere peculiar to themselves and their immediate vicinity—an atmosphere which had no affinity with the air of heaven, but which had reeked up from the decayed trees, and the gray wall, and the silent tarn—a pestilent and mystic vapor, dull, sluggish, faintly discernible, and leaden-hued.

Shaking off from my spirit what *must* have been a dream, I scanned more narrowly the real aspect of the building. Its principal feature seemed to be that of an excessive antiquity. The discoloration of ages had been great. Minute fungi overspread the whole exterior, hanging in a fine tangled web-work from the eaves. Yet all this was apart from any extraordinary dilapidation. No portion of the masonry had fallen; and there appeared to be a wild inconsistency between its still perfect adaptation of parts, and the crumbling condition of the individual stones. In this there was much that reminded me of the specious totality of old woodwork which has rotted for long years in some neglected vault, with no disturbance from the breath of the external air. Beyond this indication of extensive decay, however, the fabric gave little token of instability. Perhaps the eye of a scrutinizing observer might have discovered a barely perceptible fissure, which, extending from the roof of the building in front, made its way down the wall in a zigzag direction, until it became lost in the sullen waters of the tarn.

Noticing these things, I rode over a short causeway to the house. A servant in waiting took my horse, and I entered the Gothic archway of the hall. A valet, of stealthy step, thence conducted me, in silence, through many dark and intricate passages in my progress to the *studio* of his master. Much that I encountered on the way contributed, I know not how, to heighten the vague sentiments of which I have already spoken. While the objects around me—while the carvings of the ceilings, the sombre tapestries of the walls, the ebon blackness of the floors, and the phantasmagoric armorial trophies which rattled as I strode, were but matters to which, or to such as which, I had been accustomed from my infancy—while I hesitated not to acknowledge how familiar was all this—I still wondered to find how unfamiliar were the fancies which ordinary images were stirring up. On one of the staircases, I met the physician of the family. His countenance, I thought, wore a mingled expression of low cunning and perplexity. He accosted me with trepidation and passed on. The valet now threw open a door and ushered me into the presence of his master.

The room in which I found myself was very large and lofty. The windows were long, narrow, and pointed, and at so vast a distance from the black oaken floor as to be altogether inaccessible from within. Feeble gleams of encrimsoned light made their way through the trellised panes, and served to render sufficiently distinct the more prominent objects around; the eye, however, struggled in vain to reach the remoter angles of the chamber, or the recesses of the vaulted and fretted ceiling. Dark draperies hung upon the walls. The general furniture was profuse, comfortless, antique, and tattered. Many books and musical instruments lay scattered about, but failed to give any vitality to the scene. I felt that I breathed an atmosphere of sorrow. An air of stern, deep, and irredeemable gloom hung over and pervaded all.

Upon my entrance, Usher arose from a sofa on which he had been lying at full length, and greeted me with a vivacious warmth which had much in it, I at first thought, of an overdone cordiality—of the constrained effort of the *ennuyé* man of the world. A glance, however, at his countenance convinced me of his perfect sincerity. We sat down; and for some moments, while he spoke not, I gazed upon him with a feeling half of pity, half of awe. Surely, man had never before so terribly altered, in so brief a period, as had Roderick Usher! It was with difficulty that I could bring myself to admit the identity of the wan being before me with the companion of my early boyhood. Yet the character of his face had been at all times remarkable. A cadaverousness of complexion; an eye large, liquid, and luminous beyond comparison; lips somewhat thin and very pallid, but of a surpassingly beautiful curve; a nose of a delicate Hebrew model, but with a breadth of nostril unusual in similar formations; a finely moulded chin, speaking, in its want of prominence, of a want of moral energy; hair of a more than web-like softness and tenuity;—these features, with an inordinate expansion above the regions of the temple, made up altogether a countenance not easily to be forgotten. And now in the mere exaggeration of the prevailing character of these features, and of the expression they were wont to convey, lay so much of change that I doubted to whom I spoke. The now ghastly pallor of the skin, and the now miraculous lustre of the eye, above all things startled and even awed me. The silken hair, too, had been suffered to grow all unheeded, and as, in its wild gossamer texture, it floated rather than fell about the face, I could not, even with effort, connect its Arabesque expression with any idea of simple humanity.

In the manner of my friend I was at once struck with an incoherence—an inconsistency; and I soon found this to arise from a series of feeble and futile struggles to overcome an habitual trepidancy—an excessive nervous agitation. For something of this nature I had indeed been prepared, no less by his letter, than by reminiscences of certain boyish traits, and by conclusions deduced from his peculiar physical confirmation and temperament. His action was alternately vivacious and sullen. His voice varied rapidly from a tremulous indecision (when the animal spirits seemed utterly in abeyance) to that species of energetic concision—that abrupt, weighty, unhurried, and hollow-sounding enunciation—that leaden, self-balanced, and perfectly modulated guttural utterance, which may be observed in the lost drunkard, or the irreclaimable eater of opium, during the periods of his most intense excitement.

It was thus that he spoke of the object of my visit, of his earnest desire to see me, and of the solace he expected me to afford him. He entered, at some length, into what he conceived to be the nature of his malady. It was, he said, a constitutional and a family evil, and one for which he despaired to find a remedy—a mere nervous affection, he immediately added, which would undoubtedly soon pass off. It displayed itself in a host of unnatural sensations. Some of these, as he detailed them, interested and bewildered me; although, perhaps, the terms and the general manner of their narration had their weight. He suffered much from a morbid acuteness of the senses; the most insipid food was alone endurable; he could wear only garments of certain texture; the odors of all flowers were oppressive; his eyes were tortured by even a faint light; and there were but peculiar sounds, and these from stringed instruments, which did not inspire him with horror.

To an anomalous species of terror I found him a bounden slave. "I shall perish," said he, "I *must* perish in this deplorable folly. Thus, thus, and not otherwise, shall I be lost. I dread the events of the future, not in themselves, but in their results. I shudder at the thought of any, even the most trivial, incident, which may operate upon this intolerable agitation of soul. I have, indeed, no abhorrence of danger, except in its absolute effect—in terror. In this unnerved, in this pitiable, condition I feel that the period will sooner or later arrive when I must abandon life and reason together, in some struggle with the grim phantasm, FEAR."

I learned, moreover, at intervals, and through broken and equivocal hints, another singular feature of his mental condition. He was enchained by certain superstitious impressions in regard to the dwelling which he tenanted, and whence, for many years, he had never ventured forth—in regard to an influence whose supposititious force was conveyed in terms too shadowy here to be re-stated—an influence which some peculiarities in the mere form and substance of his family mansion had, by dint of long sufferance, he said, obtained over his spirit—an effect which the *physique* of the gray walls and turrets, and of the dim tarn into which they all looked down, had, at length, brought about upon the *morale* of his existence.

He admitted, however, although with hesitation, that much of the peculiar gloom which thus afflicted him could be traced to a more natural and far more palpable origin—to the severe and long-continued illness—indeed to the evidently approaching dissolution—of a tenderly beloved sister, his sole companion for long years, his last and only relative on earth. "Her decease," he said, with a bitterness which I can never forget, "would leave him (him, the hopeless and the frail) the last of the ancient race of the Ushers." While he spoke, the lady Madeline (for so was she called) passed through a remote portion of the apartment, and, without having noticed my presence, disappeared. I regarded her with an utter astonishment not unmingled with dread; and yet I found it impossible to account for such feelings. A sensation of stupor oppressed me as my eyes followed her retreating steps. When a door, at length, closed upon her, my glance sought instinctively and eagerly the countenance of the brother; but he had buried his face in his hands, and I could only perceive that a far more than ordinary wanness had overspread the emaciated fingers through which trickled many passionate tears.

The disease of the lady Madeline had long baffled the skill of her physicians. A settled apathy, a gradual wasting away of the person, and frequent although transient affections of a partially cataleptical character were the unusual diagnosis. Hitherto she had steadily borne up against the pressure of her malady, and had not betaken herself finally to bed; but on the closing in of the evening of my arrival at the house, she succumbed (as her brother told me at night with inexpressible agitation) to the prostrating power of the destroyer; and I learned that the glimpse I had obtained of her person would thus probably be the last I should obtain—that the lady, at least while living, would be seen by me no more.

For several days ensuing, her name was unmentioned by either Usher or myself; and during this period I was busied in earnest endeavors to alleviate the melancholy of my friend. We painted and read together, or I listened, as if in a dream, to the wild improvisations of his speaking guitar. And thus, as a closer and still closer intimacy admitted me more unreservedly into the recesses of his spirit, the more bitterly did I perceive the futility of all attempt at cheering a mind from which darkness, as if an inherent positive quality, poured forth upon all objects of the moral and physical universe in one unceasing radiation of gloom.

I shall ever bear about me a memory of the many solemn hours I thus spent alone with the master of the House of Usher. Yet I should fail in any attempt to convey an idea of the exact character of the studies, or of the occupations, in which he involved me, or led me the way. An excited and highly distempered ideality threw a sulphureous lustre over all. His long improvised dirges will ring forever in my ears. Among other things, I hold painfully in mind a certain singular perversion and amplification of the wild air of the last waltz of Von Weber. From the paintings over which his elaborate fancy brooded, and which grew, touch by touch, into vaguenesses at which I shuddered the more thrillingly, because I shuddered knowing not why—from these paintings (vivid as their images now are before me) I would in vain endeavor to educe more than a small portion which should lie within the compass of merely written words. By the utter simplicity, by the nakedness of his designs, he arrested and overawed attention. If ever mortal painted an idea, that mortal was Roderick Usher. For me at least, in the circumstances then surrounding me, there arose out of the pure abstractions which the hypochondriac contrived to throw upon his canvas, an intensity of intolerable awe, no shadow of which felt I ever yet in the contemplation of the certainly glowing yet too concrete reveries of Fuseli.

One of the phantasmagoric conceptions of my friend, partaking not so rigidly of the spirit of abstraction, may be shadowed forth, although feebly, in words. A small picture presented the interior of an immensely long and rectangular vault or tunnel, with low walls, smooth, white, and without interruption or device. Certain accessory points of the design served well to convey the idea that this excavation lay at an exceeding depth below the surface of the earth. No outlet was observed in any portion of its vast extent, and no torch or other artificial source of light was discernible; yet a flood of intense rays rolled throughout, and bathed the whole in a ghastly and inappropriate splendor.

I have just spoken of that morbid condition of the auditory nerve which rendered all music intolerable to the sufferer, with the exception of certain effects of stringed instruments. It was, perhaps, the narrow limits to which he thus confined himself upon the guitar which gave birth, in great measure, to the fantastic character of his performances. But the fervid *facility* of his *impromptus* could not be so accounted for. They must have been, and were, in the notes, as well as in the words of his wild fantasias (for he not unfrequently accompanied himself with rhymed verbal improvisations), the result of that intense mental collectedness and concentration to which I have previously alluded as observable only in particular moments of the highest artificial excitement. The words of one of these rhapsodies I have easily remembered. I was, perhaps, the more forcibly impressed with it as he gave it, because, in the under or mystic current of its meaning, I fancied that I perceived, and for the first time, a full consciousness on the part of Usher of the tottering of his lofty reason upon her throne. The verses, which were entitled "The Haunted Palace," ran vety nearly, if not accurately, thus:—

I.

In the greenest of our valleys,
By good angels tenanted,
Once a fair and stately palace—
Radiant palace—reared its head.
In the monarch Thought's dominion—
It stood there!
Never seraph spread a pinion
Over fabric half so fair.

II.

Banners yellow, glorious, golden,
On its roof did float and flow
(This—all this—was in the olden
Time long ago);
And every gentle air that dallied,
In that sweet day,
Along the ramparts plumed and pallid,
A winged odor went away.

III.

Wanderers in that happy valley
Through two luminous windows saw
Spirits moving musically
To a lute's well-tunèd law;
Round about a throne, where sitting
(Porphyrogene!)
In state his glory well befitting,
The ruler of the realm was seen.

IV.

And all with pearl and ruby glowing
Was the fair palace door,
Through which came flowing, flowing, flowing
And sparkling evermore,
A troop of Echoes whose sweet duty
Was but to sing,
In voices of surpassing beauty,
The wit and wisdom of their king.

V.

But evil things, in robes of sorrow,
Assailed the monarch's high estate;
(Ah, let us mourn, for never morrow
Shall dawn upon him, desolate!)

And, round about his home, the glory
  That blushed and bloomed
Is but a dim-remembered story
  Of the old time entombed.

VI.

And travellers now within that valley,
  Through the red-litten windows see
Vast forms that move fantastically
  To a discordant melody;
While, like a rapid ghastly river,
  Through the pale door;
A hideous throng rush out forever,
  And laugh—but smile no more.

I well remember that suggestions arising from this ballad led us into a train of thought wherein there became manifest an opinion of Usher's which I mention not so much on account of its novelty (for other men[1] have thought thus), as on account of the pertinacity with which he maintained it. This opinion, in its general form, was that of the sentience of all vegetable things. But, in his disordered fancy, the idea had assumed a more daring character, and trespassed, under certain conditions, upon the kingdom of inorganization. I lack words to express the full extent, or the earnest *abandon* of his persuasion. The belief, however, was connected (as I have previously hinted) with the gray stones of the home of his forefathers. The conditions of the sentence had been here, he imagined, fulfilled in the method of collocation of these stones—in the order of their arrangement, as well as in that of the many *fungi* which overspread them, and of the decayed trees which stood around—above all, in the long undisturbed endurance of this arrangement, and in its reduplication in the still waters of the tarn. Its evidence—the evidence of the sentience—was to be seen, he said (and I here started as he spoke), in the gradual yet certain condensation of an atmosphere of their own about the waters and the walls. The result was discoverable, he added, in that silent yet importunate and terrible influence which for centuries had moulded the destinies of his family, and which made *him* what I now saw him—what he was. Such opinions need no comment, and I will make none.

Our books—the books which, for years, had formed no small portion of the mental existence of the invalid—were, as might be supposed, in strict keeping with this character of phantasm. We pored together over such works as the "Ververt et Chartreuse" of Gresset; the "Belphegor" of Machiavelli; the "Heaven and Hell" of Swedenborg; the "Subterranean

[1] Watson, Dr. Percival, Spallanzani, and especially the Bishop of Landaff.—See "Chemical Essays," vol. v.

Voyage of Nicholas Klimm" of Holberg; the "Chiromancy" of Robert Flud, of Jean D'Indaginé, and of Dela Chambre; the "Journey into the Blue Distance of Tieck"; and the "City of the Sun of Campanella." One favorite volume was a small octavo edition of the "Directorium Inquisitorium," by the Dominican Eymeric de Gironne; and there were passages in Pomponius Mela, about the old African Satyrs and Œgipans, over which Usher would sit dreaming for hours. His chief delight, however, was found in the perusal of an exceedingly rare and curious book in quarto Gothic—the manual of a forgotten church—the *Vigiliœ Mortuorum secundum Chorum Ecclesiœ Maguntinœ.*

I could not help thinking of the wild ritual of this work, and of its probable influence upon the hypochondriac, when, one evening, having informed me abruptly that the lady Madeline was no more, he stated his intention of preserving her corpse for a fortnight (previously to its final interment), in one of the numerous vaults within the main walls of the building. The worldly reason, however, assigned for this singular proceeding, was one which I did not feel at liberty to dispute. The brother had been led to his resolution (so he told me) by consideration of the unusual character of the malady of the deceased, of certain obtrusive and eager inquiries on the part of her medical men, and of the remote and exposed situation of the burial-ground of the family. I will not deny that when I called to mind the sinister countenance of the person whom I met upon the staircase, on the day of my arrival at the house, I had no desire to oppose what I regarded as at best but a harmless, and by no means an unnatural, precaution.

At the request of Usher, I personally aided him in the arrangements for the temporary entombment. The body having been encoffined, we two alone bore it to its rest. The vault in which we placed it (and which had been so long unopened that our torches, half smothered in its oppressive atmosphere, gave us little opportunity for investigation) was small, damp, and entirely without means of admission for light; lying, at great depth, immediately beneath that portion of the building in which was my own sleeping apartment. It had been used, apparently, in remote feudal times, for the worst purposes of a donjon-keep, and, in later days, as a place of deposit for powder, or some other highly combustible substance, as a portion of its floor, and the whole interior of a long archway through which we reached it, were carefully sheathed with copper. The door, of massive iron, had been, also, similarly protected. Its immense weight caused an unusually sharp, grating sound, as it moved upon its hinges.

Having deposited our mournful burden upon tressels within this region of horror, we partially turned aside the yet unscrewed lid of the coffin, and looked upon the face of the tenant. A striking similitude between the brother and sister now first arrested my attention; and Usher, divining, perhaps, my thoughts, murmured out some few words from which I learned that the deceased and himself had been twins, and that sympathies of a scarcely intelligible nature had always existed between them. Our glances, however, rested not long upon the dead—for we could not regard her unawed. The disease which had thus entombed the lady in the maturity of youth, had left, as usual in all maladies of a strictly cataleptical character, the mockery of a faint blush upon the bosom and the face, and that suspiciously lingering smile upon the lip which is so terrible in death. We replaced and screwed down the lid, and, having secured the door of iron, made our way, with toil, into the scarcely less gloomy apartments of the upper portion of the house.

And now, some days of bitter grief having elapsed, an observable change came over the features of the mental disorder of my friend. His ordinary manner had vanished. His ordinary occupations were neglected or forgotten. He roamed from chamber to chamber with hurried, unequal, and objectless step. The pallor of his countenance had assumed, if possible, a more ghastly hue—but the luminousness of his eye had utterly gone out. The once occasional huskiness of his tone was heard no more; and a tremulous quaver, as if of extreme terror, habitually characterized his utterance. There were times, indeed, when I thought his unceasingly agitated mind was laboring with some oppressive secret, to divulge which he struggled for the necessary courage. At times, again, I was obliged to resolve all into the mere inexplicable vagaries of madness, for I beheld him gazing upon vacancy for long hours, in an attitude of the profoundest attention, as if listening to some imaginary sound. It was no wonder that his condition terrified—that it infected me. I felt creeping upon me, by slow yet certain degrees, the wild influences of his own fantastic yet impressive superstitions.

It was, especially, upon retiring to bed late in the night of the seventh or eighth day after the placing of the lady Madeline within the donjon, that I experienced the full power of such feelings. Sleep came not near my couch—while the hours waned and waned away. I struggled to reason off the nervousness which had dominion over me. I endeavored to believe that much, if not all of what I felt, was due to the bewildering influence of the gloomy furniture of the room—of the dark and tattered draperies, which, tortured into motion by the breath of a rising tempest, swayed fitfully to and fro upon the walls, and rustled uneasily about the decorations of the bed. But my efforts were fruitless. An irrepressible tremor gradually pervaded my frame; and, at length, there sat upon my very heart an incubus of utterly causeless alarm. Shaking this off with a gasp and a struggle, I uplifted myself upon the pillows, and, peering earnestly within the intense darkness of the chamber, hearkened—I know not why, except that an instinctive spirit prompted me—to certain low and indefinite sounds which came, through the pauses of the storm, at long intervals, I knew not whence. Overpowered by an intense sentiment of horror, unaccountable yet unendurable, I threw on my clothes with haste (for I felt that I should sleep no more during the night), and endeavored to arouse myself from the pitiable condition into which I had fallen, by pacing rapidly to and fro through the apartment.

I had taken but few turns in this manner, when a light step on an adjoining staircase arrested my attention. I presently recognized it as that of Usher. In an instant afterward he rapped, with a gentle touch, at my door, and entered, bearing a lamp. His countenance was, as usual, cadaverously wan—but, moreover, there was a species of mad hilarity in his eyes—an evidently restrained *hysteria* in his whole demeanor. His air appalled me—but any thing was preferable to the solitude which I had so long endured, and I even welcomed his presence as a relief.

"And you have not seen it?" he said abruptly, after having stared about him for some moments in silence—"you have not then seen it?—but, stay! you shall." Thus speaking, and having carefully shaded his lamp, he hurried to one of the casements, and threw it freely open to the storm.

The impetuous fury of the entering gust nearly lifted us from our feet. It was, indeed, a tempestuous yet sternly beautiful night, and one wildly singular in its terror and its beauty. A whirlwind had apparently collected its force in our vicinity; for there were frequent and violent alterations in the direction of the wind; and the exceeding density of the clouds (which hung so low as to press upon the turrets of the house) did not prevent our perceiving the life-like velocity with which they flew careering from all points against each other, without passing away into the distance. I say that even their exceeding density did not prevent our perceiving this—yet we had no glimpse of the moon or stars, nor was there any flashing forth of the lightning. But the under surfaces of the huge masses of agitated vapor, as well as all terrestrial objects immediately around us, were glowing in the unnatural light of a faintly luminous and distinctly visible gaseous exhalation which hung about and enshrouded the mansion.

"You must not—you shall not behold this!" said I, shuddering, to Usher, as I led him, with a gentle violence, from the window to a seat. "These appearances, which bewilder you, are merely electrical phenomena not uncommon—or it may be that they have their ghastly origin in the rank miasma of the tarn. Let us close this casement;—the air is chilling and dangerous to your frame. Here is one of your favorite romances. I will read, and you shall listen:—and so we will pass away this terrible night together."

The antique volume which I had taken up was the "Mad Trist" of Sir Launcelot Canning; but I had called it a favorite of Usher's more in sad jest than in earnest; for, in truth, there is little in its uncouth and unimaginative prolixity which could have had interest for the lofty and spiritual ideality of my friend. It was, however, the only book immediately at hand; and I indulged a vague hope that the excitement which now agitated the hypochondriac, might find relief (for the history of mental disorder is full of similar anomalies) even in the extremeness of the folly which I should read. Could I have judged, indeed, by the wild overstrained air of vivacity with which he hearkened, or apparently hearkened, to the words of the tale, I might well have congratulated myself upon the success of my design.

I had arrived at that well-known portion of the story where Ethelred, the hero of the Trist, having sought in vain for peaceable admission into the dwelling of the hermit, proceeds to make good an entrance by force. Here, it will be remembered, the words of the narrative run thus:

"And Ethelred, who was by nature of a doughty heart, and who was now mighty withal, on account of the powerfulness of the wine which he had drunken, waited no longer to hold parley with the hermit, who, in sooth, was of an obstinate and maliceful turn, but, feeling the rain upon his shoulders, and fearing the rising of the tempest, uplifted his mace outright, and, with blows, made quickly room in the plankings of the door for his gauntleted hand; and now pulling therewith sturdily, he so cracked, and ripped, and tore all asunder, that the noise of the dry and hollow-sounding wood alarumed and reverberated throughout the forest."

At the termination of this sentence I started and, for a moment, paused; for it appeared to me (although I at once concluded that my excited fancy had deceived me)—it appeared to me that, from some very remote portion of the mansion, there came, indistinctly to my ears, what might have been, in its exact similarity of character, the echo (but a stifled and dull one certainly) of the very cracking and ripping sound which Sir Launcelot had so particularly described. It was, beyond doubt, the coincidence alone which had arrested my attention; for, amid the rattling of the sashes of the casements, and the ordinary commingled noises of the still increasing storm, the sound, in itself, had nothing, surely, which should have interested or disturbed me. I continued the story:

"But the good champion Ethelred, now entering within the door, was sore enraged and amazed to perceive no signal of the maliceful hermit; but, in the stead thereof, a dragon of a scaly and prodigious demeanor, and of a fiery tongue, which sate in guard before a palace of gold, with a floor of silver; and upon the wall there hung a shield of shining brass with this legend enwritten—

> Who entereth herein, a conqueror hath bin;
> Who slayeth the dragon, the shield he shall win.

And Ethelred uplifted his mace, and struck upon the head of the dragon, which fell before him, and gave up his pesty breath, with a shriek so horrid and harsh, and withal so piercing, that Ethelred had fain to close his ears with his hands against the dreadful noise of it, the like whereof was never before heard."

Here again I paused abruptly, and now with a feeling of wild amazement—for there could be no doubt whatever that, in this instance, I did actually hear (although from what direction it proceeded I found it impossible to say) a low and apparently distant, but harsh, protracted, and most unusual screaming or grating sound—the exact counterpart of what my fancy had already conjured up for the dragon's unnatural shriek as described by the romancer.

Oppressed, as I certainly was, upon the occurrence of this second and most extraordinary coincidence, by a thousand conflicting sensations, in which wonder and extreme terror were predominant, I still retained sufficient presence of mind to avoid exciting, by any observation, the sensitive nervousness of my companion. I was by no means certain that he had noticed the sounds in question; although, assuredly, a strange alteration had, during the last few minutes, taken place in his demeanor. From a position fronting my own, he had gradually brought round his chair, so as to sit with his face to the door of the chamber; and thus I could but partially perceive his features, although I saw that his lips trembled as if he were murmuring inaudibly. His head had dropped upon his breast—yet I knew that he was not asleep, from the wide and rigid opening of the eye as I caught a glance of it in profile. The motion of his body, too, was at variance with this idea—for he rocked from side to side with a gentle yet constant and uniform sway. Having rapidly taken notice of all this, I resumed the narrative of Sir Launcelot, which thus proceeded:

"And now, the champion, having escaped from the terrible fury of the dragon, bethinking himself of the brazen shield, and of the breaking up of the enchantment which was upon it, removed the carcass from out of the way before him, and approached valorously over the silver pavement of the castle to where the shield was upon the wall; which in sooth tarried not for his full coming, but fell down at his feet upon the silver floor, with a mighty great and terrible ringing sound."

No sooner had these syllables passed my lips, than—as if a shield of brass had indeed, at the moment, fallen heavily upon a floor of silver—I became aware of a distinct, hollow, metallic, and clangorous, yet apparently muffled, reverberation. Completely unnerved, I leaped to my feet; but the measured rocking movement of Usher was undisturbed. I rushed to the chair in which he sat. His eyes were bent fixedly before him, and throughout his whole countenance there reigned a stony rigidity. But, as I placed my hand upon his shoulder, there came a strong shudder over his whole person; a sickly smile quivered about his lips; and I saw that he spoke in a low, hurried, and gibbering murmur, as if unconscious of my

presence. Bending closely over him, I at length drank in the hideous import of his words.

"Now hear it?—yes, I hear it, and *have* heard it. Long—long—long—many minutes, many hours, many days, have I heard it—yet I dared not—oh, pity me, miserable wretch that I am!—I dared not—I *dared* not speak! *We have put her living in the tomb!* Said I not that my senses were acute? I *now* tell you that I heard her first feeble movements in the hollow coffin. I heard them—many, many days ago—yet I dared not—*I dared not speak!* And now—to-night—Ethelred—ha! ha!—the breaking of the hermit's door, and the death-cry of the dragon, and the clangor of the shield—say, rather, the rending of her coffin, and the grating of the iron hinges of her prison, and her struggles within the coppered archway of the vault! Oh! whither shall I fly? Will she not be here anon? Is she not hurrying to upbraid me for my haste? Have I not heard her footstep on the stair? Do I not distinguish that heavy and horrible beating of her heart? Madman!"—here he sprang furiously to his feet, and shrieked out his syllables, as if in the effort he were giving up his soul—"*Madman! I tell you that she now stands without the door!*"

As if in the superhuman energy of his utterance there had been found the potency of a spell, the huge antique panels to which the speaker pointed threw slowly back, upon the instant, their ponderous and ebony jaws. It was the work of the rushing gust—but then without those doors there *did* stand the lofty and enshrouded figure of the lady Madeline of Usher. There was blood upon her white robes, and the evidence of some bitter struggle upon every portion of her emaciated frame. For a moment she remained trembling and reeling to and fro upon the threshold—then, with a low moaning cry, fell heavily inward upon the person of her brother, and in her violent and now final death-agonies, bore him to the floor a corpse, and a victim to the terrors he had anticipated.

From that chamber, and from that mansion, I fled aghast. The storm was still abroad in all its wrath as I found myself crossing the old causeway. Suddenly there shot along the path a wild light, and I turned to see whence a gleam so unusual could have issued; for the vast house and its shadows were alone behind me. The radiance was that of the full, setting, and blood-red moon, which now shone vividly through that once barely discernible fissure, of which I have before spoken as extending from the roof of the building, in a zigzag direction, to the base. While I gazed, this fissure rapidly widened—there came a fierce breath of the whirlwind—the entire orb of the satellite burst at once upon my sight—my brain reeled as I saw the mighty walls rushing asunder—there was a long tumultuous shouting sound like the voice of a thousand waters—and the deep and dank tarn at my feet closed sullenly and silently over the fragments of the "*House of Usher.*"

A Novel

THE VOICE OF BUGLE ANN

MACKINLAY KANTOR

THE VOICE OF BUGLE ANN

MACKINLAY KANTOR

1

HER voice was something to dream about, on any night when she was running through the hills. The first moment she was old enough to boast an individual voice, Springfield Davis swore that she would be a great dog, and within another month he had given her the name she carried so proudly.

One of her great-grandfathers, many generations removed, had followed Spring Davis away from home when he went off to join General Claiborne Jackson and his homespun army among the prickly-orange hedges, so there was logic in the inheritance which put that trumpet in her throat.

She was slender, like hounds of the Spaulding line, and not as sprawling or cumbersome as the good-natured, long-tongued Walkers. Any one in Missouri who knew anything about fox-hounds had heard of the Davis dogs, but somehow there never came to be a Davis line. It was all in the family, and there existed a haughtiness in the old man which wouldn't permit him to have Davis dogs running anywhere except in the ranges along Heaven Creek. That was why Bugle Ann was still a maiden at five years, long after old Calhoun Royster or the Lanceys would have seen to it that she carried on her business in life.

And Spring Davis was prudish past the point of ridicule, though no one would have dared to laugh at him. He hated the common word for a female dog, and would not let it touch his tongue. He called his she-dogs ladies or girls, and there was a firm beauty about him when he spoke to them. You wouldn't think that a man like that could ever be tried for murder, or become a convict.

Those things did happen to Spring Davis, at eighty-two. They didn't affect him as they would have affected most men of eighty-two. Whenever he heard the gongs and whistles which sent him about his gray routine at

Jefferson City, he must have banished those sounds from his consciousness. He must have imagined instead that he was sitting by a fire at the edge of Bachelor's timber, listening to the dogs as they hunted out of Chilly Branch Hollow, with Bugle Ann's cry echoing against the blackness of the sky.

2

"Bake," said old Cal Royster, "put some wood on."

Baker went to the woodpile beyond the red circle and found a piece of rotten stump. "We'll have a good moon by next week," he said, and jammed the wood upon the coals.

"I don't give shucks for moonlight," exclaimed Cal Royster. "Give me a black-dark night, when the fox ain't shadow-shy. Any fool ought to know that. I don't know where my boys get such notions as moonlight nights."

Across the fire, Spring Davis tapped his pipe against the heel of his boot. He stopped, suddenly, head tilted to one side. The firelight turned his shaggy mustache and eyebrows to fluid metal.

"Listen," he said. "Getting sweet."

His son, Benjy Davis, rose to his feet. He moved like an Indian; so did his father. There was something of the Indian in Benjy's twenty-year-old face, tanned and narrow and bony.

His black eyes glittered. "He's a mighty sweet fox if they've had him away over toward the river! We ain't heard a sound for twenty minutes."

There were five men around that fire at the edge of Bachelor's timber. Four of them—Spring Davis and his only son, Benjy, and Calhoun Royster and his oldest son, Baker—were the most ardent fox-hound men in the county. The fifth man was no hound man at all; he was a new insurance agent from Wolf Center. He had eaten supper at the Davises', and he was beside that fire only by invitation and sufferance.

He inquired, "What do you mean, Mr. Davis? 'Getting sweet.'"

"It sweats," Spring told him. "The fox does. They can smell him better after he's been running awhile. That's 'getting sweet.'"

Now even the agent's untrained ears could detect a faint distraction amid the common night sounds—the hush of sleeping forests that never sleep, and which is really no hush at all. The sound came from over past the Armstrong place, far past Chilly Branch and across the ridge beyond, and it was as eerie and elusive as the calling of wild geese.

"You'll hear her in a minute," whispered Springfield Davis.

The confused murmur became a tiny baying: the tongues of many dogs, eager and striving in spite of their two-hour run.

"That's Toul Sector," Bake Royster declared. Bake had been in the war, and all the Royster dogs were named Toul Sector or Border Service or General Bullard or some such name.

"It's not Toul Sector," said Benjy. "Not that nearest one."

Calhoun Royster's tone showed the jealous annoyance which he displayed frequently with the self-assured Davises. "It's no Bugle Ann, neither," he snorted. "Nor no Bill Bryan, nor Cox, nor Frances Cleveland, nor any Davis dog."

"Reckon it is a bit turkey-mouthed for one of ours."

Old Spring Davis loved to hear Cal swear in his beard. So he continued, "I'll tell you, Cal. It's an Armstrong dog. They've picked up an Armstrong as they come past."

Royster stood with head wiggling on his humped shoulders, his bearded lips hanging open as he tried to take that baying apart and examine it. "What Armstrong dog?" he demanded. He seemed to be weakening.

"I'd say it was Jackie Cooper, that little pale-faced two-year-old."

Old man Royster listened a moment longer. He gave a defeated snort. Then his ire mounted. "Where in hell's Bugle Ann, anyway?"

"Maybe she'll quit, and come in," muttered his son.

Benjy whirled, and for a moment the insurance agent thought that he was going to strike Bake Royster. "No Davis dog ever come in without being called, before a fox holed," Benjy said. "Except one. You remember him. We shot him the next day."

Spring nodded. "Easy boy. . . . Guess there's bound to be a black sheep in every tribe, though this dog was white. Don't you folks worry about Bugle Ann. You'll hear her soon enough."

"Pshaw, scat," said Bake, uneasily, "I was just joking."

On such a night as this, with clouds covering the stars and no southeast wind smothering the scent, you could tell that the hounds were running with their heads high. They skirted the eastern boundary of Chilly Branch Hollow, and straightened out along the higher ridge which swung toward Bachelor's woods.

All the men were on their feet.

"You talk moonlight," Royster chided his son. "Never get a fox to keep the high ground except on this kind of night. Lose half the sound when them dogs get in a gulley."

There was a turkey-mouth among those ringing voices; old Spring had been right about the Armstrong dog. The Royster dogs were mainly chop-mouthed, and they sent their clipped, bristling bay like a volley across the wooded plateau.

"I don't hear her, Pa," whispered Benjy Davis, with some concern.

The old man held up his hand. Suddenly a new cry was born amid all the hissing of excited crickets.

For some reason, the Wolf Center insurance agent felt the hair prickle on his neck. . . . This was no hound-voice such as he had ever heard before, and he would never hear its like again. It was a bugle—the Davises had a rare poetry in their make-up, thought young Mr. Mayor of the National Emblem Liability. He stood there with his nails cutting his palms, and listened.

"That's her, all right," came Cal Royster's admission, "but why's she kiting off by herself? If she hain't lost it, I'm loony."

Spring Davis repeated the word, "Lost," and smiled into the fire. . . . There had never been a sound like that in the Heaven Creek country until Bugle Ann was born; even now the trumpet-cry knew its own pride, and swung off toward the southeast, far ahead of the *owk-owk-owk-owk* with which the Royster dogs threatened.

The old man whooped, without any warning: "Now, there they go after her!"

Left, around the last spur of Bachelor's woods, the welter of hounds went sweeping after Bugle Ann. Her cry soared ahead—high, round, with that queer and brassy resonance which made you think that ghosts were out there somewhere, sounding Taps without any armies to follow them.

Springfield Davis came back to the fire and squatted on his heels. "You see," he told the insurance agent, "Bugle Ann was running that same fox night-before-last. I reckon she remembered how he likes to feint west along a little draw that's over there, and then double back and cut his own trail. It's a common fox trick if the fox has got the nerve to try it, and easy for him to work when the scent's heavy."

"I'm afraid," said Mr. Mayor, "that I don't understand."

"Well," said Cal Royster, somewhat reluctantly, "the average dog is bound to foller the way he's headed, if the smell is hauling him."

They were silent for a moment, listening to the baying as it swam fainter and fainter into the darkness.

"I'm afraid I don't understand any of this," Mr. Mayor cried with honesty. "I came from the East, just this year. They gave me this Missouri territory and— Fox-hunting! If you hunt every night or two, I don't see how you have any foxes left."

Bake Royster added more wood to the fire, and Benjy Davis brought up the sandwich sack. "We never kill the fox," said Spring, sharply. "We don't ride no horses, nor wear funny coats and caps. We raise dogs, and train them."

Waken, lords and ladies gay, thought Mr. Mayor in his baffled mind. *All the jolly chase is here, with* . . . "But it's really just a race between fox and dogs, then?"

"Fox holes up when he gets tired, and the dogs come home."

"And the same fox will run again, another night?"

"There's quite a slew of them around. Plenty of mice and ground-squirrels for them to eat; they never bother no hen roosts. Yes, they run again. Night after night, and year after year."

Benjy opened a battered vacuum bottle and poured a cup of coffee for his father. The gray-headed man touched the hot tin cup with cautious fingers. "Year after year," he repeated, dreamily.

The insurance agent choked over a bacon sandwich. "Are you folks—and you also, Mr. Royster—the only people who do this sort of thing?"

Spring Davis looked up from the fire. "Young man, did you ever hear of Old Man Spaulding? Reckon not. Or Gentry German, Parrish, or Colonel Trigg?"

"I suppose," Mr. Mayor replied, "that those are dogs."

"Those are men who made fox-hound history in America. And Wash Maupin, and Robert Rodes, and James Kanatzar. You see, sir, it's a matter of breeding good dogs—and understanding them—and—kind of loving them. It—" He broke off suddenly.

Cal Royster blinked at the gems of flame which shone through the whisky flask in his hand. "Speaking of names, Spring," he began, "you ought to take our friend here, over to the Armstrongs. You see, mister, Ed Armstrong is mighty religious and his boys are mighty the other way."

"Always going to town," put in Bake, "to dances and moving pictures and rotation pool, and things."

His father insisted, "But they do hunt. They name their dogs after moving picture actors. Old Ed Armstrong, he names his after religious folks. Until you've heard the Armstrong pack after a good, sweet fox, you hain't heard a thing. All turkey-mouthed, or squawl-horn-chop-mouthed at the best. Until you've heard Billy Sunday and Jackie Cooper and Dwight L. Moody and Zasu Pitts and Hoot Gibson and Mary Magdalene all driving a fox at once, you never have had no treat give to you."

"They're good bench dogs," said Spring Davis. He didn't like to hear too much laughter directed at the Armstrongs. "They mostly got stylish tails and compact feet and good stifles. If you like bench, the Armstrong dogs just hustle in the points."

He held up his hand, and Cal Royster put away the whisky bottle.

"Coming in," Davis prophesied. "I can get it, from 'way south, at the top of Heaven Creek."

Benjy swore; his face was very dark. "Blame fox won't give them more'n three hours any more."

"That's a fact," nodded his father. "We'll have to try farther up Heaven Creek to-morrow."

Mr. Mayor burst out, "Good Lord, do you do this all night, every night? When do you do your farm work?" He began to understand why Spring Davis had been unable to renew his fire insurance policy.

"Not every night," said Springfield. "Sometimes it rains. Or just the opposite, sometimes the weather's been too dry. Or we get long damp spells—too damp—or we get low southeast winds. We don't come out every night."

"Mr. Davis," cried Mr. Mayor of the National Emblem Liability, "how old are you?"

Spring smiled into the fire. "Seventy years ago this season, I ran off to join the Confederate army. I was only twelve, but I had done a sight of fox-hunting before that."

The hounds came closer, and once more Bugle Ann's blare was riding high above their hooted chorus.

"He's striking for his hole," Bake said. "In a minute he'll hand them the raspberry."

Spring Davis leaned back and closed his eyes. He drew a deep breath. "Waited seventy years to have a dog like that," he whispered to nobody in particular.

The fox uttered his shout of defiance—that strange yelp which was half a cat-cry, half a dog-bark, and wholly insulting. Then baffled shrieks told that he had holed.

"Fetch the horn, Benjy," ordered old Davis. "I don't want her sporting around."

Cal Royster bristled. "This ain't August nor yet February. You talk like our dogs was a pack of hoodlums."

"I just like to have her to home, Cal."

From beside a rolled up sweater, Benjy Davis brought a battered army bugle and gave it to his father. The old man wet his lips, fitted the mouthpiece carefully beneath his shaggy mustache, and blew two notes: the *ta-da* of galloping Valkyries, forever a summons and a challenge.

"Will she come for that?" Mr. Mayor asked in amazement.

"Always."

Benjy peered toward the crossing at Heaven Creek. "Looks like some other folks are coming, too."

The dull, yellow lights of an old Ford were rocking toward them, and they could hear the chatter of its motor. "That'll be Tom and Delbert, I reckon," said Cal Royster. "Don't know what's got into them. Been to see the Lancey girls again. They'd ruther spark around with two flibbertygibbets than be out with the dogs."

Slowly the Ford rattled up the hill, and stopped at the wood road. The two younger Royster boys got out with cheers of greeting, which were stilled hastily when they saw a stranger at the fire.

"How's the calf market?" taunted their elder brother.

"Never you mind," grunted Delbert Royster. He and Tom were sunburned, strapping youngsters who would have looked happier in overalls than in the Sunday suits they had worn for their squiring.

Their faces were unwontedly serious, and neither of them headed for the sandwiches.

"What in time ails you two?" demanded Cal.

"You heard about the old Camden place?" countered Delbert.

Every one except the insurance agent looked automatically toward the northwest. A mile down the valley of Heaven Creek stood an abandoned house and farm buildings, which in daylight showed plainly from their hill.

"I did hear that somebody was moving on it," said the father.

"Some of the Camdens, coming back," added Baker.

Old Spring Davis stood fingering his bugle. "The Camdens was great dog people in their day. That's twenty-thirty year ago."

"Well," said Tom, "we heard about it over at Lancey's. It's a son-in-law of the old Camdens, and his name is Terry, and he aims to raise sheep."

For a long moment no one spoke.

"Fence," said Spring Davis. There was an odd whine in his tone.

Delbert brought out a sack of Bull Durham, and began to make a cigarette. "Martin Lancey was at the lumberyard to-day, and this Terry was there. He was ordering posts and wire. Wove-wire, Lancey said."

"Hog-tight, bull-strong and horse-high," added Tom.

A coal popped in the fire, and a shower of sparks blew up.

Spring Davis said, thoughtfully: "Man's name is Jacob Terry. I remember him."

"Sure enough," agreed Calhoun Royster, "and he married Effie Camden. I heard she died, up in Jackson County. Had one daughter, seems to me."

Spring Davis put down the bugle. His knee-joints creaked as he stood up. "I wouldn't call this Jake Terry a pleasant man. Once he whipped a horse with a piece of board . . . going to put up a wove-wire fence, hey?"

"They're moving in, this week," went on Delbert. "Mrs. Lancey said there was a light in the house early to-night."

Something twitched outside the last reaches of firelight, and Spring Davis went down on one knee. "Come on, little lady," he cried. Bugle Ann trotted into the light, her long ears flapping, her elbows plastered with mud. She was a small hound, but with a strong, well-arched coupling, and she carried her tail like a banner.

Davis took her in his arms. "This here's the angel song you heard, Mr. Mayor."

"She didn't come very prompt," scoffed old Royster.

"Prompt enough," said the veteran. "She set out there past the light, until she was sure about that car. You didn't know the Royster boys would come driving up in their smoke-wagon, did you, honey?"

She wiped his chin with her limp tongue.

"What do you feed her?" asked Mr. Mayor.

"Best cornmeal, bran, and pork cracklings," answered Benjy. "Ma boils it to a thick mush. All our dogs get that."

His father rubbed Bugle Ann's head with his stubbled chin. "I puke out," growled the saturnine neighbor. "Spring, you're plumb foolish over that dog."

The older man shrugged. "I've run dogs for seventy-odd year, but I never heard a voice like this. Nor did you, Cal, nor anybody else. She's galloped forty-five mile to-night. She's the sweetest-mouthed hound in Missouri, and sometimes I reckon I don't deserve her."

Baker asked, "What do you say about the fence, Spring?"

The other hounds were coming in—tan and white, wet ears, drooling jowls—a muddle of tails and snorts and sneezes in the firelight. Benjy took charge of the Davises. There were six of them out, this night, and he handled them with skill and deference and firmness . . . his father still held Bugle Ann wrapped in his gaunt arms.

"I reckon," decided Spring, "that we'd better make a visit on this Jake Terry tomorrow. Call the Armstrongs and Lanceys and everybody together; even get the Pettigrews down from Big Panther Creek. Nobody has ever put up such a fence in these parts, and this is a mighty poor time to start."

Again Mr. Frank Mayor prayed for information.

"First place," explained Davis, "a fox hates such a fence. He's liable to shy off and leave the country because of it. But some of the foxes do like it, and that's even worse. Because a dog runs about fifteen mile an hour—and he hits a wove-wire fence in the dark. The fox is little—he's gone through without choking to death. The dog is liable to get killed."

He rubbed the home-made collar on Bugle Ann's neck. The collar plate was made from a silver dollar stamped flat, and silver dollars were none too plentiful with Springfield Davis any more.

"You can't get good hunting in a country where they put such fences across the fox range," Baker Royster summed up.

Bugle Ann was snoring happily in old Spring's arms.

Mr. Mayor had to drive all the way to Wolf Center, and he didn't arrive at home until four A.M., and his wife was worried to death. He told her that he had just attended the strangest fox hunt in the world; it was a kind of fox-hunting in which no killing took place. He was a discerning man, but in this case he spoke too soon.

The men of the Heaven Creek neighborhood waited upon Jacob Terry the next day.

3

That was June. By July, everybody knew that young Benjy Davis was tarnishing some mysterious code which existed among them all, and which no one of them could have explained or accounted for. Benjy was keeping company with Jacob Terry's daughter, and he made no secret of it.

She was named after her mother's people: Camden. She was eighteen, and she had the shaded hazel eyes of her mother's family, the dainty nostrils and firm lower lip which had marked the Camdens as quality folks when they first came to that country on horseback.

From her father Camden inherited the Terry stature, the Terry red hair. All Heaven Creek hoped that she hadn't inherited his surliness, loose tongue and ugly disposition. Benjy believed that she hadn't.

The crisis began to develop, one night when the grass still reeked from a July flood, and the southeast wind would have drowned any fox-smell which rose from last autumn's leaves. Springfield Davis sat on the front porch with his shoes off, and Bugle Ann dreamed on the step beside him.

Spring noticed that Benjy disappeared immediately after the evening chores were done, and later he smelled shoe polish. About eight o'clock Benjy came around the corner of the house, and he was wearing his good trousers and the blue necktie which Grandma Duncan had sent him for Christmas, and which he had never worn.

"It's a wet night," Spring said. He began to fill his pipe.

"I reckon the wind will change," said Benjy. "But anyway it's unlike to dry off the grass before midnight."

Spring put his hand on Bugle Ann. "If it does dry up enough, Cal will be out."

"I'll listen when I get back," Benjy told him. "If I hear you up in the woods, I'll come over. I thought," he said, "that I might go with Camden Terry to see the moving pictures in town."

McKee's Crossing was five miles to the north. . . . Spring thought, "I've counted, each time they was together. This is eight times." He said aloud, "That's a long way for a buggy. You plowed pretty steady all day, too."

"I wanted to lay-by that slow corn," Benjy said. "Camden can drive her Ford. We talked about it out in the field, when she came past to-day."

"Well," his father muttered. He thought, "So I was wrong. Nine times." He cleared his throat. "You might bring me a sack of Sweet Burley from town."

Benjy waved good-by. "I'll bring it," he said, and went away like a war-chief in the dusk.

A long while later, Spring leaned down and blew softly against Bugle

Ann's ear, and she roused up to wash his face for him. The April pups, by Billy Bryan out of Miss Wilson, came to tumble across his lap. "I reckon there would be no way to stop that," decided old Davis, "even if I wanted to. She looks more like the Camdens, and they was fine folks. Used to have a beautiful line of Irish-Maryland stock. I hope Benjy has sense enough to pay for the gasoline, if he rides in a Terry car. He will, though."

He sat for hours, thinking of Jacob Terry and how he had greeted the deputation which waited on him a few weeks before. They were men with sober faces, but they were not men who would shoot unless they were called by a certain name, and that was one curse which Jacob Terry had not dared to invoke. He had talked some of shooting dogs, but people didn't believe he really meant it. No man who had married a Camden could be perverted enough to shoot a fox-hound wantonly, they thought.

The fence was solidly in place: bull-strong, hog-tight and horse-high, just as the Royster boys had foretold. It ran across the creek, up the west slope of Heaven Hump, swung its yellow posts to the north and went down hill for another half mile. On the other two sides it paralleled Heaven Creek and Welsh Run. Jake Terry hadn't bought many sheep yet, but folks said that he was dickering here and there.

It seemed that recently he had inherited some money from an elderly aunt, and likely he would run through with that just as he had done with his wife's share of the Camden property.

When that woven belt of wire encompassed the slope of Heaven Hump, the Davises and Roysters had gone up into the woods and had dug out all the nearer fox dens. Several foxes were captured alive, and later were liberated miles away, east of the Armstrong farm. Their dens were broken in, or stopped with bowlders and saturated with chemicals. Now it was hoped that no fox would venture toward that menacing wire sash. The north range of Heaven Creek became a victory for Jacob Terry.

As a matter of fact, the foxes were quick to learn what Terry had done to the hills. Certain of them seemed to take a fiendish delight in slipping through the meshes, whereat the dogs would howl and scramble perilously, knotting themselves in the wire squares.

This night, Spring Davis dozed on the steps until after eleven, and his wife slept on the sofa in the living room. Mrs. Davis was thirty years younger than her husband, eighteen inches shorter, a few degrees less talkative, and she knew that after his dogs Spring loved her well. . . . The breeze did change, and when the old man awoke he found a steady west wind breathing its dryness against his face.

He went out into the yard and felt of the ground. He sniffed several times. Bugle Ann came behind him, stretching and yawning.

"I think a fox would hang on the high ground, after all. The scent'd be fairly free. Reckon you wouldn't have to grind your nose against the ground, little girl," said the master.

She swung her tail, and lifted her muzzle. "Now, hush!" he said, and waited with delight for her to disobey him.

She blew her trumpet.

"What is it?" called Mrs. Davis, sleepily.

The other hounds were answering, from out by the barn, and far in the southwest you could hear the Royster hounds casting about. "We had bugles in the rebel army," said Spring, "but I tell you, Adelaide, I waited a long time to hear the noise that this little girl has got snuggled inside her, all ready to let out when God is willing."

"Are you going up the creek?" asked his wife. They didn't say "down the creek" any more.

"I reckon I will. Cal is out. I hear General Bullard; sounds like he's striking. Will you fetch me a snack, while I get the lantern?"

She had a lunch ready when the old man came up from the corncrib, with his hands full of Frances Cleveland and Billy Bryan and Old Hickory. "I can't mind more than four, what with Benjy gone," he told Adelaide, and put his lunch in his pocket and the bugle under his suspender strap. He went across the cabbage patch, with the rest of the Davis dogs wailing their grief behind him.

"Poor little folks," he commiserated. "You'll just have to be patient, I reckon. Benjy sure is gone a long time. It must be a mighty good moving picture."

He saw the Royster lanterns opposite the line fence, and he let the dogs loose, one by one. Bugle Ann shot into the lead. "You find the pack, little lady!" Spring shouted at her. "Find the pack if they come nigh. They got a long jump on you."

Cal Royster chuckled in the shadows. "Talk like she understood every word you said."

"I wager she'll be up with them inside thirty minutes," Spring responded. "And anyway, likely she does know what's what. How could she help it, with that silver cornet the Lord beqeathed her?"

Del and Thomas were off with the Lancey girls again, but Bake and old Cal and Spring Davis all waded Heaven Creek and went up on the south end of the Divide to build their fire. The bugs were bad, and it was more of a smudge than a camp-blaze.

"What's become of Benjy?" asked Bake, who knew well enough what had become of Benjy. "Is he still taking that mail-school lesson about new ways of farming?"

"No, that's been done up for some time," Spring replied. He hesitated, then said: "He's gone to McKee's Crossing to the Wednesday night moving picture." This seemed neither the time nor the place to elaborate on his statement.

4

The hounds came down the valley soon after midnight, with the fox at a tantalizing short lead. The men descended the Divide when the baying sounded first from above them, and they felt rather than saw the truant varmint squeeze past them into the north.

White blur after white blur—like snowy hands whisking before the eyes—the dogs went by.

Cal Royster voiced the apprehension of the others when he spoke. "Fox'll go right up Chilly Branch Holler," he said, and Spring hoped that he was right, for it was hard to forget the menace of the wire which lay beyond.

They heard the dogs crossing Chilly Branch near its mouth, and then Bugle Ann singled out ahead of them all, booming up the steep terraces of Heaven Hump. And Springfield Davis recognized another sound in the universe beyond: the faint clatter of an old Ford rocking along a narrow lane.

He thought, "So they're back from the moving pictures. I hope to God the fox switches east to the hill-top. The girl looks more like the Camdens than she does like Jacob. I reckon most of my dogs would be small enough to squeeze through that fence without getting hung up."

Then Bake cracked out, savagely, "They never went up the Hollow. Let's get over there!" and he lumbered away through the darkness. The two older men fumbled after him until their feet touched a deep cattle trail at the base of the hill, and then they could travel rapidly.

They splashed through the rapids near the mouth of Chilly Branch, and far ahead the hounds were rearing and yelling against Jacob Terry's hog-tight fence. One dog (he must have been Wound Stripe, and well-named, for Bake Royster swore about it) ki-yied, and told the world that an end of the wire had been sharp and gashing.

When the men reached the fence, waving their lanterns, the fox was long since gone. The pack danced and strutted in hysteria beside the barrier.

Wound Stripe's left fore-leg was drenched with blood.

"Bugle Ann ain't here," muttered Cal Royster.

The lantern beams had gone their anxious round.

"No," Spring Davis replied, "reckon she sailed right through." He walked up to the fence and tested its strength with his shoe, and prepared to climb over. You couldn't see his face in the lantern light.

Bake was thirty-four, and heavy enough, but he was standing inside Terry's sheep pasture before old Springfield had managed to put his stiff legs astride the fence. Baker was thinking that Benjy should be there, and probably the others were thinking the same thing. . . . The far-away chugging of the Ford car had ceased, but a bright light moved rapidly toward them from the Terry farmhouse.

Sheep scampered here and there in distracted little coteries, appearing suddenly, and vanishing into the thick night amid a rattle of hillside pebbles.

"She'd come up to me, if she was inside the lot," said Spring. "It's possible she squeezed out at the other side, too."

Cal Royster put his arms in the fence meshes, trying vainly to stop their trembling. "She ain't giving voice no more. Maybe you better use your horn, Spring."

The old soldier had the bugle against his lips when Jacob Terry loomed up the hillside, an electric flashlight in his fist.

"Get out of this pasture," Terry said. He did not yell, and there was added menace in his voice on that account.

"Look out," Cal Royster warned. He saw a shotgun in the curve of the farmer's arm.

Spring Davis turned around and took down the bugle. He rubbed a finger across his mouth. "Jacob," he said, "I come in here after my dog."

"If your damn dog is here, he's got no good business among my sheep." Terry held the flashlight steadily on old Springfield's face, and somehow Bake Royster thought of big searchlights he had seen weaving above the Argonne woods, on another night when hatred paraded on a grander scale.

Spring told Terry, "It's Bugle Ann. She wouldn't hurt your sheep, but she's small enough to come through your fence when a fox brings her here."

In the next silence, they listened for her voice, but could hear only the thudding of sheep which scampered along the slope. The rest of the dogs panted and mourned outside the fence.

"Get this straight, old boy." The flashlight held its unblinking stare in Terry's hand. "I'm gonna raise sheep, and I don't care a stink for all the dogs in Missouri. You keep yours off of my land, or they'll get a dose of Number Ten shot in the high end."

Benjy got there a moment later. He had left Camden at the lane entrance, and he had started across a spur of the Davis timber when he heard the hounds working straight down the creek. He had no lantern; the woods were black, so was the creek valley, and it had taken him longer than he anticipated.

Somehow there had been a menace in the entire evening, from the moment when Camden first cried against his clean green shirt.

He asked, "What's the matter?" and his voice sounded like a youth's voice, breaking as it essayed the inflection. He snatched Cal Royster's lantern and investigated the hounds outside the pen. "Pa," he called, "where's Bugle Ann?" and then he came over.

Terry took a couple of steps closer. "There's more than just dogs that give me a peeve, anyway, and you know what I mean. Get out, all of you, and don't bend down my fence when you go over it, neither."

"One of my hounds got cut open," said Bake Royster. "I don't reckon you could be decent enough to staple down those ragged ends of wire, could you? Well, I'll sure come around and staple them for you."

Terry called him a name, and turned the muzzle of the gun toward him, but Benjy stepped out to meet it. He swung wide and openly, for he was not a trained boxer, but he was quicker than a cat in any movement. His fist lifted Terry off his heels and threw him heavily.

The shotgun flew wide; it was still uncocked, and that kept it from going off.

"Take care, Benjy," was all his father said. There were grief and resignation in Spring's voice.

Terry rolled over and got up on his haunches.

"Don't you make a pass at me!" Benjy cried. "If you've killed Bugle Ann, I'll sure kill you."

"No," Spring said, "that'd be my job. But he hasn't, Benjy, he hasn't. . . . I'm plumb certain she went out the other side." Then, all in an instant, he stepped back and flung his arms high; one hand held the bugle.

He appealed, huskily, "For God's sake, listen to that!"

. . . She was far beyond Heaven Hump, far in the timber that blanketed Welsh Run. And she must have passed successfully through the north fence of Terry's pasture, for she had found the fox-smell again, and she was telling the whole state of Missouri about it.

It was a bugle, and every man knew that he would never hear its like again after she died.

Bake Royster had Terry's shotgun, and Benjy had his flashlight, and together they eyed the big farmer. "Terry," said Bake, "it's mighty fortunate for you that she's out there running safe and sound."

"You talk smart enough," whispered Jacob Terry. "Four against one! It's easy to talk smart."

"Your having this gun kind of evened it up."

"I'll even up any of your dogs, if they come on my land again." He went on to say what kind of dogs they were.

The hunters returned across the fence—all except Benjy.

"Come on, boy," Spring ordered him.

"Here's your light," said Benjy to Jacob. "I reckoned you had something else to say."

Terry came close to him. "I'm not afraid of no Davises," he bellowed, "but I like to choose my friends! Don't you come near Camden no more—hear me? I'm particular about who my little girl goes places with."

"I reckoned that was it," replied Benjy. The others knew from the drawl with which he spoke that he was enraged almost beyond control. "Well, you can go to hell and fry in your own lard. You know well enough that fox-hounds don't go around pulling the hide off of sheep."

The man's voice rose in one shouting shriek. "Why, you young black-snake, I'll kill every God damn cur that steps on this grass!"

"Jacob," Spring called to him, steadily enough, "I can't speak for the Roysters or Lanceys or Armstrongs or anybody else. But if you shoot a Davis dog, I'll blow you clean to glory. Now come out of that hog-pen, Benjy Davis."

Benjy climbed over the fence. Terry turned off the flashlight, and stood there like the black stub of a tree, watching him. "How about my gun?" he asked. "Are you folks going around stealing honest people's guns, too?"

"Here," said Bake. He clicked the breech and threw something far into the valley. He passed the shotgun back through the fence. "Both barrels empty. If you look careful, down by the creek, you'll maybe find the shells."

"Remember what I said!" yelled Jacob Terry. "I got an old cistern needs filling in, and I'd just as soon fill it up with dog-meat."

Spring Davis said nothing more, but Cal Royster spat out his tobacco and declared that nobody would forget a word that had been said. He doubted Spring Davis's ability to blow Jacob Terry to glory, and remarked that another destination would be more easy to promise.

They gathered up the dogs and went back to the Divide. Their fire was nearly out, but Bake soon kicked it into activity, and his father found some dry wood stowed away in a hollow basswood at the head of the ravine.

They waited until two-thirty o'clock, and still Bugle Ann didn't come back, nor did they hear her metal baying any more. Baker took all the Royster dogs home to their straw beds, and then returned to the fireside. The Davis animals lay near the fire and sprawled like the dead, as only hounds can ever do, but there was a nervousness haunting their dreams, and you could imagine that the eldest of them moaned in his sleep for Bugle Ann.

Benjy sat like bronze, his arms locked around his knees. From where he watched, Cal Royster studied him and wondered if a strain of Shawanee had not been dropped into the Davis blood a century before. . . . The whisky got lower and lower in Cal's flask.

Spring Davis walked up and down outside the firelight, tramping a path from the basswood to the nearest clump of hickory sprouts. Once he came back to the fire and spat into the coals.

"Wonder how far the gamest fox would travel, if he set his mind to go in a bee-line?" he asked, but Cal Royster couldn't tell him. Then Spring climbed to the highest point of the Divide, and awakened the dozing whip-poor-wills with his urgent bugle.

5

In the darkest half-hour, immediately before the sky above the Armstrong farm turned gray, the men heard Jacob Terry's Ford beginning to hiccough. By that time they were scattered far and wide through the hills, but Bake Royster was on top of the Divide. He saw the car lights twist out of Terry's barnyard, and stop for awhile, and then go on, smudging away toward the county road.

Bake listened until the car had chugged in the direction of McKee's Crossing. He had started back toward the fire, when a gnome with a lantern waylaid him at the edge of the timber.

"Bake," whispered his father's voice, "I heard a yip."

He asked, "What kind of a yip?" with the unreasoning annoyance of a young man who shuns the mumbling vagaries of the aged.

"A dog yip," said Cal. "I was down the crick, plumb inside Terry's pasture again. And I heard it, up toward the house."

"Just once?"

In the growing fog of dawn, the old man clutched Baker's arm; his fingers tightened and relaxed. "The dog was struck dead, if you ask me. Terry might of done it with an ax, so's Spring wouldn't hear the gun."

Far along the upper twist of Chilly Branch Hollow, Spring Davis's bugle chanted stubbornly. . . . Bake felt stuffed up inside, as he considered what his father had just told him. "Benjy went to take his dogs home, Pa. You wait here for Spring, and I'll go for Del and Tom."

"Don't bring 'em back direct," commanded his father. "Send Tom across fields for the Lanceys, and have Del take the car and go up to the Armstrong place. He can ring the Pettigrews from there. I wish to God I was rich and could afford a telephone."

Bake swallowed. "You want the whole tribe?"

"We can't go off half-cocked, boy. Maybe it was just a notion I had, or something. I would of sworn it was a yip—just one quick one. Don't you dare tell Spring about it. But if that little bitch—"

"Lady," muttered Bake, not realizing he had said it.

"If she's hung up on bob-wire somewhere, we got to find her soon. It'll take a sight of searching. She never was one to try and dig up a fox-hole. Maybe she got clear over east on the slab, and some foreigners picked her up in a car."

Bake started for home like a good soldier, with crisp obedience in his mind. At all this talk of killing, he began to tremble inside with a nervousness which had never possessed him since his discharge from the U. S. Veterans' hospital in 1921. *Too much* . . . his big feet found the trampled mire beside Heaven Creek . . . *too much of that sort of thing.* Just now he didn't like the name Springfield. It didn't make him think of a town there in Missouri, but it did make him think of a rifle. Cartridges began to glint in his mind: pointed clips of them, clicking one against the other in a webbed pouch.

Suddenly, he thought he could feel the cold solidity of a Springfield bolt in the curve of his right index-finger.

He decided, "She's got to be caught in the wire somewhere. It'll be the best thing that could happen."

He routed Tom and Delbert out, and sent them flying. His mother and Lucy stood in their nightgowns and stared at him with cold, pale eyes, and said they'd do the milking if the men weren't back in an hour and a half. . . . There was a mess of cornmeal in the smelly summer kitchen, stirred up in a huge crock, and Bake took it out to the hounds. Halfway to the barn, he imagined that he heard a frightened voice yapping: "I'm runner–Brigade Headquarters–where's Sixtieth Infantry?" and the rifle bolts clicked in a machine-gun chorus. His throat was dusty, and he smelled pepper in his nose, as if some one had given him a blow that fractured the little blood vessels inside. . . . Then he pulled his nerves together, and went on to feed the dogs.

On the Divide behind his farm, Spring Davis came back to the dead fire with the sunrise smoking behind him. He walked, not like an old man who has been up and on his feet all night, but like a solemn pontiff who has sat in the cruelest judgment.

"It's the first time she ever disobeyed the horn," he said to Cal Royster and Benjy, who were waiting for him.

Cal kicked his empty bottle into the ashes. "Spring, you ought to drink at least a cup of coffee and maybe have a snack, before you go further."

"Why," said Spring, "I don't need–"

Benjy said: "They'll be gathering at the house. Bake and Tom and Del are getting folks."

"I heard her," said Spring. "So did you. She had got through that second fence. I heard her plain, over past the outside of his pasture."

"Sure we heard her," crooned old Royster, "and if she ain't found by high noon–maybe just got a toe caught somewhere, or something, like when she was a pup–I'll give you a four-headed Shorthorn rooster!"

Benjy looked at his father. "Anyway, you got to stop by the house first."

Spring nodded. "Guess that's so. Come along with you."

Roy and Joe Lancey were sitting on the well-curb when they got to the house, and Tom Royster was up at the kitchen door, talking with Mrs. Davis. The Lanceys stood up, awkwardly, as untutored men do at funerals, when Spring strode across the yard.

"Ma," asked Benjy, "you got some coffee?"

She nodded. "I kept hearing the horn, even after you was here, Benjy. The dogs have been just wild. I got a big coffeepot on the stove, and a couple skillets of eggs for anybody that wants them."

Bake Royster was coming across the south pasture, and another Lancey —Patterson, the sixteen-year-old one—was advancing up the front road on horseback.

At the back step, Spring Davis surveyed the men in his yard. His eyes were hot enough, but it was a slow and sturdy heat, infinitely ferocious. . . . An orange sun lifted above the Divide and found a whole jewelry store scattered over the clover behind the yard fence. All the remaining Davis dogs seemed to sense the import of this hour, except the April pups. They were smelling around Roy Lancey's legs.

"How about the ears on this one?" muttered Roy.

"They're well set," said Joe, "but she'll never have a stylish tail."

Cal Royster cackled, "Don't ask me! I ain't much on bench, but I'm the darndest Homeplate Judge you kids ever seen." The men all tried to laugh, as if he had said something very funny.

They heard the drone of the Armstrongs' old Studebaker from the road, and the rattle of Delbert Royster's Ford behind it. . . . When Spring Davis came out of the house five minutes later, there were thirteen men in the yard, including Benjy.

Spring had a lever action 30-30 Winchester in his hands. He tried it a couple of times, sliding shells into the breech, lowering the hammer with his thumb while he released the trigger, and flicking the cartridges out again. The sun discovered the Winchester; for a moment its barrel looked like mother-of-pearl.

"I'd just as soon go alone," Spring said, mildly.

Benjy cried, "No."

"You might say I'd prefer it."

Benjy said, "I'll go with you."

Cal Royster tried to make an explosion of laughter, but it was only a vague squawl. "Why, of course we all got to go with you, Spring. It'll take all the men we can raise, to comb real thorough. Maybe that fox took her—" His throat crackled.

"Maybe the fox went clean to the Indian River," supplied young Tom, and there was a murmur of assent.

Spring clamped the rifle under his arm. "Very well, neighbors. . . . I might be wrong, but I reckon I can learn in a hurry when I get there." He stepped down into the yard. "Good-by, Mother," he said to his wife, and in the doorway she made a sound. The pups scampered to meet him, ears flopping and tails swinging. "Get 'em into the crib or kitchen or somewhere," he requested of the world, and kept going.

The unkempt mob of men started after him. Benjy hustled the pups into the kitchen, and his mother hooked the sagging screen door.

Down in the barn, Frances Cleveland began to bay, and her relatives took up the song. Benjy sprinted ahead and opened the plank gate for his father; the old man headed along the edge of the cornfield, but after twenty yards he struck off between the green fronds, his feet sinking deep into the damp earth and leaving the prints of his heel-corners bright and compressed.

The neighbors followed, all of them; they talked a little about corn. The thinnest corner of the Davis timber swayed forward to meet them, and beyond that lay the lane, and beyond that the Terry house.

They came out into the jet lane, with its golden, morning pools of mud and the grooved ruts where Terry's Ford had plowed through. Nobody tried to avoid the deeper mire; the farmers marched in uneven phalanx behind Spring Davis, and anybody would have guessed that the old man didn't know whether he was walking through mud or last year's oat stubble.

Cal Royster had fallen to the rear, but not through choice. A little pageant walked with him, and impeded his footsteps . . . it was when he was eighteen, some fifty years earlier, and the neighbors all went up Welsh Run to prosecute Big Cass Strickland when he beat his two children to death. They prosecuted him at the end of his own wagon-harness, wrapped around the limb of a white-oak tree, and he hung there seven hours before any one cut him down. . . .

You couldn't see a soul moving in the Terry yard, and now the men believed most certainly that Jacob Terry had gone far away in the Ford, before dawn. Bake Royster and his father began to watch for tracks, as soon as they came opposite the weed-grown orchard, and it was impossible for them to conceal their search.

Cal felt Spring Davis turning and staring at him, and he held his face closer than ever to the ground.

Then all the men had stopped. Benjy Davis came back and stood between the two Roysters, with his hands clamped over his hip-bones.

"The pack never got up this high," he said. "They weren't out of the creek valley, except on the other side."

"No," whispered old Cal. "We was just a-looking."

Benjy grabbed Bake's shoulder and turned him around. "What do you know, Bake?"

"It ain't me," said Bake. "It's Pa. He heard it. I didn't."

Cal stammered, "Now, Benjy Davis. My ears are mighty old and mighty tricky. I can't depend on them no way."

"You better speak up," drawled Benjy. Spring Davis had come back to stand beside them; the rest of the neighbors waited in uneasy silence beyond.

"Well," Cal told them, "it did sound like a yip."

"Up here?" persisted Benjy.

"It was kind of in this general direction. I guess it was a short while before sun-up."

Benjy turned to his father, and tried to take the gun. The old man pushed him away with sudden and amazing strength. "You remember, boy," he said, as if there wasn't another man within twenty miles, "how she got her foot caught in that rat-trap before she was weaned."

Bake Royster yowled, without being asked. "Sure, sure! Everybody knows that. But one gone toe never bothered her, because it happened when she was young enough. You'd never pick her as belonging to a Casual Outfit."

"All right, Father," Benjy Davis said. Nobody had ever heard him say Father before. "I reckon any tracks that are here would be like cement in the mud. Quite–" He hunted for the word. "Quite unmistakable."

"I'll warrant you," his father replied. Spring drew down the lever of his Winchester the barest part of its arc: there was a shell in the breech. He clicked it back. Then he turned and started east along the lane, with his eyes boring against the ground.

Benjy looked at him as if he were just seeing him for the first time. "Wait," he cried, and the old man turned. Benjy brought out a sack of Sweet Burley, its blue seal blazing in the fresh sunlight. "I just remembered that you wanted me to bring this from town, and I been carrying it in my pants all this time."

Spring nodded. "I'm obliged, Benjy." He thrust the tobacco into his hip pocket. "Before Cal talked about that yip," he told his neighbors, "I had been quite divided. I thought that probably she was in wire, or else somebody had stole her, over on the slab highway. Just possibly."

They didn't find any tracks until they came to the yard gate, almost directly in front of the house. Then there were a few. The imprints were made by the feet of a hound coming from the east, coming slowly and wearily a few inches outside the thick grass which bordered the wood road.

Everybody moved off upon the turf, and let the Davises handle this matter in their own way.

Benjy stood looking into the deserted barnyard, but his father got down on his knees and examined the smoother patches of drying mud near the intersection of the wheel ruts.

"How about that toe?" asked the boy.

"I think so," answered Spring, haltingly. "I'm not right certain: so many car wheels, and other tracks. She must of turned off on the grass at this point. . . . Wait'll I find a good one."

Then at last he stood up, and took the rifle in both hands. "Oh, I reckon it would stand in court," he declared. "Just like fingerprints and such. That gone toe is as plain as copper plate. And the tracks don't pass this gateway. She did get this far, on the way home."

A drop of water bobbed over his crusty eyelid and spent itself in a quick streak on his face, dividing and splitting when it came to a nest of wrinkles.

Benjy said, "She was all alone, and likely the fox holed over in Lester's timber near the creek mouth. She knew this old wood road come back, and was easier traveling. She knew enough not to go through those wove-wire fences unless a fox took her that way."

"Cal Royster," said Spring, "you owe me a four-headed Shorthorn rooster." He faced the Terry house for the first time.

Old Ed Armstrong cried, "Now, Springfield. Now, Brother, wait a spell! The Lord don't smile on wrath in unguarded moments of haste."

"You and the Lord can hold your horses," Spring said, without turning his head. "If I'm looking for rats in my granary, I don't set down and pray on it."

Benjy pleaded, "Give me that Winchester, Pa."

"Pshaw, scat," said his father, and started into the farmyard. "You never bred her, did you? She was mine."

Benjy swung around and glared at the neighbors. "He don't want to go in with a whole parade. I'll stay by this gate. Don't nobody try to come past me."

"Spring!" howled Cal Royster. "He's gone! Spring, I tell you he went away in the car. We all heard it go. We—"

"If he ain't at home," said Benjy, "Pa'll wait."

Jacob Terry came out on the kitchen porch. In the barn lot, his two cows were lowing: they had not yet been milked, and none of the neighbors was surprised to know that Jacob had put off his milking until that hour. There were young chickens on the porch, and in the yard below.

Terry held his shotgun in his hands; of course there had been plenty of other shells in the house. Number Ten shot, Baker remembered. Little bright lights flickered in Bake's eyes, and again he smelled that pepper of a painful smash against his nose.

"Get out of here, you old devil," said Terry.

"What'd you do with her?" asked Spring. His tone was flat. "The tracks are to the gate. Did you haul her inside, then?"

Terry mouthed, "I never killed your damn dog, but I'll put some slugs through you if you don't get out of here." He began to hoist the shotgun toward his shoulder.

Springfield Davis fired from his hip. Terry dropped the shotgun and looked surprised and horrified; a dishpan behind him rang like a gong, and fell from its nail, rolling unsteadily across the floor of the porch. Terry's knees bent; he tried to get hold of his chest, and failed. He fell forward into the mud below the porch, with his arms doubled under him.

A lot of half-feathered chickens scurried away from him, peeping shrilly. When the men had rolled him over, they found that one chicken was dead beneath him—crushed flat when he fell upon it.

Benjy went into the house, but Camden wasn't there, and he was dumbly grateful—even in this calamity, and in the mystery of her absence. But the Ford was gone. She must have driven away in it.

That afternoon, after Springfield Davis had ridden to Wolf Center with the Sheriff, the authorities were able to telephone to the Camdens up in Jackson County. Camden Terry had arrived there about noon, but had driven on to an isolated farm belonging to a bachelor uncle. It was twenty-four hours before she could be notified and could complete the return trip as far as Wolf Center.

On the first day when people sat in the big, hot room among the scarred oak desks, Benjy Davis thought Camden looked prettier than she had ever looked before. Her pallor was the cold pallor of hepaticas; her eyes were excessively deep and shaded and secret.

Benjy didn't look her way when he thought she might be looking at him, but he studied her often when she was watching old Spring and the Coroner and the other people. Her story was calm, distant, told without emotion—it might have been translated from some ancient book. Yes, she had been with Benjy Davis the night before the shooting. Yes, she knew that her father had had trouble with the neighbors over his fence and their fox-hounds. She knew that there had been threats. . . . After her father came back to the house from the sheep pasture, they had engaged in an argument.

He had slapped her; just once, she said; not very hard. She packed some clothes, and took the Ford. He dared not stop her, because the Ford was hers—not his. Her Aunt Nancy had given it to her after Uncle Newt died; Aunt Nancy couldn't drive.

(She didn't look at Benjy, either, when she thought that he might be observing her. Sometimes their glances crossed, but never seemed to meet and hold. Each understood that Jacob Terry was still between them, standing or lying dead, it didn't make any difference. In a way, Spring Davis also was between them now. And Bugle Ann.)

Her voice continued soberly, a little-girl voice. She thought that she wouldn't stay with her father any more, after that night. She drove up to

Jackson County, and went out to Uncle Elnathan's place, and that was where the news had reached her.

Benjy Davis and the Royster boys spent days in going over the Terry farm, both before and after the sale of farm animals and machinery and household goods. They couldn't find a trace of Bugle Ann's body, even though they took up wooden slabs and explored the old cistern. She could have been buried in any loose earth of the barnyard or hog-lot, and no one would have known the difference.

Spring Davis was tried in September; the trial was in no way notable except for the oration on fox-hounds by a young attorney who volunteered to assume the defense without pay. The young attorney quoted, "Senator Vest's Tribute to the Dog," and added tributes of his own. He discussed fox-hunting as practiced in Missouri, and offered a biographical sketch of Old Man Spaulding, who was still alive in those days. In the eastern part of these great United States, said the young attorney, fox-hunting was an Anglicized pose of the idle rich, and they had many strange fetishes, not the least of which was the custom never to refer to a fox-hound as a "dog." They were all "hounds." Most of his listeners thought that very odd, but they did remember with interest how Spring Davis always called his female dogs Little Ladies or Little Girls.

Fifty years before, certainly, he would never have been convicted. But in this age you must not kill a man, even when another man talks of shooting and has a shotgun in his hands. It was proved that Spring Davis went into the Terry yard armed and ready to kill—he said as much himself. It was proved that Jacob Terry did not fire the first shot, nor did he have his gun at his shoulder when he was struck down.

The most important *corpus delicti*—the body of Bugle Ann—was not available. In short, no one could swear beyond all doubt that Jacob Terry had killed her. Spring Davis had usurped the prerogatives of the Sovereign State of Missouri, and the Sovereign State of Missouri brought that out very pointedly.

Girls made fudge for Spring while he was in jail; women sent in basket dinners. He gave the fudge away, of course, and some of the dinners. There was muttering at his conviction, and men talked darkly of a jail delivery. But such a rebellion belonged fifty years in the past. Springfield Davis went to Jefferson City and served three years, eight months and twenty-one days, and then he was pardoned by the governor.

6

During the first June which Spring spent in prison, the voice of Bugle Ann came back to ring across the dark valleys. Adelaide Davis was the first to hear this banshee, and she ran and told Benjy, and then they were both awake. Over on the next farm, Cal Royster started from his bed screaming, "Bake! Bake! It's her—" and even the youngest Lancey, who was up with a toothache, declared that there was no mistake in the identity.

And from that night rose the sprout of a legend which spread itself over the whole county, and farther than that. It was the legend of a white dog—lean, like hounds of the Spaulding line—who bugled her way through the brush at night, who ran with her head high, calling and hunting for the master who had been carried away from the hills he loved.

They said she ran at the head of a silent pack in which there were thirty-hour dogs, all the great and noble sires who had galloped those ranges before the Civil War. There were the hounds brought into Missouri when Daniel Boone came, great sword-mouthed brutes who could pull down a deer if they wanted to. But they all ran silently—their feet made not even a whisper in the dryest leaves of last year, and their baying was not the kind which ordinary people could hear. Only if you were about to die, you might hear them crying all at once.

But the Davises and the Roysters and one Lancey, and even old Ed Armstrong's hired man—all had heard Bugle Ann on that solitary night, and though they didn't hear her again, it was said that Benjy Davis spent more hours roving the woods than was wise for a young man with a farm on his hands.

No one lived at the Terry farm now. Shortly after Springfield Davis had gone to the penitentiary, men from McKee's Crossing came and took down the hog-tight wire fence. When questioned, they declared that a lawyer had told them they could have the wire and posts if they'd take them down. It was easy to pry out the staples, and they bore the wire away in huge rolls atop their trucks. But the posts were another matter; they quit digging after they had uprooted a few. Still, the wire was the main thing.

And there were those who swore that the pack led by Bugle Ann could go through a hog-tight fence like so much dishwater, but young Benjy Davis was hard to convince. After he had searched and yelled through every ravine between the Indian River and Big Panther Hollow, he declared that it had all been a mistake. Bugle Ann lay somewhere beneath the fresh weeds that grew in Terry's hog-lot, and as for her baying—it was another dog, that was all.

"It was her," insisted Adelaide Davis. "If your Pa had been here, he would of got up out of bed and gone for his lantern."

"Well," said Benjy, "I did that, didn't I?"

"But she quit giving voice," his mother said, "and whoever stole her took her away again." Her hands shook, in their cerements of bread dough. "Or else—"

He chided, awkwardly, "I got to get out to the field. . . . It's mighty unnatural to believe in ghosts."

Then he returned to his cultivator seat, and combed the black earth of the cornfield; he combed the rows early and late, and this year he had planted extra acreage. It was too bad, perhaps, for the price of corn got lower—so low that Benjy said there was no sense in selling. He didn't sell his corn, but he did sell the April pups of the year before, to the Lanceys. He took a corn-crib in payment—one fairly new. They moved it over to the Davis place with teams and cables and turnstiles: a three-day job. The Davises were hard put to scratch for a living, and that new corn-crib did look like a lot of foolishness.

Benjy stored his 1933 corn, too, and then came the next summer and the drouth, and corn at seventy cents. . . . Benjy carried an important slip of pink paper out of the office of the Wolf Center Farmers' Grain Company, and shoved it under a grille at the Wolf Center Savings Bank.

Mr. Mayor came after him and talked of insurance, but the only expenditures which Benjy was known to have made were subscriptions to *The Red Ranger* and *The Hunter's Horn.* You couldn't expect the library at the state prison to have those periodicals in stock.

It was the night of Wednesday, September 26th, when Bake Royster came around to the Davis place and got Benjy out of bed. Bake could remember the date forever; that day, sixteen years removed, marked the opening of the Meuse-Argonne offensive. Bake had a great head for names and dates.

He looked green around the gills when Benjy padded out across the kitchen in his night-shirt, and wanted to know what was up.

"I've found something," announced Bake. "Found it in the dark, and I guess you better come and see it."

Benjy's sharp glance made a hole in Royster's face. "I'll get my clothes, Bake. Keep soft, so's not to wake Ma. Her sciatica has been bothering her again."

He came out promptly, and sat on the back step to draw on his shoes. "Where is this—what you found?"

"It's clear in the east side of Bachelor's timber, where the Bachelor used to have a shack. It's a smart piece, but I got my lantern."

"I better take mine, too," said Benjy. He brought a square, scarlet-enameled electric lantern from the porch shelf; Bake thought of that check for the seventy-cent corn.

They went across the yard, with the white disk dancing around their feet and ahead of them. "Maybe you'll want a spade, too," muttered Bake.

"A spade?" Benjy stopped and looked at him in the dark.

Bake said, "Or else a grain sack."

After a moment, Benjy replied, "I'll get a sack, I think," and he found one hanging inside the barn door. Together they crossed the garden patch, and up across the Divide they could hear the Royster dogs and a couple of Armstrongs working intently north into the tangles along Chilly Branch. One or two of the Davis hounds wailed at them, but half-heartedly: the Davis hounds had forgotten what a black-dark night was like, with a fox spraying his oily perfume through the thickets.

"Wound Stripe and Toul Sector had him across the corner of Bachelor's," explained Royster. "Some young dogs was along with them, and that little Elsie Janis got herself twisted in some rusty wire. That's how I come to go down there and–"

He gargled in the dimness, and added with an attempt at being casual, "Tom and Pa are there now."

When they crossed Heaven Creek (its widest pool could have flowed between your shoes, after the drouth) Baker began to remonstrate with Benjy Davis.

"I don't see what ails you, Benjy. It's a shame to have good stock tied up and molting away the way yours are."

"You can't sashay around the woods all night, if you're busy farming," the younger man told him.

Bake growled, "Now, I know all about that corn! You don't need to rub it into me. But you ain't had nothing but dried-up crops to worry you, this year, and since the fall rains began to come there's been *beaucoup* fox around here."

For awhile Benjy climbed the incline without speaking, loose pebbles rolling down around Bake Royster as he plodded an arm's length behind. "No stomach for it," Benjy said, at last, and Baker knew that was really the explanation. "Not until he's out of that damn place. I can't set beside a fire and listen to the baying, and know he's at Jefferson City in a cellhouse."

It was eerie, passing through the oak woods, with a few katydids throbbing in secret dens under the stiff green leaves, and occasional yellow leaves sailing down into the straight electric ray. There was a feel of frost in the air, and Bake kept thinking of what he had found an hour before . . . a dog like Bugle Ann could take a thousand ghost hounds across the prairies among the stars, and still her baying would come back to you. Bake had ceased worrying about Springfield rifles and cartridges in webbed pouches, long before; sometimes still he thought of Jacob Terry and the chicken which had been crushed beneath his tumbling body, and he wouldn't get enthusiastic about half-feathered chickens ever again, especially if they made a shrill peeping.

But the death of Jacob Terry had come with its own certain violence, justified and canceled by a rifle bullet, the same as the many deaths Baker had seen in the valley of the Meuse. In Bugle Ann's passing there was too much mystery for any man to ponder. Any man who had ever been a patient in a government hospital.

The Bachelor's cabin was nothing but a heap of mossy shingles and broken crockery among the hickory saplings, for the Bachelor had left the country before Bake Royster was born. Some of his wire existed still: thick, old-fashioned plaits of bent rust amid the stumps. And near one of those barricades Cal Royster and young Tom waited with their lantern.

"Pa," called Bake.

"I'm right here," said the old man. "Evening, Benjy." Tom Royster didn't offer any greeting; embarrassment had frozen him into silence.

Benjy stood beside them and took what Cal Royster handed him. It was a leather collar, now stiff as iron with winter and summer and rain and mold, but the flattened silver dollar on it was unmistakable—you could even scrape away what had gathered over it, and see the Liberty head all flatly distorted, with its crudely-scratched legend.

The men waited silently.

"Where's the rest?" asked Benjy, after a long time. He slid the collar, with leaves still clinging to it, inside his shirt.

"Right here, in the bushes. They're a little scattered."

Benjy got down on his knees. If you had seen him, and had not known why he was there, you would have thought that he was praying. . . . Cal Royster had a vague notion that he ought to remove his hat, but Cal had never done such a thing for a dog.

"How long would you say?" asked Benjy presently.

The others murmured, hazarding several opinions. You couldn't tell much about bones. Maybe a doctor could. Animals had been there, probably, and birds. Maybe a year, maybe two, or three, or—

It was the collar which first had attracted Bake's attention. He saw it sticking up out of the leaves while he was releasing Elsie Janis from the wire. The young hound had left some of her blood there, from a lacerated elbow, and it seemed strangely appropriate to have that ground moistened with the blood of a fox-hound, even if she wasn't a Davis dog.

"The point is," said Benjy, speaking slowly and gravely, "whether she was here all the time, that night, or whether she come later. Somehow or other. The point is whether we heard her voice two year ago last June, or whether—"

Cal Royster said, "By God, it was her voice. Reckon I heard it."

"And by God," whispered Benjy, "those were her tracks at the edge of Terry's barnyard, in July of 'thirty-one."

"So what?" asked young Tom. It was slang such as he always picked up at the moving pictures, but it seemed unusually apt.

Benjy said, "I reckon there's nothing I can do except tote her home in the grain sack. I'm glad I didn't bring the spade, Bake, because now I'd be tempted to use it: just seem like a lot of old sticks, somehow, and I always did think a dog skull was powerful ugly."

They helped him pick up the relics, and he carried them back home while Bake Royster went ahead with the electric lantern. The men brought a shovel from the woodshed and buried the fragments, grain sack and all, beneath the sweet-crab tree at the corner of Mrs. Davis's little orchard. Benjy washed the collar and wiped it clean, using several dish towels in the process, and then he took it upstairs and hung it over the pointed, upright support of his bureau mirror, on top of his five neckties.

He told his mother the next morning, and of course through the Roysters the story was well around the neighborhood before noon. But Benjy and his mother were positive that no word of it would reach the ears of Springfield Davis at Jefferson City, and they were correct. It was the sort of a tale which might not be welcomed in print, so the *Weekly Clarion-Advocate* held no mention of it. No person except members of the family carried on any correspondence with Spring Davis, anyway, and thus the old man did not learn of how Bugle Ann's skeleton had been found until after he was released from prison.

It gave Bake Royster a fever, however, and he spent four days in bed. His family thought it was a kind of flu, but Baker knew the truth. He'd lie there at night, until he got over it, and watch the whole insane puzzle exploding before his eyes. Desperately he tried to align the formations—to put each separate element in the nook where it belonged; and this was lunacy to attempt.

Camden Terry: take her, now. She was living up in Jackson County, folks said, and she had never offered to sell the farm. Just let it grow to weeds. Nobody seemed to know whether or not she was married, and naturally it would take a hardy soul to mention her name to Benjy. Bake reckoned that Benjy had been mighty sweet on Camden.

Everybody had seen the tracks at Jake Terry's gate; there was no doubt about that missing toe. Not another hound in the neighborhood had a toe gone. So there were her tracks, and why would Bugle Ann have gone across Heaven Creek from the Terry farm—why would she have climbed Heaven Hump, or gone through Chilly Branch Hollow, and south into the timber land to get herself strangled in the Bachelor's wire? Spring Davis was making the hills quiver with his trumpet, and people all knew how Bugle Ann would come to such a summons.

No, she must have lived somehow, somewhere—and then she must have come back to the woods she loved, on another night, in June of 1932. Then they had heard her calling, and then she had met her death, alone beside the windfall of curling shingles.

No, she must have been a ghost, all along. It was not natural for any dog to have a voice like hers, and perhaps she had been sired by one of the silent pack which followed her so willingly in popular imagination. Even now her bones lay wadded in the Davis orchard, but Bugle Ann was up and gone, baying in ranges where no horns could ever summon her, and it would be death to hear her bugling again. . . . It was this surmise, however hysterical, which comforted Baker Royster and let him sleep with no more fever. Yet it was hard for him to forget how Benjy Davis had looked in the lantern light, coming down from the Divide with that sack of bones swinging from his shoulder and Bugle Ann's collar nestling inside his shirt.

7

They had less than twenty-four hours' warning, the next June when Springfield Davis was sent home from the penitentiary. There hadn't been such a tornado of festivity in the neighborhood since Delbert Royster and LaVonne Lancey were married two years before, and even then the Davises could not have felt very festive.

At five-thirty P.M. of the great day, Benjy and Bake started for McKee's Crossing in the old Royster car, but the fan-belt parted and as a result the train was just pulling out when they careened up to the station. They saw Spring Davis sitting there with a straw suitcase beside him.

His hair and mustache were snow-white and his face sagged, as if its fleshy sub-structure had dried up. His pointed shoulders came forward more noticeably and tried to meet across the front of his chest, but otherwise his appearance was the same as it had been. Benjy expected him to be as pale as a tallow candle, but he was not; Spring explained later that he had worked out of doors a good deal. The worst thing about the whole prison experience, he thought, was having so many of the convicts call him Pop.

He was eighty-six years old, and walked stiffly, and sometimes he'd open his mouth for a moment before he could say anything when he wanted to talk.

They got him into the car, with twenty townspeople staring quietly at him, and started for home. Spring didn't talk much on the way. He took off his old slouch hat and let the wind blow his hair—soft as milkweed silk. Once he said, "I see they've cut down that willow-row on the Collins place," and again, "Well, there's no use in my not saying that I was surprised—terribly surprised. It come so sudden! I didn't expect them to let me out for years and years."

He glanced keenly toward the Terry place as they passed its burdock-grown lane, and he seemed about to ask a question. But the next moment the north field of the Davises had swum past, and the car was crunching in at the gate. Adelaide Davis was just opening the screen door: others of the neighborhood women huddled behind her, and a lot of men were squatting on their heels beneath the cottonwood tree. Benjy always remembered how Cal Royster snapped his knife shut and put it into his pocket before he turned. Cal had been whittling a toy dart for one of the Lancey kids.

A long table had been arranged beside the peony bushes, and you could smell everything from fried chicken to beet pickles. After the greetings were made, Spring said that he'd like to put on some other clothes, and Benjy went behind him as he toiled up the narrow stairway to the hot rooms under the eaves. Spring's old work-clothes were there, but washed and smooth and foreign to him; he would not feel at home until his crooked knees and elbows had made their appropriate dents in the cloth. Mrs. Davis had disposed of his old suspenders, and he couldn't get a satisfactory adjustment on the ones he was wearing. He came into Benjy's room for help, and the first thing he saw was Bugle Ann's collar hanging beside the mirror.

If he lived to be a hundred, Benjy would never cease blaming himself for that.

Finally, after working his mouth for a long time, Spring managed to say, "Then you did find her. You never wrote it to me."

"Pa," Benjy groaned, "now you set down, Pa. Set down." And at last the old man sank deep into the narrow feather-bed.

He wanted to know, "Where was it? Where?"

"Up in Bachelor's timber. We never found her until last September."

"Bachelor's," echoed Spring. And then: "No, no, couldn't have been there."

"It was right beside the old shack," said his son, as gently as he could.

Spring stared for awhile. Downstairs they were yelling and laughing, and LaVonne Lancey Royster was ringing a dinner bell. Out in the yard, old Billy Bryan began to challenge with excitement.

"Then Terry never did it," said Spring.

"Maybe she run up there—after he shot her—or—"

The old man hissed, "Ah, stop your foolish talk!" His eyes were wet and blazing. "Nevertheless," he declared in a rapid whisper, "I'm thankful I done it when I did, for certainly I'd had to do it sometime. He meant it, Benjy. He would of killed her in a minute."

"Sure he would!" cried Benjy. "You don't think anybody in this world is blaming you, do you?"

Springfield had the collar in his hand, turning it slowly around and around.

Benjy mopped his perspiring forehead. "Pa," he began, "that ain't the whole story. There was a time, first June after you went up there—"

He told briefly of the dog's bugling which had echoed in the woods beyond Heaven Creek, and how the neighborhood had taken it, and of the phantom pack which was said to hunt so silently at night, unattended by any hunters.

Spring blew his nose when Benjy was through. "There was a time when I would of laughed my head off at that," he said, simply enough, "but I've had plenty time to think, these last four years. There were funny things in the War, boy, and there's been funny things other times. My mother knew that brother Rufus was killed by a snapped log-cabin, long before they ever brung her the news. She saw it in a kind of dream. . . . I don't say you heard Bugle Ann up there in the timber, that night, but you did hear something. Mighty often I thought I heard her, clear off in Jefferson City."

Then they went downstairs and out into the yard, to the fried chicken and other food, and all the talk, and all the people.

Supper stretched far into the dusk; then the table was cleared, and women began chattering and packing their baskets in the vicious heat of the kitchen. The men sat on the front porch and on the grass, and children shrieked at mysterious games among the berry bushes.

They had tried to enthrone Springfield Davis in the big splint-bottomed rocker, but he preferred to sit with his angular spine against a porch post. The dogs came to pay their respects; there was no one of them that he loved well enough to let it sleep across his lap, though Benjy watched hopefully.

In the first hush of twilight, when conversation had labored away from fox-hunting a dozen times, Spring astonished the crowd by rising to his feet and walking slowly down into the yard to feel the grass.

"It's not real wet," he said, so distinctly that all could hear him, "but there's a promising feel of dampness between the blades. When did it rain here?"

Somebody coughed. "Must of been night-before-last."

The pipes and cigarettes glowed spasmodically, and in the kitchen the younger Lancey girls were trying to harmonize with *Sometimes I'm happy, sometimes I'm blue.*

"This night'll be black-dark and that's a fact," came from Cal Royster.

Spring stood listening to the girls' song. "Radio," he muttered. "Well, we had radio music up there, too." He called to Royster, "Cal, I've been smelling at black-dark nights for nigh onto four years."

"I didn't think you'd feel—" Bake started to say, and then he chewed his nervous lip.

Spring Davis echoed, "Feel what?" He looked like a tall, guerrilla ghost in the thickening dusk, and the scent of June flowers was heavy as at a funeral. "Why, when a relative dies we all go on living, don't we? We all have to. I'd like, just as quick as possible, to set beside a fire again."

Benjy stood up. He felt his knees quivering. "The dogs are rusty, Pa. You know I've been farming pretty steady."

"They'll get the kinks out of their noses, once a fox is good and sweet," said Spring. It was as if he alone were trying to whistle up the courage of his neighbors. "I hate to see a good, sticky night go to waste. And there ain't any southeast wind."

There was a stir among the farmers, and more than one stood up. But for all their eagerness a certain delicacy possessed them now. They realized that this pathetic rite—the first journeying of old Spring to the hills of Heaven Creek—was something sacred to the Davises and Roysters, who had hunted together time out of mind.

"I'm afraid Gabe won't look after that colt proper," said old Ed Armstrong. "Awful hard to keep a hock bandaged." The Lanceys spoke of a big day in the field to-morrow, and Henry Pettigrew made lugubrious mention of his rheumatic knee.

"Well," Bake Royster announced, in a sweeping gesture of exclusion, "looks like everybody else has to go home and do chores or go to bed early, but Pa and I might trail up in the timber a spell with you, Spring."

Davis said, "Fetch the hounds, Benjy. I don't reckon we'll need a snack to-night, we're so full of good supper."

In half an hour the four of them had crossed the narrow clover field and were wading the valley darkness: Spring, Benjy, Cal and Baker. A solid bank of clouds rose slowly out of the west, and rain would come before morning. The air was one great, mossy cellar of humidity.

On the high crest of the Divide, the hounds went loose—four Davis dogs and five Roysters. All of the Davis dogs were elderly hounds whose voices Spring Davis knew as well as his own name. The white blots went speeding, zigzagging toward the shadows where foxes most often made their path.

The men sat on their haunches and waited.

"One's struck," said Cal, when a haunting moan came from the hilltop. The moan stopped suddenly. "No," Benjy grunted, "you just thought so. If that was Toul Sector . . . has he run on his own trail lately, Bake?"

Bake grinned, in spite of himself. "Not for a good month. Wait awhile."

The insects skirmished around them. At last little Elsie Janis found exciting evidence; she talked about it. Billy Bryan and Old Hickory joined her, and the whole mob went hooting melodiously toward the south slope.

"Good voice she's got," said Spring. "She one of your new ones, Cal?"

"Just small fry," replied Royster, with pride which he couldn't conceal, "and she'll run as long as a fox makes tracks."

Baker thought, "Good voice? Well, the old guy said so," and yet Bake was well aware that her yelps were not qualified for a chorus of the best Royster voices, let alone to bring praise from the man who had bred Bugle Ann. He wondered whether it was merely a mistaken kindness on Spring's part, or whether the old man had really lost his ear. Three years, eight months and twenty-one days were an awful long time.

Bake began to hum *I stood in the jailhouse*, and stopped in horror when he realized what he was humming.

He heard the bubbling of his father's whisky bottle. "Let's have a fire," Cal ordered.

The first curling flame, nursed tenderly through drying twigs, showed Benjy Davis something which made him catch his breath. He had to build the fire higher before he was sure. . . . Yes, old Springfield had gone upstairs before he left the house, but Benjy hadn't given it any thought at the time. And now he saw that the old man wore the battered bugle, tucked neatly beneath his suspender strap.

Stiff little needles rose on Benjy's scalp. He kept fooling with the fire.

"They're well toward Big Panther Holler," Cal estimated.

Spring inclined his head critically. "Yes, that's a bee-line fox to-night. Doesn't let no crops grow under his feet." He spoke without a tremor of madness, but his old bugle glowed and shimmered and caught dull flashes from the firelight at every snap of the flames.

Then Benjy saw the shaking of Baker Royster's hands, and he knew that Bake too had seen the trumpet. . . . The son thought crazily, "Christ in the Mountains, what would we do if he stood up and started to blow that thing?"

Bake was shivering with the same wonder. This was June . . . he knew the month, and the year, and the farm—he knew every scrap of sod beneath his feet—and yet the first blast of that horn would turn the commonplace world to madness. No person could estimate what tribes might come sweeping through the underbrush in answer.

After a few moments, it was impossible to hear the dogs any more. They had gone deep into the crooked defile of Big Panther Creek; there was no telling just when they might return. The Roysters knew this fox well enough: their dogs had run him frequently during the year. He was a bee-liner from the word Go, as Cal often remarked, and he'd just as soon venture into the next county as not. But always he holed at the south end of Bachelor's timber, so they knew the pack would come howling back eventually.

No one talked. The log on the fire shrank to the thinness of a charred bone, and Benjy arose to see whether he could find another one dry enough to burn. There was a V of discarded fence posts nearby, and under their shelter perhaps—

He stopped, frozen in his tracks as the sound pierced him. It was a faint and elvish cry, half lost amid the buzz of tree-toads, and it might have been fathered by one of those night-hawks which rode high overhead. . . . Still, it never came from the throat of a bird, and in the first second Benjy wondered what sort of a throat it had come from.

Before the sudden blurring of his gaze, he watched his father's head lifting, nodding. Spring's mouth had opened slightly, in the reflex of one who listens without half knowing. . . .

Again the thin, silver measure—the horn of something which searched the forest away over beyond Heaven Hump. Bake Royster crawled up on his elbow, and his face became yellow instead of red in the firelight.

"Benjy," whispered Spring Davis, "I reckon she's struck."

The young man made a harsh sound. "It's a dog," he said. "Fox-hound that belongs to— Running all off by himself, that way. I reckon he's an Armstrong."

The sockets beneath Spring's eyebrows were blank and dark and empty; the weaving shadows did strange things to the contour of his face. He said, "No Armstrong ever had that kind of music in him." Then, creakily, he was on his feet and fingering the lip of his bugle.

"For pity sake," mumbled Cal Royster, "it's just a kind of echo. . . ."

"Cal," said Spring, "if she comes real close to us, I'll blow the bugle for her."

Benjy didn't know why she should have been up again, loping through that timber. It was her voice, of course—no other dog had ever lived with such a melody hidden in its throat. He ventured to suppose that Bugle Ann had loved Spring Davis, much as a woman might have loved him, but it was a cruel and selfish devotion which would rob them all of their sanity, and never let them live in the same world with other men again.

He was repeating, again and again, "Pa! Pa—set down—set down—" and that was the same plea he had made in the bedroom.

Old Spring laughed at them all, and he seemed to tower against the sky. "Are you plumb certain that was her collar, Benjy? . . . I reckon nobody but God seen her bones hop up out of the orchard to-night."

He ceased speaking, then, because the dog's howling was closer and more distinct, as if the trail had swung toward the Hollow; even now the fox might be leaping the gorge of Chilly Branch. But Bugle Ann had learned the last trick of any fox that ever jumped.

Bake Royster was trying to stand up, but for the moment his legs wouldn't support him. He thought, "She won't need any help to-night. Spring Davis is in the woods, and naturally she knows it." When he was far off in the penitentiary it had been kind of the Boone dogs, the hounds buried and dust a hundred years ago, to come out and hunt with her and cast in enormous circles to locate the scent . . . big, gobbling shapes, they could drag down the fastest deer in the hills. They could make the black bears afraid of them, and every catamount would slink along the tree-tops when they went by.

In sudden relief, Bake wanted to laugh out loud. He had hoped that she was a ghost, all along, for that made the whole tale so much easier to understand.

"Sweet mouth," he heard old Davis saying, "the sweetest mouth that ever lived."

Cal groped for his friend's arm. "Now, Spring," he quavered, "you got to get holt of yourself."

Spring laughed.

That clear, baying voice rocketed against the cloudy ceiling, and came down to wash all around them.

"Get holt? Why, I bred the most beautiful tune ever played in these parts, and I ain't ashamed! Maybe you laughed when you seen me bring this bugle, but I reckoned it would come handy." He paused, grinning slyly, and nodding again as the round pealing broke loose anew.

Then, from blackest distance and seeming to rise behind the hound notes, sounded the yell of a bugle. It blew the same chords which Springfield Davis had always blown for his dog.

The hound's cry ceased, quickly, and the woods seemed to hold out empty hands.

The men looked at one another, pale face reflecting pale face, and for the first time you could see Springfield's eyes. They were bright with bewilderment, and with rage.

Once more the *ta-da*, the shrill witchery and command of it. The strings of old Davis's neck stood out tight against his skin. "I never done it," he cried. "I never gave no one else leave to blow her in!"

"Where was it?" asked Bake, hoarsely.

"Up on Heaven Hump, or past," Benjy answered him. Then he started away through the timber like a runaway steer, with Bake after him.

8

Spring and Cal stumbled cruelly in the underbrush, until the younger men called to each other, remembering, and came back to help them.

Only when they had worked their way across Chilly Branch and had crept to the summit beyond, did any one say a complete sentence. It was Spring who spoke.

"Put out your lights," he ordered. "I see another fire."

A faint ruddiness lived in the north and east, and they went toward it. Benjy grasped his father's arm, pulling him along. The old man moved like a wooden image, but he breathed steadily, and Benjy was certain he'd never drop dead in those woods, no matter who or what they found beside that fire.

Again the tree-toads buzzed; the crickets sawed and chuckled, and betty-millers came to kiss the hunters' perspiring faces; these creatures could be merry and could exalt their whispers again, with all those mighty trumpet notes echoed beyond recall.

The woods thinned away. Here was a clearing, stockaded with lonely fence posts, where once Jacob Terry's sheep had lain down in a green pasture.

A black shape grew against the distant core of firelight.

"It's a woman," said Bake.

For a moment he weaved, dizzy, as in the dawn before Jacob Terry was killed.

Camden Terry sat beside the blaze. She was motionless, even as the dry sticks crackled under approaching feet; she must have been expecting this invasion, all along. A dog was with her. The dog bayed, briefly, and Springfield Davis whispered, ". . . World, and they that dwell therein," and his arm tried to twist out of Benjy's manacling grasp.

The girl looked up at them. Benjy thought that she was more beautiful than ever—more beautiful than that day in court, for the fire made red gilt of her hair. Her eyes held dignity and fearlessness, but undoubtedly she was waiting for some immense judgment.

Spring stepped up against the fire, and looked down at the hound which crouched within the curve of the girl's arm. "You blew them notes," were the first words he said, for he saw the bugle in Camden Terry's lap.

She said, "Yes. Twice. Yes, I did."

"That hound . . ." His throat went to pieces on the word. He seemed to build it up again. "What dog is that?"

"I raised her."

"But it's got—her voice."

"Yes, I know. I used to hear her."

He said, scornfully, "I tell you, God never made no two hound-voices alike. Same kind of mouth, and all. He never."

The girl looked up at him. "This— She was hers. She's Bugle Ann's. She's by Proctor Pride out of Bugle Ann. There were four more, but only this one had the real bugle-mouth."

Springfield staggered. Benjy held him. "She never had no pups," said Spring, thickly.

Camden passed her hand over the little hound's ears, and the dog watched Spring Davis with soft, sad eyes. Her nostrils reached out for the smell of him. . . . Camden Terry stood up; the bugle rolled across the ground. Firelight made her blue dress seem purple, and it did kindly with her eyes, and for a moment Benjy couldn't breathe.

"Mr. Davis," the girl said, "my father never killed her."

Spring cried, "Aw, we know that! The boys found her skeleton over by Bachelor's, and they heard her voice in the woods, but I still say she never was bred to any dog."

"That night—" Camden's voice was very low; her hands struggled together. "I drove out of the yard, just like I told in court. She was coming past the gate; I couldn't see her in time. I couldn't— It was an awful sharp turn. . . . I got out and picked her up. . . . She wasn't dead, and even —hurt—she— She didn't seem to blame me. I was afraid there'd be trouble over it: Bugle Ann's being hurt."

Somewhere in the world beyond, Cal Royster was saying, "Car lights.

They stopped for a minute. Then they went on. It was when I heard the yip."

"This hound never was hers," Spring Davis snarled. "Where in hell did it get her voice?"

"Wait, Pa," said Benjy.

The girl's hands separated; the fingers flattened stiffly together. "I took her along in the car. The rest of my folks didn't know I'd brought her; just Uncle Elnathan. I told them I had found a run-over dog, on the way, and I hustled her out to Uncle's place. . . . After we heard what had happened, I didn't dare tell the truth. It would have been worse for you, if the jury knew Bugle Ann wasn't really dead at all."

She gasped, "Oh. I hated Pa. He killed my mother with pure meanness. It's the awfulest thing in the world to have a father you've got to hate."

Spring eyed her grimly, and told her to go on.

"Well, it was Bugle Ann's shoulder and leg. . . . She was kind of crippled, but I nursed her to health. When she came in heat in February, I bred her to Proctor Pride. He was a Spaulding hound; the only good one Uncle had, any more. There were five pups. But this was the one—like her."

Camden paused, and there were tears all over her face, but this time it was Benjy who asked her to go on.

"She waited till they were weaned. Then she left one night—there was a moon— She wasn't dried up yet, and she wasn't strong enough to run. But she did go away. We traced her fifteen miles, next day, and then lost her for good. Likely she was heading for home when she struck a fox, and you folks heard her. We never knew she was dead, for sure, but I always thought she'd been killed trying to get back home."

Spring exclaimed, "Benjy, I got to set," and his son eased him quickly to the ground. . . . Cal Royster fumbled around. It took him a long while to find his flask, but at last he did find it.

Soon, Spring opened his eyes and nodded at the girl. "You see," he murmured, "they let me out of Jefferson City."

Her chin trembled. "I knew. That's how I come to be here tonight. I thought you'd maybe be out in the timber."

Benjy stared at her with fierce intensity. "*You* knew. How did you know? They don't talk those things around."

"Well," she told him, "I knew beforehand."

Benjy said, "It wasn't a parole. He was pardoned."

"Yes. The parole board. Sometimes they—kind of recommend. Folks write letters. And talk."

He had taken her hand—both of her hands. He came between her and the Roysters, and he seemed even to have forgotten his father. Camden said, rapidly: "Jacob Terry was my father. I'd like to forget that, but it counted for something when they come to considering and— All my folks weren't Terrys," she cried at him. "Half of them were Camdens, and Camdens mean something in this state, even yet. Some of them are in the legislature."

Bake Royster exploded, "My God! You done it, didn't you?"

She shook her head. "No. I couldn't of done it myself. I just—did what I could. They all knew what kind of a man my father was. And I told them about Mr. Davis."

Inch by inch, the hound had hitched forward to sniff around Spring Davis's feet. At first the old man twisted his legs away, but finally he lay still and watched the dog. "I'm all right, boy," he muttered to Benjy, and then he raised up on his elbow. His eyes took in the whole color and shape and hide of the hound; they studied her slenderness, her strong and well-arched coupling, the stifle built far out from her body. . . . The hound sneezed. She looked at old Davis with curiosity, and then stepped across his legs with tail waving politely, and smelled him from the other side.

"I reckon she could run," said Spring.

"I trained her to the horn. Same as— It seemed like the best thing to do." Camden looked at Benjy, and he nodded slowly, and his face came close to hers.

Spring asked, "What do you call her?"

"Little Lady."

The old man said, "Got a deeper tan, but it's spotted much the same." Stiffly, reluctantly, he put out his hand and touched the hound's muzzle. His eyes were still hard and dry, but he whispered, "Little Lady. You got quite a mouth, Little Lady."

Cal Royster was crying like his own grandchild, but more quietly. Bake took him away from the fire. "Come on, Pa," he grunted, "we got to get out of here. I think I hear the pack coming north again." Baker was certain in his heart that before the other hounds had ever come in, Spring Davis would have sent Little Lady out with Camden and Benjy, to see what she was made of. He prophesied to himself that she would run as long as any fox made tracks; she would be a twenty-hour dog, given to mighty journeyings and chasings, but always she would come back to those black-dark hills when the bugle called her home.